NDOKI

TRAPPED IN THE WEB OF WITCHCRAFT

By
Charles H. Harvey

Copyright © 2007 by Charles H. Harvey

Ndoki
Trapped In The Web Of Witchcraft
by Charles H. Harvey

Printed in the United States of America

ISBN 978-1-60477-074-2

All rights reserved solely by the author. The author guarantees all contents are original and do not infringe upon the legal rights of any other person or work. No part of this book may be reproduced in any form without the permission of the author. The views expressed in this book are not necessarily those of the publisher.

Unless otherwise indicated, Bible quotations are taken from the Holy Bible, New International Version NIV. Copyright 1973, 1978, 1984 by International Bible Society. Used by permission.

www.xulonpress.com

cover by Mark Harvey

Dedicated to **Frances**
who has been my priceless companion
for more than fifty years

TABLE OF CONTENTS

The Unthinkable happens in a Congo village...11
Titi's Home village in Angola..13
Life changing experiences at Lufu school 55
Panic and escape 111
Shaped by a wise grandmother in Kiula 133
The last days of the old matriarch..203
Harrowing journey with a guerrilla patrol 213
Congo-Zaire...225
The devastating robbery that changes everything..247
Refugee reunion 259
New life on the way...287
Arrival in the village of Dimba...293
From worry to grief..317
Eight years later 361

PROLOGUE

It is my intention to give the reader and insider's view of the life and thinking of a young Angolan girl from her childhood right through into her young adult life.

I hope to help you get a feel for her thinking as you participate in the events that invade and trap her life in the insidious web of Kindoki witchcraft prevalent in the countries that surround the western region of the great Congo River.

Most of the place names, character names, and geography of parts of Angola and the Congo have been altered.

We call this a novel because apart from the basic true story, the author has created most of the small details that involve and surround Titi, our heroine. Decades of in depth involvement with a clan related to this young person provided the information for the accurate depiction of the culture and worldview that molded her thinking.

Every significant event or insight into the rich culture entered the author's reservoir of detailed knowledge through a lifetime of interaction with the people.

There is a deliberate effort to help the reader to get an accurate apprehension of what Titi's eyes have seen. Through her eyes it may become possible to acquire a deeper understanding of a world view held by countless thousands of people across the continent of Africa. The information is accurate for at least one clan of the Bakongo people of Western Angola and the Congo. The regions were once part of the ancient Kingdom of the Congo. Most customs and beliefs are simply reported or described as one local might report to another. The narrator is intended to report events as though he were from the region, and understood and respected local traditions.

The author spent more than three decades working among the Bakongo people in both Angola and Congo-Zaire. Scores of trusting relationships allowed valued African colleagues and friends to reveal their convictions and beliefs in a way that disclosed the yearnings, joys, sorrows and sometimes, the terror of their hearts.

Unfortunately, the web of witchcraft grows rapidly in the climate of suffering, poverty, and social upheaval. Like a virus, it mutates to become effective in changing circumstances. Witchcraft is probably more pervasive now than any time in the past century.

I hope that you may be enabled to discover the dignity of these people whose patterns of thought may be new to you.

Charles H Harvey

THE UNTHINKABLE HAPPENS IN A CONGO VILLAGE

Anxiety dominated their little one-room hut. The yellow glow from the lantern gave just enough light to disclose the terror in the young mother's eyes. Some evil force seemed to be sucking the very life from her baby boy. It was the fourth day of frighteningly high fever. Little Makiese vomited up his malaria medicine each time they tried to get it down him despite their disguising its bitterness with wild honey. Petelo, the young father, offered a stabilizing presence because of his deep love for Titi and their baby.

Titi sensed that her precious baby was losing the battle. Not only was he burning with fever, but also his breathing had become shallow and alarmingly rapid. She had watched babies die before. Terror and helplessness gripped her very soul. Every fiber of her consciousness was convinced that some ndoki (witch) was snatching her baby from her, right before her eyes.

"Babies don't die unless someone is making it happen," she whimpered.

Petelo perceived that death was perilously near. In desperation he went out into torrential rain to call in their kindly neighbors to join the vigil. The tumultuous roar of wind and rain removed all possibilities of simply shouting for help. To make matters worse, the local nurse had left on the market truck five days earlier.

A gust of wind wrestled the door from Petelo's hands causing it to slam shut. Immediately, little Makiese began to convulse.

"The witch is attacking freely now that I am alone! Who can it be who wants to suck the life from our precious child?" Titi sobbed.

She placed the baby on her knees so she could see him better. Again he convulsed violently. Suddenly his breathing stopped as his little arms flailed out accusingly. In the same terrible moment that she recognized the signs of death, it dawned on her terrified heart, that her baby's last gestures were accusing her!

"So I'm the ndoki (witch) killing my baby! 'The vumbi (corpse) never lies!' His little hands just accused me!"

Screaming into the gloom, she flung herself onto the earth floor, weighed down with the double burden of grief and shame. She was writhing there with Makiese's limp body in her arms when Petelo returned with the kindly old couple from next door.

"Fwididi! Fwididi! (He's just died! He's just died!) I'm the ndoki (witch) who killed him! Nkaka (grandmother) must have bewitched me during the last wild days of her existence. I've destroyed the life of our wonderful baby boy! Let me die too! Let me die too!"

For a tragic eternity, Titi screamed uncontrollably, until her vocal chords could no longer produce a sound.

Petelo sobbed freely with a broken heart, but never raised his voice.

The old couple spontaneously joined in their grief. They had watched two of their own children die in the years gone by. Little Makiese was like their own grandchild, so their grief was profound.

Titi's self-declaration of witchcraft caused them to look at each other helplessly with alarm written all over their expressive faces. Titi's totally unexpected confession could only bring devastating trouble, even scandal, to this little home and the whole village. They had never heard a grieving mother make such a confession in all their many years of life.

How has it come about that this keen, young, woman became convinced that she herself was the killer witch guilty of snuffing out the life of her very own precious baby?

In an effort to answer this question, we shall examine Titi's childhood and youth, intent on observing the dramatic factors, which have shaped her understanding of life.

Countless dramatic scenes that her young eyes have observed and absorbed have shaped Titi's thinking. Walking beside her will enrich our understanding of her heritage and grant us an appreciation of the fears engendered through her encounters with the occult world of traditional kindoki (witchcraft) and its pervasive web. To understand her, we need to attempt to see, and appreciate, what her eyes have seen.

TITI'S HOME VILLAGE IN ANGOLA

A combination of old forest and mature fruit trees surrounded the little village of Mbungu on its isolated hilltop. A steep hillside path led to the stream that supplied drinking water, as well as splendid washing and bathing opportunities. The nearest market town, Lufu, was eight hours distant on an old road that had not seen a vehicle in years.

After the war for independence from Portuguese colonial rule began in Angola in 1961, the colonial authorities hounded all the inhabitance of isolated villages to move to the main truck road. The village elders of Mbungu kept inventing excuses to stay where they have always lived. The fact that the village was so small, combined with the dangerous state of the log bridges, kept government Jeeps from bothering them. White men did not like walking long distances. To the villagers' delight, the elders were never hassled enough to oblige a move. The civil war more than preoccupied the Portuguese administrator at Lufu, allowing the village of Mbungu to enjoy the isolation it preferred.

Mbungu boasted of its own claims to importance. The huge sanda tree where notable chiefs met to settle important disputes was considered to be famous. Three men found guilty of witchcraft, were executed and buried in the ground directly under the tree at the time of its planting by Chief Mbungu, the village founder. Only a powerful man could manage to execute others and bury them so as to enhance the power and prestige of his 'palaver' or judgment tree. The present chief was feared and respected because of the powerful "teki"(witchcraft idols) he managed. Mbungu was valued and respected by the elders of the region, if not by the colonial powers.

Sanda trees were used as "palaver" (discussion) trees, because they grow rapidly, offering considerable shade in as few as three years. Under the old sanda tree at Mbungu, a hundred and fifty people could find shade for any gathering.

Even the little children knew of the sacred and mysterious nature of that tree. An "nganga"(shaman) had to be called before anyone dared to remove the branches that sometimes fall during a tropical storm.

The giant mango trees were almost as old as the sanda and have produced fruit for a century. Together with the impressive nsafu and avocado trees, they formed an enclosure for the chief's compound.

Not a half-mile along the valley there was a twin hilltop covered with a veritable jungle of trees, including some old fruit trees. The impressive forest was considered to be sacred because it contained the cemetery of the ancestors. No one except important shamen was allowed to enter the vine-covered path that led to the heart of it. The shaman entered only when he needed to consult the deceased elders, seeking advice on special occasions. The normal village cemetery was located in a field on the edge of the sacred forest.

The Luadi River in the valley was too wide to bridge with logs. A hanging bridge crossed over the gorge cut in the rocks by the forces of flowing water. Years ago, the Portuguese placed two steel cables to form the support for the pole covered passage way. The talk of gold that stimulated the hanging of the cables never materialized but the bridge they built was carefully maintained, and formed a vital link used almost every day especially during rainy season floods. The Luadi drained a number of streams and brooks in the valley.

Across the hanging bridge to the southwest lay a generous expanse of savanna grassland mixed with sparse forests in the valleys. Manioc or cassava, mbika squash, grown for the edible seeds, corn and peanuts produced bountifully in the small forests and grasslands. Beans thrived on the hillsides at the edges of the valleys. Tomatoes, sweet potatoes and sesame seed flourished too, when planted in appropriate locations. Near the water, there were always dry-season gardens with lots of collards, cabbages, onions, garlic, and peppers. Bananas graced the same hillsides as the beans. Little Titi knew nothing about food shortages.

Beans and peanuts were the major cash crops sold or traded for clothing, salt, kerosene, sugar and tea at the Lufu market. Folk grew their own coffee as well, trading it at the market whenever they had a surplus, or needed cash. Dried coffee beans kept well and were often sold at times of financial emergencies.

There were fruit trees behind each little house, as well as a grove of healthy palm trees providing palm nuts, cooking oil and palm wine. The river offered a modest supply of fish, while hunters had reasonable success on their hunting expeditions. Little wonder folk resisted any thought of leaving their isolated village that had raised healthy children for generations.

At first glance, Titi's world appeared to be idyllic and secure as she played happily with a little band of neighbor children in and around their village. She loved babies, and nothing pleased her more than to have an older child or mother permit her to carry a tiny one on her back. At five, she knew just how to adjust and tie the cloth so that the baby was kept secure She kept up with the others, even on the steep path down to the river.

Countless hours were spent on the shallow side of the river where everyone gathered to wash dishes and clothing. Children often washed everything they owned, spreading their garments out on the tall grass to dry, while they splashed in the river. Occasionally, they had the luxury of soap. As soon as a child was old enough to toddle down to the river, she was expected to learn how to swim.

It took several months for Titi to acquire the special skill needed to churn the water in such a way that it actually sounded like drums. The little girls sung lustily while they drummed in unison, enjoying their exclusively female bathing area.

The boys played in the river too, just a shout away. They washed their clothes the same way as the girls. In their play, they sometimes dammed a little tributary brook, placing their long woven fish traps in the opening they made. More often than not, they cooked and ate part of their catch right on the spot.

If they were lucky enough to have hooks and lines, the older boys fished for catfish in the deep pools on the far side of the river. Catfish were considered as family food, so the lads carried their slippery catch home like trophies from the hunt.

At a shout all the little girls dressed, gathered the basins of washed dishes and water containers, then trudged back to the village. They would be back later. The bathing spots were places of social gathering all day long. Little girls seldom bathed with the elder women, nor boys with the elders among the men.

Whenever an adult voice shouted "Kku maza?"(At the water?), children in the water responded. "Vingila fiote!"(Wait a little!) They dressed quickly, and then shouted for the elder to proceed.

As soon as they were able to carry a small basket of firewood, little girls spent part of most days with the older girls and women, working in the fields.

Traveling with the men, boys learned hunting skills, as well as the location of the grasses, leaves and vines used for house construction. Ever since the civil war began in Angola in 1961, boys learned about politics and the inner conflicts of guerilla warfare for their own good.

Girls and women grew, prepared, and cooked the food for everyone. Older boys ate with the men in the talking huts, while girls ate in the cooking huts with the women and small children. Because they went everywhere with their mothers, all the village gossip eventually reached a little girl's ears.

Small girls could almost slip out of sight in the dark corner of a cooking hut lighted only by the fire, and a small door. When women folk talked in low tones about the intrigues of inter-personal relationships, little ears were often listening quietly. Pregnancy, sterility, curses and blessings, dreams and visions, sinister witchcraft, and the power of fetish protections made by the shaman were all fascinating topics. Little minds were indoctrinated with traditions through the intensity and seriousness of a thousand overheard conversations. Sooner or later, most little girls saw things just about the same way their mothers.

Her own mother was not necessarily the first to tell her each time she had a miscarriage. Other little girls heard the news from listening to their mothers. Through these grapevines, Titi became convinced that her mother was losing her babies because of witchcraft practiced cunningly by her Nkaka (grandmother). Hatred and resentment exploded inside when she heard her mother complaining.

"That old ndoki witch is 'eating' (snuffing out the life) of my babies while they are still forming within me. She wants their power to live longer."

In their cooking hut, Titi shuddered as her mother's friend repeated a well-known saying. "Babies don't just die, they are always 'eaten' (killed by a ndoki witch)".

She yearned for a little brother or sister so intensely that she sometimes shunned her grandmother and would not even allow their eyes to meet. The child believed with all her little heart that her old witch grandmother was destroying her hopes of having a little brother or sister because of her hateful, selfish witchcraft. The elderly grandmother, Mambu, lived nearby in the village of Kiula.

Cookhouses were homes for little children, girls and women. Thatched roofs and leaf-covered walls were relatively easy to construct and could be enlarged to provide enough space for numerous sleeping mats. Women slept where they cooked, unless they were invited by their husbands to spend the night with them in the main house. If a man had more than one wife, he constructed a separate cooking hut for each wife and her children.

Titi slept with her mother except on the occasions when her mother was asked to sleep in the house with her father. She was keenly aware of the patterns of her mother's life, especially her relationships with her father.

The last time her mother gave birth to a still-born baby, Titi remembered vividly the circumstances leading up to the sad event. For more than two nights, she was awakened by her mother's outcries.

"Leave me alone! Leave me alone! You know we don't have the money for your dress! Leave me, let me keep my baby!" Her mother's nightmare experience was so vivid that they both remained awake the rest of the night.

"She was right here in this room again and she wants to take my baby," Titi's mother sobbed as she stoked the fire to remove the darkness.

"Why does my Nkaka want to 'eat' your babies?" Titi sobbed.

(The verb "dia" (to eat) was used to describe a witch's act of sucking out of life forces, producing physical death by occult power.)

"When we were married, part of the bride price was to have been a "wax" for my mother," explained her mother. "Dresses called "wax" are the most expensive material that is sold. Your father did not have the money. The war has made that kind of cloth almost impossible to find. Your grandmother wants her dress! She is getting revenge. She probably consumes their life force so she can live longer as well."

"Your Nkaka is an exposed ndoki witch. The shaman disclosed her horrible secret in a public trial. In the old days she would have been thrown off the cliff at Mongo Konde. It is a pity that they don't do it any more! The Portuguese no longer allow that old custom. No one in her village really talks with her any more."

The very next night after their conversation, Titi's mother complained of severe stomach cramps.

"That witch is at it again. She will not leave me until she has this baby too"

Not long after the first rooster crowing, (about 2:30 a.m.), the cries of her startled mother awakened Titi again.

"Leave me alone! Leave me alone! You ate one baby and that's enough. Leave me alone!"

During the heated exchange between her father and mother the next morning, Titi only listened.

"She is threatening to eat this baby. She has done it before and she is threatening to "eat" this baby too, if you don't get her the dress you promised."

Zoao replied sadly, "Pemba, you know that we used all the peanut and bean money for medicine and salt. I couldn't even by you a cheap dress this year. Everything is very expensive since the war began."

"It is too late anyway," Pemba sobbed gently. "I feel the pains already."

Titi cringed as her mother cried out in hot anger, while pounding the earth with her fist.

"Let that witch be cursed and die suffering, even though she is my own mother!"

Titi had never seen her mother so filled with hate. Normally she was sweet and pleasant. Her act of pounding the ground with the cursing gesture demonstrated more naked hatred than she ever dreamed her mother could possibly harbor.

Just after Zoao went to call the shaman, Titi watched another outburst from her mother as she ripped off a narrow cloth belt from under her skirt.

"That nganga (protective shaman) has lied to us again. We paid him three goats and brought him some of my mother's hair to make the protective charm. He put his magic materials in this baby goat's horn that I have worn faithfully for three years. He said this nkisi (fetish charm) was supposed to kill my mother if she dared to touch me as a witch. It was all useless because I am beginning to lose the second baby!"

Angrily, she threw the tiny goat horn with its belt right into the fire.

"No one can protect me from her," she sobbed, sinking back on her mat.

When her father returned with help, he took Titi away with him. They were silent as they walked to his cousin's house.

"Pemba is losing another baby. Will you please take care of Titi today," he asked with sadness.

News about life, death, and illness traveled quickly. Within a couple of hours, Pemba was on her mat in her cooking hut, surrounded by most of the women and girls in the village. Titi slipped back into the melee of women.

Suddenly a hush swept over the group. Titi's heart pounded when she saw the reason. One of the women spoke quickly to her mother, who could not see what was happening.

"The ndoki witch that ate your other baby is coming. That hypocrite has to come so she can try to appear innocent!" the woman said.

Titi's heart was pounding. *"Mother told me to always be polite with my grandmother so she would never have any desire to kill me."* The thought alone made her break out with sweat all over her little body.

Everyone was very polite with the elderly suspect.

"Mother, it is good of you to come. I've lost another baby. It was dead before it was born," said Pemba.

"Pemba, you are my child," replied her mother. "Of course I came as soon as I heard."

After this formal exchange took place, the conversation ended. No one said anything because they all thought alike. Even the old lady herself, who had been snubbed now for several years, knew that they all thought she had provoked the birth of the stillborn. She had learned to say nothing at all. Once a person is accused of being an ndoki witch, there was no way to prove one's innocence. The old lady no longer tried. Total rejection by her family and neighbors caused deep lines in her face, reflecting the bitter rejection she felt every day of her life.

"Everyone is being polite to her. They are afraid of her just as I am," Titi reasoned in her troubled mind as she reached out to greet her grandmother formally.

"Titi, you are growing so quickly, I hardly recognize you. I haven't seen you since the last rainy season."

As soon as her grandmother shifted her glance, the little girl slipped outside where she felt much safer.

The women from nearby villages moved out quietly to go get some food for the meal they would need at the wake they would hold that evening. Zoao did not enter the house during this time but he used his reserve money to buy salted fish from a neighbor. He gave them to the women to cook with the beans.

At dusk the old 'ndoki witch,' Titi's grandmother, hobbled back to her village of Kiula, to the relief of everyone else.

Three days later, Titi was pleased to be sleeping beside her mother again after the wake.

"May I sleep right beside you, on your mat?" Titi asked softly, the first night they were by themselves. "I wasn't afraid the nights so many people were around, because I knew that no ndoki witch would come then. What will keep us safe now?"

"The old witch should be satisfied, she has already taken two of my babies before they even had a chance to begin life."

Titi enjoyed the increased affection she felt from her mother in the weeks that followed the loss of her stillborn child.

"I feel safer when I am close to you like this," Titi confided.

The Owl incident

About two months later, both Pemba and Titi were frightened awake by the hooting of an owl very near their house. Huddling even closer to her mother, Titi asked the question that was on her mother's mind too.

"Mother, who is the ndoki witch after now? Does she always strike after the owl hoots?"

"The owl is a prophet and we are never sure of his intent. Sometimes the owl is only a messenger, while some owls are ndoki witches in disguise."

"Could that be Nkaka taunting us?"

"Only a special shaman would know exactly how to interpret the intentions of the owl we are hearing at the moment," Pemba whispered.

Titi's father, Zoao was a skilled hunter and the owl awakened him too.

"You are never satisfied are you?" Zoao thought. *"You have been dried up and wicked for years. Are two of our babies not enough for you? Who is it you want this time? Are you after Titi now? If I can get my sights on you, that will be all I need. If I can shoot you, owl, I have a gut feeling that the old hag will be found dead over in her village!"*

Zoao loaded as heavy a charge of gunpowder as he thought his gun could support. He rammed the wadding into place, followed by a good number of small nails and more wadding. He was ready, but must wait for a little morning light.

Creeping through the darkness, Zoao followed the sound of the owl, hoping he can get a shot at it in the first glimmer of morning light. His keen eyes spotted the shadowy figure flitting among the foliage of a giant mango tree. The hated bird was seeking a good spot to hide during the daylight hours.

His keen eyes searched a long time before he had a clear view of his prey. When he pulled the trigger, the supercharged muzzleloader discharged a deafening blast that left the hunter in a cloud of black smoke. The big owl fell to the ground despite trying to grasp the branches through which he passed. Excited, and angry, Zoao pounced on the large flailing mass of feathers that clawed him with razor sharp talons before he managed to plunge his hunting knife right into its heart.

Zoao was obsessed with getting even with the one who had sucked the life out of two of his babies before they were even born. Venting his hatred, he actually crucified the owl, his enemy. Cutting and splitting a hardwood sapling the size of his thumb, he pushed the sharpened end right up through the body and out the head. With the concentration of all his powers of hate, he thrust the other half of the sapling through the breast of the bird forming a cross. With great satisfaction he pushed the vertical shaft into the ground right at the cross roads of the village path, and the trail to the river.

"I hope I got her, that wizened up old hag. If I didn't get her, at least I got her messenger".

His was the satisfaction of getting vengeance. Zoao was counting on the tradition that maintained that killing the animal form also killed the person who was operating as a secret killer witch in disguise.

Anxious to know the result of his killing the owl, he devised a way to get his answer. He asked Pemba to send some kind of gift to her mother. Quickly, they wrapped up a nice piece of dried antelope to send to her.

Titi actually understood that the real purpose of her trip to Kiula was to find out whether or not her grandmother had survived the shooting of the owl. She was not very frightened to go to her grandmothers whenever she was asked to do something that would curry favor with the old woman.

Running down the private path that leads to the river over behind her grandmother's little house Titi found the old lady busy putting her manioc in the water to soak.

With the warmth of real affection, the aging woman clasped her granddaughter's hand in greeting.

"I wonder if this little one loves me?" thought the old woman. *"All the others are against me and believe I am a killer ndoki witch just as the ngombo (shaman) declared four years ago. The shaman always accuses elders with white hair. Is it a crime to become old? With all the accusations, I wonder if I have actually become a witch, because of someone else's spell? Could it be that I do evil things while my body is asleep?"*

These thoughts rushed through the grandmother's mind even while she was holding Titi's hand in hers.

Titi always felt confused whenever she was alone with her Nkaka.

"She looks so happy to see me. The frown has gone from her face. I don't feel afraid any more. In my heart I want to trust her. I can't believe that she killed my mother's babies. How can I ever know what to believe? None of the adults trust her and they all call her "ndoki" My father hoped that I would find that she died when he shot the owl. For now, I will just go by what I see, and what I feel in my heart. I will help her with her wash then carry up some water for her. Everyone advised me to be nice to her so she will not want to harm me," Titi reasoned in her heart.

She promptly forgot all about her anxious parents who had warned her to come back home immediately. Seated by the fire, Titi and her grandmother ate roasted peanuts and sweet potatoes for their late breakfast.

Picking up a partially finished sleeping mat with beautiful patterns in it, Titi asked a question. "Nkaka, how did you learn to do such beautiful work?"

"My mother taught me when I was still young like you. In my day, a girl could not hope to get married unless she developed many different skills needed by a village homemaker. Having a reputation for making beautiful sleeping mats was felt to be a great help in attracting a desirable husband."

"My mother is so busy with her gardens that I don't think she will ever find the time to teach me how to make beautiful mats, will you teach me sometime?" Titi asked.

"Of course I will," the old lady replied with obvious delight.

Titi was all smiles as she left for home.

"Titi! Titi!"

The little girl was startled by a voice coming from the trees.

"Over here," Zoao shouted.

He had been cleaning the top of a palm tree cutting off all the branches at the level of the fruit and blossoms, preparing it for palm wine production.

Zoao was so anxious to hear of the fate of Titi's grandmother that he had come almost to the edge of the next village to make his palm wine. It gave him an excuse to get the news as soon as his little daughter returned.

"Well, how is your Nkaka?"

For a moment Titi was surprised at his concern until she remembered the ugly sight of the crucified owl.

"She is not sick or injured, as you expected."

Titi's soft reply let her father know that she had understood her mission. She was young but very perceptive.

Titi continued her walk home, leaving her father working in the top of a palm tree. Serious thoughts troubled her mind as she followed the winding footpath.

"I know it is my father's duty to protect me from the ndoki witches. Only someone from my mother's luvila or bloodline can ever harm me. Does Nkaka's survival prove that she is not an ndoki witch? The owl is crucified at the cross road but Nkaka is not even ill! Some will say that the owl must have only been a messenger. Why do I enjoy being with her so much if she might want to harm me? She seems so wise and full of interesting ideas. She knows all about growing food. She makes beautiful baskets and mats, even pots. People come from far off villages to buy the medicine she makes from leaves and roots. She is certainly a wise old lady.

Titi had never known her great grandmother Nkaka Ndimba, who had been a special shaman. Pemba had often spoken about that old lady's abilities to treat eye diseases, skin eruptions, and all the illnesses related to legs, feet, and walking. It was not surprising that Titi's own grandmother had learned much about traditional medicines from her mother.

"Perhaps my Nkaka is one of the good witches who uses her powers to help people," Titi reasoned, and began to talk out loud as she often did.

"It is sad that so many old people are witches, and use their power to live a long time. I am terrified whenever Nkaka comes to me in dreams. When I awaken, I fear her and want her dead. Why would she come to me and frighten me when I am asleep?"

Titi was so lost in her thoughts that she slowed down and spent more time talking with herself than walking.

"I still love to be with her when she is in a good mood. She always seems happy to see me. My heart keeps telling me that ndoki witch or not, she wouldn't harm me. Mother and the elders are sure that she ate (killed) my baby brothers because she has never received her share of mother's bride price. How can I know what to think?"

The sight of the crucified owl at the cross roads in the village made her little heart churn within her. *"Father's hate is so deep. When he pushed those sharp sticks through the owl, I'm sure he thought that he was getting even with Nkaka for sucking the life out of his two baby sons."*

The most disturbing proof of her grandmother's witchcraft was her repeated nocturnal visits which terrified her mother in the dead of the night. She always appeared just at the onset of the killing pains that expelled the baby before its time.

Pemba was taunted by these horrible witch visits, which ripped away her peace and made her afraid to fall asleep again for fear of experiencing a return visit.

Everyone believed that real ndoki witches always traveled at night, even over long distances, leaving his or her sleeping body at home. Repeated visits from someone while one was sleeping were always considered to be far more serious than occasional dreams. Such repeated dreams carried a lingering terror with them. Titi could never forget the look in her mother's eyes whenever she had one of these terrifying encounters with her own old mother-turned-witch.

"What should I think? I know that mother saw my Nkaka come as a killer witch. She heard her threatening words and lost two babies the same horrible way!"

Titi frequently talked to herself when she was alone.

Gardening with her mother

Titi knew her mother intimately having been with her night and day ever since she was born. As the only living child, she was her mother's special treasure. Pemba delighted in teaching her little daughter just about everything she knew herself. By the time she was seven or eight, she had a rich store of knowledge of seasons, seeds, and soil. She was a great help and companion to her mother in the family gardens.

Every year, Zoao cleared a new forest area about three hundred paces square to be used for crops. His major task was the felling of the large trees. Eventually, everything else was slashed and left to dry for two or three months before being burned. Initially, there was far too much moisture in the large hardwood trees for them to burn in a brush fire. After a year or more of drying, the large trees often became firewood.

Corn and peanuts were the first crops harvested from a virgin field. Some areas could produce beans for a couple of additional years too. For the final seasons of tilling before abandonment, manioc or cassava was the most important crop. The new fields were always cultivated by family effort and became a source of security and pride. Working up a new field was hard work because of the many roots that seemed to fight with the hoe.

Women often worked together in little cooperatives, preparing one member's fields at a time. It was always a race to get all the fields ready for planting before the November rains began. Although still quite small, Titi had her own work cut out for her too.

"Titi, we want you to mother our children while we work. Our little ones always ask if you will be there when we are working together at this time of the year," one of Pemba's friends explained.

Since she had no little brothers or sisters of her own, Titi enjoyed caring for a half dozen little ones. A wee one fastened on her back would always fall asleep because of her movements.

If one of my brothers were alive, I would be caring for my very own family, Titi reasoned.

The women worked to the rhythm of their own songs. Titi often danced around to the same rhythm while helping a fussy little one fall asleep as it bobbed on her back.

The women came to the fields at first light, while it was cool. Titi was responsible for making the fire and cooking the food that would be eaten about mid morning. She always carried some coals from their fire at home in order to light a fire in the field. The trick was to wrap the coals in several layers of green leaves, leaving enough exposure to keep them alive without burning themselves out. Matches were rare, so women were always borrowing live coals from anyone with a fire.

At peanut planting time, most women would have saved enough peanuts for planting and a few for eating while they worked. It was a small girls task to carefully roast the peanuts in a pan that was kept moving over the fire. Sweet potatoes, or manioc chunks could be boiled in a pot or carefully covered with coals and ashes so they would bake just right. Titi was a good little cook and never seemed to burn the food she was cooking in the coals.

Often, some lady would smack her lips, as she ate, and say, "Titi you are a great little cook".

It was an honor to be praised by your mother's companions and friends. It certainly pleased her mother.

Mealtime was always gossip time. As soon as discussion of farming conditions was ended, talk always seemed to center around who was expecting a baby, who lost one, or what alliances were being formed between men and women they knew. The greatest shame was reserved for any woman who could not get pregnant even after a secret shift in partners.

"Having a healthy baby is the most important achievement for any woman". Titi whispered to herself. She knew that her mother felt ashamed to have only one living child after ten years of marriage.

The Diviner

One morning the breakfast talk in the field was all about the ndoki witch market, which supposedly gathered mysteriously after midnight, under the village sanda tree. According to tradition, killer ndoki witches meet at such a market to exchange portions of human flesh from the persons they killed through their witchcraft. It was a grotesque meat market of sorts. All of the women knew of people who had been found guilty of taking part in the market but no one had ever seen the action, except in a nightmare. These horrible dreams were accepted as valid sources of insight into the occult around them, a sort of revelation.

After the untimely death of local youth, a renowned nganga ngombo, or divining shaman, was summoned to do a witch-hunt in the extended family of a woman from the farming group to which Pemba belonged. The witch-hunt would take place under the village sanda tree allowing Titi to watch along with everyone else, if her mother gave her permission. Now that she was old enough to care for babies and complete many other responsible tasks, she could expect to be allowed to watch the fascinating trial.

The purpose of the nganga ngombo was to determine exactly who should be blamed for the youth's death. Anyone suspected of the occult crime had to be related to the victim through the maternal bloodline according to strict traditions.

A trial was always dramatic because in the end, someone would be condemned. The magical methods and supposed supernatural powers of the shaman were intended to increase the observers' confidence in the shaman's prowess, insight, and credibility.

The unique rhythm of the shaman's small wooden drum, a miniature replica of the local talking drums, could be heard long before the he actually reached the village to make his impressive entrance. The drum was a circular cylinder of special, dark maroon wood with a slit carved in it, the long way. Through the slit, the wood was chiseled out in such a manner that striking one lip of the drum made a high sound, while striking the other produced a lower tone. The shaman sang in a monotone in his secret language to the rhythm of his drum.

Titi found a good location which would enable her to watch this famous shaman called Disu, (Eye) as he rounded the bend at the bottom of the hill.

His clothes were a dull, dark, reddish color, dyed from a special wood used for traditional ceremonies. Around his neck hung a long necklace that reached to his knees. It consisted of many large seeds found only in the deep forest. Each seed represented some outstanding magic feat of divining. His hair was covered with the skin of a small, squirrel-like, animal.

On his shoulder the shaman carried his magic bag containing a wide variety of animal and bird parts, skins, skulls, and dried flesh. Dried cat's eyes, and nose, implied that the shaman had a kind of supernatural vision and sense of smell. Everyone knew that the shaman was capable of contacting the clan's ancestors in the ancestral village, the land of the dead.

About three paces back, two young female apprentices solemnly followed their master. They were dressed much like him, but had very short strings of beads.

To become a shaman's apprentice each would have needed to demonstrate that the 'ngombo spirit' could possess her, empowering her to perform a frenzied dance climaxing in a state of trance. They were, after all, ndoki witch hunters. They had to have access to occult information. They themselves were perceived to be ndoki witches capable of penetrating the secrets of other troublesome witches. The experienced ngombo (shaman) encouraged those he felt were possessed by the right spirit, to become his apprentices. Those he perceived as simply mentally unbalanced were sent home. Often the apprentice spent a year or more under the master's tutelage, learning the secrets of divining, or witch hunting.

Most extended families were pleased when one of their number seemed to have received the necessary spirit presence to qualify as a shaman. This person would be a good source of income for the clan and ought to be able to protect his or her own people well. Some clansmen were nervous and held mixed feelings when one of their own became an apprentice to the ngombo shaman. The most frightening factor was the rumored tradition that required the apprentice to offer his master the life of a blood relative to provide the occult powers needed to become a credible witch hunter.

Titi was apprehensive as she approached the gathering under the big sanda tree. The painted faces of the ngombo shaman and his apprentices, their strange language, and the odd, bent over stance, unnerved her. Every minute gesture was both mysterious and impressive.

Old Disu, the ngombo diviner, surveyed the entire audience person by person. Tension was greatest in the circle of the direct relatives of the small boy who had been victimized.

Even though Titi had no reason to be afraid, the stare of the ngombo gripped her when he focused on her with his phenomenally powerful eyes.

"I mustn't blink, or turn away, but his eyes seem to be looking right through me. I know that I can't possibly be a suspect. Why does he keep looking directly at me with those cold menacing eyes?" she wondered.

Titi maintained her stare until the shaman shifted his focus to another. She felt relieved, but the fear of the ngombo shaman was forever burned into her young mind. The terror of that encounter will long outlive the excitement of watching others squirm under his spell. All this happened before the shaman had even been formally presented.

"We have called the ngombo shaman, Mfumu Disu (Chief Eye), because we must discover who ate the boy Dimba Diambu whose body we put to rest in the cemetery yesterday. We cannot rest at peace when someone is eating our clan!"

Following these few words of introduction, the old clan chief proceeded to kneel on one knee before the invited shaman who was sitting in a ceremonial chief's chair.

After clapping his hands three times, and waiting for a three clap response from the ngombo shaman, the old clan chief made his formal request.

"Our vumu (branch of a clan) is being eaten for no reason at all. They are dying before their time. You are in touch with our ancestors. You understand the darkness. Expose the ndoki witch in our midst! We are tormented!" declared the old chief.

After this formal request, a snow-white chicken and a jet-black rooster were presented to the shaman. The gathering clapped gently, indicating a consensus that his services were needed.

The ngombo shaman was not called to investigate every death. He was called when there was a feeling that some renegade witch was killing at random, menacing a whole group of people. It was always costly to call in the expert. He usually left with a half dozen goats, and many prized chickens. Old clan tensions would be heightened to the boiling point. Hatred might be nourished to the point of physical combat.

Three drummers working with the ngombo arrived during the preliminary formalities. Moving into the large open center space reserved for them, they began their rhythmic and somewhat hypnotic beat.

One drum was six feet long, and about twelve inches in diameter. A leather strap around the drummer's waist held the drumhead between his legs just above his knees. The way the end of the drum was carved and held made it an unmistakable phallic symbol. The tight drumhead resounded with a resonance that enabled the full length of the drum to resonate with sound.

Shorter, and much larger, the base drum had a deep mellow sound. A half-pound blob of pitch in the middle of the drumhead helped produce the desired rumble. The third drum was a unique shape, larger in the middle than at either end. A network of tight bands going from top to bottom made an attractive design. This particular drum would only be employed when the shaman was endeavoring to address the deceased ancestors.

Rising to his feet in a most dignified manner, the shaman nodded first to the chief, and then to his drummers, who changed their rhythm. All eyes were on him as he began to sing quietly and do a kind of shuffle in front of the inner circle of close relatives seated according to strict protocol. Anyone under the stare of the skilled ngombo's penetrating eyes will never forget the experience. Some of the clansmen trembled visibly when caught in his gaze. After a tense half hour, both the rhythm of the drums, and the dance of the old ngombo, began to approach the level of frenzy. At that stage, the two younger apprentices joined the dance while singing songs in the strange, secret, language of their profession.

At a strategic moment, the shaman's wife appeared with a large clay cooking pot covered with a banana leaf, secured by a vine tied just under the rim. Following his wife, the shaman left the gathering after announcing that he needed to consult the elders from the land of the dead. The drums, the clapping and dancing were to be continued vigorously while the diviner was eating and talking with the ancestors in the sacred burying ground over on the hillside.

Just before going off to the sacred cemetery, the shaman led the people in the singing of a traditional song known by everyone. They were asked to sing it repeatedly, until he returned. In their song, the people appealed to their deceased elders to reveal their wisdom to the shaman.

It was dusk when the shaman returned with an empty pot, and a knowing smile on his face. The large pot of food had been eaten. There were many finger marks evident in the orange colored moamba that stuck to the sides of the large pot. Obviously, the shaman had met with the ancestors from the land of the living dead.

The crowd erupted with resounding shouts of joy because the venerated ancestors had met with their shaman just as they had been pleading. The guilty killer witch would be exposed!

The two young women apprentices danced excitedly, almost in a state of frenzy. Their necklace beads flipped wildly as they integrated with the rhythm. Within this charged atmosphere, the shaman ceremoniously opened his bag of sacred objects, tossing them dramatically on a raffia mat. He began a concentrated study of his weird collection of bones and animal parts, bird skulls, eagle talons, viper fangs, dried cat's eyes and noses, rodents, and monkeys' skulls.

Small sacks with protruding feathers, old coins, and giant seeds from the deep forest were all part of the mysterious mix. An impressively large jungle snail shell completed the inventory of tools considered to be useful for the interpretation of the supernatural world.

The drums throbbed hypnotically as the old shaman rejoined the dance. Throwing his arms in the air periodically, his clanging milunga (iron and copper wrist bands) introduced a new tension in the charged atmosphere.

Titi and many others trembled, when quite unexpectedly, the shaman screamed, provoking all other sound and motion to stop.

The relatively tiny voice of a handheld wooden drum pierced the pregnant silence in an eerie, haunting manner. The shaman carefully opened a small gazelle skin bag revealing a rather large seed from the forest. Chosen from among the many unusual items on the mat, the giant seed was his choice for this trial.

With a flourish the old shaman showed everyone that the seed was suspended on a fine string that passed right through it. Whenever he held the string vertically, the seed fell freely to the hand below.

Three frightened people were called forward as prime suspects. They had been selected through his supernatural observations.

One at a time, these very nervous people were called to kneel before the shaman who then held out his seed on the string allowing it to drop to the hand held below.

Holding the string vertically, the seed fell freely as everyone expected. Three times the seed test was performed; and three times it dropped freely either from left hand to right or vise versa. The suspect was dismissed. The test was performed before the second trembling subject with the same expected result.

Titi found herself holding her breath when the test was given to the third suspect, a woman in her early sixties.

"My heart is pounding so hard I'm afraid that everyone will notice me," Titi felt as though she was watching a snake, head in the air, about to strike a trembling field mouse.

The whole audience let out a gasp when the seed falls to the middle of the string and will not budge any further, even when the shaman rattled his bracelets as he shook the seed to make it fall. No matter what he did, the seed slid to the middle and stuck there.

To remove all doubt, a released person was called back. Under the same apparent circumstances the seed fell easily. Turning again to the woman in question to repeat the test, the seed appeared to be stuck in the middle of the string and could not slide either way. There was no doubt; the killer ndoki witch had been uncovered!

The triumphant shaman accused with precision. "You ate the head of the boy called Dimba! You sold his heart at the ndoki market, which meets right under this tree! He is not the only child you have " eaten" over the years."

The delighted crowd began to hiss at the guilty woman.

Trembling, the accused spoke. "In my heart I am not a ndoki witch. I saw the proof that the shaman gave; the seed would not fall. I know he talked with our ancestors. I must be guilty, but I do not feel guilty in my heart." She began to weep bitterly. "If I ate him, my mind knows nothing about it."

Titi clung to her mother while the relatives of the accused witch bound her hand and foot. It seemed that everyone, young and old, was straining for a chance to kick or strike the sobbing woman. Titi followed her mother's example and kicked the 'witch' like all the others. Many of the most violent were still wearing the white mourning headbands from the funeral. A strong young man pulled off his belt to whip the accused with the buckle end, until her face was covered with blood. Spoken curses, hatred and rejection hurt the woman even more than all the physical abuse.

The 'ndoki witch' was hardly even conscious when she was levied a fine of three goats and a pig, to be paid to the family of the deceased victim.

"She must take the vow or be killed," the agitated shaman shouted.

The chief called for silence.

In a barely audible whisper, the pathetic figure repeated the vow as required.

"I am a ndoki witch and, if I ever try to eat (kill) again, may I myself be the first to die! I swear, before you and all the ancestors; I vow I will die before I harm anyone."

Titi was both angry and confused as they walked home in the darkness.

"No one called the ngombo when my little brothers died inside you, declared Titi. "How do we know that Nkaka ate them? How do we know that the witch we just kicked is not the one who killed my brothers? After all she is in our blood line."

"You may be right," her mother answered after a long hesitation. "The elders taught us that a cunning ndoki witch can "wear" someone else's body while traveling at night to commit crimes. Sometimes this happens, but only a skilled ngombo could really know for sure. All I know is that I saw my own mother laughing, taunting, and making threats about revenge for the unpaid bride price. That is what I saw, child."

"Kindoki (witchcraft) is like a trap. It fans the fires of hate and deception, and stimulates the very worst that humans can think or do. The ngombo shaman is a vital part of that network of lies and deception that captures our minds. When they do what we want, we get vengeance on our enemy. When they destroy the life or reputation of someone you trust, or you, yourself, you see them as masters of deceit.

"If that woman came, wearing my mother's body, and saying what mother might say, I could easily have been deceived, and hate an innocent person."

Titi became silent and pensive. "I had no idea that a ndoki witch could wear someone else's body as a disguise. Is that the same idea as someone turning into a crocodile, or a wild pig, or an owl?"

"I suppose it must be the same. You went with your father when he caught the big wild pig in his pit trap. When that pig was running along the forest path, he had no idea that under the brown leaves ahead of him there was a deep pit with sharpened stakes in the bottom. He had no idea that he would fall and die, impaled on those stakes. The whole world of kindoki is a trap that captures you, body and mind. Once your heart is convinced that someone is out to harm you, a mixture of hate and fear obsesses you. Your troubled heart can dominate you entirely, especially after darkness falls. Your terrifying dreams become reality, and sleeplessness exhausts you night after night."

Titi sighed; "I would love to believe that Nkaka is not guilty of destroying my baby brothers. Everything I have heard about her frightens me, but when we are together, we get along wonderfully well. I don't want my grandmother to be a killer ndoki witch!"

"Just imagine how I feel child. Your Nkaka is my mother just as I am yours!"

"Is the ngombo shaman ever wrong?" Titi inquired with sad sincerity.

"Oh Titi, that is the problem. Only an ndoki can know the secrets of occult power. Remember, the ngombo is always an ndoki witch who has been hired to betray his fellows! Normally, folk call in an ngombo who is not from their bloodline, so they can be safe from his witchcraft. You can never really trust someone who is an ndoki."

"He made me hate the person he found guilty," Titi replied thoughtfully. "We both kicked that woman with hatred when we had our turn. I did not really know her, even though you say she is a distant relative."

"I have heard the elders say that every ngombo is a master of deception. As far as we could see, the seed test was fair, but we could have been deceived too. The ngombo shaman is not a person we like. We want the benefit of his or her power to expose the killer witches in our midst. They often display miracles to convince everyone of their power and authority. Sometimes I have had my doubts. Would you trust a wild civet cat from the forest to protect our chickens?"

Titi's hearty laugh was her response.

"What about the trial we just watched? That guilty old woman is one of our distant relatives. She submitted to the ngombo shaman's judgment, but she claimed that she had no knowledge of her action. She seemed to say that in her heart she had never tried to kill the victim."

"What else could she say?" Pemba reasoned. "How could she deny the powerful evidence of her guilt? Who would have believed her? If she did not admit to guilt, and make that vow, she would face some form of execution. You would hear that she died of poison in her food put there by people who feared and hated her. When accused by a renowned ngombo shaman, it is better to admit guilt, even if you feel innocent. You can never prove your innocence! Who would that crowd have believed?"

"Everyone believed the ngombo just as we did," Titi concluded.

"I heard the elders say that it was different before the Portuguese took over with their laws. That distant aunt of ours would have been executed, or sold as a slave to a far off tribe where she could not practice her witchcraft as an outsider."

"When my babies died, your father confronted my clan. Our bloodline follows the women only. Your grandmother, your mother, you, and your children are all of the same blood. Your father is an outsider, so he can try to protect you. Our bloodline cannot touch him."

"Thank you for teaching me so much today, mother," Titi said thoughtfully.

"Our elders always say that a child should be taught on the way to market. They felt that children should be taught what they need to know before problems arise. I will always be trying to teach you."

Titi remained silent for a while as they walked home in the darkness. *"If the curse our old aunt placed on herself has power, then she can't harm any more people in our clan,"* Titi reasoned.

"We would actually feel better if she died, wouldn't we, mother?"

Her mother gave no reply, but her silence was in fact an agreement.

"I just wish there were some way we could be free from the constant threat and dread of ndoki witches," Pemba said with a sigh as they reached their little house.

Titi pulled her mat a bit closer to her mother as they settled down to sleep in the comfort of their cooking hut. Her mother stirred up the sleeping embers in the fire, and put a small piece of wood on top so its flame would light their room while they were falling asleep.

Titi's mind was still racing, as she re-examined everything that had just happened.

"The eyes of that ngombo shaman seemed cold and ruthless. I felt his frightening power when he looked at me. He didn't blink, or look away, even for a moment. I felt as though he was looking right inside me. There were lots of finger marks inside that big pot. He and his wife could not have eaten the food themselves. I'm sure he really met with our bakulu (ancestors) in the sacred forest. Certainly our ancestors would know exactly who the killer witch was, because they see everything."

"Child, I think we will be free from attack from ndoki witches for a while now," Pemba sighed. "Perhaps my mother is innocent after all. No one is ever sure about these things."

Both fell asleep in their little cooking hut, while the glow of the fire gave out its comforting light.

They had been sleeping soundly but the crowing of the rooster on the roof of their hut awakened them with a start. The basin of supper dishes sat on one side of the door and the basket of water gourds on the other. The rooster was still strutting on the roof as Titi put the basin of dishes on her head and followed in step with her mother who had fastened on her big pack basket containing three very large water gourds.

As soon as Titi and her mother had washed their faces, arms and legs, they begin their routine tasks. Titi washed the dishes in the river, while her mother went to the spring to get the cooking and drinking water for the day. The drinking water "boiled" up from an underground source that formed one of the many feeders of the river.

By the time her mother came back with her heavy load of water, Titi had the dishes washed. She had been busy scouring the pots, first with sand, and finally with the special "sand leaf" which grew at the waters edge. The long pointed leaf had tough little hairs all over it, so that its surface felt like a cat's tongue, while its edge could cut like a knife.

Firewood found near the spring, filled her mother's pack basket, leaving it up to Titi to climb up on a fallen log so she could position two large gourds so her mother could carry them. She placed one on top of the wood, and the other on her mother's head. The third gourd was carefully placed in the large basin of dishes and cooking pots that Titi would carry. Without her mother's help, she could not have placed the loaded basin on her own little head. Together they climbed back up to the village, greeting their friends as they went.

"Mother, everyone I met at the water was talking about the trial! I heard one woman tell another that she was sure the condemned woman will soon die because of the thrashing she had yesterday."

"It will serve her right if she does. People will be relieved to see her dead!"

Titi was very conscious of the hatred expressed in her mother's voice. The ill will in her heart cast a somber shadow over Pemba's face.

Back in their cooking hut, they prepared breakfast. It always surprised Titi that she could find some live coals in the ashes of a fire that had been extinguished for hours. It didn't seem to require many puffs, until a little flame appeared. From a new flame to a hot fire was a matter of a few minutes. Titi boiled their coffee. Because they grew their own coffee that was one thing they always had on hand. There was plenty of fufu (cooked manioc flour) from the night before. Making the coffee, and roasting the peanuts was all Titi needed to do before calling her dad. He often ate his breakfast sitting just outside the cooking hut in the comfortable, hide-covered folding chair he had made.

Perhaps there may be a new baby

Titi was pleased when her father joined them inside by the fire. Pulling a small bag of sugar from his pocket, Zoao spoke with a grin.

"I've been saving this sugar for a special day. Now that the ndoki witch has been exposed, and forced to curse herself in public, I hope we will be left alone. She could well be the one who 'ate' our babies. If she doesn't die from the thrashing she got, she'll be poisoned, is my guess. Let's put some sugar in our coffee to celebrate!"

"She must be the one who sent the owl I killed. I'm almost sure of it! I'm glad we have the nkisi (protective charm) buried under our cooking fire. I paid plenty for it in Luanda. It is not safe to live in these parts without protection form witchcraft. Now that the ndoki witch has been exposed, perhaps we can get a son who will live."

While Zoao was talking, Pemba mixed up a bit of pounded pepper paste to add flavor to the food. Titi noticed a little smile crossing her mother's face when her father spoke of wanting a son. She remembered vividly, the vow her father had taken after they lost the second baby.

"I will put no more seed in your belly until the killer ndoki in your family has been stopped!" Zoao had said with determination.

It had been a full year since her mother had been invited in to sleep with her father.

"Perhaps I will get a little brother or sister yet," Titi mused with a smile.

When she returned from playing at the river, Titi found her mother is in a very pleasant mood.

"Your father caught us a large cat fish and I am making a mwamba (palm fruit gravy) to go with it. You arrived just in time to make the peanut butter I need to put in the gravy. I have cooked saka saka greens from the fresh new leaves that grew immediately after the first rainfall. They are as tender as raindrops. We are all going to eat well this evening!"

After Zoao had eaten all he wanted of the delicious meal, he exploded with a spectacular burp, expressing his appreciation. Everyone was in a happy mood in total contrast with the combinations of fear, surprise, and deep resentment that had enveloped them for so long.

Titi was putting the dishes and pots in the basin ready to be carried to the water, when her mother came by. "I will be sleeping with your father tonight," Pemba whispered with a smile that showed even in the dim light of the fire.

"I'm not afraid to be alone now," Titi answered quietly. "I'm so happy that father feels released from his vow."

Although she slept a bit fitfully, being alone for the first time in a year, her sleep was sweet.

Their own little rooster was the very first voice to greet the night at the regular rooster roll call around two in the morning. It was the beating of his wings, predicting his shrill crow that briefly awakened Titi. The rapid reply of twenty or more birds crowing from every direction offered a sense of security within the village that encouraged sleep.

A distant village drum announces a death

Before she was actually back into a sound sleep the sound of a chief's talking drum caught her attention.

"That drum is from the far side of the valley. The ndoki witch is dead! We will never know just how she died but she is dead and that is what counts. Whether she died as a result of the thrashing, or because of poison in her food doesn't matter now," Titi reasoned.

Titi found herself singing part of a folk song that expressed her feelings.

"She is dead she is dead,
the ndoki witch is dead.
Put her in the grave with a pot on her head
because the ndoki witch is dead".

Only when her feathered friend screeched his morning wake up call at five o'clock did Titi arouse from her untroubled sleep.

Trotting off with the basin of dirty dishes and pots perched on her head, Titi carried a medium sized water gourd in her little pack basket. She soon joined with other little girls on the early morning river run. Before she has finished washing the dishes and pots, her mother arrived with the large water gourds.

It was good to see a new contentment in her face. She had felt helpless to do anything that could convince her husband to try to have another child. It was always the wife's family that snuffed out the life of babies through nocturnal exploits of secretive ndoki witches. The early morning drum announcement of death would have comforted her mother's entire extended family. The message of the drums also confirmed Zoao's decision to be freed from his vow.

All clan members attended the wakes and funerals of their blood relatives.

"I guess everyone will be content at this wake. No one will be crying over the death of that ndoki witch, will they, mother?" asked Titi.

"Her children and husband may be very sad. Not only is their loved one dead, but also a blanket of shame will have fallen on many. She was a distant of aunt in my mother's bloodline and I hardly knew her. We have been losing our babies before they were even born, so we are glad to know that one secret killer can harm us no more. It is possible that others will not feel the way we do."

The dead witch's wake

"She looks so meek and frail" Titi whispered when she saw the shrouded body that exposed only the somber face. Her words at her trial returned to haunt her memory. For a fleeting moment, Titi felt sad, and wondered if there could have been a mistake.

A quiet voice filled with hatred caught Titi's attention.

"You, with your innocent looking face, you deceived us! You ate my only brother! You did it and now you have been caught. You thought you could go right on killing! Now you know!"

On looking more closely, Titi recognized the speaker as being a member of her mother's farming team. Caught up in a sea of quiet articulate resentment, Titi soon added her little voice. Raising her arms Titi poured out her feelings.

"You ate my little brothers before they ever took a breath of air. You terrified my mother. Curses on you! May you find no rest and be rejected in the land of the living dead!"

Another bitter person took up the refrain quietly. "If you had been innocent, you would not have died so quickly! The ancestors knew you all the time, but you will never see them!"

"You were a good wife all through the years. We raised four children together. You never left my side. We slept in the big bed together. How could you leave to do ndoki witchcraft without my knowing? Whenever I called you in the night, you always answered. You never left your body! I know you are innocent and the ancestors will know it too."

The elderly husband of the deceased wept silently, his lined face a wistful picture of sorrow.

The two older boys were far away in a guerrilla army somewhere and could not even be informed of their mother's death.

A teenage granddaughter expressed her grief. "They killed you for nothing, for nothing. They killed you for lies. You have been a good grandmother. You taught us, you loved us, and you protected us. Who will protect us now?" The protest dissolved into tears and uncontrolled sobbing.

All night long Titi heard conflicting sentiments. Those who were truly mourning were given the freedom to express their grief. That was their right. Most of the negative remarks were reserved for whispered murmuring among the women packed close together on sleeping mats.

By nine the next morning Titi was relieved to hear that everything was ready for the burial. She watched as the men lifted the body and placed it in the coffin. Suddenly, a howl of frantic protest pierced the air from the genuine mourners.

The chief of their clan proceeded to place a large clay pot of hot red peppers over the dead woman's head, just before nailing on the coffin cover. The faithful husband, her daughters and granddaughters wept bitterly when they saw the nganga shaman supervising this final act of indignity and total rejection.

"Ndungu peppers blind the eyes of her ghost; confuse her thoughts! Burn out any desire to travel or torment the living!" He chanted as the lid was nailed in place. Some folk present clapped their hands in applause.

Almost immediately, the youthful pallbearers began to move toward the special isolated burying place. Her husband and daughters, together with other truly sad mourners hoped for a burial without further incident. They knew that the burial of a convicted ndoki witch might be complicated.

The procession began in an orderly fashion with family members and villagers in the appropriate order according to the rather detailed traditional protocol. Just as the pallbearers were passing the last house in the village, and turning down the path to the cemetery, everything changed. Suddenly the pallbearers shouted like maniacs startling everyone. It seemed as though some unseen force was pushing them in the opposite direction.

Titi's eyes grew large with fear when she realized that the pallbearers and coffin were zigzagging toward her, apparently out of control. She and her mother jumped back just in time to let them pass.

"Why is the vumbi (corpse) pulling them back?" Titi asked with a pale face.

"Perhaps the woman is innocent," someone shouted, answering her question.

"The corpse is looking for the ndoki witch who killed her," shouted another.

In the end it took over an hour to reach the cemetery with the team of pallbearers bathed in sweat. It was frightening to watch the vumbi (corpse) pulling the young men this way and that.

"The elders were wise when they put a pepper pot on her head or we would have been troubled constantly by her ghost," Pemba reminded Titi. "Killer witches are not allowed to go to the afterlife in the ancestors' village for the living dead. She is condemned to be a ghost forever. She is not acceptable for either the living or the dead. Only the pepper and the powers of the shaman can keep ghosts of her kind from troubling us."

Titi and her mother did not stay for the gathering that followed the funeral. Pemba knew that some would be celebrating this death with excessive drinking and behavior that would not be good for young eyes.

Easing into greater responsibility

February, or 'the second moon' as it was called, was everyone's favorite month. A whole variety of delicious foods became available. Nguba za maza (boiled peanuts) were a very special treat. The secret was to pull peanuts that are fully-grown, but not totally mature. They were simply washed and boiled in salted water.

"Mother, I'm sure that the peanuts on the higher ground, must be ready by now. Please may I pull some to see? I will only pull a small basket full if they are ready."

Off she ran to the very first patch of peanuts they had planted. To her delight, they were perfect. Carefully she selected the most mature looking plants and soon had enough for the evening meal.

"I love pulling these plump peanuts off the roots. I think that these very peanuts are ones I planted," Titi talked freely to herself as she had often heard her mother doing. "I will run down to the water and wash all the mud off so that all we will need to do is boil them when I get home."

"Our peanuts are beautiful this year. Look at these!" Titi shouted, holding up her little pack basket which was almost filled with plump bright peanuts. "The rains came just at the right time for us. Remember, we got them planted just four days before the first rains of the season?"

"Catching that first rain always seems to make a big difference in the early peanuts. It was worth all our work, wasn't it, Titi?"

Zoao sprawled out in his chair near the door of the cooking hut. Titi and her mother sat on their low benches just inside. Their family often ate together this way.

"Papa, I think we have some of your favorite foods tonight."

Titi spoke with enthusiasm as she heaped her father's plate with fufu, sweet potatoes, saka saka greens, and caterpillars in palm fruit gravy. She placed a little pot of pounded fresh peppers by his side so he could spice up the meal as much as he wished. When the main meal was over, each plate was refilled with a mountain of warm "water peanuts" boiled in their shells.

Then, with obvious delight, Titi brought a surprise for her father.

"This is for you. I found them in the very top of a tree."

She presented him with the first nsafu fruits of the season carefully roasted in the ashes under the cooking fire.

"Mother let me climb the tree so we could surprise you."

Zoao sighed with deep satisfaction. "You two must have some too, I'm to full to eat them all."

A smug little smile lit up Titi's face when her mother told her she would be sleeping with her father again.

"I think our good food persuades him to invite you to sleep with him," Titi whispered with a giggle. "Make us a baby, please."

The abundant rains that produced good crops made the weeds grow well too. Most of the women and girls worked hard in the fields every day. No one minded the hard work when they were eating well.

Pemba and Titi were all smiles as they carried home a good feed of fresh corn for their evening meal, the first of the season. Harvest time pays back for all the hard work.

Whenever they were working, Titi was constantly asking her mother questions. That was the only kind of school available, especially since the wars for independence began.

"Is it true that some people can make marks on paper that are just the same as talk? How do they do that?" asked Titi.

"I really don't know how they do it. I have often wished that I knew. Ask your grandmother. She knows more about reading and writing than I do."

After a few weeks passed, Titi was asked to take a piece of antelope to her grandmother. Zoao caught an antelope in a snare and was not obliged to share it with other hunters as he did when they hunted in a team. He felt it was wise to keep as good relations with the old lady as he could, since no one knew for sure the degree of her ndoki witch activity.

An important question

"Nkaka, how do people put words on paper?" asked Titi.

"Let me show you something," the old lady replied as she disappeared behind her little mat wall. "Your grandfather, who died before you were born, knew how to read and write letters."

Displaying a little package of faded envelopes, she spoke proudly. "These are the letters he sent me from Luanda. I had to go to another village to find a person who could read them to me. It was wonderful to have him talk to me from the paper! I think you are smart enough to go to school and learn for yourself. You are old enough now. I hear that they have a good teacher in Lufu. I will talk with your mother."

"I would love to be able to read and write, and know how to use money like some of the girls from the city that I have heard about but I'm afraid I would be frightened to be so far from home," Titi replied wistfully.

After the peanuts had been harvested, there were lots of weeds trying to crowd out their precious manioc plants. They had been planted along with the peanuts because they did something to the soil to make the manioc grow better. Working at her mother's side Titi was a good little helper.

When they stopped for a little rest, Titi had a big question to ask her mother.

"Do you think I could learn to read and write? Nkaka showed me the letters my grandfather sent her from Luanda many years ago. She said that the letters actually carried his talk to her."

Pemba hesitated a long time before she answered. "I will talk to your father about this. It is too big a decision to make alone in these troubled times."

After supper Titi listened intently when her mother began to discuss the question of school with her father.

"I guess our little girl is growing up; she asked me about going to school today."

For some reason, Zoao was not surprised at the question and replied with little hesitation.

"It would be a good thing for her to learn what they teach in school. You have already taught her most things a girl needs to learn from her mother. In these days a girl who can read and write can marry a more capable husband. You have taught her so well that she knows more about women's work than many older girls."

"She makes better sleeping mats than I can," Pemba replied with a smile of satisfaction. "How I would miss her, and all the work she does to help me, but I can't keep her home just because I have no other children to bring me joy."

Zoao smiled, "Perhaps we will have a baby this year."

These were happy moments partly because they seldom shared their thoughts and hopes with one another. Normally, men talked with men and women talked with women. Marriage was usually more of an honoured contract than a loving relationship.

After Titi and her mother were on their mats ready for sleep, Pemba told her little daughter about the conclusion she and her father had reached.

"We think it would be good for you to begin school when we come to the ninth moon. (September) Your aunt, Mama Nkenda, in Lufu, has asked me several times to let you stay with her so you could go to school. She has noticed how bright and helpful you are. What do you think about going to Lufu so you can learn in school?"

"I would love to go to school but I am very happy here at home with you and papa. You are a wonderful mother. You teach me everything and answer all my questions. I have noticed that most other mothers don't have the patience to teach or answer questions the way you do. You have taught me some things that only a few of the older girls seem to know. You trust me and let me try things. I like working at your side, mother. If I should go to Lufu, I would miss you very much."

"Child, you can't imagine how much I will miss you," Pemba said with a deep sigh.

"I want you to have a happy life with a good husband and many children," she said with a warm smile. "You could marry an educated husband if you do well in school. You might marry a nurse or a schoolteacher. You will be the first girl in our clan to learn to read and write. Your children and grand children will be proud of you, and so will your parents. We will make plans for you to go."

"This is the best peanut crop in years," Pemba remarked to Titi as they sat beside a high stack of pulled peanut plants, removing the peanuts from the roots.

"That light rain yesterday really made the peanuts easy to pull out without leaving any behind in the soil. We will be able to send a big sack of peanuts with you when you go to my sister in Lufu. The soil there is not as rich as ours. This is one way we can help her feed you enough to help you grow."

"Mother, I will miss your good food as well as you," Titi replied thoughtfully.

After harvesting the peanuts and corn, manioc was planted in the few places where it had not been planted earlier. It was good to allow the pieces of manioc stock to make strong roots during the rains so they would stay alive during the long dry season.

"The pieces of manioc stock cut for planting should reach from your fingers to your elbow. Plant the cuttings so the head is inclined toward the rising sun so they will grow well. True or not, that is what everyone believes. The peanut crop leaves something in the soil that seems to give the casava or manioc a good start. To get the full benefit, the manioc needs to be planted immediately after the peanut harvest if it was not planted at the same time. With you to help me, our work becomes easy." Pemba reminded her.

"Mother, is putting words on paper by making marks, white man's witchcraft?" asked Titi. "I heard old mama Lina say that down at the river. They were talking about your sending me to school."

"Your grandfather told me that writing is like making little pictures that your friend understands. He said that it took lots of practice to learn to make the pictures well enough for others to read. He told me that it took plenty of work and no witchcraft at all, unless you want to call cleverness witchcraft. Sometimes, the women we farm with call you fi ndoki (little witch) because you know how to do so many things. That is their way of calling you clever."

"If I seem clever, it is because my clever mother is always helping me learn." Titi replied with a warm smile.

"How long will it take us to harvest our mbika (edible squash seeds)?" Titi asked her mother as her nimble fingers extracted the seeds from another dry squash.

"Our yield is good, and I think that we may be able to fill two big sacks. It will take us another couple of good day's work, I think."

The annual fish kill

"Will we finish in time to go on the fish kill?" Titi asked anxiously. "I think that I am tall enough to go with you this year."

"You have been growing as fast as a corn stalk. You are right. We will go together. I'm sure we will finish this work in time to get prepared for the trip. We both want to go, and our fingers know it too."

As soon as they returned from the field, Pemba lifted down her big fishing basket from its hook under the peak of the little cooking shack. It was black from the smoke of hundreds of cooking fires.

"The smoke keeps the bugs from eating the reeds in my basket. I have had the same one now since before you were born."

"How will I get a basket? I have never had one yet," A worried frown crossed Titi's face.

"Don't worry child. We have just enough time to make you a new one before we go. I will show you how to do it and you will know for the rest of your life," Pemba answered reassuringly.

"Mother, with all the things you are teaching me, you are turning me into an ndoki witch in the eyes of others."

"It is sad, but quite often, jealous lazy people call clever ambitious people killer witches. In their thinking, the only explanation for someone's success is witchcraft. According to our elders, people give permission for a certain kind of shaman to take the lives of family members, in exchange for the power to succeed in some way. By the same tradition, the suspect is successful in his or her exploits because he has the benefit of the spirit power of the sacrificed person's life. Success raises suspicion in some minds."

"People are sure that your grandmother is an ndoki witch because she has always been very successful in her farming. It is difficult for a lazy person to imagine that my old mother works so hard. Sometimes I think people have thought your grandmother uses witchcraft because she fishes and farms better than most. She carefully follows everything her elders taught her. She is more clever than most men, and some people resent it."

"She catches fish when no one else can," Titi says in support of her mother's explanation.

As soon as their fieldwork was finished, Pemba took Titi down to the swamp so they could make her first fishing basket.

"Mother, I have never been here before, even though it is not far from home."

"This place is called the Crocodile Swamp. In my youth there were crocodiles here. The hunters kill them off periodically. In my mind I know that a crocodile could slip up here from the river. It is still not a place to come alone."

Titi's eyes were like saucers. "Isn't this the place where father shoots the big land lizards?"

Pemba nodded as they moved into a thicket of fine thin reeds.

"These reeds are perfect for making fishing baskets. They are hard to cut, that is why we sharpened our machetes well on the way down. See those stubs. Other women have been here too. The fish kill will take place at the time of the full moon, and that is just two days away."

"Mother, aren't those reeds over there the ones we use to make soft mats?"

"You are right, Titi, but, we get taller reeds from another area when we are making those kind of mats."

It only took an hour to gather all the thin reeds they needed. On the way to the village, they stopped by a fallen log to make the basket. Working in the forest, all the unwanted bark and debris was left in the wilderness to return to the earth.

"There is a fine, smooth sharpening stone over there by the path. We need the tips of our machetes very sharp to finish our work."

With the tips of their machetes well sharpened, they set to work scraping off the bark before splitting their reeds. After they had split all their reeds, Pemba showed Titi just how to weave them into a large mat.

"After we have finished binding the edges of this stiff mat, we will fold it up loosely. Finally, we will sew up the ends with the very fine reeds that have been split into four parts"

They soon produced a large basket with a big open mouth. Before leaving, they closed the mouth of the basket with a reed to make it easier to carry.

"My child, what I just showed you and what you helped make is exactly the same design that my mother taught me. I will show you just how to use it when the day arrives."

"Mother, I heard some of the women talking about needing a blessing to catch fish. Do we need a blessing of some kind?"

"You heard correctly, my child. Tonight we will go to the house of Mama Ndona to seek her blessing. She is a shaman who specializes in everything that has any connection with water. Some people call her Nganga Nsimbi (shaman of the water spirits). She knows how to deal with those spirits. The special place where we will fish is the place my mother showed me years ago. No one else has ever come there during the kill. We will be in a thick, forested area where the stream makes a swirl around a huge bank of rock. Certainly, the bisimbi spirits live in the whirling pool. We will need their help and blessing."

"What will Mama Ndona do?"

"She will give us each a nkisi, (sacred magical object) and fasten it on our skirts. As long as we show respect to the bisimbi, they will help and protect us. After all, they can heal all sorts of diseases connected with the water. Eye infections, skin sores, boils, stiff joints, even swollen legs may all be healed by these unusual spirits. Certainly, they must have power over fish."

"Did you ever catch sight of the bisimbi, mother?"

"Only once in my life, I think that I saw one of the mysterious little water people with its long hair. It was dusk and the harder I looked the darker it became, so I was never sure."

" Mother, is it true that the bisimbi make twin babies in a pregnant woman?"

"That is what we have always been told. That is why little twins are taken to the Mama Ndona for blessing as soon as they are born. She puts the white dots on the mother's face and matching dots on the baby. In the ceremony, she gives her blessing.

"Whenever a twin dies, she must be called at once to stop the dead twin from returning for the living one to take him to the bisimbi hideout where the spirits of twins stay. The spirits of dead twins are always seeking to be born again in another set of twins."

"Now I understand the importance of our visit to Mama Ndona."

The water spirit shaman, Mama Ndona

A little stream was visible from Mama Ndona's tidy house. When they arrived, she was sitting under her Sanda tree weaving a mat. Somewhat older than Pemba, she wore two big white dots, one on each cheek. There was no need to explain their quest. Most of the local women came to her before they went on the fish kill. She accepted the required white chicken graciously and shut it up in her special enclosure that seemed to be full of white chickens. Invoking a blessing, she put a white dot of paint in the middle of each forehead.

"Don't remove the mark until after the fish kill. If one of you falls in the water, and the paint is washed away, quickly transfer some of the other's paint with your wet finger to the one who has lost it."

From inside her house, Mama Ndona brought two little cloth sacks.

"Each of you should tie this little sack to a corner of your skirt that will be in the water while you work. You will kill many fish!"

As they left the impressive little compound, Pemba explained why Mama Ndona was so powerful.

"She is a twin herself, and the daughter of a noted bisimbi shaman who died when I was your age. Believe me she has power!"

Titi felt safe, blessed, happy, and excited, as she lay on her mat waiting for sleep.

"Tomorrow we are leaving at the second rooster call. About noon we should reach the village that grows the poison beans. We will gather and carry baskets of those beans to the banks of the Luadi River. We will need to help cut the bean pods and stack them on the bank. All of our beans will be stacked in one giant pile. We will sleep with all the other people beside the waterfall. Moonlight will light our way to our special spot when we leave there at the first rooster call. At that time, strong men will push the huge pile of beans into the river. The Luadi will get much narrower as we travel up stream."

The detailed explanation of procedure brought Titi to a new state of excitement.

"How long will it take for the first stunned fish to arrive at our special fishing spot?"

"Titi, that is a good thing about our spot; the first fish will arrive with the daylight. We will rest a while after we arrive at our fishing spot because we will need to wait for the morning light."

Poison beans.

Picking and transporting the poison beans was hard work. Then came the difficult task of cutting up the beans with machetes so the juices would be easily released in the water. Titi did as much work as some of the grown women. Pemba was delighted to overhear two women she hardly knew talking about Titi.

"That child is doing more work than some of the grown women from our village. Some women bring their daughters along so they can grab more fish. Not that Titi, she is certainly earning her right to a share of the kill".

Before they went to sleep, Mama Ndona, the water spirit shaman, performed a ceremony by the waterfall. Along with palm nuts, she threw in a hand full of poison beans to authorize the fish kill.

All the women were exhausted and fell into a deep sleep as soon as they had eaten their prepared lunches of kwanga (manioc bread) and mbika (squash seed loaf). Titi snuggled close to her mother.

The moon was bright overhead when the rooster gave his expected signal. In no time, all the women were rushing down the trails on both sides of the Luadi River to find a good spot.

Titi and her mother were off like antelopes. Pemba knew exactly where she was going but she wanted to slip into their secret spot unseen.

"When we come to three large nkamba trees growing very close to each other with the roots of the middle one obstructing our path a bit, we will have reached the spot. If there is anyone near us, we will walk past and return when we are sure we're not seen."

Titi felt excitement rising in her heart. "How do we find our way when we leave the trail? This moonlight doesn't shine much in the deep forest."

"Child, I have been going there ever since I was your size. Once we push under the branches of the big trees, we will find a narrow trail cleared to the water's edge. The moment you see our spot, you will never forget it."

The secret place

They hurried along for about two hours with Pemba leading the way.

"Follow me right under this middle tree. You will need to push your basket ahead of you and crawl like a wild pig. We have never cut any branches because it would disclose our secret place."

"No one would ever suspect that there is a well-cut trail so near the main path," Titi observed as she scampered down the moonlit path to the water's edge.

"Your grandmother helped her mother clear this path when she was a girl. This is our part of the river, our own secret fishing place!" Pemba pointed out.

Looking down from the bank, Titi looked at their special pool located behind a huge rock face that jutted out into the river. The large rock face caused the water to flow up stream, before it could flow back down again.

"That pool at the edge is quite calm and just shallow enough for us to spot everything that enters it. There is a grassy spot near the pool, too, where we can rest. The first fish will not reach us until just after day break," Pemba explained.

Despite their excitement, fatigue quickly pulled them both back to sleep as they huddled together under the two cotton covers they had been wearing as part of their clothing. There were no roosters to call them in the morning but they were awakened with a start. A piercing scream sounding like the shriek of a terrified person thrust them violently into breath-holding consciousness.

"What is happening?" Titi shouted, as she wrapped both arms around her mother. "Is someone being killed right beside us?"

Catching her breath, Pemba explained the scream. "Somewhere, near us, a little screech owl has probably captured his breakfast. Look over there on the far bank"

In the predawn light they barely made out the shape of the little owl tearing apart the rodent he had captured.

"The elders say that little rodents like that squirrel are paralyzed with fear when they hear the screech. They don't move a muscle, and the little owl kills them easily."

"I know his scream paralyzed me. My heart is still pounding. Why have I never heard that kind of owl before?"

Pemba smiled as she explained, "These owls live in the deep forest far from villages. That is why we seldom hear them. Today, he was our wake-up rooster. Without him we might have slept until noon."

Dry branches for their fire were plentiful. Being very careful to cut some pieces of wood into very thin slivers, Titi had no trouble starting her fire with just one of the matches from her mother's precious little bottle. In just a few minutes she had set up three stones with their tin kettle on top. The pieces of wood, burning at one end, soon had the water boiling. They began sipping their sugarless coffee.

Pemba wandered casually toward their special pool, then shouted suddenly with excitement.

"Quickly! Toss me my basket. There is a big fish in the pool and he is stunned."

Opening her basket as she ran, Pemba slipped into the pool very quietly. Holding the basket with both hands, she slid it into the water and crept to one side of the pool. The cold water was up to her hips. Suddenly, she moved like lightning with a scooping motion under the water, then up and out.

"I've caught him, I've caught him!" she shouted as she headed for the bank. "He is a big one. Mama Ndona's blessing and charms have worked. We will have fish!"

Titi was delighted to see her mother's first catch. "That fish just paid for half of the chicken we gave Mama Ndona."

The water was cold, and Pemba was pleased to finish her cup of hot coffee. The joy of anticipation lit up their faces. They quickly ate their kwanga loaded with chunks of peanut butter so full of ndungu peppers that it was as hot as the coffee.

They were far too excited to waste a moment.

"Mother, let's get fishing. I can't wait!"

Down the banks they rushed to get a look at their pool. They spotted a number of smaller fish, shaking and trembling because of the effects of the poison beans.

To facilitate their work, Pemba cut two six foot saplings and sharpened the large ends. The rods were pushed into the bottom of the pool so as to support their pack baskets, one on each rod.

"When we catch fish, let's dump them into our pack baskets and go back for more," Pemba explained excitedly.

Shorter than her mother, Titi could not see the water around her quite as well. Her arms were shorter too, but within her line of vision, she became a skilled fisher.

"Mother, look at the fish I just caught!"

Titi had captured what turned out to be the largest fish of the day. To make sure it didn't escape, she carried it up the bank where she gutted it with her machete, so it could not possibly get back into the water.

The work was difficult, but exhilarating, lasting until about noon when the fish stopped coming into their pool. By then, women located all along the river had captured many fish. Other lucky fish, recovered from the poison, and rushed off to their hiding places.

As soon as the fishing ended, Titi and her mother began the task of cleaning and scaling their fish. Each fish was split open after cleaning. Their precious salt was rubbed into the flesh. By mid afternoon all the fish had been prepared.

All the fish were then placed on green sapling racks so they could be smoke cured and partially cooked at the same time. It took a major effort to prevent the fish from spoiling in the continuous hot weather.

"Mother, let's stay over night so we can make sure our fish don't spoil."

Pemba nodded in agreement, thinking to herself that her daughter was already thinking like a wise adult.

Finally, all the fish were near the fires so they decided to have something to eat because they had been forking for a very long time without rest.

"We still have kwanga and peppered peanut butter, but I am hungry for some fish. Could we please eat some?" Titi asked with anticipation.

Pemba found two medium-sized fish that had been leaning so near the fire that they were almost cooked.

"Let's hold these right over the fire. I'm sure they will be fully cooked in just a short while."

The aroma of cooking fish was marvelous and, within twenty minutes, Titi and her mother were eating their kwanga bread with fresh, delicious, fish. The meal assured them that all their work had been well worthwhile.

"Our pack baskets will be more than full. We will need to lengthen the sides with saplings to hold the overflow. We don't dare come home in the day light with so many fish or some will be jealous and accuse us of witchcraft. It seems silly after all our hard work, but false accusations can ruin our lives."

"Why do you think we caught so many fish, mother?"

"We did all the right things, Titi. We got the help of Mama Ndona. I took a calabash of palm wine and poured it on the grave of my grandmother, the one who first fished here. I asked her for her blessing from the land of the living dead. I explained that we needed to have fish to sell so you could go to school. We will take a cooked fish to her grave when we return. It is good to have our ancestors on our side."

Titi nodded, drinking in the precise explanation.

"Let's keep drying our fish until midnight. Every hour we keep them in the smoke and heat, we reduce the weight we will need to carry. We could never have carried all the fish without drying them some. We have the light of the full moon. Even if there are clouds, we can easily travel on the main path. We must reach home well before the second rooster call. If we take turns tending the fires, we can each get some sleep."

They had put their wet clothes on the poles near the fires. As Titi wrapped herself in her warm dry cloth she felt happy all over. After all, she had participated successfully in her very first poison fish kill. Her mother was treating her like a young woman and not just a young girl. She was fast asleep in minutes.

"How long did I sleep?" Titi asked with alarm in her voice, finding herself surrounded by total darkness, except for the fire light and moon beams.

"You slept long enough to gather your strength. Now it is my turn. Call me when the moon is right overhead."

Pemba was exhausted, too, and fell into a deep sleep.

It was thrilling for Titi to be left in charge of everything while her mother slept. *"I feel as though I'm almost a woman,"* she thought as she carefully tended the fires and turned the fish. *"I will even decide just when we should leave."*

She was thankful for the abundance of dried branches. Keeping the fires burning was not a problem. By carefully turning the fish so both sides were exposed to the glowing coals and fragrant smoke she made sure that no fish could spoil. Pemba had made special racks from saplings so the really big fish could be placed directly above the coals. Titi needed to watch carefully to make sure the little saplings did not catch on fire, and allow the fish to fall in and get burned.

The screech owl screamed several times, but always at a considerable distance. The screams still make her shudder because they sound like the screams of a tormented child. There were not many clouds, so the moon lit up the whole forest. When the beautiful full moon was right overhead, Titi called her mother gently. It took a minute or two for her to respond. Once she opened her eyes and saw the full moon overhead, she responded quickly.

A secretive return home

"I guess it is time to pack up, and get on our way," Pemba yawned.

Fortunately for both of them, the fish had dried considerably during their many hours over the coals. They shrank in size as well. Even so, it took very careful packing to get all the fish stashed in the two pack baskets. The dried saplings used for processing the fish were ideal to lengthen the sides of their baskets. Pemba carried the heavier load but Titi was heavily laden as well. She tied their kettle to her basket. Before shouldering their burdens, Pemba hid the two fishing baskets because they were much too awkward to carry along the trail with their loads of fish.

Because of their heavy loads, the trek home was exhausting. While they rested part way up a long hill, Pemba reminded Titi that the reason she was walking so quickly was because they needed to arrive home before anyone was awake to see their huge catch.

"Your grandmother always caught lots of fish too. Of course, she fished right where we did. That was one of the reasons others called her ndoki witch long before the trial by the ngombo shaman."

"Is Nkaka a witch, or did she just work harder and use her cleverness?"

"Titi, I don't really know. She certainly is much more clever than most."

"We gave a special chicken to Mama Ndona so we would have the help of the bisimbi water spirits to catch lots of fish. She is a kind of ndoki witch, paid to help us. Lots of people pay the shaman to do things for them that require skills in witchcraft. Some people pay to get revenge on their relatives, or even to have them killed, so they can make use of their spirits in their exploits. They are not killer witches themselves so they engage those who are. We paid Mama Ndona to help us, but we ourselves do not have her powers."

Titi trudged on in silence while she continued to think about all her mother had said.

"Is all death brought about by ndoki witches?"

"Almost every death is the result of ndoki action. There are very few exceptions except, perhaps, the death of a contented, fulfilled, old person. Titi, this is our last hill!"

Pemba had been talking and puffing as they climbed the long hill. "We will be home well before the second rooster call."

They stood motionless for a long time in the shadows at the edge of their village. Everyone was still asleep, so they proceeded in the shadows right up to their own little cooking hut, slipping inside exhausted, contented, and unnoticed.

Titi had a plan. "Let's go down to the river with all the other women as soon as the rooster crows. We both need to bathe and wash our clothes. We will carry water back like everyone else. No one will notice anything unusual about us. No one needs to know that we were drying fish until midnight. I will carry down some dishes just as though we ate here last night."

Pemba nodded her agreement. They actually dozed off for about an hour before their resident rooster called all the villagers from their sleeping mats.

Pemba and Titi wandered down to the water to do the morning chores. They were glad to have a bath and wash the fish and sweat smells off their bodies and their clothes.

Most of the women had caught fish and were washing away fish smells too. Pemba asked no questions but she was curious to know how many fish other people caught.

"I will stay behind with the children and ask some questions," Titi whispered when both of them were bent down washing their feet.

While her clothes dried a bit, Titi joined a group of girls who were playing in the deeper water.

"Did your mothers get lots of fish?" Titi asked in a nonchalant manner.

"Mother brought home twenty and some of them are big too!"

"We caught fifteen." another little voice added.

"We have eighteen, but no really big ones. I guess we will all be eating fish today," the happy youngster added with a smile. All the little heads nodded with delight.

Titi was only a few minutes behind her mother going up the hill to the village but she found her fast asleep. In no time, she was sleeping soundly as well. They did not budge until noon when Zoao knocked on the door.

"I was a little worried about you," Zoao confessed. "I guessed that you had lots of fish and stayed behind to dry and smoke them."

Pemba smiled. "Look over there under the cloth!"

Zoao's eyes grew wide with surprise. "I guess you did catch lots of fish. You must have twice as many as you ever had before."

"Remember, we had two women fishing this year!"

Titi smiled as her mother bragged about her to her father.

During the afternoon Titi took gifts of fish to a few elderly people who were too old to fish. Her grandmother was exceptionally delighted when Titi took her their largest fish, the one she had caught herself.

"I caught this big fish myself right in the spot where you fished when you were a girl. I want you to enjoy the first fish I ever caught from your pool."

"Before my joints got stiff, I went every time we poisoned the stream. I caught lots of fish too!" she whispered with pride. "As you have seen, you don't have to be a ndoki to catch lots of fish there."

There was a merry twinkle in her eyes as she remembered.

As she hurried back home, Titi was deep in thought. *"I think that my Nkaka was a clever, hard worker, just like my mother and I. Mother and I got so many fish, folk would call us ndoki witches too, if they ever found out. I can see that only a qualified shaman could know which people really are killer, ndoki witches."*

Watching the shaman or nganga ngombo declare that one of her relatives was a killer ndoki left a deep impression on Titi. She recalled that the only ones who doubted the decision were the people who knew and loved the old woman. *"I would never want to think that my mother or father were killer witches,"* Titi reasoned with a shudder.

Many people were smoking their fish outside. The delicious smell of cooking fish filled the village. Pemba and Titi smoked some of their fish outside too, but most of their fish were being processed inside the cooking hut just to keep their secret. Their plan was to sell their fish in the Lufu market on Saturday.

Taking fish to Lufu market

Pemba and Titi both packed their pack baskets carefully for the eight-hour walk to the Lufu market. They would go Friday and come back Saturday afternoon. Their baskets each had small sacks of peanuts on top so the number of fish would not be evident.

"I can't wait to go to market with you," Titi told her mother. "Going to market and carrying a load shows that I am getting older; doesn't it?"

"You think like a young woman," Pemba answered. "Sometimes I forget that you are still quite young. Our loads will seem very heavy before we get to Lufu. Eight hours of walking with a load is a hard day's work. On the fishing trip, you proved that you are both strong and willing. I imagine that our fish will be sold to some merchant going to Luanda."

"Will father come too?" Titi inquired.

"He needs to buy some gun powder for hunting. He will not be able to help us carry the load because there will be many on the trail. I think he will be carrying a calabash of palm wine. Can you imagine the shame and gossip if someone saw him carrying a woman's pack basket?"

On the travel day, several people from their village traveled together with their market loads. Zoao walked behind with the other men, while the women and girls carrying loads set the pace. All the women and girls wore old work clothes for the long journey. They planned to wash at a stream and change their clothes shortly before actually arriving in the market town. Because they had very heavy loads, the women and girls actually did very little talking on the way. On the other hand, the nearly empty-handed men talked constantly.

The women folk stopped to wash and change their clothes at a good bathing spot on the on the outskirts of Lufu. Titi felt her heart pounding with excitement as the market town came in sight.

"When I'm going to school here, I will be able to go to the market every week. I will only miss the market when I am back in our village visiting you," exclaimed Titi excitedly.

"Don't talk about that yet. I hate the thought of being separated from you," Pemba confided.

Titi was looking forward to getting to know her mother's sister, Nkenda. She would call her "Mama Mbuta" or older mother, because she was older than Pemba.

Welcome at Pemba's sister's home

"We will go directly to my sister's house to store our baskets."

"You were right, mother. The baskets have become heavier and heavier. Now, I can hardly lift mine."

Both mother and daughter had a good laugh as they wearily walked the last ten minutes of their long arduous trudge.

Mama Nkenda had no way of knowing she would have three tired and hungry visitors arrive in the late afternoon. As always, she was delighted to receive her kinfolk from the village. She expressed surprise when she saw how much Titi has grown since the last time she had seen her. There was lots of room in her rather large house and cooking hut.

Titi noticed that there is a second cooking hut right beside the one they were in. She had forgotten that Tata Sami had married a second, younger wife during the past year.

Pemba inquired about the health and well being of all her sister's family. Nkenda asked Pemba about the health of their mother and then asked questions that lead to a recounting of the village gossip.

"Sami buys salt fish in Luanda and supplies four dealers in the four major markets between Luanda and Lufu. He should arrive here tonight on the market truck. He will be bringing a supply of salted ocean fish for tomorrow's market. He is well, but I don't see him too much since he married Lala. She is much younger and shares his bed when he is here. He is good to me, and gives me everything I need. Before he married Lala, he gave me a beautiful wax, (expensive Dutch print cotton for dress making) the best that money can buy.

"A man is always attracted to his younger wife for the first year. Our children are grown up and away from home. I am too old to have more children. Lala is a nice girl. She grew up in Luanda, but her parents were from Lufu. She reads and writes, and knows how to keep track of all of Sami's accounts. She is a great help to him. Lala's father is one of the largest fish dealers in Luanda. He buys directly from the Portuguese dealers in Southern Angola."

By the time darkness had settled in, a large pot of beans and a basin of fufu were on the low table.

"Beans taste so good with salt fish in them," Pemba remarked.

"A steady supply of beans and salt fish is one of the advantages of being married to a merchant," Mama Nkenda replied with a grin.

After supper Titi slipped next door to meet Lala who was still busy cooking a special meal for Sami. She had cooked beans and fufu, which are basic. Saka saka and fumbwa greens, his favorites, were still in process of preparation. She was busy making the necessary peanut butter to be cooked with the greens, when Titi dropped in.

"I'm Titi from the village of Mbungu, and Mama Nkenda is my Mama Mbuta." Titi explained while protruding her lower lip in the direction of her aunts cooking hut. "I hope to come here next month so I can go to school."

"That will be great!" Lala said with obvious enthusiasm.

She seemed pleased to have her company.

Later when they were all stretched out on their sleeping mats, chatting in the dim firelight. Titi listened intently when her mother brought up the question of school. Mama Nkenda's response was immediate and very positive.

"It will be wonderful to have a bright young girl in our home. With my own children all gone I get lonesome. Sami's work keeps him traveling most of the time. I certainly wish I had had a chance to go to school. If I could read and write and do arithmetic, Sami would not have needed a second wife as much. Titi will be very welcome here. We have a great teacher called Pedro. He seems anxious to have girls get schooling too."

Pemba reflected before she replied to her sister. "Most men would have more than one wife if they could afford them. Older men like Sami would love to have a younger wife who could still give them children. Be glad that you get along well with both Sami and Lala. He will be back with you as soon as Lala has a baby."

"You are right Pemba, but I feel left out these days. Lala knows all the modern city ways. She is good to me, but I still find it hard to share my husband of twenty-five years, with a young woman who is younger than my youngest child. I can't wait until Titi comes to live with us. Lala will be a great help to her too. Soon she will be needing help with her new baby."

Titi was very pleased with all she had heard. It was nice that Mama Mbuta would allow her to be friendly to Lala despite her mixed feelings.

Two market trucks arrived during the night. Sami came on the second one and went straight to Lala's cooking hut where he enjoyed the good meal. He must have been exhausted because Titi heard him go into the big house to sleep alone.

As usual, Pemba and Titi got up with the familiar rooster call. Although in a new place, the routine was familiar. Mama Nkenda had lots to do on market day, so extra help to wash dishes, get water, and prepare a fire, was most welcome. Certainly, Pemba and Titi knew just how to help, and were anxious to get to the market themselves.

"Mother, there is milk and sugar in the tea. Look, there is lots of bread too," Titi squealed.

"Sami always brings us bread from Luanda. There is a baker in Lufu, but Luanda bread is better," explained Mama Nkenda.

Titi had only had a bit of bread a few times in her life when her father had brought some from the Lufu market.

"On this trip, Sami brought me a large tin of powdered milk and a five-kilogram sack of sugar. It is great that you are here when we have these treats."

"We brought you a taste of food from the village," Pemba said as she handed her sister the largest river fish they had.

Mama Nkenda smacked her lips. "You remembered how much I loved to go fishing and eat my fill," she said with a happy smile, as she smelled the smoked fish with delight. "I am thankful for the salt fish Sami brings us. I know I am lucky, but no fish tastes as good as a big smoked fish from our river."

Coming close to her mother, Titi whispered a request. "May I take a good fish to Lala?"

Pemba gave her unreserved approval. Lala was both pleased and surprised when Titi brought her the fish.

"I hope we can become good friends when I come here to go to school".

"I would love to have you as my friend. I miss my little sisters in Luanda. I need a lot of help to know how to live in a village. My father's home in Luanda has water that flows from a pipe right inside the house. We had electric lights that are very bright. We cooked on an electric stove, so we didn't need wood or kerosene. I really can't explain how we lived there but it was much different. I am in a kind of school too, learning the things you already know. Perhaps, we can help each other. I have gone to school for eight years and know about city life. You understand all the secrets of the forests, the streams, and the fields. You understand how country people think. Perhaps you can help me with my baby when it comes in a few months."

Titi was delighted with their short conversation. But soon she hurried back to her mother's side, because it was time to go to market.

Titi's eyes got very big when she saw the large crowd of people with all sorts of things for sale. Most displayed their wares on mats. Venders selling things that came from the city displayed their goods on little folding tables. A whole section of the market consisted of little shop huts with roofs that offered protection from both sun and rain. Lufu market, on the edge of the little town, became like a small town itself with the huge influx of people and produce on market day.

The secrets of selling profitably

Pemba borrowed a very large white basin about three feet in diameter. All their fish were stacked inside according to their sizes. Mama Nkenda and Titi had lifted the heavy basin up on Pemba's head. They had just entered the market when a young merchant from Luanda began asking questions about the fish.

"When did you catch these fish?"

"Five days ago," Pemba replied. "We finished smoking them the day before we left for market."

"May I examine one?" he asked. After just a moment of feeling and sniffing, the merchant made an offer.

"I will give you a twenty kilogram sack of salt for the basin full."

Pemba was surprised and confused. She had planned a price of each size of fish that she had expected to sell one or two at a time. She can't figure out whether this was a good offer or not. Just at that moment, Titi spotted Lala coming. Running to her side she asked for her help to determine whether the deal was good or not. Without actually coming over, Lala began to calculate.

"How much do you pay for a glass full of salt in the village?"

"We pay five escudos for a little glass full like the one that lady is using for sugar."

"I know you can get one hundred and fifty glasses from one sack." Lala calculated for a moment. "Take it! That is a very good price, more than Sami would pay. Advise your mother to accept the price. Ask to see the sack of salt before she agrees. Sometimes these merchants remove salt and sew up the sack in a way you can hardly detect. Check the sewing carefully on both ends and the sides. Look for little holes that have been mended. If the sack is perfect, make the deal."

Titi ran to her mother and whispered Lala's advice.

"Put a five kilogram bag of sugar with the salt and it's a deal," Pemba told the buyer.

"Come on, lady, I have to make a living too. No sugar, but a good bag of salt."

Titi was puzzled when her mother said calmly. "We will just go sell our fish as we had planned."

She began to walk away without looking back.

"I will give you one kilogram of sugar. That is all I can afford."

"It's a deal," Pemba answered.

The merchant called them to one side and went for his salt. Titi examined the sack carefully.

"This end of the sack has been opened and sewn up with different thread. Bring us a full sack or we will not trade."

"That little one is a smart one!" the merchant whispered to his partner. "The fish are really good, so we may as well get a good sack now as later. Hand me a kilogram of sugar too. That village woman knows how to sell in the market!"

The sun was not far up in the sky, and their selling was almost finished. As they were carrying the sack of salt back to the house, Titi asked a question.

"What made you think that merchant would pay you some sugar too?"

"I could tell by his eyes that he really wanted our fish. He will probably sell them all to some rich person or a hotel. I am glad that your sharp eyes exposed their trick with the bag."

"What would we have done without Lala? She knows many of the tricks of the market. She already knew just how many glasses of salt we could get from the sack. As soon as I told her the price of a glass in the village, she knew in a moment that it was a good deal for us. I really want to learn in school so I can calculate things like Lala can."

Once the salt was safe in Mama Nkenda's house, Titi and her mother hurried back to the market to sell their peanuts.

"We sold our fish so quickly that no one from our village ever saw how many we had."

Zoao found them in the peanut area of the market.

"What have you done with the fish?" he whispered. A big smile lit up his face when he heard of the deal they had made. He had already sold his palm wine for a good price too because of its quality.

Selling peanuts when everyone else is selling them was not so easy. However, people who bought carefully noticed that their good soil had produced very large delicious peanuts. Most of their peanuts were sold for seed, and were purchased by other peanut growers.

Cash from the sale of peanuts in her possession, Pemba went over to a stall selling school supplies. Titi was delighted when her mother bought two attractive notebooks and a lead pencil.

"If we have the money, we need to get cloth for a new school dress for you. Your dresses are badly worn. Your father gave me some of the money he got for his palm wine so I think we will have enough."

Titi's heart started racing with excitement as they looked at cloth. She had never chosen a piece of cloth for herself before. It didn't take long for her to find a length of cloth with big yellow butterflies on it.

"Mother, could we buy this piece?" Just as her mother was having a good look at the material, Lala came along.

"Lala, what do you think of this piece of cloth? Titi needs a new dress for school."

Lala liked her choice. "I know how to sew, so I could make you a dress just like the school girls like to wear."

Pemba began serious haggling to get the price to match her money.

"This is all the money I have, so it is all I can pay."

The lady counted the money quickly without touching it.

"I need to go home now, so I will sell it for whatever is in your hand."

Titi's face brightened with her excitement and delight.

"After we have sold some salt, we can send Lala the money for the thread and buttons."

Since it was late in the afternoon when they finished looking around the market, they decided to sleep over night and head back home in the morning. Titi's mother and her aunt, her two mothers, enjoyed chatting while they prepared supper. Time flew by and it was bedtime. Everything had been so exciting that Titi could not fall asleep immediately. She found herself remembering all the events of the day. Her new cloth lay right beside her on her mat. She could smell that special scent that only seems to be found in unwashed new material. *"I will have a nice new dress just like the girls wear in Lufu, when I come here for school,"* she mused.

In no time at all, the night passed, and the morning roosters began rousing the whole world with their noise.

Heading home again

Breakfast didn't take long. Titi savored her big piece of bread and the taste of sugar and milk in her tea. It was just daybreak when they said goodbye to Mama Nkenda. Titi ran over to Lala's cooking hut to thank her, and say goodbye to her as well.

"We will send the thread and button money next market day. There is always someone coming this way," Titi promised.

"You will have your pretty dress before long," Lala promised with a warm smile.

Just as they were leaving Titi's aunt gave her a warm hug.

"I can't wait for you to come and live with me," she whispered. "Don't expect sugar and milk, or bread very often. Most of the time our breakfast is just like yours in the village. Remember, your mother's girl is my girl too!" When Nkenda smiled, Titi noted that she really resembled her own mother. Reassured, she had no fear about coming to Lufu for school.

Zoao arrived after the women had finished breakfast, and was served the same treats of tea, with sugar and milk, together with a generous piece of bread. In no time they were on their way. Zoao was carrying a new glass wine jug to help him in making and selling his palm wine.

Titi carried the sugar and food for them all, while Pemba carried the heavy twenty-kilogram sack of salt. Fortunately she was accustomed to carrying big loads. The basket of fish topped with a small sack of peanuts had weighed even more on their trip to Lufu. On the big hills, Titi sometimes carried her mother's basket for a short while.

When they were all alone, with no one else around to see, Zoao carried the salt and let Pemba carry his valued glass jug. He was a willing helper but other men would have derided him if they discovered that he sometimes carried his wife's pack basket. If someone came upon them suddenly they had agreed that he would pretend that he was simply lifting the heavy pack basket up onto her shoulders as he made a quick transfer.

Darkness was impatiently waiting for the last hint of light to fade as they reached the river below their home village. After soaking their feet and washing their faces and arms they climbed the riverbank quickly and were happy to be home again.

Zoao sat on his chair, while Titi and her mother sat near him on a mat as they all ate the last of their travel food.

"Lufu market is right on the Luanda truck road. It will be exciting, I am sure I will learn many things both in school and out of school, but I will miss you both very much."

It was too dark to see the tears that begin to trickle from her mother's eyes as her little daughter spoke.

Cooking a special treat

Titi was searching for wood the next day, when she discovered a whole patch of fumbwa (wild greens). Growing on a low vine, the leaves are tedious to pick and even more bothersome to prepare. Perhaps that is why fumbwa was such a favorite green.

Setting down her basket of wood, Titi removed her outer skirt cloth, which covered her threadbare inner skirt. Before long she had a great bundle of the treasured leaves piled in her cloth.

Arriving home, she brought in her bundle of leaves and asked if she might make a pot of fumbwa.

"Titi, it is a lot of work and you have never prepared it before but if you make fumbwa, we will certainly help you eat it."

It had slipped Titi's mind that she would need to make peanut butter too to prepare her treat. The process had several steps. The peanuts had to be shelled, skinned of their brown covers, and then roasted just right over the fire. Pounded until they were crushed, they were finally rolled into a paste between a round stone and a flat piece of hardwood.

By mid morning, Titi had made more than enough peanut butter for her fumbwa.

"Sharpen this kitchen knife just as sharp as the stone can make it. Half the secret of making good fumbwa lies in cutting the leaves in very fine shreds. Hold as many leaves as you can between your finger and thumb. Cut all those leaves at the same time when you make your shreds. I was much older than you the first time I tried. Smaller fingers find it harder to hold the leaves tightly for shredding, but I am sure you will succeed," Pemba spoke reassuringly.

It took a good while for the tough fumbwa leaves to surrender, but eventually they were beautifully coated in a mixture of palm oil and rich peanut butter in a bubbling pot. A broad smile crossed Titi's face when she tasted her product. She could hardly wait to see her father's reaction to her effort.

On a separate fire, Pemba's pot of beans had been boiling gently most of the day. When the beans were almost tender, the water was poured off and the beans were plunged into boiling palm oil. Once the beans were simmering again, small chunks of smoked fish were carefully stirred in for the last half hour of cooking.

While her mother was finishing up the beans, Titi was busy pounding the dried manioc in the su (large wooden mortar), which had been made from hollowing out one end of a hardwood log so as to leave a cavity as large as a pail. The bottom of the su was tapered so that the food being pounded moved toward the center. The pounding stick (pestle), used to crush the food, was made of very dense wood, four feet long and about three inches in diameter. Although only three inches in diameter, the pounding stick weighed ten pounds or more. The white flour from the su was always passed through a sifter so that all the large fibers stayed behind.

The last step in supper making looked easy when done by an experienced cook. It was a matter of making a sort of porridge by stirring cassava or manioc flour into boiling water. The stirring began with the pot on the fire. The flour was stirred with a wooden paddle until it became thick. The pot was then lifted off the fire, and kept from turning by the well-callused feet of the cook, as she applied more and more effort to the paddle while thickening the mixture with more flour. Only experienced folk could get the mixture just right.

Titi could cook a small pot of fufu but she did not have the strength for cooking a larger amount. Younger, tender feet found the pot too hot to hold. The thick protective layer which had grown on her mother's feet allowed her to hold a very hot pot between her feet without getting burned.

The way her dad smacked his lips told Titi that her first fumbwa was a great success.

"Kedika (for sure) any boy who wants to marry Titi will pay us a big bride price. As soon as he tastes her fumbwa he will pay willingly," he said. They all had a good laugh.

"You see, your father and I will both miss you when you are off at school."

Signs of approval for Titi's schooling

Sleeping alone in the cooking hut, Titi had a vivid dream. In her dream she was sleeping in her aunt's large cooking hut in Lufu. An old lady, whom she had never seen before, came in carrying a smoked fish.

"We want you to learn to read and write, my child," she said with determination.

Quietly, the old lady placed her right hand on Titi's head and blessed her.

"You will learn well!" Her words were spoken as a blessing.

Titi's dream was gentle, yet of profound importance. She was not awakened by the dream but all the details were fresh and clear when she awoke in the morning.

"I've been blessed! I've been blessed!" Titi shouted.

Pemba was awake and heard her from inside the main house. Hurrying out to the cooking hut she found Titi aglow with delight.

"What have you seen child?"

Titi repeated her dream excitedly. "Mother, could the old lady who blessed me have been my great grandmother– the one who was the first to discover our fishing pool? I know that she died before I was born but she looked just the way you described her when we were fishing."

"Child, you have just been blessed by your ancestor! Who could ask for a better sign? Even your ancestors want you to go to school."

Pemba was delighted that her departed grandmother had come back to bless and encourage her only daughter.

"Where is the fish she brought me?" Titi asked concerned.

"Titi, do you remember the huge fish you caught? That must have been her gift to you. Child you have been truly blessed! Our plan for your schooling has the support of our ancestors. She must have been pleased with the smoked fish I took to her grave."

Titi's encounter with her great grandmother became the talk of the village. Everyone was convinced that whenever someone from the land of the dead appeared in a dream, it was a communication from the ancestors. These messages were highly respected whether good news or bad.

When the day was ended, and Titi was about to sleep with her mother beside her, she whispered, "With my great grandmother's blessing, I am no longer worried about going to Lufu School."

Protection

Time seemed to fly, and before they knew it, there was just one week left before Titi would be going off to school. One important step remained in her preparation. Zoao felt that before she went to live in another area she needed a protective fetish charm made specifically for her by a powerful shaman.

Many people came to a special old man in a nearby village. Everyone knew that he inherited and manipulated three powerful teki (dolls used in witchcraft rituals). The one called Pungu was supposedly able to move about by his own power. The protective fetish charms he fashioned received their power from his famous Pungu. The transferred power was intended to keep a person safe from all ndoki witch attacks.

Zoao was convinced that giving the shaman his big black goat was well worth the investment if his daughter could be kept safe while she was away at Lufu for schooling.

On the agreed day, Titi and her parents arrived at the shaman's enclosure leading their goat. As was expected in the presence of such a powerful person, Zoao approached the wiry old man very respectfully, dropping to one knee and clapping three times. Only after the shaman responded with three claps did Zoao make his request known.

"Mfumu, (chief) we have brought you our only living child. Killer ndoki witches have destroyed two others. Our daughter is going to Lufu to live with her aunt while going to school. We want you to protect her from killer witches. We have brought the large, black, female goat which you requested." Once Zoao has spoken, he terminated his request with three cupped handclaps to indicate that his request was finished.

The family was invited to enter a dimly lit room located off the inner lupangu (enclosure). Asked to sit on low benches, they found themselves within the shaman's little worship area filled with mysterious fetishes and rather frightening objects of worship of all sorts.

Some teki idols had their faces painted white representing the ancestors. There was a large pile of animal horns, each of which has been stuffed with special items. Many had feathers protruding from them.

The oldest looking teki idol was particularly grotesque, bristling with rusty nails, and other sharp pieces of metal, its eyes seemed menacing. Zoao and Pemba both knew that that kind of idol was used to curse people at the request of a client. Every sharp object penetrating the figure represented a secret curse that had been placed on someone with the intention of causing suffering or death. The threat and oppression of evil seemed to penetrate their souls. It was impossible to escape the web of evil they felt. Fear grew in their hearts the longer they looked around. This famous teki was reputed to be capable of killing victims who lived far from the region.

"Will the famous walking teki demonstrate his power to move while we are here?" Titi wondered as she waited with a pounding heart. She wondered which idol it was that could walk.

Tapping out the rhythm on a miniature nkoko (talking drum), the old shaman began to sing in a monotone. This seemed to be the signal for the shaman's helper to begin drumming on a small ceremonial drum, which he had carefully heated over a littlell fire so as to tighten the drumhead made of antelope skin.

The drumming was soft, but very resonant. The shuffling of the shaman's feet became almost hypnotic because his ankle rattles shook in perfect rhythm with the pulse of the drum. The faster the drum beat, the faster the old feet moved. Before too long the heads and toes of Titi and her parents were moving in total harmony with the intriguing rhythm of the little drum and lithe old dancer. The whole process eventually put the expectant little family into a hypnotic state ready to respond to the Shaman's directives.

Slowly and deliberately the old shaman removed a decorated basket revealing the renowned walking teki idol in the shadows on the far side of the little room.

The famous idol was dressed like a chief, wearing a long skirt with a red border along the bottom and up the exposed edge. A tiny raffia chief's hat accented his contorted little face with cowry shell eyes. The dirty white color indicated that the image represented someone from among the ancestors, the living dead, from beyond the grave.

Their hearts were throbbing as they watched the drama before them. At the command of the shaman, accompanied with hypnotic drumming, they all saw the idol move with a life of its own. No matter what the explanation might be, their experience was dramatic and unforgettable. All three became totally convinced witnesses of the shaman's occult prowess.

Gradually, the rhythm of the drum began to change, the old shaman chanted softly as the drumming faded away to become peripheral rather than the focal point of the activity.

From a small, finely woven basket carried in his pouch, the shaman withdrew a baby goat's horn. The hollow end had been filled with selected magical materials kept in place by a piece of black cloth held tight with a finely braided raffia string. The string fit in a small groove carved for that purpose, assuring that the cloth cover would never slip off. The solid end of the wee horn had been skillfully drilled so that a length of finely braided raffia cord could pass through it, permitting it to be worn like a piece of jewelry.

"Your daughter must wear this nkisi (protective charm) at all times, even in the water. Titi, let me tie this around your waist next to your skin. No ndoki witch will dare to harm you. This teki has been empowered by the ancestors through Mpungu, my most powerful teki. Anyone who tries to attack you will suffer the revenge of Mpungu. All the ndoki witches are afraid of my Mpungu. They will not even attempt to harm you! You just saw a demonstration of his power. You are safe! Yenge! (Go in peace)."

Titi had been trembling from the moment she saw the Mpungu teki moving about before her. As the shaman approached her to tie the fetish charm on her body, she was afraid the sound of her heartbeat was so loud it might offend him. She remained totally speechless all the way home. Finally, after sitting on her mat for a half hour, she was able to speak.

"No ndoki witch would dare confront the powers of Mpungu acting for our ancestors. I know I will be safe at Lufu. I don't think I will ever be afraid again. Father, thank you for paying your best female goat for my protection. I know you must love me a lot."

"The nkisi charms your mother and I wear were made by this same master shaman", Zoao explained.

The whole family was shaken by their experience and they were deeply convinced that they had done the right thing.

How could one fail to dream after such a profound encounter with a master of the spirit world? That night Titi saw the Mpungu teki moving around the cooking hut. In her dream, her protector was big and strong and danced just like the shaman. When she awoke in the morning, she felt for her fetish charm and was relieved to find it hanging right below her belly button where the shaman had placed it.

"Mother, I saw the Mpungu moving around in here in our cooking hut last night."

"So did I!" Pemba replied excitedly, " We've seen the proof of your protection."

"Do people protected by Mpungu ever die?" Titi asked her mother thoughtfully.

Pemba was silent for a long time, and then replied honestly, "I think that almost everyone around here wears protective charms made by our shaman and his Mpungu, but death continues. We don't have many really old people."

"All I know is that I feel much safer wearing my fetish charm for protection."

The travel day approaches

" Mother, do you think Lala will have my dress finished in time for school?"

"Lala likes you, and she likes pretty clothes. I am sure she will have your yellow butterfly dress waiting for you."

"Isn't it great that the money from our salt will pay for all your schooling until you come home in the twelfth month. With the food we will send and the energetic help you will give her, I'm sure you will not be a burden for my sister Nkenda, your Mama Mbuta."

As the day for travel to Lufu approached, Titi and her little girl friends talked of the future. Titi dreaded saying goodbye to the girls who had shared all of her spare time. Actually, the little friends felt somewhat sorry for Titi.

"I'm glad my parents are not making me go off to school like your parents are doing," the oldest girl said with a frown.

"I know I couldn't stand sitting somewhere most of the day instead of playing or going to the gardens. I think I would go crazy. I would be afraid to be so far from home," the smallest girl remarked while her friends nodded in agreement.

Titi was quick to reassure them with her reply, "Believe me, I really want to go to school to learn to read and write. As you know, my great grandmother visited me from the land of the dead. She blessed me and told me she wanted me to go to school."

"Anyway, we will miss you lots when you are in Lufu because you're the one who always thinks of interesting things to do. We will come to market whenever we are allowed. That way, we will see one another and hear all about your school." All the girls nodded in agreement. The thought of meeting at the market cheered them.

Pemba asked one of her friends who was going to Lufu market if Titi could travel with her. She herself would go to Lufu with some food supplies for Titi as soon as she or Zoao had something to sell. Her friend agreed readily. Most of the village women were fond of Titi.

Titi's little bag had been packed for several days. Her few clothes were carefully wrapped around the new notebooks her mother had given her. She was pleased with her mother's wise purchase of two sturdy plastic bags to keep her clothes and books dry in the rainy season.

"Mother, I have sharpened my machete as sharp as I can on our fine stone, just in case they don't have one like that in Lufu. I sharpened my hoe on the big stone at the river. You said we would probably need to help build or repair our classroom. My pack basket is ready with my clothes and my notebooks. I have all the food I will need. We have the big kwanga loaves and peanut butter for Mama Mbuta. I have everything ready except the money to help pay the teacher."

"Let's tie the money in one corner of your diputa (rectangle of cloth used as a wrap around skirt)," replied her mother. "Since you will be wearing the cloth, it can't get left behind. Titi, I would say that you are ready."

LIFE CHANGING EXPERIENCES AT LUFU SCHOOL

The walk to Lufu took the full day. The woman, with whom Titi was traveling, was carrying a very heavy container of palm oil intended for sale in the market. Titi could not even lift it, and there was no way to divide her load. They had to take more than the usual eight or nine hours to get there. Despite leaving before daylight, they arrived just before dark at seven. Near the equator the sunset came around six thirty in the evening, all year around.

Mama Nkenda, Titi's aunt had been watching the path for several hours before her little niece finally appeared with a smile that blossomed the moment their eyes met.

The beans were already cooked and her aunt was about to make the fufu, when Titi remembered the fresh kwanga bread in her pack basket.

"I've brought some kwanga loaves we made yesterday. They will go well with your beans."

Her aunt clapped her hands. "Your mother makes kwanga in exactly the same way as my mother. With your good quality manioc your kwanga is the very best; I can't wait. Let's eat some right away. When my boys were small, they loved to eat kwanga from my home village."

"Walking all day has made me hungry," Titi admitted.

"As soon as the beans warm your stomach, your eyes will begin to ask for sleep," Mama Nkenda predicted.

Her aunt was right. A very long day, the onset of total darkness, and a warm contented tummy seemed to nudge Titi right to her sleeping mat near the fire.

"Sleep well, Mama Mbuta," Tit whispered with slurred speech. In an instant she fell asleep. Lala came in to visit, bringing the butterfly dress she had made for her but she was too late.

"Make sure she comes over for her dress in the morning. I want to see the happiness in her face," Lala requested.

Having slept so soundly from early evening on, Titi responded quickly to the shrill call of the rooster. Before she was even asked, she was headed to the water with the dishes and a plastic water jug. Arriving back quickly, because she didn't know anyone at the streamside, she surprised her aunt.

"I didn't even hear the rooster call, and you are back with the dishes and water. I haven't even lit the fire yet." They both laughed and soon managed to get the water in the black pot steaming over an aggressive fire.

"Lala came over to see you last night, but you were asleep already. She wants us to come right over because she has something to show you."

As soon as Titi and her aunt entered Lala's cooking hut she greeted them and turned quickly to open a large metal trunk. From it she brought out the most beautiful little dress Titi had ever seen. Her eyes grew wide and her whole expressive face lit up as she squealed, "My butterfly dress!"

Until that day, Titi had never owned a dress. Like most of her friends, she wore a little rectangle of cotton print. When used as a wrap around skirt, it flipped over the cord fastened around her middle. When she was working or playing hard she wore no shirt-like garment at all like most of her playmates. When it turned cooler, or she needed to look more respectable, she wrapped her whole body with one piece of cloth, tying two of the corners behind her neck. Many small boys and girls dressed exactly the same way. Small boys yearned for trousers and shirts while little girls dreamed of blouses so they could wear their cloths like skirts. Dresses only appeared when relatives from the city brought them as gifts. It is not surprising that Titi was ecstatic about the pretty dress, which fit her perfectly.

"My dress is just like the ones some of the older girls wear on market day. Lala, you and my mother have been very kind to me."

As soon as Titi was finished admiring her new dress, Mama Nkenda took her off to the teacher's place to have her enrolled in the school. They found him sitting under the shade of the big mango tree beside the Chief's house where he occupied a room. Not more than nineteen, Mama Nkenda remembered that her youngest boy was about the same age, and he had already been a soldier for two years. A church in Sao Salvador, a fair distance west of Lufu, had sent Pedro. They had asked him to operate the little school for them but his income had to come from the parents of the children.

His unpretentious friendliness made both Titi and her aunt feel comfortable. Pedro smiled reassuringly as he spoke.

"It looks as though we may have around thirty children this year. Has Titi ever been in school before?"

Titi noticed that the teacher didn't seem surprised that a girl her size had never been in school.

"We have a number of children beginning school this year. With the war going on these past few years, most children have not had a chance to go to school. This is especially true for children from villages located far from the truck road. Of course, many thousands of children fled to the Congo as refugees during the first few years of fight for independence from the Portuguese."

Mama Nkenda gave Pedro the required sum of money for the first term.

"Come to school as soon as you hear the bell ring at seven tomorrow morning. Please bring along your machete and hoe because we will have a lot of work to do."

The first day at school

Titi was ready long before seven and had time to spot other children waiting for the same bell. Like magic, the bell seemed to call children from everywhere.

Soon, all thirty children formed a half circle around their youthful schoolmaster. Titi found herself in the midst of a little collection of seven girls. Looking around, she realized that most of them were about her age. She began to feel more comfortable.

The young teacher spoke encouragingly. "I can see it in your faces, we are going to have a great school. Those of you have been here before understand that we have a lot to do to get our classroom ready. We need new thatch for the roof and the walls need to be plastered with mud again. We only have seats for fifteen, so the others will need to make their own. Children who were here last year will work with the new students so everyone knows what to do."

Pedro chose six of the older boys to go off and cut nianga (thatching straw). A second group of boys was sent off with a couple of big boys to find crotch sticks to support the bamboo pieces that would become their seats. All the girls, and the remainder of the boys, were given the task of stripping off all the grass and shrubs in the schoolyard, all the way out to the trees that outlined their property.

"I want this yard to be so clean that not even a baby snake will be able to find a place to hide," Pedro explained.

The children worked enthusiastically all morning until Pedro sent a boy to ring the school bell. The bell was actually a bent truck rim banged with piece of a broken axle shaft. The loud gong brought everyone back together.

"Today, you have worked really well. Tomorrow, I want the third grade children to help all the new pupils when they gather bamboo for their seats. Pair up in teams of two. Bring pieces long enough for two to sit side by side. This sapling is the length we want. Each of you should cut a sapling for your measure. Remember, fat bamboos make the most comfortable seats. I need every girl to bring a pail, a basin, or a big gourd for carrying water. We need to plaster the walls with mud tomorrow. School is dismissed so you can do your work."

The children scampered home carrying their machetes and hoes, happy with their first day at the school.

A new friend leads the way to a bamboo grove

"Where does the bamboo grow around here?" Titi asked her new friend, Matondo.

"Come with me right now, and we can cut our piece of bamboo. At the same time we could get some water for supper," Matondo suggested cheerily.

Machetes in their hands and water gourds in their pack baskets the girls followed a narrow path down a very steep part of the hill. The hundreds of exposed roots that crisscrossed their path kept this short cut from eroding in the rainy season.

"Old folk don't come down this path because it is so steep and rough. We kids like it because it is so short. It has become our own path."

After a rapid, almost reckless, descent, they arrived at the water's edge on a bend in the little river. It was a tropical paradise. Unusually long vines hung down from the tall trees that towered well above the top of the hill they had just descended. Titi was surprised to discover that the trees she could see on the north side of the village watered their roots from the same little river that provided water for them all.

The tall broad-leafed water plants all seemed to be looking up toward the sky. With light only available through long narrow openings in the canopy, the surroundings remained dark and shaded, even in full daylight.

"See the bamboo over there on the far side of the stream," Matondo explained as she pointed. Before the girls crossed over the shoulder deep stream, Matondo gave Titi some basic instructions.

"The only danger here is from pythons and water snakes. The undergrowth is so dense that it makes a hiding place for small animals and wild pigs. Water snakes will get out of our way if we throw stones ahead of us. They are only interested in the small animals. The big pythons are not afraid of us but they prefer to eat small pigs. Do your best not to behave like a wild pig and you will be fine," Matondo warned with a giggle.

"I'm glad there isn't much current in the water," Titi observed.

"Wait until you come here after a big rain. No one could even think of crossing it then," Matondo cautioned.

Both girls threw stones and branches into the water for at least five minutes before they stripped to cross the stream.

"We need to cut the bamboo so it will fall across the stream, toward our clothes, that way it will fall almost to the ground before it gets caught in those vines."

"The bamboo grows to be very big is this place Matondo, I think we will be able to make a very fat, comfortable, bench."

Getting the small bamboo cut and out of the way so they could get at the large one they wanted was hard work. A bamboo has prickles on it at every joint. These prickles can really irritate your skin when you brush up against them. The girls managed but they were itchy too. Cutting through the tough outer skin of the bamboo proved difficult, even with the girls taking turns. Once they managed to cut a hole into the hollow bamboo, the task was half done. Soon their tree had been cut off its base. It is no surprise that the cut bamboo only gave way slightly. It was held upright by all the other trees and vines.

"We need to use a long vine to pull it over. We will make a knot in the vine, then push it up the trunk as far as we can, using a small bamboo pole. Once we have the vine in place we will go out into the stream and pull it toward us. There is one very important rule. As soon as the bamboo begins to fall toward us, we must dive under the water, and stay near the bottom until it has crashed."

After some hard pulling, the tree broke loose and began to fall toward them. In a flash, the girls went under the water, hugging bottom, just as the tree crashed above them.

"I'm sure glad you knew what to do," Titi said with quivering lips.

"A girl our age was killed here about five years ago. A tree fell on her and she drowned. Our mothers taught us what to do after that sad tragedy. Since then, the bisimbi shaman comes here each year to make a deal with the water spirits who manage these waters. Trees that grow on the water's edge belong to them, you know."

It was much easier to cut into the bamboo when it was in a more horizontal position. The girls decided to cut out two pieces just in case the teacher didn't allow them to sit together. Once they finished cutting out the second chunk, they simply left the rest, knowing that other children would find it a lot easier to get their bench seats. After all, they did have the two largest pieces for themselves.

"We should tell the smaller girls about the bamboo we cut," Titi suggested as they started up the steep hill with their water gourds in their pack baskets, and their chunks of bamboo on their heads. There was no more fear of prickles from their pieces of bamboo now because they had trimmed them with their machetes and scrubbed off all the prickles with hands full of sand.

As they started up the steep hillside, Titi stopped and laid down her bamboo.

"I can't carry both the water and the bamboo. Let's carry the water home and then return for our bamboo."

Matondo was puffing too, and agreed easily. On the way through the village to deliver their gourds of water, Titi and Matondo saw several of their schoolmates.

"We have cut down a big bamboo. Come down with us and cut out your own chunks and we can come back up together."

One of the girls had a very long sharp machete she had borrowed from her mother. With that sharp tool, the bigger girls soon cut out the necessary pieces for the others. It was a happy little crowd that climbed back up the hill, stopping only a few times for rest. The loads seemed to become lighter after they joined together to sing a rhythm work song their mothers often sang when they cleared fields together.

"It is nice to have friends," Titi recognized as the little troop carried up the round green benches on which they would sit all year. Before they went their separate ways, the girls agreed to meet at the edge of the market so they could arrive at school together the next morning.

Master Pedro happily welcomed the seven girls when they arrived together carrying their bamboo bench seats on their heads. Indeed these were industrious children. Before they came to school each of them had gone down to the river, washed all the dishes and pots so they would be allowed to bring their mother's basins to school as their teacher had requested. They appeared fresh, bright, and enthusiastic, carrying the bamboo on their heads, a basin or pail in one hand, and tools in the other. At the bell, the little army of pupils gathered outside their school.

"I am so very thankful for your willingness to work. The sooner we finish our repairs, the sooner we will be able to begin classes. Today, I will work with the boys who brought the thatching straw to repair the roof. I would like the other boys who brought crotch sticks to dig holes with your machetes. We need to place them in the ground, ready for the bamboo benches. Girls, please bring lots of water so you can make muck and plaster the walls."

Within minutes, every child was at work. The little school building was constructed exactly the same way as many village dwellings in those parts; the children knew how to do what needed to be done.

Titi and Matondo were a little older than the other girls and became the natural leaders of the plastering team. It took some careful work to produce their mucky plaster. Too much water would make muck that would become too runny to use. Too little water and their plaster would not stick to the woven walls. Their task was to completely plaster the skeleton of their school building, wherever it was exposed. They were a muddy mess by the time they had finished, so the teacher let them go early. They could bathe in the river before they arrived home. Before leaving however, Titi and Matondo placed their fat bamboo bench seats in place over the crotch sticks positioned by the boys.

"Let's put our benches side by side so that whether we sit on the same bench or not we will be near to each other," Matondo suggested.

They tried out their seats and were very satisfied. While they were still testing their seats, the teacher came in.

"I see that you two have become friends already. You may sit together in class as long as you don't talk too much."

The girl's smiles expressed their delight.

"Titi had never been in school before, and you are a good student, Matondo. You are the best reader in our school. I am sure you will be a great help for Titi.

"If we finish the roof today, I think we could begin classes tomorrow. The first big rain will show us who the best thatchers really are. We should have three whole months before the big rains test our work."

Titi and Matondo decided they should take their tools home and inform their mothers before they went down to the river to get cleaned up and wash their clothes. It would take quite a long time for clothes to dry so they were sure they would be gone quite a while. Mama Nkenda laughed heartily when Titi appeared from school totally splattered with mud.

"It's not hard to guess which work you were doing today," Mama Nkenda observed.

"Mama Mbuta, may I please have some soap to wash my clothes?"

When her aunt gave her the soap she also added more clothes to the wash.

"Let's go down the steep path because the elders will not bother us there," Matondo suggested.

With basins on their heads, the two girls scampered down the steep path as sure-footed as the little goats that played in the village.

A lesson on the use of soap

Titi proceeded to soap her clothes and pound them on the trunk of a fallen tree that lay half submerged. The white suds made a trail in the little river.

Matondo had been taught by her mother just how to make a little soap do a lot of work. First she rinsed her clothes in the river and wrung them out a bit. The things that were not very dirty, she gathered and began to wash in the soapy water in her basin. Each garment had as much soap wrung out of it as possible so there were suds to help wash the rest of her washing. Dirty things soaked in the soapy water in the basin while she rinsed the soap out of her cleanest things. After each article was washed, rinsed, and well wrung, it was spread out over the tall grass to dry. Only after Matondo finished washing the dirtiest of her wash was she ready to throw out her soapy water. Titi watched with astonishment.

"Matondo, you have washed more clothes than I and most of your cake of soap still remains for another day. You just taught me a lesson about making the soap last. From now on, I will wash your way. Your mother has taught you something very helpful. Some of your dirty clothes were beginning to wash themselves when they soaked so long in the used suds.

"Mother lived in Luanda for almost two years. They had to buy both water and soap, so she learned how to conserve both," Matondo explained.

Their chores finished, the two girls lathered up their own bodies especially their hair. Setting their cakes of soap on a leaf, the two girls jumped into the deep hole just below the big old fallen log. In an instant all the white suds disappeared exposing hair, as black as the night, and bodies of a glistening chocolate color. Both girls had bead-covered cords hanging around their hips. These bright cords supported their little wrap around skirts whenever they wore them. Each girl was wearing a protective fetish charm around her middle as well. The protective charms were noted but not discussed.

Before crossing to the far side, the girls were careful to throw stones and sticks to frighten off the snakes.

"Do you know how to do water drumming?" Matondo asked.

Titi replied by beginning the rhythmic pawing of the water in front of her, which resulted in a repeated sound that resembled a drum. Immediately both girls were drumming together to their mutual delight. Katunk, katunk, katunk, the girls drummed, their sound lifted up through the funnel of tall trees.

"Watch the little girls come now," Matondo predicted.

From half way down the hill they heard the little girls voices. "Ku maza, ku maza?" The little girls shouted politely, asking if the bathing spot was occupied, knowing full well that the big girls were there.

"Luizeno (Come along)!" Titi and Matondo replied in unison.

The little girls came bounding down. Within minutes there were seven lithe bodies bobbing in the cool water. The five smaller ones tried to do water drumming like Titi and Matondo but their hands and chests were still a little too small. Spotting their cakes of soap, the girls all wanted to lather their bodies.

"The soap isn't ours so we can't let you have it, sorry." Matondo explained.

"Ka diambu ko (No problem)!" the little girls replied in unison. They all understood how precious soap was.

Titi found herself curious about the protection devices the other girls were wearing. They each wore cords around their middles, more or less like hers. One little girl had half a dozen raffia chords each with a different kind of protective charm attached. Each child was protected from ndoki witches.

As soon as their washed clothes were a bit dry, the two older girls hurried back home sure there will be chores awaiting them.

"Let's pound out our fufu flour together under our mango tree," Matondo suggested.

The experienced girls pounded rhythmically as they sang. Pounding in the same su (mortar),they needed to work in rhythm so that when one pounding stick was crushing the manioc chunks, the other would be in the air and vise versa. Somehow hard work seemed easier when they joined in the pounding of each other's pile of white dried chunks of manioc root. Matondo's sifter or tami was a fine one, so each girl carried home very well sifted flour for the evening meal.

"I'm preparing some saka saka greens for supper. I have more time to cook things that require patience since you came," Mama Nkenda explained. "Today, you have washed the dishes, carried the water, washed our clothes, and pounded our fufu flour. All those tasks were mine before you came and began to help. Certainly, your mother must be missing your help these days. Titi, I really enjoy your company too. When I am all alone I worry. My two boys are off fighting in the guerrilla forces far away. It has been more than a year since we have had any news from them. We never know when bad news might come to us.

"Our daughters went to the Congo when the first wave of refugees left these parts. Their husbands resisted the Portuguese, so it was not safe for them to stay. We have no idea as to where they are or how many grandchildren they have given me. Sami is not with me very often either. It is always dangerous for him to travel to and from Luanda. I am very thankful that you are here with us this year."

Titi listened carefully because she was eager to understand the thoughts of her mother's older sister. She was comforted to know that her aunt was genuinely pleased about having her around.

"It is my turn to cook for Sami. He came in on a truck this afternoon, after traveling all night. He is asleep right now and he will be starving when he awakes. Would you please make some peanut butter for the saka saka? I did not expect him today, so I am rushing to prepare a good meal for him. We will all enjoy the food. I will help get the peanuts from the sack."

Opening one ear of the sack, Mama Nkenda let the peanuts flow into a basin until they had enough. Titi started working immediately first shelling and then roasting the peanuts to a golden color. They needed to be pounded then crushed. Before long she had rich peanut butter ready to be mixed with the hot saka saka.

"Peanuts make everything taste better," Titi reasoned while she worked.

Presently Sami appeared at the cooking hut door. "The smell of that saka saka with peanut mwamba (gravy) brought me to my feet and reminded me that I am starving."

"Everything is ready," Titi and her aunt said together.

"I see we have some new hands at work in the kitchen. If the mwamba is good, I think we should let her stay," Sami said with a twinkle in his eyes.

He shuffled to the house and lit the pressure lantern because darkness had fallen suddenly, as it always does at the equator.

Her aunt served Sami the hot meal and stayed by his side until he had eaten his fill and produced a loud burp of satisfaction. Now the women might eat as much as they wished because the man of the house has been well served. As soon as she finished eating, Titi went to her sleeping mat and fell asleep. It had been a day filled with activity and she would be off to the water in the morning again once the waking rooster gave his call.

After a good night's sleep, Titi always awakened the moment the rooster began to crow. It was the big flap that preceded the crow that called her from her slumber. On this market day, Titi was on her way to the river before the rooster had finished his tenth wake up call. Sami needed a good breakfast before the market activity got started. When she returned with clean dishes and pots, and a large plastic jug full of water, her aunt already had the fire going and was roasting the peanuts. Titi took over the peanut roasting while her aunt put a small pot of water on to boil.

"Sami brought bread from Luanda, so breakfast will be easy today. We even have sugar and milk!" Mama Nkenda whispered.

The smell of roasting peanuts brought Sami to the door with a smile on his face. "Soon you two will be calling the rooster in the morning. It is a great help to have breakfast ready so early because some of my customers are waiting for me already."

Pulling his old antelope-covered folding chair up to the door, he found his breakfast waiting for him on the little table.

"That is just the way I like it, hot coffee and hot peanuts," Sami said with a grin of appreciation.

Sami ate bread often, and normally carried sugar and milk for his coffee. Hot coffee just the strength he liked it and fat roasted local peanuts were his favorite breakfast treat. There was no time for him to linger on market day, so he was gone in a few minutes.

Sami bought dried salt fish from the big dealers in Luanda and supplied the small merchants at the markets. Lala knew just how to weigh the fish and calculate each person's bill. No one was allowed to buy on credit, so the business moved rapidly.

Lala was the one who took Sami's receipts from the purchase of fish in Luanda and calculated the price they needed to receive for a reasonable profit. He could do this calculation in a makeshift way, but Lala kept them from making any serious mistakes.

Some of the fish they sold would be resold immediately in the market. Other buyers used fish as part of barter deals they made when they brought farm products from the producers. A fixed sum of money plus a dozen salt fish would seal a transaction a lot faster than cash alone.

Once Sami had eaten, Titi and her aunt ate more leisurely enjoying the luxury of bread with milky, sweet coffee.

"Titi, your fast legs make it so much easier for me on a day like today when Sami is so rushed. You have done lots already. Now just go to the market and have a good look around."

Walking in the market and feeling grown up

Her pretty, yellow, butterfly dress made Titi feel very special as she strolled through the market. She had worn the dress the first day of school only, and decided that it should be reserved for special days when she would not be doing any hard work that might soil it. A coin in her deep pocket made her feel that she could buy something, if she wished.

Feeling grown up, Titi moved along looking carefully at everything. She knew that she looked nice in her pretty dress. Her aunt allowed her to rub some Vaseline on her face and arms so they shone.

"Just imagine, here I am walking through Lufu market all by myself," she whispered to herself, as she scanned the crowd for someone from her home village.

"Kiesi, Kiesi!" Titi shouted with excitement. It seemed so good to see someone from her village of Mbungu. The old friend had come with her parents but was allowed to go around with Titi. Arms linked, they looked at everything that sparked their interest.

" Are my parents both well?" Titi asked as though she had been gone a year rather than just one week.

"They are fine, but I heard my mother say that your mother really misses you. We all miss you. You always helped us have fun. Your dress is very pretty. Did you get it for school? I would be afraid to go to school. I don't think I could ever learn to read and write."

Titi laughed. "You are right about my dress. I have it for special occasions. I wore it when I went to meet the teacher. This is the first time I have had it on since then. It's the first real dress I ever had. My uncle's second wife made it for me. She learned to make dresses in Luanda."

Just at that moment, they came upon Titi's new friend Matondo, who was busy selling her mother's huge kwanga loaves to buyers from Luanda. As soon as there was a quiet moment, Titi introduced her two friends to each other.

"Why is it that people rush to buy your mother's kwanga when there are so many others selling them as well?" Titi inquired.

Matondo was pleased and proud to answer. "My mother has been selling here since I was a tiny girl. We make our kwanga loaves very carefully. We soak the manioc for four days instead of the usual three. That removes all the bitterness. We make sure that all the fibers are removed. These were wrapped and cooked just last night. Folk prefer the taste and texture of our loaves. She makes sure that the quality is always the same, so she has lots of customers. Of course, some jealous women say that mother must be an ndoki witch because she sells so successfully.

"I know that we sell well because we work harder to make good kwanga. My father was killed by the Portuguese because he was a village chief. Mother works very hard, but now I am old enough to help her a lot. She would like to be able to send me off to learn to be a nurse some day."

"It is a pity that good, hard-working people, like our mothers, get accused of being witches simply because they do something well. I guess that it has always been that way and there isn't much we can do about it," Titi observed with a sigh.

Once they arrived at the dress material section of the market, the two girls needed a long time to look over the pretty patterns. They choose what they would buy if they had the money.

"Look, here is your butterfly material. I think I like it best of all. Maybe, sometime, I will have enough money to buy a piece of cloth, and you could get the same lady to make a dress for me. Then we could be twins," Kiesi whispered wistfully.

At one booth, a medicine man sold traditional remedies every market day. In addition to a wide variety of leaves, fruits, barks, seeds and roots, he carried a full array of items a shaman might request. There were monkey skulls, dried cat's eyes, skins of a variety of little rodents, together with dried lizards, snake skins, birds feet, and assorted bird feathers, including the tiny red ones worn in the hair of a chief.

He had a supply of buffalo tails to make the symbolic fly swatters carried only by elders. Lion's teeth, leopard's claws, and coveted leopard's skins, were rare and expensive. It was a very special pharmacy, and a popular spot. White balls of special, naturally occurring clay were the only product both girls had ever actually used. It was a well-known remedy for stomachache.

"It would take a lifetime to learn how to uses all these things," Titi observed.

"I am sure that is why we need to go to skilled people when we have problems," Kiesi concluded after a long reflective pause.

Right next to the old shaman was a lady selling modern medicines from Luanda. Her most popular medicines were worm pills for the relentless intestinal parasites, chloroquine for malaria, and aspirin for headaches. She had a good supply of injectable medicines and antibiotic capsules to be purchased primarily by the traveling nurses who treated people in a whole circuit of villages.

"I smell the perfume stand," Titi noted, sniffing the air.

There were beautiful toilet soaps, perfume in pretty bottles, and all sorts of cosmetics the girls associated with women from the city and the prostitutes who traveled with the truck drivers. The adjoining table was filled with a variety of pretty jewelry, the kind that ordinary people could afford. The girls were not to interested in cosmetics but the earrings, necklaces, rings, and beads they found fascinating. They hadn't any money to spend, but they abounded with imagination.

The lady was accustomed to seeing girls and women looking at the things they could not afford.

"Be sure you marry a rich man," she advised. "He could give you all these things and more. It is too bad I married a poor man." She quipped with a hearty laugh.

There were far too many people examining the second-hand clothes for the girls to get any chance to look things over.

"We haven't any money anyway, so let's move on before we want something we can't have," Kiese proposed, walking away.

Second-hand clothes were a great help, especially for children and young people. Older women hesitated wearing foreign clothes. For the men, trousers and shirts from anywhere were fine for them. The two blouses Titi owned had been chosen here by her mother, not long before school started.

Titi was very pleased when Master Pedro called to her by name.

"Titi, don't forget to save your money for school supplies," he advised with a smile.

"Don't worry, we haven't spent any money at all. We are just looking. There is no market in our village."

Sami and Lala travel to Luanda by truck

Sami and Lala both went to Luanda on one of the market trucks. Titi and her aunt both helped get things ready for their trip. Sami had purchased two hundred large kwanga loaves to be sold in Luanda at the big market there. They were placed in sacks, twenty to a sack. The sacks were sewn closed, so there would be no casual theft on the way. It required two strong men to thrust those heavy sacks up to the top of the loaded truck. Kwanga could not travel under other merchandise. To make a living, a merchant like Sami needed to have something to sell at both ends of his journey.

The truck lumbered off into the sunset, loaded with food from the countryside and the merchants who would sell their products in the city or turn them over to relatives who handled the retail selling. Because of the armed conflict, truck travel was always dangerous.

"Perhaps, some day I will see the big city of Luanda when all the dangers of war are passed," Titi whispered to herself as she stood beside her aunt watching the truck as it ground up over the hilltop.

The second week of school

"Perhaps today I will begin to learn to read," Titi imagined as she responded to the Monday morning cry of their rooster on the roof of the cooking hut. From the water she happily joined her new friend, Matondo, for the strenuous climb from the stream to the village.

"How long does it take to learn to read?"

"It took me quite a long time, because I was only seven when I started. You are older and eager to learn. Another big difference is that you will have me to help you. I had no one to help me because no one in our house knew how to read."

"My parents have never gone to school either because our area has never had a school. If Mama Mbuta hadn't taken me in, I could not have gone to school either. I hope I will be able to learn," Titi confided with a hint of desperation.

"In the years I have been in school, I have never seen anyone fail to learn when they had a strong desire. I have no doubts at all about you, Titi."

Reassurance filled her heart as a result of Matondo's expression of confidence. The first week of school had been totally occupied with the preparation of their little classroom. She had no idea of what to expect, but she was excited.

The first day of real classes

At the sound of the first bell, the children rushed to the school and lined up at the door. When the truck rim was struck again, its sound initiated an orderly entry to their prearranged seating. Titi and Matondo stood by their prize seat, the largest bamboo in the room. As Pedro moves to the front of the classroom, they spoke in unison "Bon dia Senhor Professor" literally "Good morning, teacher". They were asked to take their seats.

The teacher began with a strange request.

"Please put you hands on your laps, close your eyes, and I will pray to God.
Dear God, we thank you for the world you have made.
We thank you for every living creature you have created.
We thank you for each other, and our loved ones at home.
Please help and bless each one of us as we study together.
Please help each of us to do what would please you today.
Please help any who don't feel well, or are nervous.
We ask for your blessing in the name of Jesus. Amen!"

Titi observed her teacher through her partially open eyes. She noticed a serious earnestness written on his face.

"Does Tata Nzambi (God) listen to what our teacher says?" Titi asked Matondo in a tiny whisper. Matondo nodded silently in response.

The faded blackboard had numbers written on it.

"I would like grade three to add up these sums as your first work for the day. When you have finished, please review the times tables up to six. The times tables are written on the backs of your notebooks. Later, I intend to test you to see how much you remember."

Matondo placed her little notebook on the board she had brought, and began to copy the numbers from the blackboard. Titi admired the neat work her friend was doing. Watching her balance her writing board as she wrote helped her understand why Matondo had said that they would need to construct their own desk.

"Grade two, please review your two times table. Copy it in your note books as you review it."

"I wonder if others can hear my heart pounding?" Titi worried, as she joined the other seven children who had been called up to the front of the room.

"I'm sure that the whole idea of school is quite confusing for you who have come to school for the first time. As you can see, the boys and girls who were here last year all understand my instructions. Next year, you will be in grade two and the ways of school will be perfectly clear to you then.

Looking directly in their eyes, Master Pedro makes a request. "Trust me, children. I will help you all to learn how to read and write. It will take quite a long time but you will learn, beginning today."

Titi looked around at her beginner's class. At least one boy named Makiadi was as old as she. The other children were a variety of sizes, but all younger.

The letters a, b, and c were written carefully on the board.

"Written words are made up of parts called letters. First we will learn all about the letters and then later we will use them to make words. Please hand me your new notebooks and I will write the letters a, b, and c at the top of the first page. Your first work is to try and copy what I write."

As soon as Titi tries to do her work, she discovered the need for some kind of a firm flat surface on which to rest her notebook while she worked. Matondo quickly loaned her little writing board when she noticed her friend's frustration. She had already finished her own work. Titi was puzzled when she noticed Matondo holding her hand up until the teacher nodded in acknowledgement.

"May I please use a reading book because I have finished my work?"

Their teacher only owned a few books but he willingly picked out one that he felt was suitable. Matondo looked very pleased.

Before she began to read her book, Matondo showed Titi just how to hold her pencil and draw the letters slowly. Titi worked very carefully and persistently. A half hour later she was making very acceptable letters. The teacher walked about the room helping each beginner. When he looked at Titi's work, his face registered his satisfaction as he gave her three more letters to make. She watched him very carefully and began at once to make her copies. Learning how to hold the pencil for the first letters was a great help. It was much easier for her than for many of the younger children. Skills like mat weaving had trained her fingers to do fine work.

The mystery of words

Right beside her, Matondo was struggling to read her book. She whispered when she read. Sometimes, she made funny sounds, which, when put together faster, suddenly became recognizable words. It dawned on Titi that her friend knew a special sound for each letter and that each word she placed her finger under, was a little bundle of letters. In fact, she recognized that some of them were the very ones she had been practicing. When the school day was over Matondo explained the mystery of words.

On the front cover of Titi's notebook, Matondo wrote the word Titi. Pointing to the t, she made the appropriate sound. Doing the same thing with the letter i, she asked Titi to put the sounds of t, and i, together.

"Now, make the sounds of t, and i, together two times." To her surprise she sounded out her own name.

"That's my name! That's my own name! I can read my name!"

Matondo laughed with delight. "There you are; you just read your name. You have learned to read one word, and it happens to be your name."

Titi, Titi, Titi, she wrote again and again. "I can read and write my name! Is this how all words are made?" Her eyes were sparkling because they had discovered the key that would open countless doors in the future.

"If I learn all the letters, and all their sounds, I would be able to read, wouldn't I?"

"You are right! That is the secret! Do you know that it took me a whole year to discover what you just recognized? It amazes me that you have understood this basic idea so quickly, on your very first day of classes. Believe me, you will learn quickly! There is a real advantage to being a little older when you start school."

In the weeks that followed Titi made an enormous effort to learn to recognize as well as reproduce all the letters of the alphabet. She made considerable progress in knowing the sounds that were associated with every letter she mastered.

"I love helping you, Titi, because you are so anxious to learn. You are smart, too!" Matondo added, as she quizzed her friend again and again on letters and their sounds.

Later that night, her aunt commented, "I looked at your notebook and, although I can't read, I can see that your work gets better and better toward the back. I bought you some more notebooks so you can write as much as you need. How I wish I could have gone to school when I was young like you."

Titi was very encouraged by her aunt's words and obvious delight.

"It is thanks to you, Mama Mbuta, that I am here in school," Titi replied with sincerity.

One day Master Pedro asked her to remain after school for a few minutes.

"Titi, I am very pleased with the progress you are making with Matondo's help. Helping you is improving Matondo's reading skills as well. As soon as you know your numbers from one to twenty, I will promote you into the second grade."

Titi was both pleased and embarrassed by Master Pedro's words.

"Thank you for your words of encouragement. I will do my very best. The people who go to Luanda keep saying that the war is going to get worse. I want to learn all I can while I have the chance."

"You are right Titi. I keep wondering when some bunch of soldiers will come along and force me to join their army."

Master Pedro was speaking very seriously. Titi realized that with civil war was on everyone's mind. Her teacher was just the right age to be grabbed up as a soldier.

A quick visit home after eight weeks of school

After eight full weeks of school, there was a national holiday approaching which fell on a Monday. Matondo agreed to go to the village with Titi. They felt they could travel with market people on Saturday, visit, and return Monday. A good friend of Titi's mother was asked to inform her mother about the plan. The very next market day, a hunting companion of her father assured Titi that her family was delighted about her planned visit.

Thursday afternoon, Titi was totally surprised to see her mother arrive with a group of market women. She came to accompany Titi and Matondo the next day. All that remained was getting permission from Matondo's mother.

Just as they expected, they found Matondo's mother hard at work with her manioc, getting it made into kwanga loaves for the Saturday market. She was pulling the fibers from her pealed manioc. It was soft and pliable after several days of soaking.

A very large iron pot, capable of holding a full barrel of water captured Pemba's curiosity. Such pots were relics of the Portuguese colonial period when they used big iron pots for the production of palm oil.

"I haven't seen one of those big iron pots since the days when the white men ran the shops at Makela," Pemba remarked with admiration.

"When the first white men fled in the sixties, my husband worked in the Nogueira store in Makella. As he left, the white man told him to take anything he wanted. He chose to bring a two-wheel cart made with car wheels, and he put this big pot in it along with a few little things. Coming up the last hill into Lufu he had to get five other people to help him pull the cart. The cart and this pot have enabled us to make a living since those troubled days. When my husband was pulling the cart toward Lufu, he met hundreds of people fleeing to the Congo in the opposite direction. He had only dared to travel at night because the white soldiers were on a rampage."

Pemba, Titi, Matondo and her mother, all joined forces to prepare the kwanga loaves for market. Matondo's mother began wrapping the white mass carefully in the leaves she had gathered. Others worked wherever they were needed. After carrying water to fill the pot half full, Titi began the task of arranging the wood fire so the water in the pot would come to a boil. The pot had four long cast iron legs that stood on flat rocks, facilitating the building of a fire right under the center of it.

"What a great pot to own in a market town," Pemba remarked.

"My Jose was killed when Matondo was only a baby, but the pot he brought us with so much difficulty has helped us ever since it arrived. If the wars ever end, and the British missionaries return to the Sao Salvador hospital, I dream of sending Matondo there to learn nursing."

With the four of them working together, all the manioc was neatly wrapped and tied, ready for boiling in the giant pot by late afternoon.

"Thanks to all of you, all I need to do now is to boil my kwanga, and everything will be ready for market. Now there is no reason why Matondo can't go off with you. I am so pleased that she has Titi for a friend. Last year some of the older boys told her that she could never find a husband if she had the reputation of being clever in school. Titi and Matondo seem to encourage each other. Matondo will need a good letter from her teacher if she ever goes to nursing school. Master Pedro is actually from Mbanza Kongo or Sao Salvador, as the Portuguese named the town, the very place the mission hospital is located."

A baby on the way

Mama Nkenda was just returning from her fields when Titi and her mother arrived at her cooking hut. Pemba's visit was a total surprise. The sisters hugged each other and danced around with delight. Soon Titi's two mothers were seated on a mat telling each other all their latest family news. Suddenly Mama Nkenda shouted out a question.

"Kedika?"(Is it true?)

Titi had been busy preparing supper. "Is what true?" she interjected.

"Your mother is going to have a baby!"

Now, it was Titi's turn to shout an incredulous, "Kedika, mama, kedika?'"

"My child, it is true, it is true!" Mama Pemba replied joyously.

"Do you think we will have twins because of all the time we spent in the pool managed by the bisimbi spirits, when we were on the fish kill?"

"Do mothers know such things ahead of time?"

With her heart bubbling over, Titi pounded the manioc into flour in record time.

"Zaoa sent this meat so we could celebrate my news," Pemba explained as she removed a generous piece of partially smoked mpakasa (buffalo) meat from her basket.

They enjoyed a delicious meal, but before they had finished eating, Pemba's eyes were beginning to close. She had walked for eight hours, and helped make kwanga for another three. A few minutes after supper, Titi smiled to see that both her mothers were asleep.

Titi lay awake longer than usual. She was delighted with her mother's news of a baby, but that would mean that certainly she would not be free to come to school for a second year. Her mother would need her when the baby came. At least, she would be able to finish the school year, because her mother said the baby would not come until the rains had ended.

"I shall learn to read and write this year. Both Matondo and my teacher will help me," she said to herself.

With her mind firmly made up, she fell into a deep sleep like the others.

In the morning, Titi was wide-awake just before the rooster sent out his clarion call. She arrived at the river in a matter of minutes only to find that Matondo had arrived a minute before.

"It looks like a great day for traveling."

By the time Titi returned, her mother had the fire burning and was waiting for the water. To celebrate their visit, Mama Mbuta brought out extra sugar and the can of powdered milk to mix with tea rather than the routine coffee. There was plenty of food from the night before to give them a hearty breakfast.

"Sweet, milky tea!" Pemba sighed as she sipped, eyes closed with delight. "I don't usually eat until mid-morning after I have been working for several hours."

"That is what I used to do until Titi came to live with us. She needs to eat well before going to school. I'm getting spoiled because I eat again in the field too." They all laughed and recognized their good fortune.

"Mother, don't forget that we must leave just as soon as we return from school at noon. Leaving immediately after class, we will only need to walk a couple of hours after dark."

Titi and Matondo talked about their trip all the way to their little school.

"Mother is sending enough kwanga for our trip," said Matondo.

"My aunt has given us three tins of sardines. They will be perfect with your mother's kwanga," Titi said excitedly.

The girls reached the school before the second bell. Master Pedro was writing some arithmetic problems on the blackboard- He greeted them with a warm smile, hardly looking up from his work.

"Please, Master Pedro, may I tell you something important before the other children arrive?" asked Titi.

Pedro's face became serious as he beckoned the girls inside.

"My mother is going to have a baby after this rainy season. This will be my only year in school so I must learn to read and write this year."

"Titi and Matondo, you may count on me. I will do everything I possibly can to help you learn. With the rumors of increasing conflict, everyone is facing uncertainty. We will do our best, and you will see that God will help us."

With this encouragement ringing in their ears, the two girls stepped outside and got in line, just as the bell sounded.

Pemba, Titi and Matondo left at noon just as planned. The long walk allowed them lots of time to talk about everything that came to their minds. After about two hours of walking, they stopped by a small steam to eat some of their kwanga and sardines.

"It has been ages since I have tasted sardines," Pemba recalled. The girls smacked their lips in appreciation of every last drop of oil and fish.

"This is the very first time we have ever eaten them," The girls remarked in unison.

"I suppose it is." Pemba said thoughtfully. "When I was a child, all the stores were run by white men. They often paid us in merchandise when they bought our palm oil or palm nuts. Once in a while we were paid with tins of sardines. We were delighted even though our parents may have wanted something else."

On the way home they met several folk from their village who were on their way to market. Everyone was in a hurry, so they only spoke to each other as they passed. Because they had no loads, they made great progress and reached Mbungu only one hour after dark. Zoao was delighted to see them all. He had already eaten at a relative's house. Hunting since before dawn, he soon went off to sleep. Eating by firelight, the three travelers quickly ate their last kwanga and tin of sardines. Once they had eaten, all three soon slipped into dreamland.

For the next two days, the two girls became carefree villagers again playing for long periods in the cool waters of the Luadi River. On Sunday, Titi took Matondo to meet her grandmother, who was delighted to see them. They carried water and wood to help her that afternoon. Matondo perceived that both Titi and her mother Pemba got their cleverness, and many of their expressions, from the old white-haired lady. Titi's grandmother was very interested in knowing just what they had been learning in school. She was curious to know the tribal connections of their teacher too.

Titi seldom had long chats with her father, but they did spend a couple of hours together Sunday afternoon.

"I am planning to accompany you girls back to Lufu tomorrow. These days, you never know when you may meet up with a band of soldiers of some sort. There are too many stories of girls being kidnapped by some of these undisciplined boys who are not from these parts. I will need some help from you as well. I have finished smoke drying a lot of mpakasa (buffalo) meat.

"The animal was a big bull. I gave some to our relatives as well as a quarter to the land chief. I still have all we can carry for Sami to sell in Luanda. He said he could always sell that kind of meat. He will not be expecting me, but I know I can trust him to pay me as soon as he is able. We will leave at daybreak, and take our time with our loads."

The girls were so accustomed to hard work that the prospect of heavy pack baskets did not worry them. Titi was happy with the prospect of many hours to learn from her father's conversation. She will probably not see him again until she returned at Christmas.

The trip was a good one. They arrived well before dark giving the girls time for a good sleep before the next school day.

The intense effort of Titi and Matondo, coupled with constant coaching from Master Pedro, meant that both girls learned far more than even Master Pedro had thought possible. He felt that by Christmas time Titi would be approaching the third grade level.

The rains always began in late November so peanuts and corn needed to be planted before the first rains fell. Titi and Matondo saw each other every day at school but both were very busy with work in the fields after class. Well-timed planting was crucial for everyone. Once the rains started the work became a little lighter.

The mango project

The very first fresh fruit of the rainy season was mangos. Matondo knew all the trees of the area. Many mango and other fruit trees were more or less abandoned when people fled the ruthless killings of the Portuguese in the early sixties to become refugees in the Congo. For some reason, certain mango trees produced fruit well before others.

The two girls were high in a tree eating their treasures when an idea struck them. "Let's pick mangos and sell them to the Luanda merchants. I am sure that Sami would buy all we can pick. He will let us have the sacks we will need too."

The girls picked a small basket of fruit and take it to Sami. His answer was very encouraging.

"I will buy all the good fruit you can pick, and I will pay you half of the price I get in Luanda. With so many people living as refugees in the Congo it has been hard to get good mangos. As you know, the best fruit is picked by the hands of skilful tree climbers."

Delight and excitement lit up the girls' faces as they planned their strategy.

"I am light and love to climb. It would be safer for me to go out on the limbs than for you, Matondo. I could pick the fruit and toss it to you. That way we will have the very best fruit."

"Your plan sounds fine to me. Because I have lived here all my life, I can find the best fruit trees. We will risk shaking off the fruit only when we are sure there is lots of grass or hay to break the fall. Adults will pick some mangos too, but their fruit will be bruised," Matondo reasoned.

"It is to our advantage to supply Sami with fruit that will bring the best possible prices in Luanda. I am sure that he really will give us half as he promised," Titi assured her friend.

The first tree Matondo located for their harvesting was right beside a spring that flowed into the river.

"Look at those beauties," the girls shouted in unison.

Up the tree like a monkey, Titi was well aware of the dangers of breaking off the fruit laden branches, and getting seriously hurt. She only ventured out on a limb when one hand was grasping another branch strong enough to hold her weight. Where this special tree was located, it caught the sunlight all day long ripening the fruit long before the fruit on shaded trees.

Titi decided to climb to the top and work her way down. They were a great team. Titi tossed her fruit accurately and Matondo seldom missed her catch.

"How much do you think we will earn?" Matondo shouted as the pile of mangos grew around her.

"I have no idea, but I am sure we can trust Sami. He likes me and asks me questions about schoolwork, every time he comes home. He knows your mother and he knows that you are helping me at school."

By dusk, the two girls have picked enough mangos to fill three big jute bags at Sami's house.

"These are perfect. They will be the first fruit from the north. How many mangos can you get in a sack?"

The girls counted as they filled the last sack. Titi could not count high enough but Matondo reported that there were two hundred and twenty mangos in the sack.

"I will give you four hundred escudos now, and more if I do better than I have calculated. I know that they will bring a good price especially if there are very few in the market. I will get my money back," Sami said with a laugh. People in Luanda go crazy when they see the first mangos, and yours are perfect!"

The two girls just looked at each other in amazement.

"I think we could each buy a new kitambula (kerchief) for our mothers to wear on New Year's Day. We might even have enough left over to buy some kind of blouse from the used clothing lady," Titi suggested as her eyes danced with excitement.

"Lots of people will be wanting to buy new kerchiefs at Christmastime. Let's choose ours the very next market day," Matondo proposed.

"That will be tomorrow, so let's be among the first at Mama Veronica's table."

The two girls laughed when they met at the kitambula table because they arrived at exactly the same moment. Mama Veronica was just opening her metal trunk. In a few minutes, the rows of saplings behind her table were covered with neatly arranged kerchiefs.

"How shall we ever choose from among so many?" Titi whispered.

"If we know the different prices, that will help us decide," Matondo explained as they asked Mama Veronica about prices.

"Each row has its own price," the cheery lady explained as she posted the prices. I don't haggle over the prices of my things. People who know me know that my prices are fair and that I will not change them."

Matondo was the one who could read the prices and make the calculations.

"I think we should choose from the bottom two rows if we hope to buy anything else."

"How can we choose?" Titi asked again.

"Aren't we both a lot like our mothers? Let's choose the one we would like for ourselves. I'm sure our mothers will be pleased."

Titi agreed with her friend and began to really enjoy the task of choosing between the fifteen different patterns. To their total surprise, both girls chose identical patterns.

"We have been together so much that we actually think alike," Matondo remarked with a giggle.

The girls happily gave the money to Mama Veronica and received their treasures.

"The pattern you chose is my favorite too," Mama Veronica said with a smile, as she put each kitambula in a little plastic bag.

"Without a doubt we will need to negotiate the price of any used clothes. I have watched them many times whenever I have been in the market," Matondo cautioned.

"That lady from Luanda who sells used clothing is clever. Whenever she thinks someone really wants something, she asks a higher price and will only bring it down a little. I have never had any money before, but I have figured out how to buy from her. Choose three or four things that you like. If there is something you like best of all, never let her know. Listen to her offer, and offer her about half that much and refuse to pay much more. When you go to her several times with several different things that tricks her into offering the normal price. She will know that girls like us don't have much money so she will not ask for quite as much."

"How did you learn all those tricks?' Titi asked in amazement.

"I think that you sometimes forget that I grew up here, and I have been around on market day for years." Matondo reminded her friend.

"If I find a blouse, I will hand it to you and you can negotiate for both of us," Titi proposed.

"We must go there separately and give no hint that we are together. When I throw things back on the pile in apparent rejection of the price, you pick them up so that no one else will get them. Hold the things. Then lay them down again when I return. By then, she may give a better price or accept my offer. Once she notices that I know the tricks of the trade, she will sell more reasonably."

Their simple buying strategy worked, and, at the end of a half hour, they each had their precious purchases bought at normal, rather than inflated prices. The girls were ecstatic because it was the very first time in their lives that they had purchased something with their very own money.

"I am so glad that you know how to buy in the market," Titi said with admiration. "We even have some money left. Let's hope that we can sell some more mangos next week. The price will be lower because more and more mangos are ripening every day."

The girls wandered over to the shade of a big sanda tree to reexamine their purchases. They were totally satisfied.

"I will be wearing my blouse and mother will have her new kitambula when we go to church on Christmas day," Matondo remarked dreamily.

"There is no church in our area," Titi explained. "I guess that mother and I will wear our new things when we eat our big dinner on New Year's Day. If father has good luck hunting, we always have a feast to begin the New Year."

"Do you know that our teacher, Master Pedro, leads a kind of church in our school each Sunday?"

"What do they do? I have never been to any church meeting," Titi wondered.

"I have gone a couple of times. They read from big black book they call God's Word. At times they close their eyes and someone talks to God. They call that prayer. They sing songs that tell about how God can be trusted to care for them. Master Pedro explains the part he read from the book. Sometimes they pray for sick people or people with problems. They all shake hands and go home. I suppose we could go sometime."

"My grandmother says that pastors and church leaders are nothing but deceptive ndoki witches. She says that they tell people to abandon the kind of protective fetishes like the ones we are wearing. She told me that she once saw one of these pastors burn a whole basket full of fetish charms and teki gods. She said that he was not harmed in any way. and concluded that he must have been a powerful ndoki witch to do what he did."

Matondo was quiet for some time after hearing Titi tell about her grandmother's opinion. After a pause, she gave her own opinion.

"Master Pedro is a wonderful person who is always helping others. He prays and teaches like a pastor. He certainly does not seem like a deceptive ndoki witch to me!"

Time flew by as the girls continued with all their activities. Their second sale of mangos did not bring them quite as much money but it was well worth the effort. The girls decided that they would do the same thing again the following year.

On the last market day before Christmas, Titi made arrangements to go back to their village with Mama Fiote, the mother of one of her good friends from back home. Because they could get caught by heavy rains, Titi took a bit of her money to buy another thick plastic bag. She packed everything that needed to keep dry in her bag, which was tied tightly with sturdy string. The bags her mother had given her were getting worn from being carried to school so often.

The journey home for the Christmas break

Titi prepared her pack basket for the trip. Matondo's mother gave her a big kwanga, and Mama Nkenda let her prepare both peanut butter and mbika paste, for her travel food. She was just arranging things when Lala came in to say goodbye.

"I am going to miss you while you are home in your village. Here is some of my favorite fish for your lunch. It is the kind you like with hot peppers."

Titi was pleased. *"I will be traveling with a whole group, so it will take longer to get home. I am always twice as hungry when I am walking all day,"* she told herself.

At noon Titi went to the market to join her traveling companions. Her pack basket was carefully packed and ready for the long walk. They met under the sanda tree where Titi spotted Matondo, who had come to say goodbye.

"Boas festas," (Season's greetings) Titi shouted to Matondo, as she waved goodbye, using the greeting they had just learned in school.

Titi was the only child in the midst of seven women. They had sold their leftover peanuts for planting purposes. Any peanuts that were left to be sold in December always brought a great price, so the women were satisfied. Each one had some sort of little treasure tucked in her basket. Their humble purchases were a modest recompense for their hard work in the fields, and sixteen hours of walking on the long market trail.

With the sun right overhead, the travelers perspired profusely. Returning from the market, there was no way to escape that hot sun.

Traditions about thunder and lightning

"Look over there at the black clouds. The rains will be cooling us sooner than we want." Everyone agreed with the words of Mama Fiote, who was their natural leader.

Suddenly, there was an ear-splitting crash of thunder, accompanied by a blinding flash of lightning.

"It is a good thing that we are walking in the forest during a storm like this. Open fields are dangerous," one of the women observed.

"I don't worry about God's lightning. It is the lightning that is directed by ndoki witches that I fear. I wear this teki doll carved by a great shaman. It protects me from the only ndoki witch in my luvila (bloodline) who is able to throw lightning at us. I feel safe, but it cost me my best female goat. Ever since my little brother was killed by lightning when he was just Titi's size, I have worn this protection. It was well worth the price.

"My little brother died when he was out gathering nsafu fruits during a storm. He was picking up the fruit blown off by the wind out under his grandmother's tree. That miserable old ndoki witch never allowed the children to climb the tree until the nsafos were black with ripeness. She zapped him on the spot. The lightning came down through the tree and killed him. There wasn't even a mark on that beautiful, strong, young, boy!"

"Everyone knew that his old Nkaka (grandmother) killed him. Just that morning she warned the children to stay away from her tree. That night her goats were all killed and her peanut harvest burned. Folk were not satisfied with that revenge so she was beaten mercilessly. While a young man was whipping her with his belt, the old wretch kept crying out, 'my grandson, my grandson, I loved him and now he is gone!' Her grief sounded genuine enough, but we all knew she was the guilty witch. I spat in her face that day! She looked pitiful, lonely, and powerless, but we all knew it was just a good show put on by a killer witch.

"Proof of her guilt came in the dead boy's mother's dream. In her dream the old grandmother laughed in her face and repeated the word lightning. There was a wicked delight in the old witch's face when she boasted. 'I killed him without leaving a single mark on his body.' The old wretch laughed ruthlessly. She disappeared shouting, 'He will never steal my fruit again!'"

"That old hag didn't last more than a couple of weeks. She couldn't walk after all the beatings and no one took her any food. Many danced with joy at her funeral. Her head was covered in a huge pot of peppers, so her ghost has never troubled us. Those kinds of people always pass on their powers to someone else. That is why I wear this protection."

Titi had many questions in her mind but she chose keep quiet and listen carefully to the adult conversation.

When the wind began to blow rather abruptly, they all knew that a deluge of rain would follow. With no villages near, they were surprised to find a banana tree. In any case, they quickly cut off all the giant leaves to serve as umbrellas. The cloud burst began just as the last leaf umbrella was cut. The widest part of the leaf was placed on their heads while the other six or seven feet stuck out behind like a portable shed roofs.

Titi began to shiver when the rain drenched her after being so very hot. She cringed every time there was a flash of lightning.

"That is God's lightning so we are safe," Mama Fiote pronounced.

Recognized as the accepted lightning authority. Her emphatic statement helped Titi to relax again, while vigorous walking warmed up her lithe little body. As the storm increased its intensity Titi found herself reaching to touch her protective fetish. She felt comforted to find it in place.

"I wish I could just fly home like a bird," Titi whispered to herself.

The whistle made by sucking in air in a special way caught everyone's attention.

"Look at the stream in the valley." Mama Fiote shouted. "Our crossing tree has been swept away in the current of the flash flood!"

"The water will not be down until morning. I guess we will need to spend the night here," an older woman said with a sigh.

Within a few minutes of continued walking toward the swollen stream, Titi spotted a possible solution.

"Look! there is another big tree that this wind has blown down. We can cut a trail across it. It will take quite a while to trim off the big branches but we could probably finish before dark."

Each woman carried a sharp machete in her backpack. Working together, as they were so accustomed to doing, they make a new trail to the far side before nightfall.

"Now we are leaving a path for others to follow." Mama Fiote concluded.

"Let's eat something, as soon as the rain has passed by," the eldest woman suggested.

Everyone laughed because the rain stopped falling exactly when she finished making her suggestion.

"We had better do whatever Mama Ndudi requests. After all, she stopped the rain because she is hungry," someone said.

They all had a good laugh, including the one they were teasing.

"Now that you have seen my powers to stop the rain perhaps you will all show me more respect," the old lady replied with a good-natured grin.

I think I will just eat all I want now, because mother will have food prepared at home," Titi reasoned.

Matondo's specially prepared fish, together with her mother's kwanga, and her aunt's goodies were indeed tasty. Titi found herself thinking of the three thoughtful people who gave her the lunch, and this, too, brought satisfaction. She had not even known these kind people four months ago.

The dark clouds had made it seem like night, but when the wind blew the clouds away, they were all surprised to see that the sun was still shining. Puffy white clouds with pink tummies raced across the sky, enjoying their last run before sunset. Darkness fell like a blanket as soon as the crimson clouds blew away.

"We have moonlight," Titi shouted.

She really didn't like walking in total darkness. Trudging along the moonlit path brought back memories of the fishing trip she had enjoyed with her mother. *"It was on that fishing trip that mother allowed me to become a grown up capable of doing a young woman's work,"* Titi reminded herself.

At one point, they were on the top of a rocky hill, which was higher than the surrounding trees.

"There is our village on the top of that next range of hills. They must be having a bonfire for us to be able to see it so well," Mama Fiote surmised.

Although the village is still more than an hour's walk away, everyone began to walk faster just because home was in sight.

"They are baking the bricks that should have been baked in the dry season. With all the young men away because of the war, they are baking them now. The bricks will be cool enough to build within ten days. I love the look of the bright red bricks when they are removed for construction." one of the women explained.

"It is a good thing that the men built a roof over that big stack of dried bricks that formed the oven. A rain like we have come through could have ruined weeks of hard work," a quiet woman observed. "I heard that our village chief is adding a piece on his house.

"The Portuguese have ordered that all chiefs should live in brick houses with metal roofs," the quiet voice explained.

"I don't think our chief should worry. The white men never even leave Luanda these days, and who would blame them, after all the killing."

Once more, it was Mama Fiote who proved to be absolutely right, when they arrived in the village.

Home for the holidays

It was about three hours after sundown, when Titi finally slipped into the firelight of her mother's cooking hut. Mama Pemba grabbed her daughter, giving her a big hug, while plying her with a whole barrage of questions.

"When I saw the big storm passing over the hills, I wondered how you were making out in all that lightning."

"As you know, Mama Fiote knows lots of things. She informed us that we were seeing God's lightning, and not the frightening kind sent by killer ndoki witches. She seemed to know all about it, and made us all feel better."

Holding her daughter at arms length, Pemba sighed. "You look wonderful, my child. You can't imagine how much I have missed you"

While Pemba was still speaking, Zoao came rushing in having heard the excited voices. Holding out his hand to grasp Titi's little hand firmly, he spoke quickly with a little embarrassment.

"Welcome home Titi. I have missed you every day you were away."

Zoao's eyes told Titi of the love his words and hands could not express adequately. She felt overwhelmed by the spontaneous affection shown by both her parents.

"Your food has been ready for hours. Eat, child, you must be starving after that long walk. I have just made fufu and beans with saka saka in peanut butter gravy."

Titi recognized that the peanut butter gravy was special because it was past most of the planting season and a couple of months before the new harvest.

"Mother, our baby is growing, just look at you" exclaimed Titi.

Pemba was keenly aware that her tummy told the world she was expecting a baby, after years of waiting.

"No one cooks food just like you do, mother. Now that my hunger is gone, my eyes are asking for sleep. I have many things to show you and tell you tomorrow."

Sniffing the air, Titi remarked. "Papa, you smell of palm wine."

"I have been working with the crew that is firing the chief's bricks. He rewarded us with some of his best palm wine. Like you, my eyes are asking for sleep. We will all talk tomorrow."

At the pre-dawn call of their rooster, Titi slipped back into her old routines. The breakfast fire was crackling by the time she returned from the stream with clean dishes and two gourds of water.

"Titi, child, it is wonderful to have your help again. Your father went hunting with the other men; so we can all have meat for the holidays. They are good hunters. We always have meat for the first meal of the New Year."

"While I was down getting the water, I heard three shots. I'll bet we have meat already."

As soon as they had finished breakfast, Titi asked about the day's work plans.

"Without your help Titi, my field work is behind. My first peanuts are up, but the rest are not even planted yet. We need to get them in the ground before the short dry season comes next month. I know that planting this late is risky. The little peanut plants may die during the several weeks that we don't expect any rain. If their roots are well established they will survive. I think we should risk it, and plant our seed today."

"Mother, you have always been wise with our gardens. Together we will get the peanuts planted before sunset."

"Let's have a cup of coffee, then we will hurry off to work."

Titi remembered that they only had sugar and milk for tea on New Year's Day so she was prepared for plain tea. Sipping the tea, Titi looks up in surprise.

"What kind of tea is this? It is so good."

"Don't you remember that we can make tea from avocado leaves when they are young and tender?"

In an instant, Titi was over digging in her precious plastic bags.

"Here is some sugar for the holidays," Titi whispered with pride. "Put a little in the tea for both of us."

"How did you manage to buy sugar?" Pemba asked with surprise.

Titi explained her mango business to her astonished mother. Reaching into her bag, she took out her special gift.

"Sugar is not the only thing I bought. Here is something for you to wear on the first day of the New Year."

Seeing the beautiful kitambula (kerchief), her mother's eyes lit up, and then glistened with tears.

"You are a wonderful daughter, so thoughtful, and so unselfish. I am very proud of you".

With the kind words, her mother gave her a very tender hug. Titi felt great joy filing her heart because of their mutual love.

"Your sister is a lot like you, mother, but she can never take your place. I may as well show you all my surprises. Do you like my new blouse?"

"You didn't accept a gift of clothing from a boy, did you? Accepting a gift like this is like a promise to marry. You are much too young!"

Titi began to laugh. "I'm not that dumb, mother! Matondo and I each bought a blouse with some of our mango money. I paid for it myself. Don't worry; it will be a long time before I accept a gift from a boy. I still have some money left for some notebooks and pencils. Matondo and I make a great team. I climb and pick and she catches the fruit when I toss it. She knows where all the best trees are located. Tata Sami gave us half of the price he got in Luanda. He supplied us with the big shipping bags too."

Showing her mother her latest notebook Titi explained. "This is your name, mother, and the next name is father's. I can make all my letters now, and all the numbers to twenty. Very soon I will begin to read. Both Matondo and master Pedro help me all they can. I have explained to my teacher that I must learn all I can this year because I will be helping you after the baby comes. With all the trouble in the land, Master Pedro says that he doubts that he will be free to teach next year anyway."

There were tears in her eyes when her mother replied after a long silence.

"You have thought out everything, haven't you? What can I say? I am sorry about the babies I have lost, but I would rather have you as my daughter than a dozen who only bring home heartaches." They sipped their sweet avocado tea in precious silence.

"Mother, we must get to work. The sun is climbing." Catching sight of her mother's silhouette in the doorway, she laughed. "Mother, you have a fat tummy and it makes me very happy."

Shortly, they were in the peanut field, hard at work, and singing as they moved to the rhythm of a familiar work song.

"These are perfect planting conditions. The earth is still moist from the rain, and the sun is hot. Some of these peanuts will begin to sprout before the day is ended," Pemba observed with confidence.

Titi was still not as skilled as her mother, who also had a growing baby in her middle, which created a degree of handicap. Under these special conditions, mother and daughter were able to fly along together, just like the two ears on a goat. Their songs kept them going on their routine for long periods. Dig, plant, cover up; dig, plant, cover up. Eventually they had a quarter of the field finished.

"I'm hungry and need a rest. I will wait over by the spring. Please climb that tree and get us some ripe mangos."

Without even climbing, Titi found some beautiful fruit that had fallen because of the wind and rain. The ripest fruit falls in a windstorm. Titi returned with her basket half full.

"I haven't had any mangos yet this year. This tree out in the field is one of the first to ripen around here." Without delay Pemba was enjoying the fresh fruit.

"Tree-ripened mangos are the sweetest, and the windfalls are always at their peek in ripeness."

Titi's voiced was muffled as she spoke because she was talking around the big juicy mango in her mouth. After a half dozen each, they were completely satisfied, and ready to take up their work again. Mangos are very sticky, so they both went to the little spring-fed stream to wash their hands and faces with the clear spring water.

"If we keep going at the same speed, we should finish planting in time to find a good load of fire wood before we go back home."

Nodding as she hurried to keep pace with her skilful rested mother, Titi kept going.

"I have dreaded trying to plant this field of peanuts. My back always aches more and I go much more slowly when I am alone and feeling sorry for myself. I love having you by my side. I was my mother's youngest child and never felt very close to her. Mother and my sister from Lufu often did things together and left me with the younger children in the village. Not only are you my daughter, but you are also my best friend. I feel free to express all my feelings with you. Not many mothers can say that."

"You should remember that I have benefited from being your only child. When a mother hen has only one chick, she can hide it under her wings even when it is half grown."

"So I remind you of a mother hen," Pemba replied with a laugh.

"Look, mother, our field is planted! We haven't even a dozen peanuts left. You took a big risk when you used your peanuts for my supper last night."

"Let's go over to this year's new field. There is lots of firewood because of all the trees and bushes we cut to clear it. We will take a look at the progress of the peanuts and corn we planted side by side."

The new corn was knee high, while the peanuts had several leaves and were at least three inches tall, looking very healthy.

"This is a beautiful field. Perhaps we could plant beans here when I come home for a week about a month before the rains end. Beans would really grow well in this virgin soil."

"I will not be much of a farmer by then," Pemba reminded her daughter while patting her growing tummy. "I may be able to prepare the ground, but I will certainly be needing someone who can bend to do the planting."

The new field was crisscrossed with fallen, charred trees and large branches. All the leaves and small branches had been burned at the close of the dry season. The fresh wood ash mixed with the soil contributed to its fertility.

"These trees are getting dry, and harder to cut. There is an excellent sharpening stone over there under the kapok tree. We can't cut these trees with anything less than very sharp machetes," Pemba advised.

Soon the chips were flying, and a good pile of logs, about two feet long, was waiting to be loaded into their pack baskets. They had to help each other get loaded. By the time they reached the hill to their village, both of them were whistling through their teeth, from the strain they were feeling. As they moved toward their little cooking hut, they stopped for a moment to admire the little clouds crossing the sky with their glowing tummies. It had been a wonderful day.

"Your father will be tired when he gets back from the hunt. I guess that the early morning shots were not lucky ones. If you will pound the flour, I will get the water boiling for our fufu. We will just eat it with peppers and salt. Tomorrow we will eat better."

"I will prepare the fufu flour, but don't forget we have mangos too," Titi replied cheerily.

"Do I have some good cooks?" a voice spoke from the darkness. "I have brought home some special meat. We shot two wild pigs which we divided between only three hunters."

Zoao's message brought squeals of delight from Titi.

"Papa, you have cooks. Just bring us the meat."

"We have meat to begin the New Year, and we can eat it with our daughter. I'm glad I married a good hunter," Pemba said, flashing a big smile as she began to prepare the meat for cooking.

"You will find that the meat for supper is all cut, washed, and wrapped in leaves. Now, Titi, show me how you can cook." After making his request, Zoao collapsed in his hide-covered chair to wait.

Cutting the heart and liver into small pieces, Titi placed them in a cooking pot with water, several cloves of garlic, and a little salt. While the meat was boiling, she poured palm oil in a second clay pot, setting it on the fire as well. When the oil was boiling she slipped in one of the dried onions that hung from the drying rack. At just the right moment, the water was drained from the cooked meat, which was sent sizzling into the hot palm oil.

Five minutes later Titi announced, "We have meat for the tired hunter. Bring him his fufu."

Both mother and daughter were pleased to see Zoao smack his lips as he ate.

"I'm not tired any longer, and I see that I have two wonderful cooks, although I only married one."

Pretending great formality, Titi brought her father his first feed of new mangos for desert. The whole family was exhausted, but very satisfied. The meat was hung on wooden hooks in the cooking hut, and they all prepared to go to sleep.

"We are assured of good dreams tonight," Zoao remarked as he went off to bed.

Titi and her mother did not fall asleep immediately. They relived the day in their minds.

"In the years gone by, only a chief or the hunter himself ever tasted the delicious organ meats like heart and liver. You have a kind father who is willing to share his special meat with us."

"I guess I must be the daughter of a chief tonight," Titi replied.

"Well, tomorrow, the chief's wife and the chief's daughter will need to dry-smoke our meat so it doesn't spoil."

As they lay on the two sides of the fire, they could see their store of meat hanging on the smoke blackened hooks to dry out as much as possible. Sleep came easily.

After breakfast, Zoao taught Titi just how to smoke-dry their meat. First, they made a rack of rather large, green saplings. This was placed across two green poles, supported by crotch sticks, like the ones they used in school to hold up the bamboo seats. This arrangement kept the meat about three feet above the source of smoke and heat.

"Pound the rock salt into powder in the su in the same way as you pound fufu flour. Next, we must rub the fine salt on all sides of each piece of meat. The trick is to keep the fire at its present level. Too hot, and it cooks the meat quickly on the outside. Too low a fire fails to dry the meat and keep it from spoiling. We are trying to dry out the meat until there is no moisture left in it at ll. We need to keep turning the meat so that it is drying from all sides. If we do it properly, it will last for a while. When we have finished, we will hang the meat up over the cooking fire so it is dried and smoked a little every day. Meat that is not fat, keeps the longest. Wild pig has a lot of fat so it can't be kept as long as mpakasa or antelope. The meat we want to eat soon should be cooked slowly by placing it a bit closer to the fire."

All of these instructions, Zoao gave to his bright-eyed daughter. He spoke to her as he might have spoken to an adult. Titi was keenly aware of the respect her father was showing her.

Once all the meat was in position, and the fire was just right, Zoao spoke again. "Tell me all about school," he requested.

Titi excused herself and ran into the house to get her plastic bag of treasures. Opening her notebook, she showed her father how she had learned to write all the family names. She showed him her pages of careful practice in letter and number formation.

"Father, the teacher has placed me with the children who are in school for the second year. I expect to be able to read and write by the time the school year ends. I am learning all I possibly can because I know mother will need me when the baby comes. Master Pedro tells us that he could easily be picked up for one of the armies. I am working as though this will be my only year in school. Matondo, the girl who came home with me once, is a great help to me. She keeps teaching me, even when we are working and sometimes when we are playing."

Displaying her new blouse, she explained about their mango business to her father's delight. When she explained their blouse-buying strategy, her father laughed out loud.

"You are a little Zombo," he said with pride. "Our tribe is famous for our cleverness at buying and selling."

Titi spent the whole morning tending the meat, under her father's supervision. Once she had to run to the forest to get more wood for the fire. In the afternoon, her father tended the meat, while she went to the water with the family wash.

"*It is great to be back at our own river. Being home feels wonderful,*" Titi mused as she washed their clothes.

"*Ku maza?*" (Is someone at the water hole)? a shrill child's voice inquired.

"*Wiza, wiza!*" (Come come!) Titi shouted back, recognizing the familiar voice of a former playmate. She appeared carrying a basin of clothes too, so they did their washing together. Dila was full of questions and observations.

"What do you do at school? You have been gone a long time. Is it fun? Are there any other girls in school? My mother says that school is for boys. You lived in Lufu near the market. Did you eat bread every day?"

Titi answered each question honestly, and the little girl was very interested in her answers.

"Dila, I had all those same questions before I went to school. Both my mother and my aunt from Lufu felt that I should go to school. There are seven girls in our school and you have already met my best friend, Matondo, when she came here with me. My uncle Sami often brought us bread from Luanda but we certainly didn't eat it every day."

"School work is hard, but it is not like working in the fields. It is something like learning the skills to make decorative mats. You learn slowly by doing things over and over. I've seen your beautiful mats, and I am sure it took a long time to learn how to make them. First, you learned how to prepare the reeds. You made plain mats with no designs at all. Learning how to finish the edges took a long time. You are probably still learning how to put designs in your mats. You will be inventing different patterns for the rest of your life. Once you began to be able to make pretty mats, making mats became fun. Learning to read and write is something like that."

"Do you learn to make mats in school?" Dila asked with enthusiasm.

"No, we don't make mats, but we learn to draw little designs on paper in a very special way. When we make our designs correctly they can communicate a story to people who have learned to read them."

Drawing her name in the sand, Titi explained that anyone looking at that word would say her name.

"Making the drawings is called writing. Knowing what the writing means is called reading. I am learning both to write and to read in school."

"My cousin in Luanda goes to school. Could you tell her something for me on a paper?"

Titi gave a big sigh. "By the time the rains are ended, I will be able to write to her, but I don't know enough yet."

"Can you speak Portuguese yet?" Dila inquired.

"I can't say very much in Portuguese yet but I am able to talk some with the merchants from Luanda. Mama Lina sells jewelry, and we talk sometimes. She cannot speak Kikongo. I help her with Kikongo and she helps me with Portuguese. As soon as I am able to read and write in Kikongo, our teacher will begin to teach us more Portuguese."

"It must be great to be in the market every week," Dila said wistfully.

"It is interesting to see people from so many different villages. There are many stories to be heard. Not everyone speaks Kikongo the way we do. Some even laugh at the way I speak. Sometimes I become afraid when the Portuguese soldiers come along with their big trucks, especially the one they call the blindado (armored car or tank) with its big guns. Most of the soldiers are white, but some are called Bailundu. They are black, but they don't speak like us at all. They use the Portuguese language to talk with other people. Whenever they walk through the market, they carry their guns in a position that is ready for shooting. My aunt says that they are afraid of being attacked by some of our local soldiers who could be hiding in the market. I always feel better when they have left."

"My uncle says that many white soldiers have been killed in the past fourteen years. There hasn't been any war in Lufu since I went there. My uncle says that there have been many killings along the road to Luanda. He says that most of the villages along the roads have been abandoned for years. They went north to the Congo where they are called refugees. Uncle says that the road to Luanda has only been open again for about two years He never rides in the cab of a truck because attackers always kill the people in the cab first."

"I often hear people whispering about kimpwanza (independence). I don't really know what it means except that our own black people will become the bosses of everything. Some say that we will see this change very soon. My father says that our village is safe because the road to Lufu is so bad that trucks can't pass. He says that after kimpwanza all our young men will come home from what ever army they are with."

Dila was quiet for a long time after this conversation. Eventually she spoke very quietly.

"My father says that he would never want to kill anyone. He said that he could be obliged to go to war, if men with guns force him to go with them. I am so glad they have not come for him yet."

"Dila, what have you been doing while I was away at Lufu?"

"I suppose that I have just been doing the things I always did. I spend a lot of time taking care of my little brothers. Whenever mother needs my help, we take the children to the fields for peanut planting and harvest. Things don't change much here in the village. All of us miss you. Last month we had fun catching zenzie (fat edible crickets). They seemed to be fatter this year. Now that I am a bit older I catch more. One night I caught twenty five."

"I bet they were delicious," Titi replied, licking her lips. "Around Lufu, the soil is different and there seem to be very few crickets. I haven't eaten even one this year. I think that they can't dig their little burrows in the hard clay we have there."

"Mother and I made a good number of simple sleeping mats which my cousin took to Luanda. She has not returned yet, so we don't know whether we will earn anything or not. Our main reason for making them was to help my cousin pay her way on the truck. She had to go to Luanda to inform the family about the death of my uncle Ndongo. He was chief of our clan and we had an urgent need to appoint his successor."

Dila's precious soap was rapidly disappearing as she pounded her clothes on the 'washing rock'.

"Let me show you a way to save on soap that my friend Matondo taught me."

Dila was convinced quickly that washing clothes in a basin conserved all the suds that normally flowed down the stream. With a broad smile, Dila began to put her clothes out to dry.

"I think that you should become a teacher. Already you have taught me something you learned at Lufu. I was afraid that you might not want to be friendly with us after going to school. Soap is so hard to get, and now we can make it last twice as long. Please keep teaching me things. It is nice to learn new ideas. While our clothes are drying, let's play water drums."

The two girls quickly waded out in the water until it came up to their chests when they were in a crouched position. Both were expert drummers and soon the water was making a deep drumming sound as the girls churned it against their chests in a well-known rhythm. The whole valley echoed with their joyous drumming.

They hadn't been drumming long before five more little girls appeared at the water's edge. In a matter of minutes, these little friends have washed their clothes, too, at the washing rock. They didn't have soap, but they did their best. As soon as their washing was spread out on the grass and bushes, they joined the fun, filling the morning air with giggles and laughter.

"Who is the best frog?" one little one shouted, as she made a giant hop from the washing rock. All the girls joined in the competition, and little Lina was proclaimed 'Mbuta Kiula' (Chief frog), because she even jumped further than the bigger girls.

When dark clouds cast a deep shadow over their water hole, the girls scrambled to gather up their clothes before the deluge. A deafening clap of thunder sent them scampering to the cave, just as the rain began to pour down. There was an outcropping of limestone that created a shallow cave in which they often took shelter during the frequent thundershowers. As the girls rushed in, something dashed out past them.

"Mbambi!" ("Giant land lizard!") they shouted in a chorus of squeals and shrieks.

The green lizard looked like a small crocodile about four feet in length. They knew it wouldn't harm them, but they had been startled enough to make their hearts pound. They watched him dash into the water, and out of sight.

"I bet that he is the one that has been killing our chickens," Dila said excitedly. "We have lost four in the past two weeks. Mother spotted his tracks. Now father will hunt him down. He will tether a chicken down here and wait with his gun. We will have a feast when we get him."

"I saw one of those guys kill one of our chickens once," a little girl piped up. "That mbambi stood perfectly still except for wiggling the very tip of his tail. The dumb chicken thought she had found a juicy grub and ran to grab it. In an instant, that critter slapped the chicken with his tail with so much force that she didn't even struggle when she was carried off."

The deafening crash of thunder roared at the same terrifying instant that a fork of fire hits a tree within sight of their shelter. "Tufwidi, tufwidi!" ("We are dead, we are dead!") they shouted in unison. As quickly as the storm had come, it passed as the wind chased the clouds away, exposing the bright sun. The girls ran like startled gazelles up to the village, right past the burning tree.

Worried mothers showed deep relief when the startled girls appeared safe and sound.

"We heard you playing down at the water and we feared that the lightning had struck right there," One worried mother explained as she hugged her little one.

"Luzolo lua Nzambi kaka!" (It was God's will!) she exclaimed. Everyone knew that if the lightning had been sent through witchcraft, someone would have died. They were all pale from the fright.

Zoao had protected his meat, as well as the fire, by placing a large roofing sheet over everything, during the downpour. The thinner pieces of meat were actually cooking, so there was a wonderful smell in their yard when Titi came back with the clean clothes.

While her mother finished the saka saka greens, made from the tender rainy season new growth of manioc leaves, Titi pounded out the fufu flour.

"I think that today is Christmas, according to our teacher." Titi announced as she brought in the flour.

"It looks as though we will have a feast both for Christmas and the first day of the New Year. The meat smells so good I can hardly wait."

The palm fruits were already cooked and cool enough for Titi to be able to separate the fibers from the delicious gravy. Eventually, some of the meat would be cut small, then boiled in the palm fruit gravy mixed with a bit of peanut butter.

Zoao was now sitting right by the cooking hut door.

"When the white men ran the stores at Lufu they used to tell us that we should eat as well on Christmas day as they did. It smells as though we will be following the old customs of Lufu tonight." His face displayed his special look of satisfaction.

"Master Pedro told us that Christmas is for the celebration of the birth of Jesus, someone very special."

"I think Jesus must have been a Portuguese man. They celebrated his birthday by drinking a lot of red wine which came from their home land," Zoao explained.

"My friend Matondo told me that our teacher has a church service in the school each Sunday. I have never gone because I knew that our family has no connections with church. Do you think I should go sometime to find out what they do?"

After a silence, Pemba advised Titi to seek the advice of her aunt from Lufu. "She could give you a better answer. All I have ever heard is that missionaries and pastors are really ndoki witches much like our shamans."

After another pause, Zoao spoke. "A man told me that you must offer the name of a family member to be sacrificed before a priest or pastor will let you join the church. They get extra powers when they abduct the spirits of the offered relatives. They are shamans from the white man's world. Just like other ndoki witches, they can't suck any life out of other people's clans without some clansman's permission. This is why our people become very worried when one of our clansmen joins up with the church. We risk being betrayed into the hands of powerful people."

By the time everything was prepared, the delicious smells were making everyone hungry. Zoao lit the lantern, and lead the procession to his table where all the pots were placed on one end while he sat at the other with his plate ready to be filled. He sometimes ate alone, and sometimes in the moanza (chatting hut) with other men. Titi and her mother waited until he had eaten his fill. Then, it was their turn to eat. They carefully carried the pots to their little kitchen. Pemba stirred the fire, then joined Titi on the other kitchen bench, which enabled them to sit about six inches above the floor. The pots were arranged around them, easily within their reach.

"When we have good meat, it isn't hard to cook a good meal. The gravy filled with little pieces of meat makes everything else taste great," Pemba said with satisfaction.

With the fufu at just the right consistency and plenty of rich gravy, like most folk in their village, they ate without cutlery. The method was simple. They formed balls of fufu about the size of a small egg made a deep dent with a thumb so the ball became a little bowl. The little fufu bowl was dipped in the gravy, or beans, or whatever served as gravy. The bowl with its delicious contents makes a delightful mouth full. Both mother and daughter smacked their lips as they ate their little feast in total contentment.

"We always use spoons in Lufu but I really like our village customs much better," Titi confessed.

The evening was warm and the moon was shining, so Zoao brought his chair just outside the door of the cooking hut so he could enjoy his family.

"It was nice that God prepared a nice pig in his forest so we could celebrate Christmas well. Once more I have been well fed by my two cooks. Next Christmas, we will eat together with my new son who will join us in a few months. Pemba, you are a good wife. You have given me a wonderful daughter, and now you are preparing to give me my son. We have lots to celebrate."

Pemba smiled. Women seldom receive words of praise or appreciation from their husbands.

They heard the village girls out dancing and singing in the brilliant moonlight, but Titi decided to stay home. Eventually weariness beckoned the household to sleep. Lying on her mat beside the glowing embers, Titi asked her mother about her health.

"Mother, is the baby growing well inside you? Are you still feeling strong? I think about you often."

"My child, there is no need to worry. I seem to be fine. I get tired more easily when I am working in the fields. To be honest, I worry sometimes because the other two babies died when I was close to the normal birth time. When I remember that the killer of those babies is dead, I know she can't touch this baby. Unfortunately when one witch dies, another always seems to be there to take over. Death and illness are always stalking us. Until a child is five or six years old it can become a victim of death very suddenly. I am glad that your father is always willing to pay for our protection no matter how much the shaman requests. I believe that I am safe."

"Mother, I feel sure you will be safe this time and I will get my little brother or sister at last. Other children my age have several brothers or sisters. I still have to borrow the other's babies to carry on my back. I hate ndoki witches."

"No more talk about death! There are some advantages to being the only child. I have had time to teach you everything I know. Girls with little brothers and sisters can't go to school because they are needed at home. You are going to be able to read and write just like the girls from Luanda."

"Mother, do you think I will ever know as much as Lala does?" Titi wondered out loud.

"You are learning to read and write and that is more than any other woman or girl in these parts. You are very wise to learn all you can this year. Zoao is sure that big changes are coming."

The fire slowly burned until only a few coals were left to glow in the darkness. By that time, both mother and daughter were sound asleep with smiles on their faces.

Every day she was home from school, Titi kept at her mother's side or ran off to do her bidding.

"It seems so good to be working by your side, mother. I miss working in our fields and watching our crops grow," Titi confides.

Pemba laughed, "Do you know that some of the women are jealous of me. They ask me how I manage to get you to do so much work without complaining. I tell them that the secret is mine alone, and that I am not allowed to tell them. Some of them have said that they want their son to marry you." Titi and her mother had a good laugh together.

Because of the rainfall in the week that followed Christmas, the peanuts they had planted came through the ground quickly. They looked beautiful, but still needed more rain.

"I'm afraid that the short dry season may have arrived a week early this year. We could have as many as six weeks without rain. These little plants cannot survive that long. Just one more rain and I think they could survive. Of course we knew that risk when we planted. At least, the early peanuts are very strong."

"Don't worry, mother. It will pour rain the day I go back to Lufu. The peanuts will be great, but I will be drenched," Titi laughed as she spoke.

New Year's day was a feast day as long as anyone could remember.

"Our elders didn't have calendars so this feast must have been invented by the white men too," Zoao speculated.

In their village, no one paid any real attention to Christmas. A big meal to begin the New Year was considered to be a necessity for good fortune.

Zoao went hunting very early the day before New Year's Day. Even though they had a good store of dry smoked pork, he was anxious to capture a good fat nsizi (large ground hog-type rodent) for their feast. Noticing the signs that the nsizi were beginning to eat their peanut plants, he made a plan.

"If I can't get a chance to shoot one, I will put a trap on their trail from the forest to the peanut patch. A soaked cob of seed corn may entice them inside. When they pull on the corn, a whole load of heavy rocks will fall on them and kill them. One way or another, nsizi is what I want to eat on the first day of the New Year," Zoao explained.

"Let's go gather a good supply of tender manioc leaves for our saka saka. We can bring back a good supply of wood at the same time," Pemba suggested.

"We need a good supply of ripe mangos as well," Titi remembered, as they passed near their favorite tree.

"Go after those beauties at the top. Toss them, and I will catch them like your friend Matondo. I'm afraid to climb as long as the baby is inside me. I don't want to do anything to harm him. Losing two babies has brought shame enough. I would be lost if I didn't have you. A childless woman like Mama Dina is not respected at all, and brings shame and sorrow to her clan. As the elders used to say. 'A woman who can't give birth is not a woman at all. She is nothing but a boba (a peanut shell that has no peanuts inside)"

"Mother, let's not talk about sad things. Let's talk about the feast we are going to have. We can do something about the way we prepare food, but we are always going to be haunted by fear of ndoki witches."

Titi climbed the mango tree, like the expert she was, and her mother positioned herself to catch the fruit on the ground. Titi's dress caught a branch in such a way that it was very difficult to set it free. Finally she pulled it off completely, and threw it down to her mother. They both giggled like schoolgirls as she continued to pick and toss mangos while wearing nothing but her well-worn panties.

"I just have enough of last season's peanuts to make the peanut butter gravy we need for our fumbwa greens," Pemba reported. "I found that a few got left behind in a fold in our big peanut sack."

"Now we have everything we need to accompany the nsizi meat father has promised. We are going to eat like kings and queens and your baby will grow too."

Pemba's face lit up with a happy smile. It seemed as though the gloom had been purged from her soul by the power of heart-felt laughter. By sunset, on the day before the feast, Pemba and Titi had everything gathered.

"If father doesn't get a nsizi, we will just put some of our delicious pork to soak."

They had a good hearty supper of fufu and beans ready for that evening. Pemba had put the beans on to boil in the morning, and a neighbor lady kept the fire going throughout the day, so they were juicy and tender. They were just about to eat when Zoao came into the firelight.

"Here is the meat I promised," the happy hunter declared with a grin. "I used the soaked corn the way my grandfather taught me. The new corn will not be ready for another six weeks or more, so I guess they were hungry for a taste. The soaked corn smelled enough like the fresh that they were tempted. I caught a big one and a small one in the same trap."

"Right now, we have beans and fufu for everyone. Tomorrow we will have a feast." Titi announced.

"I think I will eat right here in my chair. That way we will all eat together," Zoao suggested to the delight of Titi and her mother.

Fully satisfied with a good meal of fufu and beans, they were all ready to sleep within an hour of Zoao's return. Deep sleep was just what they all needed.

The rooster's scream only provoked the opening and closing of Titi's eyes on the first day of the new year.

"Boas festas, mae. (Season greetings, mother) ". Titi called out in the darkness.

"Obrigada (Thanks) " Pemba replied, surprising her daughter.

Little giggles blended happily. Titi had no idea that her mother knew any Portuguese at all. She had learned basic greetings in the shops run by the Portuguese in her youth.

"I don't really know Portuguese. When I was your age, we learned that saying thanks was a harmless reply to anything the Portuguese trader or his wife might say to us. That is about all I know."

"Did you have good dreams, my child?" Pemba asked, changing the subject.

Titi began to laugh when she remembered her dream. "I dreamed that a whole bunch of nsizis came in and slept by our fire!"

"Two of those critters did sleep here right up on the hooks. Chances are they will never wake up at all," Pemba said with a grin.

By mutual agreement, they had no plans for fieldwork on this holiday. As soon as it became light they would go leisurely to the water, have a good wash, and return with their water supply for the day. The remainder of the morning would be dedicated to food preparation.

Zoao skinned and dressed the two rodents as soon as Titi brought him a basin of water. The two fat animals together weighed as much as three or four chickens. They certainly had lots of good of meat.

"I would like to take a good chunk of cooked meat to my old uncle this afternoon. He is too old to hunt any more," Zoao explained to Pemba who nodded in agreement.

Zoao suggested that they bring his table outside and eat their feast together under the shade of their nsafu tree. They had two chairs and Titi turned the su upside down, so she had a fine stool that was just the right height. The nsizi meat was deliciously tender, to no one's surprise.

"As we eat, we are protecting our peanuts. I hate to think of how many little peanut plants these two could have eaten. I will set the trap again when I get back from Lufu," Zoao commented.

"We are going to see many changes this year." Pemba said thoughtfully.

"I get my son this year," Zoao agreed with a merry twinkle in his eye.

"I expect to be able to read and write before the dry season comes," Titi predicted.

"I hope a bunch of soldiers doesn't come and force me to join them."

"Father, don't even talk that way," Titi protested.

Zoao had planned to take Titi back to school. He decided he would take his hunting gun in to the gunsmith for some repairs at the same time. He knew that their stock of preserved wild pig meat would sell for a good price right in Lufu because there was none of that kind of game in those parts.

Titi's backpack was filled with smoke-dried pork. Zoao carried his gun and a hunting bag, which was well stocked with pork as well. No one found it strange for a man to carry a hunting bag. They wouldn't guess that he had such a heavy load. Titi was strong, but she was still a young girl and her father did not want her to carry too heavy a load.

"I will be back for a few days in about three months time. By then, you will be really big. Please don't work too hard because we all want a healthy baby," Titi instructed.

Both Titi and her mother turned away quickly to hide their tears from each other as they parted. When they were about to go down the hill, Titi pointed up and laughed. Very dark clouds were gathering. It was obvious that the peanut-saving rain she had predicted would soak them on their journey.

Back in school determined to learn

The school and work routine began the morning after their arrival. She found herself even more determined to learn, because it was abundantly evident that learning to read and write was now or never, for many reasons. The short separation seemed to strengthen the strong bond between Titi and Matondo. They were indeed kindred spirits with strong wills and ambitions. They seemed to spur each other on to greater achievements. These girls were a delight for their teacher Master Pedro.

"I absolutely must read the beginner's book this month," Titi told Matondo with a firm resolve.

Every spare moment found Titi making her letters and repeating their sounds. Her dedicated effort to learn the alphabet with all its sounds paid off when she made her first attempt at reading.

"I can't believe it. I am actually reading. The words that I don't know I can sound out."

By the end of January, Titi could read her first little book without making more than one or two mistakes. Master Pedro was a little afraid that, with all her determination, Titi might have memorized the little book. To be sure, he asked her to read it backwards one afternoon after the school had been dismissed. When she read the whole book backwards without a single mistake, he was convinced and handed her the second reading book.

"You are a delightful pupil and I am determined to help you all I can," Master Pedro told her sincerely. "When I see how much you have learned already, I am sure that keeping this school running is worth the risks I am taking."

Turning to Matondo, Pedro had a word of encouragement for her too. "I am very pleased to see the clever way you have been coaching Titi. It seems to me that while you are helping her, your own work is progressing very well too. My guess is that both of you will help lots of other people to learn to read and write in the years ahead."

Matondo was embarrassed, but very deeply encouraged.

Once she had mastered the whole idea of reading, there was no stopping Titi. She read from the little books constantly, whenever she had time to do it. She discovered that the more she read, the better she could read too. When it came to mastering her numbers, she attacked them with the same determination; however, she was so fascinated with reading that her math suffered a little.

A fall from a palm tree that affected the whole town

All the children were startled to see men rushing through the schoolyard. A well-known local man had fallen from a palm tree. Everyone knew the man who had fallen. He made palm wine which required a lot of hard work to be done while suspended from a belt carefully made belt made from vines and fibers.

The men soon returned and the larger of the two was struggling to carry Mateus on his back. Three boys bolted from the schoolroom when they recognized that their father was being carried to the nurse's house.

"Papa, Papa, did you fall?" The boys called out in anguish, as they ran with the men. Soon the whole village, including the school children, was gathered by the local nurse's home and clinic. Upon examination, the nurse discovered a broken arm, a very bloody head cut but, more seriously, his legs dangled lifelessly, indicating a broken back.

Mateus' wife pushed through the crowd. "He's dead! He's dead." She sobbed after seeing his state. She began to roll on the ground, giving full vent to her grief, as though he were already dead.

From his meager supplies, the nurse gave Mateus an injection to help with his suffering. He sewed up the head wound and got the bleeding stopped.

"He must be carried to the hospital at Kengi. I have done all I can for him here," the nurse said quietly.

Because the whole village was on the spot they soon made a kipoi (a chair bound to two carrying handles). Several teams of carriers volunteered, so no one would become exhausted.

The men went through the high hills because they knew there were no trucks until market day. They got him to the doctor but he died a few hours later. They buried him rather than struggle to carry a decomposing body back to the village. Four days passed before any news got back to Lufu.

All the school children were deeply concerned for Mateus because his boys were classmates. Titi was all the more concerned because her father made most of his living working in the tops of the tall palm trees too.

Frightening accusations in the dark of night

It was on the night before market day that Titi and many others were startled awake by the shouts of an angry man.

"I smell a vumbi (corpse) and I know the smell of a dead body! The ndoki witch who ate (killed) the body I smell will die. His children will be orphans. Let the ndoki die! Let him die! Let his children wail and cry just like the family of Mateus. Let them cry for their dead father too!"

The menacing voice only faded as he walked toward the far end of the little town.

Trembling as she cried out into the darkness, Titi asked out loud. "Who is going to die?"

Her aunt had been startled out of her sleep too, so she answered. "That is the diviner shaman, the ngombo who has been hired to discover the ndoki who provoked the death of Mateus. He claims that the guilty witch split Mateus's climbing apparatus. He is shouting in front of Mateus's brother's house. He is claiming that Lucas caused his brother to fall from the tree even though he was in Luanda when it happened. Lucas just arrived on the truck this evening. The ngombo is claiming that the smell of a corpse has lead him to the house of the killer witch."

Titi and her aunt, now fully awake, strained to hear all the ngombo was saying.

"You, ndoki. You took your brother's life because you were jealous of him. He produced a lot more palm wine than you could. He wouldn't let you sell his wine in Luanda, because you spent his money each time. You slept in Luanda, but you flew here and cut some inside strands in your brother's climbing belt. You flew back in the night so no one would catch you. The smell of death is all around your house. It is the smell of a corpse that leads me. You can't hide the stench of a corpse from an ngombo like me. You too will die, mark my words, you will die!"

The words of the Ngombo shaman frightened Titi so that she trembled all over, and told her aunt about her fear. Mama Mbuta lit the fire, so there was light in the room to help calm their thoughts.

"It is not our affair, Titi. Nothing will happen to us. The ngombo shaman has the power to smell like a cat. That is how he located Lucas, the one he accused and cursed. I am sure he too will die soon. That ngombo shaman is always right. I have seen him work before."

Titi seldom cried, but she was sobbing when she spoke to her aunt. "I wish we could be free from ndoki witches. You never know who they might be. I've been afraid ever since the ndoki witch sucked the life from my baby brothers. I'm afraid for my mother, now that she is going to have another baby. It is hard to trust the minkisi (protective charms) we wear. Everyone wears them, and everyone dies. I'm sure Mateus was wearing protective charms when he died too."

Mama Mbuta remained silent for a considerable length of time before she replied.

"Titi my child, I wish I could tell you that you are wrong. You have thought things through, just like the rest of us. You are right. The men who buried poor Mateus said that he had a half dozen minkisi (protective charms) on his body. As you thought, he was not really protected. He is dead."

"The cycles of hate and fear just keep going on and on. Now all of us will have bad dreams because of all we are hearing. From now on the children of Mateus will hate the children of Lucas, the one just accused. You will see. The children of Lucas will stop going to school because they will be called bana ndoki (witch's children). The hatred nourished here tonight will last for years to come."

After a long period of silence interrupted only by stifled sobs, Titi asked a hard question. "Is there no solution, Mama Mbuta?"

"Titi, you ask very difficult questions. Your mother has taught you to think like an adult. Because you already think like a grown woman, I will answer honestly. Our ancestors and elders have tried to free us from kindoki (witchcraft). You have noticed that sooner or later everyone dies in every generation."

"Why do ndoki witches kill babies?" Titi asked plaintively, still trembling.

Mama Mbuta thought carefully before giving her reply. "I think that you could just as well ask why cats eat mice, why owls travel at night, or why pigs love a mud hole. That is how they are! That is all I know. Our elders and the chiefs of our clans all claim to be good ndoki witches who only use their powers to protect the clan from evil witches. The shaman must first be an ndoki witch in order to know how to do his work of accusation. Far too many people will be accused of witchcraft before they die. We don't really know whether they are guilty or not. An ngombo shaman is not really someone we can trust. I don't think that there really is any way to get out of the constant fear of witchcraft. We will just get the best protective charms we can find, and hope that they work for us. Worry does not help. Anger makes things worse. Only kindness can keep us from being hated before our time."

Titi understood her sincere reply her honest, hopeless, yet practical reply. She felt drained in the morning.

"I had a frightening dream. In my dream a strange cat walked through Lufu sniffing at every door. When he came to Lucas's door, he howled and howled. He came back along our side of the village still sniffing at every door. He stopped for a long time in front of our door. I was terrified that he had found an ndoki among us. Finally, but he went on past."

Down at the water everyone seemed tired and upset. Each one was struggling with fears and anguish just like Titi.

"Did you hear the ngombo last night?" one girl asked.

"Who could miss hearing him and all his frightening talk?" another replied.

"How do you think Lucas will die, now that he has been cursed?" an adult voice queried.

"We don't know how he will die, but he will die," another woman declared. "There is no doubt about that."

On Monday, Master Pedro had a hard time getting the children to settle down to do school work. Even Titi and Matondo were tired from sleeping poorly all weekend. Being very practical, he dismissed the children to run home to get their hoes and machetes.

"Today will be a good day to clean the whole school yard. Cut every blade of grass. We don't want to leave any place for a snake to hide."

The work was hard, because Master Pedro insisted on thorough work. They were making great progress until a small boy began crying uncontrollably. It took quite a while for the lad to explain his problem.

Sobbing all the while, the little lad finally explained his problem.

"They keep calling me and my brother bana ba ndoki (witch's children). My daddy is not an ndoki witch! The ngombo shaman is a liar! My daddy did not kill my uncle. He is not an ndoki witch. You all will see!"

The teacher summoned all the children to gather around. "In my school, I don't want to hear the word 'ndoki' used at all. The school is for everyone. I don't want to hear that word again."

Even as he spoke, the wise teacher knew that the children of the accused man would probably never be back in school.

As Titi and Matondo walked home together, Matondo complained. "Why do the problems of kindoki (witchcraft) haunt us everywhere, and all the time?"

"I think that it is because death, or tragedy is always happening to someone. Our elders tell us that ndoki witches cause both death and tragedy. We can't have one without the other. We might as well ask why water is wet or why rotten mangos are slimy. We should remember that lots and lots of days go by and we don't even think about kindoki witchcraft. Haven't we enjoyed many very happy days?" Titi reasoned with a smile.

"Tata Lucas seems so kind and thoughtful. Can you believe that he killed his brother so cruelly? I can't help but doubt that the ngombo shaman told the truth."

Titi nodded in agreement. "We don't really know the truth. The best thing we can do is to work so hard at our schoolwork that we don't find time to even think about this sad problem."

Right after supper, Titi's eyes began to close in the firelight.

"Off to sleep with you. You look tired enough to sleep without dreaming tonight. Don't you think that we have lost enough sleep over things we can't change?" Mama Mbuta said cheerily.

The wake up rooster was still crowing when Titi called out to her aunt.

"You must be some kind of shaman. Just as you predicted, I didn't dream about anything. It is a wonder I even heard our rooster."

"A person doesn't need to be anyone special to learn from life experiences. I have noticed over the years that when my body is very tired from fieldwork I sleep without disturbing dreams. When my head is tired from worry, conflict, or excitement, I don't sleep well and I dream about the things I had on my mind. Ever since Mateus fell from the palm tree, everyone has been worked up, thinking about kindoki witchcraft. Your wise teacher ordered you to work hard with your hoes and machetes until your bodies were tired. He helped your bodies become hungry for sleep."

Titi nodded in agreement with her aunt. She was quiet for a while wondering if she could ever become as wise as her mother, her aunt, or her teacher.

At school the atmosphere seemed back to normal, except for the absence of the two sons of the man accused of being a witch. Titi and Matondo had agreed on the way to class, that they would work especially hard, so that their minds would not get tangled up with frightening ideas. All morning Titi struggled to read her second little reading textbook. For over an hour Master Pedro observed that Titi was concentrating with all her will power. Her lips kept moving as she sounded out the new words. Each time the letters finally released the word hiding within them a contented smile came to her face. Her concentration was such that she didn't hear her teacher calling her name.

"Titi, I would like you to come up by my desk and do some reading for me."

She had never read before the class because Master Pedro had left reading help up to Matondo's coaching. She began reading at the beginning of her book with relative confidence because of all the effort she had made. Her reading was almost flawless. She expected her teacher to stop her after a couple of pages. Instead, he had her read page after page for almost a half hour until she had finished the whole story. When she looked up, she suddenly realized that the whole school had been listening because they clapped spontaneously when she stopped.

"I have never seen anyone learn to read so well in such a short time. Matondo, you are a gifted teacher indeed. I know that Titi did not know one letter from another when she first came. I have been busy teaching the younger children."

Titi was feeling more and more embarrassed with all the sudden attention, but her heart was singing because of her longing to be able to read. Matondo was smiling broadly when Titi came back to their seat.

"Thank you for teaching me so willingly, and so well," Titi whispered.

"It was fun to please and surprise our teacher. I have really enjoyed working with you. I have never had a friend like you. Thanks for trusting me. I have never helped anyone learn to read before," Matondo whispered shyly.

The new desk

After school, the two girls decided how they should celebrate their success as teacher and pupil.

"Let's make a desk to work on at school."

Both girls had been doing all their work on balsa boards they laid across their legs. Some of the older boys had made desks out of carefully bound saplings, supported on crotch sticks.

"Remember the balsa log we split to make our lap boards for school? Most of that log is still there in the forest. We can cut off a chunk the length of our bamboo seat. After that, we will split out a plank for our desk top." Titi had the whole plan in her head.

It didn't take long to find the log, but cutting off a four-foot length was very hard work. Their machetes had been dulled by all the yard work done the day before. Chopping alternately from both sides they succeeded, while producing a lot of sweat.

"We will need to carry this log to my uncle because our machetes are too dull to split it ourselves. He is a carpenter and I am sure he will help us split out our plank." Matondo suggested with confidence.

As the girls approached the sanda tree that shaded his carpenter's bench, they could see that he was busy chiseling out a large su (mortar) for food grinding.

"What are you two up to now?" He asked with a grin. "I suppose the mango business is over for the season."

Matondo called her father's brother, Papa. "Papa, we would like you to split out a plank for us so we can make a desk for school. We cut off the log but we were not able to split out the plank."

"You have chosen a nice, straight grained log. It should split well. I have split a lot of these to make coffins for people. Balsa is about the only log that a person can split into planks with a machete or an axe."

With careful aim, he split the log easily with his axe. He split it about two inches from the center. Standing the larger piece on end, he placed his long machete in such a way as to split off a two-inch plank, if it could be persuaded to move through the log. Once the machete had been driven into the log with the back of his axe, he proceeded to bang first one end then the other of the sharp tool until a fine plank split off to the girls' delight. They began to thank him but he held up his hand.

"I'm not finished yet," the carpenter said.

From his house, he brought out a long wooden plane. Placing the plank on his bench, he began to smooth it with powerful passes with his plane. The girls marveled to see the big curly wood shavings that pushed up from the slot ahead of the metal cutter in the middle of his tool. After a few minutes work, he handed them an incredibly smooth plank, perfect for their desk.

Addressing Matondo, her pleasant uncle had a little confession he wanted to make.

"I did not agree with your mother when she sent you to school. I felt that the best place for a girl was at her mother's side where she can learn how to farm, cook, and raise children. You have been a great help to your mother. You know how to do a woman's work. I didn't believe that a girl could learn to read and write. I have never been in school, but I thought that school was only for boys. Last market day I had a long talk with your teacher. He told me that you two are learning faster and better than the boys. He told me all about you both. He is totally satisfied with you. Your idea of making a desk with a balsa plank was a good one. I thought you should know the reasons why I wanted to help you."

Both girls had been very quiet and kept their eyes down cast to show respect to an elder. Matondo broke the silence.

"Papa, some day, I will help you when you have become old and need me."

The uncle was silent until he reached out quietly and puts his hand on each girl's head very deliberately so they know that he was offering them his blessing. The girls felt his sincere blessing, which brought deep joy to their hearts.

"We can cut the crotch sticks for our desk tomorrow. Right now we had better hurry home and help with supper preparation."

"After all the troubled days, it is nice to have had such a wonderful day," Titi said quietly as they went their separate ways to get their water gourds.

Each girl carried a large water gourd in her pack basket as she scampered down the hill after school. With their well-sharpened machetes, their mission was to find four crotch sticks, and two supports, so they could finish their school desk.

"Look! I have found just what we need." Matondo shouted while pointing out the location with her lower lip. In a very short time they cut the pieces to size. The small trees they cut to get their crotch stick legs also supplied the cross pieces that would sit in the crotches to support their precious board. Carrying both the load of water and desk parts slowed their ascent. Walking at a slower pace gave them time to think about their project.

Titi had a plan. "I think that we should make two holes in our plank right over each of the four crotch sticks. That way, we can tie down our plank on all four corners."

Matondo nodded in agreement.

"At home, I can use the ram rod from Sami's hunting gun. I can heat it in the fire, and burn the holes right where we want them," Titi suggested with excitement. "We should go to school early tomorrow. We will need to put in our desk before school starts."

The hot iron melted through the relatively soft wood. They only needed to heat the iron a dozen times to make the planned holes. Satisfied with their project, Titi heated the iron one more time, then carefully burned a large 'M+T' on the under side of their desk. Sami kept heavy cord to sew up his sacks of fish, so the girls were able to get some strong cord to secure their desk top to the legs. Everything was ready.

The next morning Titi made the trip to the water so quickly that she provoked an unusual question from her aunt. "Did you glide down to the water like a big horn bill bird and bound back like a gazelle? I was up with the rooster but you are back before I have finished lighting the fire."

Titi laughed with her typical good-natured giggle. "I left while the rooster was just flapping his wings and clearing his throat. Matondo and I want to go to school early so we can make our desk."

The two girls arrived at almost the same time. It took longer to dig the holes for the legs than they expected. They were still tying on their plank when their teacher arrived to put some work on the blackboard. By the time he had finished, their dream desk had become a sturdy reality. He was surprised to see the smoothness of their desktop. Feeling its smoothness, he recognized that the good desk would improve their writing.

"I have never seen such a fine desk;" their teacher said enthusiastically.

"Master Pedro, you helped us get this smooth board;" Titi announced with a mischievous grin. "It was your talk with Matondo's uncle that made him want to help us with our desk. He smoothed the plank, all because you told him we were learning faster than boys."

Master Pedro smiled as he ran his hand over the girls' smooth desktop. "I just wish I could get boards like this to make a new blackboard."

Even the boys admired the new desk. They had made desks with saplings, but still needed to put a writing board under their work to write.

The girls were delighted with the convenience of their new desk. It was perfect, until the girl sitting ahead began wiggling it with her back because she was jealous. Fortunately, Master Pedro saw her mean actions. She was banished from the classroom and obliged to kneel outside in the hot sun while balancing a rather heavy flat stone on her head. When her teacher saw that she was drenched in sweat, she was allowed back inside.

"If you are jealous of the girls, why don't you get someone to help you make your own desk? Just don't trouble them again." Master Pedro said quietly.

There was no more trouble, and both girls discovered that their printing was considerably improved.

Lucas and the shaman's curse

It was several weeks before the two sons of the condemned Lucas returned shyly to class because of their teacher's persuasion. The day before they returned, Master Pedro endeavored to prepare his class for their return.

"We all know that the ngombo shaman has accused Lucas of being the ndoki who ate his brother. Lucas has been cursed. His boys fear that they will lose their father. Don't blame the boys for anything their father may have done. The boys are suffering, so please be kind and help them feel welcome to our school."

Everyone had remarked that Tata Lucas seemed to become thinner every day since he was publicly shamed, cursed and condemned. Walking with the two boys, Titi remarked on the thinness of their father.

"It is no wonder that my father is thin," Little Lucas blurted out. "He doesn't eat anything. He is afraid to climb a palm tree because of the curse. Over and over he tells us that he is innocent. He confesses that he got drunk in Luanda and lost all his brother's money. He said that the malavo (alcoholic drink) he drank was made from bee's honey and much stronger than he imagined. Sometimes I have seen my father crying. He says that he has no way to prove he is innocent. He says he is cursed, and must die. I believe my father is innocent, but that will not stop the curse."

Big tears began to stream down the little boy's face as he poured out his heart. "If he doesn't eat, we know that he will die. None of us can persuade him to eat. The curse is killing him right before our eyes."

The little lad began to sob again, but he allowed Titi to comfort him because she seemed like a big sister to him.

Her heart was very heavy. "*Is the ngombo always right?*" She wondered as she wandered home.

Looking longingly at the unripe fruit in the nsafu tree, Titi complained to her aunt.

"Why is it that those nsafu fruit stay red so long instead of turning black so we can eat them? I'm hungry for nsafu. The fruit in the tree beside father's house back home was almost ripe when I was there for the year end holiday."

Mama Mbuta laughed as she gave her answer. "I grew up near your village, and I know how you feel. I have learned that there are trees that always ripen early and others that are always late. This tree is a late one."

On the way to school, Titi told Matondo about her hunger for nsafu fruit.

"Back home we have huge trees planted by my great grandfather and others of his generation. We had fruit to eat from the end of the little dry season right through the next four months of rains."

"I think that I can help you." Matondo answered with the special crooked smile that often preceded the proposal of some sort of scheme. "Remember the abandoned village where we picked mangos? There are a number of good nsafu trees there too. This should be a good year because there was very little fruit last year. Let's go over and see if we can get a good bunch of fruit."

"Could we sell them like we did with the mangos?" Titi wondered out loud.

"My mother told me that the elders had special rules for nsafu fruit. We may eat all we like but selling the fruit is forbidden. The ancestors actually planted those trees around the village. They didn't just grow there by themselves. We must respect the rules made by the ancestors who planted the trees."

The girls followed an abandoned pathway to a small hill located above the old village site. Before them they encountered a little clearing around a gigantic, old nsafu tree.

"Look at those big black ones up at the top." Titi shouted, as she began to climb.

"Shake the tree hard when you get to the top. Only the ripe fruit will fall. Falling won't hurt them."

Titi shook the tree with all her considerable force and the fruit fell like raindrops.

Matondo shouted. "Stop, we have all we can eat." The girls nearly filled their pack baskets.

"If we had a fire, we could cook some right here," Titi exclaimed with glee.

"Well we don't, so we had better hurry home and make a lot of people happy."

Partly from compassion, but mostly because of curiosity, Titi decided to take some nsafos to the home of little Lucas, her friend from school. Entering the smoke-blackened kitchen, Titi found the lad squatting listlessly by the fire. When asked if he would like some fruit, the little lad perked up when he spotted several big fruits in Titi's hands.

"I sure would!" he answers. "I wonder if my dad would eat some?" The two children scraped around a bed of coals preparing a spot for roasting the delicious fruit.

Little Lucas's mother and a friend came in from the bright sunlight and didn't even notice the children in the corner. The two women continued their conversation.

"He is getting weaker by the day. He will not eat anything. He drinks a little water, but that is all. He only moves when he must go outside. He says that he feels the curse in his bones. We all know that every ngombo shaman must be a witch himself in order to do his work. His curse is fatal! Over and over he keeps saying that he is dead."

The heartbroken woman began to sob.

"He has been a good husband and a good father. What can I do? I'm too young to be a widow for the rest of my life. Most of his family fled to the Congo with the first flood of refugees when they ran from the Portuguese guns. He has no elders to help him. I don't know who could persuade him to eat again. Do you suppose Sami would try?"

At the mention of Sami, Titi looked up and realized that the silent woman was her aunt. "I will ask him when he gets back from Luanda on the truck. I know that he and Lucas often traveled together."

The women went outside again without ever noticing the children. When the fruit was roasted Lucas took a big black nsafu to his father. To the little boy's delight, he ate it slowly, thanking his namesake for the good fruit.

Back at her aunt's house, Titi explained that she had been in the cooking hut when Mama Lucas had poured out her heart. When Sami arrived Mama Nkenda asked him what could be done to save the condemned man's life. Titi reinforced her aunt's plea.

"To fight off the curse of a powerful ndoki like that particular ngombo shaman, we need to get a protective fetish charm made by someone more powerful. I know of a renowned shaman in Luanda who could save him if we brought him a bunch of hair from Lucas. He will insist on two good goats as payment."

A little over two weeks later, on a Sunday evening Titi overheard another conversation between her aunt, and Lucas's wife.

"The day after Sami brought that fetish charm from Luanda, Lucas asked me to cook a rooster. He told me that he had an important dream. In the dream, his brother Mateus came back from the land of the dead. He told Lucas that he wanted him to live and help care for his orphan children. That nganga shaman from Luanda must be very powerful!"

"Not many men could persuade someone from the land of the dead to come and visit someone in the land of the living to set them free from a curse," Mama Nkenda observed thoughtfully.

"I feel sure that he will live now. It was well worth the two goats. I will tell Sami myself, how thankful we are," The relieved neighbor promised joyfully.

Titi felt greatly relieved to hear the Tata Lucas was eating and gaining strength. She was fond of the whole family.

A wise answer to a hard question

"How does one shaman stop the curse of another?" Titi asked her aunt.

"Child, there are many things we will never understand. I always keep in mind some wise words of my old mother. 'Words are like poison in a cup. If you drink it, you will die, but if you leave it in the cup, it will not harm you at all.' Do you understand?"

Shaking her head slowly, Titi asked for the explanation.

"Lucas swallowed the words of the ngombo shaman and the curse began to work immediately. Between Sami and the Luanda shaman, hope began to grow in the frightened man's heart. Real trust in the fetish charm from Luanda helped him to vomit up the words he had swallowed in his heart. Hope changed his dreams so they confirmed that the curse had been broken. As soon as the words of the curse were vomited, he began to recover. Words can kill and words can heal. Be careful to examine words carefully before you swallow them."

Titi remained silent for a while, then posed another question. "Are you telling me that part of the power of a curse is the acceptance of the curse by the victim?"

"That is one of the most important things that your grandmother taught me when I was still a young woman. Life has shown me that she was very wise. It seems to me that courageous people live longer because they don't swallow words of false accusation, threats or curses."

Titi posed another complicated question after considerable thought. "Is my grandmother an ndoki witch, or just a very courageous woman?"

Mama Mbuta continued to talk with Titi as though she were a young woman, and not simply a child.

"Our family distrusts her because they are not sure of just how to understand her. She has always been a clever, courageous, ambitious, hard-working woman. Some say that proves she is an ndoki witch. Others would claim that it explains why she shouldn't be considered a witch at all. The ngombo says she is an ndoki witch, but some of us doubt the decisions of many ngombo shamans. Only our ancestors know the truth, because they see everything from the land of the dead."

"We always end up with doubts don't we, Mama Mbuta?" Titi concluded.

Her aunt nodded in agreement, still surprised by the perception of her young niece.

After supper, Titi roasted nsafu fruit for everyone, her aunt, Sami, and Lala. Her father had taught her just how to roast the fruit in the ashes just below glowing red coals. At just the right moment, she pulled the fruit from the bed of ashes, blowing them clean, before putting them in a bowl for everyone.

"I like it when the outside skin becomes hard like an egg shell. That part is bitter, so I pull off the outside and just eat the inside," Sami explained.

The loud delightful sound of smacking lips confirmed the happy acceptance of the young nsafu-cooking expert.

"Matondo and I picked these nsafus in the old abandoned village of Malala. She said that the people fled to the Congo after the Portuguese killed the chief and his brothers back when the trouble began in 1961. We imagine that this fruit must be from the chief's tree because it is so delicious."

At school, many children followed the model of Matondo and Titi's school desk. Some were simply split planks, made as smooth as possible, with a machete. Others had their tops planed by a carpenter. Looking at the improved desks, Master Pedro observed that the two friends were a major influence in the little school.

A surprise for the teacher

The two friends organized a surprise for their teacher. In exchange for several feeds of nsafu fruit, the carpenter agreed to plane three large boards for a new blackboard at the school. It was a struggle to carry in the balsa log because it was twice as long as the first one they brought for the desktop. When the boards were nailed together, they carried the finished product to their classroom after class. Pleasantly surprised, Master Pedro had no trouble guessing who might have brought the new board. It certainly made his work easier because he was able to leave written work up until he was really ready to erase it.

"How did you manage to make the white boards black?' the delighted teacher asked.

"It was the carpenter who had the idea of exposing the boards to heat from hot coals. It took skill to have the boards turn black without catching on fire."

Master Pedro found this trick to be very interesting.

"Whenever I meet up with other teachers, I will tell them how to make black boards without paint."

Time flew from Christmas to the Easter vacation. The two school pals both improved their reading skills by constant reading. There were only three reading books available. Titi read the first two little books while Matondo read and reread the third. Titi began the third book, but made slow progress because there were many new words. Matondo began to read a little book in Portuguese, in preparation for her next grade, which would be taught entirely in that language. She found it interesting when she encountered market words that she knew in the text she was struggling to read. Often she could read a new word but had no idea what it meant. Master Pedro helped her after class. Titi stayed with her, learning the new Portuguese words whenever she could. The merchants from Luanda spoke Portuguese in the market most of the time. Some of them understood Kikongo but were obliged to answer in Portuguese. The school children used what Portuguese they knew even when playing in the schoolyard. Peer pressure pushed everyone.

Lala was a great encouragement to Titi as far as working with numbers was concerned. Titi was amazed to watch Sami tell her the weight of the fish he had bought so she could calculate the right price for a kilogram. Although reading and writing were her top priority, Titi knew the value of understanding numbers and did her very best to learn the tables written on the back of her notebook.

Matondo was the one who helped her friend understand multiplication. Taking six palm nuts she arranged them in sets of two and proceeded to show Titi that three times two was just the same as adding the twos together. It was then, that she saw the value and purpose of memorizing the multiplication tables. Titi often tested Matondo on her times tables once she knew her numbers well. She found the times tables difficult to learn.

"How can you keep all the answers separated out in your head?" Titi questioned.

"You must learn about numbers the same way you have learned about letters and words. It will take a lot of hard work; there is no easy way," Matondo lamented.

"Before I came to school, I could not imagine that thinking, and remembering could be work. I get tired when I try hard. Isn't it strange that we can get tired without even moving our bodies at all? Running home after school seems like a rest," Titi concluded.

Preparing for a short visit back home

"I can't wait to see my mother walking like a village duck." Titi stuck out her tummy, and began to walk like a pregnant woman, laughing gleefully, as she performed the imitation for Matondo.

With her tiny reserve of money, Titi decided to buy a little sugar for her mother and father.

"I want all the sugar my money can buy," she declared cheerfully to an elderly market lady she knew.

The old lady calculated. "I can give you three heaping glasses and a matabisho (bonus)."

Titi nodded her approval, and the kind lady filled her glass very generously. The bonus was almost half a glass. Titi's satisfied smile and little curtsy rewarded the kind old lady.

"There aren't many children as polite as that little one," The old lady remarked to her neighbor, out of the side of her mouth. "It is nice to see a school girl thinking about her parents. You are a good girl, Titi; I wish I had a granddaughter like you. My granddaughter lives in Luanda. She never comes to see me or send me anything to let me know that she thinks of me."

"When I get home, I will take a glass full to my grandmother," Titi said to herself. *"No one would ever bring her sugar. Almost everyone is convinced that she is an ndoki witch.. I still wish I could know for sure."*

The month of April was always a stormy month with torrents of rain, high winds, and lightning. Titi, as well as the two ladies from the market, wore their work clothes for the long walk. Things that needed to be kept dry were carefully protected with plastic bags in their backpacks. Fast walking kept them warm even when they were drenched.

The ladies had sent peanuts to be sold by relatives in Luanda, who had paid them in advance with bags of sugar, sent to Lufu with the market truck. Because the transaction was settled easily they were able to leave half way through the morning, early enough to reach home in good time.

True to their hope, they arrived in the Mbungu just at dusk. Titi began to laugh when she caught sight of her mother carrying a load of wood toward their place. She was waddling exactly as she had imagined. At home, she hugged her mother and laughed when the large tummy kept them apart.

Men don't make much show of affection. Titi knew that her father's feelings had to be observed in his eyes, and felt in his prolonged handshake. She was not disappointed.

"You certainly put lots of peanut butter in the mwamba gravy," Titi observed while smacking her lips appreciatively.

"As you remember, this is a great time of year with lots of food. That rain which soaked you on your way back to school after the New Year saved those late peanuts we planted. The boiled peanuts waiting for us came from that very plot."

It was difficult for Titi to explain her progress at school because neither of her parents could read nor write.

"I can write letters to people now and read their answers. Matondo and I send letters to one another every day just to gain experience. We write in between the lines of finished school work, so that we don't waste any paper."

"Before you return to school, I will get you to write a letter to my sister," her mother was excited about the whole idea of writing to her sister.

The fire cast a pleasant glow as mother and daughter prepare to sleep.

"Mother, are you really well? Does the baby move inside?" Titi asked with a tone of concern.

Grinning happily, Pemba asks Titi to place her hand on her rather large, tummy. Just as Titi placed her hand gingerly, the little one inside made several distinct kicks. Tears of delight flowed down Titi's cheeks as she felt the distinctive movement of her little brother or sister.

"Now I am sure I will sleep well with wonderful dreams." That is exactly what the exhausted schoolgirl did.

There were lots of boiled peanuts left for the morning meal. It was nice to have both her mother and father together for the simple meal.

"My son is in there," Zoao said happily, as he pointed at Pemba's tummy. "He will be a big boy by the time he decides to come out and meet us. Since that old ndoki died, we have had peace."

"By the size of the boiled peanuts, that crop looks ready to harvest. May I help?"

"To tell you the truth, Titi, I have been counting on your help. As soon as we get a day or so without rain, we will harvest them. It takes a lot longer to dry peanuts when we have to put them out and bring them back in to dodge the rain. I will need you to pull out the plants. I can separate the peanuts from the roots. I really can't do very much now because I can't bend over far enough." Pemba explained.

Two days later, the perfect weather came, and the plump peanuts were pulled out of the earth rather easily, leaving few behind. The peanut plants were put in stacks to dry. When Titi had everything pulled and piled, a sudden shower washed off all the earth, leaving the almost white peanuts fully exposed to any drying conditions that might come during the next day or so. The bright sunshine did its work the afternoon the crop was pulled, and all morning the next day. When dark clouds threatened rain, Titi put all the peanuts in one huge pile and covered it with a sheet of plastic just as the deluge began.

Drying out by the fire, Titi asked her mother what they did years ago to protect peanuts in the rainy season.

"Before the arrival of plastic, we had a struggle to save our harvest some years. When your grandmother was a girl, they only grew enough peanuts for their own use. Now we try to grow enough peanuts to sell. Everything changed when food began to be reckoned as money after the regular arrival of trucks in the markets."

When the weather cleared, Titi and her mother set to work pulling the peanuts from the plants. It was surprising just how much the peanuts had dried in those few hours of bright sunshine. In the course of the day, they discovered that they had four small jute bags full of peanuts.

"When these are dried, my guess is that they will fill two of the big market sacks," Pemba estimated. Titi made three trips, while her mother brought only one sack to their house, because of the awkwardness of her walk. They were delighted with the harvest that had been salvaged by one strategic rain at the beginning of the short dry season.

"I have lost strength because of sitting in school every day," Titi was actually trembling when she finally reached their cooking hut with her last precious load of peanuts. She had just laid down her third sack, when the rain began falling in torrents. The downpour continued until late at night.

Zoao came in the door and sat to dry out by the fire. "You were just a little ahead of me. I went to the peanut field to help carry, but you had already left. I have some beautiful nsafu fruit for supper. We have just one tree that bears fruit this late in the rains. If we had some boiled peanuts to eat with the nsafus, I would be totally satisfied. These nsafus are from old Mfumu Kubukubu's special tree. I always bring him meat from the hunt, and he shares his nsafus with me.

He has some frightening fetish charms tied to his tree. Fortunately they are harmless when I pick fruit with his permission. No one ever tries to take his nsafus, even though the tree is a considerable distance from the village. About ten years ago, a young man tried. He even bragged about it when he had drunk too much palm wine. Two days later, his stomach became swollen until it was fatter than your mother's. He died in agony. Since that time, no one has even thought of stealing the old chief's fruit."

Nsafus induce sleep, so the whole family fell asleep around the fire despite the sounds of torrential rainfall. The next day was filled with bright sunshine and there wasn't a cloud in the sky.

"I think the weather has changed, so we must get our peanuts spread out to dry. They seem beautifully mature, and I expect that they will dry in about two weeks of sunshine," Pemba predicted.

Thieves, monkeys and men

Certain that the heavy rains must have exposed some peanuts that stayed in the ground when the plants we pulled, Titi and her mother went back to the field. Dotted all over the field were the uncovered peanuts, exposed by the rain-provoked erosion. As they arrived they startled a troop of monkeys, whose watchman screamed from his treetop.

"We just arrived in time before that band of thieves was able to get started."

Titi and her mother gathered almost a basin full for their effort.

"I just thought of a great story to spread. I could tell people that those monkeys are really your helpers from the land of the dead," said Titi. "As a secret ndoki, you use them to get your fieldwork done."

"Would anyone believe me if I spread such a story?" Titi wondered.

Mama Pemba nodded. "People would believe your explanation because it happens sometimes."

"It wouldn't be difficult to discredit someone would it, mother?"

"Destroying someone with a lie is not hard at all. I think it happens all too often," Pemba concluded with sadness.

They told Zoao about the troop of monkeys with the hope that he might be able to shoot one or more. The kind of monkey that robbed their crops was delicious as meat. He made a plan to go hide near the garden well before daybreak so the scout would not see him entering the field.

"I need to try and guess just how those monkeys are thinking in order to stand a chance of capturing one of those wily thieves."

Anxious to help while she was home, Titi looked for jobs to do each day. Her mother asked her to dig up a good quantity of manioc and put it in the water to soak. Before she even left for the field, she heard a resounding gun shot.

"You will see our meat before I do. Your father is a great hunter. There is no chance to shoot twice at a troop of monkeys. You should meet each other on the path."

The smile on her father's face told Titi that she would have a taste of fresh monkey before returning to school. Zoao displayed a good-sized young male.

"This fellow was their scout. He was climbing a tree right near to my hiding place. He is still young enough to be tender."

Titi noticed that her father had tied the tail around the monkey's neck forming a carrying handle. A large leaf covered the face so no one had to look into such a human likeness.

The monkey had been well fed from people's gardens, so the meat was exceptionally tasty.

"Lala told me that in Luanda it is only the rich who manage to eat this kind of meat. We may not have much sugar, milk, or bread, but we have lots of other food that only the rich can afford."

The whole family gathered together at mealtime because they treasured the days of Titi's visit home from school.

Always curious, Titi asked her father a question. "Is it true that some ndoki witches can turn themselves into monkeys?"

Zoao replied with an illustration. "If monkeys had ruined our peanut crop, we would suspect that they might have been ndoki witches in disguise." Zoao paused before continuing with his answer to his inquisitive child. "Sometimes, ndoki witches turn themselves into monkeys. On other occasions, a troop of monkeys is managed by an ndoki witch. The monkeys are his slaves because of his powers."

"Has anyone seen someone while he was turning into a monkey, or changing back to become a person?"

Once more Zoao hesitated before answering, weighing in his mind whether he should answer Titi as an adult, or give her an evasive answer. He decided to give a full answer.

"Five years ago, a hunter from a village near here was shot by another hunter. The man who died was called Duma. Nani Zeyi was considered to be the best hunter in these parts. He shot far more game than anyone else and he was accused of shooting Duma, another very successful hunter.

"It seems that Tata Duma had made a kind of a nest up in a tree, where he could wait for game to pass by. Animals don't expect danger from above. That was one of the hunting secrets he taught me one day. Nani Zeyi was watching the trees because he was hunting for monkeys. When he caught sight of a big one moving very slowly, he took careful aim and fired. To his horror, the big monkey turned out to be Tata Duma shot through the heart. Apparently Tata Duma was an ndoki witch, who could turn himself into a monkey when he traveled in the forest. His magic enabled him to creep up on the many animals he killed. He was the one man I knew personally who was judged to have been an ndoki who turned into a monkey when hunting in the forest."

Titi's bright little mind was spinning. "Couldn't Nani Zeyi have shot Tata Duma by mistake?"

"That is exactly what many thought. The ngombo diviner who judged the case made a clever decision. He knew that many people were jealous of Tata Duma because he was so successful in the hunt. People didn't like him. He was dead and could not speak for himself. Declaring that Nani Zeyi had shot an ndoki witch, set him free."

"Is the judgment of the ngombo always right?"

"I don't rightly know, child, but the ngombo is the best authority we have to settle cases like that."

The peanuts were becoming lighter each day as the hot sun dried out the moisture. After three days of good drying weather, they actually began to rattle inside their shells. This was the first measurable sign of progress. Peanuts that don't get adequately dried can make people ill. By the time Titi was ready to return to school, she was able to take a basket of peanuts that could finish drying in Lufu.

"Titi, we will go to Lufu with the marketers. I have some dried meat to sell. I like to see people in the market so I can know about the political situation. Folk from Luanda hear what is happening everywhere. The meat money will pay for your last months of school." Titi was pleased that she would walk back to Lufu with her father.

In the quiet of the cooking hut, as the embers gradually faded, Titi and her mother have their last bedtime chat.

"Big changes are coming, Titi. I will give birth to our baby just a short time after you return from school for the dry season. I know I will really need your help. I hope that you will be able to go back to school after you help me for a year. It will be wonderful to have you back home again. I am so glad that you have already learned so much.

You are clever like your grandmother. She knows more about every part of village life than anyone I know. She is a very clever gardener and catches fish when no one else can. Our history, the stories of our ancestors, all our customs, taboos, and our rich proverbs, are all stored under her white hair."

"You too are able to learn all sorts of new things. I am proud of you, and only wish that people were not so jealous of clever people. If you can be clever and humble, you will be fine. If your cleverness makes you arrogant, you will not have a good life.

"I worry about the war too. The road to Luanda has only been open a year or so now. Before, there were too many ways to blow up trucks and kill people. I have heard so much talk about kimpwanza (independence). They said we would live like the white Portuguese but that will not happen. All the white people have left the small towns, and more than half of our people have fled to the Congo as refugees. All I know is that life has become more and more complicated since I was your age. I want you to learn all you can, but I want you to remain the same wonderful, thoughtful person we have always known."

"Mother, I want to grow up to be like you. When I have children, I want to be the kind of mother you are. I'm glad our village is small and on a road that trucks can't pass so that we can stay out of the war."

"Titi, my child, soldiers can reach our village without trucks. The only time I wish we lived in a town is when we need a hospital. When we get seriously ill, we die because there is no modern help."

"Do you worry about having the baby, mother?"

"Yes child, sometimes I do. We have the shaman to protect us but we have far too many ndoki witches who are ready to suck life out of our babies or us. Losing two babies one after the other has put fear in my heart. I have protective fetishes tied to my body, like you. We have teki (protective images) to protect our house, but often I don't trust those things. They did not save my other two babies. I am not telling you these things because I am more afraid than others. I think most village mothers feel the same as I do. The days you are here are my happiest days. Titi, in a few short years you will be a woman too so I want you to enjoy being a young girl learning all you can"

There was a long pause, and her mother began the deep breathing of sleep. Titi stayed awake a while thinking over the many things her mother had said. She realized that her mother had opened her heart to her. It was a very special talk that helped her understand the joys and fears that filled her mother's soul. No one had ever talked so intimately with her before about such important feelings.

A rapid trip back to Lufu and school

Market people generally left very early during the rainy season with the hope of avoiding the afternoon thunderstorms. Titi found that she really had to make her feet fly to keep up to the pace that her father and two women set. About mid-morning, they reached the banks of a stream where they decided to eat while they had good fresh water to drink. As usual, her mother's kwanga bread had its deliciously familiar taste. Eaten with stiff chunks of peanut butter laced with ndungu peppers, it was a satisfying meal. Before they moved on, they each filled their small calabashes with water because they would not pass over another stream until they were almost at Lufu.

No one was overloaded. The women were carrying prepared mbika (squash seed) loaf. Zoao had a large chunk of meat in his hunting bag, and Titi carried a second piece of dried meat together with her precious peanuts. Walking at their pace, in single file, it was not easy to carry on conversations, but they managed anyway by raising their voices.

"What is all this talk of kimpwanza (independence) we keep hearing about at the market? People have talked about that ever since the war with the Portuguese began in '61, almost fourteen years ago. Nothing good has ever come from that idea yet," the brightest young woman remarked.

"I think that you should give your question to someone from Luanda, "Zoao recommended.

"I'm glad the road to Luanda is open again after such a long time. It is nice to be able to trade again in the market," she observed.

"That road could be closed at any time." Zoao pointed out. "One of the reasons I am coming to the market is to get some idea of what is happening in our country these days. Kimpwanza has caused incredible suffering so far. Thousands have died. All the white traders are gone from the north. Hospitals and schools have been closed ever since thousands fled to the Congo in those early years. Sometimes I try to listen to the news on the chief's radio, when he has batteries. Those people on the radio talk Portuguese too fast for me to follow. So many of our young men have died, or been away so long that we don't know whether they are alive or not. I agree that this whole kimpwanza idea has only brought suffering, death and destruction."

Fortunately, there was no morning thunderstorm, and the fast walking brought them to Lufu, just as the warning wind blew dust clouds around the town to warn people of the deluge waiting to fall from the billowing black clouds. Titi and her father just reached Mama Nkenda's house a moment before the violent thunderstorm began. There was such a roar on the metal roof that no one could talk; so Titi and her dad fell asleep while the thunder roared and the lightning flashed. After an hour or so the storm passed completely and the washed world was again bathed in late afternoon sunshine.

Titi gave her aunt the good piece of dried meat that had been prepared for her. Zoao went into Sami's house where he was refreshed with palm wine, and private conversation. Sami knew what was happening and often lowered his voice to a whisper, when telling Zoao things that were not general knowledge.

New threats of approaching conflict

"There will be big changes before long. There is going to be serious war between FNLA and MPLA (the two major political forces in the north at the time). Holden feels cheated by Neto. Tension is rising in Luanda. When MPLA decides to slaughter the northerners, we will see a kind of war that we haven't seen yet."

"Will the fighting come up this far?" Zoao whispered his question.

"If Holden's forces lose in Luanda, it will come here. Holden's FNLA can't defeat the MPLA, with all the equipment they were given by the Portuguese".

Sami cupped his hands when he made the next statement at a very low whisper. "I've heard that the MPLA is getting a whole battalion of Cuban Soldiers to fight on their side. If they come, they will have all their own trucks and tanks."

Zoao pursed his lips and whistled, showing his alarm.

"You can never be sure about these kinds of information. If anything happens, we will head for the Congo and we will send Titi back to your village. I will not go to Luanda again, speaking Kikongo is becoming more and more dangerous there. All the police and soldiers are Kimbundu speakers. Some of the Kimbundu people are on our side, but the ones with the government of MPLA are threatening us already. You are lucky you live in back country far from the truck road. Once the rains end in late May, I am expecting trouble."

Sami and Zoao ate supper together. Sami offered Zoao a good sleeping mat saying that he knew he must be tired. Zoao was soon fast asleep with the sleep that comes from fatigue, because he certainly didn't have peace of mind.

The last two months of school

Matondo and Titi met at their favorite booth on market day. The lady, who sold jewelry, simple cosmetics, and lots of pretty things, welcomed the girls because she knew she could trust them.

"What is this?" Matondo asked holding up a peculiar kind of soap called Ambi.

"I don't think you girls will need this kind of soap. It is so strong that it turns a black person's skin white! Look at the faces of the truck driver's dumba (prostitute). See how white it is, almost like a white person? To get white like that, they scrub their skin with ambi. They think they look more beautiful that way, and they want to be picked up by truck drivers so they can buy and sell in the markets without paying for their passage."

The whole idea of scrubbing your face and arms white struck the girls as hilarious. No one but the market lady knew why they were laughing.

Titi whispered in Matondo's ear. "Look, their legs are the same color as ours. I think they need to buy more soap." This observation set the girls laughing again.

"I'm glad I don't need to be pretty like that," Matondo said quietly.

"Just wait a few years, when you girls are trying to attract husbands, you may be surprised to see what you will be doing to be considered pretty," the jewelry lady predicted.

The girls talked about everything they had done during the school vacation. Both had been helping their mothers. Titi spoke about her mother, and how big she had become. "She will have her baby a week or so after I come back from school".

"They say that we Bakongo (northern tribes) people are no longer safe in parts of Luanda. Many people are coming back to this region. My uncle came here last night. He said that there are killing teams, just like when the white Portuguese went on their killing spree back in '61. The only difference is that now the killer soldiers are black men from the southern tribes."

" If there is trouble coming, that just means that we must work all the harder at our schoolwork," Matondo mentioned quietly. The girls shook their special handshake, used for serious commitments to one another.

Their teacher knew that the girls needed a lot of help with the Portuguese language. In fact, he used Portuguese with them from Christmas on. They could read and write in their Kikongo language, but they needed knowledge of Portuguese to be able to read the most interesting books he owned. The girls agreed that they would try to talk with each other in Portuguese until the school year ended. This turned out to be a real struggle even though it enabled them to progress considerably in the last two months.

Serious trouble erupts

The last day of school came far too quickly for the girls. Master Pedro gave a letter in an envelope to each child. "Please give this letter to your parents, so that it will be carefully put in a safe place. This letter tells your next teacher what you have already learned, so he will know how to teach you."

"Children, I am sorry to say that serious fighting has broken out in Luanda. A whole division of foreign, Cuban troops has come to make sure that the Communist MPLA party governs our country. I listened to my radio this morning. As I am talking to you, our people are being killed. Trucks can no longer go from here to Luanda. Unless our FNLA soldiers can hold them back, the Cuban soldiers and MPLA soldiers will be heading north."

Master Pedro shook hands with each child as he gave out the envelopes. When he came to Titi and Matondo he gave them special words of encouragement.

"You girls are both gifted, and intelligent. You should continue in school if you get a chance. Titi, you are well along in grade-three work. Matondo, I have placed you half way through fourth grade. I am thankful that we made it to mid June without being interrupted. I have been called into the army. We may not see each other again."

All three had tears in their eyes as they shook hands with full hearts.

"Before we separate, let me pray for us all."

With closed eyes, Master Pedro poured out his heart for the school children he had learned to love.

"Dear God, you know every one of us, and you really care about us. I know that you would like to guide each of us by placing the Spirit of Jesus, your son, inside our hearts."

Opening his eyes, their teacher prayed for each of them by name.

"Lord we all need you, especially in the days we are facing. Help each of us to trust you and call out to you for help and wisdom. I pray in Jesus name, amen."

Titi had never heard anyone but her teacher pray to the God who created everything. When he mentioned her by name it touched her deeply, and she remembered his prayer for years to come.

"He talks to God as though he knows him and is sure that he is being heard," Titi remarked. "I would love to be able to trust in God the way he seems to."

On their way home, the girls saw trucks coming into Lufu loaded with more people than they had ever seen on a truck before.

"They are fleeing from Luanda." Sami explained to Titi as soon as she entered the door.

PANIC AND ESCAPE

Titi stood in solemn silence as Sami spoke to their household.

" The war is coming this way. Cuban troops with trucks, tanks, and big machine guns are too strong for our FNLA soldiers. They are retreating, running for their lives. We too must leave immediately. Leave everything! Grab some food and hurry out to the market. The truck I have hired is waiting right now.

Titi, you must head for home at once. Take something to eat. Take a sack of my salt. I can't take anything with me. There will be no salt for a long time. We are heading for Lukala in Congo Zaire, where I have relatives."

There was no time to say goodbye in the panic that followed. Titi only managed to embrace Mama Nkenda for a moment, long enough to say; "You have been a wonderful mother to me and some day I will join you in Lukala."

Titi left with her schoolbooks, clothes, and a whole sack of salt. As she walked through Lufu, she was appalled at the confusion and panic that had taken over. An old man refused to get on the truck. "I refuse to die in a foreign land!" he moaned.

Titi watched the family weep because they were obliged to leave him behind. Warned by the people who had barely escaped being killed in Luanda, a combination of panic and reason pushed people to follow the advice to flee while they could.

Titi's load was heavy because of the salt. She took a kwanga, and some salt fish for travel food. As she walked, she found herself weeping uncontrollably, as she left Lufu behind. Machete in hand, she began her long lonely journey. Her hope was to reach home before it was too dark. By mid afternoon she arrived at the banks of the brook with the tree bridge. Stopping to eat and rest, her thoughts turned to Matondo. She wondered if they would ever meet again. Tears filled her eyes, as she realized that her life would never be the same again.

Her thoughts turn to her teacher. "If he joins the FNLA army. He could be killed by those advancing Cubans," Titi found herself worrying out loud.

She was sobbing quietly, when she became aware that someone was watching her. Looking up, she couldn't believe her eyes.

"Father, father, you have come!"

With a smile lighting her tear stained face, she embraced her father. In a rare show of affection, he drew her to him.

"We heard what was happening on the chief's radio, so I left this morning, to come and get you."

"What is making your basket so heavy?" Zoao asked her.

Titi recounted all the events of the morning. "Sami told me to bring a sack of his salt because he said we would be without it for a long time."

"Sami was a wise man to get out with his family. Not many are wise enough to leave riches behind. You, my child, are a brave girl."

Zoao put more than half the sack of salt in his hunting bag leaving Titi with a normal load. "Let's move as quickly as we can, as your mother is very worried about you."

"We will follow Sami's advice and stay right in our village at least until after the baby is born. By then we may know what will be best for us." Zoao reasoned out loud.

"How is my mother?" Titi asked anxiously.

"She seems fine, and her baby must be a big one by the looks of her."

Since they were walking quickly, they really didn't try to converse much more. There was no danger of rain because the dry season had begun. They arrived about two hours after nightfall.

Clasping her daughter's hands, Mama Pemba repeated over and over, "You are safe, you are safe! How did you get here so quickly?"

"Our brave little daughter was half way home, resting at the stream when I met her. Sami had warned her to hurry home. She was carrying a whole sack of salt that Sami gave us." Zoao said proudly.

Of course the whole story was repeated not only to Titi's mother, but also to the chief and a number of village leaders, who wanted to know just what was happening in Lufu.

The weary travelers ate a good meal of beans and fufu before they went to bed. Zoao slept in the cooking hut too, because it was cold enough to make a good fire inviting. He kept the fire burning all night long. He was doing a lot of thinking. War was changing their lives again. He thought of how fortunate they were in their village to be well off the truck road with rich forests and gardens to meet their daily needs.

"We survived the long years of the war with the Portuguese; we will survive this war too," he kept mumbling to himself.

The stress of the previous day left Titi exhausted, and she didn't even hear the regular wake up call. It was almost noon when she finally aroused, feeling confused, as to where she was, and especially the time of day. A kindly neighbor had brought sufficient water for breakfast but the supper dishes were still waiting to be washed. Outside, she found her mother making palm fruit gravy.

Home in Mbungu with new challenges

"You were so tired that we just let you sleep. Come and have some roasted peanuts to give you some strength. I don't know how you managed to carry that twenty kilogram sack of salt, along with your other things, as far as you did." After eating a good number of her mother's fat peanuts, she revived.

"I will run to the water now, at least I can do that for you. Later this afternoon I will bring in some wood, or do anything you want."

The village girls laughed as they watched Titi coming down to wash dishes so late in the day.

"Did you sleep until now?" They asked in surprise. "I would have been afraid to come from Lufu all by myself."

"Well, I was afraid to stay in Lufu with all the confusion that was going on there," Titi replied.

For the next half hour, the girls asked all about her experience until they ran out of questions.

"Are you going to live back here now?" one of the older girls asked excitedly. They had all missed her while she was away in school.

"My mother will soon give birth to our baby so I will have lots of work to do, but I will be here." Her friends were very pleased.

Returning with clean dishes and pots, as well as a supply of fresh water, Titi sat down beside her mother for a little while before she returned to their newest garden spot to get firewood. In the dry, cool season, called Sivu, they used more wood, because it became much cooler especially after the sun went down.

"It was hard to leave Mama Mbuta's house in Lufu. They had so many nice things. There were five sacks of salt, ten five kilogram bags of sugar, and a big sack of dried fish. I wanted to bring us sugar, but I just could not carry any more than the one sack of salt."

"You made a good choice, salt is far more important to us than sugar. Meat goes bad so quickly without salt."

"Do you know that you were born in the first month of the dry season eleven years ago? Already you are becoming a young woman. You know how to do every kind of work we village women do. I can hardly believe that you learned to read and write in just one year. I am very proud of you. I overheard an older woman saying last night when you came home that she would rather have one child like you than a dozen like many of the children she knew.

"I notice that your breasts have begun to show just in this one year. Once a girl has breasts everyone knows that soon you will be able to give birth. Before long, men will be asking to marry you. Now that the war is getting worse, young men will be in a rush to marry and father children. They don't want to die without leaving at least one child to keep alive their memory. You will need to be wise."

Titi laughed at first, then sobered when she answered. "Mother, everything you said is true, but I have such a hunger to learn in school that I will not even be tempted to marry for a long time. You may trust my words, mother, I am determined to learn more before I consider marriage."

"I brought home some fish hooks from the market. My friend, the jewelry lady, gave me a little metal box with ten good hooks and some line. We made a deal. I was supposed to send her three good-sized catfish in payment. She would keep on sending hooks and line in exchange for the fish. I'm sure she is on her way to the Congo now, and I may never see her again. All my friends and relatives from Lufu are gone. It is hard to believe."

Zoao was present when Titi talked about the hooks. "Let me have a hook and I will catch us a good fish for supper. I have line but lost my last hook when a big catfish got away with it." Off he went on his mission.

"Mother, you are so big now, do you suppose you will have twins? We were fishing in the bisimbi (water spirits) hideout. Perhaps they changed your pregnancy to twins as you told me they could do."

"The ama (traditional midwife) has felt me with her hands and is sure that there is just one big baby. Titi, sometimes I feel afraid. You were small but I really struggled to help you be born. My bones are small, that is why I wonder. There are no doctors anywhere now, if the baby gets stuck. I don't want you to worry, but I want you to know what I am thinking. You are the only one to whom I have ever shown the thoughts of my heart. I will give birth very soon now and I am so glad you are here with me."

Her mother was quiet for a long time and then spoke very quietly and deliberately. "If I should die, I want you to go live with your grandmother. You two get along well. I know that I accused her of eating my babies. Now I am sure that that ndoki aunt of mine who died destroyed them. I'm sorry I trusted the Ngombo diviner instead of my mother. Perhaps some day you can tell her how I feel now. We have always spoken of 'Ndoki a mwini' (witch of the sunlight) as well as 'Ndoki a fwa' (witch of death). I believe that she is of the sunlight. She will soon need someone to help her in her advanced age. Already her knees are getting very stiff. My older sister from Lufu has now gone to the Congo. Yes, I want you to go with her if anything happens to me."

It only took one teardrop in her mother's eye to start Titi into quiet sobbing. The two held hands warmly for a long time, unashamedly reaching out to each other for support. This was a precious time for both mother and daughter. Such intimacy was uncommon because of ingrained fear and distrust. No one ever knew which blood relative was a secret killer witch.

"We are both alive and well," Pemba said, breaking the spell. "Let's enjoy every day we have, and laugh some while we are doing it."

"I wish there were more people around to whom we could open our hearts without fear," Titi sighed. "Did you and my grandmother ever talk like we do?"

With sadness in her voice her mother replied negatively. "Mother had already been accused of being an ndoki witch while I was a bit younger than you. I was afraid to ever show her my heart."

"I just can't get around to do very much these days so you need to become the woman of the house. Just do what you see needs to be done. I can cook and tend the fire but not much more.

"There is no manioc soaking at all, but the sweet potatoes planted after the early peanuts were pulled should be about ready to eat now. If they aren't ready, you could pull some malanga (a large leafed plant with a turnip sized root that tastes like potatoes). I would love to have some sweet potatoes with fish and peanut butter laced saka saka. I am sure you father will bring us a fish."

Titi did what was necessary during the afternoon. As she went about their gardens, it was easier to know just what was ready and how she should carry out her duties. It became evident that her first task would be to put sufficient manioc to soak, so they could soon begin to make fufu again.

Returning in the late afternoon, Titi's basket was loaded with sweet potatoes and firewood. A bundle of manioc leaves covered the top, and flopped over her head like a green hat. The cherished catfish had been in thick smoke all afternoon. Somehow her mother had made a good supply of peanut butter. Titi put the sweet potatoes on to boil and set to work at once making the saka saka.

"We will eat well tonight," she said, with a smile on her young face.

Appearing again just before supper, Zoao explained that the chief's youngest son, Afonse, had just arrived home.

"He grew up in Luanda, speaking Kimbundu like a native. He was an MPLA soldier, and came north with the Cubans. While the soldiers were sleeping in Lufu, he slipped away to come here. He was afraid that someone who knew him would make his leaders suspicious that he was not a native Kimbundu speaker. He hid his uniform in a plastic bag in the forest.

"He confirmed that there was a blood bath in Luanda as the MPLA and FNLA fought for power. He said the arrival of the whole division of Cubans, complete with their own food supplies, took away all hope from the FNLA. Most people in Luanda just hid in their houses, or began to flee to the countryside. The city became more calm after a week because the FNLA soldiers retreated to the north with a combination of Cubans, and MPLA, in pursuit.

"According to Alfonso the only people left in Lufu are a few old people, too feeble, or too stubborn, to leave. Alfonso felt that it should be safe here for a long time yet. He said that the MPLA and Cubans wanted to capture Mbanza Congo from the FNLA and force them to become refugees in the Congo Zaire. Most of the villages along the main truck road are abandoned. His guess was that many were in the forest, while others will be pushing through the wilderness to seek refuge in Congo Zaire."

The cooking fire always felt good in the cool season, so Zoao ate in the cooking hut with his family.

"I am going over to the chief's house to find out the latest news of the war. His son Alfonso understands Portuguese perfectly, and can easily explain what we hear on the radio. I may brag a little too, about enjoying the food cooked by my two women."

The first pains of childbirth, prelude to tragedy

When Titi was awakened by the usual rooster call, she found her mother fully awake but leaning against one of the malunzi (upright house supports) of the cooking hut.

" Mother, how long have you been having pains?" Titi asked with alarm in her voice.

"The pains began with the first rooster call, and they have been getting more and more frequent. I think that the process of labor has really begun. You should call Mama Tadi, because she likes to be with the person giving birth from the beginning. She will bring in her special teki (doll like object of worship). She says it will give me strength to give birth."

Titi looked more worried than excited, when she made her trip to the stream. As she went down the path, she felt an ominous oppression. "I should be delighted, but instead I just feel afraid. Her baby is much too big for her small body. I wish I could trust the protective fetishes. Why do I doubt, when I should feel secure? It is good that the baby is coming during the day, when ndoki witches don't like to expose themselves." She mumbled as she hurried along the path.

At the water's edge, she met up with several other girls, but decided not to say anything until she had called Mama Tadi. She wasted no time in chatter, but returned as soon as her work was done.

"Giving birth is wonderful, but it is frightening too. Some young mothers have died here in my own lifetime. Everything would be perfect, if we only had a way to stop ndoki witches from spoiling life," Titi talked to herself all the way to the house.

"I will put the water on for coffee, and then go call Mama Tadi as you said. I don't think I will be doing much in the fields today."

It was broad daylight when she arrived at Mama Tadi's house. She was a widow woman, and all her children were grown up and married. Her grandchild, who lived with her, was roasting peanuts when Titi arrived. "I've come to get your Nkaka (grandmother). Where is she?" The bright little seven year-old looked up from her spot beside the fire.

"She went to the water but I think she will be here soon." Titi sat on the very low stool beside the little girl.

"My mother is going to give birth today. That is why I came to call your grandmother."

"Nkaka will not be surprised that you want her help. We have all noticed how big your mother's tummy has become. Nkaka has been expecting your call. I'm sure she will be over as soon as she eats.

Satisfied that the little girl was both bright and reliable, Titi hurried back home. As she came through the door, her mother was in the middle of another contraction that seemed to last a considerable length of time. "Please bring me some breakfast, I think I will eat it standing because it is so much more comfortable."

Titi turned the big su (mortar) upside down to make a tiny table near her mother. Taking an aluminum plate she placed a good-sized sweet potato, a pile of peanuts, and a mug of coffee within easy reach.

While her mother was still eating, Zoao came in. He had been out collecting his palm wine. From his hunting bag he produced a dozen huge nsafu fruits, so ripe they were jet black. Tit was surprised that there are any nsafu left in the forest. As her father sat down to eat, Titi slipped the fruit in under the coals.

"These nsafu will give you strength to buta (give birth)," he said with an encouraging smile. The words weren't out of his mouth when a hard contraction contorted Pemba's face.

"We should call Mama Tadi. It will not be long now, " he said anxiously.

"She is on her way," Titi affirmed with certainty. "Are you afraid, father?" Titi queried, looking right at him.

"I'm more excited than afraid," he answered, carefully hiding his emotions. "I expect to have my little hunter before the day is over."

They were savoring the delicious nsafu fruit, when they heard Mama Tadi at the door, clapping her hands as a request to enter. Pemba herself welcomed her to come sit by the fire. The old lady looked all around, then let her gaze rest on the expectant mother. Zoao excused himself and stepped out, knowing that he no longer belonged inside.

"Would you like a hot nsafu?" Titi asked, holding a big one out to their helper. "My nsafos were done two months ago. This is a treat."

The old midwife was still savoring her nsafu, when Pemba had another strong contraction. She watched quietly, with keen observant eyes. "The baby is on his way, we will see him before nightfall," she predicted quietly.

"Now just let me feel the baby between the pains;" she said as she reached out to examine the enlarged abdomen. "I feel him kicking right here, and I don't like that because it means he is coming feet first. Babies are intended to come head first." She sounded calm but concerned. "I see you have a new mat for the birthing. That is good."

"We will need all the help we can get," The old midwife mumbled to herself as she removed her little teke (carved image) from her raffia bag.

Carved from dark wood, the image was a likeness of a pregnant woman, with large breasts. The abdomen had an opening that was covered by a small piece of mirror held in place by black pitch. The old lady explained that her grandmother had left this powerful teki.

"It protected me when I was born, and it protected me each time I gave birth myself. Behind the mirror in the cavity, my grand mother's hair and fingernails are kept secure. I will address her in the land of our ancestors, and she will send us the power we need."

Chewing some nkaso nut, (cola nut), the old lady spit on the encrusted face of the figure and began to recite her prayer.

"Mama Moyo, come and help us.
Your child is ready to be born.
You are remembered and respected.
Come and help us, come and help us.
Your child wants to join us.
Let your child be born.
It is far too soon for him to go to you.
Stop the ndoki!
Remove the curse!
I am your child Tadi.
I follow in your footsteps.
Curse anyone who wants to eat this child.
Cause him to die tortured.
Help your child to be born.
Bless this child with your spit-covered hand."

Titi sat in rapt attention as the old lady held the teki and spit chewed cola nut on the rather grotesque face each time she repeated her prayer. After each ritual spitting, she expressed her request. "Utudimba, utudimba" "(Hear us, hear us!)" she pleaded.

All are relieved that someone in their midst knew how to call on the supernatural power of the ancestors. Zoao would not begrudge delivering her requested goat in payment.

Any birth in the village was of interest to all the women and girls. They surrounded the cooking hut to watch, help, and give advice until the baby was born. Because the contractions were so strong and regular, all the women stayed in from their fields — sure the baby would be born by noon.

Their conflicting advice made it confusing for Pemba. One group of women was coaching her to push, with every contraction. Mama Tadi, however, spoke quietly. "Save your strength until I can see that the way is open."

The vocal majority was urging her to push, so push she did with all her strength. Mid morning, her waters broke and a cheer went up from the assembly.

At noon, a rather large foot protruded through the birth canal. By then, the excited women were shouting in rhythm. "Push, push, bring the baby, push, push!"

Mama Tadi grasped the leg and pulled to no avail. "The baby is big and he is coming the wrong way, He is caught in the birth canal and can't get out," she muttered.

Titi's heart was racing, because it was obvious that the baby was stuck. Her eyes caught her mother's eyes, and in them she perceived deep fear. They were in trouble!

All afternoon, her mother pushed with her considerable strength, but it was in vain. In the late afternoon, her mother began to loose consciousness at times, as a result of the pain and exhausting effort.

The women gathered in a conference and Mama Tadi gleaned a consensus. "Our traditions say that inability to deliver a baby can be because of the unfaithfulness of the woman giving birth. She must confess her unfaithfulness to her husband in order to survive. She must expose any unresolved problem between herself and her husband's clan."

Pemba understood the tradition. In her frail state it was hard for her to respond. "Before you and all my ancestors, I vow that I have never been unfaithful to Zoao!"

The women nodded, and were satisfied with her reply and vow. All the village women knew that for years Pemba had accused her mother of being an Ndoki witch who was eating her babies. They knew as well, that the previous year one of Pemba's aunts was discovered to be the ndoki killer indicating that her mother was innocent.

"There has been no public reconciliation between them," Mama Tadi concluded. "Until there is a witnessed reconciliation between them. The baby will not move."

Titi hated to leave, but knew that she was the logical one to call her Nkaka to come save their baby. Even at her fastest walk, it took almost an hour for her to reach her grandmother's village of Kiula.

"What is wrong?" her Grandmother asked immediately, seeing the deep anxiety in Titi's face. "Is it Pemba?" Nodding in affirmation, it didn't take long for Titi to explain her mission.

"Mama Tadi thinks that lack of witnessed reconciliation between you and my mother is blocking the birth. Mother told me herself that she was sorry she believed the ngombo rather than you and that she no longer blames you. She may have told you all that privately, but Mama Tadi feels that you need to be reconciled publicly. Please come."

"Of course I will come, Pemba is my own flesh. She has already asked me for forgiveness here in my house. That is all I ever wanted." The two began to walk as quickly as her grandmother's stiff legs permitted.

"The people around here are convinced I am a Ndoki witch quite apart from my relationship with Pemba. I want to be by her side. Titi, run back and catch the white chicken. I need to take it with me. I will keep walking because you can easily catch up with me."

It took some fast running to catch the suspecting fowl. Following instructions, Titi tied the chicken's feet, then procured the pack basket, a sleeping cloth, and her grandmother's sleeping mat.

"This time of day I am not so stiff. In the morning I can hardly move. In any case, it will be dusk when we reach your village."

When she saw Titi with her old mother at her side, Pemba's face lit up a little. Titi was relieved to see that her mother was still conscious.

"Mother, I am so glad you came. You know that we are reconciled, but Mama Tadi said that since I accused you publicly, I should ask for your forgiveness publicly as well." Pemba's voice was just a whisper, but Mama Tadi followed the exchange very carefully.

For all to see, Titi's grandmother spit on her right hand before she placed it on her daughter's sweat covered head in a formal blessing.

After complying with the urgent request, the old lady put her two hands together in the traditional manner of group greeting, and spoke quietly. "Kimbote kieno. (Salutations to all of you) Thank you for surrounding my daughter with your concerned presence. It is true that for a number of years Pemba and I lived in a broken relationship after the ngombo accused me of eating her two babies. In anger I declared the Pemba was no longer my child. I know that rejection of that kind acts as a curse. You need to know that she and I have been reconciled ever since my cousin was found to be the active ndoki witch in our clan. I am prepared to follow the traditions of our bakulu (ancestors) so that there can be no impediment for the birth of this baby."

After delivering her little speech, the concerned old woman sat next to her daughter's head, as she lay stretched out on a mat.

After the contraction, Pemba whispered feebly, but audibly. "Mother you gave me birth, and I want everyone to know that you have helped me all my life. You would have helped my other children too, if your sister (cousins are all called sisters) had not eaten them, and blamed you. You are my mother!"

Pemba's mother pulled her skirts up above her thighs, and then sent Titi to bring earth, from under the Sanda tree. Titi was quick to obey, and was soon back with the requested soil. Sitting next to her grandmother, her young eyes were wide open in rapt attention.

The old lady put the earth on her folded skirt, right close to her stomach. She proceeded to brush the soil down so that it fell between her legs. She was acting out a birth process, symbolically. As the soil dropped between her legs, she intoned her blessing.

"Pemba, you are being born once more from my body. You are flesh of my flesh. You are truly my daughter." Grasping Pemba's hand, she held it up as high as it could go, while repeating the words, "You are my daughter and I bless you."

Silence fell over the whole group. For many, it was the first time they had seen such a meaningful ceremony of reinstatement. True reconciliation was so seldom seen that they were thrown into deep reflection.

Mama Tadi broke the silence. "We need our elders to teach us a better way to live." No one doubted the profound validity of what they had witnessed.

"Ntondele, ngudi ami. (Thank you my mother)." Pemba's breath was swept away by a painful contraction, forcing everyone back to the reality of the impossible situation they were all facing.

Mama Tadi examined Pemba after the contraction and was obviously alarmed to see that the umbilical cord had come out beside the protruding leg.

"The lifeline is in danger," she said. " I must try to push the baby back up inside and turn him around so his head will come first."

With her eyes burning with tears, Titi watched the whole scene. Her bright little mind told her that if the lifeline had come to the outside, her little brother was already dead and she became afraid for the life of her mother, who was fading in and out of consciousness.

When the contraction ended, Mama Tadi pushed the baby's leg up into the birth canal as far as she could manage. Before she could accomplish anything, the next contraction pushed everything back out. The lifeline, as she called it, came out further than before. An ominous hush electrified the room as Mama Tadi prepared to try again.

Someone proposed the calling of the Nganga shaman to put a protective fetish on the protruding leg to thwart whatever ndoki was holding back the child.

The stark words of Mama Tadi stifled that idea. "The child is already dead, and we don't put fetishes on a vumbi (corpse)!"

Titi was sobbing audibly when she felt an arm go around her. Looking up, she saw the compassionate, wrinkled face of her grandmother. Her eyes were filled with silent tears too. In her heart Titi knew that their worst fear was unfolding right before her eyes. The baby was already dead and her beloved mother was dying.

The only source of light was the well-fed fire. On occasion a kerosene lantern was lit to help Mama Tadi see better. They had only a tiny bit of fuel, so it was quickly extinguished when not essential.

The deep darkness of the cool dry season was oppressive because the cloud cover excluded the meager light of the moon and stars. Witchcraft was felt to be a far greater threat in thick darkness. Titi felt the menacing darkness penetrate her very soul.

"Your mother is still alive and we must try to encourage her," her grandmother whispered as though she was reading Titi's thoughts.

As the struggle to give birth dragged on, Pemba became more and more feeble. Her contractions began to fade. Mama Tadi decided that she would make one last effort to turn the baby. The lantern loaned by the chief was lit. A good look at Pemba made it obvious that she had no reserve strength left. When Mama Tadi pushed the baby's leg back up in the birth canal, a huge flow of blood from internal bleeding obliged her to stop almost immediately. Pemba would surely die from her bleeding. Mama Tadi sopped up the blood with a cloth, which she placed in a basin. Solemnly she put a blanket over Mama Pemba, who was no longer conscious.

The village women had been coming and going all afternoon. Fires had sprung up in several sheltered spots where they planned to spend the night. The men were gathered on the south side of Zoao's little house around a generous fire. Pemba was not yet dead but everything was setup in the format of a wake.

Men and boys stayed together as did the women and girls. Zoao was kept constantly informed about his wife. His stock of palm wine was a most appropriate means of expressing his gratefulness for the solidarity of the men. Several of the men present had lost their wives in a similar situation.

Because the afterbirth had separated with the baby still inside, most of the women understood that the end was imminent. The moment she placed the blanket over Pemba, Mama Tadi had acknowledged the obvious hopelessness of the situation.

"Kiadi! (Sadness!)" she whispered looking over at Titi and her grandmother. "I can do no more!"

All were silently awaiting the end. Suddenly Pemba began to shake all over for a few minutes only to fall motionless.

Her old mother, with Titi by her side, put her ear to her daughter's mouth and nose. "Fwidingi! She has died this moment!" the old lady announced with a grief-laden voice.

Suddenly, the little cooking hut and the whole yard erupted with a tumultuous outburst of collective grief. The whole village knew simultaneously that they had just passed over the thin line from a vigil to a wake.

The wake

Mama Tadi tied a kerchief under Pemba's chin so her mouth will not be locked open by the natural changes brought on by death. The screaming and sobbing continued uncontrolled for a half hour or so, and then gradually changed into a choral like, rhythmic wailing chanted in a minor key.

Mournful wailing rose and fell throughout the night. The arrival of additional mourners from other villages caused renewed crescendos of shared feelings and hopeless grief.

The chief's large talking drum (nkoko) proclaimed the death officially. The earth trembled as the huge hollowed log echoed out a clear message that could be heard by the whole cluster of villages in the area.

When the death announcement was drummed for someone you loved deeply, the drumbeat shook your very soul into the acknowledgement of death's reality. Titi's sad little frame trembled with each drum vibration.

Titi sobbed uncontrollably for a long time in the arms of her grandmother who wept silently and internally. "No one ever had a better mother than I did. She understood my every thought and dream. The ndoki didn't even let us see the face of my little brother," Titi whispered after a long silence.

Her grandmother's feelings ran far deeper than her display of grief revealed. She was the elder in charge of the proceedings. Even while she comforted her sobbing grand daughter, she carefully closed Pemba's eyes so they would not be left staring at people when the rigidity of death took over.

After a couple of hours had passed, good friends brought water. Ever so gently, Pemba was carried out to the back side of her cooking hut. The Chief's lantern was lit once more. Titi helped her grandmother and neighbors bathe the mortal remains of their loved one, then procured a fresh new mat and her mother's best clothes. When they had finished the preparation, they carried her, mat and all, to the front of the main house. The one bed the family owned was set about ten feet in front of the door.

Pemba's frail body, still supported in the mat, was placed on the bed. The lantern was hung so it illuminated her face. Village women circled the bed, but Titi and her grandmother sat beside the head of the bed as principle mourners. The first ring of women around the bed were all blood relatives of some degree. When she selected clothes for her mother's funeral, Titi lovingly placed the new bandana on her mother's head, the one she had given her during the Christmas vacation.

The events of the day were overwhelming and sometime after midnight Titi fell into a troubled sleep from pure exhaustion. From midnight until dawn most everyone slept some. There was always someone awake. People took turns, so that Pemba would never be left alone until she was buried.

When Titi awoke from her troubled sleep, she looked around in bewilderment as though she were in the throws of a terrible dream. Suddenly it all registered with a new clarity. Her sobbing turned into a frenzy. She threw herself on the ground, rolling and screaming out her grief.

"Now I have no mother to love me, to teach me, to comfort me. How will I ever marry? My children will have no grandmother. The ndoki witches have eaten all my brothers. Why could they not have left my mother? Have they no pity? How could they force out all her blood right before our eyes?" Other bitter words were swallowed up in shrieking cries.

No one interfered with Titi's expression of grief until she began to pound her head on the earth crying out. "Take me too, let me go with her! Let me go!"

One of her mother's friends, who knew Titi well, held her head in her lap for protection while she wept out of control with cries of bitter hopelessness.

"They will never leave us alone. The ndoki witches have laughed at our protection, at the total weakness of the Nganga Shaman we paid. No one tells the truth. We are surrounded by evil forces we can't stop!" she sobbed.

"Come child, we must go over to our beloved Pemba. Her nose is dead and she no longer breaths, but her ears still hear. She will miss us. Come child," her grandmother whispered.

In the very early morning Titi's grandmother danced a slow dance of grief, chanting a sort of eulogy which included memories, both good and bad.

"You brought me happiness when you were born.
As a child you brought us laughter.
As a little girl you brought me comfort and help.
We planted and harvested together.
Together we made mats and fashioned pots.
When I was sick, your food gave me strength.
You wept with me when your brother died.
You wept when they said I was an ndoki witch.
When the white soldiers killed your father,
You never left my side.
My baby, my youngest, you have left us.
Who will care for me now?
Nkenda has left me too. She is in the Congo.
In the end you knew I did not eat your babies.
We forgave each other after all of those bitter years.
They took you with the baby still inside.
They have no shame as all.
You were the clever one.
When I taught you to garden, you did it well.
When I taught you to fish, you never forgot.
I taught you mat weaving and you surpassed me.
You tried to give me other babies, now I have only Titi.
You have left me your only child.
She is alone when she needs you most.
Tell our elders, tell my mother, I'm coming soon.
Cursed be the Ndoki who sucked out your life.
Let him die in agony.
Don't let them bury you without disclosing.
Who is the guilty ndoki witch?
May all his children and grand children be sterile.
Kiadi! Kiadi! (Tragically sad, tragically sad!)"

Slowly the old woman danced out her pain.

By the time her grandmother had poured out her grief, Titi had given full vent to her sadness and bitterness as well. Quietly the two survivors sat down by the body of their loved one. Choruses of wailing that came and went like the waves of the sea took up their lament. There was profound empathy in the united weeping of women who have wept with one another so often throughout their lives.

Early in the morning Titi was asked to locate a bed sheet that had been used by her mother. Having done so, all of Pemba's blood relations were handed a narrow strip torn from the sheet. This narrow band was tied around the forehead to identify the mourning family. Zoao was the only non-relative to wear the white mourning band. The only other times Titi had worn this band was at the funerals for her baby brothers.

"Now I am wearing the white band for two people at once. Grandmother, how can they be so ruthless? It pains my heart to know that the killer will be with us today wearing a white band because the ndoki witch is always from among our blood relations. What kind of person would eat (kill) my mother with a partly born baby within her? The ndoki who did this must be found! I hate him! I hate him! I hate him!"

Titi's spoken words expressed the feelings of the whole circle of women who were gathered around the remains of a person they loved. The agonizing thought that tortured Titi's inner most being was the fact that the ndoki witch was probably already among them, wearing the mourning band like all the others. How could anyone ever really trust a relative? She realized that the trust and intimacy she had with her mother was without reserve. There was no one who could ever fully take her place. Filled with disturbing thoughts mixed with profound grief and exhaustion, Titi fell into a troubled sleep again for less than an hour. Suddenly a dreadful nightmare jolted her awake.

"Mbuta Mbanza, the one who ate my little brothers, just came to me laughing and said, 'You can't destroy us all, you can't kill us all, can you?' She laughed and laughed until I awoke."

It was Titi's old grandmother who gave her a quiet explanation. "My Child, Mbuta Mbanza is right. All through the years our elders have tried to punish and dispose of all the ndoki witches. Some were burned alive in the market place. Others were thrown off cliffs. Large numbers were sold as slaves. Our wisest elders and most renowned shaman never succeeded. Death continues to stalk us like a starved leopard. One ndoki always seems to be replaced by another."

All the women who heard the explanation nodded their heads in sad agreement. "Fwa tufwanga kaka! (Die, we all die!)" they chanted the simple proverb in unison.

The very old chief Kizolisa was too frail to come over in the darkness, as he had wanted to do. He was the chief of the bloodline (vumu) of the deceased, and lived in the most distant village of their cluster. Until he came, Titi's grandmother was the most senior elder.

Upon his arrival, he and his younger assistant took charge of arrangements for the burial. With the dawn came a large number of people who heard the drum in the night.

Because the Portuguese had been gone from the north for many years, it was very difficult to find lumber for coffins unless there was a crew that sawed lumber by hand. Most of the young men were either in one of the armies, or waiting out their years as refugees in the Congo. The end result was that there were no planks available for Pemba's coffin. The only way left for coffin making was to split planking from balsa type wood that could be split by the skillful use of the axe and the machete. The very practical old chief ordered that such a simple coffin be made at once. The financial resources of the clan were in his hands so he used his authority to dispatch three grave diggers to do their work. Two youths were dispatched to the forest to find the kind of vines they would use to lower the coffin into the grave.

Even before the old chief arrived, men from the village had gathered more than enough bamboo and palm branches to construct a shelter about fifteen by twenty feet square. The shelter protected the area occupied by the deceased and the first circles of mourners.

All the male members of their clan were called to meet under the local sanda tree for consultation. The old chief's assistant had a notebook in which to record all the contributions brought into their circle. Many of the men had brought palm wine. Normally there would have been gifts of money, but their unusual situation with the war made cash contributions rare. The older folk brought the traditional gifts of blankets and sheets, a number of which would be buried with the coffin. Many of the blankets were never removed from their wrappers because they would be reserved by the clan chief to be given at future funerals. Blankets and sheets served as the currency of funeral courtesy.

Men sipped palm wine or a stronger drink made from sugarcane. There was no wailing among them. Their role was more functional; assuring that the burial took place in an acceptable manner. Men would dominate the session of inquest that invariably followed the burial. At least Zoao was surrounded by men, some of whom had lost their spouses on some previous occasion.

The women folk continued the wake in an orderly fashion. A wave of mournful wailing arose each time someone arrived who had not seen Pemba since she died. There was a lot of movement as women built fires and prepared food for the large number of people who had gathered. By ten, breakfast food was available. Titi had no appetite and only ate a few peanuts someone brought her.

All through the night Titi only glimpsed her father from a distance. She knew that eventually he would need to hold the elders of her mother's clan responsible for the untimely deaths.

Mid afternoon, Mfumu Kizolisa made an announcement. "Everything is prepared. We shall complete the burial before sunset."

Four men wearing white headbands brought over the new coffin and placed it beside Pemba's body. When she saw the coffin, Titi was reminded of the beautiful desk she had left behind in Lufu. It too had been constructed with split balsa planks. For a few minutes her mind wandered back to the happy days of school. She wished her teacher, Master Pedro, could talk to her now. She thought of her close friend, Matondo. *"She doesn't even know that my mother has died with my baby brother still inside her."*

"In just a few weeks, I have lost everything that was precious to me," she whispered to herself. *"The war took away all my school friends, our market, and our way of living. The ndoki witches have taken all my brothers and now my mother too."* With all these thoughts going through her mind, and with her tired eyes closed, she was unaware that her mother's body was being placed in the coffin.

Chief Kizolisa and her grandmother were deciding which items should be placed in the coffin. Titi whispered in her grandmother's ear with some urgency. "Nkaka, could we place the baby's clothes in the coffin too? I know right where mother has been keeping them. This way she will have clothes for my little brother in the ancestral village on the other side."

The old grandmother nodded her approval and Titi hurried to get the clothes. She soon located the tin trunk her mother had purchased from the Portuguese shopkeeper, before any of the wars had begun.

"This is my little brother's funeral, too," Titi stated as she carefully placed the baby clothes in the coffin. Everyone was pleased with the idea. The coffin was finally closed and six middle-aged clansmen with white bands on their heads, headed up the procession to the cemetery. Because it was a long walk, they carried the coffin on their shoulders.

Some of the women had milking drums. Others had bibandi (ordinary drums). One woman had an ngongi (welded gong), which she beat rhythmically, with a metal spike. An energetic young woman kept rhythm with a shrill sports whistle from Luanda. The procession was long because almost everyone from the cluster of five villages along the river had come. The death of a mother and child in childbirth was considered to be a major tragedy. Folk sang traditional songs as they walked toward the cemetery located on the edge of the sacred forest.

Suddenly the pallbearers stopped and begin turning the coffin in circles. "The vumbi (corpse) is searching for the ndoki killer!" they shouted.

Everything was thrown into chaotic disorder. Zoao, Titi's father, screamed toward the coffin. "Show us the ndoki! My children have been eaten and now they have eaten my wife too. It is too much! We can't let the ndoki escape or he will want to take my only living child!"

Because her quiet father was shouting with such articulate anger, it dawned on Titi, that he feared that she herself would be the next victim.

In a frenzy, the pallbearers began running back toward the village past the startled crowd. Unexpectedly, the coffin and pallbearers were bearing down on the old chief Kizolisa who was walking behind because of his infirmities. With an audible thud the old chief's assistant was hit so hard he fell to the ground. Five times the coffin was dropped on the writhing body of the man in his late fifties. The pallbearers tried to move away but were drawn back as though pulled by a powerful invisible force. As suddenly as this drama began it was finished. The pallbearers walked back to the head of the procession and lead it to the open grave.

The freshly dug grave was right beside the poinsettia tree that had been planted between the graves of Titi's baby brothers. The mound of fresh earth seemed very large and the grave looked grotesquely cavernous. It was time for selected people to say their farewell to Pemba and her baby.

Nkaka, Pemba's mother, was the first to speak. Kneeling in some soft earth by the head of the coffin, she spoke quietly, with feeling.

"Pemba, my child
I carried you in my vumu (abdomen).
I carried you in my arms.
I carried you on my back.
Whenever you were ill, I couldn't sleep.
I danced when you were married.
The bakulu (ancestors) will tell you that I didn't eat
your babies. I wept when they died.
I wept when you turned your back on me.
I wept when the ngombo diviner lied.
I wept with joy when we were reconciled.
Forgive me for my failures.
You have shown us your killer.
Titi and I will be together.
Ask the bakulu (ancestors) to help us.

Ask the bakulu to protect us from war.
Wenda mbote! (Go well!)"

Zoao came up very quietly and knelt where Nkaka had been kneeling.

"I'm sorry, I'm sorry! Wenda mbote!"(Go well.) Pemba, I will miss you. You have been a good wife. You always did everything I asked. I know you didn't want to leave me. They tore you away from me. Thank you for Titi, I will do all I can for her. Thank you for showing us your killer before you left us. Your luvila (branch of a clan) is filled with wanton ndoki witches. I gave my goats, my chickens, and my money, to buy protection. No Nganga shaman was ever able to stop them. The expensive fetish tied to your body did nothing at all. I couldn't stop them!"

An even greater hush settled over the assembly when Titi knelt to say good-bye to her mother. She felt nervous until she remembered that her mother could still hear her. This was a special occasion to talk with her. Closing her eyes, Titi pictured her mother alive and well.

"Mother, I find it really hard to say good-bye to you. You are a wonderful mother, and I have felt your love as long as I can remember. You have taught me everything you could. I loved working by your side. We succeeded with planting our peanuts even though it was too late. We will be eating them until next dry season. You taught me about fishing when I was still younger than most girls. I'm not afraid of the screech owls now, because you showed me how they hunt. You always answered my questions as though I were much older. Mother, you trusted me to do many things, and I always tried to do what I thought you would want. I will keep on the same way. You made me so happy every time I came home from school. I can read and write because you wanted me to learn. I will help Nkaka as much as I can. Mother, I will try and live so that you will never be ashamed of me. Wenda Mbote (Go well), my mother. I will always love you."

When Titi finished her farewell, all the women looked at one another nodding in deep approval as if to say; "Now that was an example for all of us."

The hunters shot their guns in the air, advising the ancestors on the other side that a respected person was being sent into the world of the living dead. The cemetery was the acknowledged gateway to the world of the ancestors and all who live on the other side.

The coffin was lowered into the grave accompanied with many quiet sobs. Chief Kizolisa nodded his head as he was handed the shovel to begin the actual burial. The sound of the earth falling on the coffin served as a cruel reminder of the reality of death. Titi and her grandmother were among the first of the long line of kinfolk and friends who participated in the burial by throwing earth on the coffin.

As soon as the relatives had all participated, younger men set to work to fill in the grave. No one would leave until the grave was in order and the simple wooden marker carrying the name of the deceased had been put in place. The grave was always dug in an East-West orientation. If ever one were to rise from the grave, he would be looking toward the sunrise.

Pemba 1946-1975. The simple marker recorded. Titi read it solemnly.

Before they left the gravesite, all the pallbearers washed their hands from a calabash of water, which was crushed when they finished.

The main circle of mourners went down to the river. Nkaka called Titi to her side. "Come, this is our first walk to the river. We have done all we can, and Pemba is at rest."

All the women wearing white head bands followed as the elders lead the way to the river for the actual, as well as ceremonial, washing. Out of respect to Pemba, none of them had washed, combed their hair, or changed their clothes since they came.

At the river, Nkaka, Pemba's mother, set the pattern with Titi by her side. "Bakulu (ancestors), together we have sent you our loved one. We have sent her lovingly and respectfully. We ask you to care for her now as we cared for her when she was among us. The smell of death is on us all. Bisimbi (water spirits), we come to your waters to wash the odor of death from our bodies and our clothes. We want to return to our villages cleansed. Grant us all cleansing and health as we plunge into the waters that washed our ancestors before us. Bless us all!"

Titi felt something much deeper than water cleansing as she plunged into the water beside her grandmother. Quietly her grandmother placed her hand on Titi's dripping hair. "Bakulu (ancestors) cleanse her of death, and bless her with life!" Her grandmother's blessing brought release from profound gloom.

"Nkaka, I feel clean again," she whispered to her grandmother.

Although their clothes could only be dried later, they all washed their clothes with water, and put on the clean clothes they had brought with them.

"We will sleep in this village three more days, or until the elders have finished discussing the cause of your mothers untimely death. After that you will come home with me," her grandmother informed Titi.

As they approached a cooking fire, Titi noticed a warm smile on her grandmother's face. The smile sent healing into her broken heart.

Once they returned from the water, cooking fires were fanned into action. Several groups of industrious women made the final preparation for the evening meal. The beans and meat were cooked. For the most part, it was the fufu that had to be prepared in large quantities. The savory smell of the pots of goat meat was most inviting. The clan had supplied two large goats. The men had plenty of palm wine.

Chief Kizolisa walked about making sure that the clan resources were providing a generous feast. There was a festive mood. A good meal to end the funeral was equivalent to a good send-off for the deceased. The local chief supplied two metal tubs to facilitate the cooking. Being the beginning of the dry season, there was plenty of food. Any leftover sweet potatoes would help out with breakfast. Some young women were roasting peanuts, while others were cooking palm fruit, all intended to transform the mountain of saka saka into a treat. The old Chief was very satisfied. Because of the respect for Pemba, people had wanted the feast to be a fitting celebration of her valued life.

"Our ancestors will see our esteem for our daughter and will certainly receive her well," the elder declared.

Titi had no heart for celebration, and was not expected to do any cooking. The family and neighbors were anxious to participate. Her Nkaka was busy supervising the cooking while not expected to actually do it because of her status as an elder.

Watching her grandmother from the sidelines, Titi was amazed to see her interacting with other people. Normally, she isolated her self totally. She wondered whether her grandmother would return to isolation after the funeral. Perhaps it was because she had a right and a duty to fulfill her role that she moved about so comfortably. Possibly, the public ceremony of reconciliation had made some difference.

Most people brought their cups and plates to funerals. A few children would eat off banana leaves. The small children were gathered around large pots of food set on a mat, within easy reach of everyone. Like puppies, the children ate as long as there was food available. Their communal bowl was filled more than once until their tummies began to hurt from sheer volume.

A squealing, struggling pig was brought into the cooking area. His feet were bound together. A pole had been thrust under the tied feet, and the poor creature was carried upside down. As his throat was cut with a sharp machete, a final helpless squeal pierced the air while its lifeblood soaked into the sand. Pork was a treat, and folk would eat some more once the pig was chopped into pieces and cooked in two very large pots. Most people loved pork. However it was cooked separately because it was taboo for some people who lived under the protection of a teki god called Masasi.

Out under the sanda tree, chief Kizolisa doled out the ample supply of palm wine brought for wake and celebration. Everyone who could walk was present. Weddings and funerals were the primary occasions for community gatherings. The men sat or squatted in circles around the wine and talked about the things of common interest. There was a lot of talk about the civil war that had called away most of their young men to all sides of the conflict. They all missed their market in Lufu because through it they kept informed about everything that was going on. Most of the produce they were accustomed to selling found its way to Luanda, where it helped relatives to eke out a living reselling things in markets big and small. All communications with relatives in the big city were now completely broken.

Still early in the evening, Titi and her grandmother retreated to the familiar cooking hut. Both fell asleep on their sleeping mats as the fire warmed the soles of their feet. Eventually, all the women slept in, or around the hut, still maintaining their community of mutual support. Women who were not a part of Pemba's clan went to their homes at first light.

Only the members of Pemba's bloodline stayed for the inquest that followed the funeral. They were descendents of three original mothers of long ago, Tadi-goma, Tadi-mwini, and Tadi-luka. These three ancestral mothers were sisters. Traditionally, there was intense rivalry between these three vumu (literally wombs). Each was anxious to be predominant in terms of numbers of descendents. Although they were all from one original mother, each subgroup always suspected one of the others whenever there were tragic deaths.

Chief Kizolisa was a member of the Tadi-goma line, the same as Pemba and her unborn baby. Diambu, the man singled out by the vumbi (corpse), was a leader of Tadi-mwini branch of the family. It was not a total surprise when Diambu was exposed by the corpse, and injured by the repeated banging of the coffin. They were long time rivals of the Tadi-goma people. The Tadi-mwini line had been dominant until a dozen of their young men were killed in the war with the Portuguese. Tadi-goma witchcraft was felt to have been the underlying cause of the death of these young men who died when a grenade exploded in the hut where they sleeping.

Verbal battles between the rival family branches soon became evident when they assembled for the final inquest of Pemba's death. Fortunately, Chief Kizolisa was both wise and esteemed as a leader. Under the influence of excessive palm wine, men were prone to overstatement but nothing too damaging was allowed to stand unchallenged.

Chief Kizolisa's handclap called the gathering to order. The men sat in a semi circle on chairs, benches and logs. Most of the women sat directly behind the men. When everyone was quiet, the chief recounted all the events leading up to the death of Pemba and her unborn child.

Every minute detail was reported. When he had finished, he requested the reporting of any details that others felt should be added.

Zoao clapped, asking permission to speak. "I was married to the departed for twelve years. In all those years I have only had one living child." With his two hands held together he pointed to Titi. Ndoki witches have eaten all our children except this one. Not only did the Ndoki witches of your clan eat three of my children, but now they have eaten my only wife while she was still of an age for bearing children. I have been cheated, I tell you, cheated!" His voice rose in a mixture of anguish and resentment.

"I know that you can not bring back the dead, but I insist that you allow our one child to live and bear children. It is your duty to protect her! The girl is all I have. I insist that you punish the one accused by the corpse. The vumbi (corpse) never makes a mistake when accusing its killer. Why is Diambu not here in this assembly? If he is left alive, he will eventually eat the whole Tadi-goma branch of your clan, and my daughter is in the Tadi-goma line."

Clapping his hands three times and bowing his head to Chief Kizolisa, Zoao spoke authoritatively. "Mfumu, (chief) protect my child!" With one more bow, Zoao asked permission to leave the gathering because he was from an outside clan.

Addressing the Tadi-mwini clan branch, Chief Kizolisa spoke sharply. "Where is your leader, Tata Diambu?"

There was a total silence. Finally one of the men asked permission to speak. "My neighbor is a hunter and he told me that while he was attending his snares he saw Diambu and his family heading north before dawn. My neighbor said he was afraid to call out an alarm because he feared the fetishes of a killer witch like that man. I reckon he has fled to the Congo where he can hide among all the other refugees."

A murmur of discontent pervaded the whole assembly. A frown of consternation swept like the dark cloud that precedes a violent thunderstorm. Nkaka noticed that Titi had begun to tremble.

"Don't be afraid child, now that Diambu has been exposed, you will be safe. We will have him cursed. He will not live long now. Our Tadi-goma branch has a powerful teki (fetish statue) capable of assuring our enemy a horrible death with suffering. There is no doubt about it my child."

An elder from the Tadi-mwini branch of their clan clapped for permission to speak. When he spoke he used a complicated traditional proverb. For a full half hour, the elders bantered in a contest of proverbs, which encapsulated their traditions. Apparently all possible avenues of opinion were aired. At the first lull in the contest, Chief Kizolisa convoked a secret consultation of a half dozen elders who would "drink water", or in other words seek a consensus.

While the elders were in conference, Titi whispered to her grandmother. "Nkaka, I speak our language, but I didn't understand any of the proverbs the elders used in debate. Why could I not understand? I knew all the words, but nothing made sense for me."

Her grandmother smiled as she replied. "Did you have secrets with your good friend Matondo there in Lufu? Were you not able to say just one word that reminded her of a whole escapade you experienced together?"

A smile of comprehension lit her face. "If I said 'mango' to her, she would think of our whole money making project. When we walked around the market we watched people who were clever at negotiating. When we had understood just how they carried on their dealings, one of us would wink and say 'mango'. That meant that one of us had figured out how they were making their profit. We then moved on, and whoever had captured their secrets explained it to the other.."

"Titi, you have just explained how those elders debated. Sometimes an elder would only speak three words but everyone recalled the deeper meaning intended. Many people here did not follow the debate either. The elders did not wish to be understood by the crowd. You could say that proverbs are, sometimes, the secret language of our elders."

When the elders returned, Chief Kizolisa outlined the proceedings. "Your elders will consult with you, then meet together in secret with me before the sun goes down. My drum will call you back together for the final session."

Titi and her grandmother met with the elders of their Tadi-goma branch of the clan. Chief Kizolisa spoke in a low voice. "We all know that we have enemies, and I want to discuss our defense. Some of the elders want us to call in Nganga Masumu to curse Diambu or deliberate about his guilt or innocence. The vumbi (corpse) does not lie! We all saw how the pallbearers were overcome, and controlled by the power of the corpse. Their faces looked like the faces of men under the power of a curse. They were driven! The spirits of our outraged ancestors took over their minds and bodies. We must stop Diambu and I trust no one but ourselves and the powerful teki our ancestors left with us for our protection."

The wise old chief saw that there was a clear consensus. The women were dismissed for food preparation while the men considered other issues the family needed to settle.

As the women walked away, Titi broke their silence with her observation. "I am not as afraid now, since I have heard our chief speak so confidently. He confirmed what you told me earlier when he said, 'Diambu will never be well again; you can take my word for it!' Does the vumbi (corpse) always choose its killer accurately?" Titi wondered out loud.

"Our elders have always claimed that the vumbi (corpse) never lies. Not every ngombo (diviner) agrees with other diviners. You can't always trust the decisions of a ngombo but as far as I know, it is true that the vumbi (corpse) never lies."

"I watched the pallbearers very carefully, and they certainly seemed to be driven by some powerful force. I was very afraid." Titi confided.

"I noticed the same power you observed. At times the pallbearers plot a plan together to accuse someone. When it is a plot, they don't look driven in the way we saw. Those men were driven by an outside power, so I believe that Diambu was truly the killer witch who ate your mother and her baby. That is why I am sure He will be trapped by our elder's curses. He will become like a living dead man. The vumbi does not lie, and our Tadi-goma clan knows how to destroy an exposed killer witch!"

Titi trembled as a shiver went through her body at the thought of being in Diambu's shoes. "He deserves what will happen to him because he ate my wonderful mother and my baby brother!" Even as she spoke, she felt a knot in her stomach formed by pent-up hatred, resentment, and grief all wound up together.

The position vacated by the affair of Diambu had to be filled and announced while everyone was present. It was important that everyone feel that he or she had been consulted before the elders made any pronouncement. Chief Kizolisa was skilled at orchestrating the whole process of decision-making. He never called the people together to hear his decision until a consensus had been found that allowed them to go on with their lives, despite their rivalries. With the war changing their lives, it was important to have wise leaders they could trust. They never knew when they might be forced to flee conflict, like so many others along the truck roads. In fact many had already decided to escape to Congo Zaire and join those who fled in the sixties.

The sound of the drum called the assembly together again under the spreading branches of the sanda tree. The new assistant chief was presented and approved with applause.

"We have agreed that Titi, the only child of Pemba, will live with her grandmother now that her mother is gone. This will assure us that Titi will be well instructed in the skills and traditions of our elders and ancestors. Her strong young body will be a great help to her grandmother as well."

Nods of approval showed that the consultations had been well conducted. Titi herself felt a new surge of security because she had just been placed in her grandmother's home with the consent of those who knew what they were doing. She was very pleased that her mother's dying wish had been granted, despite all the derision her grandmother had experienced at the hand of these same people. She knew that her father would be free to visit her because he no longer suspected her grandmother for the deaths of his children.

Well before sundown, the crowd had totally dispersed. Titi gathered up her things into one of her mother's pack baskets. A couple of Pemba's basic cooking pots were chosen and carried home by Titi's weary grandmother.

SHAPED BY A WISE GRANDMOTHER IN KIULA

"My life will never be the same again," Titi sighed, as they took the path to her new life with her grandmother. Only a few weeks before, she had been a very happy schoolgirl anticipating the birth of a new baby in the very house where she had herself been born and loved.

"I have lost too much!" she whispered to herself in a voice too low for her old grandmother to hear. *"I have lost my school and all my friends in Lufu. Even if the war ends soon, many will never return. I will never have a mother again. I will only hold a baby of my bloodline when I give birth on some far off day. Because of the war there are many young widows who would be glad to marry my father. Everything I treasured most is gone forever. I am so glad I still have my grandmother. When she is in a happy mood, she reminds me of my mother. There is really no one left to help her but me. Her children are either dead or refugees in the Congo."*

It took over an hour to reach her grandmother's little house, so there was time to contemplate this big, unexpected, change.

A rustic home in isolated surroundings

Her grandmother's house was shrouded in shadows by the time they arrived. The type of construction was typical of the whole area. Upright poles, spaced a foot apart, had reeds woven through them making the house look like a large basket, with a thatched roof. The whole interior of the construction was sheathed with overlapping leaves that reached from floor to roof. The long leaves had been split at the center vein. These veins appeared in neat, vertical, lines two inches apart, because of the careful overlapping of the rather wide leaves. One of the interior walls was covered with a beautifully woven raffia mat, while on the opposite wall her grandmother's reserve sleeping mats hung like tapestries.

The scene on one exposed mat was that of a hunter shooting a large mpakasa (buffalo). Her grandfather had very skillfully woven that mat. A double wicker chair sat under the extended roof that served as a verandah. Titi had never noted before just how skilful her grandparents were. None of the younger men could match this double seat made years ago by her long deceased grandfather.

The makuku matatu (three cooking stones) were actually made from three identical termite mounds that looked like mushrooms out in nature. These cooking stones were baked hard by years of cooking fires. The stones were a mass of little tunnels that once formed the residence for industrious insects. Because of the tunnels, the fairly large stones were not too heavy to move to accommodate a variety of pot sizes. Directly above the cooking stones was an artistically woven loft, placed high enough that one could pass under without bending. The loft was smoked to a glossy black from years of cooking fires. This was a perfect storage place for peanuts, coffee, baskets, and mats, because the daily smoke supply kept out all the hungry insects, which might otherwise destroy such things.

The more she looked around at the careful workmanship, the more she appreciated the craft skills of the grandfather she had never seen. The wood used for construction was all of a sort that termites refused to infest. The two malunzi (upright logs) that formed the support pillars for the roof were made of kwati, a tough wood that even resisted grass fires. Such trees stood strong as iron long after they had died. It was the hardest, most durable wood in the whole region. Titi's new home was old, sturdy, and beautifully constructed by a master builder.

To her delight, her grandmother cleared off a section of the loft, so that Titi could store her little treasures from Lufu, which were still in their protective plastic bags. She wondered when she would open those treasured notebooks again.

They were both still exhausted by the petulant days of unending grief and anxiety they had experienced together. As they stretched out on their mats beside the glowing fire, Titi was entertaining very practical thoughts.

"Nkaka, I have much to learn before I can be of any real help to you. I don't even know where your gardens are located. You will need to show me everything. I am young and strong, and I will help you every way I can, but I will need you to teach me about the way you like things done. I really want to learn about our traditions so that I will be able to pass them on to others. You are our clan's elder, and there is no one but me to listen to your wisdom. My mother told me that you do everything better than most people. I'm glad the clan decided that we should live together."

"You are the only sunshine in my life, child. Your mother was so proud of you, and so fond of you, that I expected you would spend all your young years helping her. My heart is broken by her death, but I am delighted that you will be with me as I grow too old to fully take care of myself. When your mother talked about you, I thought she was exaggerating. I see for myself that you are clever and willing to learn. You are very much like your dear mother. Many young people have no desire at all to talk with their elders.

"The false accusations of a deceptive ngombo shaman have kept us apart too long. As long as your family felt that I had eaten your little brothers, they wouldn't let you spend much time around me. I am so glad that your mother and I were reconciled before she went to our ancestral village through death. You can't always trust the ngombo diviner. Some are wise, and powerful, while others only pretend and live off bribes. Titi my child, I am old, but I still have many unanswered questions. Long experience has helped me to sort out the true and the false, at least to my own satisfaction. We will talk every day. It is wonderful to have someone I love, sleeping right here by my fire." By the time the fire had burned to a soft red glow, they were both asleep.

The voice quality of the nearest rooster changed a little from place to place, but the wake up call in every village, was always crowed on the same schedule. After Nkaka's roosters raucous serenade had ended, the elderly grandmother and Titi exchanged morning greetings cheerily. They both felt greatly refreshed from sound sleep.

"Today, I will begin to show you around. We don't have much in the house to eat. I took all my dry manioc when I was called to your mother's side last week. It is a good thing we brought back kwanga from the wake. We have peanuts, some dry mushrooms, and a good supply of dried beans. We will be fine, but we need to prepare the manioc I put to soak, the day I left. We will not have fufu ready for a week, no matter what we do."

Titi scampered down the steep path behind their house, which led straight to the water. The path was quite short, but very steep. Roots exposed by erosive rains, served as irregular steps. The stream was deeper and narrower than the one by her mother's house. It looked deep enough to sustain fish. "Nkaka will teach me how to fish here, I'm sure," she said to herself, while looking for the spring that supplied drinking water.

The steam came from a deep forest so the fish had never been killed by poison as in many small rivers. On her way back from getting the water, she spotted a large dry branch that had fallen, and broken into pieces that she could carry. Her mother had taught her to always be on the look out for firewood. It was great to have found a good supply, so very near home. Gathering firewood was difficult for her grandmother, because of her stiff and painful joints.

Her grandmother had the breakfast fire burning when she returned. Unloading the water containers she smiled at her grandmother. "I spotted some good firewood, I will be right back. Mother taught me that good firewood waits for no one."

Titi bound a good load of wood together with vines. She carefully placed the load on her head, by bracing one end of the bundle against the steep hillside, while she put her head under the middle.

"Oh child, I am glad for your help! I would need to make six trips to carry that much wood, now that I am old and stiff. Your mother taught you well."

In the afternoon, Titi put all their clothes in the big white basin, so she could do the wash at the stream. "It's a pity we don't have any soap," she mentioned quietly.

"We have soap, but I must teach you how to use it." Her grandmother explained, pulling a bottle out of her pack basket, when they had reached the water. "This is liquid soap made the old way. Put this much in a half basin of water and mix it well. You will have suds enough to wash all these clothes, if you wring out each piece, after washing it in the suds. When you have put everything through the soapy water, then you can go out to that smooth rock and pound as you rinse in the water. When the suds are gone, your clothes are ready to be laid out to dry on the tall grass."

Titi was amazed at the washing power of the liquid. "How did you make this wonderful soap?"

"Some day, I will show you. I boil palm oil together with water that has been changed by wood ashes. The big job is getting the palm oil and preparing the ashes- water. When I have the money, I buy the palm oil from one of the men who make it here. This is the only kind of soap we had, when I was a girl. They told me that the first white settlers showed our people how to make this soft soap.

"Come, I will show you the spring where I soak manioc. I put some to soak before your mother died, but I think it will still be good even if it is mushy. We will pull it out carefully and let the water run out a bit before we try to put it in the basin."

The main reason for soaking manioc three days or more was to remove the natural cyanide that is found in the tubers. Sweet manioc may be eaten fresh because it has no poison however, the more popular bitter manioc must be well soaked before it may be eaten safely.

Titi staggered a little, when she put the basin of soggy manioc on her head with the help of her grandmother. Fortunately she did not need to carry her load too far. Her grandmother had a drying rack over by the path. After it was dry, they would they carry the miteki (dried manioc sticks) up to the house to be pounded into fufu flour.

As soon as the soggy manioc was spread out to dry, Titi washed out the basin in preparation for carrying back their dried clothes. By the time they were ready to go up the hill again, Titi noticed that her grandmother had gathered a considerable load of firewood in her pack basket.

"My joints work better in the afternoon, and I have always made it a habit to never climb that hill empty handed." She would do as much work as she could, as long as her health allowed, that was sure.

Half way up the hill they stopped for a little rest. "Now that I am living with you, I think I should cultivate a field of manioc so we will have enough. When I am hungry, I eat a lot! If you agree, I will ask my father to come over and cut down the big trees for me. My mother taught me how to grow and care for the kinds of food we grow. Please correct and guide me whenever we are working together."

"You have a wonderful idea, one of my biggest problems in late years, has been finding a man to cut the big trees in any fields I have wanted to clear. I know that your father blamed me for eating your two little brothers. Perhaps he knows by now that I was innocent. Perhaps he will clear a field for you, even if he would not want to do it for me. You have a good plan worth following."

Once they had reached home, they were glad to put down their burdens. "I think that you should bring up a small load of our wet manioc. It will have drained a lot by now. We could make up some of it into kwanga loaves which we can eat until the rest is dry enough for pounding into fufu flour."

The errand didn't take long, Titi was soon back with the manioc as well as a good bundle of wrapping leaves, that grew near the water's edge. Soon both of them were mucking in the soft manioc to pull out all the fibers that would spoil their kwanga.

Titi went for water while her grandmother tied up the loaves of kwanga into neat leaf covered packages bound with threads made from fine vines. The extra firewood came in handy to boil the water in the big pot, used for cooking kwanga. By dusk, the pot was boiling merrily. Nkaka prepared gravy made of palm oil and dried mushrooms to accompany their kwanga for the evening meal. Hot, red, ndungu peppers from a bush behind the house gave a great flavor to their mushrooms. They both discovered their appetites; when they finally sat down to eat by the light of the fire. The new 'team' savored their simple meal, after their first day of working together.

The cool dry season made the fire most inviting. Two rather large pieces of wood were placed so the ends would keep one another company, as they glowed red from the carefully made fire. To increase the heat all they needed to do was to push the burning ends closer together. Pushed close enough they burst into flames whenever needed.

Both were very tired and fell asleep without pursuing any further conversation. Their sleep was so sound, that neither had any dreams to report the next morning when they were awakened by the pre-dawn alarm.

"Child, we had kwanga last night so there is only the mushroom pot to wash. Let's sleep some more." They both fell sound asleep once more. They had both gone through a heart-rending, and exhausting period of anxiety, anger, and grief. When they finally awoke, sunshine was seeping through the cracks in the door.

"Would it be all right for me to go back to my village and get some of the peanuts mother and I planted?" Titi asked.

"My child, those were all eaten during the wake and funeral. It is always that way. Don't worry my child. I am old, but I'm still a good farmer, we will have plenty of food, for this first year that we are living together. With your help, we will even have enough food to help folk in need, like old Tata Mbwa. He is old like me, but he is sick and never had any children. I always give him food. There are several people that this village sustains. We always have enough. Come take a look at our reserves for yourself."

Pulling aside the mat that served as a door to her little private storeroom, the old lady pointed with pride to her five demijohns full of dried beans. Each glass wine jug held ten liters. The beans had been lightly coated with palm oil before the jug was corked. No weevils could destroy her treasure.

"We have beans to eat, and beans to plant. I have learned a few secrets about growing beans. I plant them on an incline in the valley. Excessive rain runs off. Should the rains fail, there is enough moisture in the ground to support them for a long dry spell. Around here they call me 'Ndoki witch,' because I always have success with my beans, whether there is too much rain, or too little. The customs I follow have been passed down from mother to daughter since the time of our ancestors."

"Mother told me that the word ndoki can mean diela or wisdom. She told me that some people called ndoki are simply wise people who followed clever customs. Mother said that not all ndoki were evil killers."

"Once more I must say your mother taught you well. Jealous or lazy people are far too quick to call wise people, 'ndoki witches' of the worst kind. They have never known just how much wisdom and hard work can accomplish. They strive for success through magic, or someone's occult powers of kindoki. The young granddaughter was keenly aware that her grandmother's reserves of beans were exceptional.

"Let's put some beans on to boil while I take you to see our crops. I feel strong and well today. When I feel well, I do all I can."

Behind her grandmother's house was an open cooking and work area that was protected by a well-made, thatched roof. Because one side had no wall at all and the other walls were very low, big logs were used for any slow cooking. The smoldering ends of two large pieces of wood kept a pot boiling for hours. In the afternoon, they would finish cooking the beans with a few hours of constant, intense heat.

"We will just eat peanuts and coffee this morning, because we will eat well tonight."

"What kind of special food will we eat this evening?" Titi queried.

Learning how to use Nkaka's special fish traps

"You will just have to wait and see," the unfathomable grandmother quipped with a mischievous smile. Just above the cooking fire were two smoke covered fish traps. She smiled when she pulled them down. "As soon as you can find a half dozen ripe palm kernels from under that tree behind the house, we will be on our way."

Rushing back after a few minutes Titi had a dozen over ripe palm kernels that had fallen to the ground. "Are you going to set your fish traps, Nkaka?"

"No, I'm not going to set them, but you are."

A mixture of surprise and pleasure lit up Titi's pleasant face. "Setting my fish traps is becoming too difficult for me now that my joints are so stiff. When the water is as cold as it is in the dry season, I can't stay in the water without suffering for days. I intend to show you exactly what to do. We will have fresh catfish for supper; I feel sure."

After they arrived at the stream, Nkaka took the lead along a tiny path that followed the course of the stream along the high bank formed by the hill. After a short walk they arrived at her little bean garden.

"Right down there in the stream is where I have had great success in catching fish with these traps. Do you see where the water rushes between those two large rocks? Right beside the rocks, the water is very deep. I like to place the traps so they sit on the bottom, right in front of those rocks."

Reaching in behind a tree, Nkaka pulled out two flat stones, about the size and weight of three large axes. Carefully she pulled out lengths of handmade rope. "We will open the little door, and place the flat stone inside the trap. See, there is a woven basket to hold it in place. Put the palm nuts in the little basket on top of the stone and secure the door. Fasten the rope to the front of each trap.

"Carry out one trap at a time. Your feet will find a large flat rock under the water. When you find it, stand there and put your trap down on the bottom. The current will carry it toward those big rocks. When you have let the rope out until the knot reaches your hand, the trap will be in position and you will wade to shore and hand me the rope so I can tie it to this tree root. Do the same thing with the second trap. When we come back, I hope to find at least one good fish. When the fish swim in the opening they enter easily through the funnel-shaped entrance. Most fish can't get back out. We will have fish for sure because I am a ndoki witch, you will see." There is a broad grin on her face.

Titi was all smiles as she stripped off her clothes so she could place the traps precisely as she had been instructed. Once her feet found the large flat rock under water, she felt confident. In no time the two traps were set.

They continued to walk along the little footpath that followed the twists and turns of the stream. At regular distances they encountered other little bean gardens until they had passed by five in all. The last little garden was filled with the rich green leaves of sweet potatoes.

"Let's dig enough potatoes to do us for a week. They will not last much longer than that." Soon they were heading back with the potatoes all washed and snuggled in their pack baskets.

As they retraced their steps, Nkaka remarked that she preferred to farm in small gardens alongside the stream. "I guess I am a river person. The Bisimbi water spirits treat me well, but they never gave me any twin babies."

Titi filled the remaining space in her pack basket with some good firewood. Although her load was heavy, she found herself hurrying as they approached the spot where they had set the fish traps.

"You will need to go back in the water to pull out the traps. You must pull them straight toward you. If we tried to pull in the traps from the side of the stream, the traps would get caught in some jagged rocks that we can't see."

In just a few minutes, Titi was stripped and up to her breasts in the cold water again. "We caught a good one," she shouted with excitement as she carried the trap to shore. Her grandmother smiled knowingly.

"I told you we would eat well this evening."

Grasping the rope, Titi waded back to repeat the process with the second trap. "We have two more cat fish." she squealed.

"I told you that the Bisimbi water spirits are good to me. Let's clean them here, there is no point in carrying their guts up the steep hill to our house."

As they walked along together, Nkaka spoke quietly. "Titi, you are the only person, beside your mother, who knows the secret of how I catch fish when no one else has any luck. My grandmother fished here and taught me just as I have taught you. Sometimes I have caught as many as six fish at once. I haven't fished for a long while now because the current is too strong for me. Of late, I have only been able to fish at the end of the dry season when the water is low. Now we can eat fish again! As I told you, we will have lots of food as long as we have our health."

"Nkaka, I am thrilled to be allowed to share our family fishing secrets. I feel as though I know my ancestors when I remember that I am fishing just the same way they did. Thank you for trusting me. My mother has already shown me your special fishing place where you caught fish during the times of the big poison fish kills. Mother was a lot like you. We caught so many we came home in the dark so no one would accuse us of being ndoki witches."

Penetrating talks about ndoki witches

"It is a sad truth my child. If we catch more fish than others, or harvest more beans and peanuts, some will call us ndoki witches. There is a saying, 'Any smart ndoki witch can become a killer witch.' Our elders always valued the wise people among them. They were chosen as chiefs, as shaman diviners, and healers. There were wise women, who were very helpful when mothers were giving birth. We had people who were skilled at reconciliation. They were peacemakers. Wise women served as Mama Ndona to help heal us and to enable us to negotiate with the water spirits.

"We had powerful shamans who made our teki idols and got revenge on our enemies. Others made the minkisi charms, which we wear as protection against killer ndoki witches. All these wise people were considered as being some sort of ndoki. People simply felt in their hearts that these successful people possessed special powers that could be misused. There is always a measure of distrust toward any person excelling in whatever he or she does in life."

"Nkaka, with all their knowledge, and powers did anyone ever succeed in stopping the killer ndoki witches from destroying lives?"

There was a long silence before Nkaka gave her reply to her perceptive grand child.

"Child, your questions amaze me. They are the questions older people have in their hearts but never allow past their lips. To put it simply, every one of these elders died. Not even the king of the Congo (Ntotila) escaped death. Most death seems to be provoked by ndoki witches, but they too die like the rest of us."

Titi brought up another difficult topic with quiet sincerity. "Nkaka, I wish mother had not turned her back on you when my baby brothers died. We could have been good friends sooner, and I could have helped you sometimes."

"Truly, child, I was very sad when your mother rejected and distrusted me for almost eight years of your life. The past is gone. We must do the best we can right now. I don't blame your mother. The ngombo diviner pointed his accusing finger at me. Everyone believed the diviner. When I was feeling lonely and rejected, I sometimes wondered if the ngombo diviner was right about me. I wondered if I had killed my grandchildren because someone had made me a killer ndoki secretly without my knowledge or consent. It happens sometimes that people are tricked into becoming Ndoki witches. Sometimes pieces of mystic human flesh are slipped into the food of an innocent person and they become something they themselves fear."

" How is it that ordinary people become ndoki witches?"

"There are many ways, my child, and the subject is a very unhappy one. Let's hurry home and make a good supper, I'm sure that is something we will both enjoy."

The pot of beans they had left on the fire was still hot, even though the logs were no longer glowing because they needed to be pushed together. Titi fixed the fire, while her grandmother prepared the fish for smoking.

"Catfish taste a lot better when they have been smoked a little.," she said out loud to herself. It wasn't long before green saplings were producing a cloud of smoke to flavor the fish placed on a rack above them.

Their supper was a great success. They had kwanga, sweet potatoes, and beans with smoked catfish mixed in with them. After their supper, eaten by firelight, they were tired, but very contented. Titi realized that while she had lost her mother, she now had gained the trust of her grandmother. She knew that it was quite unusual for someone her grandmother's age to treat a young girl almost as though she were an adult. With their tummies satisfied and their bodies tired, sleep found them easily with the fire glowed between them.

Titi slipped down to get water and firewood as soon as the rooster crowed. She was surprised that his vociferous crowing right over their heads did not awaken her grandmother. As she climbed up their private path from the stream, it suddenly dawned on her that she really did not know the people of their village at all because they always used the village path that lead to a different little river. Although she had been in the village four days, she really had not had time to meet anyone. No one had dropped by to visit either, confirming the reality that her grandmother lived in isolation.

The fire was burning brightly, a little pot of coffee sat boiling when Titi returned from the stream with water, clean dishes, and firewood.

"Child, don't carry so much at one time; the wood will be there tomorrow. On our path to the water, it is very seldom that anyone but us will ever use it. The main path to the water is in the middle of the village. Have you ever met anyone on our path? I neglected to tell you, that you would probably enjoy using the other path. It is a little longer, but not so steep. If you begin to use that path, you will soon meet everyone but me. I have used my own path for years now since long before your birth. You see, most of the villagers really don't want to see me.

"I just keep to myself as much as I can, but there is no need at all for you to live that way. I would rather have you make lots of friends. Many years ago, there were four more houses near ours. One by one our neighbors died and the houses fell down, so that is why we are here alone. Those folk were very old when they died, so they were thought to be Ndoki witches too. Our little corner of the village was called Zandu (market) because they claimed that we held a witches' market between us. Most of the present inhabitants don't even know this piece of history, and that is just fine. You need to meet the other children. They will be wondering how you are getting on living with an old witch."

Her grandmother had a mischievous smile on her face, when she made the last remark.

"Our fish is almost cooked as well as smoked," Titi noted, as she restarted the smoking process. "If you feel well today, I would like you to show me your manioc field. We need to get some soaking for next week."

"You see, I need you to remind me of things, I must be getting old when I forget to soak manioc. I feel fine, so today will be a good day to go over there. My manioc patches are on the far side of the stream on the other side of the hill."

As soon as they had finished their sugarless coffee and with peanuts and kwanga, they were off down the trail. "While we are over by your manioc gardens, I would like you to show me just where my father might clear the new field, we talked about."

"You haven't been with me a week, and you have almost everything settled. That is good, very good. We are going to get along well. You remind me of your mother. How I missed her company after the diviner destroyed our relationship. I was so very lonely until now. It is wonderful to have you by my side."

To cross the stream, they walked along a long fallen tree. Titi was pleased to see the dexterity of her grandmother, as she crossed over the stream. She stepped with confidence, like a young woman.

"My fields are located just over the top of this hill. The soil is good, but I have a problem with wild pigs digging up and destroying my crop. I came across one in full daylight. The look in his eyes made me uneasy. I felt he was an ndoki witch in the form of a pig. I detest having my fields ravaged, just because someone is jealous of me. I bought protective fetish charms from the Nganga nkisi (shaman who makes protective fetishes). I hung them in some of the trees and he never came back! That is what makes me think that the leader of those pigs was a person transformed into a wild boar."

"Nkaka, how do people transform themselves into animals?"

"Child, there many secrets about ndoki witches that we don't understand. We really don't know how it is that they can travel long distances at night to torment or suck the life out of people who live several days walk away. We don't know why they never travel in the light of day. How do they get into a locked house while you are asleep? Why do they become mice that eat your peanuts, or chew the calluses on people's feet at night while they sleep? Where do they get the tiny airplanes they use for travel sometimes? How do they get into your dreams disguised as someone else? Just how do they do their killing? What kind of mystic human flesh do they sell in their markets? How can an ndoki witch eat someone's heart and leave no scar? How do some ndoki witches direct lightning so that it kills the person they want to kill? Titi, I am old but I cannot explain these things any more than I can explain how the seasons change, or how the sun, moon, and stars manage to do what they do. There are many things I do not know. I know about the many things ndoki witches do, but I don't know how they do them."

Titi was surprised that her grandmother admitted so openly that there were many important things that she could not understand. Her mother had told her on one occasion, that old men like to pretend that they know and understand the strange things that happen. They are afraid that they would not be respected if they admitted to their ignorance. It was troubling to think that someone as old and wise as her grandmother had no explanations for all these mysterious issues.

Stopping near a heavily forested area, Titi's grandmother asked a question. "Do you notice anything special about this patch of forest?"

"Yes", Titi answered after careful observation. "All the big trees are the same size."

"You are right my child. When I was your age we grew bananas there. All those trees are younger than I am. Once cleared it would make a great spot for a new field of manioc. If we can get the trees cut, we would have a great supply of good firewood too. The soil has rested so long, it will be like virgin soil again."

"For some reason, I really enjoy working in the fields and watching things grow," Titi noted.

"My child, you remind me of your mother so often. When a child works well at her mother's side, her mother's hopes, joys, and ambitions, seem to flow in and become a part of her innermost heart. It seems to be the same between boys and their fathers. Bad traits and ambitions seem to be communicated the same way.

"Whenever you want to marry a boy, you must find out about his parents. Sometimes, you can learn more about a boy by observing his parents, than by watching the boy himself. When we chose spouses for our children, we were deeply concerned about knowing the customs of the parents. It is good to set your heart on a boy whose parents are friends of your parents. This is why we have the system called vutula menga (return blood). According to our traditions, you get your blood from your mother. All who share the same bloodline (luvila) of mothers are considered to be brothers and sisters, totally inappropriate for marriage.

"Your father is your protector and has an important role in your life. His family and bloodline (luvila) have no connection with you. You may marry any of your father's relatives. If your mother's line has been marrying into your father's line for years, then most parents will want you to find your spouse somewhere among his relatives preferably his sisters' children. Families and clans which have intermarried, following the vutula menga tradition, are more adept at resolving conflicts because both sides want the marriage to be a success."

"Our school teacher at Lufu said that it is not good to follow that vutula menga (marrying first cousins in the father's clan) tradition. He said that doctors know that a baby's blood is formed by both the father and the mother. The doctors say that cousins on my father's side are just as much my brothers and sisters as are the cousins of my mother's clan. He told us that that God's book forbids the custom of marrying what he calls first cousins from either family. He advised us to marry someone who is not related to either our mother or our father."

"Your teacher may be right. Our elders said that it was good to follow the vutula menga custom occasionally, but not always. My grandmother advised me not to marry into my grandfather's or father's clan because I might bear children with mpeve zambi (mental problems). Perhaps your teacher's book and the doctors are right. I have noticed that families that marry back and forth frequently, because of the lower bride price, often seemed to have stupid children who never became wise."

"Nkaka, I love to talk with you. I feel as though I am back in school again." Tears trickled down her cheeks when she remembered how willingly her mother had answered her constant stream questions. She had observed that most mothers did not want their children to ask too many questions.

"Mother trusted me and answered all my questions when she could. I miss her! But you, Nkaka, are like an older copy of my mother."

"That is what Nkaka means, I am your mother's mother, you know. How many rainy seasons have you seen my child?"

"I am almost twelve years old now. I have been a young woman now for almost a year. Since that time, my mother told me that my body could grow a baby."

"My child, don't rush to get married. Let your body grow strong and your breasts develop so that when the time comes you can feed a baby well. Don't be in any hurry to live with a young man."

"That is exactly what my mother told me too. I dream that some day I may be able to go back to school. I can read and write now, and I brought all my note books with me so that I can keep on learning."

"You are a wise girl. Now just stay that way! I know that you will."

As they walked back together with a load of manioc to be soaked, Nkaka took Titi over to see her little banana plantation. Once more she was very surprised to see the large number of banana trees.

"Nkaka, how do you do so much work at your age?"

"I do a little work every day. What else have I had to do? I have been a very lonely person for years. This white hair is like a curse. When your hair is white, your old friends are dead and the young people are afraid of you. Let's cut down that stalk of bananas and divide it, so we can carry it home. Our loads will be fine, after we put all our manioc to soak."

"I guess I feel a kind of loneliness too, although for different reasons. My life has changed too much far to quickly. My eyes have been scrubbed with tears. First I lost my teacher and all my school chums. I have never had a friend like Matondo. The whole town fled to the Congo, including your daughter my Mama Mbuta. I was afraid coming back home alone, but my father met me half way. You know all that happened after that. We cried together when my mother and her baby died. Nkaka, you have had to replace all of them for me."

"Once we get the work in hand, you will soon find new friends here. I guess that we are leaning on each other. I have shown more of my heart to you than to anyone else. Your grandfather was a good man and did his share of the work, but who ever opened her heart to a man? Men need to talk with men, and women need to talk with women. That is how it is, but I surely missed him when he was killed by the Portuguese soldiers, the year before you were born."

With all the talking, they were home before they knew it. "Let's boil some of our plantain bananas for supper. They will go well with some of our smoked fish, especially if I prepare the fish with moamba, so the bananas will slide down well," Nkaka suggested with a smile.

In the part of the village where they lived, there were many palm trees planted by the folk who had homes there years before. Some of the palm trees were being tapped for palm wine, while others had not been trimmed for years, and looked like old men needing a haircut. The old trees did not bear much fruit, and no one could harvest it because of the untrimmed branches. Small rodents, monkeys, and birds all enjoyed the abandoned fruit. In their squabbling, they often knocked mature palm nuts to the ground. Titi quickly found enough ripe palm nuts to make the moamba for supper. Fortunately, she also found a young tree, with a whole stalk of palm fruit close enough to the ground that she was able to cut off with her machete.

Titi came back carrying the beautiful stalk of mature palm fruit on her head. "Where did you find that?" Her grandmother asked, with obvious delight in the tone of her voice. She was pleased to learn that there were three more stalks forming.

The fruit was a deep orange color, just right for their cooking plans. It wasn't long before thirty or forty nuts were boiling merrily in the pot. After about twenty minutes, the pot was set aside to cool. Later skillful hands would remove the fibers that looked like orange hair, leaving behind the gravy they needed. Titi had already removed the bones from the smoked fish, so some of it was added to the moamba, making a delicious, thick, fish gravy.

Plenty of good food soon satisfied their discriminating palates. The meal was a great success, leaving them both satisfied. Two lonely people had joined hearts with unusual openness. Grandmother and granddaughter had truly bonded to their mutual surprise and delight. Despite the difference in age, they had kindred spirits. Relaxing by the fire after supper Titi's grandmother repeated what she had said earlier.

"When you go down for water tomorrow, take the path that is in the middle of the village. Everyone but me uses the same path to the stream. You will have a chance to become acquainted with the girls and women of our village. They all know who you are because of the funeral. Let's go to sleep. I feel we will have pleasant dreams."

Because they fell asleep early, Titi was awake before the rooster. Her thoughts turned to her father. "Father is all alone. He lost my mother. He lost the hope of a son, and he even lost me!"

Tears ran down her cheeks as she remembers it all. "I will ask Nkaka to let me take my father some fish moamba. I could visit my mother's grave on the way and I could ask father to help clear a field for us. I will talk to mother even though I know that she can only give me answers if she comes in my dreams."

All her grieving, and planning ended abruptly, when the rooster makes three loud flaps followed by his shrill wake up crowing. Titi was catapulted into the new day listening for the answering roosters from the whole village below.

Their rooster, perched higher than all the others, somehow felt it was his duty to call first each day. Titi laughed to herself when she heard the first reply. The call was that of a young rooster just learning to crow. His voice cracked like a teen-age boy.

"That's what I am," she said to herself. "I am a little rooster learning to crow, only I am a girl."

Following her grandmother's advice, she took the basin of dishes and her water container down toward the path that everyone used. As she scampered down the hill, she soon found herself in a little stream of women and girls headed for the water, each one on the same mission. She felt strange because she had never been with these folk before. Because of her eagerness to learn all about her grandmother's little world, Titi was just entering the life of the village for the first time after living there a number of days.

"Will they know who I am? Will they shun me as an outsider? I don't even know where to go for drinking water." All these thoughts jostled one another in Titi's mind. At the water's edge, it was the older women who opened up the conversation.

"You must be Pemba's daughter. You look just like she did at your age. Your mother and I played together when she was small." All the women had known her mother well and had been at the funeral.

One grumpy-faced woman blurted out her thoughts. "It's too bad that a nice girl like you has to live with an old ndoki witch. They say she didn't eat your mother, or your brothers, so she will probably won't harm you. Don't let her make you an ndoki too. All she has to do is slip some of that mbizi (meat) she gets at the witches' market into your food. The ngombo said she is president of the witches' market that meets under the big sanda tree in front of the house. Watch what you eat! It's a wonder she even let you come down with us. She never comes. She knows that we all know what she really is. But none of her doings are your fault, so you should just come down every day. You look so much like your mother; it is good just to see you. Your mother was everybody's friend."

After shaking hands with all the women, Titi quickly joined the girls. As soon as she arrived, they helped her to feel welcome.

Dina, a girl about her age asked an important question.

"Did you really learn to read and write when you were at Lufu? I used to sleep at your friend Matondo's house whenever we went to market. She told us that you were learning very quickly."

Titi was very surprised to learn that Dina actually knew her best friend from her Lufu school days.

The children plan a village school

"Titi, would you please teach us whatever you know? I saw your school at Lufu, and I wished I could learn too. My aunt was a schoolteacher in Luanda before she fled to Congo Zaire. The one time I saw her, she told me about the importance of school. Mother and father can't read and they don't feel that school matters very much. I would just love to be able to read and write like some of the women I saw in the market."

Titi felt drawn to Dina, in the same way she had been attracted to Matondo.

"You would need to get permission from your parents and the village elders, and I would need permission from my grandmother. If everyone is in agreement, I would love to help others to learn what I have learned".

"Great!" Dina squealed in total agreement. There was so much infectious joy in Dina's eyes that Titi bubbled with excitement.

"See you here tomorrow!" Dina said as she hurried up the hill with her load.

Looking up from her task of roasting peanuts, Nkaka spotted the twinkle in Titi's eyes immediately. "Tell me what you are scheming to do in our village now."

"How do you know I have something I might want to do?" Titi asked in surprise.

"You see, I had a little girl who was just your age once. You even look like her. Whenever she was excited about anything, her eyes told the secret just like yours do."

"Down at the water I just met everyone. One girl my age named Dina knew my friend Matondo at Lufu. She used to stay at her house whenever they went to market. She knew I was in school with Matondo. She just asked me to teach her the things I learned. I told her I would ask your permission and she said that she would ask her parents, and the village elders." Titi was so excited that her words all tumbled out together.

Her grandmother laughed heartily. "You show your excitement exactly the same way as your mother did when she was your age. It is though she has come back to cheer me in my old age. Do you think you could teach others the things you have learned? If you can, I think you should. I'm shut out of village life but you aren't. I'm cut off forever because I can't prove my innocence. I don't want you to be cut off at all. Teach them if you can! Your mother was unselfish too."

Titi's tears of joy expressed her gratitude for having been placed with a grandmother filled with vision and imagination. With new enthusiasm, Titi carried water, chopped wood, put manioc out to dry, pounded fufu, and helped with the cooking.

"You have been teaching school all day, I've seen it in your eyes." Her grandmother observed, as they ate their supper by firelight. "It is a good thing to dream of doing something worthwhile. Years ago, I taught school too. I taught eight little girls, including your mother; I showed them how to make clay cooking pots. They are all grown women now and some of them still make pots. In better times they sold their pots in the Lufu market."

"Nkaka, I would love to be in your school. You know many things I would love to learn. Perhaps you could teach us if we ever organize a little school."

"I doubt that the parents would let their children be taught by an old witch," Nkaka surmised.

Stretched out on her sleeping mat, Titi continued to dream aloud with all her teaching ideas. Finally she realized that her grandmother had fallen asleep despite all her talking.

Excitement awakened Titi before their rooster's scheduled morning outburst. Her pots and dishes were all thoroughly washed and her calabash filled with drinking water, before Dina came running down the long hill. The broad smiles on both girls' faces assured the possibility of achieving their mutual dreams. Dina was still breathless when she began spilling out her findings.

"There are five of us who want to go to school. The village chief says we can have our school down near the sanda tree. We can start meeting under the tree, because it is dry season. Once our little school gets going, we can build little by little. The chief himself will bind on the thatch, if we bring in the bundles of elephant grass from the valley. I saw your black board at Lufu and I am sure my father would smooth out planks for that. After all, he is the village carpenter. There is just one big problem, we can't get notebooks from Lufu or Luanda any more because of the war."

The girls could not imagine any solution for their notebook problem.

Nkaka did some food preparation while Titi washed their clothes and carried in a good supply of wood. She had promised that in the afternoon they would try their luck at fishing again.

Nkaka could no longer do the work involved in fishing, but she loved to be part of the team. Titi prepared everything just as her grandmother had shown her. Her grandmother was satisfied to see that her little granddaughter had remembered every detail. Because she knew exactly what to do, it only took a few minutes to pull the traps out from their hiding place, prepare them, and then slide them to their position.

"I can see that with your help we can fish all year around. With fish, we can buy some of the things we may need but we can no longer sell them in Lufu market."

Leaving the traps behind, they went down to the sweet potato patch and soon gathered all they needed.

"We will plant more manioc in November just before the rains begin. A growing girl like you needs lots of fufu and saka saka to be healthy and strong," Nkaka suggested.

They were both anxious to pull up their traps. "Don't be disappointed, child. You know we have only been gone from here a short time."

As soon as Titi began to pull the first trap, she felt it jerk. "We have something. I can feel it. It's a big catfish!" Titi shouted with glee as she scrambled to the bank. Rushing back out to pull the second trap, they were rewarded with a long, fat eel and the skin of a small catfish. Evidently the eel had gone in after the trapped catfish, and eaten nearly all of it in the hour or so the trap had been there.

"Eels are hard to catch, because they don't like palm nuts, and they often find their way back out of the traps. I have sometimes found only the skin of a fish but no eel. I think the bisimbi spirits are fond of you. They are letting you catch lots of fish," Nkaka affirmed encouragingly.

The eel kept squirming in Titi's basket despite her earlier efforts to kill him. "Even with his guts removed, he is still moving." Titi reported with a start, when the eels tail somehow touched her ear. "I feel as though I am carrying a snake.

"Nkaka, could we make some eel moamba for my father? He loves eel, and mother used to make it every time we got one. I was thinking that I might go to visit him tomorrow. Dina has relatives in the village too and she is willing to go with me. I know that the low palm tree has lots more palm fruit for us to cook with. I will gather the palm fruit and make the moamba if you will smoke the eel. I don't need to go before tomorrow afternoon."

Nkaka nodded, giving her willing assent.

The two set to work just as soon as they reached home. They agreed to smoke the eel overnight, before cooking it. Since there were plenty of palm fruits, they decided to make a moamba gravy for both fish.

The sweet potatoes were delicious and her grandmother had a surprise to complete the meal. While Titi had been busy with chores and gathering wood, she had prepared a generous loaf of mbika (squash seeds). The seeds were stored in demijohns like the beans. She had cracked off the outer shells with her teeth, pounded the inner seeds in the same su (mortar) used for grinding up peppers. Hot peppers and salt were added to the mix that was wrapped in leaves like kwanga, and then boiled in a pot. A little chunk of mbika loaf with each mouthful of sweet potato made a perfect combination.

"If you hadn't brought that salt from Lufu, our food would be rather tasteless," Nkaka recognized.

The supper meal was a happy one, and while they were eating, Titi mentioned the big problem of notebooks for their school.

"Everyone could write on the black board with dried manioc sticks, but they will need to learn to write small letters like I did with a pen and paper when I was in school at Lufu".

Surprisingly, Nkaka proposed a solution. "I think I know just what you can do. Once I went with my father to the mission at Sao Salvador. He was admitted to the hospital for treatment of his terrible cough. I did the cooking while he was being treated. One day I went to take a look at the mission school. The teacher was a white missionary woman who invited me to sit in one of the seats. I think she was anxious to get little girls to go to school. Almost all the pupils were boys. The children were all writing on slates, which are a kind of flat stone that forms in layers. They wrote on their slates with thin pieces of slate that left a white mark like on a tiny stone blackboard. The white marks could be wiped off with a bit of damp rag. I noticed slate rock, just above the clay bank, that we used to make pots years ago. I think Dina would know where to find the clay. That kind of slate rock can be pried off with a machete. You could each have a slate for writing."

Titi was very encouraged with her grandmother's solution to their school problem.

They had lots of firewood and green leaves for the slow process of drying and smoking the fish, so the big eel was well on the way to becoming delicious. By noon the next day, Titi's surprise meal for her father was cooked, and carefully placed in a basket, with a white cloth to cover it. Food gifts were always covered with a cloth to show respect.

Dina arrived ahead of time and met with the full approval of grandmother's perceptive eyes.

"We plan to be home before dark. If we don't find my father, I will just leave his food with the woman who lives next door. I don't know where he may be eating these days. I will visit mother at the cemetery too. I want to tell her about everything."

On the way to her former home village, Titi and Dina talked about their plans for a school. She explained about her grandmother's suggestion of using slates. Dina remembered the location of the clay bank so it would not be difficult to locate the slate rock.

Titi visits her mother's grave

The cemetery was just outside the village of Mbungu, right beside the footpath they were following. The girls went reverently to the fresh mound that was a part of her mother's grave. A smooth board carried her full name and the date of her death. Titi fell to her knees right by the marker that was located at the head of the casket.

"Mother dear, I miss you. I wish you had not been forced to leave us. I have so much to learn that you could have taught me. How is my little brother? Do you have enough milk for him? I wish I could hold him. Don't worry about me. Nkaka, your kind mother, is wonderful to me. She is a lot like you. I'm so glad you told us that you wanted me to live with her. She misses you too. She has shown me all of her gardens. She has even taught me how to catch fish. Mother, we are going to start a little school in the village where I will teach the children everything I learned. Thank you for sending me to school. I am bringing smoked eel with moamba gravy for my father. It is made just the way you used to make it. He must miss you terribly. I will try to come to talk with you quite often."

During Titi's whole visit at her mother's graveside, Dina sat quietly beside her. Many thoughts were coursing through her mind too. She talked to herself very quietly. "I am glad that my mother, my sisters and brother are all alive and well. I'm glad I don't need to live with my grandmother. I need to be more helpful to my mother, and kinder to my little sisters, and brother." The girls left as quietly as they had come.

It seemed very natural to turn into to her old dooryard. All the palm branches had been cleared away so that the house and cooking hut looked normal.

"My father makes palm wine and he should be home soon."

The door to the cooking hut hung open, it looked forlorn, and abandoned. "I don't know just where my father may be eating these days, but I imagine that he still keeps his wine and his equipment here. He may be eating at his sister's house. He was always good to mother although he was angry at our clan for destroying all his sons through witchcraft," Titi recalled.

While the girls were chatting, he appeared carrying has climbing equipment and a large demijohn of white milky palm wine. The moment he spotted his only child he set down everything and ran with arms open for her embrace. Her father had always been on the quiet side, and he seldom embraced her. Titi knew he loved her. More than once he had walked all the way to Lufu to get her. They had not really been able to talk since before her mother died. Men and women grieved differently, and apart for each other.

"Titi you can't imagine how lonely I am without your mother and you. I'm glad you are with your grandmother. You need each other. I miss your happy face and your chatter. I feel so lost when I look out to that abandoned cooking hut."

"Papa I am going to start a little school in grandmother's village. I have agreed to teach them all I know. I am so glad you encouraged me to go to school. Dina here will be one of my pupils."

"I am sure you will be a great teacher, Titi. You learned so quickly yourself."

"Papa, I was wondering if you would be willing to come and clear a field for me so I can plant manioc and other food. We must grow more food now that there are two of us eating from grandmother's fields. She too old, and I am a little too small to cut the trees myself, but I want to learn."

Without a moment's hesitation, her father accepted her request. "Now is just the time to do that kind of clearing while the dry season is just in its beginning. That gives the brush a chance to dry well and be burned before the first rains come. Does your grandmother want me to come after all I have said against her over the years?"

"She gave me permission to ask you. She understands that you were only following the decisions the diviners gave. There is no problem at all. Everyone around her village still considers her to be an ndoki witch so it is hard for her to find anyone to help her. If you help her, you will be helping an old lady who seems to like me. She is always saying how much I remind her of my mother."

"There is another reason why I would like to begin clearing the field very soon. One of the UNITA officers came by the other day and they want me to join their army. I don't really have a choice. If I don't join, I will be in danger. Furthermore, I don't want our land to be run by foreigners like the Cubans. I will come in three days to begin clearing the field. When it is finished, I will join the army. I don't want to kill anyone, but I do want people like you to be safe."

"When I am there clearing the new field, perhaps you can cook some more food that smells like that pot you brought."

Both girls laughed and got up to leave so they would be home before dark.

"Wait a minute," he said. "I think I have something that will help out your little school." He slipped into the house and came out with a package all wrapped in plastic. He held out a large package of new notebooks. "I bought this package of note books in Lufu along with these pens so you would be able to go to school another year. Now that you are the teacher, you can probably use them."

Titi and Dina looked at each other and then at her father with total astonishment written all across their faces. "Papa we have no notebooks or pens at all. Now we can really start our school. We will use these very sparingly. Nkaka thinks we can make slates for most day-to-day work. In any case, we can start our school almost immediately whether our idea about slates works or not."

"I'm so glad I bought those school supplies a few months ago when I sold my buffalo meat at Lufu. The smile on your faces is all the reward I could ever want. Seeing you Titi will always remind me of your wonderful mother."

The two girls practically ran back to their village. They were very anxious to share their good news with the other girls who wanted to form a school. As they hurried home, they made a plan. They would both work hard in the fields all the next day, so they could go look for slate the day following.

"I think it would be good if all the girls go together to look for slate. Each one could bring a pack basket and a machete. Let's all meet here after breakfast tomorrow if everyone gets permission to go."

The girls were so busy that they did not see one another until the morning of the day of their planned expedition. They met at the river, while doing their morning chores.

The girls all agreed to the plan, and scampered up the hill with their basins of clean pots and dishes together with the fresh water for morning tea or coffee.

As Titi hurried home, she had many thoughts going through her mind. *"I'm pleased that I am really going to be a teacher. I will try to teach exactly what I was taught. My books will have to do for everyone. I am so glad that Master Pedro gave me my little reading book that last week of school. I guess he knew that he would be forced to join the army. Teaching others will be a great review for me. I think my mother understood me when I talked with her in the cemetery. I feel that part of my heavy burden is gradually lifting"*

At home, her grandmother had been planning too.

"I think that we will need to go fishing tomorrow so that we will have good food for your father when he comes, " Nkaka told Titi. "I'm glad he is willing to come. It worries me that he is going into the army, although I am not surprised. War is bad, but we can't let foreigners rule us again!"

The firmness in her grandmother's face made Titi feel more confident that her father was doing the right thing.

"Child, I want you to take some of this peanut butter with you to eat with the kwanga. The trail will be difficult because people don't make many clay pots these days. All the young women prefer metal pots. I still like bananas to be boiled in clay pots because they turn all black in metal ones."

"That must by why Mama Mbuta's bananas were always black when we ate them at Lufu." Titi recalled. "Nkaka, some day I want you to teach me how to make good clay pots."

The slate expedition

Titi placed her machete, her short peanut hoe, and her food in her pack basket. All five of her future pupils were waiting excitedly for her, when she arrived at the water's edge as planned. Dina knew the way so she led the group as they hurried along the narrow footpath in single file.

The first hour of their trek was relatively easy because they were traveling along well-used paths that lead to people's gardens. They walked right past the fishing rocks, but Titi did not even look down at the stream for fear of betraying her secret. Once they had passed her grandmother's last garden, the trail became much more difficult to follow. They had to cross the river, but the old log that had been used for a bridge had rotted. The only way across now was to follow a long fallen tree that had not had any of its branches trimmed. It took a lot of slashing to get across the river.

"At least this will be waiting for us on the way back!" Dina remarked as she mopped her brow. "Once we are up the hill, the old trail turns right because it always follows the river."

The trail was in bad shape, so the girls took turns going ahead to cut brush out of the way so they could pass. They had been traveling laboriously for more than an hour, when Dina asked everyone to stop and listen. They all heard the waterfall so they knew they were almost at their destination.

"Let's go on in silence the rest of the way. From the top of the waterfall, we may just see the bisimbi playing down below where the water hits the pool at the bottom of the falls," Dina suggested. "My grandmother told me what to do. I have brought some ripe palm fruit which I am to throw over the falls when we ask the bisimbi spirits permission to remove the rock we have come to gather," Dina explained.

After a final half hour of strenuous travel, the sweat covered girls stood in awe, looking silently at the spectacular sight below them. The vegetation was of a rich deep green color because of the constant mist that billowed up from the gorge below. The whole stream crashed over the waterfall to the sunken valley. Unfortunately, everything around the gorge was hidden in thick mist.

"We certainly will not see the bisimbi this time. I think that you might see them when the river is almost dry, at the end of the dry season," Dina speculated.

Today they could see the dense virgin forest with treetops that stretched half way up from the famous Forbidden Valley, located far below them. The sight was breathtaking.

"This was a place where our ancestors came to losa bandoki (throw witches). Because it is a place used for the execution of witches, no one goes down to that part of the valley. Your grandmother could tell you more about this place, Titi."

The girls sat in spellbound silence watching an eagle circling far below them, yet, well above the forest beneath it. When it settled on its large nest in the top of a tall tree, they could imagine the baby eagles squabbling to grab the prey brought in for them.

"Let's look for the slate rock." Titi whispered, breaking the spell. "Nkaka said it is directly above the clay bank. Show us the clay, Dina, and we can all begin our search."

Dina lead the girls to the clay bank, which was light gray in color without even a hint of vegetation. "It is no wonder that my grandmother's pots are so durable if they are made of such pure clay," Titi pointed out.

It only took a few minutes for the girls to locate the flat black slate rock outcropping. With their hoes, they cleared off a good area of the strange rock that was naturally formed in layers that could be pried apart. Titi grasped a small piece of the rock and proceeded to write her name. To their surprise, black stone rubbed on another black stone left a white line. Working their machetes under the edges, they managed to free rather large pieces of flat rock. With practice, they became more and more skilful at releasing larger and larger pieces before they broke. Dina found the best technique of all. She found that she could cut a groove in the rock with her machete, influencing the slate to break on that line, when she carefully pried up on the other side.

After a half hour each girl had a pile of slates from which she could choose several of the largest and smoothest.

"If we take a few more than we need, I think some of them might be used as our first blackboard. See, I have drilled a hole in this one with the point of my machete, so we could attach them to the wall. Now that we have cleared the trail here, we can return when we need to. It would be fun to come here for clay, and get some of the older women to show us how to make pots," Titi added.

The girls packed their chosen slates with leaves between them to keep them from breaking.

"We need to get small narrow pieces to use as pencils," Titi remembered.

Dina found that she could cut strips with the sharp point of her machete. Everyone followed her example.

"Lets eat now," pleaded the smallest girl.

Each girl laid out the food she had brought. Dina had a little loaf of mbika. Lisa opened a medium-sized kwanga. Diela displayed a piece of antelope meat. Little Tina brought out a ball of fufu carefully packaged in leaves, and a small packet of minced peppers to accompany it. Kwilu produced a small kwanga. Titi set out her generous package of peppered peanut butter. Dina divided everything six ways, so they each had the same amount. Sharing equally was something every child was taught at home, and it contributed to their harmony.

After enjoying their little feast, they all went to the water's edge for a drink. Refreshed, with their baskets carefully packed, the girls decided to walk back to the high spot again where they could look down on Forbidden Valley once more. While they were watching, the eagle brought a fish to her young ones. Looking down at the mist-covered caldron where the speeding waters smashed on hidden boulders, Titi expressed her thoughts.

"Our ancestors had a good idea when they threw ndoki killers over the edge here." She pictures her mother's escaped killer as she spoke.

"It is a good place for killing enemies, unless you are the one to be thrown," Lisa replied. "My great grandmother was killed here, and my old grandmother still claims that the old lady was killed as a victim of a ruthless nganga ngombo (diviner).

"Not everyone killed here was a killer ndoki," Dina suggested.

With this sobering thought, the girls all walked silently until they could no longer hear the sound of the thundering falls.

The return trip was relatively easy, enabling the girls to thoroughly enjoy one another's company. When they reached their log bridge, the girls decided that they would clear a path to the river and have some fun in the water while they washed their sweaty clothes.

The cold water cooled their fun a little, so they came out of the water much sooner than they had expected. While waiting for their clothes to get a bit drier, the girls arranged themselves in a circle on a gigantic boulder and begin trimming their slates with their sharp machetes. The strips cut off made slate pencils when sharpened. Someone discovered that they could smooth the surface of their slates by rubbing them vigorously with very fine sand from the stream. By the time their clothes were dry, they each had a couple of very acceptable slates ready for the first day of school.

As they trudged the last hour of their journey home, they made some plans. Dina proposed that they should make benches for everyone including their teacher. She had examined the seats in the Lufu School and agreed that she was willing to help her friends make their bamboo benches.

"Because of the work we must do for our mothers, I think we need about three days to make our benches," Dina calculated with an enthusiastic tone.

The slate adventure knit the whole group of girls together into a little club that included their teacher. It was a great beginning for their proposed school.

Nkaka was very satisfied when she saw the slates Titi had made. Her idea had worked, as she hoped it would.

"I think that you should catch us some fish for your father's meals when he comes. We will kill a rooster on the day the work is finished. I have no doubt that you know just how to set the traps."

Titi was very pleased with her grandmother's expression of confidence. Her own mother was the only other person ever allowed to fish in Nkaka's special spot.

"Do you think the bisimbi spirits know me by now?" Titi inquired.

"Take the bisimbi some of our ripe palm nuts, and you will know sooner or later. I will stay at home and make some mbika. My old joints will not let me do much else today. You can set the traps and leave them overnight. On your way back, please bring us some manioc leaves. The leaves are no longer tender, without the rains but they are still good food"

Titi was very tired from the day's journey, but so excited about setting the traps all by herself that she forgot her fatigue, as she scampered off down the path. Darkness was approaching as she returned with a good supply of manioc leaves for saka saka. It pleased her to remember that her father will be coming soon. The leaves would last because of the cooler weather.

After supper, it was Titi who couldn't keep her eyes open. She fell asleep almost immediately, and, as a result, she was awake before the rooster, thinking about the activities of the day. After her morning chores, she planned to gather lots of wood, put some soaked manioc out to dry, gather sweet potatoes, and check her fish traps.

Titi headed down the path to the river before the rooster crowed. When all the schoolgirls arrived early, they had a good laugh.

"I bet that all of us went to sleep early last night," Titi suggested with a grin. "I know I did." Smiles and nods said it all.

"We hope to get our benches started today," Dina reported.

"I am getting my work done so we can receive my father who is coming to clear the big trees for our new field. I think that he may arrive tomorrow. Nkaka estimates that it will take him about three weeks. I will want to work with him as well, and help prepare his meals. Our school may get delayed a little."

After breakfast, Titi went directly to the spring where their manioc was soaking. Very carefully she cut each root into four sections, and placed them on the rack to dry, noticing that by the next day the other manioc would be ready for pounding. She knew very well that her father preferred fufu, to any other form of manioc. As she went to gather sweet potatoes, she passed by her traps set the previous evening. It took a lot of self-discipline, not to stop and check them out. The desire to pull up the traps pushed her to work rapidly in the sweet potato patch. The potatoes were at their very best, so it did not take long to fill her basket. Boiled sweet potatoes with peanuts would make a great snack for her father when he was clearing the big trees. Titi marveled again at the generous supply of food her aging grandmother had growing in her various gardens. As soon as her pack basket was as full as she could carry, she rushed back to the fishing site.

Her heart was racing with her excitement as she stripped to go after the traps. She shivered from the combination of cold water and cool morning air. Her hands trembled in anticipation as she drew in the first trap. It contained only the skin of a catfish. "We can't eat that," she grumbled.

The second trap seemed heavy, so she knew she had something. It turned out to be an eel even larger than the first one they had caught. It was a force to be reckoned with. She carried the trap a good distance from the water and carefully split the eel's head, in an effort to make it manageable. It took quite a stretch of time for the critter to stop moving. Proceeding to clean out his gut, she was not surprised to see that his stomach was full of chewed up fish, the one he had stolen from the first trap. She was pleased that she had caught the very kind fish her father liked most.

Her grandmother was delighted with Titi's success. She felt all the more motivated to walk out to the proposed new field to perform the required rituals that would make everything ready for Zoao's efforts to clear a new farming area.

Walking at a steady pace, Titi and her Nkaka soon reached the intended field. Carefully, her grandmother attached a protective fetish at the entrance to the field to protect anyone working in her forest. Earlier in the week, her grandmother had made a visit to the old cemetery where she poured a calabash of palm wine on the grave of the first ancestor of their clan in those parts. She had asked his permission to open the new field. Because she lacked the support of the living, the elderly woman valued the support of her ancestors and was always careful to keep all the traditions.

She was consoled with the thought that the ancestors knew that she was not a killer witch. They knew that she had never taken anyone's life intentionally. They were witnesses to her open condemnation of two relatives who were bringing dishonor to their clan. They understood about the time she had warned the culprits that the bakulu (ancestors) would not leave them unpunished if they did not change.

The ancestors themselves snuffed out the lives of the transgressors within a month of Nkaka's warning. The ancestors knew very well that they themselves had put the curse on the men, and not her. They knew that that incident caused her to gain the unjust reputation of being a killer ndoki witch. She was always confident in asking for the blessing of the ancestors because she was one who constantly honored them, and followed their rules. They alone knew of her basic innocence.

It comforted Titi to know that her grandmother had done everything necessary to protect her father.

Knowing that her grandmother needed to keep a little fire burning for most of the dry season, Titi decided to carry in all the wood she could for the remainder of the day. Going down their private path to the water, she was encouraged to see the quantity of good wood available. It had been such a struggle to find wood at Lufu. Here the only challenge was cutting and carrying it.

For the cool season, large pieces of reasonably long logs were the best sort because one could keep a fire smoldering by just keeping the two burning ends the appropriate distance apart. Titi recognized that there was far more wood than she could actually carry. Her aging grandmother had only been able to carry home the smaller pieces.

Often Titi was only able to carry one large piece at a time. On many occasions she put one end over her shoulder and let the other drag on the ground. By the end of the day she herself was surprised by the size of the pile she had stored in the outside shelter behind the house.

Titi was coming in with her last big log, one that dragged on the ground a little, when her grandmother came out to advise her to come in. A clicking sound from the back of the old woman's throat was the deepest expression of astonishment in their language. Clicking her throat and nodding her head, she took both of Titi's hands, and looked directly into her eyes with intense affection that surpassed words. A woman who had worked hard all her life was delighted to see a child with a quality of work habits found in few adults.

"How did a young girl like you ever carry such large pieces of wood? Ngeye fweti kaka kala Ndoki!" ("You just must be a witch!"), she whispered with a big laugh, and wink of her merry eyes.

" Nkaka, do you talk to yourself when you are working alone?"

" Yes, child, I have talked to myself for years. I have not had anyone else to talk with me. Why do you ask?"

"Well, I have noticed that I talk to myself all day about everything I am thinking. I remember that my mother talked to herself too, so I just wondered if the whole family did that. Sometimes I even sing some school songs in Portuguese."

"I see that your big eel is being smoked very carefully," Titi noted.

"Why do you call it my big eel? You are the one who caught him."

"Nkaka, I just remembered, while I was talking to myself about fishing, that the one who is taught to catch fish must give his first fish to the teacher. I want do things correctly so the ancestors will bless me." They both laughed again.

"Child, no one has laughed in this house for years. You have brought laughter back into my life. I didn't expect to ever laugh again. You may be sure that your mother is laughing too, because she knows all about us. It is good to live in a way that pleases those who live on the other side. In that other world, our ancestors always know the truth. They never let a killer ndoki into their world. Try to live in such a way that your mother will always be proud of you."

"Father said that he would come tomorrow. I think we are ready for him. We have plenty of wood and a good supply of food, including the smoked eel. I told the girls that we really couldn't begin school until after father finished clearing the field. They have worked hard and begged me to come tomorrow morning for a little while just to try out their facilities. I think that perhaps I should spend a little while with them before my father gets here. What do you think?"

"You say the girls have been working hard on their little school. It will encourage them to have your approval and hear your first lesson. I will have some food ready for your father when he comes. If he is ready before you get back, I will send him down to the sanda tree to find you. He will be most interested in your little school."

Before she went to sleep, Titi looked over all her notebooks and decided how she would begin her lesson. The very thought of teaching someone else excited her.

Their plan was to meet at the school right after an early breakfast. Dina was to be the bell ringer. Striking an old axe of her father's that hung on a wire called the children to school. Her father was going to tell her when it was seven o'clock.

The Kiula village school opens

Titi arrived at the school just as Dina was striking the old axe with her father's hammer. It made a good bell sound that could be heard in the whole village.

Under Dina's supervision the girls had created their own little one-room schoolhouse. The walls were made from long palm branches planted in the ground. The girls carefully dug small deep, holes with their machetes, placing a palm branch in each hole. The branches were quite close together and offered total privacy. Saplings were placed on both sides of the palm branches and bound together as far up as the girls could reach. This kept the palm branches in a permanent position, creating a rather attractive green wall. Inside, they were totally protected from the wind, as well as curious eyes.

Bamboo seats mounted on crotch sticks were perfect replicas of the Lufu School. Three large slates had been pierced and hung from the binding saplings so that they were suspended at eye level. Dina's father was smoothing balsa boards for their desktops. They had made a very attractive and functional little school and were justly proud. Titi could hardly believe her eyes.

The five girls sat quietly in their seats until Titi stepped up front. "Bon dia nossa professora, (Good morning teacher)," they said in a chorus of very acceptable Portuguese.

The Kiula School was officially open. Dina had obviously observed the Lufu School very carefully. She had asked a lady who once lived in Luanda just how a teacher should be greeted, and then drilled her little colleagues thoroughly, while they were building their classroom.

From the beginning, the roles were very clear. In the classroom Titi was to be called "nossa professora" (our teacher). When the roll call was read, each child was taught to stand and say, "Estou present. (I'm present). Dina had done all this formal organization very skillfully. She had worked very creatively to make their little school a success from the very beginning.

Titi spoke to the girls from her heart. "All of your work and planning tells me how much you really want to have a school in your village. I should say our village because it is my village now too. If you desire to learn to read and write as much as I did last year, you too will learn. Some will take longer than others, but that is not a problem.

"As you know, I have only been to school for one year. I should be in school with you, with someone having more schooling here to teach us all. I will do my best to help you learn. All my notebooks and the little reading book from which I first began to read are our only resources. Real teachers go to school for many years before they are allowed to teach others but I will do what you asked me to do.

"You want to learn, and I am willing to teach you everything I know. I know you will learn and so will I. I think that it is a good idea that when we are inside we will behave as a teacher and her pupils. Outside this room we will simply be six friends from Kiula village."

"My teacher, Master Pedro, always began school days with prayer. When he prayed he seemed to talk to Nzambi Mpungu (God almighty) the one our ancestors always said had made everything. He always talked to God in Kikongo, our own language. I will pray as he did but I don't really understand what he believed.

"We bow our heads and close our eyes when we pray. I will try to say, the kinds of things he said.

"Powerful God, you made the whole world and everything we see. You made us too. Please help us in our school to learn what we should. In Jesus name, Amen.

"When I say 'amen', the prayer is over and we may open our eyes. Everything my teacher believed was written in a big black book with gold letters that said Biblia Sagrada (Holy Bible). It was written in funny old fashioned Portuguese and I never understood it."

For the next hour Titi explained how letters joined together to make words. She showed them how to make the letter t and the letter i. She taught them the sounds of the two letters. When they could say the sounds for the two letters she wrote, Titi on one of the slates and asked them to put the sounds together and raise their hands whenever they thought they had figured out the word. Lisa waved her hand, followed rapidly, by each of the other four. Finally Titi asked for their conclusions.

"It's your name!" Lisa said with excitement. The other children all agreed that it was their teacher's name.

"You are all right! You have just learned to read a word; that was the first word I learned to read as well. On other days we will discover how to make each of your names. I see my father has arrived and I must go. Please practice writing the two letters we have studied today. Make lots of them on your slates until you can make them easily. I will leave the letters written on our black board. School is dismissed until the next day we can meet"

The girls were visibly excited. In one hour Titi had taught them a very basic idea that was totally new to them.

Zoao took a careful look at the new school. "You certainly have worked quickly. It was just a few days ago that you were telling me of your plan. It will be wonderful for these children to go to school. Our villages in these parts are fine in many ways but we have always lacked two things. We have never had schools, and we have never had a trained nurse or dispensary."

"Father, I will take you to the chief's house. You know him anyway. The chief showed me the room where you can sleep while you are helping us. I will bring your food to you. I understand that, according to our traditions, you shouldn't stay with your mother-in-law and me."

"When I was walking down here, the chief called me over and showed me the room. He is very pleased that you are going to teach the children. I already put my bag in there so we can go right to the field as soon as you are ready."

They walked together to Titi's grandmother's house where Zoao ate a hearty breakfast in the outside cooking shelter. Zoao and her grandmother spoke in a friendly manner so everything was off to a good start.

The sun was just burning through the dry season haze when Titi showed her father the field they needed to clear.

"This will only take a couple of weeks or so of hard work because none of the trees are too large. I think this field must have been cultivated years ago."

"Nkaka says that she remembers when her mother's banana grove was located here, so all the trees are younger than she is."

Zoao had a reputation of being a good axe man. She watched in admiration as his axe bit into the sides of the hardwood trees with real precision. While he worked with great energy, Titi organized a little rest spot. She made a good fire, found stones for her water pot to sit on, and pulled a chunk of dry wood over to make a seat. After her dad had been working hard for about two hours, she called him over to have a lunch of some of his favorite things. She knew he liked cold sweet potatoes, hot peanuts, and hot coffee.

"Come and rest a little," she called.

"You know exactly what I like to eat when I am working, don't you?" He began to eat his sweet potatoes with a few warm peanuts to give zest to each mouthful.

"Sorry, I have no sugar for the coffee."

"Who has sugar these days?" He answered with an understanding laugh.

"Father, do you think I could learn to cut with an axe like you? You are going away in the army so I think I should learn. Next year I may need to clear another field. I know it could be done with a machete, but an axe would be much better if I could learn to use it. With all the young men in the army, we girls need to learn to do what has always been considered to be men's work."

"If you could find an axe a bit lighter than mine, I think I could help you learn. Most of your skill will come from practice. You already know just how to cut a tree with a machete. You really do the exact same thing with an axe. It takes a lot of practice to manage to get your axe blade exactly where you want it." Her father's words and attitude encouraged her.

"Nkaka has an old axe that my grandfather used years ago. It is covered with rust, but I may be able to get it prepared."

"An axe needs to be as sharp as a very sharp machete, to really do its work. A sharp axe is safer than a dull one because it bites into the wood rather than bouncing off and harming you. I am sure you will be able to help me. After all you are accustomed to all kinds of field work."

While her dad was eating, Titi went over and counted the growth rings on one of the big trees. She counted seventy-one or two rings on three different trees. "Grandmother must be about eighty-three or four years old. She remembers working in the fields when she was a little girl, and they cultivated fields for about five years."

"Numbers of years don't mean much, child. Some people are old when they have not been living many years, while other people stay young, and well, like your grandmother who has been living a long time. Your mother is already in the village of her ancestors, but she hadn't lived as many years as I have."

"I will run now and help grandmother get supper. I will bring it down to you after sun down. It is great to have my own father clearing my very first field."

Titi had her water calabash with her so she carried water up the hill on her way home. She thought that her grandmother might need it to finish her cooking.

"Nkaka, could I borrow grandfather's axe? I want to learn to cut trees like my father. He said he would teach me, if I could find an axe lighter than his. He said that I should sharpen it sharper than a sharp machete. If father and all the other young men go away in the army, women are going to need to learn to do men's work. Don't you agree?"

"My child, you think just like your mother and me. I always wanted to be able to do every kind of work including the work done by men. Look at me. I have not had a husband since before you were born. The first years after your grandfather died I cleared the big trees myself. The last few years I paid a young man to do the work for me. I paid him in smoked fish that he sold in Lufu to buy the things he wanted. Certainly you may use the axe. It is a bit rusty, because I have not used it for five or six years now.

To remove the rust, rub the axe in the dry sand beside the river. When you go to sharpen it use the big stone on the top of our hill. When you have done all you can, bring the axe to me, and I will show you how to finish sharpening it with a special stone your grandfather and I always used."

"I will run down to the river now, and bring back a load of wood when I come. Do you have enough dry manioc for tomorrow?"

"We have enough dried manioc for two days, so just bring the wood if you like."

The axe cleaned up quite easily because it had palm oil spread on it before it was put away. She rubbed wet sand on the rustiest spots. Within a half hour her axe was shining like new metal. Loading her basket with wood, Titi climbed back up the hill to the big sharpening stone. The axe was not too dull because it had always been properly sharpened. After a half hour of very careful sharpening, she had the axe as sharp as most machetes.

Her grandmother was pleased with the restoration of the axe.

"Come, and I will show you how to finish your job," Nkaka offered.

From behind the dividing mat, she heard her grandmother opening one of the metal trunks. When she came out, she had a small stone that had been purchased in Luanda years before.

"Put a little palm oil on the stone, and move it in a circular motion like this until the whole blade is smooth and as sharp as you can make it. Turn the axe over and do the same on the other side. When you are almost finished, rubbing your thumb on the blade will tell you where you need to do more sharpening. You will know when it is really sharp. As you can see, this stone is very fine, compared to the big stone on the hill. When I was making mats or baskets, I used this stone to sharpen my machete so I could do fine work with it."

Titi worked diligently, while her grandmother went over to a tree and picked some large leaves.

"When your work is finished, the axe blade will cut this leaf without tearing it at all when you draw it over the blade."

It took a lot of polishing before her axe passed the split-leaf test. When she succeeded, she had no doubt that she had met her father's requirements.

"You will soon learn, I am sure of it, because you are already skillful with a machete. I will finish the supper, but I need you to run down and get a basket of sweet potatoes before dark." Handing her some ripe palm fruits she added. "You must go by our fishing place on the way to get the potatoes. Set the larger trap, both eels and catfish seem to take an afternoon nap and they look for food in the late afternoon when they get moving again."

Titi shivered when she went out into the deep water to set her trap. Still wet, she pulled on her clothes because she didn't have the time to wait until she dried off. Going down the path quickly, and quietly, all the way to the potato patch, she surprised a big fat thief, a wild pig.

The pig looked right at her, but did not move because the breeze carried Titi's scent away. She was very close, when he grunted in a startled way and ran off into the underbrush like lightning. He had looked right at her, but didn't move, until he smelled her presence. He had eaten a good number of sweet potatoes and dug up many more with his snout.

" Ngulu evo ndoki? (Pig or witch?)" She wondered with a pounding heart. "My father will take care of this thief," she whispered to herself, as she filled her basket with the potatoes the pig had dug.

Titi was back at her fish trap within a half-hour.

Into the cold water she waded courageously. As she pulled the trap to the surface she saw as large a catfish as she had ever seen. *Grandmother knows just how to fish. I'm lucky to have such a teacher,*" she told herself.

It didn't take her long to split the fish's ugly head and remove all his gut. If it had been warmer weather she would have wrapped him in leaves without cutting him because he could live most of a day out of the water.

Her grandmother was pleased with the big fish. "Your father's supper is just ready this very moment. He will be hungry."

Hurrying down to the chief's house, she noticed that her father was sitting down in a wicker chair on the verandah. He had just arrived from his work.

"Papa I hope you are hungry. I have brought you lots of food."

"My child, I think I could eat an elephant right now."

As her father cleaned up the last bit of moamba gravy with a ball of fufu, Titi sighed a happy sigh.

"Nkaka will be happy because you ate all the food."

In affirmation of her observation, her father produced a voluminous belch in appreciation. Laughing, she teased, "I will tell grandmother what you just said," referring to the belch.

"There is a fire in the chief's talking hut, and no one else is there. Let's go over and sit by the fire."

Two large logs encouraged each other's glow and produced a comforting heat.

"Papa, there was a big pig in the sweet potatoes just now. He looked right at me with his mean little eyes. He didn't budge until he could smell me. Then he bolted into the underbrush."

"Was it a male?" Her dad asked with deep interest.

Titi nodded affirmatively, "He had big tusks that came out each side of his mouth.

"If you ever run into a female with young, be prepared to defend yourself, because she might attack."

"Papa, how do you know whether a pig is just a pig, or a ndoki witch?"

"The elders say that a pig that is a man in disguise will turn into a man again when he is shot. They say that if you kill a crocodile who is really a ndoki witch, the animal will die in the river and the man will die the same moment in the village."

"Papa, did you ever see one of these miracles with your own eyes?"

"No, I have never seen them myself but men I trust have told me that they have seen these things. I'm sure your grandmother knows all the traditions. Her fetish charms would stop an ndoki witch but they wouldn't stop a simple pig. I will borrow the chief's rifle tomorrow and I will need you to lead me to the same field. What way does the wind usually blow over there?"

"The evening wind blows from the potato patch toward the path. I think that is why he did not move until I was close," explained Titi.

Titi laughed, and asked her dad another question. "Do I smell so badly that a big pig will run away from me?" She actually understood well all about animal's acute sense of smell.

"No matter what other work you may be doing, make sure that you come for me so we can get there at the same time as you saw him today. If he had a good feed of sweet potatoes, he will be back. My tired back tells me it is time to go to sleep. I will see you tomorrow. All that good food is making my stomach smile and my eyes grow sleepy." He held Titi's hand fondly when she shook hands before she headed home.

"My father is a good wise man," she whispered as she scampered across the village to her grandmother's house. Because of the cool season she could see flames dancing in every open door she passed at that early evening hour.

Once she was snuggled under her covers, Titi told her grandmother about her father's plan to pursue the fat potato thief.

"Your father is a great hunter. Perhaps we will have pig meat by this time tomorrow."

Titi made no reply to her grandmother because she had fallen asleep.

Next morning, when she went to do her regular chores at the river she saw all her little pupils.

"We can hardly wait for your field work to get finished, so we can have school every day," little Lisa protested.

There was a lot to do before she could join her father. She needed to make sure her grandmother had everything she needed for the big evening meal for everyone. The only special thing she needed was a fresh supply of palm fruit so she could make a moamba gravy for the big catfish she had smoking over a smoldering fire. Finding a good supply of palm fruit just prior to her father's visit really helped with the cooking.

Once she had gathered the required fruit for her grandmother, Titi put both her axe and machete in her pack basket along with boiled sweet potatoes, roasted peanuts, and the old metal coffeepot. The last thing she did before leaving was to put some coals in a piece of broken pot, so she could light her father's breakfast fire. When the Lufu market was open there were lots of matches around, but many things had changed.

It was mid morning by the time Titi had the coffee boiling and the peanuts hot for their hearty breakfast. They normally ate twice each day, at mid morning and again about seven in the evening.

"I see we have something extra today. What has your grandmother made?"

Nkaka had made a package of catfish spiced with hot peppers and moamba. Titi heated the leaf bag on the coals so her father would taste it at its best. He dipped his sweet potato into the mixture and then smiled as he took a bite.

"The food is so good, I should take my time finishing this job."

Learning to cut down big trees

After her dad had almost finished his meal, she showed him her axe. The first thing he did was to run his thumb along the blade.

"Your axe is sharper than mine. Did your grandmother show you how to do it?"

Titi nodded her head.

"There are not many things she hasn't done in her lifetime," said Titi. "She loaned me a special stone for the final sharpening. She said that my grandfather bought the stone in Luanda"

"You know, child, knowing how to sharpen an axe like that is more than half the secret of cutting large trees. There are lots of men who still don't know how to sharpen their axes. Come on over and I will show you a few things you need to remember. The rest will come with practice."

Moving to the base of a tree Zoao taught Titi the basics about undercutting and directing the fall of a tree.

"Probably the most important thing to remember is to prepare the area around the tree for your cutting work. Cut all the little bushes and vines so that there is absolutely nothing that can catch your axe when you swing. Many people are seriously cut every year because they don't take the time to trim around the tree they want to cut. Always cut your tree so that the wind will help push it where you want it to go. Always stand a long way back when your tree starts to fall. Watch me cut the next three trees, then go try one yourself."

Titi watched her father very carefully and, after he had cut his third tree, she went off to cut her own. She knew exactly what she wanted her axe to do, but found it difficult to place her axe accurately. Her father cut down five trees before she finally had the pleasure of watching her rather large first tree fall to the ground.

"My axe just doesn't want to obey me," Titi moaned.

"Did your pen obey you the first time you tried to write?" Her father asked with a grin. "How did you teach your pen to obey?"

Titi smiled with understanding. It took a lot of practice for her to learn to manage her pen. It was going to take time to learn to chop with an axe too, but she would learn all she could, as long as she was able to work beside her father. By late afternoon, she could see that she was chopping a lot better than when she first began.

"I am happy to see that you have carefully followed all the things showed you to keep yourself safe. Just being careless one time can cost you your life, or make you a cripple. You are doing better than I did when I was your age."

Hunting down the sweet potato thief

"Father, it is time to catch the potato thief with the beady eyes."

With the chief's rifle over his arm, Zoao followed his daughter down the path that would eventually lead to the sweet potato patch, and perhaps some fresh meat. The shadows were getting long when they arrived near the potato patch. At that point, Zoao lead the way with his gun cocked and ready.

Titi's heart began to pound when she spotted the large wild pig. He was so greedy that he didn't even look up. They were looking at the creature from a full side view. He was still pigging out on sweet potatoes when he was blasted from the muzzleloader rifle.

The big animal leapt into the air, and fell down dead. They both rushed forward and Zoao adeptly cut the creature's throat with his machete. Needless to say both hunters were delighted. They suddenly had a generous supply of meat and the sweet potato crop was rescued. Zoao reckoned that the boar was traveling alone or he would have had his companions with him after his first big feed the day before.

One of the lead balls had ripped through the pig's spine damaging a minimum of meat.

"He will bleed well because his heart is still pumping. That will make the meat much easier to conserve," Zoao explained. They pulled the pig around, so his head was in a hollow permitting the best possible bleed. The bleeding ended after a few minutes, and Zoao slit the animal's stomach so they could remove all the innards. Titi carefully wrapped the heart, kidneys, liver and intestines, in leaves, then placed them in her basket.

"I will turn the intestine inside out and wash it thoroughly when we get to the river," she told her dad.

Zoao looked for a long slim bamboo near the river. Titi found thin vines. Front and back feet were tied in pairs and the bamboo was thrust between the trussed legs. The pole was placed on their shoulders with the dangling animal much closer to her dad so Titi would end up with the amount of load she could carry.

"We will carry the pig to the chief's house. He is entitled to half the meat because it was shot with his gun. He must have the heart as well."

We know it is an animal, and not a person, but it is good for the chief to be a witness," Zoao explains.

They stopped at the riverside, to thoroughly wash the intestine. Everyone liked pig intestine but only when all traces of the pungent smell of manure had been washed away. The inside of the intestine was very smooth so it was not too difficult to get it clean.

As they walked toward the village Titi remarked. "We both smell like a pig, I think we will need some of Nkaka's ashes soap to really get clean. Anyway, it is well worth it."

The two weary hunters rested several times, coming up the hill. When they reached the village they walked briskly and proudly to the chief's house in the middle of the community. As they approached, the smile on the chief's face got broader.

"You got him, you got him!" he exclaimed. "Those critters are hard to get especially if they crawl into the underbrush after they are wounded. A wounded boar is mighty dangerous too. They can slash a man to death with those big tusks."

Feeling the point of one of the large tusks that came out of the side of the animal's mouth, the chief commented, "You are a great team of hunters. This girl of yours is very special. Today she is a hunter. Tomorrow she will be a schoolteacher. You need to know how pleased we are to have her in our village."

"Chief, we have come to bring you your half of the pig. Without your well-made gun, we would have nothing. We respect you as Mfumu a ntoto (land chief) as well." As they spoke, Titi handed him the heart, making a curtsy at the same time.

The chief showed his delight.

"With my three wives and our children we can use the meat. I haven't given them any meat for a long time," the grateful chief explained.

Both men examined the animal and were agreed that the severed spine had paralyzed him instantly.

The chief lowered his voice. "If anyone dies with a bullet in his neck we will know he was a Ndoki, won't we?"

They had just finished cutting up the boar when Titi came back with their supper. The chief had already eaten but he invited Titi and her father over to the talking hut to eat their supper. Titi held the pots for her father to serve himself generously. After her father had been well served, she served herself. They were both ravenously hungry, but Nkaka had supplied an abundance of delicious food.

After sweating so much from carrying the heavy animal up the steep hill, Titi and her father shivered a little in the cool breeze. The fire felt great.

Titi recognized that it was real honor to have been invited by the chief to a place reserved for men and boys. The conversation involved a detailed account of exactly how they had shot the wild pig. Titi remained totally silent, knowing that she should only speak when asked a question. Wishing to slip off home to get some sleep after such a hard day, she whispered to her father.

"Titi would like permission to leave now because she has worked very hard today. I have been teaching her how to cut the big trees. She wants to learn how to do it because, she has noted, most of the young men are either soldiers or refugees in the Congo. She likes to teach school a while every morning as well."

The chief readily nodded his ascent.

"I have not forgotten my promise to build you a real school house with a roof before the rains begin." There was a broad smile on Titi's face as she curtsied once more before going out into the darkness with the white basin of empty pots. Her father would bring their portion of meat in the morning.

For the second night in a row, Titi fell asleep talking. She began to tell her grandmother about her tree cutting, and the exciting hunt, but she fell asleep in mid-conversation.

The next week and a half was filled with constant activity. Titi divided her time between assisting her grandmother with food preparation, and helping to clear their new garden space. They thoroughly enjoyed generous portions of pork. With salt in short supply they decided to use up all the meat for Zoao's meals. Conserving meat for a few days did not require too much salt. Between the pork, and smoked fish, Zoao felt he had never eaten so well before in his life.

By the time the field was fully cleared, Titi felt she had gotten to know her father better than she ever had before. As long as her mother had been alive, she quite naturally spent all her time with her mother. There were tears in her eyes when she said goodbye to her dad, knowing that he was joining the army— a difficult, and dangerous life with the UNITA forces.

The first morning after Zoao left the village, the axe bell rang cheerfully, calling the children together for school. Actually, the bell was more of a formality because the children were all gathered at the school well before Dina rang the bell. Once the class had begun, each girl brought up her slate to display the work she had done while the school had been closed. Titi was amazed. Her friends were making their letters very skillfully.

Little Lisa explained their secret of success. "Dina sits in your seat and runs the school for a while every morning."

Dina smiled sheepishly. "I didn't want us to lose time while you were working with your father, so we met for a while every day. We have smooth boards for our desk tops too, but we wanted you to show us how to fasten them to the legs."

Titi thanked all the children, especially Dina. As soon as they began their studies with Titi again, Dina raised her hand.

"Each of us would like to learn to draw our own names just as we have learned to draw yours," she requested hopefully.

"That is exactly what I plan to do because as soon as you can print or "draw", as you say, all your names, we will learn the letters that remain."

Titi wrote all of the names on the largest slate hung up at the front of their little room.

"Since Dina is the mbuta (elder) among you, we will begin with her name. It is a little more difficult than my name, but, now that you can handle your slate pencils, it will not be too difficult.

"While my father was here, I learned to use an axe to cut big trees. The first days I had a terrible time getting my axe to go where I wanted it. After lots of trying, I was doing quite well in the end. It is the same with learning to make your names. Teaching your fingers to go where your mind wants requires a lot of patience. You need to remember that writing any of the words we speak is done in exactly the same way as the way we write names.

"In order to learn to write your names you will learn how to draw each letter and remember the sound it makes. Some people draw letters more easily than others. To understand what I mean, I would like each one of us to try to draw a goat. I will try too."

For the next few minutes everyone was at work. When most had finished, Titi asked each one to hold up her work. Little Lisa's goat was by far the best. Titi's goat looked as funny as any of the other children's.

"You see. We don't all draw as well as Lisa. I think Lisa will probably make good letters sooner than the rest because she can draw more easily than the most of us. We will not all learn to write our names as quickly or as well as some of us. What we need to remember is that we will all be able to draw or write our names some day. Each day try to do better work than the day before, but don't worry if your work is not as nice as the work of the person beside you. When it comes to learning the sounds of each letter, we can even work at that while we are outside the school."

The village chief visits the little school

Three claps outside the door caught everyone's attention. The village chief wanted to visit them. Titi motioned for all the children to rise. She invited the chief to enter and have a seat on her bench at the front. The Chief entered quietly. In a soft voice he asked the children to be seated. Titi sat down beside Dina.

"Children, you have made me very happy with your school. I have been sitting under the tree listening for quite a while now. Your teacher is very wise. Even at my age, I learned what reading and writing is all about this morning. You will learn a lot here. I am very pleased with the way you all behave and show respect to your teacher. I watched you all make this little school and I am proud of you.

"When I was a boy about your age, or a little older, I worked for a Portuguese merchant at Lufu, called Santos. He always spoke to me in Portuguese and so did his wife, so I learned Portuguese from them. I worked for both of them. He taught me how to write my name. He wrote it, and I struggled for a long time to draw my name the way he had written it. I like the way some of you said, draw your name. I learned to draw my name. No one taught me about letters or their sounds. I only learned to draw my name the way Mr. Santos had shown me. I yearned to learn how to read. Mr. Santos had fifteen or twenty books. I wanted to learn to read, but I had no one to teach me.

"You have built your own school shelter, and it is a good one for the dry season. If you keep on attending regularly, I will see that you have a roof over your heads before the rains begin. Perhaps you can persuade a few more children to come to school. Little boys need to learn too. Boys will be embarrassed to join a room full of girls unless they are sure they are welcome. I just wanted to let you know that I am very pleased with what you are doing. If ever you need my help, please come to me."

The children all stood respectfully until the chief had left. They were all very excited to hear his encouraging words.

Titi began helping the children to make the 'd' that started Dina's name. She spent time with each child, helping her to draw a straight line with a mug handle on the bottom. It was not an easy letter to make, but they all tried, with some doing better than the others. Printing a good letter d on each slate, she encouraged them to practice whenever they found time. Class was dismissed, so they could each run home to help their mothers.

Nkaka was making kwanga when Titi arrived.

"You are just in time. I can't finish my kwanga, until you bring me some wrapping leaves from down along the river's edge. My legs are too frail today, even to carry up the leaves. I'm getting old, and my bones and joints are as old as my white hair. You have arrived to live with me right when I am beginning to really need help. I don't know what I would do this cool season, without your help. Now tell me how school went today."

Titi told her about everything that happened that day. When she heard about the chief's visit and promise to build a roof, she made the clicking sound in her throat that expressed her hearty approval.

"I wish I could have gone to school when I was a girl. The missions had schools and residences where village children could live while they went to school, but I was always needed at home so I never went. In my day, parents sent boys to school, but not little girls. The missionaries wanted schools for girls, but the elders did not agree to that for a number of years. As I have told you, girls in my day learned about farming, mat making, pottery, basket making, fishing, and child rearing.

"The elders saw no need for girls to read and write. Some of them wanted to think that men knew things that a woman couldn't learn. They were just beginning to have more girls' schools at the mission, when the wars interrupted. We intended to send your mother to school when the war broke out between us blacks, and the Portuguese, who wouldn't let the missionaries stay to do their work.

Did the ancestors pray?

"Nkaka I have a question. Master Pedro, my teacher, opened each school day with prayer. Sometimes he read a little from his big black book, but I could not understand the funny Portuguese that was in it. Sometimes he prayed for children who were sick. Did our ancestors pray to God?"

"My grandmother said that Nzambi Mpungu (Powerful God) did whatever he wanted to do and all we could do was to make the best of it. We were taught that Nzambi (God) made everything. But we knew nothing more about him so we never prayed to God. We made our requests to our ancestors just the way you went to the cemetery to talk with your mother.

"We had teki (little carved gods) to whom we made requests for protection. We still do that. Some special teki are kept in the hands of the shaman. These little gods can punish, or kill our enemies. Both your mother and I taught you to respect the bisimbi water spirits. It is because of your respect for those spirits that we have kept catching fish, even when no one else managed to get any.

"We show respect to our ancestors in many ways, and they in turn, can help us. When we went to get clay, we always threw something made of metal up into the surrounding grass. That coin or nail was a little gift to the ancestors. Men drinking palm wine always throw a little on the ground for the ancestors. We were taught just what your mother taught you. No one ever tried to talk to Tata Nzambi (God)."

"Why would Master Pedro try to talk with God?" Titi wondered out loud.

The big black book kept for its protective power

"He probably studied at the mission school where they teach a lot about God from the big black book they call the Nkanda Nzambi (God's book) in our language. I have my great uncles book in my metal case. It was given to my mother when he died. From her, it came to me. I have never read it, and none of my children learned to read. I have been keeping it for someone who could read. I will give it to you. You may be able to read it."

"I would love to own a big book of my own. Certainly I will try to read it. I know I could read the words but I might not know the meaning of those Kikongo words, written many years ago."

While they were talking, they managed to wrap all the kwanga loaves in leaves tied with fine vines, as well as put in the big pot to boil. Titi and her grandmother both washed the sticky manioc from their hands, and stepped inside the house. Her grandmother went directly to her little private storage space. Titi never went near that area behind the mat division. She heard one of the old metal trunks being opened. The Bible had been stored in the trunk that contained the family protective images or teki.

"My mother felt that this old book had magic power, just like the other fetishes, kept to protect the family," Nkaka explained.

Titi opened the big black book very carefully. On the first page she found the hand written name of W.H. Bentley. Titi sounded out the name B e n t l e y.

"Who was that person?" Titi asked.

Her grandmother was surprised to hear the name Bentley.

"My great uncle worked for this man. I heard that he was sent home from the white man's house because he was stealing things. Perhaps he stole this book because the white man treasured it. I have heard that that white man spoke Kikongo as well as the elders and the King. I heard that Mfumu Bentley (Chief Bentley) was the white man who changed the bible from his own white man's language to the Kikongo of our kings. He wanted our people to know the secrets in this book. None of my family could read a book so full of words."

Moving nearer the door to get more light, Titi leafed carefully through the perfectly preserved book. She found a carefully folded paper filled with very fine handwriting.

"Who could have written this?" She wondered, but she could not read any of it because it was not written in Kikongo or Portuguese.

"Nkaka, it is wonderful of you to let me have this book. I can read many of the words but you would need to tell me what they mean. Perhaps I can read some of it to you some day if we have time. Right now I know I need to put some manioc in the spring to soak and get some sweet potatoes at the same time. We still have enough wood."

She did a lot of talking to herself, as she went to the far field to pull manioc and gather leaves. She kept wondering about everything that black book had seen in the years of long ago. The afternoon flew by. Titi's hands did the work but her mind was thinking about many things, especially her bible and the ancestor who may well have stolen it.

She was glad when she had carried up her last load of wood to the house and sat down by the fire with her grandmother. "It has been a good day, and I think I have the field work done up in such a way that I will be able to teach each morning, and still give you all the help you need."

"Can you imagine how hard it was for me when I did not have your legs to do the running, or your arms to do the lifting?" Nkaka asked.

The firelight was not quite bright enough for Titi to read her new but very old book. "Perhaps some day I will find someone who will help me understand the teachings in this book."

"You were so busy and so tired, when your father was working in our fields, that I never did hear how you made out cutting big trees. Did you manage to learn to use that axe you sharpened so well?"

"Nkaka, I did learn to cut down trees. While I was cutting down one, my father could cut down four or five. The last two days I did quite well and my axe finally began to obey me. It would take me a long time, but I believe I could clear a field now."

"It is always good to know how to do things, you never know when it may become very important."

It seemed strange not to be rushing to take food to her father.

"I miss my father now, more than I missed him before he came," Titi said wistfully. "I do hope that I will not lose my father too!"

Her grandmother simply remained silent because she knew how dangerous war could be.

It was good to be able to talk for a little while after they had both laid down on their sleeping mats. All the other nights, sleep had come the moment she pulled her cover over her head.

Some boys want to go to school too

There was a surprise when Dina banged the school bell. Two shy boys were waiting near the doorway to their little school.

"Please could we come to your school?" the boys asked very submissively. "We are sorry that we made fun of the girls when they started making the school. We would like to learn to write our names too." The boys were each about eight years of age.

Titi asked the boys to wait over by the big tree while she talked it over with the other girls. The girls whispered among themselves and in a few minutes, Dina spoke for them all.

"We know that these are good boys, and we think they should be allowed to learn, they are like our brothers."

Broad smiles replaced the worry lines when the boys heard the verdict.

"May we come in now? We will sit on the floor until we make our bench this afternoon."

It turned out to be a great morning in school as Titi thought of new ways to explain the mystery of reading and writing. She remembered that none of the children had ever seen anyone write at home.

Titi had just told the children that they could go home when they were all surprised to see most of the adults gathering under the near by sanda tree. Since other children were going to the meeting with their parents, Titi and her school children decided to go too. They sat together on the ground.

When the little assembly was complete the chief rose to speak. Looking over the gathering, the chief expressed his appreciation that each of their village's twenty-three houses was represented. Titi realized that she represented her grandmother's house.

The chief organizes the construction of a permanent classroom

"We should build a school house before the rains come. I want each household to bring two bundles of long thatching grass and place them behind my house." The chief then proceeded to give out other building material assignments to assemble the poles and saplings that were needed for the normal kind of construction.

One might think that the chief was acting as a dictator when in fact; he had talked with every family privately, before the assembly.

"I would like to ask the parents of the children who attend the school to allow their children to help our young teacher by giving her a hand with field work every Saturday morning. This will make it easier for her to teach, without getting behind with her own work. We all know that her grandmother is not able to do much field work any more."

There was a congenial nodding of heads accompanied by affirmative whispers. They all liked their village schoolteacher, even if some of them had no use for her grandmother.

The dry season flew by, and true to his promise, a neat little schoolhouse was built very near the old one. The eaves were made very long so that the walls would be protected from the blowing rain. Windows were simply openings, but they were well protected by the long eaves. One day the chief came to Titi to find out whether there was anything lacking in the new classroom. Titi explained the advantage of the few balsa-topped desks they had made in their little school. She also mentioned that smooth balsa boards blackened with heat made great black boards at Lufu.

"I worked as a carpenter in Luanda and still have my tools. You will have your blackboard and desks. I have a little table that I will put up front for you Titi, now that we have a roof for the school."

Titi felt very encouraged. The new school building complete with simple desks was finished by mid September, several weeks before the first rains could be expected.

Before they entered the new school the chief organized a feast. People brought all kinds of good food to the long sapling tables which were built under the big sanda tree. To everyone's delight, the chief had one of his largest goats killed to provide a true goat feast for everyone. The school children sang three songs in Portuguese before the proud villagers. After everyone had eaten very well, and the men, mostly old men, had had generous amounts of palm wine, the chief stood to make a speech.

"We have built a good school house by all working together. You know that it is well built because you built it yourselves"

The chief began a dialogue with his people.

"Who made this school? Who made this school?"

"We did! We did!" replied the village.

"Who teaches our children? Who teaches our children?"

"Titi! Titi!" the village responded.

"We all know that Titi is teaching our children. We have never had a school in these parts before. We know she is young, but she has the responsibility of an adult. She teaches our children and she must grow the food for her grandmother and herself. They have no one else to help them. Titi and her father cleared a new field. I tell you that she helped clear it because I went out to see the work one day and this girl was chopping down big trees like her father. She had her father teach her because he has gone off to join the army himself, joining the other young men from these parts. If you women folk could join together and work up the soil in that new field, I am sure that Titi and her pupils will be able to plant it."

The women moved closer together and whispered for a few minutes. Dina's mother stood with quiet dignity and made a simple announcement.

"Next Saturday morning all the women and girls will work together so our little teacher will not have to worry about her food." There followed a general buzz of agreement.

When Titi looked around, she was surprised to see that her grandmother was there in the outer circle seated on her mat like the other women. A quiet, dignified smile graced her wrinkled old face. She knew that some individual women believed in her innocence but had been powerless in the past to break with the negative consensus of the village. Through Titi, some of her secret friends had the opportunity to give the kind of help that elders sometimes received, when they were in need. They all knew that if they could cling to life, one day they too would become old.

"Your mother sees, and she is proud of you. She is certainly proud of you! You have my blood in you, and I am proud of you too," the proud grandmother affirmed as they walked back through the village to their little isolated house.

Over and over her grandmother kept repeating these words quietly as she walked. Just outside the house the grandmother took Titi's hands in hers.

"Child I am proud of you, but I must warn you. Sometimes it is dangerous to receive so much honor when you are still so young. I see two dangers. You could become proud and begin to look down on others as though they are not worth as much as you. You are not a bit like that, and I believe you will always remain humble. The second danger is that of jealousy. When people see your success, some may well assume that you are using kindoki (witchcraft) power to achieve so much. It is good that many women will prepare our field. In that way they will not be surprised, when you have a good harvest. That field is a good one, and we will have a good harvest if anyone around here does."

Dramatic blessing

In a final dramatic gesture Nkaka spit on each of Titi's hands and held them as high in the air as they could reach. Holding her hands up the old woman solemnly gave her blessing.

"Bakulu beto (Our ancestors) Listen to me! This is your child. You know she is both kind and obedient. She shows respect to her elders. Our village chief trusts her, and is helping her to teach this generation of children. Watch over her! Continue to give her good thoughts, and good words! Protect her from ndoki witches! Prepare a good husband for her! Give her many healthy children! Bakulu elders, listen to me! She is worthy! You will see! You will see!"

When she had finished with her blessing, their arms were lowered gradually. Titi went on her knees, looked up, and spoke very slowly.

"Nkaka, Thank you! Thank you! Thank you! I shall try to bring you honor. I shall do my best to live according to the will and customs of our ancestors."

Her grandmother gently reached down and took her right hand drawing her up to her feet, relaxing her hold only when her granddaughter's hand was fully extended above her head.

Titi had heard about the blessing of an elder, but she had never seen it happen. Her heart was pounding. She felt as though she had just been honored before a gathering of her ancestors in that village on the other side of the grave. This was a day that would leave a mark on the rest of her life! Titi could not imagine that her mind could possibly quiet down enough for her to sleep, but it did. And she didn't stir until the rooster called. As soon as she awoke she was excited all over again.

"Nkaka, Nkaka, I was in the village of our ancestors, they shook my hand and the old ones each blessed me like you did. My mother was there, and she was the one who introduced me."

"Child, now you are really blessed. Our ancestors heard me, and they gave you their blessing in response. I am not surprised that your mother was among them. Your dream was sent by our ancestors. Your blessing has been confirmed. Often we are afraid to see the dead in our dreams. Your dream should bring you peace, not fear."

"Nkaka, I feel as though I am a part of a very large and honorable family. In this life they have been scattered because of the war and death. I have now seen that mother is there safely settled among them."

The whole experience raised a new set of questions in Titi's inquisitive mind. Was it the chief's unexpected words that stimulated her grandmother to bless her? The dream had been marvelous; did it hold any hidden meaning? Her life was changing in so many ways.

One day Dina made an important observation. "Your breasts are becoming like a woman's, just like mine." They had been drumming in the water while their clothes were drying. "The change has come to both of us during this dry season."

Both girls knew that adults classified girls by their breasts. When your breasts were noticeable you were no longer considered a child. Suddenly in the space of a few months, a girl moved from childhood into young womanhood. As soon as a girl with monthly signs developed breasts, she could be considered for marriage.

"Nkaka has noticed the change, she has given me her blessing at a very important time in my life." Titi said to herself. Upon further reflection, she realized that the chief would not treat a child like an adult. He had noticed the changes in her body that led to a reclassification.

It was Dina who had said that she was glad that there were no young men bargaining for them. "I want to learn many things before I am forced to consider marriage. It is wonderful that I am going to learn to read and write this year," Dina said dreamily one day.

With the extra help, the chief had arranged for her, Titi found that she had a bit more time to improve her own reading and writing skills. Everything she taught was a kind of revision for herself. When all the children were working at their desks, she practiced her own writing and printing. She was very thankful for the books Master Pedro had given her on the last day of school. One book was written in Portuguese and she could read parts of it, but some words were a mystery for her. One day she had and idea. She remembered that the chief had spoken Portuguese as a young man. Although he couldn't read, he could probably tell her what some words meant.

The chief often sat under the sanda tree in the comfortable chair he had made. It was like a white mans folding chair but a buffalo skin replaced the fabric. The buffalo tail, which he always carried as his badge of authority, and as a fly swatter, had come from the same animal.

Titi ran over to the chief as soon as she let school out. She explained her dilemma. "I can read Portuguese but I don't hear it (understand it)."

"Well, I can hear Portuguese and speak it, but I can't write it or read it."

"I would like to read my story book to you because you may understand the words I have never seen before," Titi explained.

The Chief was delighted because he understood the meaning of every word Titi read. Each time he explained a word Titi wrote down the meaning in Kikongo in one of the precious notebooks her father had given her.

"My dictionary will be very small, compared with the fat one Master Pedro had at Lufu. Nonetheless, it will help me to help the children when they begin to read Portuguese some day."

The Chief found it amazing that Titi could read a word she didn't understand.

Nkaka's joints predict rain

As Titi and her grandmother were having breakfast in late October, the old lady made an urgent proposal.

"I can feel a change in my joints. The rain is coming in a couple of days. Can you get the help of your school to plant peanuts in our new field. Peanuts that drink the first rains grow the fattest. The best way to use the new field will be to plant peanuts and corn at the same time. After we have pulled the peanuts and eaten the corn, we can plant manioc. This is urgent. Try and do it tomorrow.

"Pull down that blackened sack from up there on top. I will shell the peanuts and pull the corn from the husk while you are at school. They are both in that same bag."

Titi pulled down a sack that was almost totally black from the daily coating of wood smoke. "I think we could plant either today or tomorrow whichever you wish."

At school, Titi asked the children if they could help plant her peanuts and corn in the afternoon. They all were sure they would be allowed to come.

"How does your grandmother know when the rains are near? My mother is not planning to plant for another week or two," Dina wondered.

"She tells me that her joints let her know when the rain is on its way. I don't really know, but I am sure she is a good farmer so I want to follow her advice."

Dina shrugged her shoulders and reasoned that it was is great idea to plant Titi's field before they were needed to help their own mothers. They all agreed to meet at the river right after school.

Titi was pleased to see that every pupil had come including the boys. The women had worked all the soil very thoroughly just a week or two before. Titi had worked with them. All the branches had been gathered and burned in such a way that they set fire to treetops that were lying everywhere. The large trees were all over the place. They would be removed little by little for firewood or burned after they dried in a year or so.

The task was to plant peanuts and corn in all the available spaces between the trunks of the large trees. It was most unusual to have little boys doing field planting. That was a task reserved for girls and women. The schoolgirls treated the boys like little brothers and showed them exactly how to plant. Actually, they were all pleased to be able to help their teacher.

When the work was over, Titi had a surprise snack. She had lots of boiled sweet potatoes and a good supply of peanuts roasted by her grandmother during the morning. Many homes only had seed peanuts left so the children were delighted.

"By working together, we really got a lot done." Little Lisa observed, and all the others nodded in agreement.

"We don't know what to wish," Dina said. "If it rains immediately it will be before our own peanuts are planted. If it is more than ten days before the rains come, these seeds will spoil. We can't change the day of the first rains, but I am going to suggest to my mother that we plant tomorrow, and get the benefit of Titi's grandmother's wisdom." The other children thought Dina had a good idea.

"If you like, I can cancel school and everyone can plant tomorrow. That way, you will all be away on the same day," Titi suggested. All the little heads nodded in consensus again.

"If it rains in the next three days, we will all know who to ask next year when we are trying to decide when to plant our first peanuts." Lisa observed.

With no class in the morning, Titi took the time to wash all of their clothes. She greeted her friends as they went wearing their work clothes, trailing their mothers.

The following day, everyone was back in school. Mid morning, a dark cloud began to sprinkle a light rain on their dry world. The school roof did not leak at all. It rained gently for three hours. The children were actually happy to run home in the rain.

"Thank your grandmother for the message from her aching joints. All our peanuts are drinking the first rain thanks to her," Dina admitted.

Some of the adults were pleased, while others, who had not planted their seed, complained indignantly, "I'm not going to be lead by any Ndoki Witch." Secretly they wished they had followed her leading.

About dreams

Some time later, Titi confided to her grandmother, "Ever since the day you blessed me, Nkaka, I keep having dreams that include my mother. They are not frightening dreams. I just wonder why they come so often. Where do dreams come from anyway?"

"My grandmother once told me about three main kinds of dreams, that come from three different sources. Dreams like the ones you are having come from our deceased ancestors in the land of the living dead, the ancestral village. Normally they come from people like your mother who knows and observes you. We must consider these dreams carefully because they are intended to encourage, or warn us. I think your dream has come as a result of the blessing I asked the ancestors to give you. Your mother is the only person among them that you know. You keep seeing the one you know best.

"There is another kind of dream that is very frightening. In those dreams, we feel threatened and in danger. It could be a dream about being bitten by a snake or about being choked, or beaten mercilessly. Dreams like that are all initiated, or managed, by ndoki witches. Because an ndoki witch can get into our house, or into our dream, our local judges will condemn anyone, you can identify, who bursts into your room, or your dream, with an evil intent, especially if the experience happens several times.

"I'm sure you know that ndoki witches can leave their bodies behind and travel long distances to torment, or eat (kill) a victim. They only travel in darkness. Sometimes at night you can see a light in sky that passes in the blink of an eye. That is an ndoki traveling. Sometimes they travel and attack disguised as a ferocious animal, or even a bird or insect. It is because they are near you, that your dream experience is so frightening and dangerous. When you are being choked in a dream, it is because someone is there doing it to you in a mysterious way. All Ndoki witch dream encounters are dangerous. The good thing is that if you survive and wake up, you have been warned, and can seek protection.

"Some people experience a third type of dream, especially people who know a lot about God and the Black book. These people see God or Jesus, or Mother Mary or some person mentioned in the bible. These people claim that they get messages from God in their dreams. Those dreams should be obeyed. Our ancestors can send us dreams that direct our decisions. Religious people say God does that too. I don't know, because I never believed anything but the beliefs of our ancestors.

"Some dreams are silly and have no meaning at all.

"There is one important principal I have observed both in myself and others too. Whatever preoccupies your mind, dominates your dreams as well. To give a simple example, when I was thinking about getting our peanuts planted, I dreamed about planting peanuts too.

"Nkaka, why is it that we can only be attacked by ndoki witches from our own blood line, or by ndoki witches sent by blood relatives?"

"I think you are beginning to see that our ancestors left us in the same trap that tormented them and brought them conflict, treachery, deception, and death. I have no understanding of how it all began, but I do see that we are in a kind of trap all our lives. You are asking about that trap. You think like an adult, so I will answer you to the best of my knowledge.

"Everyone wants certain things in life. We want to live, raise children who live in harmony with us and, in their time, bring many grandchildren into our lives. We don't want to be hungry, and we fear sickness because it leads to death. We want to be respected. You, my child, are enjoying respect right now. I lost the comfort of respect when I was accused of being an ndoki killer. When people can't get respect based on love and esteem, they search for respect through power.

"Power that does not grow out of love and esteem must be acquired either by becoming a ndoki witch or from negotiating with some powerful person who is reckoned to be a powerful. I have concluded, that Nzambi Mpungu (Almighty God) made us with powers to bless and powers to curse. Blessing assures life and reproduction, while curses cause death, tragedy, and sterility. These powers seem to be at work within our blood relations.

"Often, blessing, cursing, and sterility can find origins within the father's clan. The father's clan can't take a life. His job is to protect his children from the ravages of witchcraft coming from their bloodline (maternal). As I see it, the powerful ndoki witches of our bloodlines have us trapped. They can eat us (kill) when they decide to, unless we employ kindoki (witchcraft) power that outwits or over powers them. There is a constant power struggle in the unseen world. You, Titi, are appreciated at the moment. No relative will attack you out of hatred. In fact, most of your relatives have left these parts and gone to the Congo. Perhaps, some ambitious relatives might want to suck your superior intelligence to use for their own ends some day.

"Someone could be required to give a ruthless shaman the right to capture your spirit in return for protection from some death threat. Child, I hate to admit that you can never trust any relative completely. We are always watching over our shoulders in regards to clan members. They help us, and they also take our lives. I don't blame your mother for distrusting me. Older persons are always suspect because they are at a point where they might pay any price for their own survival. This seems to be how Tata Nzambi (God) created us."

Vumbi, Nkaka's source of protection

At this point, Nkaka went to her private store place, opened a trunk, and came back carrying a hideous statue almost two feet tall. The statue was shaped like a pregnant woman. Its face was a dirty white. Just below the breasts there was a piece of mirror held in place by dark pitch. The eyes were made of small white cowry shells.

"My eldest aunt passed down this teki (god) to me. The sharp pieces of metal driven into the abdomen were intended to kill unborn babies. The intent was to kill a baby within someone, so it could be reborn in a women who wanted desperately to become pregnant herself. This Teki has been used to kill. For a teki to have that much power, one or more people had to die to enable the shaman to empower it. Every life that has been taken to empower this object had to have been of our own bloodline. This teki called Vumbi (corpse) protects this house. She embodies the spirit power of those who died, when she was made, and is imbued with power captured from the victims. Other ndoki witches are afraid to come here because they are afraid they may become victims of Vumbi.

"Nkaka, is it because of your teki, that you have lived so long?"

"Yes my child, I am protected and so are you. My Vumbi will only kill someone who tries to kill me. If I were heartless, I could have her kill others. Do you see the trap? In order not to be eaten (killed), I manage a teki who will kill my enemy. When people want something badly enough, they will sacrifice someone else to get what they want. Up to the present, Vumbi has protected me, but I have no way of knowing when some ruthless shaman may have a more powerful teki. We are never totally safe."

"How does a teki get empowered?" Titi asks very seriously.

"My dying aunt gave me this explanation. The Shaman (Nganga nkisi) who prepared Vumbi demanded the death of two family members who were known to be ndoki witches because of their roles in life. One was the chief of our clan, and the other was a renowned diviner (Nganga Ngombo)."

For a long moment her Grandmother was silent. Finally she spoke again.

"It is time for me to tell you some of our mbumba za kanda (clan secrets). My great aunt poisoned those two powerful men. To kill them, she boiled the skin of a chameleon (Lungwena) and proceeded to put the poison in the calabash from which they were both drinking. Everyone recognized that they must have been poisoned when they died the same day. Since both of them were hated, feared, and felt to be responsible for many clan deaths, the whole thing was covered up. The word spread around was that they had poisoned each another. The clan was delighted, and hid the affair from the Portuguese authorities of the time."

"The Nganga nkisi who was preparing Vumbi captured those two powerful spirits with the help of our ancestors through a secret process I don't understand. Vumbi became as powerful as the two spirits captured to empower her."

Nkaka lowered her voice to a whisper.

"There is a cavity behind this mirror. Hair from the men who were killed is stored in there. Their power was captured. I don't know how they did that. The one who gave me Vumbi said that I am protected as long as I believe I am protected. You see me. I am an old woman. Why would I not trust Vumbi?"

"Nkaka, didn't that Chief and Ngombo have their own teki and fetish charms to protect themselves?"

"I am sure they had protection against the power of ndoki witches. Poison is something else. They were not killed by witchcraft but by poison," Nkaka explained.

"How did your aunt who owned Vumbi die? Titi inquired.

"How well I remember how she died because I lived with her for a couple of years before that fateful day. She was old, like I am now, when five little children died in our village in an outbreak of measles. The ngombo diviner claimed that my aunt was the guilty ndoki. At the trial she had to take a public oath to save her life. She had to vow that if she ever practiced witchcraft again that she would be cursed and die. Within six months she became insane, caught by her own curse.

"She died with her feet held in a special log arrangement. A log was split, notches were cut to the size of her ankles and the two halves were rejoined with spikes. She could not harm anyone. After the restraint, she only lasted two weeks. When she was buried a large pot of hot peppers was put over her head so she could not torment or frighten people after she died," Nkaka concluded thoughtfully.

"Thank you for entrusting me with such important clan history. I know that I am too young to be told, but we are not living in normal times," Titi pointed out.

"While we are talking, I must tell you the family branches (luvila) that you should know. We are from the luvila (clan or line) called Tadi. Our founding mother was Tadi, and she had three daughters (vumu) wombs. Each vumu became in turn, founder of a sub branch, Tadi-goma, Tadi-luka, and Tadi-mwini. We are descendents of Tadi-goma. The two powerful men, who were poisoned to make this teki Vumbi, were both from the descendents of Tadi–mwini. The descendents of Tadi–mwini, are potentially our enemies. They are always seeking revenge for the deaths of their two most powerful members.

"The man accused of your mother's death is from the Tadi–mwini line ! Someone may tell you that he is from the Tadi clan like you. You must always find out which vumu (sub group) he is from. You must always be careful of any of the descendents of Tadi-mwini. Always try to find out which branch of Tadi a relative is from. If he is from Tadi-goma like you, you have found a brother or sister. If they are not from our branch, do not trust them and do not tell them that you are from Tadi–goma."

"It seems to me that all teki and all protection fails eventually because everyone dies sooner or later," Titi concluded.

"You are right my child. Our struggle is to try to die later rather than sooner. At my grandmother's funeral an elder spoke wisely when he told us that we all must pass over the kiamvu (bridge) called death. He noted that powerful protection may change the day of death, but it can't change the fact of death itself."

"How can we be sure we are safe?" Titi asked plaintively.

" I am afraid that we are only be as safe as we believe we are." Patting her teki called Vumbi on the head she said quietly. "She has kept me a long time. I am sorry that I have no other answer."

The cowry shell eyes of Vumbi seemed to glare at Titi, demanding respect from this young girl who knew all her secrets. Titi did not feel comfortable. She shivered, feeling some dark, restless, evil and menacing power. She could find no confidence of protection. She was relieved when the Vumbi was back in the darkness of her grandmother's tin trunk.

"It is always revenge that provokes suffering isn't it, Nkaka?"

"Clans like ours are divided by desires for revenge." Nkaka nodded affirmatively, with obvious heaviness of spirit.

In her dreams that night Titi saw Vumbi hovering over her. Her heart was pounding like a dance drum, so frantically, that it awakened her. Getting up immediately, she rebuilt the fire so it would produce a maximum of light. All sleep had been erased from her eyes. She sat up wide-awake until, eventually, nature aroused her grandmother.

Told of her dream, Nkaka showed visible relief. "You are included in Vumbi's protection. Your dream was your affirmation. I had the same experience years ago when I was introduced to Vumbi, and the whole story. The teki came to you so you would know that you are a member of the protected group." Titi felt somewhat relieved.

On her way to the water, Titi felt unusually weary. "The adult world is filled with secrets and problems." She told herself out loud. She realized, that in fact, she would never be a real child again. It was not pleasant to think that every child born in a bloodline inherited conflict from the moment of birth. The cheery faces of the schoolgirls brought back a sense of well being again.

The little school continued to be a great success. Not a single child had any thought of dropping out. The pattern of the rains was very predictable. It rained mid morning and mid afternoon almost every day until the beginning of the short dry season early in January. School went from eight to twelve most days. The rain always brought relief from the ever increasing heat.

The men of the village had done an excellent job in building their school building. No matter how hard it rained, the long overhang kept water from entering the open windows.

The warm rains were producing good growth in their peanut patches. Those who planted the same time as Titi and her school children were happy with their decision.

Titi was the only one who planted corn before the very first rains. As a result her corn was beginning to ripen by mid January. Several times, she brought fresh corn to be cooked and eaten at break time. Mangos were ripe again, some early nsafus were ripe, and the manioc leaves had become tender and juicy once more. With everything green and growing, hungry caterpillars were collected to supplement their generous food supply.

Their village seemed more isolated than ever before, with Lufu the market town abandoned. All food was for eating, as it had been in bygone years. The children seemed healthy, except for the malaria that came with the myriad of mosquitoes hatched in the ubiquitous ponds of surface water.

By February the peanuts were fat, and ripe. Everyone loved peanuts, both fresh, and dried. Good food seemed to enable the children to learn better. By the time the peanuts were ripe, the children could make all their letters, and identify their sounds. They could write each other's names. Some knew their numbers to fifty. As Titi expected, Dina was as anxious to read as Titi had been the year before at Lufu, so she spent time with her each day after school. Dina expected to be able to read and write by dry season.

Both the early and normal rains were abundant. Sometimes the waters in the river were so high, that Titi did not dare to venture out to set the fish traps. With plenty of caterpillars they really didn't miss the fish. The warm weather was much kinder to her grandmother as well. She enjoyed going out to her gardens where she actually did a lot of work.

Following the example of Master Pedro, Titi made sure that the children were comfortable with their own language before she introduced much Portuguese. She taught them to speak a selection of useful phrases, but she purposely did not write them on the blackboard for fear of confusion.

When the children had made enough progress with basics, she copied some of her first little Kikongo stories onto the black board, from her own notebook. The children found that sounding out the letters and recognizing the words was like a game, of which they never seemed to get tired. Paragraph, by paragraph, they went through the first story. To encourage them, Titi gave a pen and notebook to each child so the story could be copied, and kept. They were all very proud of their notebooks, so judiciously purchased by Titi's father before Lufu market closed.

At home, the children began to read to their delighted parents. All the little songs in Portuguese that Titi had learned in her year at school soon became part of the repertory of her little school choir. Their chief, who had worked in Luanda and at Lufu, could speak Portuguese, and he enjoyed teaching the children several songs as well.

Civil war casts a long shadow

The trickle of people leaving for Congo Zaire was gradual, but it ate away at their total population. Gradually, the villages around Kiula became peopled by old people, women, and children. All the healthy young men of military age were either in one of the armies, or in the Congo. Sometimes the elderly made long treacherous journeys because they no longer had any adequate medical help in their villages.

There was increasing tension between the armed groups, especially when the Cuban's made it possible for the MPLA to rule the country as a communist state without having any fair elections. Tribal issues separated the military groups as well. The MPLA were primarily made up of part of the Kimbundu people who lived in and around Luanda. Many of the people from around Kiula had relatives who had lived in Luanda for years. There were many Bazombo, as they were called, in the MPLA army, which they had joined to fight the Portuguese. UNITA had its headquarters in the south of the country, in what the Portuguese called Bailundu country. The mother tongue of the founders of UNITA was Umbundu.

The major group from the north was called FNLA with roots in the old kingdom of the Kongo around Mbanza Kongo. Young men from the Kiula region were to be found in each of these military groups. In some military engagements they ran the risk of killing one another.

Titi's Father was with UNITA because he did not want to be in a party allied with the Cubans. Neither could he stand the thought of being commanded by some arrogant person from Mbanza Kongo, their historic masters. Titi had no word from her father since he had joined UNITA the previous year.

Often UNITA and FNLA soldiers collaborated despite their tensions. They both saw the MPLA as their mortal enemies to be killed on sight.

When wounded soldiers from one group or another came home to the village, everyone was nervous. There was always the risk that a patrol from an opposing force might come through. Harboring the enemy could cost your life, especially, if there were no local boys in the patrol. The war in the bush country was one of "kill or be killed."

In the school, with children from seven different homes, it was almost impossible for anything to pass unnoticed in the village, without the school children learning about it from one another.

Wounded soldiers seek refuge

Two young men with relatives in the village were MPLA soldiers. They were wounded when UNITA soldiers carried out an ambush in Lufu. Seriously wounded, they were left behind and presumed dead by their unit. Scrambling into the river, the two boys hid, staying in the water with their heads obscured by foliage and rocks. One lad had serious bullet wounds in his hip, while the other had been shot through the shoulder. They were starving, and desperately weak, when they crawled into Kiula under cover of darkness. Helped only by the light of a partial moon, they moved like phantoms from shadow to shadow, until they reached the chief's house. They slipped into the same room in which Titi's father had once stayed.

Down at the water's edge Dina whispered into Titi's ear. "Two wounded MPLA soldiers came to the chief's house last night. Mother was behind our house having a pee in the shadows, when they passed so near, that she could have touched them. Their eyes were on the clearing ahead. One has a bad leg and the other a paralyzed arm. They carried Kalasnikof rifles, just like the one her brother had in Luanda. The chief heard nothing when they slipped into his little guest room through the outside door. Our chief is in a tough spot. He will want to help them, but he could be killed or beaten severely if soldiers from UNITA or FNLA catch him."

The two girls shifted the topic to school as soon as they saw others approaching.

The Chief was awakened early, by the unusual growling of his little hunting dog. Those dogs can't bark, so growling was the only alarm signal they could give. When he opened the door, the little dog went immediately to the room where the two boys had hidden. Once the chief had opened the door, the little dog was satisfied that he had alerted his master, and ran out to sit under his tree.

A glance at the uniforms, and he knew the young men were MPLA soldiers. "Did anyone see you enter the village?" he asked in a whisper.

"No one, we are sure! Chief. We haven't eaten for a week. We hardly made it here after the fight at Lufu. The river is flooding and has carried away the log that served as a bridge. Antonio has good legs, so he pulled a vine rope across the river while holding a log under his good arm. He had a terrible time grabbing the bushes on this side but he did. My arms are both good so I pulled myself across on the vine rope. I tied our two rifles onto the end of the vine and we pulled them across too. Crossing the river took a whole day. We had to rest a long time to get the strength to move on. Chief Luz, you can save our lives, or let us die."

There was a long silence. "We are pleading for our lives! "We know that UNITA will kill all of us, if we are found, but we don't know what else to do."

The chief had listened attentively looking at the boys intently as they made their plea. Quietly he proposed a plan.

"According to all the traditions of our ancestors I must risk myself to save you. Here is what I will do. I will brick in this door explaining that now that we are older we don't need so many guest rooms. I will not put a door from your room into my house. I will loosen some bricks in that inner wall so you can come through whenever you must. We must get rid of your uniforms and I will bury your rifles When you are well again, you must go to Congo Zaire as refugees with the rest. You must not fight again!"

The two young soldiers were relieved, and amazed at his wisdom. They gladly accepted all his conditions.

"There is one more condition. My first wife must agree so she can prepare your food. Your MPLA soldiers killed her only brother in Luanda, so they could rob his little store. Her heart is very bitter toward MPLA."

"Please remind her that we were rounded up by other soldiers and forced to join the army against our will. Remind her that our uncle is from this region. Ask her to come and see us. No doubt she has a mother's heart."

The chief was impressed with their thinking too. While drinking coffee with his wife, he mentioned casually that two young visitors had come during the night.

"They are both injured. They want to meet you."

"Are they soldiers?" Mama Tedika asked suspiciously.

"Come see for yourself," he suggested.

When she saw the MPLA uniforms she stiffened, her face registered her bitterness. Looking more closely, she saw the young faces, and heard the boys plead in unison. "Mother, we need your help badly." Her heart melted and she went back into the kitchen to prepare some food for them.

"She has accepted you. I will tell her the plan. I will not come to this door again until I come with bricks to fill it in. I will loosen some bricks on the inside so we can give you some food and so you can slip outside at night," the chief whispered.

People were accustomed to seeing their chief do many different kinds of work because he was a skilled workman. By nightfall he had filled up the doorway with some bricks he had stored in his back yard. As far as the soldiers knew, they were safe and totally undetected. Only Dina, her mother, and Titi knew they were in the chef's house. They all knew that secrecy was absolutely necessary in wartime.

Hardly a week had passed, when a patrol of eight UNITA soldiers came and searched the village without a word of explanation. They looked in every possible hiding place including the private storage place in Titi's grandmother's house. They searched every room in the Chief's house except for the room with no door that escaped detection. When they had finished their search, they informed the chief of their mission.

"We were looking for two wounded MPLA soldiers but we reckon they drowned trying to cross the river."

The chief was relieved when they didn't even ask about the room without a door.

"Please forgive us for searching without permission. We have learned that we can't trust anyone these days. This is the worst kind of war when blood brothers can end up on opposing sides! We say that we are fighting the Cubans, but often, we end up killing our brothers, from our own region," the UNITA patrol leader explained.

The evening the patrol left, the chief and his wife were surprised, when Dina and her mother brought a good meal.

"This is for the boys, you can't feed them all alone."

The chief tried to look surprised but Dina's mother spoke quietly.

"I was in the shadows of my house when they arrived. I watched them go to your house. Titi knows, but no one else. We will help feed them until they leave."

The chief explained his terms of acceptance and Dina's mother was very satisfied.

"I knew you would do what was right," she affirmed.

"The younger boy still has bullets in his shoulder. When they are strong enough, they need to go to Congo Zaire to get them removed," the chief confided.

Titi brought fish, whenever she could, to help feed the young men. After six weeks, they were both strong and the lad with the bad leg could walk with a limp. The day before they left, the chief called Dina and her mother, as well as Titi, to meet the boys they had been helping. Antonio and Lucas were deeply touched to actually meet all the people who had helped them recover. As Antonio looked at Mama Kiadi, Dina's mother, his mouth fell open.

"You look just like my mother!"

"You look familiar too," she replied. "I had a funny feeling when I saw you in the moonlight the night you came. I have a number of relatives in Luanda. What is your luvila (blood clan)?"

"We are part of the Zinga clan."

"Then we are family." Mama Kiadi affirmed with tears in her eyes.

"Gracas a Deus! (Thank God!)," the two lads said in unison. "Together you saved our lives!"

The meeting was brief but unforgettable. They slipped away in the moonlight just after midnight. By morning there was no trace of them, and no one ever mentioned them again. Titi was thankful that her father, a UNITA soldier, did not show up during that period. It was ironic that the two wounded MPLA soldiers were hidden in the very room where he had slept, while clearing the new field. Afterward, there was a new bond between the chief and the three who kept his secret.

The chief learns to read and write

In late February the chief asked Titi to teach him to read and write if she could. In exchange, he helped her with spoken Portuguese. The lessons took place in the chief's talking hut, which consisted of a low roof with a generous overhang and open walls. The furniture consisted of two wicker chairs made by the chief himself. The village talking drum was housed here, and served as a seat as well. There were cooking stones, and a place for a substantial fire. In the hot rainy season they needed fires for cooking only. The wise chief always made sure that one of his wives was present during every lesson.

Ever since the opening of the school, the chief often sat under the sanda tree, listening to the school sessions. When the rains began, he asked permission to put his wicker chair at the back of the classroom. He understood all the lessons but needed private supervision of his drawing of the letters. As time went on, he learned to write the names of all the children. Because he learned the sounds of all the letters, he began writing a list of the names of everyone in his village, household by household.

Apart from Titi's one little reading book, the only books in the village were bibles. Titi had her Kikongo bible in and Dina's mother's owned a Portuguese bible that came from Luanda after her brother was killed.

They sometimes endeavored to compare the two translations using one to help understand the other. They were both trying to read about creation, from the first part of their books. It became evident that the chief needed glasses to see the small letters. Of course, there was no way to buy glasses.

One evening, when Titi and her grandmother were talking about the chief's progress in reading, Titi mentioned his need for glasses.

"I have your Grandfather's glasses in my trunk. Perhaps they would help him. Your Grandfather bought them years ago in Luanda. I think he bought them so he would look important like the white men who worked in offices." She explained with a little grin.

"Chief Luz is a good man, even though he believes I am a ndoki witch. He is convinced because the ngombo diviner was very impressive. The magic performed by the shaman at my trial was amazing. It has made me wonder sometimes."

She left that topic abruptly and went off to get the glasses.

The glasses, as well as their case, were in perfect condition. Obviously they had been used very little. Titi was anxious to see if they would help her friend. If times were normal, she could have taken them over immediately to test them by lantern light. However, since the trouble at Lufu the previous year, no one had any kerosene.

"Nkaka, what did you use for lights at night before the white men began to sell kerosene?"

Torches to replace kerosene

"We used torches at wakes, weddings, or any kind of celebration when I was a child. In the deep virgin forest, there is a tree that oozes a sticky kind of pitch, which becomes hard with time. Heat the hard stuff in a pot and it becomes a sticky liquid. We wrapped the sticky pitch in leaves that would not burn easily. We bound the package of pitch to a sapling. Once set on fire, it would burn half the night. Sometimes we used those torches for night fishing, during the poison fish kill. We used them to catch zenzie (crickets) in their season too. We need some of those torches now that we can no longer use our lanterns."

"I think we should make those torches again. It would be a good thing for the school children to discover."

"You would need to go with the chief, because the trees are only found in what people call the 'forbidden valley'. You saw that valley when you got the slates. Did you notice the giant trees that line the banks, where the river emerges after leaving the falls? The pitch trees are in there. That forest is owned by the Bisimbi spirits from the gorge."

"Dina told me that that was the gorge where ndoki witches used to be thrown years ago."

Dark history about the world of the occult

Nkaka became pensive. "Many a witch has gone screaming into death in that place. People don't go there without taking special precautions. Ndoki killer witches are not allowed in the ancestral village, nor are they allowed among living people. That valley harbors their miserable ghosts. You would need an Nganga Nsimbi (water spirit shaman) or a Mama Ndona to get permission to gather pitch down there. I would not go without first getting protection from a Nganga Nkisi (shaman who makes protective charms), so you will be protected from ghosts.

"Remember that any ghost down there was once a killer. You will need to sleep there because it is too far to go and return in one day. No doubt innocent people were thrown to their deaths too, but the bakulu (ancestors) always knew the truth and received the innocent among them in the ancestral village. The bakulu only rejected selfish ndoki witches, who wantonly ate people only to enjoy their flesh."

"Nkaka, do some people eat other people just like we eat chicken?"

"Understand this child, whenever ndoki witches eat someone or get flesh to eat at the zandu dia bandoki (witches market), he, or she, is eating parts of the invisible spirit body that only they can see and enjoy. If you went to their market you could not see what they were cooking or eating. When we speak of a ndoki eating someone, we mean that he or she is consuming or enslaving their total spirit power.

"The captured spirit becomes a slave of the ndoki witch. When they eat the spirit, the body of the victim we see dies. Our elders claimed that the white men came here, so they could capture, and enslave spirits, for their own advancement. Our elders took many people to the slave traders. Many of the people they took had already been found guilty of witchcraft. In these parts they could be thrown into the gorge or sold as slaves.

"Selling slaves to work in fields stopped long ago. Sucking all the spirit power out of a person and leaving the body to die is still going on. That is what happened to your mother. The white men never understood us, and their judges always made serious mistakes. One of our ngombo (shaman) might declare that the ndoki ate the head of the victim. The accused might even admit it. The white men would sometimes dig up a grave. When they found the physical head was still present they dismissed the case angrily. They never understood, that what the ndoki ate, was the invisible, mystic spirit head. That kind of eating made no change in the appearance of the physical corpse."

"Now I understand why it can be dangerous to be clever," Titi replied with a look of discovery. "People could think that someone is clever because he has the spirits of his victims working for him in all kinds of mysterious ways."

"My child you have understood! How I wish we were not trapped in all this, but we are! Imagine the pain I have felt when people accused me of sucking the life from little children so I could catch more fish or farm better than others," Nkaka replies sadly.

"Nkaka it must have been painful to be called Ndoki a fwa (Witch of death) by people you loved."

"Everything is invisible, so there is no way to really prove innocence. Guilt is declared by someone who uses his ndoki powers to declare that he sees, or has seen, what no one else can see! Only an ndoki can catch another ndoki. It is impossible to trust an ndoki. We are trapped!" the old lady sighed.

Sleep did not come easily, or as quickly as usual. Titi found her mind was spinning. She had simply asked about making torches, but her Grandmother ended up shedding light on some of the mysterious facts of the occult. This kind of instruction was always disturbing. Part of her wanted to understand all she could about the world around her, both seen, and unseen. On the other hand this knowledge brought pain. She was gradually understanding the depth of her grandmother's isolation.

Titi awakened shouting, " No! No!"

"Why are you shouting, 'No?!'" her grandmother asked with some alarm in her voice.

"Nkaka, they were throwing you into the gorge. They were killing you for being a killer ndoki witch! I was terrified because I couldn't stop them." Titi began to cry. "I don't want you to die, I need you. I need you."

"Remember one of the laws I told you about dreams! Whatever preoccupies your mind will preoccupy your dreams. I should not have troubled you with so many heavy words just before you went to sleep. As you can see I am alive and well. I don't think that dream came from our ancestors."

The Chief tries out reading glasses

At breakfast, Titi was still talking about the glasses for the chief. "I think you have found yourself a grandfather in our chief. I hope they will help him too," Nkaka said with sincerity.

The chief had barely settled himself in wicker chair at the rear of the classroom, when Titi was at his side with the glasses in her hand.

"Nkaka sent them to you. They belonged to my grandfather. Perhaps they will help you to see the letters better."

The chief politely clapped his hands to express his thanks, holding out both hands to receive the gift. Holding out both hands was a way of saying that the gift was too generous to be held by only one hand.

Putting them on excitedly, the chief took a look at Titi's bible, the only book he had. The expression on his face became ecstatic.

"I can see every letter of every word. The letters are all black and clear. I'm sure I can read now because it has been my eyes that could not see all along! I knew you had taught me well. I can draw all the letters, and I know the sounds they make. Taking my time, I believe I can read."

Spontaneously, the children clapped with joy. All the children were fond of their chief, who came to school almost every day. When Titi remembered her grandmother's observation, she realized that he really had become the grandfather to all of them.

The continued study with the chief at his hospitality shelter was more animated than usual. All the new possibilities had emerged because of his improved eyesight. He had had no idea that his greatest impediment to reading had been his eyes.

When they had finished with their study, Titi raised the question of pitch torches. She explained how it was that her Grandmother had explained about the lights they used before they had had any access to kerosene. Once she had explained her request, the Chief was all in favor of an expedition to the forbidden forest.

"It looks as though we may need to wait a very long time before we will have any kerosene. Your Grandmother has given us a possible solution to a very serious problem. There are times when we really need a light at night."

Incredible journey into the forbidden valley in a quest for pitch

The Chief agreed that he would lead the expedition to the forbidden valley in quest of pitch. It was not long before he had initiated the preparation. They all felt the need for emergency light, so the plan to go after pitch actually interested most everyone.

They needed a shaman who specialized in Bisimbi (water spirits). Mama Ndona Simba was willing to go because she was rather curious to see the most renowned water spirit haunt in a vast region.

Makasi, the Nganga Nkisi (protection shaman), agreed to prepare special protection amulets for everyone on the condition that he receive a good supply of torches. They all agreed that the best time to go would be in the dry season, which was still a few weeks away. The parents of the school children had no objection to their children's participation in the project once they were aware that their chief would be in charge.

Unexpected advice about marriage

After supper chats made up a part of the warm relationship between Titi and her grandmother. For the old woman, her granddaughter became her window into the world around her. She was interested in every step of progress made in the school. It was as though her years of isolation had ended. She often gave Titi very practical advice.

"I have noticed that your breasts are almost fully developed. Your body tells you every month that you are a young woman who could give birth. Men will be noticing you. Please do not abandon your dream of school. In my day when I was developed like you the clan leaders were already planning my marriage. I was very fortunate because they allowed me to marry a boy I liked.

"Many girls your age were given to be the second, or third, wife of an old man. I was only about one year older than you when I was married. Right now the local boys are away in the army or in the Congo. Old men always want young women. When the soldiers return, they will all say they want to marry you. Please don't think about marriage until several more years have gone by."

"Nkaka, don't worry. I couldn't get married without your consent."

"Child, we are living in days when some young women begin to sleep with their men without consent! They soon become worried and unhappy because they are living without any blessings from their elders. It is never wise to make important decisions without the blessings of your elders! Some day soon, the young soldiers will return. They will all want to marry you or at least sleep with you. Remember my advice!"

Titi nodded in honest agreement.

Not a full week passed, until her grandmother's predictions came partially true. Three young men returned to the village. Each had been wounded in some way and had come home for recuperation. One lad had a broken wrist. His friend limped from a leg wound. The third young man had seen so much death and horror that he could no longer face being in the army. He was intending to escape to Congo Zaire, if he could regain his strength. The three young soldiers asked permission to go on the search for pitch. The young men felt sure there would be lots of wild life in that undisturbed forest. They were hungry for a good feed of meat.

In the days leading to the trip Titi did everything possible to provide for her grandmother. She brought up lots of firewood. She filled the big kwanga boiling pot with fresh water. Her Grandmother laughed.

"Do you think I am helpless? I can still go to the water and to the fields. I just go more slowly. Don't worry about me. If I were not so stiff, I would like to go with you. I have never been there. In my youth only men and special people were ever allowed to go."

Titi had a good supply of travel food in her pack basket when the group was ready to leave in early October. It was a good time for folk to travel because their fields were ready for planting, but the rains were not expected for a few weeks. She was excited when she went over to the chief's house, where the group planned to gather.

Final preparations for the trip to the mysterious forbidden valley

The chief explained how they would travel. He himself would travel with Mama Ndona Simba, the water spirit shaman, who was traveling with her two sisters. Titi and her seven pupils followed behind the chief and the three women. The three young soldiers were to come behind so they could help anyone who had a problem.

Every member of the expedition wore a tiny sack, suspended on a cord about the neck. These objects were prepared by Nganga Masasi to protect them from ghosts. Each person carried a small bag of ndungu pepper powder, which would deter any aggressive ghost as well. The same shaman loaned the chief a special teki to protect them day and night.

The carved figure had two complete faces, one on each side of its head. Mysterious sources of occult power were hidden in the cavity of the carved image. A piece of mirror covered the cavity with its intrigue. Only the Chief knew about this protective personage, wrapped in a black cloth, and resting in the bottom of his woven hunting bag.

The sun broke through the clouds just as the group arrived at the high spot, overlooking the roaring river that crashed into the mist covered caldron far below.

"It was from here that our elders threw ndoki witches screaming to their deaths," the chief explained gravely.

All stood in silence, as Mama Ndona opened her bag of sacred objects and addressed the bisimbi water spirits shrouded in the mists that hid the bottom of the waterfall from view. She chanted in a high piercing voice.

"Bisimbi, Bisimbi. We want to come down to your valley.
We ask for your blessing. We need your blessing.
Protect us with your power. Allow us to descend.
Help us gather pitch from your forest.
You rule the waters and the canyon.
You give us all our twins.
You heal our eye diseases.
You heal our skin of blemishes.
Help us to approach you with respect.
I am one of your children. I am a twin."

When she finished her chant, she went to the water's edge with a pot full of ripe palm fruits carefully covered by a well-bound banana leaf. With an impressive flourish, she set the floating pot adrift. It drifted over the roaring falls into the mist-covered canyon far below.

Just as the pot went over the edge Mama Ndona went into a frenzied trance. Her eyes were closed as she trembled violently, while her head nodded affirmatively.

"The bisimbi spirits welcome us!" she shouted triumphantly. The whole group cheered and shouted their thanks.

Only the chief really knew the path to the forbidden valley, so he led the way. They walked along the ridge that overlooked the valley for over an hour. The chief needed to pause frequently to determine which way the trail actually went. It had been unused for years and was almost completely overgrown.

It was a process of constant slashing to clear the ancient trail. Everyone strong enough to do the clearing took a turn. Eventually they came to the top of what had been a significant landslide at some point in history. A forest now covered what amounted to a steep but regular incline, which could be followed all the way to the valley. At least it was possible to climb down without needing to negotiate the kind of cliffs and gigantic boulders that formed the approach to the valley below the falls. The trail was a bit easier to locate as well, because it snaked through tall trees without significant undergrowth obscuring the old trail. After over an hour of descent, they decided to stop for a rest.

"This trail will take us directly to the river where it begins its path through the jungle. I think we are at least half way down by now. We should be able to get there easily before darkness sets in." The chief announced encouragingly because their legs were hurting from the constant effort to keep upright on such a steep trail.

While they rested, one of the soldiers went off to one side for a few minutes, and then called for everyone to come in and get a drink from the spring he had located.

In they went, clearing a path. They were delighted with the rapidly flowing stream coming right out of the hillside. Astonishingly, the stream disappeared again into the rocks and gravel below them.

"Let's have some food," one of the small boys pleaded.

It seemed like a good idea to eat. It had been almost seven hours since they left the village. Within minutes, mbika, peanut butter loaf, crushed peppers, nsizi meat, and smoked fish were spread out on leaves within reach of everyone. These delicious foods were ideal to accompany their kwanga bread. Great food, coupled with the abundance of clean cool water, restored their strength and enthusiasm.

After a few minutes of descent, the sun broke through the dry season cloud cover to brighten their beautiful world. In full sunlight, they came upon the top of a more recent landslide. A whole swath of trees had slid out of sight allowing them to look out over the canopy of the giant trees that were reaching up from the valley floor. One of these giants was totally covered with white blossoms. The view below them was indeed breath taking.

Only the chief and Mama Ndona had ever walked among such giant trees, many of which were from six to ten feet in diameter and seemed to stretch up endlessly. The towering limba trees were supported by huge buttresses roots, giving them a diameter of fifteen or twenty feet from buttress to buttress. The trees stood like giant sentinels guarding the changeless, untouched virgin forest. Normally such a forest would be relevantly silent. However, the roar of the waterfall created an eerie atmosphere.

Mama Ndona, who had learned to recognize medicinal plants, was in her glory. Ever since their rest period, she and her sisters had been constantly gathering leaves as they walked.

"I have not seen some of these plants since I was a child. My grandmother knew them all and we gathered them in this forest, when I was the size of the school children. She was one of the people thrown over those falls and I have never come back until now. I think she knew every plant in the forest. She had to be an ndoki to accumulate all her knowledge of medicinal plants, leaves, bark, and roots.

"She was only an ndoki, when measured by cleverness. I am sure she was accused falsely of being a killer ndoki. I am certain that the bisimbi spirits received her well, because she was one of their kinfolk, being a twin. I have detected her good spirit in my daughter in Luanda," Mama Ndona explained.

Finally, the trail brought them to the water's edge with the roar behind them to the right. Mist and spray from the waterfall blocked out their view of the top the plateau from which they had come.

"Just imagine the roar of the falls in the rainy season when the river is running full," someone suggested.

While most everyone was looking up toward the falls, they were startled by a gunshot near by. One of the young men shot a beautiful antelope that had been drinking from the river.

After the antelope was carried over to where they stood, the chief clapped three times for silence.

"We have arrived safely and the bisimbi who rule this place have given us meat to eat, accepting Mama Ndona's intercession on our behalf. They are watching over us along with our ancestors. We will have a good stay."

Pointing to Mama Ndona with his lower lip, the chief expected her to speak. "Our Chief is right. We are safe here. Tonight I will meet the bisimbi water spirits in my dreams. After thanking them, I will seek their permission to gather the pitch and medicinal plants from their sacred forest."

Clapping three distinct claps, the whole expedition displayed its acceptance of her words.

"We will be spending the night, so we need a good supply of wood. There are lots of dry branches around us. With a good fire, we can cook the meat, keep comfortable, and be sure that we are safe from the leopards that live in these parts. I need three flat rocks set over here by the river, where I will set up the protective teki, loaned to me by our Nganga Nkisi (shaman). Tala-tala will watch over us while we sleep, and keep us safe from the menace of any of the disgruntled ghosts of executed witches. This teki has been passed down for generations. We are safe, but no one will go further than the circle of light, until day break," cautioned the chief.

Chores were all finished just before sunset. A huge collection of dry branches was piled up against an old fallen tree at least five feet in diameter.

With the help of others, the chief built a little slate rock shelter for Tala-tala. He was carefully placed inside along with half dozen cola nuts for the Ancestors. Each of the group placed a cola nut inside the shelter as an act of submission and trust. The chief addressed the grotesque statue on behalf of all.

"Mfumu (Chief) Tala-tala, greet all our ancestors. Offer them our kola nuts respectfully. Ask them to protect us from the ghosts of the wicked ones who were thrown down to the rocks under the waterfall. You have refused their spirits and so do we. They lost all their rights in both worlds, yours and ours. Protect us this night. We have followed the tradition our ancestors left us. Grant us peace, and protection."

Under the immense canopy of the virgin rain forest, darkness was total. Everyone seemed cheered by the crackling fire. Within a very short time, generous chunks of antelope pierced by saplings were placed so they were leaning over the edge of the fire. The delicious smell of roasting meat was tantalizing. Sleeping mats circled the fire like petals on a daisy. Each person tended his own chunk of meat on its stick. Inside a half hour, the meat was perfectly cooked. Large kwanga loaves were cut into equal chunks by pulling one of the wrapping strings down through them. The antelope was fat and tender. Each piece of meat contained enough fat to mix deliciously with every bite of kwanga. The adventurers were naturally tired, but very satisfied.

Mamma Ndona explained to a group of girls, just how she planned to communicate with the unseen bisimbi spirits.

"When twins die, their spirits live among the bisimbi. Before I sleep I will recall the names of all the adult twins I have known, those who have died during my lifetime. I will talk with them and bring back any message they give me. Tomorrow I will walk up into the mist around the gorge. One way or another, I will hear from them."

As they sat around the fire, Dina asked the chief if he had ever witnessed an accused ndoki being thrown over the falls.

"I heard of a woman being thrown over here by her clan, but I didn't see it happen. All of my days, the Portuguese administered the country. People were not allowed to execute anyone, simply on the basis of a shaman's decision.

"It was different in my grandfather's day, and a good number of people were executed here. All through the years, our leaders tried to get rid of killers one way or another. Since the time of our ancestors, the poison made from the bark of the nkasa tree has been administered by the ngombo shaman. According to theory, innocent persons vomit the poison and escape death, whereas the guilty cannot escape. My grandfather said that many of the people thrown over the falls were dead from nkasa poison before they were thrown over.

"Grandfather told us that in his opinion the ngombo controlled the outcome of the trial by poison, by the quantity he put in the drink. I have heard that since the war for independence began in '61, soldiers have been executed here by their colleagues who felt betrayed in battles. I have never witnessed anything personally. I know that if those rocks under the falls could speak, they would have a lot to say."

One of the soldiers asked the chief a very serious question. "Do you think that the ngombo shaman is usually right in his judgments?"

"The ngombo are the best authorities we have when it comes to discovering ndoki witches. People agree with them when their decisions correspond with their hopes. We are very upset when decisions go against the thinking of the people who knew the accused best. An ngombo tends to be trusted, when his decisions conform to the thinking of the majority, or when he performs convincing miracles before our eyes.

"An ngombo who used to live at Lufu tested suspects with tiny white stones called tensi. The tiny stones were somehow pushed into the corners of the eyes of the accused person. If the stones then dropped out that person's nose onto a plate, he or she was innocent. If, on the other hand, the little stones moved inside the person's head causing excruciating pain, the ndoki had been exposed. My opinion is that a genuine ngombo, who has been gifted by our ancestors with the appropriate spirit, is someone we are obliged to trust when he gives a judgment. The problem is to know whether or not the ngombo consulted is genuine. That is why people will travel very great distances to consult someone renowned to have a powerful, penetrating spirit.

Another of the young soldiers posed a question of interest to all. "Chief, Is it true that there is a giant zandu dia bandoki (witches market) somewhere in these parts? I have heard that this is the most important witches market for our Bazombo people."

"The elders often spoke of this market as being located somewhere in the vast rain forest we saw from the top of the falls. They said that no one who reached it could ever come back alive, unless he himself were a killer ndoki witch. I have heard that that market is surrounded by underbrush so dense that only wild pigs and snakes can get through it. I never heard of an elder who claimed to have seen the market. The moment he made such a claim his own guilt would have been exposed."

Mama Ndona's sister clapped three times seeking the Chief's permission to pose her question. "I heard that an old chief from Congo Zaire was thrown over the falls about three years ago. Is there truth in that story?"

"I had forgotten the case of the old Congo chief. I only know what his son told me when he stayed in my house. He told me that he followed the people who executed his father. He was a secret witness, keeping in hiding all the time. This is what he told me.

"It seems that the man later known as Chief Samuel was first accused of being a ndoki witch when he was in his late teens. He and his mother were accused of eating three children during an epidemic of measles. To humiliate them, the boy and his mother were forced to dance together naked before the elders. Everyone knows that a full-grown boy cannot look on his mother's naked body. His mother suffered unbearable shame which no doubt contributed to her death within a few weeks. Some others felt she had been poisoned.

"Despite all the shame he suffered, Samuel proved to be a very clever and enterprising person. He was renowned as a hunter and excelled as a farmer. In addition to all the traditional crops, he cultivated an impressive orange grove. Local people always felt that all his apparent success was brought about by his prowess in witchcraft. He inherited significant sacred objects from his Uncle as well.

"Chief Samuel claimed that he had superior harvests of corn, peanuts, manioc, and diamba (marijuana) because he inherited very productive land from his grandfather. He became relatively rich and powerful. He claimed to be an ndoki witch, and intimidated his enemies. In the sandy soil of those parts, people tended to build reed houses. He became the most gifted, artistic builder of his tribe. In everything he attempted, it seems that Chief Samuel was very successful. Even his wife was the chief of her clan. They had a good number of healthy children.

"The accusation which probably cost him his life involved children. Lightning struck the Catholic school located a day's walk from his home. The lightning struck a school dormitory and killed six children. Chief Samuel was accused of having thrown the lightning that killed the boys. An ngombo shaman from his own region accused him of causing the deaths from lightning.

"The son felt that his father's early admission of being an ndoki may have been made simply because there was no way he could ever prove his innocence. He used the resultant situation to intimidate some of his enemies. His father maintained his innocence concerning the dormitory deaths, but as is always the case, he had no way to prove it. Local chiefs paid soldiers to throw the old chief over these famous falls.

"That boy wept, when he told me of witnessing his old father being tied hand and foot, before he was thrown into the roaring falls. He admitted that his father had an unusual amount of wisdom and power. He felt that his father received unusual powers from his uncle when he inherited all his arm bracelets, and family gods. He did not need to kill anyone to empower his milunga (bracelets). He didn't need to. He inherited all that power legitimately. The last words the boy said to me were these. 'My father had many dark powers but I will never believe that he killed all those boys with lightning! He loved my son. He could never have killed him with lightning, because he was far too fond of him.'

The chief paused after recounting what he had heard.

"You ask me about the decisions of the ngombo diviner. Who should I believe, the son of a man thrown over those falls, or the renowned ngombo who the people from his region trusted? Remember, it was the old chief's blood relatives who paid the soldiers to throw him over the falls. How can anyone be absolutely sure he knows the truth of these murky matters? Only our ancestors know the truth. If Chief Samuel was innocent, he is with them now. If he was guilty, we are protected from his ghost."

At the beginning of these discussions with their chief everyone was listening. By the time he had finished explaining his opinions, all the school children were fast asleep. It was as though the group was inside a capsule of intense darkness, which surrounded their little circle of cheery firelight. Only the light of the fire kept the mysterious at bay.

Titi's sleeping mat was placed between that of her friend Dina and Mama Ndona. In the middle of the night Dina shook Titi awake.

"I have to pee, and I am afraid to go alone."

The two friends got up and slipped off into the shadows answering the age-old call of nature. Because they had to go into the shadows, they were keenly alert, looking at everything that surrounded them.

Suddenly Dina froze. "Titi, look over there!" She indicated the direction with her finger.

Their eyes strained to penetrate the darkness. Something was moving!

"Should we alert everyone?" Dina whispered.

They decided to wait and watch. The ghost, if it was one, never came any closer. It moved almost rhythmically. Neither girl had ever seen a ghost, so they didn't know just what to expect.

The girls had no idea as to how long they had stood motionless. Someone stirred. The Chief stepped out in the shadows across the fire from them. When he returned he threw some wood on the fire and if flared up, pushing back the darkness with bright light. Their ghost turned out to be a dried palm branch, hanging by a strand, swaying with the breeze. Relieved, the girls smiled at their folly.

"If we had called out, they would have teased us forever about our ghost."

The ghost excitement behind her, Titi disappeared under her cloth, which covered her from head to toe. Soon she was drifting back to sleep. Strange sounds coming from Mama Ndona caused her pop out her head to take a look. The woman's body was twitching strangely indicating that she must have been experiencing some sort of dream. Titi guessed that the bisimbi water spirits were communicating with her.

The hooting of an owl in the distance, kept Titi from falling back to sleep. She was haunted by her childhood experience of seeing her father spitefully place the owl he had killed, on a cross, because he thought he was killing her menacing grandmother, prowling as an owl. Since that moment, owls frightened her.

Each time the owl hooted it was coming closer, apparently curious about the firelight. Finally it perched in a tree in the near shadows. When its frightening hoot was emitted again, Titi could hear an answering hoot from the deep forest. Was the answering hoot from the infamous witches market? It seemed as though the whole encampment held its breath, until their unwanted feathered visitor flew off to join its mate. Finally they could all risk going back to sleep.

At first light, Mama Ndona moved off into the mist around the waterfall. Titi and Dina followed her at a discrete distance. The experienced shaman crept into a cavern carved by the swirling waters of the rainy season. The walls were worn smooth by swirling gravel. At the time, there was only a trickle of water on the bottom. The girls watched in wide-eyed wonder, as the woman began to tremble violently in some sort of trance. She shouted ecstatically in some kind of mystic language. After ten minutes of spectacular movement, she leaned against the wall and seemed to sleep from exhaustion. It was broad daylight when Mama Ndona aroused, and began to make her way back to the campsite.

Going directly to the Chief, who was seated by the fire, Mama Ndona requested an opportunity to speak. Her face was all smiles. She spoke slowly and distinctly.

"The bisimbi are glad for the respect we have shown them. We have their permission to gather all the pitch we need together with anything else we might desire for food or medicine. The only request is that we leave them a burning torch when we leave."

The whole camp clapped three distinct claps to indicate their acceptance of her communication.

For breakfast, they ate more of what they had eaten for supper the night before. They all enjoyed the luxury of eating plenty of meat with their kwanga.

Breakfast over, all eyes turned to the chief for instructions as to where to go to gather pitch.

"I was just a boy when I came here with my father. I remember him saying that the pitch trees always grew close to the water. Father and the other men cut scars in the pitch trees. The pitch flowed, as if to cover the scars. That was how we gathered the fresh pitch. It seems to me that we also gathered large lumps of dry hard pitch that adhered to the giant trunks of the trees."

While the chief was recalling the past, someone spotted large, healed, scars on the trunks of several huge trees within sight of their encampment. On closer inspection, they found that each old scar was covered with a layer of pitch from two to four inches thick. In an hour or so, their pack baskets were full of the product for which they had traveled so far. Once they had removed the layers of dry, hard, pitch right down to the wood, fresh liquid pitch began to seep out of the bark, to begin the protection of the tree wound, all over again.

Lisa found some unusual, brightly-colored mushrooms and brought them to Mama Ndona for identification.

"These are not good for us to eat or use as medicine, but I need them." Before she left, she took the bright yellow mushrooms and left them at the foot of the burning torch, requested by the Bisimbi.

As soon as their pitch was gathered, they started on their way. It took two hours of walking to climb down into the valley carrying only their food and supplies. They knew that the climb back would be arduous. Despite the hard climb, conversation never let up. They were all very pleased with themselves for coming. It had been a memorable adventure that would be talked about for years.

Memories from the past seemed to dominate the chief's conversation.

"The pitch we are carrying was gathering over the scars we inflicted on those trees almost fifty years ago." There was a long pause before he continued. "My father came to me last night while we slept. He looked exactly the way he did when he brought me here. He told me he was pleased that I had been chosen as Chief. He even mentioned our school. He told me he had wanted to go to school to learn to read and write."

At this point, they all began to climb over a part that was painfully steep. Their toes searched for something solid to help push themselves up to the next step. Titi and her school children lead the way. They began to slow down when they realized that the elders were not as nimble as they were. When the chief caught up, he thanked Titi for leading at a good pace that took everyone into consideration.

Once they had reached the plateau, the travel seemed easy in comparison with the climb, but they were all exhausted by the time they climbed the final hill to Kiula. Each of them went straight home.

To her surprise, her contented grandmother was cooking a good big pot of meat when she arrived. "Where did you get the meat?" she asked with great curiosity.

"This meat came to me all by itself," she said with a chuckle. "This is a young python that was trying to corner one of our best hens. I cut off his head with one sharp blow of my machete."

There was pride in her voice. Not only had she defended her chickens from the early morning attack but also she had a pot of treasured meat.

"Look at the oil I have skimmed off already. That oil is great medicine for my old joints."

Nkaka explains the history of the forbidden valley

"You must be as strong as a young mpakasa (buffalo) to have carried a pack basket as heavy as that one, all day long. I have looked down into that valley from the look off. I can imagine how hard it was. Sit down an rest until supper is finished."

Sitting down by the fire with all her load off her back Titi actually fell asleep and slept soundly for about an hour. When she awoke a hearty supper was waiting.

"Did adventurers into the forbidden valley, take the teki Tala-tala when they went down there in your youth?"

"Of course they did. No one dared to go down there without proper protection. That famous Teki protector has always been kept here in Kiula village. No one ventured into that valley without arranging to have him along. Often the Nganga who managed Tala-tala went with any adventurers himself. Years ago our hunters killed elephants down there. The hunting stopped when four men were stomped to death by a wounded beast. The leopards carried away their bodies, and they were never seen again.

"Once we walked along the ridge you followed until the sound of the falls was muffled. We could hear elephants trumpeting and squealing over around the tiny lake in the middle of the sacred forest."

Nkaka explained that the forest was called sacred because in it was located the oldest cemetery of the first ancestors to settle in the whole region.

"My uncle told me that in that old village site there are huge nsafu, cola, avocado, and mango trees. He said that a whole grove of nkasa trees surrounded the chief's enclosure. Elders have always claimed that the famous witch market meets within that nkasa grove. Uncle claimed that the cemetery was unique in that each grave was marked with a carved stone replica of the person who died. Giant trees had grown up between the graves, signaling that it was indeed very old."

"Do you know why those early ancestors moved away from that rich valley?"

"They moved for the reasons most villages move. When large numbers of people began to die a terribly painful death, and no one could stop the ndoki witches from their wanton killing, the remaining survivors moved up to this plateau. Later the white men described that sickness as sleeping sickness. They gave us injections to protect us, just before the battle for independence started. The white men told us that we could catch the sickness whenever we were bitten by a Tsetse fly that had first bitten a person or an animal infected with the disease.

"I think those white men were right. The years following the treatment, no one caught the disease. Now it is coming back again. Our ngombo insisted that the sickness was provoked by ndoki witches. Many of the elders died."

"Did any shaman find a way to stop the spread of the deadly disease?"

Sadly her grandmother admitted, that nothing the traditional diviners or healers had done ever stopped the scourge.

"During my childhood many people moved out of the rich forest valleys just because of that one sickness. My child, your questions are serious ones. The elders passed down the only answers I know. I have asked those questions too. Some questions seem to have no answers. Now that you know how to read, perhaps you will find other answers. I only know what the elders taught us. Perhaps other elders of other people will have better ways to understand death, sickness, and tragedy."

After a very refreshing sleep, Titi took a larger than usual supply of pots and dishes down to the water. Her shoulders ached from their journey.

Because of the accumulated field work, and the need to wash all their clothes, the girls decided not to open the school again, until everyone had another good night's rest.

During the day, Nkaka showed Titi and Dina exactly how to transform their chunks of pitch into very useful candle torches. The special leaves they needed grew all around the village. The chief showed others how to make the torches down at his hospitality hut. In the evening torches seemed to be everywhere. Everyone was surprised by the long slow burn. Each of school children gave a portion of pitch to the Chief, so that he would have a supply for emergencies. He needed some pitch to pay back the owner of their protective teki, Tala-tala.

Going to the forbidden valley and hearing accounts of the horrendous executions that transpired at the giant waterfalls left a deep impression on Titi. Coupled with the many explanations of her well-informed grandmother, they only served to whet her appetite for examining every aspect of the teaching and practices of witchcraft. There was one recurring idea that begged for further information. As they sat shelling their peanuts for planting, Titi decided to ask her grandmother to explain more about the idea of becoming a ndoki witch, without the consent of one's conscious will.

Tricked into witchcraft

"Nkaka, at different times you have said that you have harbored the fear that you might have been made into a ndoki witch of the evil kind. You have said that you feared someone had tricked you into becoming such a witch. Tell me if you can, how in the world a person could ever be tricked into such a serious state without her consent."

One of the qualities of her grandmother that Titi respected was her lifelong habit of thinking very carefully before responding to questions. After a long pause, her grandmother began to explain.

"Some of my memorable experiences coupled with much listening to elders, and much reflecting, has lead me to some important conclusions about myself. I have never consciously endeavored to kill anyone. Twice in my life my words appear to have held some sort of frightening power.

"My maternal uncle was a wicked man, consumed with hatred and vengeance. He threatened my sister with a curse of sterility if she refused to marry an old man when she was still your age. He angered me, and I challenged him. I warned him that if he cursed my sister with sterility he himself would die. I warned him that our ancestors would not allow him to live if he cursed her. My sister married the young man of whom both she and her family approved.

Uncle hired a powerful nganga shaman to curse her. For two years she could not conceive. My miserable uncle died suddenly and within months my younger sister conceived. At the inquest concerning his sudden death, my threat to him was remembered and I was accused of provoking his death. They accused me of uttering poison words that killed him. Their term was mate mandudi (poison saliva).

"About the year your mother was born, I was menaced by an other uncle who had always blamed me for his brother's death. I don't know how he planned to do it, but he got right up in my face and snarled. 'You will die before this dry season ends!' My reply was spoken angrily too, when I told him I would count on the ancestors to see that he died first. He died before that season ended! Once more the diviner shaman accused me of killing with my words. Once more, I was accused of being capable of speaking poison words. I must confess that I was glad when each of those wicked old men died. Many others were glad to see them dead too, but not everyone. It was in those days that people began to ostracize me, and call me a ndoki witch more than ever.

"My life was probably saved by one of our elders who came to my defense. He quoted a proverb 'words are like poison; they can only kill, when they are swallowed.' His judgment concluded the affair when he said, 'Let the bakulu (ancestors) judge her!'

" It surprised me that twice my words appeared to have had the power of a fatal curse that only a ndoki can make. You asked how I could have been given the powers of an ndoki witch without willingly consenting. I just do not know the answer. It seems to me that my words killed those men, but I never tried to kill them.

" I have wondered whether someone put mystic human flesh in my food without my knowledge. At funerals and wedding feasts we all eat together. I have no way of knowing whether someone tampered with my soul that way. My child, I can only report on what I know in my heart. I know that feeling innocent in my heart does not prove my innocence either to others or to myself. I have been very careful with my words since those days.

"I haven't said so in public, but it deeply troubles me that twice my words seem to have killed. I have not worried about the people who accuse me out of jealousy over my farming, or my skills for fishing. I know that I have worked harder than most, and that I learned farming and fishing from a clever mother. The secret fear that someone made me an ndoki witch without my consent, does trouble me.

"When everyone has called you an ndoki for years, it raises doubts. I have never been able to know whether the ndoki witches that have tormented me in my dreams could have done something to infect me with their powers while I slept. I have told you all I know, and I have told you of the important things I do not know. We are protected from the ndoki witches that might want to destroy us, but we all know that that protection is not forever. One day they will get me. We are trapped!"

Zoao returns after more than two years of military service

Two years had passed by with no word at all from her father. Some of the men told Titi that they thought that he was serving in a region south of Luanda. In general, soldiers only came home when their orders brought them near enough to visit, or when they were wounded. The UNITA soldiers only operated trucks infrequently, when they captured them. Even the captured vehicles were only driven until the fuel was used up. Generally, soldiers like Zoao went everywhere on foot.

In mid-dry season, Zoao was one of a hundred men assigned the task of transporting ammunition, grenades and mines. The supplies arrived by ship to the port of Matadi in Congo Zaire and were trucked east to an isolated area on the border with Angola. On the Angolan side there were no truck roads, so soldiers on foot could cross with very little difficulty. The roads in Congo Zaire were in very bad condition, but huge, six wheel drive UNITA trucks could get through.

Zoao became a leader of the munitions transporters from Congo Zaire to Nzeto on the Atlantic coast. At the first opportunity, he came to Kiula to see his only child Titi.

Arriving at dusk, he moved like a shadow to a spot near the chief's house, as soon as he spotted the chief, he approached. The old chief embraced him warmly.

"You're alive, you're alive! Come in, and I will give you a change of clothes, and hide your gun. As far as I know, there are no MPLA soldiers in these parts, but we will take no chances."

The room he was assigned was the secret room that once protected his official enemies.

"My wife will cook for you, and I will send for Titi. She can be here with you, so you can have a good talk. She is a great girl and we think the world of her."

Titi nearly burst with excitement when the chief's eldest wife told her that her father was in the village. Fortunately they had food on hand, so she was able to leave with a well-laden basket. Titi was about to leave when her grandmother brought a clean white cloth to cover everything respectfully. In her excitement the need for the cloth had slipped her mind. Everything finally ready, she rushed out the door with her sleeping mat under her arm. Darkness hid her in her own village.

The fire in the chief's house shed a reasonable light. When Titi entered, Zoao was startled; he thought at first that she was a stranger.

"My child, how you have grown," he gasped and filled with emotion. "You look just like your mother! She looked just like you when I brought the first palm wine to ask her father for permission to marry. You bring it all back to me."

"Papa, Papa, you're really here at last!" Titi exclaimed, as she went to hug him impulsively. "I have thought of you every day and hoped you were well. Everyone has said that soldiers only come back when the war is ended, or they are wounded. I had almost given up hope. You look strong, but you are too thin. Do you not get enough to eat?"

Zoao just gazed at his daughter for a few silent minutes.

"I get enough to eat but I have lost weight because of the hard work I am doing. I carry heavy loads for long distances. You are not a little girl any more. You have become a young woman!"

Her father's observations delighted her. She yearned to be like her mother and she enjoyed being called a young woman.

"How have you been, Papa? Have you been in the killing war?"

Zoao weighed his words carefully.

"I have seen far too much killing. War is terrible with young men killing and wounding one another. I have seen far too much death. If the war ever swings through here, I want you to flee to Congo Zaire. I don't want soldiers to find you here. I have seen what they do to young women. War is worse than you can ever imagine!"

"We have a hiding place all prepared in the forest at Nkaka's insistence. All the girls know where they will hide, if soldiers come. There is no way I could leave Nkaka. She is growing feeble, and walks very slowly. I could never abandon her Papa."

Once more Zoao was silent, choosing his words. "You have your mother's heart too. She would want you to care for Nkaka, especially since she has no one else."

"Don't worry about us. We have a complete plan. We have a tiny hut made complete with secret gardens. We will survive!"

"That is enough talk about danger and war. I brought you some food and I am sure you are both hungry, and tired. Eat well, and then sleep. We will talk again tomorrow. How long can you stay?

"I can only stay one more night because I am traveling with others."

All of this time the chief had been silent, he only began to eat when Zoao began to eat hungrily.

"Zoao, you have an exceptional daughter. She has given you many good reasons to be proud of her. She is wise, well beyond her years. All of our village children can read and write now. Even in my old age, she has taught me too!"

First Zoao looked very pleased. Then a shadow crossed his face.

"It is too bad I am not here so I could learn too," he said with deep feeling. "I am so glad we were able to send her to school that year."

The chief continued his commentary to Titi's embarrassment. "Your daughter teaches, but she is always wanting to learn everything she can. She and I traded lessons you know. I taught her to speak Portuguese and she taught me to read and write it. She is constantly asking her elders deep questions. It is not every day we find young people who actually want to learn from us older people. Zoao, I think Titi should go to Congo Zaire before too long. We have no school here. One more year and she says she will have taught everything she can, unless she goes back to school herself."

Zoao was quiet again for a while eating, and reflecting.

"Chief, I want you to take my place when I am gone. I want you to advise her as you would a granddaughter. She needs a grandfather like you."

The chief gently clapped his hands three times to indicate his acceptance of Zoao's request.

"I guess I have been looking at her as my favorite granddaughter for a long time now. Thank you for trusting me."

"Papa, the chief does treat me like a granddaughter. I have felt safe in his protection these years that you have been away in the army. You look as though you need a good sleep. If I stay, I will keep you awake with my chatter, so I'll go back to be with Nkaka. There are no MPLA soldiers in these parts. I think the chief will agree that it is safe for you to walk around freely. Perhaps we could go to the cemetery together tomorrow."

Gathering the dishes and pots she slipped quietly out into the darkness with deep joy in her heart. Nkaka was still awake when she came in. Sleep did not come quickly so she told her grandmother about all the serious talk of the evening.

"I told you quite a while ago that I thought you had found a grandfather in the chief. I'm glad your father asked him to be a grandfather to you while he is away. I know that at my age, I could go to the ancestral village any time. Your father was wise to tell you to go to Congo Zaire if the fighting comes to these parts. If soldiers ever move into this village, go straight to the chief and follow his advice. If you need to flee to Congo Zaire, don't worry about me. I know that you are good to me, and that you would stick by me if you could. You couldn't help me, you know, if you were being carried off by a bunch of soldiers."

It was the only breakfast she could prepare for her father, because he planned to slip away in the moonlight, sometime before the next morning. Titi carefully roasted the fattest peanuts she could select, lots of them, to be eaten with the plump plantains taken from among the coals at just the right moment. The coffee was freshly boiled. She knew she could put it on the fire again at the Chief's conversation hut.

Zoao grinned as he poured a little bag of sugar into the coffee.

"We haven't seen sugar for years. Where did you buy that?" Titi asked with a smile on her face.

"This is not happy sugar. I scrounged it in an abandoned home when we were sheltering during combat. It was sad to see that people fled for their lives leaving everything behind. War is terrible."

Zoao savored every moment with his delightful daughter. A new bond had developed since her mother's death, coupled with long separation caused by the war.

The chief joined them, savoring the sweetened coffee with delight. He asked Zoao the crucial question that Titi had wanted to ask.

"When do you think the war will be over?"

Speaking softly, Zoao replied. "It will be a long time I'm afraid. There has been so much suffering and injustice on all sides that the desire for revenge is deep. Ordinary people with deep losses want revenge. The leaders want power at any cost. I know that UNITA forces felt cheated from power by the arrival of all these well-equipped Cuban soldiers.

"Everyone is using mines to ring positions at night so they can sleep. When the fortunes of battles push either side, we leave behind land mines that are often never retrieved. Hit one of those wires, or step on other types, and you will at least have your foot blown off. Without medical help, most victims bleed to death. My heart aches when the young boys die. Some are no older than you Titi. Every day people find new reasons to want revenge and continue the armed struggle.

" In a few days time, I will be carrying a full pack of those mines to our secret encampment outside Luanda. If we don't ring that encampment with defensive mines, we could be wiped out while we slept. In war, young men kill one another because they are afraid not to. War is terrible but right now we are forced to fight to survive. It is as though we are holding a viper (pidi) by the neck. As long as we hold him close to his head, he can't get his poison fangs in us. If we let go for a moment, he will kill us."

The chief leaned forward and whispered his next question. "Should I encourage our folk to stay here in our isolated corner, or should we make plans to become refugees?"

After a pause, Zoao practically whispered his reply. Both sides will tend to protect this village, and fight some other place. I know that I never want to kill or harm anyone from these parts. I am sure that the MPLA boys feel the same.

"Chief, we know that young men from this village are soldiers on both sides. You are fairly safe, but you must rely on yourselves for everything. Don't take sides in this conflict. People who know that you have soldiers on both sides will understand. Outsiders will show no mercy. Remember that! When your boys grow to be strong lads, send them to Congo Zaire or they will be forced to fight by someone. This war will only end if one side wins, or the people revolt against the leaders who force us to fight.

"Remember, apart from the Cubans, everyone who dies in this civil war is a child of Angola. Angola is losing her sons every day! Chief, I expect that a couple of soldiers will arrive this afternoon or evening to check up on me and see that I am where I said I would be. I know too many secrets, so they naturally want to check up on me. Whenever they come, I will leave immediately without saying goodbye to anyone. I am not a free man, no soldier is!"

When the two men stopped talking for a while, Titi asked her father another question. "Do the MPLA soldiers know about the trail you follow to carry supplies?"

"We hope they don't, but we keep constantly alert, watching for men, and those killer mines. We take turns walking ahead as scouts. It is hard, dangerous, work and we are often very hungry too. We are afraid to hunt with our rifles because that would expose our location to the enemy. I wish the war would end soon, but that is only a foot soldier's dream."

The school children knew that their teacher's dad was visiting and that their school was cancelled. Titi hurried home to her grandmother's place to tell her of their plans. When she came into the house, she saw that her grandmother had the two catfish, caught the day before, in the final stages of smoke curing.

"One of these is for his last meal here this evening. The larger one is to go with him along with loaves of peanut butter and peppered mbika to keep him strong while he walks those long distances." A satisfied expression enveloped the old woman's face as she displayed her thoughtfulness.

Titi prepared the outside shelter. Her grandfather's chair was placed by the fire with two low stools for her grandmother and herself. There were lots of peanuts to be roasted while they waited. It seemed strange to see the chief's familiar clothes coming into their enclosure. Zoao bowed and clapped respectfully when he approached his mother-in-law. Nkaka responded warmly. They asked about each other's health before beginning any real conversation.

"Mama Nzitu (mother-in-law), I want to thank you for the wisdom you are passing on to my daughter. Her mother will be comforted when she sees that her daughter is becoming the kind of person she would want. These days, I have nothing to bring you. We haven't been paid for a year now. All I have is this little package of sugar that I would like you to have."

She was delighted with his thoughtfulness. She knew that no one had had sugar for a couple of years now. Sugar was also a traditional, very acceptable gift from a son-in-law. The symbol of good will was, perhaps, more precious than the gift. The old woman remembered vividly the angry remarks in the past, when she had been suspected of being responsible for the death of his baby boys.

"Zoao, by far the greatest favor you have shown me, has been to agree to leave Titi here with me. Her help has made these past few years a happy time for me. It is like having her mother back again. Through her I am linked to the world around me and no longer locked in a prison of loneliness."

Zoao smiled awkwardly, but happily.

After a short chat Titi proposed a slight change to their morning trip to the cemetery. "Father, I need to do some work here this morning. You will want to see some of your old neighbors and relatives over at Mbungu. I will meet you at the old house around noon."

Zoao was pleased with the plan and headed off toward his home village quite happily.

Titi hurriedly did some washing at the river. While the washing dried, she hurried over to the patch of giant leafed malanga (special type of potato) and put a good supply in her pack basket because they kept well once they were mature. On the near by hillside, she gathered enough fumbwa (greens) for a meal. Her last task was the gathering of the palm fruit needed to cook the fumbwa. All her chores were finished before noon, allowing her to keep her rendez-vous with her father.

The noontime shadows had just begun to move out from under the trees when Titi arrived at the old house. It was sad to glimpse the little cooking hut where she had passed so many happy hours with her mother. The door hung open. A myriad of goat droppings showed her that it had become their refuge. The main house looked abandoned too, because part of the thatch had blown off and never been repaired. The cousin, who had moved in after Zoao joined the army, went to Congo Zaire because her son was getting old enough to go to school. There were a number of abandoned houses in the village.

At the cemetery, Zoao and Titi talked to Pemba at her gravesite, just as though she were present, but had become mute. To Titi it felt like a family reunion. Both of them felt consoled, as they walked back to Kiula village in the silent presence of a host of renewed memories. As they were about to take the last turn in the trail, they were surprised by a low whistle. Two men in UNITA uniforms stepped out.

"We must leave right away!" The older soldier said quietly.

"I'll only be a few minutes." Zoao replied.

Titi hurried to get the travel food that she and her grandmother had so carefully prepared. Zoao changed into his uniform, thanking the chief, who handed him his automatic weapon in a sleeping mat. The food slid into her dad's backpack, and she accompanied him to the waiting men. Her father looked very different wearing his uniform and carrying a weapon.

She could not hold back the tears, when she gave her father a farewell handshake. The slight quiver in his eyes told her how he felt.

"Let's hope I can see you more often now that my work should bring me through this region once in a while."

The shadows were getting longer when the three soldiers rounded the bend and walked off briskly into uncertainty.

Neither Titi nor her grandmother had much appetite for the delicious supper they had prepared for Zoao.

"War brings heartache on every side," said Titi. "Father told me that all the big villages along the truck road from Lufu to Luanda have been abandoned. The only people living in them are the old people who could not flee, and a few young mothers who couldn't travel with their very small children. Most of the houses have been burned to the ground."

"It is fortunate for us that our chief resisted the orders that demanded that we move to that same truck road. I hope I can die right here in my own village and be buried with my family."

"My heart is heavy with all the thoughts about war. It is hard to imagine having fun with so many sad thoughts troubling my heart. The further I try to see ahead, the more uncertainty I see," Titi confessed.

"My child, how can you help but be sad? You just watched your father walk off into a work that puts him in constant danger. That kind of sadness never really goes away. We will constantly be forced to live with both sadness, and joy, the same way as we learn to live with both sunshine, and thunder storms. A good sleep will help us all."

Titi's thoughts robbed her of sleep. She could not stop thinking about her father. Memories of her mother had all been rekindled by her visit to the cemetery with her dad. She had never thought much about the dangers of boys growing taller or girls developing breasts. Her grandmother's talk about her own death raised other uncertainties in her mind. In the morning, Titi found her joy returning as soon as she met the girls at the river.

"We are really sorry that you father had to leave, but we are happy about going to school today." Lisa was expressing the feelings of all the schoolgirls.

A very useful, surprise for the school

The chief brought a surprise to school the morning after Zoao left. Arriving at the school about a half hour after they had begun, he called Titi to his side. With a broad smile he handed her four storybooks, two in Kikongo and two in Portuguese.

"Your father left these books for the school. He found them in an abandoned house near Nzeto. He thought that new storybooks could brighten up your day after he left."

They really needed more reading material, because they had all read Titi's books over and over. Now they all had a challenge.

In her after class session with the chief at their usual spot, Titi struggled to read one of the Portuguese language books.

The chief suggested a change. "Could you please let me see if I can read this all by myself? When I have finished, you can read it. Then we will try to tell each other the story using Kikongo. If it is a good story, we will need to write it in Kikongo for most of the children who don't know enough Portuguese to read a book like this yet."

They agreed to the new study plan, but Titi had some important things to ask the chief.

"Avozinho, (grandfather) my father asked me to think of you as my grandfather, so I will."

The chief grinned.

"How do I make the right decisions about important things? How can I study more, and still take care of Nkaka at the same time? How can I think of going to Congo Zaire for safety, and even dream of leaving my old grandmother?"

"Netazinha, (granddaughter) remember this. Days are like bricks. They join together to make weeks, then months, and years. You will only get one day at a time. On a journey into new country you must go as far as you can see. When you get that far, you will see how to go a little further. Do what you think you should each day, and you will make your decisions just fine, you will see. Whenever I have advice for you, I promise I will tell you what I think, because that is what your father asked me to do."

Titi had started to go home when the old chief called her back to hear some more advice.

"Our elders used to say that you should teach a child before he goes to market. The wisdom was this, if a child is taught all about the market before he goes, he will not have any trouble when he gets there. Titi, you have had many people preparing you to go to market. Your mother taught you many things about life. Late years, your grandmother is teaching you. Your father gave you many good ideas in less than two short days. I am trying to teach you anything I think may help you. Child, you are being well prepared to make good decisions in the market called life. You have no reason to worry. As you get older, you will begin to realize that none of us knows about our future. Discovering how many things you don't know is part of growing up."

The four new books brought in a great new challenge to the little school. Titi and the chief worked on the Portuguese books every noon for a good long time. They both became comfortable reading them. For the chief it was the challenge of sounding out the words. For Titi it was the challenge of learning the meaning of so much new vocabulary. Together they wrote a translation of the two books in Kikongo. The whole process kept them both very interested in what they were doing.

Writing the whole translation so well that the children could make out all the letters easily was a good exercise for Titi. As soon as the children could read a story well, they were allowed to copy it into a precious notebook, so they would all have something to read. Some days, all the children were asked to write letters on their slates. Later, they exchanged their slates to get practice reading different kinds of writing.

Dina pointed out some day that in the future, when they were in different places, they would be able to write to one another.

The chief's eldest wife and Titi's grandmother taught all the children how to make pottery. They did it one day each week. When each child had several pots sun dried, they were shown how to fire them.

The method was very simple. They gathered a good supply of dried palm branches. The thick wide parts that were attached to the trunks, gave a very intense heat when burned. The older women showed them just how to pile up the palm branches, so that the pots could all be lined up with a good number of branches directly below them. Once the fire was kindled, the fire became so hot that the clay pots glowed red like coals at one point. The following day, they each picked their pots from among the soft ashes. Not one piece broke because there was not even one grain of sand, mixed with the pure clay.

Other women taught the girls mat weaving. Men traditionally made pack baskets, so that is what the chief taught the two boys to do. All in all, the little school at Kiula village became the center of their community. Although they were isolated during many war years, the children learned many lessons which helped them for the rest of their lives.

THE LAST DAYS OF THE OLD MATRIARCH

In time, Titi had taught her friends literally all she knew, and everything she herself could learn. The timestables on the back of their notebooks served as the basis of all their mathematical studies. Just when Titi was wondering whether there was any point in continuing to direct the school, her grandmother began to need so much care that she realized that her teaching days were about over. Because of the exodus of so many families, there were no new children to enter the school. Times had changed again.

It became more and more difficult for her grandmother to walk about, and do the little chores she loved to do. Far more alarming than the physical changes were the changes that began to transform the elderly woman's thinking and her capacity to communicate.

In the middle of the night, the old woman sometimes woke up terrified.

"They are after me! Don't leave me, Titi!" She would say over and over with terrifying fear filling her old eyes, distorting the once stalwart face.

In her dreams, she often felt she was flying over the water endlessly. Titi knew that this sort of dream normally foretold the approaching death of the person dreaming. At least it showed that they themselves thought they were going to die.

"That sister of mine keeps taking me out over the water. I don't want to go but she takes me! She is the ndoki witch, not me. She must be a ndoki witch to be able to take me out over the water."

The dreams often came just before dawn. When she awoke, the dreams were still vivid and she often remembered the details that had tormented her.

"Titi, the time has come. My teki that has protected me all these years is no longer protecting me. My youngest sister from Congo Zaire is getting inside the house. She wants to take my life. I can't stop her! I haven't heard from her for fifteen years. Why does she torment me now?"

Bewildered and frightened, Titi went to the chief for advice.

"Child, there is nothing you can do to protect your grandmother, if her famous teki can no longer do it. All you can do is to be there when she calls,"

The horrid statue, with it's grotesque, cowry shell eyes, had to be placed between the fire and her grandmother's sleeping mat, so he could watch over and protect her, while she slept. Every day Titi's troubled grandmother became more and more obsessed with fear. She was so transformed that she no longer seemed to be the same person at all.

One night, during a violent thunderstorm, the sound of the torrential rains awakened both Titi and her grandmother. A few pieces of fresh wood on the fire soon produced plenty of light to calm her grandmother's fears. A toad, seeing the light from the outside, was attracted to the crack in the door and began jumping against the door repeatedly. Her grandmother became frantic.

"That witch has come to get me disguised as a toad!" Nkaka screamed in panic.

Suddenly the old woman began to utter horrible curses on her family both the living and the dead.

"Be sterile, be sterile," she screamed over an over again.

Everything that came from her mouth seemed to be boiled in hate. Titi had never heard such a tirade from anyone in all her life.

Day by day, her grandmother became more and more hateful; finally refusing to eat because she was sure her food was poisoned. Titi went to the chief again, seeking advice in her terrible situation.

"Chief, it seems as though she has become totally evil. I watched her drive a nail into her teki image. As she drove the nail she cursed someone I have never heard of. These days she seems like a true ndoki witch, gone insane. Now, I am becoming afraid. When she refuses the food I prepare. Sometimes she screams at me. 'If you poison me, you will die too! You will die too!'

"She is becoming weaker and weaker. She will not let me touch her, to clean her up. Chief, what shall I do? I'm the only relative left in these parts."

The chief spoke calmly, and gave her an explanation that satisfied her understanding.

"Our elders have always said that when someone becomes insane, it is because they are suffering from a reversed curse. It happens whenever a person fails to keep a promise to allow a family member to be sacrificed in order to be granted some deep desire. If the person who took the oath refuses to allow the required death of a family member, they themselves become cursed with insanity for not keeping the promise made to the nganga shaman. My wife and I will come over to help you decide what to do."

Arriving at their little house the chief hesitated.

"I have not set foot in her house since before your grandfather died. When she was declared a killer ndoki witch by a renowned ngombo, I told her I would never come to her house again. I was so angry with her, for being an unrepentant killer. I will enter, Titi, but I am entering your house, not hers!"

Titi nodded gratefully.

As they entered the little house they could not see well because they had moved from sunlight into darkness. The old woman sat up on her mat and screamed, "If any of you touches me, Vonda! Vonda! I will kill you!"

"You want to sell me in the witches market beyond the big waterfall, don't you? Well, you can't eat me! My ancestors left me protection! I am not alone! Touch me and you will die."

Her voice became a croaking scream because her frail body could not support her mounting outrage.

Pounding the floor to affirm her curse, she croaked venom. "You call me ndoki witch, when you yourselves, are the ndoki witches. You wouldn't try to sell my flesh in the witches market if you were not ndoki witches yourselves!"

Gasping, she pitched forward onto her face and became motionless.

"I think she has just died," observed the chief's wife as she gently laid the old woman back on her mat in a reclining position.

Holding her ear close to the twisted face, the experienced woman announced quietly "Fwididingi" (She has just died this moment).

Titi began to weep in the arms of the chief's wife.

"Why, oh why should she die like this? Why would she die behaving like an ndoki witch? She was so good to me. She helped me every way she could. She saved my life, and gave it back meaning when my mother died. I never wanted to see what I have seen these past two weeks. I don't want to believe she was an ndoki witch! Now I have lost everyone in my family. I am alone without kinfolk! I don't even know whether my father is living or dead. I have lost my dream that my grandmother was not an ndoki witch.

"These last weeks were filled with her anger and spitefulness. Her twisted wickedness has spilled over my memories like maggots in a piece of antelope."

Titi broke into sobs, not loud wailing, but the kind of sorrow that originates in a broken heart.

The chief slipped out, leaving Titi to pour out her grief in the supportive presence of his wife of many long years. He walked through the village announcing the death of Nkaka Mambu. The news was a surprise. Because she lived in isolation so much of the time, they were unaware of her rapid decline. There was no one left of the old woman's generation, no friend who knew her from childhood.

The death of the despised old woman brought no sorrow related to her passing, but the whole village rallied to comfort Titi whom they dearly loved. The older women simply took over and guided Titi, so she could fulfill her duties, as the sole close relative. She was led through the ceremony and practical necessity of bathing the corpse.

The men, mostly older men, set to work digging the grave and making all the required physical arrangements The chief conferred with Titi, making suggestions all of which she accepted.

The chief promised, "She will be buried with dignity. She is the oldest resident of this village. For years she lived in her husband's village until she had to come back here to care for her mother."

As they talked, folk began to bring the palm branches for the outside shelter they always built to protect the mourners from the sun.

Caring people surrounded, and comforted Titi. Dina, who had become closer than a sister, was right at her side. The little school became Titi's family. She certainly was not allowed to feel alone as the storms raged in her heart. By sundown, the Chief reported that everything was proceeding without any problems.

A pitch torch lit the site for the wake. Going through another funeral of a loved one brought back the memory of her mother's death. The prolonged civil war had radically changed their region in those few years. Some villages had gone to Congo Zaire en masse. All the villages had been depleted. There were no young men except the feeble minded and handicapped. The only young women having babies were those who had made alliances with the older men in their desperation. No one could remember ever having seen the funeral of an elder where the only blood relative was a grandchild.

The school children supplied mountains of wood and the village women dutifully spent the night associating with Titi in her grief. In death, the old woman's face seemed to lose the temporary lines of bitterness and fear that dominated her last two weeks of existence.

She looked much more like the person who had loved her unstintingly, since the crisis of her mother's death.

Titi could not escape the ambivalence of emotions that had invaded her so suddenly. It seemed to her, upon reflection, that during the final weeks of her life, some malevolent force had manipulated the Nkaka she loved. It seemed as though the hatred and darkness that had created her protective teki had suddenly taken control of its long-time mistress. It bothered Titi that, at one stage, her demented grandmother had become terrified of her, as though she saw her granddaughter as a threatening ndoki witch. The idea of her elderly loved one dying was not strange, nor unexpected. She had never imagined, however, that she would ever see her courageous grandmother end her days consumed with fear and frustrated hatred.

As the long night progressed, Titi wondered if the chief and his wife might be able to make sense of the disturbing turmoil that troubled her grieving heart.

Even the pitch torch candles that lit the night brought warm memories back to Titi.

"She always encouraged me to do everything. She taught me how to use her fishing traps. She seemed to want me to learn everything she could possibly teach me. She told me of her joys and sorrows. She talked about the accusations of being an ndoki witch. She said most sincerely that she had never practiced witchcraft with her will. She herself wondered if she may have been tricked into becoming a ndoki without the consent of her own soul."

Dina simply allowed Titi to pour out her thoughts. She asked her friend no questions, but simply allowed her to speak from her troubled heart.

The chief's eldest wife was at Titi's other side. Like Dina, she listened with very little comment. She offered only one word of wisdom.

"You shouldn't get rid of your fat goat simply because you discover he has one bad eye!" Titi nodded with comprehension. "In the past four years your grandmother expressed her love for you in a hundred practical ways. Don't condemn her because of her behavior when her mind was sick and dying."

Titi's tears began to flow more freely because she felt understood.

During the long night of the wake, Dina advised Titi to remove her braids and let her hair stick up in an unkempt manner that was traditionally supposed to express grief. To identify with her, Dina removed all her own braids too. When they tied the white mourning band around Titi's head, Dina asked to wear one too.

"She is my sister so I must mourn with her as a member of the family," Dina explained to the surprised women of the village.

Throughout the endless night, Titi was sometimes consoled, but there were many distressing moments as well when the older women frankly expressed their relationships with the deceased. In accordance with custom they danced a slow mournful dance, while telling of their good and bad relationships. The remarks could be cutting, positive, or reflective. There was no sorting of these memories, sung in a monotone voice. Some remarks were nothing but a venting of pent-up feelings of hostility.

"She always looked at me with those snake eyes of hers. Everything about her proved she was nothing but an ndoki witch. How many years has she lived alone? What woman would choose to go to the water alone every day? Who would travel her own path to the water and to her fields? Has anyone but her ever lived and worked alone? When our children died with measles, she didn't even come to their funerals. We didn't want her, and she didn't come."

The kindest women said nothing. The deceased had many enemies quite unashamed to renounce her, despite her total vulnerability.

All eyes were on Titi, when in the small hours of the morning, she decided that she had a duty to express her deepest sentiments with dance and song. Traditionally, only the elders sang. Being the representative of a whole family, it seemed proper that her voice should be heard.

"When I was small I learned to fear and detest her as the one who ate my baby brothers. In my childhood dreams, she terrified me when she appeared as a killer witch. In time a renowned ngombo shaman declared my grandmother to be innocent of deaths in my household. My frightening dreams ended the day she was declared innocent. I saw my mother and my grandmother reconciled just before my mother died. She received me in her home, as a loved grandchild, who reminded her of my mother. She taught me everything she could. We laughed together, and felt sadness together. She bared her heart to me. She told me all the history, traditions and rivalries of our bloodline.

"She encouraged me to teach school. She taught me to respect our chief. She taught me how to cook and how to fish. She taught me about our traditions. She blessed me with an unforgettable maternal blessing. She opened her heart to me.

"In the past three weeks she lost her strength, her health, and her understanding. She lost trust in everyone including the family god "Vumbi". She became terrified, in her dying weakness. She became grotesque, like the god who failed her. All the hidden wickedness of her heart was poured out against the family who rejected her for countless years.

"She loved me until these days when some evil power possessed her, terrified her and destroyed her. I saw a demon in her eyes the day she died. Her heart died three weeks ago but her body died only yesterday. I cannot judge her by the behavior she displayed after her heart had died."

Uncontrollable sobbing forced her to sit down again. As soon she regained her voice, she continued her monologue. Looking at the remains, she sobbed saying over an over.

"I love you, but I am confused. I am confused. I need help to understand you. I need our clan. We have a good clan. We have a big clan. How can a young girl think for the whole clan? How can a girl be an elder?"

Sobbing took her words away and she leaned into the arms of the chief's wife Mama Tedika, while Dina held her hands gently.

The intensity of the mournful wailing increased and deepened in sincerity. They were weeping for Titi sobbing in their midst bereft of the normal comfort of her clan. Most of them had never imagined that the dead women in their midst had been a person capable of loving and being loved. They all trusted and respected Titi and their hearts were sad because hers was broken.

Titi didn't yet realize it, but she was receiving a far deeper level of support and understanding from the little community that surrounded her, than most people receive from their own kinfolk. Being able to pour out her heart freely was a process that was bringing a deep kind of soul healing.

After she had poured out torrents of tear-washed grief, Titi fell into a deep sleep from sheer exhaustion, supported on all sides by her close friends. Eventually Mama Tedika helped her to lie down on a mat, covering her gently with her cloth as though the girl she was helping were her very own daughter. She slept until awakened by a bright ray of sunlight.

"Nkaka came to me while I slept! She smiled at me approvingly, the way she always used to. I asked her how she felt. She smiled again and said, 'You know, I'm old, but I can still do a day's work.' She was just like she always used to be. If Nkaka is all right, so am I. We can all speculate as to how she must be. She and the ancestors are the only ones who know the truth, but she has spoken to me! I'm all right now. We can all do whatever we must." Friends brought Titi a mug of coffee with roasted peanuts. She ate heartily for the first time since her grandmother's death. Everyone around her was relieved. The crisis was obviously past. The girl they loved and respected had somehow been purged of the disorienting experiences of the past three weeks.

Men had gathered under the big mango tree but they could not follow any known traditions. There was not a man from the old woman's clan in their midst. All of her clansmen were either dead, in Congo Zaire as refugees, or in the army. No one had ever seen a village funeral with no clansmen present at all. The chief had brought some palm wine for the night but it certainly was not sufficient to make anyone drunk. After breakfast, the chief proposed what should be done.

Following the chief's directives, the grave was dug, several men split out balsa boards with their machetes and Dina's father constructed a simple, traditional, coffin.

"We may as well bury her today. There is no one else coming. We can't hold any inquest into her death, because there are no clansmen present to do that. There is no reason to give her an ndoki witch's burial with a pot of peppers on her head. There are no clansmen here for her to haunt. With her love for Titi, she certainly will not trouble her. A dignified burial was Titi's only request. I think we should grant her wish. For us she is all the clan authority we have."

The men gathered there, all clapped quietly displaying a comfortable consensus. They agreed with the chief.

When the chief came over to the women, he was pleased to see Titi alert and composed. He called her to one side. He outlined the proposals of the men of the village, and quietly asked for her wishes.

"You are proposing that we lay her to rest in a dignified manner. That is all I want. I am so thankful that there is no plan to punish her with an ndoki witch's burial. Our ancestors will judge her justly. I am grateful, and accept the plans," Titi concluded.

"Mama Tedika will help you choose whatever you want to bury with her. I'm sure she has blankets in her trunks for that purpose. She would have been prepared. I advise you to make a written list of everything in her trunks. Some day your family will want to know, whenever you join them. It will seem strange for you to open her very private possessions. You are her clan. It is your right and duty." The chief spoke with quiet authority.

"We will go in and take a look right now. I am ready," Titi replied.

Opening the trunks of a private world

In order to see in the dark house, she lit one of their pitch candles. Titi felt strange entering behind the woven mat walls that enclosed her grandmother's very private world.

There were three rather rusty metal trunks that sat on four pieces of kwati (an indestructible dark wood). Small clay pots covered with lizard skins that looked like four tiny drums, sat on top of everything.

"Those are fetishes prepared by our old Nganga (shaman) for her personal protection. They are useless now," Mama Tedika explained.

A small balsa shelf supported by vines attached to the roof supported a number of teki (sacred carvings). One was a carved hunting dog complete with a dibu (wooden bell) around his neck all ready to go hunting. The dog's face was covered with a thick layer of dried kola nut spittle. This was obviously Titi's grandfather's hunting fetish.

Beside the little dog was a small statue totally dressed in the reddish cloth and the rodent skin hat of an nganga ngombo. Next to the doll was a little red hand drum of the sort carried by the ngombo in his or her ceremonies. Mama Tedika had no idea that the old woman must have been an ngombo for a while. Often people go through the whole training and initiation into the secret service of the ngombo diviner because they are seeking a cure for a chronic illness, or anxious to become pregnant.

A carefully woven raffia sack with a closed drawstring sat next to the drum.

"That would have been her bag of bones, skins, claws, and magic objects she used for divining."

The last Teki was a small figure with two faces one on each side of its head. Mama Tedika had no idea as to its use.

"Do you know the secret words, the songs, and the rules and taboos that must be used with these objects, Titi?"

Shaking her head, Titi explained that she had never even seen them before. The only teki she had ever seen was Vumbi, which was still standing on the floor beside the fireplace.

"I didn't even hear her use any formula with him either."

The fresh kola spittle indicated that her grandmother had been seeking the help of two of the teki without Titi's knowledge.

"You should not attempt to use any teki to which you have not been initiated." Mama Tedika cautioned. "I think they should all be buried with her because they are only of value to her." Titi nodded in agreement.

The top trunk squeaked when it was being opened. Inside were four beautiful dinner plates and two ornate blue glasses.

"Let's put one of those glasses on the grave, and I will save the other for my aunt in Congo Zaire. We can put the three plates on the grave. One for grandmother, one for grandfather, and one for my mother."

There was no question about the second trunk. It was filled with blankets and a wall hanging obviously reserved for her funeral. The wall hanging was a giant picture of a Lion.

"I remember when we sold those in Santos' store many years ago," the chief recalled.

The chief had entered and recognized the type of hanging from many years back.

"We used to sell all those covers about twenty years ago when I still worked in Lufu. People bought them for funerals both for themselves, and for giving to valued relatives when they died. No one ever thought of using them. We sold almost all of them to be used as burial blankets."

To their surprise, a piece of paper was folded inside of the blanket. It was a receipt signed in the handwriting of the chief himself.

"I told you I could sign my name even though I could not read or write anything else," he said with a grin.

"I would advise you to keep out one blanket or hanging for yourself." Mama Tedika suggested. "Put the others in with her as she planned. Keeping at least one is customary. She would want you to have it."

After a short hesitation, Titi made her choice.

"I will keep the one with the signed receipt as a reminder of you too."

The six colorful blankets were taken, and placed with the other objects in the coffin.

"She will be respected when she gets to her ancestors' village on the other side," Titi remarked.

"Where she goes will be the ancestors' decision," the Chief said quietly, prompting Titi to nod in agreement.

By mid-morning everything was ready. When Titi placed the covers in with her grandmother, there were remarks of admiration. None of these things could be purchased anymore, because all the old colonial stores were long gone. Some of the elders wished they could be buried as luxuriously, when their time came. All her teki (worship and protective objects) were placed in the coffin before the last blanket.

After the men had placed the lid on the coffin, Titi asked to speak. The villagers were all surprised when she stood and asked to address the gathering and the elders. It simply had never happened before.

"I understand why most of you are convinced that my grandmother is a ndoki witch. She lived in total isolation because she knew how you felt and had no desire to aggravate you. I became her window into the village. She was interested in your welfare. Her life was unbearably lonely after my grandfather died. She told me all about the past decisions of the ngombo diviner. From what she told me, I too believe that she was some kind of ndoki.

"These past few years, we have been together day and night. My own mother could not have been more kind and thoughtful. She told me herself that she had never in all her life tried to harm anyone through her powers. The evidence you heard that found her guilty troubled her too. However, she told me that she was convinced that if she was an ndoki witch, she was made one by some other ndoki who tricked her without her consent.

"She was a wonderful grandmother until the past three weeks when the power that had entered her years ago took complete control and snuffed out her life. You know that it is possible that she became insane because she would not surrender me to her tormenter. Only the ancestors know the whole truth. For two reasons I have asked that she be buried without the pepper pot on her head. She may have been tricked, and had no choice. No matter what kind of ndoki she may have been, I am the only family member who lives here, and she has already shown me in my dream that her loving attitude toward me has not changed."

The gathering had become totally silent while she spoke. They had never heard a young girl speak with such wisdom before. Initial skepticism was replaced by an affirmative consensus. They went in quiet procession to the cemetery.

Titi was the only person with the right to address the vumbi (corpse) at the graveside. On her knees by the head of the coffin she spoke simply, and convincingly.

"Nkaka, we have loved each other and helped each other since the days of my mother's suffering and death. Tell mother all about our happy days together. Let her know about all the things that you taught me, so she will not worry. Tell my little brothers all about me. Nkaka, I will miss you, I will deeply miss you. Because of the war, I am the only member of our clan here now. Please continue to help me from your new place, just as you helped me when we were together here. Wenda mbote (Go well.)"

Four men lowered the coffin into the grave by letting the vine rope slip in a controlled fashion until it sat on the bottom. The vines were dropped in. Following tradition, Titi threw the first shovel full of earth in on top of the coffin. Simply hearing the earth strike the coffin with the sound of profound finality caused her to weep unreservedly once more. There was no rush to finish the burial and Titi was joined by many who had never dreamed that they could shed a tear at this woman's passing.

Appropriately, the grave was filled in by community effort. The chief had written on the marker himself. The mound was carefully rounded. When all were finished, Titi placed the basin they had used in her last washing, the beautiful blue drinking glass, and two dinner plates, on top of the grave.

Dina and Mama Tedika saw to it that she did not walk back to the village in solitude. As they neared the village Mama Tedika's voice seemed to boom out as she addressed Dina.

"Ndoki a mwini ndiona. (That one is a witch of the sunlight,")" she said while pointing to Titi by protruding her lower lip. The lower lip was often used instead of the index finger. The wisdom and insight evident in such a young person evoked the complimentary remark.

As her grandmother's little house came in sight, a new wave of nostalgia swept over the brave girl. She had not had time to think about her own future. The women would sleep with her a couple of nights. Beyond that, she had not given herself time to think.

"I am all alone now. The only people of my clan I can visit are in the cemeteries," she reminded Dina.

In her heart, a new form of grief enveloped her feelings. She had no living kinfolk in the region.

Gradually, both of her supportive friends recognized that Titi found herself in a very difficult and unusual situation. She was approaching the age to marry in a village where there were no young men. She had no clan to consult for major decisions. In essence, she was a like a vulnerable orphan. In the past, the only people in similar circumstances were people sold into slavery, or widows whose husbands died leaving their wives too far from home to return. No one could expect her to tolerate such a situation.

Surrounded by most of the schoolgirls and a number of the village women, Titi ate the hearty meal that had been prepared for them all. Many of the women slipped home in the cover of darkness. They knew that there would be no inquest into the old woman's death. It was clear that there was no one who would contest that Titi was the sole heiress to everything her grandmother had owned. For the curious, there was nothing to anticipate, no need to stay.

It was a cool evening, so Titi and her friends decided that there would be room for them all inside the little house. She had no fears at all about meeting her grandmother's ghost. None of the others had anything to fear because they were not relatives. Surrounded by friends, including the five girls from her school, together with most of their mothers, she slept soundly.

After the rooster's shout, the whole houseful of women went to the water together. Titi passed around a bottle of her grandmother's soap so everyone could have a really good wash. Most of the women were surprised to learn that Titi and her grandmother had made soft soap ever since the Lufu market closed. Actually her grandmother had been making it for years.

On the way back from the river, Dina asked the question that was on everyone's mind.

"What do you think you will do now that your grandmother is gone?"

Obviously, Titi had been thinking about that because her answer came immediately.

"I think that I must go to Congo Zaire and join my family. I don't know just when or how I should go, but I wish you would come with me."

Dina's reply surprised her.

"We both have aunts near Lukala, wherever that is. If you leave, I want to go with you."

All the women gathered up their mats and prepared to go to their homes, all but Dina. She decided to move in with Titi. Quite often, the other older girls from the school slept there as well. Titi kept up her fieldwork because her future was still unplanned. The school decided to gather once each week to do some review work so they would not forget what they had learned. The chief usually joined them for the same reason.

HARROWING JOURNEY WITH A GUERRILLA PATROL

One day when school was over, Titi asked the chief a serious question.

"Along with some of the older girls, I am wondering how we should go about travelling to Congo Zaire? Each of the girls has relatives there and we all want to continue in school."

There was a silence before he answered.

"Sadly, I must admit that I think you girls should go to Congo Zaire so you can carry on with your lives. Every time soldiers come near our village, I am worried about you. You have learned to hide well, but one day you will be discovered and they will just take you with them. I agree that you should go, but not until you have someone who can guide you through the mined areas. It has been two years since your father's last visit. If he is still alive, it would be great to have him come by soon. Certainly, he could guide you to the border. I know the trails reasonably well, but I know nothing about the dangers of war along those old pathways. I wouldn't want to see you go alone for many reasons. Find out all you can about the names and location of all your relatives. You would be wise to pack a travel pack basket that has everything you plan to take, except food. When someone comes whom we can trust, you need to be able to leave almost immediately."

Within a week, five sturdy baskets were packed and ready for their journey of a lifetime. Only the travel food was missing. In mid October the Chief's wish was fulfilled when Titi's father and three other UNITA soldiers slipped into the village at dusk. They went straight to the chief's house. Zoao knew about the secret room, and was counting on it. He himself had been observing the village for an hour or two until they were convinced that there were no enemy soldiers present.

"We are exhausted and very hungry. We need to rest up for a few days," Zoao explained.

At the first opportunity to talk with the chief alone he asked about his daughter. He was surprised to hear of all that had happened.

"Thank you for helping her make up her mind to go to Congo Zaire. I am so glad that you insisted that they wait for an escort. There are mines everywhere. There were six of us when we left, but two of our boys had their feet blown off by the same mine. They bled to death. There was nothing we could do for them. Please tell Titi that we will leave in five days. We will stay in hiding because the MPLA have a large encampment at Lufu now. We don't dare take any chances. If Titi can find some food for us, it will be a great help. We haven't a scrap of food left."

While Mama Tedika roasted some peanuts and cut up some kwanga for the hungry men, the chief went off to inform Titi of her father's arrival and the travel plans.

The girls prepare food for a long journey

The girls set to work in a very organized manner.

"We will need all the kwanga we can carry. We will need lots of peanuts because they will keep us going when we have nothing else to eat. Two of us can get busy making kwanga both for now, and for the journey. Two of us will roast peanuts and make as much peanut butter as possible. I will try to catch us some fish and do the cooking for all of us." Titi spoke as their natural leader.

Before she went to set the fish traps, Titi had a serious talk with the chief.

"I want you and your clan to take over all of our land and crops. I know that as long as you or your nephew is chief here, you would give it back to us when we return some day. Right now I want you to come with me and learn a secret. You need to learn how it was that my grandmother caught so many fish. This is the first time the secret has left our clan. It is the least I can do for you. I am going to set traps this morning. We need fish both now and for our trip."

A broad smile showed that the chief was very pleased. Fish were very hard to catch now that they could no longer buy good hooks.

Of course Titi had to go in the water with her clothes on this time. The chief was most impressed when he saw just how the traps were set in that peculiar spot where the boulders altered the course of the stream. Titi advised him to show serious respect to the bisimbi water spirits. Before she could tie the trap rope to the tree at the water's edge, she felt the trap shake from fish movement. Pulling it back immediately, she found that she had caught a good-sized catfish. They were both delighted because they had food for the hungry soldiers.

"Please keep this secret in your family. This secret enabled my grandmother to live during her long years of living alone here. She was very clever, and she worked very hard."

Titi did not see her father to talk with him until she brought his crew a large meal of beans, fufu, and roasted peanuts, for a mid-morning breakfast. Her father looked thinner, but he looked well. He was almost overwhelmed with emotion when he saw her again. After a pause, he got right to the details of their planned travel.

Travel details

"If we have no trouble, we can reach the border in five days of hard walking. We cross over into Congo Zaire at a large border village called Kibuki. I know the driver of our truck that carries all our military supplies. The truck goes non-stop to the port of Matadi where our supplies come in by ship. To get to Matadi they must drive through Lukala where we think your aunt from Lufu is living.

"The truck seldom stops because of its secret military mission, but he makes a stop in Lukala to buy food for his family at Matadi. He buys his food from his sister. She always has everything ready to load because he only stops for five minutes. That is when you will get off just when the back is opened to receive the food. Whenever you want to send me a letter, you will give it to the driver's sister. I will look for your letter each time I am at Kibuki. I have friend who can read and write."

Patrol discipline

The heavy laden group of five young women and four soldiers left immediately after the first cock crowing, about two in the morning, in bright moonlight. Titi was too filled with emotion to dare look back after they left her little house. The girls shivered in the cool air initially, but they were soon warm from carrying their heavily-laden pack baskets at the walking speed of a seasoned military patrol. They were very excited to be on their way to a whole new life. Despite their excitement, each of the girl's faces was wet with tears as she walked away from childhood.

There were strict rules for their manner of travel. The soldiers were well armed. Two walked about three hundred paces ahead of the girls separated from each other by fifty paces. One walked just ahead of them, while the fourth was about a hundred paces behind. They traded their positions every hour. It was very nerve-racking to be the lead scout. Scouts almost always were the first to die in combat. The two fellows lost before they had arrived at Kiula were just passing to change positions when a mine hit them both. They tried never to walk beside one another because of the obvious danger. It made for a long lonely journey, because they normally dare not shout to one another in conversation.

The girls' instructions were simple. In case of attack on anyone, they were to take cover in the forest immediately. They were not to move or speak until one of their own soldiers whistled like a particular well-known bird. The birdcall was the all-clear signal. The UNITA soldiers knew that the government MPLA troops were aware of the location of their supply trail. Setting anti personnel mines was their most risk free method of interrupting travel on the vital UNITA supply route. On occasion whole patrols had been wiped out in an ambush situation. Hilly forest-covered portions were ideal for ambush.

Titi noted that her father is constantly on the alert, utilizing his hunter's eyesight, and insight. His eyes were always watching for any signs of human presence on the sides of the trail. This was not a pleasant walk, but rather a deadly serious military patrol that had already lost two of its six men. With her father in the lead, Titi feels both confident and nervous.

About noon, Zoao's hand signaled for a stop. Immediately they all took cover in the underbrush on the side of the path. To everyone's surprise he shouted, "O galo voa. (The rooster flies.") In a moment they heard the same slogan answering back as the two lead scouts embraced." It was always encouraging for two patrols to meet when they were heading in opposite directions. They could each brief the other on any danger that lurked ahead.

Zoao explained why they were late. He explained that when they had lost two men they were forced to leave the trail and travel through the wilderness. The explosion of the mine had given away their position to the government troops. Their long detour had exhausted them and depleted their food. Zoao then introduced the girls to the patrol commander.

"These girls replenished our food supplies and fed us well at Kiula." Pointing out Titi with his lower lip, he said proudly. "This one is my daughter. Her grandmother just died leaving her the only one of her clan still in Angola. All of these girls are heading for Congo Zaire where they hope they may be able to join family and go to school."

The patrol leader gave his report to Zoao. "We didn't run into any mines on this trip, but we have been informed that there is a platoon of MPLA soldiers east of Ntoto. They have opened up the old airfield. We can expect mines or ambushes any time now. I know the dangers of travelling in daylight, but I think you should travel by day so you can spot their mines if they set them. You know what it is like at night!"

There was an ever-mounting tension as the group of nine cautiously advanced through the potentially dangerous zone. Travel was somewhat slower because the scout stopped to listen at the brow of every hill and when rounding blind twists in the trail. People waiting to perpetrate an ambush have the advantage of surprise.

Daylight gave a distinct advantage when it came to dealing with mines. Experienced men could normally spot mines on the trail. Ambush patrols are often awake all night, and tend to fall asleep during the day. At least that was Zoao's hope. On the other hand, it was difficult to hide effectively during the day once you were spotted.

At tense moments, Titi found herself feeling for the familiar bump of the little protective fetish under her clothes. Somehow, it didn't bring much confidence in this new situation. It was designed to protect from ndoki witches. In her case, no family member knew she was on a trail to Congo Zaire.

Tense travel

War was a grotesque game between groups of young people to see who could catch the other off guard, and kill the most players. The five teen-age girls were experiencing the all-invasive fear of warfare. Their lives had already been profoundly affected by war. Their present experience of paralyzing fear was a totally new reality. Hundreds of thousands had known these fears already. These girls from their isolated village, deep in the bush, had never feared mines in their gardens or surrounding forests.

Since they left, their trail had wound through uninhabited wilderness, purposely avoiding all human settlements. Through this danger zone, Zoao was the lead scout most of the time because he was by far the most experienced at spotting both mines and the slightest movement of anything ahead.

It was about four in the afternoon. Zoao was moving around another bend with utmost caution when the staccato roar of a klasnikoff shattered the pristine silence and flying bullets hit the leaves in the trees above. Zoao responded in a split second of time with a burst from his automatic weapon. Everyone cleared the path and hid in the deep brush. The soldiers at the rear of the column went on tense alert. In an ambush situation, the patrol often lets the prey pass, only to attack from behind. Apart from the pounding of their hearts, there was no sound at all since the initial exchange of fire.

Just before sunset they spotted an ominous sight. Two giant buzzards began circling lower and lower right over the place where the gunfire exchange had taken place. Those scavengers could always smell death; after all, it was their way of life. When Titi spotted the birds her heart sank. The enemy had fired first and her father shot back within a split second of time. The question was who were the victims spotted by the hungry birds?

The girls' orders were simple. No movement of any kind until authorized by a soldier. Darkness fell and with it came all the night sounds of the wilderness. The haunting hooting of an owl was most intimidating. There was such a buzz of crickets and many other insects that it would have been very difficult to detect someone creeping around in bare feet.

"Remember when the enemy is close, shut your mouth and your eyes. That is all he can see of you when you are in the shadows."

Those were Zoao's instructions, given before they left. Small animals began to scamper about seeking their food after a long day's nap. When one is listening intently, every sound seems to be amplified and potentially important. With the darkness, and their immobility, they all became victims of hordes of hungry mosquitoes. In any case, there was no way for Titi to sleep until the fate of her father was known.

About midnight a night bird gave its peculiar call from a distance. To her surprise an answering birdcall came from very near by. There were long pauses between the calls and answers. "He is alive!" Titi heard one soldier's voice whisper after the third birdcall. The birdcalls continued periodically with the distant one coming progressively nearer.

Finally, almost beside her, she heard her father's voice give a number "G4046." From near by she heard a reply "M3727".

After the response Zoao spoke quietly. "I was not hit. I shot their scout. They will swarm out in the morning. We must cut across country going directly east to an alternative trail on the ridge of hills over there. We must be careful to leave no trace of our trail heading east."

After two birdcalls given successively from Zoao, all of them were off in same order in which they had been travelling. They took utmost care not to leave the slightest sign that anyone had passed through those parts. The walking was dreadful. Unseen branches often scratched their faces. They did not dare clear the trail with their machetes for fear of being followed later. A little stream running through the valley was a welcome sight. They were all parched, and drank their fill.

Avoiding ambush

Gathering them close together, Zoao explained their strategy. First they would eat and rest a little because they had been on the move since dawn.

"If their patrol finds where we moved east, they will follow it to this stream. They will expect us to walk in the stream to throw them off our trail, that is an old trick. They know we are headed north so they will follow the stream in that direction. That is why we will back track a half-hour by walking south in the stream before we move east again to find our trail. We don't dare rest very long. We need time to separate us from our enemy."

The good food the girls had prepared gave a great lift to their spirits. They were all very hungry and much more inclined to eat, knowing they were out of immediate danger.

"I think these girls should become a permanent part of our patrol. We never have really good food like this when we are on the trail."

The girls were glad that they were not just seen as a burden.

Twenty-five houses but only one roof

Zoao, still leading the way, with his boots slung over his shoulder, was pleased to find that the stream bottom consisted of soft clean sand.

"At least we will all have clean feet," he said as he distanced himself ahead of them.

Eventually they came to a path leading away from the water that obviously led to a village. All the villagers in those parts had fled to Congo Zaire during the war with the Portuguese in the '60s, and never came back.

Naturally the old path was overgrown, a sure indication that no one had lived in the village for a long time. The village had an eerie appearance in the moonlight. All the thatched roofs had been burned.

Made of brick with a metal roof, only the chief's house was intact in the whole collection of twenty-five homes.

"The Portuguese often put mines in houses like this one. Now that we are near the other trail north we can sleep here a while. In the morning we can decide whether we should hurry on, or let their men wear themselves out looking for us. We don't dare enter that house until we can inspect it in the light of day."

Huddled together at the back of the house, they slept until the sunshine awakened them. There were no roosters on duty in that village. Zoao took a look inside of the house through an open window.

"Their mine has already been detonated," he reported, "but I will check a bit more before we enter."

Zoao actually wanted to gather up the dried remains of some poor chap who had been killed when he entered some years before. He didn't want the girls to see the gruesome sight. He did explain what he had found so everyone would remember to be cautious in other abandoned villages.

Zoao shook his head in disgust. "White men often did this. First they burned the village, and then they booby-trapped the good building when they were finished with it. The man who died did not have a gun or a uniform. He was probably a former resident, perhaps even the former chief. War is totally unjust!"

Zoao had only gone as far as the bones of the victim and removed him. "Let me check out the whole house before we enter. There were two more hidden booby traps. One guarded the back door, while another was attached to a pile of tinned sardines on the table. Once he had disabled the explosive devices they were free to enter. The bonus was the stash of tinned Portuguese sardines.

There was a careful look for food growing in the abandoned gardens around the village. No one had ever seen sweet manioc tubers as large as the ones they found. The plants had simply reproduced naturally over the years.

Further search revealed plantain bananas and a giant clump of elephant foot. Behind several houses they found ndungu pepper bushes. The very last find was a stalk of beautiful ripe bananas. They didn't dare make a fire during the day, because the smoke would give away their position. One of the girls found a large clay pot in a burned out kitchen. They would eat their fill of boiled manioc at night.

"We can have a feast because we even have tins of sardines to provide us with meat," a hungry young soldier suggested with delight.

Everything was prepared and ready to be cooked as soon as darkness came. In the meantime, they all needed to get some sleep inside their temporary barracks. All were tired enough to sleep soundly in the totally abandoned village.

Zoao insisted that one soldier should act as guard at all times.

"It is good that we found food, because no one planned for extra days on the trail. The MPLA change their patrols on Sunday. The patrol we encountered will be nervous by this time. They didn't find us, so now they are the ones fearing ambush. Most of their soldiers are very young and inexperienced. By now they are frightened. The lad I shot was far too young to die, but it was a question of him or me.

"We will try to be moving on that northbound road at daybreak tomorrow. Let's eat and rest until the full moon is overhead, then we will head east to the trail we need. If it looks really unused, we can risk travelling on it in the dark. Normally people only mine trails that they know are in constant use by the enemy," Zoao explained.

Watching her father, now a skilled guerrilla soldier, she realized that he had no heart for killing. Survival was the science he had perfected. *"War is totally unfair. Young boys are forced to join the army and put their lives at risk. Young men die while the men who give the orders remain in totally secure places,"* Titi reasoned in her heart.

The full moon facilitated their travel north through the mixture of forest and savanna. Zoao was a bit surprised to find that the road north was an old abandoned truck road. Local folk and guerrilla soldiers had destroyed all the bridges to keep the trucks of Portuguese soldiers from advancing. Although almost grown over, it was a relatively easy walking.

They were reasonably confident that their road would not be mined, because it led to a destination too far east for their purposes. They could work their way west to their original trail as soon as it was safe to do so, perhaps as early as the following day. The scouts however, remained as cautious as ever watching for signs of the enemy as well as any sign of mines.

By late afternoon they were heading west over open grasslands. They were fortunate enough to find a trail heading in their direction, made by one of the large herds of mpakasa (buffalo) that roamed those parts. By early evening, they were on their original northbound trail once more.

"There is a stream nearby. We will camp there for the night. We can't risk the mines on this main trail until we can scan the ground in broad daylight," Zoao explained.

They didn't make a fire, so they enjoyed the remains of the food they had prepared in the abandoned village. They had rationed their sardines. Eating a few tins at the close of a full day of travel helped them feel well fed. Sleep was no problem for any of them, now that they felt they had evaded the enemy patrols.

From their supplies, the girls handed out peanut butter chunks, and boiled manioc, for breakfast. The regular soldiers were more than pleased with the treasures from the girls' pack baskets.

"We should cross the Benga by mid-afternoon. The other side of that river is under our UNITA control. After that, it is just a matter of hard walking for a day and we should be able to sleep at our encampment and base near Kibuki.

"This end of the trail was probably cleaned of mines by the patrol we met on the first day but we will keep alert. You die when you let your guard down," Zoao explained, as he was about to take over as scout again.

They arrived at the Benga River in mid afternoon. Zoao was on home turf now, where he knew every inch of the terrain.

"If we walk west along the river about a half hour we will come to a giant nkamba tree to serve us as a bridge. A brisk walk until dusk should have us at the first UNITA outpost encampment, where we will spend the night. This particular outpost is allowed to hunt. Sporadic shooting from a variety of locations keeps the young MPLA patrols nervous; so they keep their distance. They don't generally look for trouble unless ordered to do so by their command headquarters."

It was just at dusk when the tired travelers began to climb the hill on which the outpost was located. Zoao pulled a metal whistle from his pocket. He gave three short bursts, paused and blew two more times. As soon as a response came from the hilltop they continued their climb with confidence.

Half way up the hill, two well armed soldiers stepped out from their hiding places and asked to see their travel documents. Zoao explained everything and gave a brief report of their encounter with the southbound patrol. Sadly, he reported the death of two faithful companions. The attacks by two separate enemy patrols explained why they were eight days behind schedule.

"I would like to send my daughter and four friends on the munitions truck with driver Makengo on his return trip to Matadi. They will get off at Lukala when he makes the regular five-minute stop for food."

The friendly young officer turned on the transmitter so he could contact headquarters. The girls were very impressed when the officer began talking with someone on his radio.

"Patrol seventeen has just reported in at our outpost," reported the officer. "They lost two men on the way because of a well-hidden land mine. They were forced to travel west through rough terrain to avoid patrols alerted by the mine explosion. They encountered an enemy patrol west of Ntoto, shot their scout, and took devious routes to escape. G4046 requests passage to Lukala for his daughter and four young female friends".

A voice came crackling over the airways. "Because Makengo has a scheduled stop at Lukala, the request is granted. We are very glad Patrol seventeen has made it back. Eight days delay had us all worried. Sorry about the fallen; they were both good soldiers."

You could see the tension go out of Zoao's face. Titi and her friends were out of danger and headed to where they could carry on meaningful lives. Titi was greatly relieved as well. She felt responsible for her four friends, believing that they had only come along because she herself had decided to live in Congo Zaire.

"We're out of food as of today. That skirmish with the enemy patrol added several unexpected days to our journey." Zoao reported.

"No problem, we have lots of food here. We grow our own gardens, you know. That way we are sure of our food supply. The local people are surprised to see our large gardens. When the MPLA occupied these parts, they robbed all their food from the local people. Sometimes we have food to give away. Our food policy has earned us wonderful support from the local population. We shot a beautiful antelope yesterday, and even have salt." The young commander spoke with pride.

The release of tension, coupled with the hearty meal, prepared them for a great sleep. They were however, all somewhat excited about getting on the trail for their last day's journey to the base camp called Benga. Out of danger, this was the first day they traveled close enough together to chat. As they neared their destination the men were becoming animated at the thought of being reunited with their families after an absence of almost two months. They explained to the girls that Benga camp contained more civilians than soldiers.

"Our families live there in the safety of northern headquarters. There are no truck roads anywhere near the camp on the Angolan side, so no one dares to bother them."

Safe, where joy and deep sorrow mingle

As soon as they began to climb the hill to the Benga camp in the late afternoon, a whole contingent of women and children converged on them. As their three military companions encountered their wives and children, they were transformed into young family men.

Two young women with their children began to weep uncontrollably. It was at this moment that they first knew that their own loved ones were not going to come back again. They had heard that two were missing but their eyes confirmed their worst fears.

Titi and her friends wept with the two bereaved families. Until they saw the heart broken women and bewildered children, the deaths of the men they had never met had been impersonal and abstract. The two young women in grief were actually about the same age as Titi and Dina. One had a little baby and the other was pregnant.

"I suppose that somewhere others are grieving their hearts out because of the man my father shot like an antelope. I hate war!" Titi whispered.

The arrival of the five young women was not really noticed. Grief for the two men who died set the mood for the camp that afternoon.

As many as a hundred little huts lined the two sides of a large open space that served as a soccer field and parade ground. Two larger structures, one at each end, served as barracks for the men who had no families with them.

After an hour consumed with the expression of grief, Zoao called the girls aside to tell them that it was time to meet the commander. He was an impressive man, a bit younger than Zoao, who spoke only in Portuguese. Titi was amazed to see that her father spoke Portuguese now too. What was most pleasing, the girls were able to understand most of the conversation. They learned that the commander was from South Angola where his mother tongue was called Umbundu. Since no one spoke his southern language, he, indeed most of the soldiers, communicated in Portuguese.

"Makengo will arrive with the supply truck within the next day or so. Whenever he arrives, he may leave at zero two hours the next Monday, Wednesday, or Friday as the case may be," the young commander explained.

Zoao grinned, "That is army talk for the first rooster call. The trip will be exhausting for you. Makengo must drive fast over very rough roads. The truck is new, with six-wheel drive and huge wheels. You will not get stuck. On the day the truck goes, road traffic will all be travelling in the western direction. That makes it safer for everyone on the narrow dirt roads.

"The truck will be almost full of empty munitions boxes and sacks of beans. The noise will leave you deaf. I think that they can put a net over the boxes so they won't be falling down on you. It will be a rough ride and the truck must remain closed, except when Makengo allows it to be opened. Most people do not know that our big truck is carrying military supplies for UNITA in Angola. In other words you will travel for about fifteen hours and see nothing at all. Two of my most trustworthy soldiers will ride with you in the back in case of any kind of attack " The commander was very clear about the conditions of their travel.

Titi gave their reply. Choosing her words carefully she thanked him in Portuguese and assured him that they would follow any orders given to them. Zoao had never heard Titi speaking Portuguese before. He was amazed when he remembered that the old chief was the only person in the village who spoke that language.

"My wife will show the girls where they can sleep. She'll see that they get some food for the trip as well," the commander explained.

The commander's wife was about twenty. She was the mother of two fine children. Her face was streaked with tears.

"The young pregnant woman next door has just learned she was a widow. I knew her young husband well," the young woman explained with sobs.

"I know what it is like to travel with a patrol because we came all the way from South Angola that way. Fortunately we hadn't any children then. Death, danger, and uncertainty can make you very tired. You have another exhausting trip still ahead of you. It is not dangerous, but that truck will shake you apart. I will spend most of tonight with my bereaved neighbor. If I'm not back, you can fix your own fufu in the morning."

She spoke to them entirely in Kikongo. There was a hint of accent, but she was fluent in their mother tongue.

"How long have you lived here in the north?" Dina asked.

"I have been here since I was about your age, around sixteen."

"*She has been through a lot,*" Titi thought to herself.

Sleep does not come quickly when a dozen serious issues keep presenting themselves for intensive thought. "*I want the war to end. I want to live at home with my father, my mother, and all three of the little brothers that I never saw alive. I want to know what lies ahead for me in Congo Zaire. I'm afraid to know what lies ahead. Will all these young men in this camp kill or be killed? Is there no other life for my father? Will I ever live an ordinary life? Will I be able to go to school? Will I be able to find my aunt?*" All these issues swirled in Titi's mind eventually exhausting her as she reflected on the big change she was facing.

The commander's wife did not return at all that night. She was weeping with young widows next door. Their hearts were broken. Their families were months of dangerous travel far away, in South Angola. Their problems were so basic, yet so difficult.

"How will we raise our children? How long will the civil war keep us prisoners so far from people who speak our language or share our customs? How can it be that our husbands are buried beside a trail in the wilderness?"

The young commander's wife recognized that her situation could become just like that of her friends the day her husband's luck ran out. Sometimes her tears were for herself.

Forest people?

Although they had no soap, the four young travelers went down to the Benga River, to wash as best they could. They had just begun their washing when the young woman next to them observed that they had no soap.

"Are you forest people?" she asked quietly.

They had never been called that before, but they realized that the term described their former isolated existence.

"We have been living several days journey from here where there have been no markets for five years because of the war".

"Would you like a little soap?" she asked in a way that in no way threatened their fragile dignity. "I sold my beans last month so I was able to buy some soap. I lived like you, until I came out last year when I married a soldier."

Noticing that she was not using her big white basin, the girls asked to borrow it for a while. The small piece of soap was enough to wash all their clothes because the soapy water in the basin was used over and over. Their new friend was watching in amazement. She had always washed in the current of the river.

"Thank you for giving me my soap back. From now on I shall wash in my basin and then rinse in the river like you. I used as much soap washing one person's clothes as all five of you together.

The girls were pleased that they had something to give in return for her spontaneous kindness. When they put their clothes out to dry, it dawned on them that their clothes were hopelessly faded, compared to those of the other young women at the military camp.

Everyone on both sides of the border sold food products at the markets in Congo Zaire. Sesame seed and tiny pea beans called bwenge grew very well on both sides of the river border. Their agricultural products were transported all the way to Kinshasa, despite the exorbitant cost of trucking foodstuffs over primitive roads. As a result the demand for their produce, most young women had enough money to buy pieces of bright new cloth from the Kibuki market. For the first time in their lives, all five girls were ashamed of their clothes. Four or five years of tropical sun removes most of the colors from any kind of cotton.

"Are you going to the market tomorrow?" their new friend asked in a friendly manner.

"If we are still here, we would love to see a market again after all these years."

The girls felt clean, and presentable, for the first time since they had set out on the trail. As they walked up the path to the village with their new friend, she told them that their truck would arrive in the night and leave for Matadi about noon.

"The trucks here follow a pattern. They travel west one day and east the next. Our UNITA truck tries to arrive before the market trucks, and leave before they head back to Kinshasa. Our truck will buy beans tomorrow for our soldiers that occupy Noki, our small river port, very near Matadi. I am sure you could go to the market in the early morning.

"All of us women will be carrying the bags of beans from the market to the truck around mid morning. The men will unload the munitions during the night, and load the empty cases first thing in the morning. The truck waits about a half-hour walk from the market. All of us will be going over together. You will hear the racket."

The thoughtful Commander's wife gave each of the girls a small lunch consisting of a kwanga together with a smaller leaf package which she described.

"This is a sesame seed loaf. It will remind you of your mbika squash seed loaf. It goes well with Kwanga."

The girls were very grateful for her thoughtfulness.

"I've traveled in that truck, you will be hungry before you get to Lukala."

The girls each shook hands and bid a fond farewell to their new friend.

"Try and get some schooling before you think of marriage. We children of war are growing up without the education we need."

CONGO-ZAIRE

Their pack baskets seemed very light. All they had was a change of clothes and a few very precious belongings. They were rested and excited to be going to a market. The only other market they knew was one that used to be at Lufu. It had been years since they had been able to dream of all the marvelous things available in such a place.

They could not take their eyes from the incredible array of bright beautiful pieces of wrap-around dress material. Even Lufu, never did have so much variety. After all, Kinshasa was the textile capital for several African countries. It also seemed like a dream to see basins of sugar and salt together with tea and powdered milk. There were merchants selling bright metal pots, notebooks, pens and pencils. Stacks of white basins, pails, plastic jugs, and mountains of used clothes kept the girls pulling each other this way and that to see the things of which they had once only dreamed.

Because it was bean harvest season, most women had money. They were in fact, buying lots of things. One of the women from the military camp told them that this was the largest market in months.

"When the trucks come from Kinshasa to buy beans, the buyers bring products from Kinshasa to trade for the newly acquired money."

Sesame seed and beans were actually the only significant cash crop all year, apart from peanuts.

The girls were still looking excitedly when the whistle sounded calling all the camp women to help carry the sacks of beans to their supply truck. Two young soldiers placed a heavy sack on each young woman's head. Soon there was a long column of over fifty women gliding along the path in single file. They did not bob up and down like men when they walked. Their heads remained level and all the action took place from the hips down enabling them to glide without wasting energy by bobbing.

As they walked through Kibuki village, they passed a very large thatch-roofed building with a high steep roof. The girls from Kiula had never seen such a large building before. The low sides were open and they could see rows and rows of bamboo seats just like they had made for their school.

"What is that big building?" Lisa asked the nearest young woman from the camp.

"That is our church. On Sundays we gather here from all the villages around on both sides of the border. You should hear our camp choir! We join about eight other choirs when we sing. We sing for about three hours and then our pastor teaches us from the Bible in very interesting ways. His teaching often begins with a drama put on by the local people. I have really been helped here.

"Our pastor shows us that we need Chief Jesus to rule our hearts. The spirit of this Chief Jesus, which the Bible talks about, can change how you think, and feel inside. Too bad you won't be here on Sunday. Sometimes we have four or five hundred people. Last week there were five different people who burned all their protective fetish charms and teki figures."

Titi was very curious to hear this young woman talk so positively about the Bible.

"I can't imagine what would ever persuade people to burn their protective fetish charms," she whispered to Dina who was walking next to her.

The caravan of carriers left the road through the village taking a shortcut through the bush. Within a few minutes the big gray military truck became visible. The women passed by the tailgate where two soldiers grabbed each sack off their heads, and stacked them in the truck.

Zoao was coordinating the loading process. He signaled for the five travelers to climb up into the truck and help place the sacks of beans. Over half the truck was filed with empty ammunition boxes. He wanted the girls to sling a layer of bean sacks over the tops of the boxes to keep them from bouncing. The women who carried in the beans, left immediately, to return to the market. Zoao, the five girls, and a second guard, had to make the final placement of the bags.

At ten-o clock, Makengo, the driver, appeared, looking at his watch.

"It's time!" He said tersely. "Which one is your daughter, Zoao?"

Zoao presented all the girls as he began to close up the back. The two armed guards appeared who had been designated to sit up front with the driver. Zoao and his colleague were the armed guards for the rear.

Makengo walked around the truck for a final check. A mechanic had checked the truck, and supervised the filling of the fuel tanks. With a roar, they were off at quick pace, considering the miserable state of the roads. The girls were pleased to be travelling in daylight.

Zoao was assigned to travel in back as one of the two designated guards. The girls expressed alarm when the tarpaulin was closed so tightly that all light was shut out.

"If we didn't close this tightly, we would be unable to breathe in here because of the dust." Zoao explained, as he slithered over the load to the very front of the truck where he proceeded to open a long narrow slit in the front end of the tarp, just above the cab.

"This is our fresh air. If we were travelling in the heat of the rainy season we would all crawl up there and stick our noses in the slot to survive the heat. On an overcast day like this we will be fine. After a half-hour of adjustment, they could all see around a little, because of the slit of light at the front.

Zoao explained their situation. "This is a munitions truck carrying all our supplies for the north of Angola. The only other supplies we get are the ones we capture. This truck is on a highly secret mission. You must never discuss it with anyone, because it could cost a lot of lives.

"The Congo Zaire police let us past their check points because our license plate indicates that we are a top priority truck of their own army. We are never questioned and we seldom stop. When we stop in a few hours for a rest stop, we will not get out. We will loosen the tarp and all hang over the tailgate at once. Forget modesty and custom, we are on a military mission with strict rules.

"At Lukala the lady supplying food will help you down. When we are stopped in a town we keep very alert. We do not want anyone to be able to see inside! Mind you, there is next to no danger on our return trips to Matadi. When we head back to Kibuki, we will be loaded with strategic military supplies. As soon as we leave the paved road that goes from Matadi to Kinshasa we are keenly alert because the enemy could attack us if they knew just when we are passing. All it would take would be a half dozen well trained, well equipped, brave MPLA troops to blow this truck sky high!

"They don't dare set big mines in the roads because of the local traffic. That is why we try to make our trips very close to the times of heavy commercial traffic."

The constant roar of the big turbo charged diesel engine, combined with the whine of the gearbox, made conversation too difficult. Everyone was lulled into a state of sleep by the hypnotizing cacophony of sound. In some respects the journey seemed interminable. In a way, it passed like an undefined dream.

Paved roads and towns

Ten hours travel brought them to the paved highway joining Kinshasa to Matadi. The bouncing ended, and the gearbox became quiet, as the truck flew along at a hundred kilometers per hour.

"We will reach Lukala in a bit over an hour and a half. Then we must separate. You will all begin new lives. I will be back leading munitions carrier patrols. You have an idea now about my life. I really don't know what things will be like for you.

"Climb up and peek out the opening because in a few minutes we will be in the town of Mbanza Ngungu. You have never seen a big town before."

On the smooth road, it was relatively safe to crawl through the narrow distance between the load and the top of the truck.

As they sped through the town, the girls all emitted little shouts of astonishment, as Zoao had anticipated. They had never seen passenger cars before. No car could ever navigate the truck roads of the interior.

As in the Kibuki market, it was the bright colors of women's clothes that dazzled them. The buildings, the paved streets with sidewalks, and gas stations with pumps that put fuel directly into vehicles were almost beyond their imaginations. However, they all recognized pretty dresses when they saw them.

Lukala

As soon as they spotted the giant stacks of the Lukala Cement Company, they all began to crawl toward the back. Zoao unfastened the inside ropes allowing the rear tarp to gape enough to allow the girls to squeeze out and the bag of kwanga to be pushed in. Once the truck had come to a full stop, Zoao helped the girls slide down between the tarp and the tailgate. Their baskets followed, and a moment later the sack of kwanga was pushed up through.

"Give the note to Makengo," Mama Rosa shouted as the truck moved away into the dusk.

"Mama Rosa, we are Bazombo girls and we have come from Angola. My aunt lives here, but I have no Idea of where to look for her."

"I am a Zombo from Makela de Zombo. Most of us Bazombo live in the same part of town where I live, so you had better come with me."

"My aunt's name is Mama Nkenda She is married to Tata Sami who was a merchant trader in Angola. Sami's younger wife is called Mama Lala," Titi explained as they walked.

"Sometimes merchants, and market workers live closer to the market. Tomorrow is a market day. You can sleep at our house, and tomorrow you will probably find people you know. Angolan refugees actually live in all the villages around here. I don't think there is a village between here and Matadi without a good number of refugees living in it. My house is small. I lost my husband in the war. My three children are all in school and it takes everything I can earn to keep us alive. I'm sorry I have nothing to offer you. I know what it is like to arrive here and have no place to go. When I came, I had the three little children too. God is good and he has helped us."

Mama Rosa's little house was made of brick and had a metal roof.

"Here in Lukala the government authorities required all of us refugees to build brick houses. They reckon that when we return to Angola we will be obliged to leave some good houses behind us. The way the war is going, we will all be here a long time, I fear."

"All we need is a spot to lie down. We still have a little kwanga and sesame seed cake left from our trip. We will be fine," Titi assured their kind friend.

Everyone was awake early the next morning and the girls helped Mama Rosa carry her things to market. The girls were looking everywhere in the hopes of finding someone they knew. Titi had the greatest hope because she was sure that Tata Sami had relatives in Lukala.

The girls were drawn immediately to look at the beautiful lengths of bright print. Some merchants simply stacked their lengths of cloth in a folded format, on sheets of protective plastic. Other more aggressive merchants arranged poles or wires so the cloth could be draped in all its beauty. The girls were going from one display to another when suddenly Titi shouted.

"Mama Mbuta, Mama Mbuta!"

Her startled aunt spun around and ran to her seemingly full-grown niece, throwing her arms around her. First she hugged Titi, and then she held her at arms length to get a better look.

"You are a woman already. Is your mother here with you? I want to see the baby."

"I have a lot to tell you," Titi said quietly. "I would rather tell you in your home."

After the initial excitement was over, Titi introduced her four friends explaining whose daughter each girl was. Naturally, her aunt knew all of their mothers from the days she used to live in the village of Kiula herself.

"Dina, your uncle drives that big red truck over there. A rich Zombo owns the truck and they buy food here to sell in Kinshasa. Sami often travels to Kinshasa on that truck.

Looking at the two girls who were sisters, Titi's aunt had more good news. "Your grandmother lives in Kimpese about an hour's walk west from here." Tina's face showed her worry and sadness because Mama Mbuta could help everyone but her.

"There is a whole village of Zombo folk who live out by the Lukunga River. Their market day is tomorrow. Because we Bazombo are merchants, you can always find your kin if you just go to enough markets." The girl's confidence grew as Mama Mbuta spoke. "Lala is right near here, Titi. She will be excited to see you. After we have seen her, Sami is selling hardware over in that section near to the trucks. I can leave my merchandise with my friend. Why don't we just go over and surprise them one after the other. Sami is right near the truck that Dina's uncle drives."

Both Lala and Sami reacted the same way as her aunt. Their minds were not prepared to see a little girl who had emerged from her cocoon of childhood to become a surprisingly attractive young adult.

Sami directed them to Dina's uncle who seemed rather pleased to meet up with his fine young niece. Before they separated, Titi learned that Dina might be living in Kinshasa.

It was a busy market that day because people were still selling their beans. "Whenever the women have money to spare, they love to buy cloth. We will leave at noon because no one buys cloth in the afternoon," Titi's aunt explained.

The girls were surprised that to find that Sami had inherited a rather large house right beside the market.

Sami's house beside the market

"This house belonged to Sami's uncle who lived here for years. We lived with him when we first came over from Angola. They really got along well together. He was chief of his clan. When the old man felt that he wouldn't live much longer, he chose Sami as his successor. In addition, he told him he could have the house. He didn't have good relationships with others of his clan. We came to Lukala because of that uncle," Mama Nkenda explained.

Once they were seated in the large living room, Titi began to tell her aunt about everything that had happened since they separated in Lufu. It didn't take long to recount the two saddest pieces of news.

"Mother died in childbirth the month I returned home from Lufu. I have lived with my grandmother until she died last month. I buried her with dignity with the help of the village."

Pulling the pretty blue glass from her basket, Titi explained that the other was on the grave in Kiula cemetery. The glass was one of the very few keepsakes Titi was able to bring out with her.

At the sight of the special blue glass from the house where she had been born, Mama Nkenda broke into sobbing. She was a woman with great inner strength but hearing of the death of her beloved younger sister, and then of her mother, was too much. Tears flowed in little rivers down her face.

"You my child, stayed with my mother to the end, and you buried her all alone as far as our clan is concerned," her aunt blurted out between sobs.

Embracing Titi fondly, weeping uncontrollably, she absorbed the strength and comfort flowing from her younger sister's only child. Titi found her own grief rekindled in the fellowship of the aunt she loved almost as much as her mother.

It was the three girls who described Titi, as their village schoolteacher. They went on to explain her special relationship with the old village chief who rallied the whole village to help bury her grandmother with dignity.

"It was a beautiful funeral," the girls continued. "Anyone would have been deeply satisfied to be buried so honorably. Your clan should be proud of Titi. Certainly those of us she taught to read and write are proud of her."

There was much to discuss, far more than they could cover the first day. Because of her aunt's urgent questions, Titi did recount the details of the reconciliation between her mother and grandmother. She was pleased to tell her aunt about the satisfying relationship she had enjoyed with her grandmother up until the last couple of weeks, when some kind of malevolent spirit possessed the old woman. She explained that in her dreams, her grandmother had come to her right after the funeral.

"In the dream she was happy to see me and seemed her wonderful old self again."

"The chief acted on my request and saw to it that she was buried with dignity and not as a fearsome witch with a pot of peppers on her head."

Titi decided to tell her aunt about the ngombo's decision, which facilitated reconciliation.

"Mbuta Mbanza turned out to be the Ndoki who ate my little brothers. She acted while magically disguised as my grandmother, so the blame would be cast on her. It was my mother who asked my grandmother to take me just before she died in childbirth."

"My father joined the UNITA army about two months after mother died. His patrol escorted us out of Angola. He was guard inside the UNITA truck that let us off here last night."

Titi's aunt, known locally as Mama Nkenda, was so full of questions that Titi decided to tell her everything she thought might be of interest.

"How did you manage to get along with mother? She never seemed to be able to get along with anyone except your grandfather."

"I had such a great need after losing my mother, that Grandmother treated me like one of her own children. She often remarked at how much I resembled my mother. All I can say is that we loved, and trusted each other. She taught me so many things I needed to know. She even showed me how to operate her secret fishing traps. She opened her heart to me. When I looked for advice, she passed her wisdom on to me. What she gave me was priceless. At the same time I must say that as my strength grew, hers diminished. We probably got along well because we really needed each other."

"I am so pleased that you got to know our old mother's heart. After she was condemned as an ndoki witch before you were born, she was hated and rejected by our whole clan and she withdrew from everyone. Tell me, what were her last days like?"

"I'm so glad she came to me after she died so I could know that the last few weeks of her life she was not in charge of her own spirit. She seemed to be manipulated by a frightening evil kind of spirit. She began to fear everyone, even me. In the very end she refused to eat or drink.

A few months before she died, she told me that she sometimes wondered if she had been tricked into becoming an ndoki against her will. It looked to me as though some evil ndoki spirit destroyed her right before my eyes. It was terrible to watch. Without the support of the whole village I could not have managed. She was a wonderful grandmother right up to the last three weeks. During that last period, she seemed like a tempestuous, wicked, twisted, totally evil being."

"What did you place in the coffin?" Mama Nkenda asked quietly.

Titi explained everything; the nice clothes, the beautiful blankets and hangings, the family teki and fetishes. The Chief's wife persuaded me to keep this one cover to keep me warm."

Taking the practical keepsake from her basket, she opened it and showed her aunt.

They had been talking with rapt attention for a couple of hours, when Mama Nkenda suddenly thought of the rather depressed girls looking somewhat abandoned.

"We all need a good meal. It is my turn to feed Sami and I think I will invite Lala too. She is so fond of you Titi."

Mama Nkenda was a well-organized woman. She gave jobs to all four girls. Everything she needed for the meal, she had bought very early at the market. The girls were amazed to see that the fufu flour came from the market ready for the pot. They had never even heard of a fufu mill. Titi cut the fumbwa leaves, while the other girls shelled and roasted peanuts over a charcoal fire. Charcoal was a new concept for them as well. Mama Nkenda prepared the dried fish to be mixed with the saka saka greens. The feast was fully prepared by dusk, including a good piece of ngombie (beef) for Sami.

The girls' mouths fell open when Mama Nkenda flicked a switch, and a bright bulb hanging from the ceiling, lit up the whole room. When the electric hot plate began to glow like coals, all four girls shook their heads in amazement.

That evening was the very first time the girls had ever seen a whole family sit on chairs and eat together at one large table. Sami asked a lot of practical questions about roads and bridges. He was surprised to know how general the exodus from Angola had become.

"You were smart to come over here. Angola is going to be in trouble for a long time yet," Sami said sadly.

"Tell us about your school" Mama Nkenda insisted.

The three girls had a hard time to wait for each other because of their eagerness to explain everything well so that the family could appreciate what Titi had accomplished.

"She is a great teacher. We can all read and write quite well because of her clever ways of teaching us. She even taught our chief to read and write at his age! He helped us learn to speak Portuguese. She has been our teacher and our best friend all at the same time.

"We would never have had the courage to come out of Angola if it were not for Titi. We are so glad that you folk kept her at Lufu during the year she attended school. Now each of us wants to go to school here if we possibly can."

Sami encouraged the girls by telling them that lots of Angolans managed to attend the local schools.

"Children who speak Portuguese, learn to speak French quite quickly," he said encouragingly.

"Did your grown sons ever meet up with you over here?" Titi asked.

"The older one was killed in the war, but the other lives here in Lukala. He is growing large fields of onions over beside the Lukunga River. This time of year he stays right in his fields with some workers. They have huts there. Everything would be stolen if they didn't do that. Congo Zaire is not like Angola. Did you ever hear of anyone stealing another person's crops? Well, sad to say, that is the way things are here, and some of the worst thieves are from Angola. The war, and refugee life has changed many people," her aunt explained.

Before they settled down to sleep, Mama Nkenda told the two sisters that she had sent word to their grandmother in Kimpese.

"Tomorrow morning she will come here for you. Didi, you will go with Sami to the market at Kitobila. You can help him with his things and he will help you find your relatives if they live in those parts as we think."

Knowing that they would probably find their families soon removed a big burden from the girls.

"Girls, you need to know that most Angolans are having a hard time to make a living here in Congo Zaire. We are more fortunate than most because Sami's uncle gave us most of what you see around you. Being a refugee means that you really don't own any land. Our people are willing to farm and work hard but often they are obliged to give half the harvest to the landowner. Many parents can't afford to send their children to school. If it weren't for the help of the churches, many Angolans would not be in school."

"Our gardens are out by the Lukunga River, beside our son's onion farm. We are really lucky, because we took over Sami's uncle's good land. Many Angolan women from here have to walk an hour or two to find land to till. Most Angolans were robbed of all their possessions when they crossed over the border. Soldiers from here took everything.

"Where we crossed the border, the Commander of the Congo Zairian soldiers was actually a Zombo like us. He was only pretending to be a native of this country. Sami gave him three bottles of Johnny Walker Whiskey to order his soldiers to let us past. He accepted for two reasons. He loved whiskey, and he was afraid Sami might tell on him.

"Back in Angola, when he saw that things were going from bad to worse, Sami began to invest all his available funds in rough diamonds that showed up in Luanda from the Lunda region. They were not worth a fortune, but they enabled Sami to buy his first stock of goods to sell as a merchant in the market. Fortunately for us there was a Zombo in Kinshasa who was a diamond dealer."

Titi felt oriented by all she had been told by her aunt. The other girls had hopes of finding their relatives. They were out of the war zone. Before falling to sleep Lisa remarked that this might be the last time they would sleep together. It was a sobering thought. They slept very soundly in their new security despite their uncertain future.

The whole, normal morning routine of the village was totally upset in town. Water came from a tap in the back yard, where the dishes were washed. The electric hot plate, and the charcoal burner boiled water, and roasted peanuts. Mama Nkenda was gone five minutes and came back with bread that was still hot from the mud brick oven in her neighbor's yard. They even had the luxury of powdered milk and sugar for their coffee that morning.

The whole procedure seemed so fast, and wonderful, that the girls just kept repeating the same exclamation. "Kedika, kedika! (Amazingly true!)

Even before they had finished breakfast, an enthusiastic knock rattled the old door. In an instant, an ecstatic grandmother was united with two grand children she had only dreamed of seeing seen since they were little children. As soon as the excited family had enjoyed some coffee and bread, they were off to Kimpese.

It was because a flat tire delayed their truck, that Didi and Sami had time for breakfast at all. They left again for Kitobila market about eight. Finally, Titi and her aunt were alone after all the flurry of activity.

"Let's go out to our gardens where we can talk and work at the same time," Mama Nkenda suggested with a cheery smile.

The half-hour walk to the garden was a pleasant one. As soon as they left the last row of houses, every available space was under cultivation. Titi was shocked to see the small size of the manioc some women were harvesting.

"This soil is tilled every year and never given a rest. We never get large manioc in these parts. We work just as hard but we only get less than half the yield. It is when we are tilling poor soil that we yearn for the gardens we all left behind. I know you are a skilled farmer because my sister and my mother have trained you. If you will help me in our gardens, and in the market, I am sure we can find you a way for you to continue your schooling, when the schools open in a few weeks."

The fieldwork was heavy for both of them. When the soil has not swallowed even a drop of rain for almost five months, it becomes incredibly difficult to till.

"Peanuts and corn do well in this field. The manioc I planted the first year was a fair crop, but the soil needs a peanut crop to enrich it. We just have a few more weeks before the rains come. If we can get it ready to plant, we will watch the signs to know just when to drop in our precious seeds. I think I have some of my mother's ability to predict the rain. In this poor soil it is necessary to get the benefit of the first rains."

"The schools around here are used twice a day. Some children study from seven in the morning until noon. When one group is leaving, the others are at the door because they study from noon until five. We will try to get you enrolled tomorrow."

Titi had been tilling the soil with all her strength in perfect rhythm with her aunt who had been trained in farming methods by the same person as she.

Mama Nkenda was very pleased with their progress in tilling the soil.

"You have become stronger than I am. All the work you were doing back home has made you strong," her aunt observed.

"I really wonder how I will make out in school, and where the teachers will place me," worried Titi. "I don't know any French at all! Reading and writing in Kikongo is quite easy for me now, after the years of teaching others. I know all the times tables on the back of the notebook too. I can write Portuguese, but I'm sure it isn't spelled correctly because we had no way to check the spelling except when we tried to write down what someone read from a book."

"Don't worry about school. I have heard the mothers say that their children do most of their work in Kikongo in the primary school. People have told me that someone who speaks Portuguese will soon learn French."

"Who pays the teachers here? Is it like Lufu where we gave some money every couple of months?"

Her aunt looked a little distressed as she replied, "The government is supposed to pay the teachers but the money seldom comes for them. The teachers really depend on fees paid by the school children. Here in Congo Zaire you usually are expected to pay 'madezo mabana' (a bribe called beans for the children) before any thing is done in an office.

"When we go tomorrow I will need to put a sum of money in a closed envelope and hand it discreetly to the school secretary. Poor children can't get into school because they don't have enough money. At least you will not need to pay a bribe to pass your exams because you are smart. We will try and get you into a school run by the church. In the church schools, the teachers are not allowed to force the young girls to sleep with them in order to be promoted. That kind of a bribe we will never pay!

"Since we moved here I have begun to go to church sometimes. There are lots of young people your age in our congregation. We can go Sunday if you would like. If you go to their school, you will be expected to go to church most of the time. That seems to be their rule. Often there are more Angolans in church than local people. The women there have been good to me. Some of them remember that all their ancestors came over from Angola many long years ago. Of course there are some who think they are much better than we are, so they look down on anyone called a refugee. As far as I can see, there are many more nice people than rotten ones. There are many choirs. I'm sure you could join one of the youth choirs if you wished."

Titi was surprised that her aunt actually attended a church.

"Why did you start going to church?"

Mama Nkenda reflected a little before she answered. "After all the suffering I have seen, I decided that I needed God's help if there is a way to get it."

Registration for school

Friday morning Titi went off nervously with her aunt to be registered in the nearby church run school.

"This school was built and is managed by the same church that I attend."

Assessing the grade level, appropriate for Angolan students, was not a new experience for the secretary. Their standard procedure was to test the child's reading ability in Kikongo to give them some idea of their previous schooling. She had already admitted that she could not read French. Naturally she was nervous. She hadn't been tested for a number of years.

Given a book of Kikongo fables to read, she soon found herself reading with pleasure. The secretary was very impressed with her reading so he turned to the other major subject of mathematics. To test her he plied her with random multiplication questions. Years of repeated drilling allowed her to answer quickly and accurately. The final test consisted of writing down as a dictation, a few lines from the book she had been asked to read. She wrote naturally and legibly.

"Angolan children make good students because they are so anxious to learn. In my experience, students who speak Portuguese, soon catch up with the other students as far as French is concerned. We will let you attend with the sixth grade students. I think you will do fine."

Opening his register, the secretary frowned. "I will put her on the waiting list along with these others." He displayed a full page of names. Titi filled out the form, including her aunt's signature.

Mama Nkenda knew that reference to a waiting list was intended to extract a bribe. She folded the equivalent of a workman's wages for a week in the middle of the registration form. When the secretary spotted his appropriate bribe, he smiled.

"I'm glad you understand our procedures. Your niece is so clever. I am sure we will find her a place in our school."

Titi wanted to squeal with delight, but restrained herself until they were well away from the little school office.

"Mama Mbuta I will work very hard to catch up with the other students, I promise!"

Her aunt smiled. "I have no doubts about your determination after all you have been through. I do feel sorry for the children who can't afford the bribe. We certainly know that the world is not fair. If it were fair we would all be living in our own country and we wouldn't even understand the word refugee!"

Titi nodded sadly and added, "If the world were fair, my mother and brothers would be living and my father would not need to kill people to stay alive."

"We must find you some clothes. See that shop over on the edge of the market? They sell second-hand clothes that come here from rich countries. They might have something you would like. Once you start to school we will need to get you a uniform. You will need a white blouse and a blue skirt. If we could find you a white blouse and a skirt today, you could wear the blouse as part of your uniform."

They looked very carefully through the pile of clothes, but the white blouses were all gone. Mama Nkenda found a bright red dress that fit perfectly. Titi was ecstatic. She had only had one new dress in her lifetime, the one Mama Lala had made her for her school days at Lufu, five long, hard years ago. While Titi was admiring the dress, her aunt quietly selected a bra for her niece.

"Mama Mbuta, how can I ever repay you?"

"Child, remember that you are my daughter now, especially since your mother's death. I should have been taking care of you for these past five years. Instead, you took care of yourself and my old mother too! I will do all I can for you. We will work together."

As soon as she came through the door, Titi stripped off her faded clothes and put on the new dress. They were both delighted.

"Now that you are becoming a woman, you need to wear this bra," Mama Nkenda explained.

Titi had never even tried on a bra before, so it proved to be both exciting and embarrassing. When she put her dress on while wearing her bra she was surprised by what she saw in the little mirror. She really had become a young woman. The thought both pleased and worried her.

"Where is Mama Lala? I haven't seen her since the day we arrived at your house."

"She has gone to Kinshasa to buy cloth from the factory. She buys those five-yard pieces that women like for their wrap around dresses. At the factory there are twenty or thirty different patterns. She buys the patterns that women around here prefer. She is good at choosing new patterns that will become popular.

"Sami's uncle had two wives too, so this house was built to allow each woman to have her own part. We get along well, and work together in the market without any problems. Sami worked out a plan that seems fair to both of us. Each time we sell twenty pieces of cloth, we are paid one piece, or its value in money for ourselves. Sami pays for the electricity and all the fish and food that comes from stores. We supply all the garden food from our fields. We take turns cooking. You will probably want to help both of us."

Titi nodded with satisfaction because she had learned to like Lala in Lufu.

"I think we should go to church tomorrow. Most of the children you will be with in school will also attend. The pastor is from Manianga and his way of talking is a lot like the Kikongo many people speak over here. The Bible he reads sounds a lot like the way he talks. I have been thinking a lot about God since I started going there. Just like you, I grew up without any talk about God. The teachings we hear from the Bible make me do a lot of thinking. Perhaps I go because I love to hear the choirs.

"You should iron your dress before you go, so that it will look really nice. This electric iron is a lot easier to use than my mother's old charcoal iron that could easily drop coals on our clothes."

There was a broad smile on Titi's face as she moved the electric iron over her dress, she had never seen one before.

A new dress for a new world

Sunday morning was bright and clear. The amount of sunshine increased as the rainy season gradually approached. In her bright red dress Titi felt happily self-conscious. The bra made her dress fit perfectly. Her new profile left her feeling a twinge of embarrassment mixed with a deep satisfaction that she no longer looked like a poor refugee.

"You look so nice, all the boys will want to marry you." Mama Nkenda says smugly, as they walk along.

"My only dream is about going to school. Getting married is for older girls, not for me right now," Titi replies emphatically.

"Your thinking is right. I wish I had had a chance to go to school when I was your age. Look at Lala. Sami sends her to Kinshasa to buy the cloth we sell. She is the one who manages our business, and sets the prices. She has many privileges simply because of what she learned in school. If I had the same schooling as she, Sami would not have needed to marry a second wife. You are right in wanting to go to school. You don't need to think about marriage unless you find someone you really want to marry. It is good to be young, pretty, and smart. You can afford to wait."

The walk to church only took about twenty minutes. Their walk took them through rows and rows of identical company houses.

"These houses all belong to the Lukala Cement Company. In a couple of weeks you will hear the roar, when the big machines are started up again over there by those giant chimneys. Hundreds of men work in the factory. That is why this town developed here. Sadly they are not allowed to hire any Angolans."

Just as they turned left to go over to the white church building, the big bell began to ring.

"That's only the first bell, we will still be in time to get good seats." Mama Nkenda explains as she pointed toward the long row of classrooms behind the bell tower. "You will be studying over there when school starts. The secretary we met has an office over there too. In just a few more days you will be wearing your blue and white uniform."

Under the spreading branches of the crimson-blossomed, flamboyant tree, they spotted one of the big choirs having a last minute rehearsal. It was the famous men's choir her aunt had mentioned earlier. Wearing dark trousers and white shirts, they looked impressive. The men were putting blue, decorative sashes on over their heads as they sang. Titi became excited.

"There are women's, children's, and youth choirs too. When you hear them all sing you will understand just why lots of people come to this church on Sunday mornings."

The church building was painted white on the inside with blue trim. Titi had never been in such a large building before. A large sign was painted on the wall above the pulpit. NZAMBI I ZOLA ("God is love"), it said. The pulpit was designed so that from below you could only see the form of a cross. Big comfortable chairs covered with red upholstery were pushed back against the wall, right under the sign, on the raised platform.

"Those three chairs are for the leaders," Mama Nkenda explained.

The whole auditorium was filled with many rows of long smooth benches, arranged so there was an aisle at both ends. There were already about a hundred people seated near the front. White paper signs reserved the seating for the choirs that had not yet entered the building. Within a few minutes of their arrival, their bench filled up, as did the whole sanctuary. Of course, they followed the age-old tradition of men sitting on the right and women on the left. Only a few of the younger families sat together.

From the entrance came the staccato of bongo drums, rhythmically echoing, as the teen choir danced its way to their reserved seats near the front. Titi felt her excitement grow as young people her age begin to sing enthusiastically.

They sang a narrative about a man named Noah who built a gigantic boat on dry ground with no water near by. Despite the catchy rhythm, the story was tragic because only one family was saved when endless rain caused a flood.

After two more songs, they moved into their seats and sat down the instant the drums stopped. Before the teens singing had actually finished, the large adult women's choir began to make its entrance. All dressed alike, the women swayed in unison as a combination of small drums, and a metal gong gave them their coordinating rhythm. They sang a lively number before sitting in their designated spot.

From a side door at the front, the sound of rhythm sticks delivered the beat, as the smartly-dressed men's choir hummed in harmony. Dark trousers, white shirts with bow ties and sashes made them eye-catching, as their white-gloved director led them in a number that displayed their versatility. The men swayed from side to side and moved their feet in unison so that the long line looks like a giant centipede.

All these songs were simply entrance songs not to be confused with the music they would provide when their turn came. The ceremonial entrance of the five choirs took about a half-hour. Their smart entrance numbers simply raised one's anticipation for their official presentations that would follow.

Pastor Pangu came in with the last choir wearing his dignified black gown and a white clerical collar, giving him an authoritative appearance. He was obviously in charge of the animated assembly. For about an hour the five choirs sang in turn, to the delight of everyone. The singing and drum rhythms were outstanding. Titi had never heard anything like this in her whole lifetime. Following the choirs, the pastor and others announced all sorts of activities.

Three young people invited youth to join their group called the League. The thought of meeting lots of other young people was very attractive to Titi.

The dynamic, white-gloved leader of the men's choir led everyone in what was called animation. All the choirs, and the whole congregation joined together in song to the beat of throbbing drums. The whole congregation swayed joyously as they sang in a most animated manner.

Later Titi understood that the swaying parade of people coming from the back seats and walking up the aisles was actually the manner in which people brought up gifts of money to the front. This parade continued until every bench full of people had filed past the offering containers. A lady dressed in white held a basket to receive the gifts of all the women and girls. A white-haired man held the basket for gifts given by men and boys. Mama Nkenda gave Titi some cash to contribute when it became time for the people on their bench to join the animated procession.

"The women always win in the offering competition," Mama Nkenda whispered.

After a half-hour of universal movement, the temperature rose in the building and almost everyone began to perspire. During all this activity most of the little children escaped to play under the shade trees located along the side of the church building where they could enjoy quiet freedom.

Immediately after the offering had been collected, and prayed about, a kindly-looking deacon invited sick people to come to the front for prayer. Five people walked up and knelt expectantly, while others slipped quietly to their knees wherever they were seated. Everyone closed his or her eyes while the deacon led in prayer. His prayer was tender and compassionate. When he finished his prayer, all the deacons stood together while one of them offered a prayer that was calling for God's blessing in the lives of those who had expressed their need throughout the congregation. Titi appreciated the prayers for healing and felt a kind of security in her heart.

The last half-hour of the service consisted of a lesson based on a portion of the Bible. Titi was curious to see that the Bible in use looked just like the one her grandmother had given her. First the pastor read from the Bible, then he explained what he had just read. When he explained the reading, he made sure that people understood how the teaching in the special book applied to their daily lives. Whenever the pastor made reference to the Bible, he always called it 'God's word'. People listened very carefully because the Pastor seemed to understand the kinds of struggles they had. He seemed confident that God wanted to help people. When he had finished his lesson, he prayed for everyone before taking his seat.

After the service was ended, the combined choirs sang while friendly people began to leave or chat with one another. Titi and her aunt left the church and began their walk home.

"If that is what church services are like, I think they are a wonderful gathering of folk for a good purpose." Titi told her aunt very emphatically. " We have been here all morning but it was all over too soon for me. Do they do this every week? The choirs were wonderful. Do you know how I could join that youth choir?"

"As far as I know, you simply ask the leader of the choir. Many of those young people are Angolans just like you. Sometimes they sing in Portuguese," Mama Nkenda explained. "A life of suffering and danger seems to give people a desire to learn how to pray to God. I think that is why there are so many Angolans in the church."

Titi and her aunt worked diligently at the heavy task of preparing their fields for planting. They were both skilled workers and encouraged one another. By the time the schools were about to open, Mama Nkenda felt that their work had gone so well that they would be totally prepared when her joints told her that the rains were near.

Very nervous about school

Doubts stood on tiptoe waiting to be given a hearing, as Titi went to the school with her aunt on the first day.

"I hope I get as understanding a teacher as Master Pedro was back in Lufu," Titi said wistfully.

She remained unusually silent despite the wild activity in her mind.

"Don't be afraid. You have probably had more experience with life than your teacher. You have absolutely nothing of which to be ashamed. Remember, you may not know French but you know many things much harder to learn than a language"

Titi perceived that her aunt had the same capacity to read her thoughts as her grandmother.

The line up of students had already begun. Each child stood with an adult. They were all sizes, and all looked nervous.

"Those three were in the youth choir," Titi whispered to her aunt while silently pointing with her lower lip.

To their surprise there were almost as many girls as boys. When their turn came at the wicket, they discovered that all they were doing was paying their school fees. Upon receipt of the money they were given a receipt and a list of required supplies including five pieces of chalk for the teacher.

"Bring this receipt to classroom '6A' and you will be admitted. Buy your school supplies and line up in front of the classroom by 7 o'clock Monday morning," the secretary informed them.

Just as they left the line up for paying fees, they saw another queue formed under a tree where the school tailor was taking measurements and accepting down payments for school uniforms. Measurements were quickly taken and a numbered receipt exchanged for the cash received. He needed the cash advance so he could buy the material and set his crews to work at their sewing machines.

Before leaving the school complex, they went in search of the classroom marked '6A'. There was a long row of brick classrooms with metal roofing. The classroom in question was near the end of the row farthest from the church building.

"These are the newest classrooms built the year we came," Mama Nkenda reported.

Titi spotted a special sign with the large letters CPRA. Asking her aunt what that word meant, she noticed her brighten.

"These were built by a special group which built extra classrooms in local schools so the Angolan refugees would be given a chance to study. I was here when a Reverend Grenfell opened these very classrooms. He explained that they were built with money gathered by the churches in his homeland. He spoke in Portuguese, because he was once a missionary in Angola. Don't ever say it out loud, but you have a right to be here."

Looking inside, Titi was pleased to see large blackboards, plank benches, desks, and a good table for the teacher. She was surprised to see a cement floor in every classroom.

"I hope you learn lots in that room," Mama Nkenda's thoughts slipped through her lips.

"I bet it is hot in there when the sun shines, and noisy when it rains. I think that in the hot rainy season, my little thatch-roofed school was more comfortable than this one will be," Titi remarked with a grin as they were leaving.

"Tomorrow will be our last market day before school opens. We will need all the help we can get. Lala did not buy cloth on her last trip to Kinshasa. She knew that parents would need all their money for school rather than cloth. She bought school supplies with the money. We have lots of every item on your list. We will be very busy all day long."

A half-hour before daylight, Lala was at work organizing her merchandise for the busy day in the market. Titi made many trips with heavy boxes carried on her head. Lala had marked the prices on every package and box. The evening before Titi had helped make little receipt books. Each was stamped with a rubber stamp and numbered. Lala's stapler helped her make very neat little receipt books.

Titi had never made change in a real market before, but her friend, the chief, had taught all the girls the right way to make change. The white merchant who taught him had been very strict, so the chief was an excellent teacher. It was a delight to use the skills she had learned in her little Kiula School.

Titi was so very busy that she really had no time to chat with the hundreds of children and parents who came to buy supplies. Unbeknownst to her, she served most of her future classmates, who would, nonetheless, remember her. One of the men who bought from her turned out to be her teacher when she arrived in class on Monday. It was a relief when the market closed about three in the afternoon. They had sold most of their stock and everyone was exhausted.

After she had helped carry back the merchandise, Titi handed over her money and the receipt stubs to Lala.

"How did you ever learn to sell like that? I was watching you for a while until I saw that you knew exactly what you were doing. I went to good schools in Luanda but I could not have handled sales as well as you when I finished."

Titi explained about the old chief who once sold for Santos in Lufu.

"We didn't have many other ways to learn our mathematics. To make change you need to know your times tables and learn to add and subtract. What I did in the market made use of everything I know about arithmetic," she said with a grin.

"I can see that you will be a great help selling school supplies in the market. The children will know that you are a fellow pupil so they will prefer to buy from you."

Titi was exhausted but delighted with her day. She just wished she knew her numbers in French.

At church on Sunday, many of the children smiled at the kind, bright girl who had sold them their school supplies at the market. Those little smiles made Titi begin to feel that she belonged. As soon as the choirs began to sing, she listened in rapt delight. The rhythm and words combined to communicate a variety of ideas. Every song was a kind of story or parable about life.

Reverend Pangu presented his sermon dramatically. However, it seemed to Titi that each teaching he gave seemed to stir up other questions in her mind. Certainly from the Pastor's point of view, the Bible was like a letter from God himself.

By Sunday evening, Titi was troubled enough about school that her aunt noticed. "What is worrying you my child?" she asked gently.

"I can't speak French. When I heard people using it in the market, I seldom understood them. What will I do in the class room when the teacher asks me something in French?"

"I don't know just how the teacher will deal with you, but any teacher in Lukala will be accustomed to having Angolan children who begin the year without understanding French."

Titi's dream did not help calm her. She dreamed that she was in the classroom and all the other classmates were laughing at her because she couldn't speak French.

Despite her fears, Titi was very excited to be going to school. She dressed modestly, looking repeatedly in the mirror hanging in the living room. She knew exactly where to line up. The teacher, Mr. Bedelo, called the pupils' names from his list. He seated the boys on the right and the girls on the left. Titi was relieved to see that the children were a variety of sizes and ages. Certainly a number of the pupils were her age. She was wearing a blouse loaned to her by Lala. It hid her developing breasts so she would appear even younger than she actually was.

As soon as all the children were seated in their assigned places, Mr. Bedelo addressed them all quietly in Kikongo. He explained the basic rules that would be applied in their classroom and on the school grounds.

"There will be no whispering or talking in this room without my permission."

He proceeded to make a little speech about his high expectations. He reminded the pupils that they were the elders in the primary school and should behave in such a way that younger children would learn from their examples. When he had finished, he prayed for them all in a manner quite like the prayers Titi had heard in the church.

After the prayer, Mr. Bedelo explained his use of Kikongo.

"I have spoken in Kikongo because I wanted to be sure that everyone understood me. From now on I will speak primarily in French and so will you! I am aware that some of you are from Angola and others are from village schools where you didn't really use French. We have arranged a special class for you that will meet in the church. The instructor speaks both Portuguese and Kikongo so I am sure you will get along well. That class will meet in the church right after our courses are finished. You will need your parent's permission to attend because the teacher will need to be paid. He will tell you all about it tomorrow. How many of you don't speak French?"

Eleven pupils put up their hands. Titi felt greatly relieved, as did the others, no doubt.

The school day seemed to pass by quickly despite the language problems. Titi listened very intently for the many French words that resembled Portuguese. Listening so intently kept her mind active. She had no problems with arithmetic except that she could not express her answers using the French words for the numbers.

There were practically no textbooks available. As a result, key ideas had to be copied from the blackboard. Many concepts were simply learned by rote memory. Titi was able to repeat phrases that she really didn't understand. She knew that some day she would understand what she was saying. Mid-morning, Mr. Bedelo rearranged the seating so those children who did not understand French were seated with children who did.

"You are allowed to whisper to one another about the meaning of words." he conceded.

Before they expected it, the noon whistle at the Cement factory sounded and their studies were over for the day. Mama Nkenda was waiting for her at the door when she came home.

"Tell me, how was your first day of school here in Lukala?"

Titi explained everything that had transpired. Mama Nkenda nodded in contentment. Titi was not he only child behind in French. The teacher and the school administration had taken steps to help people just like her.

After a couple of months, Titi was able to follow her lessons reasonably well. Writing French was difficult but she could reply to simple questions. As time went on, she discovered that her understanding of Portuguese helped her more and more in grasping the meaning of French. Learning the French numbers helped her in the market. Lots of people speaking Kikongo used French numbers when they talked about money. A number of the wives of Cement Company managers spoke other African languages but did not understand Kikongo. French was a necessity with them.

There were only eleven children who enrolled in the special French studies given by an Angolan teacher. Isaac had graduated from the renowned Sona Bata Secondary School, enabling him to be of great assistance to Angolans who were changing from Portuguese to French. He remembered his own struggles in the late '60s. Titi discovered that he was, in fact, a Zombo like herself.

Lala preferred that Titi handle all the sales of school supplies because she herself was a pupil. She would teach Titi about selling cloth whenever the sale of school supplies was unprofitably slow.

After enjoying all the choirs for over a month, Titi gathered up enough courage to ask the youth choir director if she could join. His response was very positive. Choir practice and performance became Titi's happiest times of the week. She joined in time to take part in the special Christmas music.

At the beginning of December, Mama Rosa told Titi that she believed that Tata Zoao would be on the munitions truck due to pass on the last day of the month. It was good to know that her father was still alive. She decided that she would write a long letter to tell him everything that had gone on just in case he could not stop longer than five minutes. He would find someone to read it to him.

Christmas, a new experience

All of the talk and preparations leading up to Christmas were totally new for Titi. They had never celebrated Christmas in their village because there were no churches. The intensive choir preparation sparked great enthusiasm in Titi's happy heart.

Christmas Eve was a marvelous new experience. Hundreds of people gathered outside between the church and the school. Men from the factory hooked up electric lights to illuminate a raised platform borrowed from their employer. All the church choirs were there, with visiting groups as well. Each choir stood on the platform so everyone could see them when they sang. It was a warm evening in rainy season with bright moonlight and not a rain cloud in sight.

The youth choir sang a special Christmas song composed by their leader. Without doubt, their drummers and three guitar players were outstanding. The young people danced, swayed, and sang their hearts out. From the sound of the applause, they actually won the choir competition. Singing encore after encore, they were exhausted, and soaked with perspiration when they danced off the stage singing their last number. Titi wondered if they would have the strength to sing again in the Christmas morning service.

Half way through the evening, the choirs paused to make way for the dramatic presentation of the whole story of the birth of Jesus. Titi's heart went out to Mary and Joseph when they had to run off in the night to escape the soldiers who had been sent to kill all the babies in their little town. It was relief to know that they escaped in time to travel to a safer country.

If Mama Nkenda had not shaken her awake the next morning, she would have missed singing with her choir in the Christmas morning service. She was glad that everyone had heard their choir Christmas Eve because she was sure they would sound as tired as she felt. Many of the choir members slept on mats in one of the classrooms.

Titi practically ran to join her choir under their practice tree. The boys were heating the drumheads in the flames from a small pile of burning grass. The sound of the tightened drumheads was electrifying. The youth choir gathered around quickly, energized by the call of their own drums. They would sing well. They all felt it in their bones.

"We look nice in the morning light." one of the girls whispered. "Our hair designs are special. We are wearing our best clothes, and I feel like singing and dancing."

With all the energy of youth, they danced and sang their way to the front of the church when called to sing. Despite her joy, Titi, thought of her mother and Grandmother and her visits to their graves.

"I hope they are watching this morning. I know they would have loved to be here."

Happy, delighted, and exuberant, the youth choir sang with their whole beings. Even before they had finished their first chorus, the whole crowd began clapping to their very special rhythm. As soon as their chorus had been sung twice so the audience knew the words, the whole assembly joined in with them on each successive repetition, to the choir's absolute delight. Titi had never in all her days heard such singing. She had never felt the thrill of being part of anything that involved so many people. For a glorious moment she could forget all the past, and rejoiced in the fact that she was part of a youth choir that was leading a thousand people in enthusiastic singing.

All the hymns, and all the special choir songs of each and every choir told some part of the story of the birth of Jesus. The Pastor's sermon on Christmas Day seemed to echo the words of the choirs. He told about a very young woman whom God chose to give birth to a baby that was conceived by God's Spirit without her ever sleeping with a man.

It was an amazing story, but Titi felt let down when she learned that Mary, Joseph and the Baby Jesus were some tribe of white people in a far off land. She found some comfort from the fact the Mary, Joseph and Jesus became refugees to survive. It looked as though Jesus and his family were not the mean kind of whites. They suffered because of the cruelty and jealousy of some miserable baby killer called Herod. Titi was very puzzled as to how someone called the Son of God could also be a refugee.

Even Sami praised her when she came home after the morning service. Lala and her aunt hugged her.

"We are so proud of you. We told everyone that the girl in the bright red dress was our daughter."

The awareness of her total acceptance in the household was priceless. After all, she had only been with them a few short months. When she sat on the mat with Lala's little children, they all struggled to get close to their very special big sister.

The large piece of beef (ngombie) Sami brought home for Christmas dinner astonished everyone. Titi knew about New Year's festivities, but eating beef at the main Christmas meal was a new tradition for her. She had never tasted beef before. Her father had supplied them with plenty of good game during her childhood years but beef was a kind of meat she had only heard city people describe. With three women to do the cooking and plenty of delicious meat, Sami and his whole household had a delicious feast in the late afternoon. Because of all the activity and excitement of being part of the youth choir, Titi fell asleep with her empty plate in her lap. All that delicious hot food produced a sleep that took her right through the early evening into a new day.

As they walked to the fields the next morning, Titi's aunt asked her what she thought about her first Christmas.

"I will never forget the thrill of singing in that great youth choir. I enjoyed listening to all the other choirs too. Singing at funerals and weddings in the village is not at all like singing in our choir. I am so very thankful that you have accepted me as your daughter. All of these happy experiences have come to me because of you."

"You are my daughter! My sister's daughter is my daughter too! After all you have done for my mother, and our clan, I would try to help you even if I didn't love you as I do. What did you think of the Christmas drama that we watched?"

"It was a surprise to me to realize that Mary and Joseph were poor folk. It shocked me that they were not safe even in the village of their ancestors. Somehow, it made me feel better to know that Mary, Joseph and baby Jesus were refugees like us. They ran in the night, just like we did."

"The other day the pastor told us that the distance from Bethlehem to the border with Egypt was about four day's walk. Your frightening trip from our village to the border at Kibuki was a bit longer than theirs. At least they didn't need to fear mines as they fled."

Titi reflected in silence for a while before stating that she wished she would someday find a husband like Joseph in the play.

"He was really kind to Mary when her birth pains began. I can hardly imagine having a baby with only a man to help. How do you think that old man Simeon knew that a tiny baby would grow up to really help his people?"

"This whole idea of Church is new to me too, Titi. I only know what I hear when the pastor teaches us. He said one time that the very same invisible Spirit from God can guide ordinary people like us from right inside our own hearts," Mama Nkenda recalled.

Finally the day of her father's proposed visit arrived and Titi waited with mama Rosa for three hours. She promised to help her lift her sack of kwanga into the big UNITA truck when it made its five-minute stop. Titi was nearly smothered by her father's generous hug.

Handing her a heavy leaf-covered bundle he said, "Boas festas. Eat this on New Year's Day. I shot it myself." The engine roared and Zoao had to scramble to get on the moving truck.

"Thanks a lot, father. Season's greetings," Titi shouted to the departing truck.

She guessed her father had given her a big piece of mpakasa (buffalo) meat, her favorite. The smell of the smoke-dried meat was unmistakable. It was just dusk when Titi came through the door to her aunt's kitchen.

"I had no idea the truck would be so late. Sorry, I was unable to help you prepare supper. I was hunting," she announced with a grin as she put the package on the floor. "Mpaksa! (Buffalo!)" she shouted. "I haven't tasted that meat since I left Angola. Father said that he shot it himself and he wished us all 'season's greetings'."

In a flash her aunt rushed to the adjoining rooms where Sami was eating with Lala and the children.

"Zoao sent us big piece of mpakasa for our New Year celebrations," she announced joyfully.

The delight was contagious, and even the toddlers shouted with joy.

After supper, Titi and her aunt carefully spread out the generous portion of meat over the rack used for smoke-drying fish, just to keep it in good condition.

"Now we will have a New Year's feast, thanks to your father's thoughtfulness. Don't forget to marry a man like your father." Mama Nkenda said with a grin.

There was lots of fieldwork to be done during the school vacation. They were rushing to get the manioc planted before the little dry season arrived in mid-January when all the rains would stop for several weeks.

All the older women were amazed at Titi's knowledge of farming that she had learned from her clever grandmother.

"Most of the young girls nowadays only know how to make babies that they can't feed!" one older woman remarked, when she looked with delight at the young girl's approach to the finer details of gardening.

"I have three daughters with babies and no husbands!" she lamented. "It is so good to meet a girl who goes to school but knows how to farm as well. Don't rush to get married, child. Good men are hard to find. Be sure to marry a boy from Angola like yourself," she advised with a wagging finger.

"Marry a boy from Angola who has not been a soldier all his life," another cautioned.

Celebrations and budding romance

Every evening, Titi rushed off after supper to meet with her choir, which was preparing for a musical evening that would rival Christmas Eve, but on a New Year theme. The young man who led their choir had great ideas for new songs and dramatic presentations. Singing in the front row of girls, Titi began to be aware that her director's eyes were meeting with hers rather frequently. He liked the way she sang. The last practice before their special evening, the director shook hands with each choir member before they left. When he shook Titi's hand, she was aware of very special warmth in his eyes. A whole new sensation enveloped her being. She had never been attracted to a boy before.

Titi's mind began to whirl. *"Is this the feeling that influences a girl to think about marriage? Did all the other girls get the same feelings? Could it possibly be true that I have some special appeal for him?"* Titi asked herself dreamily as she sauntered home.

The market preceding New Year's Day was the most active, and animated, Titi had ever seen. Three big cows were butchered and sold right at the market. People lined up to get their pieces of beef for the festival. Even old widows bought tiny pieces of meat with a few coins carefully tied up in a corner of their wrap around skirts, just to have a taste. Sami knew that no one would want to buy school supplies so Titi was asked to help Lala sell cloth.

"We will have fun watching and helping men buy cloths for their spouses and mistresses tomorrow. I just have one rule for selling. If they are rich, I try and persuade them to buy the most expensive pieces. With other people, I try to help them buy what they can afford," Lala explained carefully.

Titi smiled to herself as the rich men came directly to the display of Dutch made, 'wax' cloths. They cost the most, but they kept their color marvelously. Any woman would be proud to wear one of those pieces that cost as much as a working man could earn in three months. Most men only bothered looking at the cloth in the price range they could afford. Often they asked Lala or Titi to help them choose. As the morning rushed by, Lala could see that they would soon sell everything. She raised the prices, knowing that every man worth his salt needed to present his wife with a new cloth for the New Year. By noon, not a single piece of cloth was left in the whole market and some men realized that they were in trouble for waiting too long.

The colors in church on New Year's Day were marvelous. Most women had new cloths to strut. Some poor women stayed away rather than feel the shame of having only faded clothes.

Rich women and newly engaged girls wore nice clothes and carried their folded new cloths like scarves over their shoulders.

Many women who could not afford new clothes wore bright new bandanas proudly on their heads.

Men wore new clothes as well, if they could afford them. The omnipresence of new clothes, and the expectation of having a taste of beef for the first meal of the New Year, made New Year's day a much larger celebration than Christmas.

Well before the church bell rang on New Year's Day Lala presented Titi with two beautiful matching pieces of cloth. One would make her skirt and the other would become a matching top.

"You helped us earn a lot of money yesterday. You earned this!" Lala explained.

In deep gratitude Titi knelt to express her profound thanks to Lala.

"How can I ever thank you?" she whispered.

"You will show me your happiness and enjoy the new clothes you deserve. We know nothing about tomorrow so just be happy today."

Titi had always worn second hand clothes bought very carefully in the market. Today she would dress like a young woman and not just another schoolgirl. She couldn't believe her mirror!

The choir director's eyes warmed Titi's heart with a lingering glance when she appeared in her new clothes feeling very self-conscious. In her heart she really felt that she was beginning a very special New Year.

The musical evening was as great a success as the Christmas Eve program. There were even more choirs taking part in what was felt to be a kind of friendly competition. Audience response was their only measure of comparison. Titi enjoyed singing in the regular church services when there was much less of the spirit of competition.

When the choir broke up to go home, she observed very carefully just how their director greeted the girls near her. There was no doubt in her mind. This young man was attracted to her. A new happiness and feeling of acceptance pulsed in her heart.

New feelings

During the sermon, Titi could not help but take notice of the many new pieces of cloth around her. Because she knew the prices of each pattern and quality of cloth she felt as though her head held a thousand little secrets. According to her aunt, the pastor spoke very well. Titi really had not listened. Along with all the other distractions, the young choir director had chosen to sit right beside her. She didn't dare to look at him, but she was very conscious of his close proximity.

"Does he feel my presence like I feel his? Will he ever tell me what he is thinking? Is this all in my mind?" She fondled these thoughts so frantically she feared they might slip from her lips.

With so many choirs and a long sermon, the church emptied quickly because everyone was thinking of the feast they needed to finish preparing back home. Titi simply nodded and fled, afraid she would reveal her feelings if she even shook hands. At home, there was indeed lots to do as the three women worked together to prepare a delicious meal with the mpakasa meat as their most attractive menu item. The whole household had its roots in rural Angola and had a deep appreciation for mpakasa meat. It was delicious, and came from the most elusive and dangerous animal in the savanna lands. They ate as much as they wanted and were thankful for their bright future.

Vacation over, Titi went back to school with renewed determination to master the French language to the very best of her considerable ability. Sami and Lala went to Kinshasa to pay for the great volume of cloth that they had received on credit. They traveled together partly for reasons of security and partly so they could transport a good supply of cloth for the next three months. The Zairian currency lost its buying power from month to month so it was wise to keep all ones available money invested in something that could be sold later. Titi helped carry some of the sacks of onions that were being taken to Kinshasa at the same time. The truck left at midnight.

THE DEVASTATING ROBBERY THAT CHANGES EVERYTHING

Home from school, Titi had just changed into her work clothes when she heard a commotion out side the door followed by the surprise return of Sami and Lala. Sami was wearing trousers and a shirt that did not fit, while Lala was wearing a tattered old work dress given her by someone.

"We were robbed just beyond Madimba! Armed robbers in military uniforms took everything! They asked for identity cards and then rounded up all the Angolans because they said there had been a revolt in Kinshasa lead by Angolans. They forced us to take off all our baggage and then ordered the driver to drive off without us. The even made us strip and took everything but our underwear. They took all the cloth money! We are ruined! The Marsavko Cloth Company can even take our house because it is in Sami's name. Those ruthless thieves forced the next truck to take them to Kinshasa with all our money and belongings. We don't even have our identity cards any more! I'm so glad we didn't have the children with us."

Sami looked gray with fatigue as Lala hugged her baby and cried uncontrollably.

"If it were not for the kindness of an Angolan truck driver we would still be there beside the road. An old widow from the nearest village felt sorry to see us stripped of our clothes. She gave Sami her deceased husband's clothes and gave me her oldest work cloth just to take away my shame. The truck driver had to pay the police a big bribe at Mbanza Ngungu because he was carrying passengers without identity cards. We have a debt to that driver on our heads too."

While they gave vent to their feelings, Titi prepared a good meal. Some of the dried mpakasa meat was still left and she felt that they needed a good meal. They were so hungry that, despite their turmoil of soul, they ate well.

"The Cloth Company goes to Matadi on Fridays to pick up supplies at the port. They will stop in here to get their money. The deal we had was that they would stop in, if we did not come to their office before Friday. I have nothing to give them; no money at all! We will lose everything! There is no way around it!"

Meanwhile out in the manioc field, Titi's aunt was becoming very worried.

"Titi is never late. She always comes out right after class. I wonder if she is sick? I must return to the house because there is something wrong. I feel it in my heart," she talked to herself worriedly as she half ran, back to their house.

By the time she arrived, Lala and Sami were eating. One glance at their clothes and mama Nkenda knew for sure that there was some kind of serious trouble. Sami and Lala began to tell their story all over again with even greater detail. Whether they realized it or not, the telling of their story helped them prepare for the stark reality they faced. They made far more money in cloth sales during the month of December than in the whole previous eleven months. Without the women's knowledge, Sami had hired an ex Angolan soldier to guard their house for the whole month as soon as the giant order of cloth had arrived.

"It is hard to imagine this kind of bad luck coming on me when our clan is so vulnerable. The others all depend on me. We should have waited for the Cloth Company treasurer to pick up the money here at the house where it was safe. Who is the ndoki witch who did this to me? Does he plan to eat me too?" Sami shouted in an uncharacteristic fit of anger and frustration.

"He might just as well eat me too now that he has taken everything we owned!"

The circle of sad frightened faces all nodded gravely in agreement. Only witchcraft could have dealt them such a blow.

"Whoever did this has more power than the protective fetishes and teki that have guarded me ever since I began my life as a merchant."

The women listened in silence because they thought just as he thought. There was a sense of impending danger, and gloom that filled their home like an ominous storm cloud. Anyone powerful enough to ruin them could destroy Sami's life as well.

Sheer exhaustion brought troubled sleep to everyone in their household, even though they feared the night when ndoki witches carry out their demonic tasks with the greatest ease.

When she awoke in the morning, Titi felt totally unsettled. On her way to school she realized that everything had changed. It was as though Sami had died and his relatives had come to claim everything, turning the women out of their home.

The dreaded moment arrived when the company truck stopped beside their house. The treasurer knocked impatiently with every expectation of being paid.

"We were robbed on our way to Kinshasa," Sami explained to the treasurer. His voice trembled to the point of breaking as he spoke.

"Don't try to pull that kind of story on me. I know the Judge in Mbanza Ngungu, so don't provoke me with any kind of story or delay. I want the money or the cloth, and I want it now! Why did you not wait for this truck? I don't believe a word of this story, you crooked, snake-eyed refugee. We are going to the Judge at Mbanza Ngungu this minute!"

Ruthless judgment

Sami was pulled out of the house like a common criminal and forced to climb up on the back of the truck suffering kicks when he fumbled.

Three interminable hours later the truck returned with the feared Judge in the cab. There were three armed policeman on the back of the truck as well. A crowd gathered within minutes. The policemen stood at the doors of the house as the judge pronounced slowly and distinctly.

"This house and everything in it is hereby seized to pay for the stolen cloth money."

A second truck appeared and men, led by the policemen, proceeded to list everything in the house right before their hopeless eyes.

"The gendarmes will use this house as barracks whenever they supervise the market. Why don't you Angolan thieves go back to your own rotten country?"

The judge climbed back up into the cab with a scornful look on his face.

By sunset, the family was destitute. Refugee friends, who had no doubt at all about the robbery, took them to their little homes for supper. They were silent, and in shock.

"The police will sell your things at the market tomorrow. We will help you buy back a few of your clothes but we have very little money as you know."

The whole household was so stunned that they couldn't even respond verbally to the kindness.

It was a very sad, subdued Titi who trudged off to class empty-handed, more from a sense of duty, than any other reason.

"Now that I come from a poor family that has been publicly shamed I wonder how many true friends I will really have." She held this little conversation with herself as she recognized that her days in school could well be numbered.

As soon as she arrived at school, her teacher called her outside where they could talk privately.

"People don't know it but I have roots in Angola too. My parents fled during the Buta rebellion many years ago. I will help you buy back your school supplies at the market sale. The pastor has given me some money from church funds to buy them for you. I will be at the market early in the morning to find out what I should buy. Once I am informed we will separate."

Titi smiled and felt hope come back to her soul for the first time since the tragic robbery.

They were at the market early Saturday morning and Titi informed her teacher. Other Angolan families came to buy back some of the very essential items. No one had much money right after the two holidays. It was hard to see their belongings being sold by the wives of the policemen from the verandah of what had been their own house. By the end of the morning, all had been sold. Their friends bought enough for them to have basic clothes and cooking pots.

By arrangement, Titi met her teacher over by the church.

"You are such a promising student and good example. I hope you are able to keep coming to class. Here is your school bag with all your note books and supplies."

Her teacher's smile was genuine and she felt that somehow she must continue to study.

The garden shack becomes home

With their meager belongings in their baskets, they trudged out to the garden hut. It was built to offer shelter during sudden rains when they were out in their fields.

"Thank God they did not take our land," Mama Nkenda remarked when they arrived.

It was comforting to see their gardening tools and a pail. With two mats, they could all sleep together on the floor.

"At least we have food right here in our gardens," Titi observed with a smile.

Sami could neither eat nor sleep properly because of the shock and public shame he had suffered. He kept dreaming about his cousin who had been a rival back in Luanda. It seems that they both were dealing with illegal diamonds from Luanda. His cousin was caught, and imprisoned, while Sami escaped. When the MPLA army opened the prisons, his cousin was released and became an officer in their army. He was a man to be feared, no matter where he was. Ndoki witches are not limited by borders.

In the ensuing days, Sami cut the small poles necessary to make an extension on their hut. His son had a couple of bundles of thatching straw. Although he had not done any thatching since he was a youth, he did an excellent job thatching their addition. A torrent of rain proved his work to be well done.

Many of the school children were poor. In that sense Titi was far from being the only one.

"I will try to gain respect through my hard work," she mused. "I will never be able to feel good about my clothes again, but then, I have only had nice clothes for a few months of my life."

At the Saturday market Titi was able to sell some of their surplus produce quickly because so many people recognized her as the one who once sold school supplies and nice cloth. The people who had purchased expensive cloth seldom dickered about her prices. They were good customers.

Sami never came to market. "Nsoni! (Shame!)," he kept mumbling whenever anyone asked him if he wanted to go.

Once their little hut was constructed, Sami spent most of his time sitting in a chair he made. He felt too ashamed to work in the gardens at what he called 'women's work'. He had no money at all, with which to do even a tiny bit of buying and selling.

"My protection has failed me. If my fetishes and teki were strong enough, we would never have been robbed. I don't trust the Zairian Witch doctors, and I can't afford the good ones. I am in danger!" he remarked to Titi's aunt.

Sami became very thin and it seemed as though his hair turned gray overnight. He sat in his chair most of the time and only slept during the daylight hours. He was truly afraid for his life. The fear of ndoki power was gradually wearing him down.

Because of the influx of so many refugees from Angola, churches and international aid agencies paid for their medical bills at the mission hospital at Kimpese called IME. Sami's wives decided that he must be examined at the hospital. They made all the arrangements and saw to it that the required specimens of body waste were available to the laboratory people. The day he was seen by the doctor he had his blood specimens given at the Laboratory before 7:30 a.m. By the time he got to see the doctor in the late afternoon, all his lab reports were in his hands. The young Zairian doctor was from a distant province. Sami endeavored to use his Lingala to communicate.

"I can't find anything wrong with you that good food could not cure," the young Doctor informed him after giving him a thorough exam.

"Doctor, I can't sleep at night and I just have no desire to eat. When I do fall asleep at night I am startled awake by horrible dreams," Sami explained hopelessly.

The nurse was Angolan and gave Sami some advice as he led him out of the office.

"This doctor is one of our best, but he can't take away your fears. Fear robs a person of both sleep and appetite. Even our white doctors cannot remove your fear of ndoki witches." Sami nodded because he knew full well that the experienced nurse was right.

Not surprisingly, Sami was even more despondent when he reached home after the rather long walk from the market place where the kimalu malu (taxi pick up truck) had brought them.

"When doctors, and laboratories can't find anything wrong with a sick person, we all know that the cause of the illness must be the activity of ndoki witchcraft," Sami reasoned.

At the hospital Sami had been given a supply of vitamins and some sleeping pills. Although he didn't eat much supper, he took his pills as he had been instructed and before long, drowsiness obliged him to lie down and sleep.

Later, the darkness was pierced by Sami's voice screaming. "No, no, Take it away! Take it away!"

Their hut was in darkness because they let the fire die during the hot months. Lala quickly lit the lantern.

Sami was covered with sweat with a terrified look in his eyes.

"Alfonso was right here in this room! He was in his army uniform and had an mpidi viper in his hand. He was about throw that deadly viper onto my naked body. My shout and the lantern frightened him away!

"I'm as good as dead. All my money, every diamond is gone but he is still angry with me because he thinks I informed on him, and got him imprisoned. Why can't he leave me alone in my misery? Can't he see that I have nothing? I guess I shouldn't be surprised. He must be the ndoki witch who has been sucking the lifeblood from my clan. Only God knows how many died in Luanda about the time we fled here to Zaire. He must be using clan lives to keep himself alive when he is in battle. After all, he is a professional killer now!"

Sami began to weep and the whole household wept with him. Their little garden hut was so isolated that no one came when they wept.

"I have escaped death so many times in these past years. What a pity that I must die in misery because Alfonso has decided to eat me like a cat kills a mouse, by tormenting it to death. It would be better if he simply shot me with his officer's pistol, rather than follow the process of gradually sucking out my life through his witchcraft."

The whole household was silenced by Sami's outburst. He had always done his best to protect them all. Both of his wives felt that he managed their lives well. Titi had been accepted like a true daughter in his warm, generous heart. They all knew that in normal times, such an impasse called for a gathering of Sami's clan to mediate the conflict. Remnants of the clan lived in Luanda and in various refugee communities in Zaire. They didn't even know where most members lived, or who was still alive. There was no solution. Sami would die sooner or later at the hand of the man who had appeared so suddenly in the dark of night.

In the midst of all their gloom, the kind of wind that precedes a thunderstorm began to howl and pull at their thatch roof menacingly. Within a few minutes, torrents of rain were falling outside. A gust of wind blew out their lantern just as a flash of lightning turned night into day. Storms often followed the course of the Lukunga river valley where they lived. The violent storm lasted over an hour and it seemed that their little abode must have been dodging the forks of lightning. The roar of exploding thunder seemed even more menacing than the lightning. No one slept as they all huddled in the new part that Sami had thatched. Somehow being thrust together brought a kind of comfort. The thunder and lightning passed on up the valley before dawn, but the rain was still so heavy in the morning that no one went outside. In the quieter gloom they all fell into asleep from exhaustion.

"Mpidi, viper!" Titi's aunt screamed. "It is here in the house. Get out, Get out!"

Her cries were so urgent that they all rushed out into the rain and mud.

"Alfonso came to me too. He held that serpent in my face. He laughed a haunting laugh and said, "Don't worry! I will throw it on Sami. He cheated me once, now he will pay!' He threw it. That is when I screamed to warn you."

Their belongings were so few; it didn't take long to thoroughly search the little hut.

"Snakes managed by ndoki witches often just disappear. I wish he would just kill me and let me die. The ancestors will judge me justly. Those Portuguese soldiers stole his diamonds, not me!"

Once more the family wept. They felt so helpless and alone in their sudden poverty and vulnerability to the attacks of a ruthless unseen enemy.

"You women need not have any fear. According to the rules of our ancestors only my bloodline is being threatened. Alfonso has no power over anyone but me. I will die because I am defenseless and living like a fugitive without any kinfolk."

In a normal village, neighbors would have rushed to their sides the moment they shrieked in the night. Their hut was so isolated that no one heard them at all.

"Today I really feel like a refugee for the first time," Lala said. "When we came we had possessions and a house to welcome us. Look at us; four adults and two children in a tiny mud hut. If lightning had struck us, no one would have known until someone came to work in the field." While she spoke there were tears in Lala's eyes despite her strength.

The powerful wind and rain had come from the northeast leaving their firewood reasonably dry under the long overhang of the southern eave of their dwelling. In no time Mama Nkenda had a fire roaring and they gathered together to warm up and dry their clothes. Titi made a pot of tea from avocado leaves. They had a little sugar, and certainly this was the day to use it. Titi knew that school would be cancelled because of the rain. Very few children had rainwear although some had sheets of plastic. The roar of rain on the metal roof of the school made it impossible for the teacher to be heard during any serious rainstorm.

By late morning the storm clouds had all blown away to be replaced by a few puffy white ones drifting in a sea of blue. Bright sunlight transformed the world into a bright world filled with life. It didn't take long for their clothes and sleeping mats to dry. The children played around Sami and the three women planted manioc cuttings with modest hope. There was something very healing about planting for the future. Manioc took a year to mature. It took some degree of faith to keep planting and planning ahead. Mid-afternoon, Lala went to get the children because Sami wanted to go find some ripe palm nuts for the family.

On the north side of the Lukunga, Sami had located some unattended palm trees. Some trees he had trimmed up to produce fruit, while others he had stripped for wine production. Working slowly he had made himself a little sanctuary where he could work at 'man's work'. He was actually surprised to find any neglected palm trees at all. It was probably because the women did most of the farming along the river and they don't climb palm trees.

Sami did not realize just how weak he had become. Walking slowly he had managed to cut down a stalk of palm fruit. He actually carried it on his head as far as the swinging bridge over the river. He sat down to rest and fell into a deep sleep from fatigue and all the stress.

The women were alarmed when Sami was not home when they arrived at dusk. Immediately the two wives set out to look for him while Titi cared for the children and prepared supper. They both knew the way to his little palm grove, but were shocked to find him on the ground near the bridge.

"He's dead!" the two women said in unison.

They were relieved when he was startled awake by their shout.

"Alfonso has sucked out my strength like a thirsty man drains a calabash of water. My strength was all gone when I reached this bridge. I don't know whether I can walk or not." Sami remarked as he struggled to his feet.

They were greatly relieved to find that some of his strength had returned while he slept. Lala carried the stalk of palm fruit while Mama Nkenda walked beside him with her arm locked on his to support him.

Dark powers invoked

When supper was finished, Sami cleared his throat to speak in what turned out to be a family conference. Rest and food had restored him enough to express his thoughts very clearly, as they sat together on their mats conversing by firelight.

"Nkenda, you have been a good wife. You gave me four children. They are good children, but they have no way to help us. Lala, your two children are small but with their kind hearts, I know that they will care for you in your old age.

"Titi, your life has been very hard for a young person. You watched your mother die, and in due time you cared for your grandmother until she too left this world. Soon you will see me die too. I have lived sixty-six years and had a prosperous life up until these days. I have been delighted to have you as part of our household. I no longer have any money to help you go to school. The only thing I have to give you is my blessing. Care for them when they are old," He charged. "The war has robbed us of our normal helpers. Titi, I see you as one of our children and I am thankful for you."

Sami talked a long time about his life, his relatives, and each of their children. When he finally finished, there was a hushed silence punctuated only by his heavy breathing.

Suddenly he pounded the earth beside him three times with his fist.

"Let that ndoki Alfonso and all his descendents be totally cursed forever! Never will any of my children marry his descendents!"

The women were stunned into electric silence.

Grasping his raffia bag of protective charms, fetishes and teki idols, Sami continued his tirade. Slowly he drew out a hideous nail studded wooden teki in the form of a man. None of the women had ever seen this teki before. Little wonder the police had been afraid to keep Sami's sacred sack!

The wood was almost black. White cowry shells filled the eye sockets. Black pitch held a mirror cover over a cavity in the middle of the carving. Nails, and other sharp pieces of metal, stuck out randomly all over the body making it look like a demonic porcupine. Every sharp object had been driven in with hate over the years. The intention had been either to kill or cause severe suffering.

With grim determination Sami pounded a three-inch nail into the carving with a stone they used in the kitchen.

"Suffer, Alfonso, suffer! Suffer long, and die! I curse you with all the powers of our ancestors and this teki made for my grandmother! Die in misery! Let your wives be barren so there is no one to remember you!"

By the time Sami had finished, he was exhausted and the whole household was trembling from the impact of the evil and hatred expressed so powerfully. Darkness seemed to permeate their very souls. It was as though they had all witnessed a brutal murder taking place right in before their eyes.

"I will die before long. Alfonso has threatened me, and breached my defenses. I have taken revenge, just as my uncle would have wished. The honor of my vumu (bloodline) has been avenged. Our Ancestors are my witnesses!"

All the women felt a powerful, frightening oppression that left them fearful and deeply depressed. What they had witnessed seemed too filled with hate to bring any relief.

"I feel as though our whole household is surrounded by a deep cloud of evil," Mama Nkenda was the first to break the silence.

"Of course we feel the evil. We know that Sami's dream and mine were in total agreement. This makes us sure that Alfonso is the ndoki attacker. Sami used the teki idol his uncle gave him to take revenge, as it was his duty to do. If the ancestors reinforce his act of revenge, it could be that Sami might be free from his attacker. In this world you have to fight evil with evil. It is all so frightening."

Titi hesitated to reply but felt she had to express her feelings.

"This battle of witchcraft is just like the war in Angola. Many young soldiers are spending their youth trying to kill each other. Father is not evil but he kills others who are probably no more evil than he. Hate causes many innocent people to suffer."

They agreed that they didn't have the money to pay some nganga shaman or ngunza prophet to reverse the inevitable. There was no question about the attack on Sami. They would just have to wait and see if Sami's curse had the power to stop his enemy.

They were all grateful for the firelight because no one wanted to face the darkness. When nature called, they went by twos to their latrine. Sleep eluded everyone, until exhaustion closed their eyelids.

The next outburst came from Titi, crying out from her nightmare. "No! No!" she screamed and awoke crying.

"Sami's horrible teki was hovering like an angry eagle right over there above Sami. It looked so horrible. What can it mean?"

A long silence ensued broken at last by Sami. "Your vision is good news. It means that the ancestors have empowered the teki to act. It is a good sign."

"Well, I never want to see that horrible teki again. Everything about kindoki witchcraft frightens and overwhelms me. Even in my childhood, I have seen the hateful, wanton acts of ndoki witches. They ate all my baby brothers, my mother, my grandmother, and family members of some of my friends. They seem to be behind everything that is tragic or evil. I have seen where our ancestors threw the condemned ndoki witches over the Great Falls to crush them on the rocks below. I have watched people being buried with pots of dried red peppers covering their heads, totally robbed of dignity. We are surrounded by evil. Killing war ravages our land. Even as refugees living in a tiny hut in the field, we cannot escape the destructive power of ndoki witches."

Everyone was relieved to see a bright sunrise. After bathing down at the river, Titi headed off to school, glad for a change of atmosphere.

"School is where I love to be. My thoughts are so different here. I am beginning to understand the French language now, almost as well as Portuguese. If I can learn to write, what I can say, I could be considered as one of the better students," she whispered to herself, without even moving her lips.

The morning flew by, filled with routine schoolwork.

"Before you return to your homes I will lead us in prayer." Titi listened very attentively to the prayer of this man she respected.

"Lord of heaven and earth, we thank you for the beautiful living things you have created. We thank you that your book tells us that you love us, even when we know we have failed you, or feel very unlovable, and discouraged. You are more powerful than any evil force. You want us to trust you, so we can live in peace despite our circumstances. Please help each of us to trust you to manage our hearts, and the details of our lives. Please bring us all back to class tomorrow. Help us to trust you just like little children trust their loved ones. We pray in Jesus name, amen."

The peace and love of his prayer touched Titi. She felt a blanket of peace and hope as strong and as real as the cloud of hatred and fear that dominated her home the night before.

With her head still bowed, Titi prayed her own prayer. "O God, if you really love me, please help me trust you and find peace in my frightened heart, I really need your help."

As she hurried home she was amazed at the new kind of peace and hope she felt inside.

"I hope it is true that God cares about us," she whispered out loud as she hurried along the path.

When she reached their hut, everyone was gone. Changing quickly into her work clothes, she decided to run to the river and try out the fish trap she had made. It was as much like her grandmother's traps as she could remember. She was anxious to set her trap by a rock formation that seemed to be very much like the special spot where her grandmother had fished so successfully back in Kiula village.

Within a half-hour she had found a promising spot. She carefully slid her weighted trap into the current. Rapidly, it was carried to the deep hole eroded by water rushing around the boulders jutting out from both banks.

For twenty minutes she stood motionless, holding the cord. She knew that the palm fruit inside her trap was just the right degree of ripeness, according to her Grandmother's methods.

Suddenly there was a tug in the trap and she pulled it back to find a large fat eel and a very small catfish. She squealed with delight as she split the eel's head with her machete. In no time she had her trophy gutted and skinned.

"God is good," she found herself saying, just as her teacher sometimes said in class.

She reset her trap and hurried on a cross path to join Lala and her aunt in the manioc field. They were surprised to see her running from a different direction than they had expected.

"Look what I caught for us."

Holding up the eel for them to see she was pleased to see encouragement written in their broad smiles. She excitedly explained everything.

"I did everything just the way Nkaka taught me, and it worked again here in our river."

"I'm sure, Nkaka is helping you," Mama Nkenda remarked. "She taught your mother all about fishing and she taught me all about farming and weaving mats. I am sure she must have loved you. It is great to have ancestors who want to help us. Perhaps we will eat well again because she wants to help you for being so kind to her."

"Why don't you run on home now and begin cooking the eel so we can eat well tonight. We are making good progress here in the manioc field, but a good meal would cheer up everyone," Lala suggested.

Sami was worried when he saw smoke billowing from their tiny house. He laughed out loud with relief and delight when he found the eel spread out on the rack.

"I thought I would smoke cook it inside because the new thatch roof needs to be smoked so the insects will not eat it," Titi explained.

Sami felt a little better and had managed to collect a calabash of palm wine. His pockets were filled with ripe palm fruits he had collected under an old untrimmed palm tree. It couldn't be climbed until its old branches were trimmed off, and he didn't have strength enough for that heavy work yet. The palm fruits on the underside of a stalk fall out by themselves when they become ripe enough.

"I have to gather palm fruits like an old woman until I get back my strength if I ever do."

It was a big job preparing food for the family, but Titi flew at the multiple tasks energetically. Everything was ready when the others came in at dusk. The atmosphere in the home had certainly changed since the night before. It was as though they had some big battle behind them.

Everyone ate heartily. They had not been able to afford fish or meat, so the eel was greatly appreciated. That night everyone slept better. Titi had the only dream to report in the morning.

"Nkaka came to me last night. She was contented and happy. 'Titi I am happy to see my spirit in you. You fish just the way I taught you,' she said. Then she blessed me like she did when I was younger."

"Your grandmother was never indebted to anyone. She has found a way to help you. I think we are going to get a lot of help from the fish in the Lukunga, thanks to you," Mama Nkenda predicted.

"From now on, school work and fishing will be your most important assignments. If there is time left over, you can help us in our fields."

With excitement in her soul, Titi ran to tend her trap just as dawn was breaking. To her delight, she had two good-sized catfish in her trap. *"Fish bring a good price in the market,"* Titi thought. *"Perhaps fishing will help me pay the school costs so I can keep on in school"*.

"God is good!" Titi found herself repeating as she hurried back home to get changed for school.

The family seemed to adjust gradually to their new circumstances. They would be poor but not hungry. Titi might be able to stay in school. Perhaps Sami would not live too long. They felt that come what may, they could face life together.

The youth choir continued to be a bright spot in Titi's busy life. Quite often Mama Nkenda accompanied Titi to church. It was difficult to be so poor, so suddenly, especially for her aunt. Once they were rather well dressed. Now their clothes were definitely poor.

Not long before Easter, the director of Titi's choir announced that the Cement Company had transferred him to Kinshasa. Titi's heart broke a little. She had such a crush on the gifted leader that she wished he would stay forever. In her heart, she had to admit that the attraction was mostly one-sided. Now that her clothes were anything but pretty, he hadn't seemed to notice her as much.

"A student from the Kimpese Pastors School will take over the choir next week," he explained. The whole choir was sad to hear of the transfer.

"No one will ever be like you," they said sadly.

"No one will be like me but that will mean that you will get a chance to learn from someone else who will have new talents. Just give him a chance. Don't waste time comparing him with me. Wait until you meet Petelo. He has sung in the famous Kimpese choir directed by Master Diawako. Wait and see."

REFUGEE REUNION

Titi was still feeling sad as she went off to choir practice Saturday afternoon. She found her heart pounding, when Petelo was presented. *"He looks just like my schoolteacher from Lufu days,"* Titi thought as her eyes grew bigger. She had heard that he was killed on the way out from Angola. When he spoke, all her doubts disappeared and she could hardly stay in her seat.

"Will he recognize me? I was just a little girl when he left." Her heart kept pounding as the choir members introduced themselves one by one.

"Are you the Titi I taught at Lufu?" he asked excitedly, grasping both of her hands while he studied her face. Her tears of joy gave the answer.

"I could never forget you. You were the best pupil I ever taught," Petelo said quietly with emotion.

Titi's heart was screaming, *"We belong together!"* although her lips didn't move. As the new choir director, he had to move on to give the formal handshake to each choir member. Just the moment his eyes were free, they flew back to Titi.

Fortunately, Petelo was a very skilled choir director, just as their previous director had said. The transition was not difficult because he was able to help them sing with great freedom, as they had been accustomed to do.

By the time practice was over it was dusk, and Titi had had to slip away a little early because of the distance she had to travel. How she yearned to talk with Petelo or Master Pedro as she had called him. She had a thousand questions and her heart was filled with unquenchable yearning.

All the way home she kept repeating her teacher's phrase, "God is good!" Over and over she said it out loud to herself.

"He remembered me, he remembered me!"

Titi's mind was spinning most of the way home until she remembered how overwhelmed she had felt when the former choir leader had spoken to her with his eyes. I need to keep calm, and not raise any expectations at home. I will simply tell them that our new choir director is the same person that taught me in Lufu primary school several years ago.

It was too dark to think of tending her fish trap. She thought she might go later when the moon was higher in the sky. Once inside, Titi calmly told her family that the young teacher they all knew from Lufu days was now studying to become a pastor, and that he had been asked to lead their youth choir because of the transfer of the choir director they knew.

"I had heard that he was shot in an ambush near the border."

"I'm glad to hear he is alive. He was the finest young teacher Lufu school ever had. You wouldn't be in school today were it not for him," Mama Nkenda pointed out.

It was not hard to cover up her excitement, because the two wives were so deeply concerned for Sami. He seemed to make progress for a few days, but had become despondent and discouraged again. His appetite could not be aroused, even with his favorite foods. The despair written in his eyes spelled doom.

The women had prepared a delicious meal complete with fish and fumbwa. He leaned listlessly against the wall, with his eyes on the ground, completely ignoring the good food before him.

Titi speaks to Sami like a wise elder

Titi felt it was time to speak to her beloved uncle.

"Who do you want to help anyway, Alfonso or us? When you refuse to eat any of this good food, you are pleasing Alfonso and helping him accomplish his desire to see you dead. Why don't you work against him, and do everything you can, to live with us as long as possible? You have always been a great merchant and clever planner. When the MPLA and Cubans armies were headed for Lufu, did you tell us all to sit on the road and die? No, you used all your cleverness to hire a truck when that was thought to be impossible. You brought your family and many others to safety. You did not die in Angola like many others.

"When you refuse to eat it is the same as if you had refused to get your family out of Lufu. Right now you are sitting there convinced that you can't fight your enemy. Nkaka told me a kind of proverb. She told me that poison could only harm you if you swallow it. She told me that curses and threatening words could only kill you if you swallow them. She was very wise and outlived most of her enemies because she refused to swallow their threats.

"Please, Sami, vomit out those threatening words of Alfonso. Eat, even if it is only to spite your enemy. We want you to eat, and do all you can to live because you love us. As I see it the choice is yours. Either try to live and get strong every way you know how, or let the words of Alfonso kill you because you choose to swallow them and do nothing at all to vomit them up!"

When Titi finished, there was a deep silence in the household.

"Titi you have spoken like a wise elder and you are completely right," replied Sami "Why should I help Alfonso my enemy? I will eat for you, Titi. I want to see your wedding whenever that day comes."

His reply encouraged them all. Titi found it uncanny that he spoke of her wedding day as though he could see the yearnings in her heart for Petelo.

"Whenever I marry you must be there! Please don't swallow any more of Alfonso's poison words. Eat our good food and help us with your wisdom."

Mama Nkenda, and Lala, looked on in total surprise.

"My mother, your Nkaka, is truly speaking through you. Certainly she would never have survived if she had swallowed the hateful words thrown at her by many of us. Titi, you have learned from the wisest of elders your grandmother and the old village chief. It is wonderful to see a young person who has been willing to learn from the very same people I spurned. I would like to think that Alfonso will die long before Sami. If he does, it will because of the wisdom you have brought us."

Sami ate a reasonable amount and fell asleep soon after he ate.

When Titi prepared to go off to tend her trap in the bright moonlight, Lala asked if she could come along. Titi was pleased to have her company. The night was beautiful. To their delight, the trap contained a good-sized catfish.

"If this pattern continues we will get through this crisis," Lala whispered with deep sincerity. "It means a lot that you accept me just as though I were you mother's sister too. If we can all work together, we will sing again some day."

Not surprisingly, Sami's strength began to return little by little. Good food, some work, and good rest worked wonders.

One morning he had a dream to report. "The mpidi serpent came after me again last night." He said somberly, casting gloom over the house. "When I threatened it with my walking stick, it fled. Titi's wisdom is good medicine."

Everyone was relieved with the encouraging conclusion to his dream. They were winning.

Each Saturday market brought them a steady little income from the delicious smoked fish they sold. Lala suggested that they prepare pieces of smoked fish in hot pepper and tomato sauce ready for eating with small snack-sized kwanga. Selling their fish as market snacks doubled their income.

"If we could just get enough money to enable Sami to begin selling again, I think he would regain his dignity and his health."

It took two months for them to gather enough money to buy a twenty-kilogram pack of frozen mackerel at the cold storage place in Lukala. Sami constructed a better fish rack from some bits of metal he scrounged from behind the cement factory. While the mackerel was being smoked, Lala made more of her delicious sauce from their own peppers, tomatoes and some salt. Their little business flourished with two or three kinds of fish available. They had mackerel from the store together with catfish and eels from the Lukunga River.

Sami didn't sell fish, but he helped plan how they would market their goods. He kept the house well supplied with palm fruit. They needed a considerable supply of palm fruit to make some of their better fish sauces. He made enough palm wine for himself and the few visitors who came by. Little by little, the sparkle returned to his eyes and he began to take long walks to visit the local merchants to try and figure out their next move. The merchants were all respectful because they knew why his commerce failed. Sometimes they were glad to talk business with him just to get his valuable advice.

A second chance

One day the gray-haired manager of the local Nogueira store called him into his little office for a talk. The old man was scheduled to enter the hospital soon.

"Would you consider managing this store while I am laid up? If it goes well, we could talk business again after I get out."

Sami was as surprised as he was pleased. The old man continued, "I saw how well you managed your cloth sales in the market. You could live in the little apartment in the back. That would make it unnecessary for me to hire someone to sleep here."

Although Sami knew that he would not earn very much money, the chance to get back into commerce thrilled him and gave him hope. The whole family was excited at this unexpected opportunity. They felt that if Lala and the children went with him, she could do the accounts and keep careful records. Titi and her aunt would stay in their hut because their fishing operation was keeping the family going, and allowing Titi to continue in school.

"God is good!" Titi repeated to herself as she headed out to choir practice.

That very afternoon Sami, Lala, and the children moved into the Nogueira store. Sami was recovering. Titi's heart sang as she anticipated another afternoon near Petelo, her beloved teacher from the past. They had managed to have several chats before or after choir practice.

Petelo

Petelo (Pedro in Portuguese) had graduated from the Sona Bata High School, which had been founded in order to allow half of the student body to be made up of Angolans. He did not have enough money to bribe the state officials, so he was lacking a state diploma. Titi found it difficult to understand what he meant when he explained that he felt that God wanted him to become a pastor.

"I had my High School diploma and was asking God to show me what he wanted me to do with my life. I had a dream in which the old pastor I knew in my childhood came to me and put his hands on my head to bless me."

"Did the old pastor say anything when he came?" Titi asked earnestly.

"Every time he came in my dreams, he always blessed me, and said I would be a good pastor. That dream must have come to me four or five different times. I concluded that the dream was God's answer to my request for guidance. I applied to Kimpese and am in my second year now."

There was great warmth in his eyes each time they talked. He was most interested to hear of the amazing progress she had made in school. He was very careful not to reveal his feelings toward her. There were always others around whenever they talked. He was very careful not to show any favoritism within the choir. Eventually Titi understood that Pedro was directing the choir as a part of his training. The Pastor was supervising him directly. Reports about his work and his comportment were being sent back to the Pastors Training School.

With so little church experience, Titi had no idea about how carefully the elders watched the behavior of choir leaders. Far too many young girls had been lead astray by these young heroes. Parents and church leaders wanted to avoid scandal at all costs. Young girls were expected to be virgins when they became candidates for marriage and the serious church folk were always suspicious of choir directors who were basically unknown. Young Pastors in training were expected to live in such a way that they maintained a spotless reputation. Titi and Petelo became reacquainted gradually without many romantic overtones.

As Titi said later, "Our eyes always spoke intimately if only for fleeting moments."

When the old manager of Nogueira came back from the hospital six weeks later, he was delighted with the management Sami and Lala had given. The inventory was completely in order, and the accounts showed everything that had been received or spent. They had run the store more profitably than he had been able to himself. Lala grew up in Luanda and had excellent ideas about ways to display the products which they had for sale.

Lala made one trip to Kinshasa to buy material for women's dresses. She had made excellent choices and some women began coming to the store when they realized that she was the same person who had been the best supplier in the market. Women liked her choices so their sales increased. The accounts were so clear that the old manager had no doubt.

"I want you two to keep running the store for me just the way you have been doing. From now we will divide the true profit equally between us. I am so glad for your help." The old man lowered his voice almost to a whisper. "Most people don't know it, but my grandparents were from the Zombo tribe like you. We Zombos are good merchants. That is why I called you in the first place. Don't tell anyone that I am a Zombo. Some local people wouldn't like that." With a handshake and a Portuguese style embrace, the agreement was settled.

Both Sami and Lala were delighted. They knew that they wouldn't earn a lot of money in that little shop but they felt vindicated. Someone in the commercial community trusted them. A whole new sense of worth transformed their outlooks. Lala was quick to remind Sami that they both had Titi's wisdom to thank. She was the one who had persuaded Sami to choose life when he had indeed already chosen death. Just as soon as they had the funds, they began to buy respectable clothes for all four of them but Titi was the first to benefit.

There was more work in the fields with Lala working in the store, but she came back to help when she could. Titi's fishing expertise kept on supplying nutritious food as well enough cash to pay for her school costs. Because they could buy sufficient soap, even their old clothes looked better. School went very well for Titi. Sami's recovery took a burden off her mind. Sharing the little house with the aunt she loved even turned it into a little sanctuary.

Titi's teacher told her he was convinced that she would move into high school for the next school year. The primary school found it difficult to classify her. Her letter of recommendation from her first grade teacher was the only document she had. They understood that she taught school for a number of years, learning her Portuguese language from the old chief she taught to read. They decided to classify her at the end of her first year in Zaire when they really could assess her knowledge.

Being a bit older, she applied herself to her studies with amazing diligence. Her teacher helped her with French as much as he could and was amazed at her capacity to take advantage of every similarity between Portuguese and French to forge ahead. Her years of teaching elementary arithmetic gave her a very solid foundation that put her at the top of her class in math. True to her teacher's predictions, she passed the high school entrance exam with a comfortable margin. She was not tall, and being only a few years older than the others, she expected that her high school peers could accept her as a normal student.

The list of those who were successful in passing the high school entrance exam was posted outside the school principal's office for all to read.

The green silk scarf

During the choir practice, Petelo congratulated each of the choir members who had been promoted into high school. When the practice was over, Petelo was chatting with his singers before they went home. He called Titi aside for a moment and slipped her a tiny package.

"Don't open it until you reach home," he whispered.

Titi's curiosity goaded her into running all the way home.

"Look!, Mama Mbuta. Petelo gave me this package and asked me not to open it until I reached, home."

Even as she spoke she was removing the paper. Inside she found a small, bright green silk scarf. It was the kind girls wore as a decorative tie back for their hair, or as a pretty splash of color around their necks.

"It's beautiful, and I have envied the girls who have them. What does he mean by giving me this gift?"

Mama Mbuta smiled. "It means that you have a special place in his heart. If you wear it, it tells him you accept his affection, and are willing for the relationship to progress. He was very wise to ask you to open your gift in my presence. He is not interested in a secret relationship with any devious intentions. However, there is a possible problem. By his accent in Kikongo, I know he is from Kongo dia Ntotila, and we are Zombos. Normally our tribes do not marry. In the Angolan war some of the Zombos have been fighting with the men from his tribe. I am telling you of our traditions. Personally, I have been very impressed with him since he first came to Lufu to teach. If you really like him and want to get to know him better, I think you should proudly wear your little scarf when you go to church Sunday. If this is your desire, I will help you in this exciting adventure for your heart."

Titi did not fall asleep quickly instead, she had a long talk with her heart. *"Petelo is kind and thoughtful. His eyes have been telling me that he is fond of me. Probably, my eyes have given him my heart's response long ago. It is true that my heart beats faster whenever he looks at me with those big, kind eyes of his.*

"I wonder why he has chosen me? There are many fine girls in our choir. Some of them are from his region in Angola. I would be lucky to have Petelo to love and care for me. He would be wonderful with children. I am still very young, and I have not finished as much schooling as I really want. He will graduate next year and villages will not want him to come as their pastor unless he is married.

"I am not even baptized. A pastor could never marry a girl who is not a member of the church. I know that I could join the baptismal class and pass the deacon's examination. I could get baptized. I have behaved well so I have no scandal connected with my name. They would let me join the church I am sure. I need to talk to him about some of these important issues. How can we ever talk, when he is not supposed to talk with any girl alone? My Mama Mbuta will need to guide me like the wise mother she is."

With her course of action resolved, she slipped into a sleep with a new smile on her young face. When morning came, Titi was pleased that she and her aunt were alone in their little abode. Hearing her aunt stirring it seemed appropriate to tell her of her dream.

"I had a marvelous dream. Petelo came and took me by both hands and looked right into my eyes and told me he loved me and wanted me to be the mother of his children. As he was speaking, my mother came by and smiled at us both. That is when our rooster crowed and ended my dream. My mother gave me the kind of smile she always used to give me when I had done something just the way she wanted me to do it. What do you think it means?"

"I think it is very clear that your mother approves of Petelo. If she were opposed she would have let you know of her disapproval."

"Today we must dig our peanuts while there is still moisture in the ground. The rains are about over. You know how hard it is to dig peanuts from dry ground. Lala is coming to help us today too. I think you should talk to Lala about Petelo while we work. She is much younger and has lived in the city. She will give you good advice and keep it all a secret too."

It was still early when they began harvesting the peanuts. Their hut had been built in the middle of their farmland initially as a shelter from the rains, but also as a way of keeping their crop from being stolen. The peanuts were literally growing all around them.

"Sami says that if he can save the money, he would like to put metal roofing on the little house," Mama Nkenda told Titi with a contented smile.

"That would be kind. In many ways it is easier for us all if Lala and her children can live at the store and help with the work there."

"We all need gardens, and I would rather live out here. If we improved the little house, Sami could come out to be with me whenever he choose."

Standing up straight for a moment's rest, Titi looked right at her aunt.

"You amaze me, not many women can get along with their husband's younger wife like you do."

Her aunt reflected a moment before she replied.

"Long ago I decided that conflict would help no one. Lala has been a great help to Sami in his life as a merchant. I like Lala, and we both respect Sami. I am too old to have any more babies. Many men simply abandon their wives when they pass the childbearing age. I have seen far to many women bitter and abandoned when they get to my age. Bitter women soon pass their bitterness along to their children. Most bitter old women are the prime suspects of being ndoki witches with all that entails.

"I am thankful for the relationships we have, so I intend to cooperate with Lala and Sami. I am fortunate. I have given birth to four living children, if the war had not taken one of them. Other Angolan women respect me. We will always be foreigners and refugees in the eyes of most of the local people. At the church I feel the most acceptance. It helps us feel a part of something."

Lala arrived in good time, carrying a special digging fork she bought at the farm center called CEDECO.

"They told me it is good for digging peanuts when the soil is getting a bit hard." She said, as she shook hands in her their normal greeting. "It feels good to get away form the store and children for a while. I know I am a city girl but I do like fieldwork, especially at harvest time. A little school girl is taking care of the children."

The digging fork proved to be a tremendous help. Deep digging loosened all the soil around the peanuts so they could be lifted out without leaving any stuck behind. They all took turns doing everything, so no one would get too tired. By late afternoon the whole peanut crop was drying in mounds spread around the field. The peanuts were reasonably fat, and the yield looked to be good. The digging fork enabled them to harvest almost every peanut.

It was quite late in the afternoon when they gathered in the hut for fresh kwanga and smoked catfish with a delicious sauce made with palm oil, peppers and tomatoes.

"We make good food together," Titi remarked with a grin. In this pleasant setting, Titi told Lala all about Petelo.

"My opinion of Petelo is based entirely on his year at Lufu. Remember that he and I are nearly the same age. I heard all the comments of the women folk at the river. Without a single exception, he had a spotless reputation both as a teacher and as a person. That doesn't happen very often!

"In the old days, families told young people whom they could marry. The city has changed all that. Young people are thrown together in their schools, in the church choirs, and in the crowded housing conditions. Wise parents help their children to evaluate the persons they choose. Rebellious young people find ways to make babies together and ask permission to marry only after the girl is pregnant. Parents are so happy at the prospect of a baby that they give permission in the end.

"Petelo is behaving honorably. He wants you to seek the opinion of your family. He seems to me to be an unselfish young many you may trust. You need to understand that there are very few men like him around. Titi, I simply trust your judgment. You are young in years but old in terms of maturity. I wish you had more schooling, but Petelo has had a lot of schooling and will be able to teach you. In addition to Pastors Training, he has earned his high school diploma."

Titi felt excitement growing in her heart as she listened to Lala. All three of her 'mothers' were giving their authorization for her to respond favorably to the young man of her dreams. Lala was not a blood relative but Titi respected her as an older sister.

"If this good weather continues, we will be able to pull the peanuts from the plants and put them out to dry on the warm earth very soon. I think we should all go have a look at our bean crop and call it a day," Mama Mbuta suggested.

The beans were a treasured crop. Everyone loved to eat them, and any surplus could be easily sold. At first glance, they looked very good until they got close to the river. The nsizi rodents were chewing up their precious plants. Larger than rabbits, and eating only plants, they are very destructive.

Lala took a few fresh peanuts and good load of manioc, then went back to the store.

Titi's mind remained centered on Petelo.

"How could I ever be a pastor's wife?" she asked her self over and over. "I have only been thinking about God during this school year. Nkaka used to say that she never prayed to God because she was sure it was silly. God would do what ever he wanted to do. She told me that our elders addressed their prayers to the spirits of our ancestors that empowered their teki idols."

"We talk to our loved ones in the cemetery. We endeavor to keep in harmony with the bisimbi water spirits. We trust our fetish charms to have spirit power enough to protect us from Ndoki witches. It has only been church people who say that they are talking to God when they pray. I am still learning what to think about the teachings from the Bible. I would like to believe what the best Christians believe, but I have not settled all that yet. He may think that because I have a reputation as a good girl, that I am a believer. I am not yet fit to be a pastor's wife. What do you think, Mama Mbuta?"

"He has not asked you to marry him yet," replied her aunt. "I think that he really likes you and hopes that you may become his wife. He is smart enough to know that he needs a chance to get to know you better. Going about things the way he has chosen, we will be able to invite him out here so you can both have good talks without raising any eyebrows. If you know that you are willing to consider him seriously, that is all you need to know for the moment. He is just the kind of person who could help you believe if you really want to. Don't worry unnecessarily!"

Before she knew it time for choir practice had rolled around. Titi took a little longer than usual getting dressed in her best. She had a broad smile on her face when she came to say goodbye to her aunt. The pretty green scarf was attractively displayed around her neck.

"I have never been anxious about my appearance before," she confessed.

Mama Mbuta gave her a tiny treasured bottle of perfume.
"Put on a few drops of this perfume. You look beautiful, my child."

Wearing the "yes" scarf

"Please put a drop of the perfume on my 'yes' scarf," Titi requested with a happy grin on her face.

"You are taking your first step toward Petelo, just as he took his first step toward you when he gave you the scarf."

Petelo had arrived early for the choir practice hoping that perhaps Titi would come a little early too if she had accepted his proposition. Mama Tabita, in her white deacon's uniform, was the only other person in the building when Titi came in shyly. The old lady was dusting the benches and never even looked up from her work.

As Titi walked up the aisle to where Petelo was standing, her heart was pounding and she was sure her face displayed all the feelings in her heart. She went straight to him and shook hands as all the choristers did. A smile dominated his whole face when he saw she was wearing his little gift.

Suddenly the handshake became filled with magic power as he held on to her hand for a long, unforgettable moment.

"Thank you for your trust. You look wonderful! From now on we have a secret. I will not look at you very often when I am directing the choir or someone will guess."

He could say no more because other choir members were coming up to shake hands.

The way he had looked at her, and held her hand told her heart everything it longed to know. A whole new set of sensations rushed through her trim little body and settled in her heart. As Petelo directed the choir she could not take her eyes off him. Fortunately, that was what the choir members were supposed to do.

When the practice was ended, Titi suddenly became aware of two other girls who were trying to capture her Petelo's attention. They were not doing anything new, but Titi was much more observant than she had ever been.

"They should be ashamed of themselves, chasing a man like that. Imagine, that man chose me, and I never chased him for a moment. All I ever did was answer his eyes whenever they spoke to mine." All this discussion was only in her mind.

Titi's farewell handshake to Petelo would have looked the same as all the others. In fact, they gave each other a very special squeeze that sent them both home dreaming.

"Was he pleased? Was he pleased?" Mama Mbuta asked excitedly the moment Titi returned.

"He looked ecstatically happy when I came up wearing his scarf. He told me I looked wonderful. He held my hand and whispered in my ear that we had a secret from now on. He warned me that he would not dare to look at me very often or others would guess our secret. Mama Mbuta, he looked more often than he ever did before."

"Titi, I am so happy for you. When I was married, our parents arranged it all. We had never talked before we were married. I am so lucky that Sami turned out to be a good man.

"You are fortunate that you both have seen a lot of each other before either of you had any thought of marriage. That doesn't happen very often. It is because you knew him long before this year that I trust your judgment. You know that you will probably be poor all your lives if you must live on his income. Money is not everything, and I know that you are very resourceful. Does Petelo have many relatives here in Congo Zaire?

"I think that Petelo and I will need to exchange letters so we can begin to answer each other's questions. I will slip him a note when we shake hands at Choir practice."

"I have never been able to write a letter so I think you have a great idea."

The uncertainties of war and refugee life produced two kinds of reactions in the thinking of most of the young people involved. Either they rebelled against tradition or embraced it as an element of identity and security. Titi had done many things that young girls had never done traditionally. She also had a deep sense of the value of being both respected and respectable. It comes as no surprise, that her letters were examples of good taste and sincerity.

Lukala June 12, 1981

Dear Petelo,

Your kind attentions have both surprised and thrilled me. I have treasured fond memories of you ever since you helped open my curious mind with your patient and wise teaching back in Lufu. That period seems to have taken place in some other world, in some distant past. No doubt we have both had many life-changing experiences since those days. When we have an occasion to have a good talk, I am sure we will have a lot to share with one another.

I am honored to wear the beautiful scarf you sent me to signal your interest in me. I am sure we each have many questions about the other. My aunt, with whom I lived in Lufu, is the only blood relative that I have located here in Zaire. Can you imagine, my whole clan consists of my aunt and myself. Do you have many relatives living here in Zaire?

Like you, I will be very careful to keep our secret as long as we both think we should. I'm glad you can say so much with your eyes. They compensate for our lack of opportunities to chat.

I have always loved singing under your direction ever since you began.

Respectfully yours, Titi

This letter was very carefully folded until it could be hidden in the palm of her hand. When she met Petelo on Sunday, she slipped him her note, when they shook hands. The surprised grin on his face gave her deep satisfaction. Apart from that moment, which went unnoticed by everyone else, Titi simply blended with the choir and sang with all her heart. The real surprise came for Titi when she took her turn to give Petelo the farewell handshake, along with all the others. When he shook her hand warmly he also transferred his note to her. It was interesting that each had written to the other. His note was not a reply to hers but rather the first of a number of letters he intended to write.

Lukala June 12, 1981

Dear Titi,

It gives me great pleasure to write to you. I have decided that I will only give you this letter if I should have the great good fortune to receive one from you.

I reasoned and prayed a long time before I offered you the little green scarf to express my intentions. Titi, you left an indelible impression on me in that wonderful year when you learned to read and write before my eyes. Your sparkle and enthusiasm spurred me on to do my very best.

Can you imagine my delight to discover that the wonderful little girl I taught in Lufu had become the beautiful young woman that you are? Because I am a few years older I suppose that I look much the same as I did in Lufu. You, on the other hand, have changed from a little girl to a woman during those same years. Despite all the changes that you have experienced, I still feel that I know you because of that memorable year when I knew you as a schoolgirl.

If it is God's will I want you to become my wife and the mother of our children. I must confess that I don't know God's will about this yet, but I want you to know that I feel strongly that it was God who brought us together this very year, when I hoped to find a wife. I would like to share learning experiences with my wife for my last year of pastoral studies.

Titi, I have no money and no family here in Zaire to help me. My uncles are all in the FNLA army if they are still alive. I have had no news from any family members for over three years now.

I want to marry you, but I am powerless to make it happen without money, and without family to help fulfil my obligations. Even after I graduate and am assigned a pastorate, I will have very little money. Do you understand my dilemma?

I would love to respect our traditions offering gifts to your family in gratefulness for them allowing you to marry me.

One of my professors, Pastor Makena, is willing to represent me like an uncle and kimpovila (spokesman) in a meeting with your family.

I can't believe that I am telling you all my limitations in this first letter. The look in your eyes, and the touch of your hands gives me the courage to ask the impossible. In the end, if you do marry me this summer, God will need to be behind it or it will never happen. I am aware that I am making a most unusual request.

Please ask God to lead you before you reply. I would love to have your yes immediately but I have the patience to wait as long as it may take for you to give me a reply from your heart.

With deep respect, Petelo Mavitidi

Sunday afternoon as soon as they returned to their little house after church, Titi read Petelo's letter to her aunt in its entirety.

Her aunt was very attentive throughout the reading and remained in total silence for a considerable length of time before she offered any response.

"Child, this Petelo is an amazing young man. Never in my life have I known of a person to be so open and honest. It is most unusual to have a young man give you all the reasons why you might refuse to marry him. To be too poor to marry and not have any family to help is most unfortunate. I have never heard of such a proposal for marriage. What he is saying is that he loves you, and wants to marry you, but he can't meet even one of the normal requirements for marriage.

"I wish he were a Zombo like us. He certainly seems like someone we can trust despite his poverty. This past year, we learned what it was to have nothing at all. I feel sure that God must have been helping us. I would far rather have a poor man I could love and trust than a dozen rich men whose word meant nothing at all. We must carefully seek advice. As he said in your letter, if it all works out for you to get married, you could certainly take it as a sign from God, I think. I will talk with Sami and Lala to see what they think. These are certainly strange days. In my youth, I never could have imagined that an older woman would ever be encouraging a young girl to make her own choice very carefully. That is what I hear my heart saying to you."

"Being a refugee forces us to change a thousand customs," replied Titi. "We have lost our land, our tribes and our clans. We don't even have our own cemeteries. We have been stripped naked. Two refugees getting married face a whole new situation. Circumstances of our refugee life strip us of our customs, along with everything else. We need guidance to think about marriage in this new circumstance. We may need to make new customs. Like you, I feel the need to think a lot. I don't know much about praying but I am going to begin to pray for God to show us what he wants. In some ways, it must have been easier to have wise elders, aunts, uncles, grandparents and older brothers and sisters making this kind of decision for a young person like me."

Her aunt spoke quietly, "Don't try to wish back the past. The way we made decisions then seemed reasonable, as long as we had good leaders. Selfish leaders ruined the lives of too many young girls by giving them in marriage to their old cronies. These days call for other ways of making decisions. Clans don't live face to face any more even here in Zaire. We know that North Angola has been fragmented like pounded manioc. A kwanga contains pieces of many different manioc roots. We refugees are like kwanga."

Titi and her aunt didn't fall asleep quickly. Each one was lost in thought. Their last conversation was about Titi's mother who died the same year that the Lufu people fled to Congo Zaire. Their chat was bound to influence their dreams.

Both slept soundly until aroused by their solitary rooster. He screamed his head off each morning and never heard an answering call because they were in an isolated house rather than a village.

"Mother came to me again last night. She put her arm around me and told me to marry Petelo, if I loved and trusted him. That was all she said before turning to walk away. Mama Mbuta, that is the second time she has encouraged me."

"I had a dream about my life when I was your age," responded her aunt. "The whole extended family had gathered to respond to Sami's clan concerning his request to marry me. The elders said that Sami was a dependable and trustworthy young man from a good family that they respected. They told me that they thought our marriage would be good for both families. They asked me if I was willing to marry him. I wanted to be married, and my family had chosen a young man, I had no desire to go against their decision so I said yes as they expected me to do."

"I have trusted Petelo since I was a school girl 11 years old. You all trusted him the whole year he was among you. Lala said that he had a spotless reputation among the young women of that period."

"Child, you are right. I remember that two different women tried to push their daughters to entice him. He discreetly refused all the food they sent his way by asking that it be given to an old deranged man kept by the village. Your mother gave you good advice when she came to you. Trust and love are the qualities that will see you through the hardest days of your life.

"If the boy has no money and no family, there is no point in discussing the traditional bride price. How ridiculous it would be for me to set a bride price all alone without my clan. I don't need to receive a bride price to give you my blessing. I will give you the blessing of your bloodline, if you want it. Be assured of that."

Taking her aunt by both hands Titi expressed her feelings. "Mama Mbuta, you are amazing. You have no money, and you could eat (spend) the whole bride price on yourself. You have honored our clan's traditions all your life. Now you are willing to do whatever will help another generation to find its way. It is your example that encourages me to keep myself as pure as you were for your wedding day.

"I see the rebellion and conflict all around me, as young people do shameful things to get even with their elders, or shame them into granting their wishes. I am a fortunate girl, I know and value our traditions, but my aunt is willing to understand today's challenges and work out ways and means to allow me to make my own decision.

"Your support is a very important to me. It would be heartbreaking for me to go against your advice. Most girls never get to talk with their families honestly and openly like I can. All the time, I hear the schoolgirls talking about the things they are hiding from their families. Thank you for being my Mama Mbuta."

"When you reply to Petelo," said her aunt. "I think you should tell him that your family would like to meet with his spokesman, his teacher, pastor Makena. We could meet him at the house behind the store next Sunday. I will go into Lukala to talk with Sami and Lala. You can begin to write your letter. I am sure you will need time to do that. I will be back in an hour or so with their reply.

"We don't have any tables and chairs here, so I would rather meet at the store. When we all listen to this pastor who has been teaching Petelo for several years, I think we will feel better prepared to know what to do. It is amazing that you may become a pastor's wife and none of us ever went to church until a few months ago. Petelo is wise to want to have you in school with him so you can learn how to be a pastors wife some day."

After a simple breakfast Mama Mbuta went off to Lukala carrying Petelo's letter inside her blouse. Titi hurried off to tend her fishing traps. She would need lots of fish to enable her to buy some of the things a bride needs. She knew that Petelo could not buy anything.

The trail along the river's edge was beautiful in the early morning. Startled waterfowl squawked their protests at being disturbed. At a curve in the river a giant mango tree leaned out over the water. From under the tree you could see up along the river for almost a whole kilometer. *"This looks like a good place to sort things out in my mind. Perhaps I should try to pray too. Petelo was the first person I ever heard praying to God.*

"None of my ancestors prayed to God unless it was the one who stole the kikongo Bible from the missionary for whom he worked. That old Bible did not look to have been worn from use. How strange it seemed to me that Petelo our teacher would just talk with his eyes closed when he prayed. I suppose it was no different from the times I talked to my mother by her graveside. When Sami addressed his teki we couldn't see the spirit he addressed. When the shaman talks to the ancestors we don't see any one. When he goes into the sacred forests he claims to meet with ancestors but he is the only one who ever sees them, if indeed he does.

"Dreams seem to be the most real communications with people we normally cannot see. If someone like Petelo, Pastor Pangu, and our deacons say they believe the Bible teaching about prayer, why should I doubt some of the best people I know?"

In a dreamy mood, Titi began to talk to herself. "I do trust Petelo. Whenever he looks at me or touches my hands, a joy comes over me. He makes me feel like a woman. I would love to have him become the father of my children."

Suddenly Titi began to laugh as she remembered the happy year at Lufu School. *"I told my girl friends that I was going to marry our teacher when I grew up. Just imagine, I said I would marry Petelo when I was eleven years old. They teased me by saying he would be married with three children before I was even old enough to be engaged."* Titi laughed a good wholesome laugh again.

"It is just possible that God has been guiding our lives just like Petelo believes."

Looking up the beautiful stretch of river, Titi felt she should pray to the God who made it. She spoke in a strong clear voice.

"Dear God, thank you for bringing Petelo back into my life. Please help me to learn to trust you as much as I trust Petelo. I would like to really trust you. Please show Petelo and me what you want us to do. I'm sorry I don't trust you as much as I should. The Pastor says that you understand our hearts. I hope so, I know that I can't pretend when I try to talk with you. Goodbye for now."

Titi felt as though some of her worries had just been removed as she hurried toward her fish traps. To her delight, she caught a medium sized catfish in one trap, and two eels in the other. The eels had eaten most of a small catfish that must have been caught first, providing bait for them.

"Thank you, Nkaka" she shouted as she reset her traps leaving the remains of the catfish in one of them. She was very sure that her old grandmother's spirit was helping her catch the fish she needed so badly.

At the store in town, Lala read Petelo's letter aloud so they could all think seriously about it. Sami was the first to speak.

"Everything we know about this young man makes us want to trust him. Sometimes I think Titi is the most mature person among us, so we trust her judgment." Sami began to laugh heartily. "The only thing that worries us is his shortage of money. We, above all, ought to know that riches can be gone in a moment. A few months ago we had nothing at all. Despite that, we have eaten every day. Titi has even continued in school and found a fine man who wants to marry her. In my mind, the only thing that is missing is money and I will never trust that stuff again."

They had a good laugh at themselves and agreed to support Titi any way they could, beginning with the preparing a meal for Petelo's spokesman some Sunday soon.

Mama Mbuta spoke for all of them when she said. "Our circumstances are totally changed. We need to question every custom we have, to determine whether it still applies to refugees like us."

The family was still chatting when a customer entered.

"My name is Makena and my wife and I have come to choose a nice piece of cloth for the girl one of our students wants to marry. He hasn't any money, but we have a little fund in our church for emergencies. We have heard that Madame Lala is a good judge of cloth. We have brought all the money we have. I am not trying to dicker with you. We would appreciate it if you would give us the best cloth you can for the money we have."

"Are you Pastor Makena from Kimpese? If you are, you need to know that we were just wondering how we could get in touch with you to invite you to come to our apartment for meal and an occasion to hear from you as the kimpovila (spokesman) for the student pastor called Petelo. You see he wants to marry this lady's niece."

A great laugh broke any potential tension.

"Imagine our meeting this way without expecting it." Pastor Makena said quietly. "Your invitation is accepted for tomorrow afternoon."

They shook hands formally all around.

Lala and Mrs. Makena looked very carefully at the cloths in their price range. Mama Nkenda was soon beside them when she realized that these folk were choosing a gift for Titi.

Lala thought a moment, and displayed the next higher price range.

"We don't own the store or its inventory but we can contribute our normal share of the profit. That will allow us to choose from among these five cloths."

Mama Nkenda spoke quietly. "Petelo's first gift for Titi was a little silk neck scarf with exactly that shade of green. Titi loves that color and apparently Petelo does too."

The three women agreed, and the cloth was wrapped.

"Madam Lala, we think the world of Petelo, and we are very grateful for your contribution to the purchase price of this cloth."

"Pastor, we will look forward to having a good visit with you Sunday afternoon."

"What better kimpovila could a man have than a Pastor of that quality. I think we are going to have a wedding in the family this dry season," Sami remarked with obvious enthusiasm the moment Pastor Makena had left their shop.

Mama Mbuta's legs could barely carry her fast enough to get back home to inform Titi of all that had taken place. *"Perhaps God is already working things out because of Titi's prayers. She said she was going to pray about it. I'll bet Petelo has been praying for a long time too," she thought.*

Titi had her fish spread out on the smoking rack, and was working on her letter when her aunt returned bubbling with news.

"Everyone has agreed to support you with whatever decision you make, Titi. While we were talking, guess who came in? Pastor Makena from Kimpese came into the store! He is Petelo's kimpovila, and he is coming to talk with the family Sunday afternoon! Pastor Makena is so nice! Your Petelo must be a very special person if a man like that has volunteered to be his spokesman in marriage arrangements!"

Titi squealed with delight. "My faith was not very big, but it is growing. I think God is helping us with this big decision. I am glad I didn't have time to prepare the fish for today's market. It will be perfect by tomorrow. We can prepare a good meal. With lots of peanuts we can prepare saka saka with peanut butter sauce."

"I must finish my letter because we have choir practice this afternoon."

Dear Petelo,

Your letter swept me off my feet. I am deeply honored to have been asked to marry you. I supposed that should you ever ask me, it would only be after we had spent considerable time discovering one another's thoughts and aspirations. It is your complete honesty and openness that has won my heart.

We could talk forever, but in the end we would simply be trying to make sure that we loved one another and were willing to trust each other totally. If I were to simply follow my heart, I think I would be willing to marry you tomorrow. However I am sure it will be of great help to my immediate household to meet with Pastor Makena tomorrow afternoon. They met today in the store because of an unusual set of circumstances. My family was very favorably impressed. The Pastor and his wife have accepted to come for a meal Sunday afternoon. Can you imagine that all this has been arranged so quickly? After my family has met your friend, I am sure that later they will want to meet with you. I will not give you any formal answer yet, as it would not be appropriate. I am simply thrilled that you want me to be yours. Do you suppose that God is at work in arranging all this?

Your affectionate pupil, Titi

As planned the young couple managed to exchange notes without being suspected by anyone. It seemed to be a marvelous intrigue that quite delighted Titi's impish mind. Although she sang as best she could, she found her eyes fascinated by a detailed study of every mood and thought expressed by Petelo's communicative personality.

When the practice was ended, Titi was torn between the desire to dash home and read her letter, and an even stronger desire to hold his hand as many moments as they dared. She actually waited to be the last to give him his good evening handshake. There was no one really near when he held her hands and whispered, "Titi, I love you." At the very same moment Titi was saying to him, "Petelo, I love you". The moment was precious, but caused them to regale in laughter in the years that followed.

Once more Titi arrived home to their little hut in the field in record-breaking time. Once again she read her letter aloud to her aunt.

Dear Titi,

I grow more confident every day that we are going to be married. I had reason to look over the membership list of the church today, and I notice that you are not a member. In order for us to be married in the church by an ordained pastor, you must be a baptized member in good standing. The Pastor tells me that you have been in church every Sunday since you arrived from Angola. I would love to have you join the baptismal class that begins next week so that we could be married before classes begin on the fifteenth of September. It will be good for you to express your faith in baptism even if you should decide not to marry me. Please marry me! Keep asking God to help us make the right decisions.

Yours, with love, Petelo

Once more, Titi's aunt was impressed with Petelo's open honesty. "No one in our family has ever been baptized. I am not sure I even know what it is all about. I think it is a kind of initiation rite you must experience in order to become a member of a Church. Once I heard very old women saying that in order to be baptized by the white missionary, a person had to be willing to sacrifice a family member to be consumed by witchcraft. In other words, someone had to die every time another person was baptized in the river. I have never heard anything like that since I was a small girl.

"In those days, the white missionaries did everything that our own pastors do now. Titi, I would like to go to that class with you. I like what I have seen of our church. There are many things I don't understand because I have never been going to church regularly until you came. We could discuss what we heard in class and that would help me. You grasp new ideas much faster than I do. You can read the Bible for yourself to examine what it teaches. I will ask Sami's permission the first time I see him. If we both believe, it would be nice to be baptized together."

Titi was very pleased with her aunt's proposal.

"Sami and Lala have been working seven days a week to improve the business in the store. They said that they are beginning to save a little money now. This weekend Sami is coming to spend some time with me after the meeting with pastor Makena. At that time you can go and stay with Lala so she is not alone in the store at night.

"I have noticed that five families have begun to make their bricks for house construction. I will be living in a village before you leave me to join your husband. I am very pleased about that. I would not have stayed here alone if there were no other houses. All the people building houses are refugees like us. Even after you are married I feel sure that you will spend many weekends with me because it is here that you have gardens and food."

Titi and her aunt agreed that they should get the food prepared for the important meeting at the store right after church. Everything that could be prepared in advance had been made ready.

Sunday morning Titi and her aunt went to church early so they could ask the Pastor to include them in his baptismal class. Pastor Pangu was pleased and surprised with their request.

Mama Mbuta insisted that she could carry all the food they had prepared in her large white basin. The three women had prepared a delicious meal. They had two kinds of smoked fish, together with both fumbwa leaves and saka saka, drenched in fresh peanut butter sauce.

Lala knew all about the proper way to set up a table for visitors that one wished to honor. She borrowed good china from the storeowner who lived nearby.

Pastor Makena and his wife were a bit younger than Sami and Mama Nkenda. They all enjoyed the good food and became more and more acquainted as they chatted.

The spokesman

"I have known Petelo since the days he arrived in Matadi as a refugee. From the beginning he was active in our church, and especially in the choir. He won a scholarship given for refugees to allow them to study at Sona Bata High School. Once more he was very active in choirs and Bible study groups during his years as a student. By the time he came to the Pastors School at Kimpese, I was one of the instructors. We have been delighted to have him as a student. Any girl who marries him will find him to be totally trustworthy.

"Any girl who considers becoming a pastor's wife needs to think seriously about what she is facing. Normally, they will not earn much money. Because they need to work with many different kinds of people, they need to be able to trust one another completely. We know Petelo rather well and we have no doubts about him at all. Quite honestly, our deep concern is that he finds a young woman who is worthy of his love and trust. We have urged him to find a wife, but you can understand his dilemma. He has neither money nor family. We are all Africans here, and we know that most families would never allow their daughter to marry under such adverse circumstances. Quite honestly he is one of the finest young men we know, and a wise family will be delighted to give him their daughter in marriage because of the faithfulness and love he will provide."

Mama Nkenda found it difficult to reply initially because of her natural shyness.

"I am Titi's aunt, and the only blood relative she has located here in Zaire. War has separated us from our loved ones. We are refugees and we understand very well what it is to be poor and have no family. We have no thought of insisting on the customary requirements for marriage. This girl has had adult responsibilities since she was eleven years of age. She lost her mother that year and moved to the home of her grandmother. She was a wonderful companion for my mother until she died a couple of years ago. While she helped my mother, she also taught school. She managed to help seven children and the village chief learn to read and write. She has managed to switch form Portuguese to French and pass the high school entrance exam. She displays the wisdom of an elder. We are amazed at the kind of person she has become. If she agrees to marry Petelo, she will be totally faithful, and we will encourage them both."

Pastor Makena smiled and asked permission to pray. There was a long silence and then he began to speak softly.

"Lord, you are my witness that I have spoken the truth today. You know how much I love and respect Petelo. Father, I thank you that this family understands the changed circumstances of refugees. Lord, if it is your will that Petelo and Titi become husband and wife, please make your will clear to the young people who must make the decision. We humbly ask for your help and blessing on all of us. Lord, we trust you to lead them and to lead us too. We thank you that you can guide their hearts. We seek your will, in Jesus name. Amen."

Mama Mbuta gave Titi a detailed report of their encounter with Pastor Makena, No detail went unreported. As she spoke, it seemed as though Titi began to glow with deep satisfaction.

"Isn't it amazing that we were able to find someone who knew the details of Petelo's life from the moment he came as a refugee?

"Mama Mbuta, we need to invite Petelo to our little home so I can give him my reply personally. I want to marry him with all my heart."

"According to our tradition, when a young woman prepares a special meal for the man she loves, the dinner tells him that she wants to marry him and his eating of the meal is his response. The giving and receiving of this special meal is a kind of covenant between you. We have everything we need. Our rooster has been reserved for a special occasion, and this is it. You can prepare a beautiful meal. All we need to do is find out when he can come. Remember the only chair we have is the one Sami made. No one out here has any chairs."

Titi smiles as she concocted a plan. "I will make a table of saplings like the one he had as a teacher at Lufu. There is lots of bamboo over by the river. I will make two bamboo benches, one for each side of the table. It will remind him of the year we met."

Mama Mbuta thought that Titi had come up with a great idea.

"I will have a table to use long after you have left me," she said with a laugh.

Titi remembered that there were perfect saplings growing along the river not too far from her traps. By Tuesday evening a sturdy table and benches had been constructed in the part of the house Sami had added. In the meantime, Mama Mbuta had woven a beautiful mat to cover the table. They were both very pleased with their work.

"I think we should invite him to come Saturday after the market is over," her aunt suggested.

"How can we invite him? I will not see him until choir practice late Saturday afternoon?"

Mama Nkenda had an idea. "You write the letter of invitation and I will take it to the church office for him. After all, he is working with our pastor full time during the school vacation. We have resolved all the problems but one."

"What is that?" Titi asked anxiously.

With a very serious face her aunt explained, "A girl, anxious to win her lover's heart, must shell a whole bowl of peanuts, remove all the brown covers, and leave the peanuts whole and not broken into two halves."

Titi laughed. "I think I have the patience to do that. My dear Mama Mbuta, it seems to me that you are as excited as I am."

"Perhaps I am; I have had a happier relationship with you than I ever had with my own children when they were your age. In those days, people just never revealed their thoughts to anyone. You know, I think your own openness has changed our whole household and me too. Sami has changed since you have been with us. From what you have told me, my old mother opened her heart up to you as she had never opened up to anyone else in her whole lifetime. I'm sure you were a big influence on each other.

"You had better start shelling your peanuts. It is a hard job you know."

"I have prepared perfect peanuts before. When we were school children in Lufu, we worked at it. Someone told us that we could never marry a good man if we did not know how to shell perfect peanuts. I had lots of trouble then, because I tried to do it quickly." They both had a good laugh about the peanuts.

Friday morning Mama Mbuta called out even before the rooster had had time to call.

"Child, since we lost everything we only own a few cheap plastic plates. We must borrow some!"

"I have already thought about that. Petelo is poor and so are we. Why should we pretend? My job is to prepare the best meal I know how to prepare. Good food will make us forget the plates. He must enjoy our food and forget the plates if we are going to be happy."

"You are totally right. Where do you get such wonderful ideas?"

"Perhaps God or our ancestors are guiding me."

On Saturday afternoon everything was prepared, the whole table and its contents were covered with a white cloth. Petelo was well aware that the formal meal itself was a symbol of Titi's acceptance of his proposal. She was dressed attractively with a dress from the market that matched her little green neck scarf. As Titi removed the covering she held Petelo in her gaze and spoke softly.

"Please accept the first of many meals I intend to serve you in our home."

After she had spoken so meaningfully, Petelo asked permission to pray.

"Dear Lord, we can see your hand in our lives. We believe that you brought us together. We ask for your rich blessing as we eat this beautiful meal together vowing our love for each other. Amen".

Petelo was delighted when he saw the beautiful meal. A look at the reed table and bamboo benches brought a broad grin to his face.

"I have never known anyone more resourceful than you, Titi," he said as he beamed at her. "Your creativity has brought us back to Lufu memories for our very first meal together. Thank you, I would rather sit at the table you made with your own hands, than at the finest hotel table in the Kinshasa."

Mama Nkenda was the servant for this special day. "Petelo, it seems that we have broken with most of our traditions and begun new ones that fit our circumstances. We should have brought this meal to you to be eaten in your solitude. We felt that eating together was a far better tradition to begin."

After her short message of explanation, she retreated to their tiny outside cooking hut.

Petelo and Titi were essentially alone for the first time in their lives. The table was narrow and it allowed them to clasp each other's hands by reaching under their feast. There was no rush. They held hands for a long time leaving only their hearts and eyes to communicate feelings that were far beyond words. Their letters had transmitted the words. They had both been yearning for this moment. Both of them enjoyed the good food, but the pleasure of each other's presence superceded every other consideration.

Before he left, Petelo reached into his little carrying case and withdrew a beautiful cloth with a touch of green that matched his first gift.

"I am delighted to give you this engagement cloth. Pastor Makena and the little Kimpese church enabled me to offer you this symbolic gift. I love you, and I want the world to know that we intend to become man and wife."

Titi was amazed, and overcome by his gift. She understood his financial situation, and certainly had not expected such a beautiful, traditional offering.

"God is good," she whispered because she was almost speechless.

Revealing their well kept secret

Titi felt very self-conscious during the morning service. She caused quite a stir in the choir when she appeared with the folded engagement cloth draped over her shoulder in the traditional manner. "Who is he? Who is he?" the girls asked in excitement.

As soon as Petelo stepped up to lead their last-minute practice before entering the church sanctuary, he paused to make an announcement.

"I am pleased to let you in on what has been our secret. Titi and I hope to be married before long."

No one had guessed about their romance. The choir was a buzz of excitement. Most were very happy but a couple of girls looked rather sad.

"How did you ever keep such a secret from us all?" one of Titi's close friends asked.

"It wasn't easy," she replied. "We didn't want to give any hints until we had made up our own minds."

They all knew Petelo was a struggling student, so they were surprised at the quality of her cloth. Petelo only made one more reference to their plans.

"The Lord provided me with the cloth, you see. I have no relatives in this country. God has provided me with amazing friends, He is worthy of our trust."

Once their engagement was official it was easier for the young couple to meet. They met before choir practice when only the cleaning deacons were present in the sanctuary and quite willing to serve as chaperones.

One old deaconess came to them the first Saturday after their announcement.

"I noticed that Titi was always the first girl to arrive each Saturday. I just wondered if you had a secret. I must say your behavior was always totally acceptable. Not many young people bother to respect our customs these days. I am very happy for you!"

It was a great relief to be able to hold hands without any embarrassment.

"Petelo, I am amazed at the peace I have about our marriage. I have spent a lot of time with older women. We seem to have more shared thoughts already than many ever have. Most never think of showing their inner thoughts to their husbands and vice versa. They have sort of contracts. The wife grows the vegetables, carries the wood and water, and gives birth to the babies. Men build and maintain the houses, clear the large trees from the fields, and try to provide meat from the hunt. They seldom seem to really talk with one another. Some learn to have affection one for the other but feel very embarrassed to show it. I never wanted a traditional relationship like that. I am very young, yet the only man I have ever loved is already someone I feel I could trust with my deepest thoughts."

"I guess we have both observed the same older generation and felt we wanted better relationships than they seemed to have. I simply feel that God has been preparing us for each other. It may seem strange to you, but I have never set my heart on any woman but you. We need a solid trusting relationship to serve people well as Pastor and wife. You have not been in the courses that are given for the training of pastors' wives in my school but God has been teaching you throughout your young life."

Baptism classes

For an eight-week period both Titi and her aunt really enjoyed the baptismal classes taught by Pastor Pangu. Neither of them had had any relations with the church before the last ten months. When the pastor asked for questions, Titi had many. However, she soon detected that her probing questions made the pastor very uncomfortable.

"I guess my deepest questions will have to wait until I have Petelo to help me understand," Titi remarked to her aunt as they walked home after church. "I will just content myself with learning all I can so I can qualify as a candidate for baptism."

While meeting Petelo during this time, she felt she should tell him about her doubts.

"Petelo, I don't think I have the kind of faith a pastor's wife should have. I have many questions and doubts. I want to have faith but I have a much deeper grounding in the witchcraft and traditions of our area than in the faith and teachings of the church. I believe many things. I am just beginning to think about trusting God. Are you not afraid to marry someone who knows so little about the faith that seems to govern your life?" Petelo paused for only a short time before giving a serious response to her understandable reservations.

"Your faith will grow, if you want it to. I am convinced that God deals with us very personally. When you yearn for something he wants you to have, he will see that you get what you need. Your faith may not grow as fast as you would like because God seems to teach us through the struggles of life. My faith has grown the most when I have faced situations in which I had no idea of which way to turn. Don't worry! Just keep asking God for faith," Petelo answered with assurance.

Sami sent word that he had been able to buy enough metal roofing sheets to cover the part of the house that leaked badly in driving rain. He asked for Titi and Mama Nkenda to come to the store to pick up the roofing because he hoped to come with a carpenter on Saturday morning. Titi and her aunt were happy to come for the roofing. It was not too heavy, but just difficult to carry on their heads in a wind. As they carried back the sheets, Titi recognized that Sami was a good husband as far as traditional standards would dictate. He had a younger wife but as soon as he had a little money saved, he was thinking about his first wife's comfort.

Baptism

The baptismal classes continued for a full eight weeks. Both Titi and her aunt felt in their hearts that they really wanted to be baptized and identify themselves with those who wanted to live like Jesus through the strength of his Spirit. The deacons were pleased with their replies on the day of their oral exam. They were baptized together with seven other people in the Lukunga River not far from their little house.

When Titi gave her public testimony on the bank of the river, she spoke with deep conviction.

"I am happy to join the church that has helped me ever since I arrived here as a refugee. I know that my faith needs to grow. I need to learn how the teaching of Jesus relates to the other beliefs I have had since a child. I really want my trust in Jesus to grow."

In her heart she felt that her Petelo would help her faith and understanding to develop.

Wedding plans

Their plans for the September 3rd wedding went well because everyone in Titi's little household was totally supportive, and Petelo had no relatives at all. There was nothing to negotiate. In the end, the young couple were able to plan everything according to their possibilities. Titi's family required none of the normal gifts. They had no possibilities of preparing any kind of big feast.

Just a week before the wedding, the churchwomen told Titi and her aunt that they wanted to help. They all understood the circumstances.

"After all, you have become our full-fledged sisters now that you have joined us," the spokeswoman explained.

"We really want to celebrate together! When all the women work together, we can organize a great wedding reception. Think of us as your new family. Trust us, you will have a wedding celebration to remember."

Petelo made arrangements to borrow the community wedding gown kept at the Pastors School. It was a beautiful gown sent from America. Titi and her Aunt altered it to fit her perfectly.

Early September was a great time for a wedding because it was a slack time between harvest time and planting. A celebration could be held outside without any fear of rain.

Titi made a major effort to catch fish the last ten days before the wedding. The river was low but that only made the fish a bit hungrier. There was a constant plume of smoke above their little home because of the continuous process of preparing fish. The plan was that she would bring the fish to the choir ladies on the morning of the wedding. The fish would become part of the reception food the women were preparing.

Petelo spent as much time as he could back at Kimpese preparing his little student's house for his bride. The house was about twelve feet square, and consisted of a one-room brick structure with a small kitchen at the rear. Petelo cleaned everything, and managed to get some green paint to paint the window shutters and the front door. A fellow student helped secure a strong wire, which they stretched from wall to wall. It supported a reed mat curtain that divided the one room into a bedroom and a living room.

"Titi has lived a difficult life. I would like to make our little home as attractive as possible for her," Petelo explained to his classmate. "My desk will serve as our table but I need to find a second chair somewhere."

Petelo had slept on a reed mat but he was anxious to have a bed for Titi, even though he knew that she slept on a mat at home. In the market he found a perfect bed made from a type of palm tree. He looked it all over, to see if he might be able to duplicate it. The construction was simple, but the special palm grew in a swampland a great distance from Kimpese.

The vendor guessed Petelo's dilemma.

"I don't want to carry this last bed back to my village. I came on a truck, but I must walk back home. You are a student in the pastor's school and you don't have the money. Take the bed and pay me three sacks of oranges from the school orange grove in April. I know I can trust you."

Petelo was amazed that he would be allowed to take the bed home to complete the preparation that he felt he should do in advance. All the other little changes they would plan together.

There was only one missing link in all the wedding preparations. Zoao, Titi's father had still not responded to either of the letters she had placed in the hands of the driver of the UNITA munitions truck the moment the wedding date was set. She realized that he could be on patrol in the interior of Angola but she yearned for him to meet Petelo, even if he could not attend the wedding. She was well aware of the long tradition of the bride needing her father's blessing in order for the marriage to be blessed with the birth of children. She had no doubt that her father would bless her, but she wanted his blessing. There had been no word at all.

Sleep eluded the young bride the night before the wedding. Her mind was filled with happy thoughts of soon being in their own little student's house at Kimpese. Petelo had not let her see it. He wanted the little nest to be his surprise.

"By this time tomorrow I will married to my teacher, the very one who changed my life," Titi talked constantly to her aunt. "We will not have any money, but that will hardly be a change for me. My fellow choir members already call me Mama Pastor. I have never even seen a church wedding so I can hardly imagine it. All I have heard sounds like a wonderful celebration. How can I get to sleep?"

Fortunately, fatigue did what her will couldn't manage. She fell into a profound sleep.

Quite early in the morning Titi and her aunt took the large basin of smoked fish, with their famous sauce, over to the church kitchen. The whole place was swarming with busy choir members decorating the church and grounds for the wedding. The men had cut and carried in mountains of palm branches. There were no flowers at that time of year but folk had brought their collections of plastic flowers to mingle with the ornate leaves that were brought from the river. Mama Nkenda was allowed to stay but Titi was ordered back home to wait.

Woven arches of palm branches decorated the paths leading to the church. Countless branches lined the white walls turning them forest green. A love seat for the couple being married was placed at the front, facing the audience. It was covered with gorgeous blankets. A palm branch canopy was cleverly erected so that the love seat looked more like a throne. White basins were placed on either side of the throne to receive any gifts people might bring. The folk had learned to love their student pastor as much as Titi's friends were fond of her. Together, the church folk would become the family the young couple needed to effectuate an African wedding.

Between them, Titi and Petelo had only three family members who would be at the wedding. The senior women's choir decided they would be seated as family on the left side of the sanctuary while the senior men's choir would be seated as family on the right. The other choirs filled in behind the special family benches. All agreed that the youth choir drummers should provide the rhythm for the long processional.

Celebration of marriage

At long last, everything was ready The women's choir were wearing their colorful matching dresses, while the senior men's choir wore blacks trousers, white shirts and bow ties. Titi had dressed in the manse beside the church, while Petelo wore a modest suit he had purchased from the used clothing merchant. His honesty and sincerity gave him a natural dignity.

The young drummers' skillful beat set the mood. Each choir sang a number as they danced up the aisle. The wedding shuffle consisted of endless repetition of two steps forward and one step back. By stepping appropriately, they could actually maintain their place without advancing at all, if they so desired. The choirs that were singing managed their stepping and swaying so that their song would finish only when everyone was in a position to be seated. This happy process lasted about an hour, to everyone's delight.

As Titi worked her way up the long aisle, she knew that, according to the strictest traditions, she should walk with her eyes down cast and a serious look on her face. Failing to enter appropriately cast doubt on the bride's character. To keep her face somber she kept remembering that her father had not been able to come. She even prayed that he would be kept safe on his patrol.

Just as she reached the front, the young bride was startled, when a big hand grasped hers. It was her father! As she turned to him, radiant joy filled both of their faces. She had his blessing! His face said it all! Her father knew Petelo from the Lufu days. Titi was able to be serious at the appropriate time but she was unable to keep up her somber pose any longer. Unknown to her,

Zoao had come to Lukala in the night and delivered the hind quarters of a large mpakasa to the church kitchen, knowing that it would provide sufficient meat for a large reception.

The marvelous choir concert lasted an hour and a half. Some of their songs and antics made everyone laugh. Others were serious and instructive. Keeping up their reputation, the senior choir prepared a whole song, which was an exaggerated version of the lives of Petelo and Titi from the time they first met. They got all their information from Mama Nkenda. At one point in their dramatic number, chosen ladies wagged their fingers as they instructed first Titi and then Petelo concerning their marital duties. They were gifted at dealing with delicate issues in a humorous and non-offensive manner.

Pastor Pangu was wise enough to have a very short sermon after such a lengthy and varied musical presentation. The part that pleased Titi the most about the church's teaching on marriage was the concept of unconditional vows of mutual support. Traditional marriages were always conditional. If there were no babies, the marriage was dissolved by both families by mutual consent. Pastor Pangu asked both Petelo and Titi to promise to continue faithful to each other whether they were sick or well, and specifically whether they had children or not. To make such vows to someone you love and trust brought a great sense of security to their relationship. They promised faithfulness until death separated them. Titi was impressed with the exclusiveness of their vows that left no room for Petelo to bring in other wives. Both of them repeated their vows enthusiastically so that, when the Pastor Pangu pronounced them man and wife, the audience clapped in loud approval.

The recessional march went relatively quickly because everyone wanted to get over to the reception meal served out under the mango trees near the classrooms. Just as soon as the last person was out, the young men began to transport the church benches over to the reception area.

The churchwomen had prepared a marvelous meal. People remarked for months about the abundance of fish and gigantic basins of mpakasa meat and gravy to accompany their plates loaded with fufu and saka saka greens. Meat was so costly that no one expected anything but saka saka. Titi's father became instantly famous because of his generous supply of everyone's favorite meat. Many of the young people had never tasted this famous game meat before because there was none available anywhere near Lukala. The servers were very wise in determining how much meat each person would receive so that, in the end, everyone had a fair share.

Two large head tables accommodated the bride and groom and their small circle of family. Pastor and Mama Makena were counted as Petelo's family. Titi was supported by her father Zoao, her aunt, Mama Nkenda, together with her uncle by marriage, Sami, and his younger wife Lala.

Beyond doubt, everyone felt they had experienced a true celebration. Sami and Lala were very surprised at the way the church people had worked together to create a memorable experience for a penniless young couple.

After the reception Titi changed into a traditional blouse and wrap around skirt made up from her engagement cloth. She wore the matching neck scarf to complete her attractive attire. Lala had spent hours creating a Luanda hairstyle for the girl she considered to be like a little sister. Many people had worked together happily to bring about a wedding miracle.

The white basins collected a surprising number of envelopes with small sums of money and notes expressing good will. All together, their wedding gifts took away the sting of poverty for a few happy weeks.

The bride and groom went to Kimpese by taxi after the reception was ended. They shared the vehicle with Pastor Makena and his wife, who directed the taxi driver to the little student house that Petelo had carefully prepared.

To their surprise, there was another little reception awaiting them at their house. A little group of Pastoral School students prepared a friendly welcome for their colleague and his bride. Several of the teaching staff came to the quiet reception. Portions of a simple wedding cake were served along with soft drinks. Cakes were rare and reserved for very special occasions. It was a most pleasant end to a memorable day.

The fresh, green paint on the door caught Titi's eye as she stepped into their first home. She appreciated his ingenuity at his construction of the reed mat divider that allowed them to have a bedroom separate from the other multi purpose room. She had not expected to find the neat new bed awaiting them. In their little room, Petelo had carefully placed his one table and chair.

"With some of our gift money, perhaps we can buy a second chair. I couldn't make a table and benches like you did, because this little house has a cement floor so that I couldn't drive stakes in the ground."

Before they got in their new bed, they sat on the edge and Petelo expressed their profound thanks to God in prayer.

When Petelo enveloped her in his strong gentle arms, Titi felt gloriously content and secure. The last time she remembered feeling this kind of peace was when she had snuggled in her mother's arms as a child.

"God is good, she whispered."

Titi had never even imagined how it would be to be held tenderly by the only man she had ever loved. The yearning that had invaded her heart when her mother died was finally satisfied. She belonged to someone who loved her.

"With God's help, I will always love you!" Petelo whispered. Those were the last words they exchanged before their extreme fatigue whisked them off into a profoundly refreshing sleep. Not even the roosters awakened them. With their windows covered with wooden shutters, neither awoke until they had slept off all their tiredness. Minutes after they awoke, the church bell sounded its first invitation to worship.

Beginning to giggle, Titi called Petelo over to the little table.

"Your breakfast is ready," she said, handing Petelo a piece of the little wedding cake. "No time to even boil water before we need to be on our way to church."

"Cake makes a very special breakfast. We may as well finish this one bottle of orange soda to replace the coffee we don't have."

The local congregation was delighted to have the young newlywed's present. They all knew Petelo but most of them had never met Titi. Listening to the different accents in Kikongo, Titi realized that there were many Angola refugees in this church community too. She could tell that some were Zombo like herself.

Life in a student village

With the pastor's school slated to begin classes in ten days, the little students' village soon became totally occupied with the bustle of returning students as well as those coming for the first time.

In those first ten days, Titi learned about her new community and its surroundings. There was a large water tap not too far from their house, which supplied most of their needs for water. Petelo went out with Titi almost every day showing her their possibilities. To her surprise, he had a field of manioc that he had planted during his first year. That was great news for her. She had thought that she would need to bring all their manioc from Lukala.

They had to walk long distances to find firewood. Because they lived very near the town of Kimpese, it seemed as though there was someone waiting for each branch that fell. Wood was going to be a problem unless they had money to buy charcoal. Titi discovered that the Lukunga River was only about twenty minutes walk from their village. Once they reached the river, she was surprised that she could walk to her aunt's little house in a little over an hour. She and her aunt had planted both peanuts and beans together so they would share the harvest as well.

It came as a bit of a shock when Petelo mentioned their need to pay school fees in order to study. It would not be an easy year, but surely the God who enabled them to get married would help them live too.

Only a few of the students' wives had sufficient knowledge of French to be allowed to attend a variety of courses intended for student pastors.

Lisa lived next door in the adjoining student house. She was curious to understand how it was that Titi could read both Kikongo and French despite having spent all but one year of her life in an isolated village in Angola. Titi explained her life history briefly, pointing out that it was Petelo who had taught her to read and write Kikongo when she was about eleven years old.

"If Petelo taught you that explains everything. All of us women who have been in his reading classes for the past two years have learned to read and write too. I wish I could have had him teach me when I was younger. You have a really good man for your husband."

Titi had not known that Petelo was teaching literacy while he carried on his own studies.

The wives who lived nearby felt a little awkward around her when they met at the stream for washing. It was only when they saw how hard she worked in her garden that they accepted her. Because Petelo had taught many of them, they felt a natural inferiority to his wife. They were impressed at the details about successful farming that she knew and realized that she had spent a lot of time working in the fields just as they had. It was her willingness to do really hard work that opened their hearts for friendship.

Anything Petelo was paid for his literacy courses went directly toward his school fees. He had no way of earning anything. It was a blessing that Titi had shared crops in her aunt's fields. Mama Nkenda helped her out by soaking and drying her manioc. It made it so much easier to carry back to Kimpese. Fresh manioc weighs at least four times as much as when it is properly dried. Titi continued to operate her fish traps on some weekends. She taught her aunt the family fishing secrets so she was able to earn enough to help them both.

"I have never been so happy since I was your pupil at Lufu," Titi whispered to Petelo as she lay his arms after a long day.

"How I wish that you didn't have to work so hard to keep us fed," he replied with sincerity. "You work so hard, just so I can study. I think that your constant work is keeping you from becoming pregnant. Everyone is watching us because, as you know, many people still feel that getting pregnant early in the first year is the only true sign of family approval. They know that I hadn't any money and that neither of us had true clan approval. Now that they are in this kind of a school, some feel that getting pregnant is the necessary sign of God's approval, too. Please remember that I do not think that way. I love you and will continue to love you whether we have babies or not."

Titi snuggled in Petelo's arms feeling deep comfort from his kind words.

"As nearly as I can tell, most of the wives here never know what their husbands are really thinking. It is as though they don't really trust one another. Each woman knows what her husband wants and expects, but not what he thinks in his heart. Petelo, God has given you a deep understanding of people. Even when we were school children, you seemed to understand just how we thought, and you used your understanding to spur us on to do our best.

"Petelo, I need a good pastor to help me because I still have many questions that I don't feel free to bring up in class. I never had anything to do with the church until this past year. All the ideas are new. I get the feeling that there may be serious conflicts with all of our traditional beliefs, which I have gathered since a child, both from observation and direct teaching.

"We lived in a world where unseen sprit forces were everywhere. Almost every spirit was filled with raging hate that could be directed against enemies and rivals. I grew up in a world of curses, vows, fetishes, teki gods, diviners, and shaman with powers to invade the very soul of a person. Death never seemed to have any important connections with God.

"Ndoki witches could be very clever people who did no harm, or malevolent, wanton, ruthless killers who would suck the life from an old person or a little child without a moment of regret. The spirit world I knew seems ruthless.

"In class, I get the feeling that I am the only one tied up so intimately with our Congo traditions. I understand now, that you were trying to teach us about God when you were at Lufu. When you closed your eyes and prayed, I remember watching you and wondering what you were doing. Petelo, my head is full of ideas. No doubt some of them need to be rejected but I don't know how to pick and choose. I can't jump out of beliefs just because someone says I should.

"I am so glad my father was able to get to our wedding. His gift of mpakasa meat and his presence assured me of his approval and blessing. Without his blessing, I would be worried that I might not ever have a baby because I have always believed in the profound importance of paternal blessing. You have said that while you would have loved to have your family present to support you, you are at peace whenever you feel confident of God's approval. His approval is enough for you, but I don't have that level of faith yet. Petelo, I am so glad that you are able to accept me the way I am."

NEW LIFE ON THE WAY

When people are healthy, happy, and working hard, time flies by. That was how it was for Titi and Petelo. Before they knew it they had reached the month of May with only six weeks before graduation.

May is noted as the month of torrential rains accompanied by thunder, lightning, and violent winds. Petelo was drenched by such a storm when he burst through the door at suppertime. Changing his clothes, he was delighted to sit down at their little table. He could smell the delicious fish as soon as he entered the door.

"It is great to be in a house that doesn't leak on a night like this. Just listen to that rain roar on our roof."

The meal looked delicious. Petelo smiled when he looked at his wife sitting happily across their tiny table. They held hands while he returned their thanks to God before eating. There was no need to rush because he would not go out into the storm again. When they had finished, Titi told Petelo that she wanted to tell him a secret.

"Petelo, I have passed my ngonda (period) by two weeks now. I think that we are going to have a baby."

Coming quickly to her side to embrace her, Petelo was delighted.

"All our critics will be silenced now. One group will feel that we must have the approval of our families, and a second group will feel God has blessed us. All I know is that your secret makes me happy. I have learned that godly people like Jesus and the Apostle Paul were blessed by God even though they had neither spouses nor children."

"The dress we bought for my graduation will still fit me in June. It will feel good to finally have a baby in my tummy when we reach your graduation day."

Graduation day was drawing near. As soon as the academic worries were behind them, almost every graduate began to wonder just where the church elders and leaders would assign him for the first pastorate or parish. Being both young and Angolan refugees, Petelo and Titi knew that they could expect to be given a tough assignment. The settlement committees waited for the results of the final exams before they made their decisions. There was no point in assigning someone who needed to repeat another year of studies.

Pastor Kwandambu came personally to inform the students from his community concerning their assignments. Petelo was assigned to the parish of Dimba in the northwest area of the Bangu Hills.

"You will find lots to do in the parish of Dimba. It is a very productive agricultural area, but the roads through the hills are often impassable during the rainy season. One of your areas is made up of Angolan refugees. To get to Dimba by truck you must go with the market vehicle that tries to go every week from Mbanza Ngungu in time for a Friday market as long as the roads are passable."

When Titi told her aunt about their posting, a sad look crossed her face like a shadow.

"We will miss you more than you can imagine. You have been like a ray of sunshine for us ever since you arrived less than two years ago. We were able to help you when you first arrived, but within a few months, it was your wisdom that rescued us. Sami is well now thanks to your strong advice. He has really fixed up my little house as you can see. Now that a village is growing up out here, I don't feel so lonely any more. Sami is very fair with me and comes to visit regularly. At least you will need to return to these parts when you are going to have your baby. Because of the distance, you will need to come a few weeks ahead of time. Travel on a big truck can be difficult if you must climb up to the top of the load."

Titi began to laugh. "Mama Mbuta, you are worrying about me already, and we haven't even left Kimpese yet. We both know that we will be doing all we can to get together. If I worried about everything, I'm afraid I would be frightened to death. Sometimes I just trust Petelo's judgment. He has been trusting God much longer than we have. He feels sure we can trust God for the details of this move. I trust him, and he trusts God. I trust as far as my faith takes me, but I rely a lot on Petelo's wisdom. Some day I am sure my faith will grow too, because it has been growing ever since I opened my heart to God's Spirit."

Graduation and travel arrangements

Graduation was an exciting time for all the seven couples who had qualified. Titi's heart nearly burst with pride when Petelo won the prize for the highest grades. Each of the wives received certificates of recognition for the studies they had completed in their own training school. Titi found herself far more excited than she expected when she responded to her call to come forward. As she walked toward the front, it dawned on her that her life was almost a miracle. Who could have guessed back in the Kiula that the year she turned eighteen she would find herself married to the teacher who taught her to read and write? Who could have guessed she would become a pastor's wife and an expectant mother? There were tears of deep gratitude running down her radiant face when she received her certificate. Petelo alone really understood all the reasons for her deep joy.

The day after graduation all the graduates were suddenly faced with a new set of problems. Most of them had very little money, yet they needed to move their families and modest possessions to some new place. A student who had visited Dimba the summer before was able to give Petelo and Titi a much clearer picture of the challenge they faced. The parish had been decimated by witchcraft. There were not many active church members, partly because the old Pastor had alienated many people before he died. Many of the local folk were convinced that the church leader was actually an ndoki witch. Most accused the old pastor of conducting a witches' market right behind the little church building under the spreading sanda tree. There were countless stories of trade in human flesh in all the grotesque details typical of the witchcraft tradition.

Mama Lukau who lived near Mama Nkenda was an Angolan woman whose relatives lived in one of the villages in the parish of Dimba. She raised many fears in Titi by telling her about all the witchcraft that cursed the area.

"Two of my grand children were sold and eaten in the witches' market that meets behind the Dimba church. We know for sure because the prophet Zulu told us himself after he was thrown into a trance by the Holy Spirit," she warned.

Petelo tried to calm his wife but that was not easy to do.

"Remember Titi, Mama Lukau received all her information from a local ngunza prophet. The ngunza is just a new deceptive role for the traditional ngombo diviner. In these parts, most accusations of witchcraft are made by people wearing crosses, who claim to be lead by God's Holy Spirit. They simply can't be trusted any more than the traditional ngombo diviners."

Inside their home Titi felt free to raise all her doubts and questions before Petelo. He explained things to her, when he was able.

"Petelo, all my lifetime we have always depended on the ngombo diviners to explain the causes of tragedy and death. I know that those people may well be deceptive, but what else could we do? How did your tribe describe the cause of death? Did they not consult the Ngombo diviners just like we did?"

"The Bible and the church have been in my area of Sao Salvador, or Mbanza Kongo, for many years. Church people were taught never to consult with the ngombo diviners. The Bible teaches that it is not God's will for the living to consult the dead in the way the Ngombo diviners claim they do.

"Most of our church leaders simply claimed that everything that happened, including death, was the will of God. I must admit that their answer was not satisfactory either. The old church leaders did not like anyone to challenge them. I know that many felt that their answer turned God into a baby killer.

"One of our teachers here at Kimpese, a big Canadian, always insisted that we should be more honest and humble when asked to explain a tragedy. 'Admit that you don't know why it happened, and trust God even when your hearts are broken.' He would advise us."

"He did not give us an answer, but he encouraged us to keep trusting God when we are stricken with grief. He pointed out that tragedies take place everywhere in the world including his country too. We were surprised when he told us that our kind of witchcraft with ndoki witches was totally unknown in the region where he grew up.

"He kept reminding us that Jesus shows us what kind of person God is. He admitted that Christian's children die, like others, from diseases and accidents. He told us that the big mission hospital at Kimpese was organized to prevent the deaths and suffering that could be prevented by modern medicine. He admitted his limitations when he talked with us.

"He would say, 'I can't prove that there is a loving God, but I believe there is. Neither can you prove that all your babies die as a result of the actions of ndoki witches.'"

"He told us that he was convinced that most African children died from causes that would take the lives of white children too, if they received no treatment."

Petelo spoke slowly, with deep conviction. "Titi, I believe that we can trust God just as well at Dimba as we can here in Kimpese. It will be more dangerous to be far from a good hospital. Our hearts may be broken sometimes, but I am convinced that we can trust God even in the face of death."

"I wish I could trust God the way you do! My fear of the spirit world of witchcraft is far stronger than my trust in God. The idea of trusting God is still new to me. My doubts and questions have often made me say that I am not fit to be a Pastor's wife."

Holding his wife in his arms, Petelo spoke gently.

"Please allow me to trust God to grow your faith. It is like a plant; it does not grow in a day. Your very questions tell me that it is your desire to have faith. The desire in your heart is a result of the living Spirit of God working in you. Trust me when I tell you that some day you faith will bloom like a flower. Please trust me when I tell you that you are not a disappointment to me. Your faith is real, honest, healthy, and growing. Faith grows when we find God meeting our needs in impossible situations."

Titi began to smile a little. "When I look back, it was God's helping us through impossible situations that has grown the bit of faith I have in my heart. One thing about me, I will be able to understand the fears and heartaches of the people of Dimba very well."

"Pastor Kwandambu has a Land Rover, could he take us out to Dimba?" asked Titi.

"I'm afraid not. He told me that he does not receive enough budget to allow him to take student pastors to their parishes unless the parish can pay for the trip. We know that our parish can't, so that way is out. There is another possibility that I am hoping might just work. The nurse in charge of the IME hospital community health programs, told me that they have a trip scheduled for Dimba. He said he could take books, pots, clothes, and us. Our nice bed and chair will have to stay here. I think it is our only possibility. They go in two days."

Titi was pleased and sad at the same time. She had counted on having a good long visit with her aunt before they went away so far.

"Well, at least we can take our sleeping mats and the cover for our straw mattress," she answered cheerily.

Petelo managed to get a sturdy carton to protect their books. Quite simply they didn't own much, but what they had was precious. The cooking pots and dishes all fit in Titi's big plastic basin. An old work wraparound was slipped under the basin, then tied in a knot on the top. Nothing could fall out. Their clothes were all packed in a flour bag they bought at the bakery. Everything was ready in a couple of hours.

Needless to say, the time flew by. There was barely enough time to say goodbye to all their friends at Kimpese. They paid the owner of a fula fula (pick up truck taxi) to take them to Sami's store in Lukala where they could be picked up early Monday morning by the community health vehicle.

Following the Sunday church service in Lukala, there were countless goodbye handshakes. Pastor Pangu called them to the front and offered a very meaningful prayer on their behalf. It was hard to leave them all behind. Titi's family all met at the store for a big meal Sunday afternoon. Lala prepared a box of basic supplies for them from the store. It contained salt, sugar, tea, cooking oil, soap, sardines, corned beef, and matches. She knew very well what it was like to leave the city and go to the country.

Monday morning, the Hospital Land Rover came along shortly after seven. The community health team occupied the seats, but their book box and bag of clothes made good seats in the back. Petelo had strong twine prepared for tying their sleeping mats and two chickens to the top carrier. In less than an hour they were in Mbanza Ngungu.

At the foot of the long hill leading out of the town, they came to a dirt road which turned north. Branch roads off that road would eventually lead them through the hills and valleys to the market village of Dimba. There had been no rain for three weeks because the dry season had begun. The water was drying up in the gigantic mud holes that bedeviled the road. With very skillful driving, they managed to crawl through holes that had entrapped large vehicles for the whole month of May. It was easy to understand why the market at Dimba was forced to be irregular during the last part of each rainy season.

Although Monday was not a regular market day, the place was a hive of activity. The people had a good bean harvest, as well as a generous supply of peanuts. Trucks had been unable to get through until Sunday morning. They had been trying to get to the Friday market but all got mired in the mud.

Three trucks were lined up, while local merchants loaded their beans for Kinshasa. Since everyone was at the market, it is quite possible that most of the region got a glimpse of the new pastor and his wife.

Petelo and Titi were still standing by the IME Land Rover with their baggage when an older couple approached them cautiously.

"Are you our new pastor?" the old gentleman asked as he extended his hand. "I'm deacon Dioko, and this is my wife, deaconess Sala. We are members of the church here at Dimba. Pastor Kwandambu sent us a letter telling us to expect you at the beginning of the dry season so we have been watching for you. Your kind faces made us feel that you are the ones who have been in our prayers."

Petelo and Titi smiled warmly as they shook these kind folk's hands.

"Thank you for your prayers. I'm pastor Petelo and this is my wife Mama Titi. It was kind of you to keep watching for us."

The welcoming couple asked the newcomers to wait a while until some of the deacons had sold their beans.

"They will want to welcome you and help carry your things." Mama Sala explained as she went back to attend to the sale of her harvest. "At my age I can't grow many beans for sale, but I do have a few.

"Your house is right next to ours, so we had better learn to get along well and not fight." Tata Dioko said with a poorly disguised twinkle in his eyes. "Go take a little look around the market. It is an old one. It was once a slave market, the elders have told me."

Petelo went over to express his thanks to the community health nurse who had been kind enough to allow them to travel with them.

"Pastor, we will be calling on you to help us from time to time, especially when we have an important immunization campaign. The local nurse is an alcoholic, and we can't depend on him. It will be good to have someone like you who can help us."

By noon the market was over, all the buyers had purchased their beans and arranged space on one of the trucks to get them to Kinshasa. Some of the small dealers paid for the transportation costs with sacks of beans. The more experienced buyers worked with money advanced by their Kinshasa customers most of whom were actually relatives.

ARRIVAL IN THE VILLAGE OF DIMBA

Four middle-aged women wearing white bandanas, which distinguished them as deacons, came over to Petelo and Titi to welcome them and help carry their things to the little manse beside the village church. To get to the village of Dimba from the market place they followed a winding path that spiraled down the hillside.

Petelo's eyes caught sight of the little old church building from a considerable distance. It was covered with rusting metal roofing. Coming nearer he could tell that the sheets were the thick old-fashioned kind that kept a building dry long after they had turned red with rust. From the outside, the building looked as though it could accommodate a hundred people or more. As they approached, three goats dashed in the open door to escape from the sun, and enjoy chewing their cud in peace. Everything spoke of neglect.

"We have not had services in the old church for over a year now, ever since old Pastor Mavova died. Pastor, we have a lot of work to do to win people back. Many of our folk joined with the ngunza (prophet) after he convinced the local population that the old man was the president of the witch market supposed to meet over there under the giant sanda tree. Some of our villages have a fair number of active believers. Dimba village and the area around us is in the worst shape. We are so glad you have come. We need a young pastor to approach our young people. You two are an answer to our prayers."

The old folk had done their best to get the little manse ready for habitation. The floor and whole yard had been meticulously swept. Metal roofing covered the front half of the house but the thatch on the back half was so full of holes that the sun shown inside, lighting the room with little shafts of light. Before they left, Deacon Dioko invited them to come over to their house for the evening meal.

After the little group left and they were alone, Titi began to sob gently. "Petelo, how are we going to live? The old folk have no money, and it looks as though they are the only active members in this village. Those other kind women were from some place else. We can plant a garden, but this is the dry season. How will we survive for all those months? Remember, I will be growing our baby all that time."

Petelo put his arm around Titi, remaining silent for a long time; he broke the silence with prayer.

"Lord you have met our needs in the past nine months in your amazing ways. Please help us both to trust you because we are totally dependent on you and the people you call to help us do your work. Please give us faith and the peace that comes with it. Amen!"

As they looked around, they saw that the communion table and two ornate chairs had been brought in from the church to provide them with a little bit of furniture. Fortunately, the little kitchen out back was covered with thick metal sheets. Titi broke into a smile when she found that a great supply of wood had been brought in to help her. She could tell the wood had just been cut by the freshness of the cut ends. Three, fire-baked anthills provided a dependable base to hold her cooking pots over the fire. A sturdy shelf in the front part of the house was large enough to accommodate all of their books and notebooks. Together they chose the spot where they would place their sleeping mats. On the wall beside their mats there was a whole line of hooks, obviously placed there so clothes could be hung up. By suppertime their little home was organized as well as they could manage.

"Titi, can you imagine how I would have felt if I had not married you and arrived here all by myself. It is wonderful to have each other. We can't see God, but in the Bible he promised to be with us always. We are facing a big adventure of faith. From what I know of God, he will use these circumstances to grow our faith. Let's go next door and eat the food God and our neighbors have provided."

Petelo and Tata Dioko ate beside a little low table in the main house. Titi and Mama Sala sat on the six-inch high, kitchen benches eating from the food pots placed on the mat.

"Once we saw for sure that you had come, we informed the deacons from all the villages in our parish that we would be having a communion service this coming Sunday. We haven't had the Lord's supper here for over a year!"

Petelo was pleased with the initiative of the thoughtful old man.

"Folk will have a good occasion to come back into the flock if they have slipped away during the past fourteen months. Those who began to follow the ngunza called Vunda know now that the man was a false prophet. He founded a big girl's choir that was expected to spend Saturday night in his village so they could sing on Sunday. Most of his Sunday services consisted of singing, and dancing with ndoki witch accusation as the most exciting feature. In the midst of wild singing and dancing, he claimed that the Holy Spirit threw him into a frenzied trance and told him who was causing death in our parts."

"When he made five choir girls pregnant the same month by enticing them to make 'Spirit babies' with him, the whole community ran him out of the area. The angry parents burned his house and meeting place. At the peak of his popularity, people came from everywhere to get ndoki witches exposed. Many of our families were thrust into sudden division, hatred and distrust.

"We have a big job ahead of us this week to get our church building ready. I think we will need to scrape off the top layer of the earth floor to get the smell of goats removed. I did my best to keep the doors closed but some enemy of the church opened up the doors every single night. There was nothing we could do. If that person takes a liking to you, Pastor, perhaps he will leave our doors alone. Most certainly that flock of goats will do their best to get back in because they know no other goat pen."

Petelo, several deacons, and some curious teens worked for three days to remove an inch or so of the dirt floor to rid the building of its stink. Titi came up with the final solution. All around the little manse there was a thick hedge of jasmine with its pungent, sweet perfume. On Saturday afternoon generous bouquets of these white flowers were tied to the windowsills.

"That has done the trick. The whole church building smells like a flowerbed rather than a goat pen. Your new ideas are helping us already," deacon Dioko observed.

At eight, Sunday morning, the precise drumming of old deacon Dioko sent out a welcome signal from the giant church drum that had been silent far too long. The final drumbeat to invite folk to enter the sanctuary would only be sounded when the old man reckoned that the majority of the congregation had arrived in the village.

Petelo wore his suit and Titi wore her graduation dress. They were both very nervous, but encouraged, seeing that about eighty adults and scores of children had come to the very first service.

Old deacon Dioko introduced them simply.

"This is Pastor Petelo and Mama Pastor Titi. They have just finished studying at the Kimpese Pastors School. They are great, hard working folk and I pray that God will use them to bring new life back into the five villages of our parish. Let's welcome them with our special clapping."

A tall young man popped up to lead in the intricate rhythm of their regional clap. They clapped together with perfect synchronization, ending after about three minutes with one gigantic clap. The united exercise brought broad smiles to most faces, and broke the awkward tension, making folk happy to be together again.

The young man, who directed the clapping, continued the process of welcome by saluting specific groups with a good round of clapping. Each group was asked to stand while the others welcomed them. All the deacons and lay pastors were made to feel appreciated with generous applause. The deacons were wearing white shirts and would have been wearing black ties if the dictator's government had not outlawed the wearing such attire. The women deacons all wore white kerchiefs with white blouses. One of the elderly lay pastors was asked to bring the opening prayer.

"Tata Nzambi, (Father God) maker of heaven and earth, we thank you that we can gather here. Last night we all died in sleep. We were like corpses and didn't know anything. We had no memory of people or possessions. This morning you brought us all back to life again and gave us the strength to walk to your house. You are powerful and good. We ask you to subdue any evil spirits in this place. Bind them and keep them quiet. Warm our hearts with your Spirit. Break our hearts of stone and open our hearts to receive your teaching. Bless this young couple who have left their home to come among us here in the parish of Dimba. Father, please fill them with wisdom and love. Protect them from evil spirits. Father, we have sinned in thoughts, words, and actions. Please forgive us. Father, we have a deep need for your forgiveness and blessing. We pray in the name of the Father, the Son, and the Holy Spirit, Amen!" The whole assembly echoed a clear "Amen."

The choir that initiated transformation

From the entrance to the church came a distinct drumbeat, followed by the united voices of a youth choir, singing as they entered. Surprise caused every head to turn to watch the group come up the central aisle, singing exceptionally well. When they were about half way up, Petelo suddenly realized that it was his old youth choir from Lukala. They had walked eight hours on the cross-country trail over the hills.

The audience was thrilled with their marvelous singing as they made their way to the front of the assembly. Their young leader asked for permission to speak.

"No doubt you are surprised to see us among you. We are Pastor Petelo's youth choir from Lukala. He did so much for us that we decided that we wanted to be here when you welcomed our beloved leader and our fellow chorister, Mama Titi."

The church exploded with enthusiastic applause and shouts of "bis, bis!" as they asked for more singing. By the time the choir had finished their second number all the local young people had crowded into the church just to listen. The choir sang three more numbers before Petelo rose to speak.

"This visiting choir has transformed our simple service into a celebration. Who knows? Perhaps by this time next year a choir from Dimba will go to sing for the folk at Lukala."

With the hope of a local choir, all the young people began to clap, showing their desire to take up the challenge.

By the time he began to speak, Petelo had their rapt attention. He spoke of the power of the Spirit of Jesus to heal the hearts of wounded people.

"God wants your wounded bitter feelings to be healed by means of his supply of love and forgiveness. Right where you are, please ask for God's help to enable you to forgive the people you feel have wronged you. Ask Chief Jesus to rule your hearts and enable you to love the people you have been hating. We need to ask for the cleansing, transforming, power of the Spirit of Jesus to prepare us to take communion together. Remember that Jesus died so that we may be forgiven. His is alive, and his Spirit is with us to change our hearts when we are helpless to change our own."

The communion service began in an atmosphere of peace and joy as the communicants came forward to receive the symbolic bread and wine. The whole assembly was unusually quiet while the communion service was completed. The local youth were surprised to see that almost all of the Lukala choir members were taking communion. The congregational singing reflected a new level of hope.

When everything was over, deacon Dioko clasped his new pastor's hand. "Pastor Petelo, God met with us today. He has heard our prayers."

Titi invited the Lukala choir to her little home as bare and empty as it was. Tears of gratitude flowed down her face as she embraced her fellow choir members. In her heart was a hopeless yearning to feed the choir that had come with such sacrifice. Didi, a close friend, looked around and understood Titi's embarrassment.

"We have brought Kwanga enough for all of us," she whispered gently. "We will just sit down on your mats and eat with you." They had just settled when deacon Dioko and Mama Sala came in with a huge pot.

"God must have lead my wife to cook this big pot of new beans and we want the choir to eat them for us."

The twinkle in their eyes and joy in their faces encouraged the young people to receive their generous gift of food wholeheartedly.

"Before we leave, we will sing a song of blessing over at your house," the young leader promised.

Titi put some of the beans in several other small pots so everyone could dip his or her kwanga pieces in the beans. Noting the confused look on some faces, she gave a demonstration.

"I know that you are accustomed to eating with spoons. Let me show you the village approach. You can do it with either kwanga or fufu. First break off a piece of kwanga. Make a ball of it in your hand. Push your thumb into it until you have a tiny kwanga bowl. Dip the tiny bowl into the beans and fill it. Pop the whole thing in your mouth and enjoy it."

They all laughed, but some remembered that they had eaten this way when they were children. It was a happy reunion.

Mama Sala had returned with a little pot of hot peppers for those who liked them. She heard the last of Titi's explanation.

"That is exactly how we ate all the time I was growing up. You can see I didn't starve either," she affirmed with a hearty contagious laugh.

"With these delicious beans to give us strength, we will make it back to Lukala before midnight. We plan to make use of the moonlight," the young choir leader explained.

Petelo and Titi were saddened to hear that the choir was returning to Lukala immediately.

"Some of us work in the cement factory so we must return in time to sleep a little before we go to the factory. Now that we are certain of this cross-country trail, we may well come back again sometime."

"I don't think that you can imagine what it means to us to think that you will have walked a total of sixteen hours just to visit our remote parish. I feel that the messages you brought in song were used of God today. You probably didn't know that this was the first public church service in fourteen months! Did you notice how many young people crowded into the gathering as soon as your singing reached their ears? I'm sure God has used you today. Please keep on singing for the Lord. When we sing just to get praise, God really can't use us. Chances are the young people will want to form a choir now. Thanks to you folk, I shall never forget the first service in my very first parish."

By four in the afternoon the choir had gone, leaving the village wistful and relatively quiet. Petelo and Titi carried back the communion table and chairs to their home. They were just sitting there remembering the day when Petelo made an observation.

"We had no idea what we would eat today. God enabled us to feed the five thousand and have some beans left over."

"Not bad for your first miracle," Titi said with a mischievous grin.

Titi took the bean pot back to Mama Sala's cooking hut where she found her talking with half a dozen women. Petelo sat down in the main house with deacon Dioko.

The old gentleman began to talk.

"Your coming has brought us hope. The past few years have been sad ones. You can't imagine how much division, hatred, and confusion that false prophet Vunda brought to this region. People can't retrieve the destructive words they have spoken. When he started abusing our girls, we knew that the Holy Spirit had nothing to do with his insights into family conflict. People knew that he wasn't a man of God, but many still believed that he had the power to expose the ndoki witches in these parts. Children have turned against their parents. Whole extended families have gone through ceremonies to divide into separate branches, cutting all relationships between them. They don't even attend one another's funerals.

We experienced more unity and goodwill this morning than we have felt for three years or more. We need you here to help us. Most of my children and grandchildren think that I am a killer ndoki witch. Through prayer I have been reconciled with two of my nephews. A third one still hates me, and would love to see me dead. God and I know I am innocent, but he has believed lies and can't help but hate me. Only God can change hearts and bring genuine reconciliation."

Petelo simply nodded with concern as the story unfolded.

"According to Vunda, our former pastor and I managed the ndoki witch market that he claimed met under the big sanda tree that we planted behind the church years ago. He claimed that we kept the spirits of the people we ate in the cabinet that contained the communion sets. We burned the cabinet but that made no difference at all."

"I'm glad that the fellowship of true believers belongs to our Lord. He will show us what to do," Petelo remarked in a quiet voice.

"Pastor, your support will be very slim unless there is a big change. My wife and I have good-sized gardens for old folk. We want you to eat our manioc until your own is ready to eat a year from now. A number of the deacons have put aside some beans for you too. We put a few beans in a jar every time we cook some for ourselves. We hope that together we can keep you supplied with beans. Some of the deacons in the other villages are doing the same thing."

While they had been talking with the door open, a half dozen children sat around on the ground listening to the conversation. Looking right at the boys, Tata Dioko grinned a little and said to the Pastor.

"I bet these boys and their friends would sing in a youth choir, if you organized one."

The positive response was immediate.

Lying on the sleeping mat close to his wife, Petelo promised that on Monday he would cut the grass they needed for their mattress.

"We have a lot to be thankful for already. Today was a great beginning. We seem to have some genuine friends and supporters. We have even been promised our basic food."

Putting her arms around him, Titi responded, "You made me very proud of you today. I kept saying to myself that that great Pastor was my very own husband. I wish I had faith like you. You knew somehow that we would have food, even though we had no money at all to buy it. Mama Sala and her friends said that they would give us manioc cuttings to plant when the rains return in November. They have already partially cleared some fields for us. They seemed glad to have a young person around. The prophet Vunda destroyed their relationships with their younger relatives.

'Did you know that your accent in Kikongo changed while you were at Sona Bata? The ladies asked me if you are a Mutando from up that way. I thought that the Angolans would identify with you after the service but I think they think you are a Mutando from this country. The ones I heard talking had a Caipemba accent."

There was silence for a few minutes and Petelo spoke again.

"I will try to visit all my villages this week. After you are settled, and before the baby slows you down, we will do some visiting together." Titi agreed that she would love to do that as soon as possible.

"The women want me to see the field they have been preparing for us. I am anxious to get a good look at the stream in the valley to assess my prospects of using my special traps here."

Turning to his sleeping position, Petelo explained that he felt he needed to meet with all the village chiefs and church leaders as quickly as possible. While he was speaking, Titi fell asleep before he could ask her to end the day with prayer.

The next morning, while the women were off getting water, Petelo asked deacon Dioko to explain where the other four villages of the parish were located. Drawing a little map in the sand, he explained that the trail leading out of the east end of their village led to the village of

Maki. The trail leading west from Maki went directly to Dumba. Walking west from Dumba lead to Nkosi while the trail south from Nkosi lead back to Dimba.

"It takes about an hour to walk from Dimba to Maki and less than an hour to go from Maki to Dumba. From Dumba to Nkosi takes less than a half-hour. Because of the hills, the journey form Nkosi back to Dimba takes about an hour." Petelo repeated the explanation to make sure he understood.

"I would be glad to go with you, especially when you meet with the village chiefs. You have met our local chief but it would be better to have a spokesman with you to seek your audience with each chief. They will feel you are showing more respect that way."

When Petelo thought a little, he was perplexed.

"You told me there are five villages in this parish. Where is the other village located?"

"I'm getting forgetful in my old age. The trail that goes to Dumba from Maki has a short side road down to Losa. It is a small village located only a short distance off the path we will be travelling. I will take my hunting gun along just in case we come across some game. There are often partridge between Dumba and Nkosi."

Petelo listened carefully as the old deacon gave a short history of each village including their involvement with the Vunda movement. In general, the younger people joined the movement and the older people were found guilty of witchcraft. The walk to Maki from Dimba took about an hour as they had estimated. Petelo was delighted to be walking through rather dense forest because he had grown up in savanna country. The forest had never been cut to any extent because there were never any truck roads constructed in this area covered with so many steep hills.

A necklace of leopard claws caught Petelo's eye when they had an audience with the elderly chief of Maki. He did not wish to receive the new Pastor until he was properly ensconced on his special chair and wearing his leopard skin apron. Elderly, and dignified, he looked the way Petelo had imagined that the chiefs of a bygone era might have looked. The very first questions the chief asked, after their introduction, concerned Petelo's identity.

"What is your luvila (bloodline)? Explain your lusansu (succession of matriarchal ancestors)."

As soon as Petelo gave his luvila as Kongokula the chief's eyes brightened, he spit on his hands and gave a paternal blessing.

"We are from the same luvila! You must be from the Mbanza Kongo region, the land of the kings," he proclaimed with pride. "My parents fled at the time of the Buta rebellion against the colonial rule when I was just a little too young to join the fight. "Speak the king's Kikongo if you can!" he ordered.

Petelo reverted to his childhood pronunciation repeating an old proverb. The old man slapped his thighs and grinned with delight.

"When I settled here in the forest there was no village at all. I planted all those big trees myself, including this sanda that covers us now! Angolan refugees built all those new houses. They are mostly from Caipemba. We didn't get along very well in Angola in the years gone by, but we get along fine now. Do you speak Kipotuki (Portuguese)? If you do, they will be on your side. Some of them are followers of Toko, but they are good people."

When they had finished a good visit with the chief, the lay pastor and his deacons were awaiting them in the little brick church. The oldest deacon was a native son, but all the others were refugees. They made Petelo feel very welcome.

"Very few of us came to the service on Sunday because we had a death here in the village and we simply could not leave. We have heard that you are from Angola. Is that true?"

Petelo told them his brief history, and explained as well that his wife was a Zombo. When he said his wife was a Zombo, the young lay pastor slapped Petelo's hand in a quick handshake of acceptance.

"If you can love a Zombo, you are capable of getting along with us," he said with a big grin. "We have all learned to pull together over here."

The friendly lay pastor was full of questions. "The folk who went to the big opening service told us that you directed a big youth choir in Lukala. Do you suppose you can help us with our choir here? We have a lot of young people who love to sing, but our leader needs training."

"I'm just looking over the work today, but I can assure you that I will do all I can to help your leader. Let me get a grasp of the parish before we try to make plans. After a good chat, they had prayer and separated.

As they were leaving the village a girl ran after them, "We want to help you start your flock of chickens so here is a pair to get started."

On the way to the village of Losa, the old deacon gave him the history.

"In the days of our ancestors, people found guilty of witchcraft were thrown off the cliff on the south side of the village. As you know, Losa means to throw. The poor victims smashed into the rocks far below. Often the accused's family was given the choice of ending a miserable life quickly by being thrown, or being sold as a slave. Most families preferred selling the condemned as slaves. The Sundi from Manyanga on the North side of the Congo River were traders. When the opportunity arrived they bought slaves from our Dimba market and traded them for cloth from the white Portuguese traders on the coast. Slaves were sold locally long after the white traders were forced to stop. Surrounding tribes bought women of child bearing age to increase their clans."

Petelo's face looked sad as he thought of the heartache these hills had witnessed.

"My ancestors did the same thing of course. I think that all the Kongo tribes have followed similar traditions. Our ancestors sold slaves to white traders, who shipped them all over the world."

In all the villages the Chiefs were cordial, but none so delighted as the one who found that Petelo was his fellow clansman. At Dumba and Nkosi, the little church buildings were filled in anticipation of their Pastor's visit. In each place he preached a short sermon, then talked with the folk who had gathered. One courageous woman described their situation.

"We no longer take communion because we followed Vunda. Pastor, we are sorry for all the heartbreak we have caused. We need help to return. We want you to come back and spend some time with us. I think we need to talk with you one at a time. Bring your wife too, if you can. We know now that Vunda was not a man of God but his miracles enticed us."

At Nkosi, their visit began with a delicious meal at the Chief's house. Fresh nsizi (groundhog) in a moamba sauce was too good for words.

"My wife will be jealous of me when she hears about this meal," Petelo said with a laugh.

"We have too many of these critters, and they are smarter than we are," the chief explained. "We have dry season gardens down by the stream. We get great prices in Lukala market, but we just can't catch enough of these nsizi. They are ruining our crops. Right now we have to keep watchmen in our gardens night and day."

They had a good meeting in the little church where people expressed the same kinds of feelings as they had been hearing.

"I have every confidence that God will heal you and your families from the wounds of hatred you are carrying. God has never stopped loving you, and He is more than willing to restore each one to a relationship of love and forgiveness. It will not happen in a day. Healing takes time. Together we can look forward to better days."

The enthusiastic way they sang the closing hymn made it was evident that their hope had begun to be restored.

Just as they expected, the two weary travelers arrived home at dusk. Tata Dioko shot two partridges, turning his trip into a successful hunt. Petelo held up the little palm branch basket woven around his hen and rooster.

"This is the game I shot with my gun." They all had a good laugh.

"Well I shot a catfish with my kind of gun," Titi replied. "My game is cooked and ready to be eaten by two hungry travelers."

The men had bathed when they came past the stream in the valley so they were glad to sit down after a busy day. Within minutes loaded plates were brought to them.

"This fufu is exactly the way I like it so you ladies must be agreed on at least one important thing."

"And just what is it we are agreed about?" Mama Sala asked cheerily.

"You must agree as to just how much water you mix with the fufu flour."

"Can you believe it? A woman young enough to be my granddaughter, and we both like our fufu to have the same consistency. That means we can eat together often. At my age I can't eat fufu made any other way."

Petelo was surprised when he saw piles of drying hay in their back yard, revealed by the bright moonlight.

"Some of the children helped me cut it. I knew you wouldn't have time. In a couple of days we will be sleeping on our mattress again."

They both smiled in the morning when their new rooster crowed out in the little cooking hut. They had both wanted to talk about many things after they were in bed. The joke was that they both had fallen asleep almost immediately the night before.

"I had a wonderful look at the parish yesterday, and met many very interesting people. There is a lot to be done, but many people really want help. That prophet Vunda really caused a tremendous amount of division and hatred. These folk are all tangled up in the fears, hatred, and desire for revenge that kindoki witchcraft produces."

"Petelo, I am afraid that I am a lot more like these people than you are. I can't imagine just how God is going to change my mind. You seem to feel it will happen. I want it to happen, but I guess I will need to have a whole set of alternative ideas to replace the ones I have gathered over my lifetime. If the folk here need as much change as I think I need, you certainly have a big job. I guess that I have seen so much power in fetishes, teki idols, curses, and shamans of different sorts that I can't help but have fear. I have seen too much, heard too much, and felt too many frightening moments. I want to believe I can trust God all the time. I want to get rid of my fears. Probably some of our traditional ideas are mistaken, but I feel many are true. I'm a pretty inadequate pastor's wife, but I am willing to learn. I still have fears, but as long as you are with me, I'm ok."

Petelo said nothing at all. For a long time, he simply held Titi in his arms gently, with great affection and tenderness.

"You know, Titi, it is helpful to have you tell me of your fears and struggles. I have never feared witchcraft like you. My parents and grandparents were all Christian believers. Your experiences will assist me to help others. I am certain that God will answer your longing for faith."

"Petelo, the way you love me and accept me just the way I am, helps me believe that God loves me too because I think He is something like you."

When Petelo noticed that Tata Dioko had a bed much like the one left behind in Kimpese, he asked if the necessary mateva palms grew near by. The very same morning the kind Deacon led him to the swampland in the valley where the special palms grew in abundance. They brought back all they could carry, then Petelo returned for a second load. The bed was finished in a couple of hours. In the meantime Titi had filled their mattress with dried grass. Together they had reproduced their Kimpese bed.

With saplings and mateva palm, Petelo constructed a good-sized table with two benches. They both felt that the communion table should remain in the church.

Before the rains returned, local men and boys replaced the thatch on the bad part of the roof in one long day's work. When the work was finished the boys had a proposition.

"Pastor we would like to have a choir by Christmas. Will you help us?"

"If you can round up fifteen young people, I will do my best."

"A number of us are away at school during the week but we are home every week end. We will recruit at school because the young people from all the villages of our parish go to the same school. We will gather a group by next Friday evening."

A choir of their very own

During the five months since their arrival, Petelo and Titi had established many good relationships. Gradually people were beginning to trust them enough to begin to unburden their hearts. Petelo preached in three of the five villages each Sunday. Wherever he preached he worked with the local choir leaders and their choirs too.

The choirs attracted the young people back to the church again. The central choir, which practiced at Dimba, was making good progress to the delight of everyone. The young people were happy to have someone organize them, and bring interesting songs with bright new rhythms. The older folk were encouraged just to see young people coming back to their church again.

Chief Kongokula never missed a service at Maki. He planted his special chair up beside the first bench and sat there in full regalia. After several months, the congregation was surprised when the old man asked permission to speak during the service. He had never asked to speak before.

Chief Kongokula burns his bridges

"God has used this young pastor to convince me. A week ago I asked Chief Jesus to rule my heart just the way our pastor has been asking us to do. I have made a big decision; today I want to burn all my fetishes and teki gods. I can see that this Chief Jesus has brought changes to my heart already. I want to be a member of his clan when I die. I notice that His clan receives people from all kinds of human clans. Everything is out under the sanda tree. I would like everyone to witness the burning."

After a prayer of thanksgiving, Pastor Petelo led the whole congregation to the sanda tree. The deacons got a good fire burning. Following the chief's instructions, Petelo placed the whole basket on top of the fire. As the paraphernalia of a lifetime of witchcraft burned, the old chief prayed resolutely.

"Chief Jesus, please rule my heart. Forgive me please, and wash out my old heart. Please lead me from right inside my heart, Amen."

The whole gathering shouted, "Amen!"

Pastor Petelo placed his hands on the head of the old chief who had been on his knees praying.

"Chief Jesus, please bless Chief Kongokula with your peace. Please forgive him for all the years he lived with his back turned on you. Please fill him with love, joy and peace for the rest of his life. I pray in Jesus name, Amen."

At this moment, the young pastor took the old man's right hand and held it above his gray head in the traditional manner of giving a blessing.

"In the name of the Father, the Son and the Holy Spirit Amen!"

While saying these words, he lifted the old man to a standing position. The Chief bowed a little and spoke distinctly through his tears.

"I feel forgiven! In the days ahead I want to ask for forgiveness from any of you I have wronged. Pastor Petelo, Chief Jesus has taken away my fear of dying."

A young deacon asked permission to speak.

"Ever since we arrived as refugees from Angola, we have had the feeling that our Chief allowed us to stay, but never really wanted us. Now we have a real father as a chief. Our own elders were unable to flee with us. Many have died. We are delighted that here in our little church, we are all belong together in Chief Jesus' clan."

The folk of Dimba Parish felt that the Christmas preparations were the best they had had for years. Each village had some kind of choir, even the little village of Losa. The most enthusiastic members of local choirs came to Dimba to become part of the central choir. Petelo and Titi worked together with the enthusiastic people who came from all over the parish.

Eventually, two choristers from each of the five villages were chosen for special training in choir directing. The idea was to improve the quality of local choirs throughout the parish.

"We would like our central choir to be a kind of 'musical mother' giving birth to other choirs for folk of all ages. All the choirs met together for concerts at Dimba. For four nights before Christmas, the choirs sang in each of the smaller villages.

A choir for Christmas and beyond

On Christmas Eve, everyone converged on Dimba for a wonderful evening of singing, as well as with an innovative presentation of the Christmas story in drama. Folk who had nothing to do with the church could not resist the offer of inspirational entertainment. Bringing folk together for a positive experience helped the villagers to rub shoulders again after years of conflict.

The Christmas experience gave the central choir considerable confidence. Folk were especially excited when they found that the pastor and deacons had accepted the Lukala Choir's request to pay them another musical visit on the third weekend in January. The choir requested that date for two reasons. The date fell in the middle of the traditional short dry season, and the Monday of that weekend was a work holiday, allowing the choir to sleep in the village before returning.

All the choirs, especially the central choir, practiced faithfully and often. They understood that when you host a choir, your own choir should sing for them too. They didn't want to be embarrassed before the great Lukala choir.

Excitement mounted in Dimba on the day the choir was expected. Beyond question, the small boys and girls were the most excited. They were posted as watchmen on the top of the hill that lead down into the village.

"Zingoma! Zingoma!" ("Drums, drums, we hear their drums!")

A stampede of choristers hurried to the hilltop so they could escort their visitors to the village.

"Let's sing some of our animation songs that we know well," Zabo Zabo shouted, as he clapped his big hands to mark the rhythm. He had evolved as an enthusiastic, creative choir leader.

There was a lull in the singing while the two choirs were meeting and shaking hands. After a few minutes, the two choirs began to sing a number of songs together. After all, Petelo had directed both choirs, so they knew his favorites. The united choirs sparked enthusiastic responses of all sorts.

Mama Sala and her crew flew into action. "Get the beans heating! Let's get the water boiling in our three fufu pots!"

The Dimba ladies knew that their hospitality reputation would be on the line until the hungry choir ate its last meal on Monday morning. They loved it, because they were all good cooks. They loved choir singing, and they had generous amounts of food already gathered in for the occasion.

Several families had volunteered their tables, which were all arranged under the spreading sanda tree behind the church. The village chief had two large Coleman, kerosene pressure lanterns that he normally rented out for wakes. He was so delighted to see a genuine measure of harmony again that he made his two lanterns available for the weekend. His oldest nephew had a large container of fuel and volunteered to keep the finicky devices functioning. In a word, they were prepared for visitors!

The experienced choir members each had brought their own plates and mugs with their initials on the back in red fingernail polish. Small boys fed the bonfire from the mountain of wood they had gathered. The bright flames competed with the lanterns to light the whole area under their giant tree.

Family reunion

Looking over the whole scene, Pastor Petelo expressed his contentment by stating clearly; "This is a real celebration!"

He had no sooner pronounced his happy judgment, when suddenly, two women grabbed Titi and all three began squealing with delight.

"Lala! Mama Mbuta!, Where did you come from?" Titi asked breathlessly.

"We started with the choir, but had to drop back and move more slowly coming through these hills."

Titi was well advanced in her pregnancy, but her family had not seen her since she left Lukala.

"You look big and wonderful," her aunt cooed, while patting Titi's very large tummy. "We just had to come to see you. Sami knows the driver of the big green Volvo that comes here to the Dimba market. He has paid our passage on it, so we don't have to walk back. I guess that means leaving about noon tomorrow."

"How are Sami and the children? Is the store still running well? Don't answer me until you are settled in our house. You must be exhausted after walking all day. Some of the young people have finished eating. Come over to the tables and meet my neighbors. You must be starved!" Titi put their two bundles in her house as they passed by.

As soon as they reached the visitors tables, Mama Sala came over. "This is my Mama Mbuta, and her husband's younger wife Mama Lala," Titi explained.

They began to shake hands as Titi explained that Mama Sala and her husband Tata Dioko had been like loving grandparents ever since she and Petelo arrived in the village.

"Their children and grandchildren live in Kinshasa so they really treat us like grandchildren."

After eating the delicious late afternoon meal, the young people stretched out on their mats over by the fire where they fell fast asleep allowing mama Mbuta and Lala to climb up on Titi's bed and do the same. After a couple of hour's sleep the young people were totally recovered from the long walk and launched into song. By midnight, every choir had had a chance to sing for the large appreciative audience. Their very best numbers were reserved for the Saturday night concert, intended to be the main event. Many of the young people would have been glad to try to sing all night, but Petelo's request for them to sleep was obeyed because of their basic respect.

At four in the morning, a powerful thunder and lightning storm took everyone by surprise. Theoretically it never rains during the January dry season, but at times it does. Fortunately, the choirs had not slept outside all night. They were all asleep on their reed mats in the church building with their chaperones.

Titi clung to Petelo, when the storm drew near with blinding flashes of lightning, and deafening thunder. She was actually trembling with fear.

"My grandmother was always terrified during a lightning storm. One of the old men who hated her, and told her so was suspected of being capable of throwing lightning on an enemy. She set up her teki as soon as she heard thunder in the distance. You say that we don't need protection like that, but I still feel afraid."

"Titi, my dear, I understand your fears, but I trust the God who made heaven and earth far more than I could ever trust a wooden doll made by a shaman. One of our Kimpese instructors taught us how lightning works. It is a force we can understand but we can't control. He explained that lightning strikes high points. He told us that lightning frightens people all over the world.

"We were surprised when he said that not a single scientist, or anyone else in his country, believed that people could direct lightning at will. He gave us some very practical warnings. He warned us not to build our houses on the tops of hills where the house would be one of the highest objects around. He warned us not to take shelter under a tall tree during a storm. He even cautioned us to lie flat on the ground if we were caught in a large open place without protection, during a storm.

"Were there many tall trees around your Grandmother's house?"

Titi remembered that there were giant nkamba trees between her grandmother's house and the stream.

"Those trees were your protection!"

"Perhaps that is why they were hit several times over the years. Even if it was, I'm still afraid. You are the only person I have ever met who didn't believe that ndoki witches could manipulate lightning to destroy their victims! Perhaps some day I will feel safe here because there are so many big trees around. Right now I am still afraid!"

The storm passed by after pouring oceans of rain over everything.

"Let's go back to sleep now because you will not need to go for water tomorrow. I put our basins and pans out under the eaves before the storm disturbed you.

Titi gave him a big hug. "Do you think I will think like you by the time I am your age?" she asked plaintively.

"I'm glad I love you the way you are and that I don't need to wait a dozen years to begin," Petelo replied with a chuckle.

In the morning, the deep rumble of the church drum startled everyone who had fallen back to sleep after the storm. Titi hurried to Mama Sala's little cooking hut to help with breakfast for their visitors. As soon as they met, they all admitted they had been frightened.

"That lightning tore a big chunk off the big Nkamba tree by the cemetery, and that is far too close for me!" Mama Sala admitted.

By nine, all the visitors had been served with coffee, roasted peanuts, boiled manioc, and boiled sweet potatoes. They were ready for excitement. All around the village, choirs were rehearsing for the great Saturday night festival.

Titi brought food over to her house for Lala and Mama Mbuta, who were just beginning to awaken as she set the food on their table.

"I'm sure that downpour will change the plans of your green Volvo. It will never get over the roads. They know for sure there are lots of early mangos up here, so they will come when they can, even if it isn't a market day. Dimba mangos sell really well in Kinshasa because they are so plump. In any case, that prolongs your visit a little. You will be able to attend the choir concerts tonight."

People from the surrounding villages began to arrive in such large numbers that it became evident that they could not meet in the old Church auditorium. As soon as Petelo gave permission, the benches were moved out under the big sanda tree. Dimba folk brought chairs, benches, and mats until everyone was seated. Village chiefs and other notable elders were all seated in the very front rows. Dozens of little children squirmed on mats placed between the elders and the choirs where watchful deaconesses in their white uniforms carefully supervised them. The natural rise in the ground allowed everyone to see and hear well. There were over five hundred people present.

As far as the appreciative audience was concerned, the choirs were the best they had ever heard. Each village clapped and cheered until they were hoarse, especially when their own local choir was singing. Each choir, including the central choir, presented its special numbers to the enthusiastic delight of everyone.

Tape recorders were busy recording all the new numbers. Later, they could alter and adapt what they heard to make a new presentation some day. Good singing seemed to generate an ocean of good will.

When the Lukala choir sang one of their old favorites, they invited Petelo and Titi to join them. They both thoroughly enjoyed singing with their friends again.

The whole evening brought great satisfaction to Petelo. He had trained the leaders of every choir. For the most part, the leaders accepted Petelo's emphasis that a choir should try to communicate the truth of the song in a way that would please the Lord. Not every choir member was a convinced believer, but the leaders were all people of faith. Intentionally there was a good message in every song.

The young people were a little disappointed when once again Petelo requested the Saturday evening concert to end around midnight. He knew that many people needed to go home to their villages sleep and put on their good clothes, before coming back to the big Sunday service and choir concert. It had been a great evening for everyone.

On Sunday morning, despite singing their hearts out on Saturday evening, the whole village was the scene of impromptu choir rehearsals in every available secluded spot. Their breakfast was ready by eight thirty. While they were gathered, Petelo took the occasion to address them.

"I would appreciate it if each choir will take time to pray as a group. You know that this whole area has suffered from the divisions and distrust that a false prophet movement brings. In you hearts, remember that you are singing for God. Many people may forget my sermon, but a large number will leave here singing some of your songs. Please ask God to help you recommend him well when you sing. We all know that far too many choirs sing only to be seen and talked about. Please sing as messengers for our Lord. We all need the help of the living Spirit whether we are singing or preaching."

Once more the gathering under the Sanda tree must have reached well over four hundred people. The expectation of the arrival of the market truck brought many on a double mission. They brought their sacks mangos with them, with the hope of avoiding double trips from their villages.

There were eighteen choir numbers before Pastor Petelo brought his message. Titi sat with her aunt and Lala.

"Just look at that Petelo beaming up there, he does love to hear these choir's sing," Mama Mbuta whispered to Titi.

Petelo began his sermon by making reference to the splendid choirs.

"We have heard eighteen little sermons in song. Please let me bring just one more before we separate.

"Listen to the words of Jesus found in Matthew chapter five verses forty three and forty four."

"You have heard that it was said, 'Love your neighbor and hate your enemy.' But I tell you: Love your enemies and pray for those who persecute you."

Pastor Petelo preaches and an old chief speaks

"Dear friends and neighbors, we are all aware that our traditions tell us to hate our enemies and take vengeance on them to make them suffer. Wouldn't it be wonderful if all of us gathered here could love, rather than hate our enemies? If that happened, many of today's enemies could become tomorrow's friends. I can hear you muttering in your hearts that no one can love his enemy. You are right, no matter how we try we can't change our hate to love. That is just why we need the Spirit power of Chief Jesus to change us on the inside. Many are trapped in hatred. We have become as bitter as meat drenched in the juices of gall when the hunter's knife cuts it by accident. We are sick of hatred in our hearts, like someone exhausted from vomiting. Only the forgiveness, and transforming power of the living Spirit of Chief Jesus can change what we can't change. Ask Chief Jesus to take over the chief's chair in your heart so that the power of witchcraft can be broken. He alone can set us free from the gnawing misery of hatred that keeps us miserable and afraid. No one but Jesus has the power to rescue us, and remove our meanness and shame."

Just as Petelo finished his short but memorable sermon, old Chief Kongokula from Maki clapped his hands requesting the privilege of speaking. Petelo quickly gave him permission.

"I want you all to know that what our Pastor has just taught is completely true. I'm sure you all heard that a couple of months ago I burned all my protective fetish charms and the teki I received from my ancestors. I asked Chief Jesus to forgive me and become the Chief of my heart. I want you to know that I sleep in peace now, feeling safer than when I had all my protection. I have found myself praying for some of the people who hate and fear me because they believe I am an ndoki witch. Chief Jesus is changing me in ways I could never manage myself. I'm not afraid any more. I'm not even afraid to die. As I became older, my fears kept increasing until the living Spirit of Chief Jesus began to change me on the inside."

When the dignified old chief regained his seat, the Lukala choir sang an old hymn. "Trust and obey, for there is no other way, to be happy in Jesus, but to trust and obey."

Not a half-hour after the service was over, the roar of the big Volvo announced its arrival at the market. Within minutes the path to the market looked like a long line of brown ants, as folk hurried to the market place with sacks mangos on their heads.

Knowing that her family would be leaving with the truck in about four hours' time, Titi busied herself preparing their meal. All three women worked together in Titi's little cooking hut. Titi had a portion of the beans that had been cooked for the choir. Lala had brought a little package of dried cod fish, which they decided to boil and place in the beans. Mama Nkenda busied herself by pounding out the fufu flour. Titi prepared saka saka greens.

"It seems like old times to be cooking together again. Titi, you seem happy. Are you really happy with Petelo? What is it like to be called 'Mama Pastor'?"

"Petelo is a wonderful husband. I could not ask for anyone better. Thank you for allowing me to marry him. He is kind and thoughtful with everyone. He is away a lot because he serves five villages and he is trying to equip the leadership in each place. He works with the lay pastors and the choirs.

"I suppose that our greatest difficulty is that he receives very little money. In the past, the head pastor was always a local man with very little training who farmed like everyone else. No one saw any real need to pay him. The tiny offerings are divided between the lay pastors and Petelo. Gradually people are noticing that Petelo works full time in their midst. Some think that because he owns a good suit, he is rich. Recently a local man, who is a schoolteacher attended the parish council meeting. He reminded them that Petelo had more years of training than he, when he heard of the pittance he was being paid. He said he thought that Petelo should receive as much as a schoolteacher.

"Later, the council made a decision give the total income from the next Matondo or Thanksgiving service. They planned this special offering to be taken up at the time of the peanut harvest. They recognized that I would want to have my first baby back where I would be close to you. If people give generously, it will really help us to pay for the truck trip.

"I should say that Mama Sala and Tata Dioko our deacons have been like family to us. We are living off their manioc this year. Many others have given us peanuts and beans. They have been careful to see to it that we are never hungry. I have caught a few fish with hook and line, but have not yet located a spot where I could employ traps. Now it is my turn to ask some questions.

"How is Sami's health? Is he able to walk longer distances? How many families live out near our little house now? Is the store business in Lukala still going well? Are you catching any fish in the traps I left with you?"

Both Lala and Mama Mbuta laughed about the list of questions.

"As you can see, Lala and I still get along well. She often stays overnight with me when we are doing fieldwork. Now that Sami is much stronger, he comes to see me almost every week. He has finished putting a metal roof on our little house. There are seven little houses in our village now. Now it is your turn to answer Lala."

Looking right at Titi, Lala gave expression to deep feelings. "Titi, thanks to you Sami is alive and well. My little children have a father. If you had not advised him with so much wisdom, I think he would have died in the months following the robbery. The little store is providing a living for us all, so I am very thankful."

Stirring the thick fufu as she talked, Mama Mbuta remembered that she had not replied about the fish traps.

"I can't wade out in the currents of the deep water during the rainy season, so I can only catch fish in the dry season. I catch some, but I don't have your magic."

Titi laughed as she asked. "Are you calling me a ndoki with special powers?"

"Perhaps," her aunt replied with a grin.

As soon as they had finished eating, Titi took her family down to the stream to have a look at her gardens that were situated on the side hills leading up form the edge of the stream.

They had never gardened in such hilly terrain.

"I can see why you folk have such good bean and peanut crops. You are down where it is moist but the fields drain quickly after a big rain."

When the truck horn sounded, they quickly scrambled back up to the village. "That is just the warning horn. They will leave in about a half hour," Titi explained.

By the time they got to the truck, it was loaded high with sacks of mangos and dry manioc.

"It is a good thing that Sami has already paid the driver for us to sit in the cab. It will be very dangerous for the people who must ride on the top the load. They risk being hit with branches." Lala observed.

Petelo was with them as Titi said her farewell.

"In a few weeks I will be with you to have my baby," Titi shouted as the truck pulled away. Mama Mbuta was in the middle, with Lala next to the window. The driver had insisted that the older woman sit next to him so no one would think that Lala was his new prostitute. Part of the payment of a truck driver often involved paying for a prostitute to accompany him. Their driver did not live that way and didn't want to give any the impression that he did.

By five in the afternoon, the village of Dimba was totally silent because everyone had left, including the marketers. Petelo helped return the borrowed table. The crew of women who had been cooking in Mama Sala's cooking hut was tired but very pleased. They remembered that the first time the Lukala choir came by surprise, they had not been able to provide much food.

"I think we will have a good reputation in Lukala now because their young people ate well. The old church roof kept them dry the night it rained. People were very happy to have them as I'm sure they could tell by the smiles and clapping. Our choirs sounded great too." All the women were nodding their heads in agreement as Mama Sala spoke.

"Titi, your husband is a great speaker. I never heard a preacher say such important things in such a short time. People smiled at one another this weekend, who haven't been civil to one another for over a year. In the past, there was always one of our five villages out of sorts with the rest of us. This time everybody came, and every village contributed food to this kitchen. Let's hope that the worst is far behind us." It was Mama Didi who was getting the nods as she spoke. "It did my heart good to have our big services right on the very spot that Vunda claimed to be the ndoki witches' market."

Petelo's reputation grew considerably because of the special weekend, increasing the number of people who wanted to talk with him when he came to their village. They had never had a pastor who knew how to relate the teaching of the Bible to their very own struggles. He always walked home at night, even when it was raining because he didn't want to leave Titi alone during any thunderstorm that might come during the night.

By the beginning of March just about every household had its peanuts harvested. Titi was not able to do as much work as usual because of her advancing pregnancy. A heavy rainstorm softened the soil the day Petelo planned to dig their peanuts. As a result they were much easier to get out. Titi sat in the shade to pull the peanuts off the roots, as Petelo brought them over to her from their good-sized plot. By the time they had finished, they had enough to fill well over three of the big peanut sacks. They put their crop into smaller sacks, because the fresh peanuts were heavy to carry. Titi would be able to supervise the drying process on the flat spot in front of their house. As she tended to their own little crop of peanuts, Titi was hoping that folk would be generous with their gifts from their peanut harvests. The special harvest thanksgiving service was just a week away.

Walking like a duck

By the end of February, Titi had slowed down in her movements. She broke out into gleeful laughter while watching one of Mama Sala's ducks. She realized that she walked exactly like the waddling creature. Both she and Petelo were becoming more and more excited about the prospects of having their first baby. They were agreed that they would follow a family tradition allowing the father to name the first boy, and the mother to name the first girl. It was agreed as well that they would keep their choices secret, until they were needed.

"In our village no one named a baby for several weeks until it was strong and healthy. The elders felt that naming a baby made it more vulnerable to ndoki witches," Titi admitted.

During their visit, Lala had agreed that she would accompany Titi to the hospital and stay with her when her time came.

Matondo or Thanksgiving celebration

The fact that there were choirs practicing for the Matondo (Thanksgiving) festival helped local people to plan for the gathering. Of course there was a friendly competition developing between the five choirs. It was friendly because they all united to form the central choir. As a result of all the keen anticipation, large numbers came to Dimba for the special weekend.

The Saturday evening choir festival was a marvelous event. It was a pleasure to see the competing groups all join voices when they merged to become the central choir. Once more Petelo requested the event to end at midnight so folk would be rested for the Sunday services.

The choirs sang their hearts out for the first two hours of the program. Folk enjoyed the singing so much that most came in time to hear the whole concert. It was the choir from Maki that brought an outstanding presentation. Their choir leader composed a song with a very catchy rhythm and theme. Their musical narrative spoke of a village, once totally divided, led into a new life by their old Chief who burned his past and surrendered to a new Chief called Jesus. Their village had gone through a major transformation in a few months. They were filled with joy and hope that they expressed marvelously through their singing.

The central choir sang enthusiastically while people brought up their harvest thanksgiving gifts. Great sacks of dried peanuts were carried to the front by dancing carriers. In the end, they had contributed over twenty sacks of peanuts together with money gifts from people who had already sold their crop. Generosity brought joy to the givers. They filled the sacks gradually right in the meeting as people gave according to their possibilities. Some of the old widow women gave full basins of peanuts. Titi had filled her big basin from their peanuts and carried it in joyfully along with the other women who were doing the same.

Petelo spoke warmly and wisely in a way that encouraged people. "The Lord loves a cheerful giver!" "This is what God's word says about giving. I have watched your joyful giving. I know the Lord will bless you. I watched the women bringing and cooking the food for the Lukala choir in January. It was their joy that pleased the Lord."

He concluded on a personal note. "Titi needs to go to her sister's at Lukala to wait out the days until our baby will be born. Now we know that the treasurer will be able to pay us some back pay. We hadn't a penny for the journey, but now she will be able to go. Your giving has lifted a burden from us."

As soon as Petelo finished the old chief or Maki asked to speak. "You say that God used our peanuts to lift your burden. I am thankful that he used the words that you spoke to lift a burden from my heart and from many hearts in my village. You moved among us joyfully and willingly. God is blessing you for your cheerful giving too."

The villagers returned happily to their homes led by their singing choirs.

Titi made a confession to Petelo as they lay in bed. "Petelo, once more you have shown me an example of your faith. Until today we had no way to get me to Lukala. I didn't see how it could happen. Your trust in God was well placed. Do you suppose I will ever learn to trust like you?"

Petelo paused before he answered. "I see lots of changes in you already. The day may well come when your faith will be stronger than mine. You will just have to wait and see what God will do with you, just as we had to wait until today to discover just how we would find the funds for you to get to Lukala.

During the rainy season, market day arrived whenever the truck got there. Folk from a considerable distance stored their produce in houses near the market so they could be shipped whenever a truck was available. There was just one old truck that could generally make it through the mud and up the hills. The big old German made Mann diesel army surplus truck, with power in all six gigantic wheels, was only stuck when some other truck blocked the road. Roaring in on time, its arrival was unmistakable.

Excited at what lay ahead, Titi and Petelo did not wait until the last moment to assure their place. When the driver saw how very pregnant she was, he assured Pastor Petelo that Mama Pastor would ride in the cab.

"The road is so rough that I will only allow one person in the cab so that I will have lots of room to maneuver this old giant."

The truck was headed for Kinshasa, so Titi would need to get into one of the little taxi trucks at Mbanza Ngungu to take her to Lukala.

In their modest fashion, Titi and Petelo shook hands to say goodbye.

"I'll be praying," he said softly just before the big old engine broke into roaring life. They found it difficult to face separation. They had not been apart a single night since they were married.

Waiting for news of the birth

Each successive market day, Petelo hurried as soon as he heard the roar of the truck climbing the Ndoko hills only three kilometers away as the crow flies. The first week there was no letter. On the market day closest to the expected birth date, the truck got stuck on a bad hill. Petelo joined prospective passengers in the difficult walk to the mired truck. They were drenched by the rain on the way over but soon began to dry out again when the sun shone again after the storm.

"Do you have a letter for me?" Petelo asked the driver with a longing in his eyes. At first the driver shook his head putting on a sad face. After watching his suffering a moment, the teasing driver handed him his letter. The young pastor trembled as he opened it.

"Dearest Petelo,
  We have a wonderful son. I hope to be back home again in about three or four weeks. If you have chosen his name, please send it to me so I can get his birth certificate before we return. He is beautiful! I can't wait for you to see him.

Your loving wife, Titi"

The driver decided to return to Lukala market because he was unable to complete his load from the Dimba market as he had expected. In a great rush Petelo wrote on the back of Titi's letter and reused her envelope. In the letter he explained his dilemma and gave her the name he had chosen for a son.

"Dearest Titi,
  I thank God for the safe arrival of our son. Please name him Makiese. That was the name of my godly grandfather! I love and miss you. I can't wait to see our son. I shall

try to send you a real letter next market day. Although I miss you, I would like you to stay with your family until you and the baby are both strong. With all the heavy rains, you may have to walk to Dimba from Ndoko Mountain.

Your loving husband Petelo. Please forgive me for reusing your envelope."

Mother and baby home at last

On the twenty fifth of April, the old German army truck was able to climb all the hills to Dimba market. The muffler shook loose on the rough roads causing the roar of the engine to travel at least ten kilometers on the still morning. Petelo and everyone else had lots of time to get to the market before the truck. As soon as the roar of the engine had stopped, Petelo was up on the high running board, hungry for a letter from his wife.

"What do you want a letter for? Wouldn't you rather receive your wife and baby," the driver enjoyed teasing him.

The whole village crowded in to get a look at the baby who was looking at the world from the safety of his father's arms. Titi's smile went from ear to ear. It took an age for each of the women to hold the baby for a few minutes. Mama Sala waited to the last, picked up the baby, and headed for the village.

"My little tekolo! (grandchild), " she cooed as she led the way home.

"We left Lukala at four this morning so I'm very tired. Makiese will want to eat several times throughout the night so please forgive me and just let me rest."

The women all understood because they too had raised babies.

When the smell of good food awakened Titi, she was surprised that Makiese was still asleep. Mama Sala had cooked the traditional rooster that Petelo was expected to provide for the mother of his baby. It was considered to be a man's duty to provide a whole rooster for the wife's first meal following the birth.

"I'm a little late, but then you have just brought me our baby today," Petelo explains with a grin.

Titi only laughed at the idea of eating the whole rooster by herself. Petelo invited Mama Sala and Tata Dioko to join them for the supper.

"Makiese told me that he wanted his adopted grandparents to eat with him," Petelo said with a happy grin.

After a prayer of sincere thanks for the safe return of Titi and her baby, they all ate heartily. The rooster was a big one that had been auctioned off, after the Thanksgiving service at the church. No one bid against the pastor because they knew that he needed a good rooster to offer his wife after she gave birth.

After supper, Titi and Mama Sala talked about caring for the new baby.

"There is one thing that worries me about babies born during the rainy season. The mosquitoes are thick at night. There is water everywhere so we will have mosquitoes right up to the end of the rains in the beginning of June. Fever is a dangerous enemy for our little ones" she sighed.

"How is your milk supply, Titi?" Mama Sala asked.

"I think I was made to raise babies because I have had plenty of milk since the second day." Titi replied with a grin.

"You look like a little tired child. When you are nursing a new baby, I think you should let your fields go a little. It is hard on you to feed a baby and work in your fields too."

"I have always worked hard, and really love to do it. Once the beans are planted my field work will slow down."

When Petelo and Titi were alone, Titi had things to discuss.

"At Lukala, my aunt pleaded with me to take Makiese to a renowned Angolan shaman who lives near Sami's old house in town. I knew that you would be very upset with me, so I didn't do it. I just hope that you have enough faith for all of us. I feel vulnerable all over again, not for me, but for my baby. Three of my mother's babies died."

"Did your mother have the traditional protections?" Petelo asked in his quiet penetrating way.

"We always had every kind of protection, especially after the first baby died. I only removed my last fetish charm just before I was baptized. It made me very nervous to do it. I had the pastor do it because of all the taboos threatening any voluntary destruction of the shaman's work."

"Thank you for resisting, Titi. It must have been hard to resist the advice of your aunt. As I see it, going to a shaman who is an avowed ndoki witch is like asking a python to guard our guinea pigs. According to tradition, he or she has offered the life of one of her family members in order to obtain the spirit needed to do the divining. It would be an insult to our God to go to the enemy for that kind of help. In my opinion, we do the very best we can and trust God for the rest. This does not guarantee that our children will not become ill. The children of faithful believers die, too. All I am sure about, is that the Lord wants us to trust him in good times and bad."

With their tiny baby sleeping right beside Titi in their bed, they both became far more conscious of the mosquitoes.

"I think there are far more now than before I went to Lukala," Titi lamented. "I always sleep with my sheet over my head, so I have never really noticed that they were around me."

"I love it when we are all home together in the early evening. Ever since you came home with the baby, I have tried to get home before dark. I worked a lot with the village choirs in the evenings while you were away. They are doing well and I think that a couple of them will probably even do better without me. Some of those young people have great ideas for new songs."

Worry a few weeks later

Petelo was holding the baby while Titi finished preparing their supper. "Titi, I'm afraid that our baby is getting thin. He is longer, but he doesn't look as strong as he did nor does he seem as strong."

"Now you sound like a worried mother."

"Do you realize that four weeks have passed since you brought home our baby. There has not been one truck that has made it to the market since the big old army truck that brought you. Someone told me that there are two big trucks stuck in the valley by Ndoko Mountain. Nothing can get through. People headed for Kinshasa or Mbanza Ngungu have to walk about twenty kilometers to get to a part of the truck road where trucks do pass occasionally."

"Perhaps I have been spoiled by living at Kimpese and Lukala. All my early years we lived eight hours' hard walking from the truck road at Lufu. We didn't feel cut off, because we had never seen trucks in our villages. Now, I feel a little worried when the market vehicles can't get through."

FROM WORRY TO GRIEF

Malaria fever

Thunder rolled off in the distance as Titi sleepily put her whimpering baby to her breast. For the first time, her little one refuses to eat and just kept on being fretful. When she put her hand under his head, she was alarmed by how hot he felt that she awakened Petelo. As soon as he felt the feverish body of their little one, he shared her concern..

"Those plagued malaria mosquitoes have finally gotten through to his little body. He is so small. We must take him to the nurse in the morning."

There was no more sleeping that night as two worried young parents watched helplessly as their little one suffered. Titi was glad that the thunderstorm rumbled off to the South, leaving her without that additional torment. At first light, both parents hurried to the nurse's home near the market. The nurse got up willingly and gave the baby an injection of anti-malarial medicine. By noon Makiese was obviously feeling much better and began to nurse a little. However, he still seemed listless and fussy. After all, it was the very first time he had ever been ill.

Makiese neither ate well, nor slept normally during the next five days. Out of anxiety, they kept their little lantern lit every night. By early evening of the normal market day, the baby was feverish again. Petelo hesitated to tell his worried wife that their only nurse had walked over beyond the Ndoko hills to try to get a truck for Kinshasa. He needed to buy a supply of medicine because the supplier who normally came with the market truck had not been there for a month. There was no point opening his little dispensary when he had no medicines.

With the reverberation of heavy rain on the metal roof and their basic anxiety about the baby, a pernicious pessimism seemed to invade their little home. Petelo did not easily become depressed, but the reality of their circumstances was oppressive.

The Thanksgiving service in March had brought in a generous offering. The peanuts were turned into cash on the first market day, and turned over to Petelo to help cover some of his back pay. The church had voted to pay him teacher's wages whenever they had the money. It was wonderful to have some money right at the moment when they were facing the considerable cost of bringing their baby into the world and supplying him with his first basic clothing and supplies. With the costs the birth, and the paying back of little debts, Petelo was once more almost out of money. The kerosene in the lantern was their last. Even if he had money, the failure of the market trucks to arrive provoked a general shortage. They had plenty of food because of the generosity of their neighbors and the high productivity of their own gardens. Petelo had hoped he could buy a big tin of powdered milk to keep Titi strong while she nursed. It cost more than they could afford.

Storms herald the unthinkable

All night long the rain bucketed down and, despite the coolness of the night rains, Makiese grew hotter and hotter. His little body felt like fire whenever Petelo touched him.

"We must go to the nurse at daybreak and pay for another injection for our baby. The fever is more than his little body can stand," Titi says with urgency in her voice.

"The nurse left the village two days ago and walked over the hills so he could replenish his stock of medicines," Petelo explained sadly.

Although he had been praying quietly all night long, the young pastor prayed out loud, expressing his burden.

"Dear God, you gave us our wonderful Makiese and he has brought us profound joy. As you can see, he is very ill and we don't know what to do. Titi is becoming worn out and frail. Our baby has been suffering for over five days now. Lord, please help him and help us too! We want to trust you, but we are finding that very hard to do because our baby only seems to be getting weaker. Lord, please have mercy on us."

As dense darkness crowded out both light and hope, the wee baby's fever increased alarmingly. The little one seemed to be breathing only in shallow gasps. About two in the morning, the roar of rain coupled with the growls of a gathering thunder and lightning storm forced Petelo to build up the fire to provide more light, despite the unwanted heat. Their lantern was flickering because the fuel was all but finished.

Worn with worry and fatigue, Titi was reaching the limits of her endurance. The storm increased its intensity. Bright lightning flashed, with shorter delays between flashes and the thunder grew relentlessly unnerving. A blinding flash accompanied by an ear-splitting thunderclap shook the ground under them. Three such terrifying flashing explosions followed in rapid succession, hitting something nearby producing a pungent burning smell. With the final blinding flash and terrifying thunder, little Makiese was thrown into a shocking convulsion, shaking violently in his mother's arms. The menacing thunder and lightning storm seemed to be paralyzed right over the village.

Despite the storm, Petelo rushed out the door to call their faithful neighbors to their aid. Death seems perilously near, and they desperately needed someone with them. As he bolted out, the wind wrestled the door from his hands and slammed it violently behind him.

The sudden crash of the wind-slammed door seemed to double the intensity of Makiese's convulsion. Titi placed her little one on her lap face up, so she could see him better in the dim light. Every fiber of her consciousness was convinced that some wanton witch force was snatching her baby from her, right before her eyes.

"Babies don't just die unless someone is sucking out the life spirit," she wailed. "Who can it be who is sucking away the life of our precious baby? You had to wait until I am all alone to finish your kill!" Titi screamed out into the darkness that surrounded them.

Another simultaneous explosion of blinding light mixed with ear-splitting thunder seemed like the shriek of death. The baby convulsed ever more violently. His breathing stopped, but his little arms stretched out accusingly for a long moment before falling lifelessly to his sides. Titi recognized the signs of death and, at the same moment, it dawned on her terrified heart that her baby's last gestures were accusing her of being the killer witch.

"So I'm the ndoki witch killing my baby! The vumbi (corpse) never lies!" She screamed into the gloom. "His own little hands just accused me!"

Totally overcome with terror and grief, Titi fell to the earth floor, clasping Makiese and screaming.

"Fwididi! Fwididi! He has just died! He has just died! I'm the ndoki who took his life!"

Petelo, followed by the drenched forms of Mama Sala and Tata Dioko, are in no way prepared for the scene that met their eyes.

"I ate him! I took his little life from him! He pointed me out as he died! I'm an ndoki witch, a hated ndoki witch! I'm trapped! I'm trapped just like my grandmother was! 'The vumbi (corpse) never lies!' "

Titi was rolling on the earth floor with her dead baby still clasped in her arms.

"He's dead and I'm the one who ate him. I killed my lovely baby boy. 'The vumbi doesn't lie'. He accused me with his hands and the look in his eyes. He accused me so I would know. Let me die, too. Let me die with him!"

Petelo sobbed openly as he knelt beside Titi and their baby. In the midst of all the expression of grief, the elderly couple remained calm. Mama Sala rushed to check the baby only to shake her head in grievous disbelief. All they could do was to pray silently and join in their own expressions of grief. Their hearts were tormented to hear Titi confessing that she was the ndoki witch, guilty of the tragedy. Their grief was compounded by the prospect of another church scandal when villagers hear of Titi's shocking confession.

Collective grief

The storm muffled all the sounds of grieving. As soon as it passed over, the wailing from their pastor's house soon alarmed the village. By dawn the little house was packed with villagers who had come to share the grief and heartache. No one was in any way prepared to hear Titi moaning her confession of guilt. No one had ever heard of a mother confessing witchcraft voluntarily.

"She seemed like one of us," Many kept repeating sadly.

One old crony added her own comment. "You can't trust those Zombos, never could!"

Deacons Sala and Dioko mobilized the church people. They took over like family. By noon the palm-branch mourning verandah had been erected before the front door. The tiny baby was placed on a low table, which became the focus of sincere expressions of grief.

Two young choir members volunteered to take Petelo's letter to Lukala so that Titi's aunt could be alerted. He himself had no relatives in Congo Zaire that he knew of. Mama Nkenda was the only relative who could be reached. There was a community effort to make all of the provisions. No one had ever heard of a funeral with only one family member expected for the wake.

The five village choirs took turns singing in the evenings. They brought real consolation to Petelo but Titi became almost incoherent because of the overwhelming weight of grief, and the sense of guilt.

Titi's aunt, Mama Nkenda, left everything and walked the eight-hour journey with the young messengers. She understood that no trucks could get through. Her heavy fieldwork made her strong enough to keep up with the two young men. As soon as she saw her aunt, Titi embraced her like a little lost child, weeping again until she lost her voice.

Final separation

The lay pastor from Maki conducted the simple funeral as best he could. There was profound sympathy for Petelo but mixed feelings toward Titi who confessed a thousand times that she was responsible for her baby's untimely death. The Dimba choir members took turns carrying the tiny coffin to the cemetery.

Titi's whispered address to the tiny coffin before burial was perceived as tragically sad.

"Good-bye, my darling baby. You know how much I love you. I am not an ndoki because I want to be. Forgive me; I will never see you again. I can't come to the ancestral village; they can't let me in. I can never be at rest while I live, or even after I die!"

After her whispered remarks, there were hisses from those who found her totally disgusting. People were astonished that Petelo seemed to care for his young wife as though she were innocent.

Deacon Dioko handed Titi the shovel and requested her to begin the burial process by throwing in the first bit of soil. Unfathomable grief distorted the young mother's face as she forced herself to throw a shovel full of earth on the tiny coffin. The sound of earth hitting the tiny coffin was an unforgettable reminder that her baby was dead, and gone from her embrace forever. Petelo was the next to throw in a shovel full of earth on the coffin of the baby he loved more than life. Mama Nkenda participated as the only family member. The deacons and choir members completed the sad task. Everyone found the death painful. The leftover earth was formed into a smooth mound. Deacon Dioko placed a small cross at the head of the grave. On the cross he had simply written the name Makiese and the date of death.

Grief and rejection mixed

Titi collapsed at the grave sight and it was Petelo who carried her home on his back, while some looked on in disgust and disbelief.

Late in the evening, Mama Nkenda tried to persuade her niece to take a little food. Petelo added his gentle persuasion. In a voice that was no more than a hoarse whisper, Titi responded to their worried requests.

"It would be better for you if I died. Do you want to keep the wife who ate your son? I know I am the guilty; the baby accused me with the certainty of an adult.

"If Grandmother made me a ndoki witch, I will keep on eating my children. I have no control over those powers. I had no idea that she had betrayed me. I loved her; and she loved me. She was changed and demented at the end. She must have put the cursed human flesh in my food, or followed some other deceptive maneuver, but I knew nothing about it until now. I refuse to make babies just to eat them. I would rather die. Get yourself someone who is fit to be your wife, one who is not a witch.

"Last night when I fell asleep, my grandmother came to me with the distorted look she had before she died. 'Tekolo, tekolo, (grandchild, grandchild,) now you will be just like me, just like me, just like me!' She laughed the crazy way she laughed just before she died. Petelo, I am trapped. I am destroyed. I should die."

Petelo cradled her in his arms as she whispered her fear.

"I'm afraid to fall asleep because she will only come again to taunt me."

The night of the funeral Petelo had a dream he found significant. In the dream Titi was crying uncontrollably just as she had actually done. In the dream Titi stopped crying for a moment and pleaded for him to help her. Still within the confines of the dream, he embraced her tenderly and told her that he still loved her and that he was sure that God would help them find some kind of resolution of their impossible situation. The next morning, Petelo awoke to find Titi basically irrational, but the resolve in his dream became the conviction of his heart.

Mama Nkenda understood Titi's troubled thinking because she recalled that her very young niece had lived through the last three horrendous weeks of her demented grandmother's life. She knew that Titi could have become the unwitting victim of the malignant spirit that sometimes manifested itself in her old mother. She felt no inclination to turn against her niece because she felt that she was probably an innocent victim of a possessed grandmother who may have found herself trapped by the same powers. She had no idea how anyone could save Titi from her ill fate.

The risk of unconditional love

The kindly deaconess Mama Sala respected Petelo enough to speak the truth to him. She called him to a quiet place out by the sanda tree.

"Pastor Petelo, we don't know what to think. Any other father we have ever known would certainly abandon a wife who confessed to eating his son. You need to know that some people have asked me if I thought that you joined you wife in the terrible process of bringing death to your child. If you are innocent, then you must reject her, or be condemned along with her."

Looking directly into the kind old lady's eyes, Petelo responded. "I love my wife whether she is sick or well. That is all. If you have ever believed anything I have said, believe that I am not an ndoki witch who participated in removing life from my son!"

"I believe you, she said, "but I had to ask for myself. I know what it is to be falsely accused. The prophet Vunda convinced people that I was guilty of taking my granddaughter's life in Kinshasa. I know that the only time you know for sure that an accusation is false is when the accusing finger points at you. Only you know that you are innocent. No one believes you, and you can never prove your innocence."

Two days after the funeral, Petelo had a talk with Titi's aunt. "I know that people have no patience with my desire to stay at Titi's side and help her. This is obviously seen as some fanatical weakness on my part. God has not stopped loving her and neither have I."

Mama Nkenda listened while shaking her head in disbelief. "In my whole life time, I have never heard of a man taking your attitude toward a self-confessed ndoki witch. I was raised in all our traditions but my heart supports you. I don't understand how in the world you can still love her. I can only conclude that the living Spirit of Jesus is touching your heart in some unusual way."

Encouraged by Mama Nkenda's confirmation, he explained to her his plan to search for help.

"One of my teachers at Kimpese is a big Canadian called Hedley. He has actually written a book in Kikongo called, 'The way out from the fears of kindoki witchcraft'. When he taught our classes, he seemed to understand our way of thinking. Despite his understanding, he proposed alternative ways of looking at our traditions. Any African counselor I can think of will simply tell me to abandon my wife and get another.

"Pastor Hedley was convinced that the Spirit of Jesus could lift a person out of the kinds of traps our traditions create. I want to take Titi to his home in Kimpese to see if there is any help for her. He and his wife often have black folk in their home. Somehow, I feel that God wants me to try this route. What do you think?"

After a long pause, she responded. "I know of no traditional solution. If you can think of any way to get help, I will be grateful. I know that if she has become a witch, it is because she had to deal with her very complicated grandmother alone, while she was still a child. I must say I never imagined that a white man could possibly help us with problems of kindoki witchcraft. If she continues as she is, without eating any food, she will soon die. Sami gave me some money when I left. I think it would be enough to get the three of us to Lukala on the market truck, if it comes tomorrow."

Petelo was deeply relieved when he heard the unmistakable roar of the old army truck. Mama Nkenda had done her best to bathe Titi, and put clean clothes on her. Just before they left for the market, Mama Sala and Tata Dioko came over to say farewell. The kindly old lady led them all in prayer.

"Tata Nzambi utufwila nkenda! (Father God, have mercy on us!) Life is a mystery to us all. We marveled at the new life in the beautiful baby that lived here among us. We are amazed that that life is over even more quickly than it began. We weep with Titi and our Pastor. They are our children. Makiese was like our grandchild. Father, we don't understand either life or death, only you understand. Only you can heal broken hearts.

"Father, you alone understand why death took that little boy from us. You know that Titi is sure she took her baby's life acting as a bewitched person, pushed and pulled by powers outside her and within. You alone know the truth. You alone know what ndoki took the child. We ask you to punish or forgive, according to your wisdom. We don't ask you to remove our sorrow, but we ask you to bring trusting peace to every one of us. There is no one you refuse to forgive, except those who will not ask. Thank you, our Father, please help these three to find your help as they go to Lukala and Kimpese."

A good number had gathered while she prayed and said amen together.

Speaking to the gathering, Petelo spoke softly. "I am taking Titi to find help. I will let God judge whether she is the guilty ndoki or not. I am sure I saw the killers myself. There were hundreds of them. Mosquitoes have poison saliva that kills more babies even than measles. I know that God forgives and transforms. How can I abandon the wife I feel sure that God gave me? I know that I am not following our tradition of hating my ndoki wife. Even if she were the enemy, God has commanded me to love her. Please pray for us. I am convinced that only God can rescue Titi. If I didn't believe that God could rescue people, I would immediately abandon being a pastor."

Dimba market had been so long without a truck, there was far more produce than the truck could carry on such poor roads. The driver allowed Mama Nkenda and Titi to ride in front. Titi was too frail to sit by herself. Petelo climbed up on the top with another twenty passengers.

The road was treacherous because of all the rains. About ten in the evening, the wheels began to spin in the muck holes of the low land that adjoined Ndoko hills. Twenty people pushing together for over a kilometer enabled them to creep through. It was about five in the morning before they found a little taxi truck that would take them from Ngungu to Lukala and

Kimpese. Mama Mbuta got off in Lukala not too far from Sami's store. Petelo and Titi traveled another twenty minutes before arriving at the IME hospital on the edge of Kimpese.

In her state of mind, the only words that had registered were 'Kimpese', and 'help'. It was not many weeks previously that she had given birth in the same hospital. She was not strong enough to protest anything. As they walked slowly past the hospital toward the residences, she was confused and pointed back to the outpatient clinic. It was only a momentary hesitation, so she trudged on, leaning on Petelo. As they moved along a busy pathway filled with people, Titi pulled her cloth over her head like a shawl. She hid her face.

Acceptance by a white family

As soon as Petelo saw the big red and white Toyota Land Cruiser with a platform on top, he knew he had remembered the right house. He had come to the house a few times because Pastor Hedley had once worked in Angola, spoke Portuguese, and administered some scholarship funds for Angolan Refugees. The lawn was carefully cut and gorgeous rose bushes bloomed right by the steps to the front door.

Stepping up on the verandah, it took courage to knock. Pastor Hedley himself came to the door. Petelo explained that he was a Kimpese graduate with a pastorate on the far side of the Bangu hills at Dimba.

"Our first baby just died a few days ago and my wife Titi is convinced that she ate him (took his life through witchcraft)."

Petelo watched the white man's eyes for his first reaction. As he had hoped, there was no sign of rejection or incredulity. Pastor Hedley seemed to sense the gravity of their situation. He invited them into their living room. Petelo looked exhausted and nervous. There was a pleading in his eyes that communicated that he had come to his last hope for help and refuge.

When Pastor Hedley addressed her, Titi could only utter a few phrases. She was relieved that this white man spoke her language.

"My baby died, my beautiful baby died, and I am the one who took his life." Her state of mind and health were obvious. She covered her face with her shawl and looked at the floor. Petelo sat there with a knowing look that seemed to yearn for comprehension of his desperate situation.

The white pastor was impressed with Petelo. He knew that most men would have angrily abandoned someone like Titi immediately. After a brief consultation with his wife, Pastor Hedley came back with a proposal.

"Please stay with us for a few days. I think we may be able to help Titi after she has rested."

Petelo was a bit surprised to be invited to stay for a number of days. He had never slept in the home of a white person before. His mind raced. *"Will we be able to eat their food? Will we feel too uncomfortable and out of place to even sleep? Do they really want to help us?"*

"We have a little guest room downstairs, with its own washroom facilities and shower. You have traveled all night and been through so much. You can move in down there, and get some rest immediately. At mealtime the choice is yours. You are welcome to eat at our table and we would be pleased to have you. If you would feel more comfortable eating by yourselves, we will bring down your food. Titi needs to be as relaxed as possible. The guestroom used to be my office when the children were home. It has it's own outside door so you may come and go as you wish."

Petelo felt a wave of relief flow through him. They both needed rest after going through what they had. It would be wonderful just to be alone with no one else at all. Titi said yes with her eyes when Petelo looked toward her for her response.

A new world

The room seemed large and luxurious to them. It was furnished with a small bed complete with a soft sponge mattress. They had a table and two chairs. The whole room was painted with glossy white paint and the floor was made with smooth dark cement. Behind an attractive curtain that stretched from wall to wall, there was a wash basin, a shower stall, and a flush toilet. One of the taps in the basin and the shower supplied hot water.

Titi actually smiled when she stepped into the shower, turned on the water to just the temperature she liked, and lathered her whole body using the new cake of Lux soap. She lathered her self with soap suds three times, then rinsed herself with warm water. She felt totally clean and considerably refreshed. *"Probably, nice hotels are like this"*, she mused. Her exhaustion obliged her to try the bed. In no time she was in a deep sleep.

Petelo thoroughly enjoyed his shower as well. On their income, scented toilet soap was out of the question. They didn't always have yellow laundry soap either. He was relieved to see Titi enjoying a deep sleep, the kind she needed so badly. Just being here, free from the penetrating stares of far too many people seemed like an answer of his prayer for peace. Before falling asleep, Petelo expressed his thanks to God. He felt accepted in the Hedley home and, in his soul, he felt the first rays of hope.

The exhausted pair slept without even stirring until Pastor Hedley knocked gently on their door. The invitation to come up for the evening meal was appealing. Initially, Titi felt very nervous. "What will I do if I can't eat their food?" she whispered.

"I have heard that lots of Africans eat in their home. They will know what we eat," Petelo replied encouragingly.

Approaching the table, Titi was greatly relieved to see fresh Kwanga and a large pot of beans. The only food missing was saka saka, and she knew that no one had the time to prepare it every day. The dessert was a new experience. Mama Fan had made mango sauce, using cooked mangos and a little sugar. Titi loved mangos, but had never heard about cooking them. *"Whoever heard of cooking mangos?"* she thought to herself. When she tasted the sauce, surprised delight registered in her face.

"I could prepare these at home." she mused. After supper Pastor Hedley prayed, asking God to heal their broken hearts. Titi was relieved that there was no probing of her problem that first night.

Back in their room, Titi thanked Petelo for bringing her to the Hedley home. "Somehow, I don't feel uncomfortable with them; I never dreamed that they would be eating our kind of food. Every window, even the door, has screens to keep out the mosquitoes. We will not suffer a single bite tonight."

It was the first time Titi had spoken normally since the day the baby died. It was good having other things to catch her attention.

"By his prayer, I think pastor Hedley feels that God can do something for me. I wish I could believe it," sighed Titi.

It wasn't long until fatigue made the bed attractive again. The bright fluorescent light gave them a new sense of security. They would leave it on all night. Ghosts and witches avoid light like the owls. Often they could not afford to keep their little lantern lit during the long nights. The feeling of basic security, the total absence of mosquitoes, and accumulated fatigue soon lulled them both into deep sleep once more. Petelo had tried to pray when they first settled in bed, but sleep cut off his words.

A bright morning sun sent its glow through the curtains at the window, gently dissolving sleep from their eyes. Glancing at his watch, Petelo shook his head.

"We just slept twelve hours without any interruption even from mosquitoes."

Despite the sleep Titi awoke to find that her grief was still pressing on her like the weight of a full basin of manioc on her head.

"My baby is dead. My beautiful baby is dead, and I'm the ndoki witch who killed him," she sighed and began to weep softly.

The good sleep simply made the reality of her situation clearer.

"Pastor Hedley can't change the truth about me, no matter how much he prays."

During her profound sleep in a brightly-lit room, her baby came to accuse her just as he did the night he died. The look in his eyes and the frantic flailing of his accusing hands haunted her memory.

There was something soothing about enjoying a luxurious shower with warm water. By the time they were called for breakfast Titi was calm.

Having breakfast where there was plenty of sugar, milk and bread brought back memories of the first months in Lukala, when Sami and Mama Nkenda had enough money to eat well. This bread came from the little wenze market in front of the hospital and was baked fresh every morning. It seemed luxurious to have all the Blue Band margarine you wanted to spread on the bread. The roasted peanuts were not quite as fine as their own Dimba variety.

The one unexpected food on the table was mango jam. Jam was much sweeter than the sauce had been. Petelo was the first to try the jam, and his face revealed his very positive evaluation. Once more, Mama Fan suggested that some day soon she would show them how to make the jam.

"We make jam and sauce out of green mangos. They come from our own trees that we planted many years ago. The school children take all the ripe fruit before we can pick them. Adding enough sugar to green fruit is the trick. Ripe fruit doesn't require as much sugar. To make jam that doesn't spoil takes quite a lot of sugar."

While everyone was still seated at the table, Pastor Hedley read some verses from the Kikongo Bible. The last few verses of Romans, chapter eight, were selected. The Apostle Paul affirmed that no kind of threatening power, not even death, could separate a follower of Jesus from his love. When he prayed, he asked God to use his powerful Spirit to help Titi and Petelo to know that they are deeply loved. Titi watched Pastor Hedley while he prayed. In her heart, she felt that he really did care about them. It was comforting to feel the depth of love expressed in her own language by someone who was actually a foreigner from far away.

Feeling understood without rejection

After the brief prayers at the table, Pastor Hedley asked them if they could return in a half-hour or so to begin discussion of their problems.

Titi felt uncomfortable as Petelo reported the details of the past seven days from the baby's illness right through to their arrival at Kimpese. They were surprised when the pastor asked for the details of all their dreams during the same period.

Titi's depth of grief and depression kept her from saying much. She did, however, point out that she felt that her repeated dream, which relived the death scene including her dying baby's accusation, was living proof that she indeed was the ndoki killer who had snuffed out her darling's life. After all, her baby came regularly to accuse her and her grandmother invaded her dreams to laugh at her, and remind her that they were both ndoki witches. One session was enough for pastor Hedley to understand the convincing experiences that kept Titi overcome with oppressive guilt that was even heavier than her natural grief.

It did not take very long for the basic picture to become clear in the missionary pastor's mind. He had lived in both Angola and Congo Zaire, working with local churches in the equipping of grassroots leadership. Problems involving the kindoki kind of witchcraft were at the root of most devastating and divisive issues facing ordinary church people. Only a small percentage of believers were really free from the inroads of witchcraft in their lives. The problem often resurfaced at times of crises, like the sudden death of a baby.

"I think that you both need more rest before we tackle Titi's burdens. You will both need to be thinking very clearly before you can handle the kind of thoughts we will need to face. Before you go back downstairs, I want to give you a copy of my book 'The Way Out From The Fear Of Witchcraft'. You probably have a copy at home, because I gave each class member a copy when I taught at the Pastor's School."

Petelo smiled. "It is because of your book and the class you taught that we came here. All of us felt that you had really listened to our people and understood the way we look at things. You understand that, if I were to follow our traditions, I would simply abandon Titi. You seemed to feel that The Spirit of God could bring a whole new kind of help for our old problems. I will read the book again. I think that you are right when you suggest that Titi still needs more rest."

"Just do whatever you would like, and we will see you at meal time. Until Titi is really rested, we will only use the time to pray, and to get to know one another."

Back in their bright little room, Titi raised questions.

"Why do these people treat me so well? I really feel that Pastor Hedley understands why I feel the way I do. When I say I am the ndoki witch who destroyed Makiese, he does not seem puzzled. If he knows what I am saying, why is he so kind and thoughtful? When we have prayers at breakfast time, I feel love that reminds me of my mother's love and your love, Petelo. Why do you keep on showing me love? I know that some people will think that you are an ndoki, too, because you have refused to condemn me. I get the feeling that you, Pastor Hedley, and Mama Fan seem to know something I don't that enables you to keep on caring for me."

"Titi, my love for you doesn't gather all its strength just from inside me. The Spirit of Jesus keeps giving me new supplies of love. I think that it is the same Spirit that gives these folk love for you. The kind of love Jesus wants to supply will even enable people to love and pray for hateful enemies. The Spirit of Jesus helps us to love when others would feel driven to hatred. Jesus' Spirit can even motivate a person to forgive someone who has wronged him and never asked for forgiveness. I remember that, when he taught us in class, he described the kind of love the Spirit can supply as being the most revolutionary force in the world. Once he told us that Spirit-given love was the only power that could rescue our Bakongo people from the trap of kindoki witchcraft."

Petelo embraced his wife tenderly. "You must believe that I do love you dearly. Wherever the love comes from, it feels like mine, and I really do love you."

"I am not fit to be loved. If you punished me, I would understand." Titi began to weep bitterly and uncontrollably. She was still sobbing when she fell asleep."

While she slept, Petelo began to read again the book dealing with kindoki witchcraft. It was a pleasure to have uninterrupted study. Eventually he went for a little walk around the house until he spotted the king mango trees with their gigantic fruit. It was still morning and the school children were all in school. To his delight, he found seven beautifully ripe fruits that had blown off during the night storm. Taking them to Mama Fan, he spoke with a laugh.

"Here, have some of your own ripe fruit for a change."

She took four for jam and suggested that he and Titi enjoy the others.

It was almost noon when Petelo came back to their room with his mangos. He had been sitting out under a shade tree within sight of the door to their room. He had left the main door open so that he would be able to see Titi if she awoke. Titi was just beginning to awaken, when Petelo came over to call her for lunch. Both her tears, and the long sleep had helped her creep back a little toward normal strength.

The noon meal was more rushed than usual because Pastor Hedley had to drive to Matadi for a meeting.

"I have a feeling that by tomorrow morning everyone will be rested enough for some serious conversation. These days have not been wasted. You were both in desperate need of peace and rest. Our first talk showed me how we should be praying. I am sure that people back at Dimba are praying too. Prayer is marvelous medicine. I will not be home until late this evening, so let's plan to meet tomorrow morning shortly after breakfast."

Titi actually fell asleep again after lunch and slept until mid-afternoon while Petelo continued his reading.

"Let's eat one of these big mangos. I certainly couldn't eat it all myself," Petelo suggested.

"Perhaps you can tell me some of the important ideas pastor Hedley has written in his book. I'm not up to reading yet but my head is clearing."

"Reading his book again brings back memories of his teaching in our class. He has always worked with a team of several Africans. They did everything together and helped each other. He knew lots of things his African brothers didn't know but they had insights into our way of thinking that a white man seldom, if ever, would discover on his own. They did counseling together in the villages and towns helping people deal with their problems. Whenever he spoke, he gave us several illustrations from his personal experience. I have never heard anyone describe what he calls our rules for relationships before. I guess it surprised me when he told us that most other people in the world live by different rules from ours."

Titi's requests help with Pastor Hedley's book

Partly from memory, and from readings in the book, Petelo began to summarize the teachings about traditional attitudes and thinking.

"You treat people well, as long as you feel they are treating you well. You reject people who seem mean, or people suspected of posing a threat in terms of kindoki witchcraft. You consider people guilty unless they can prove that they are innocent. Seldom does a suspect ever prove his innocence. Dislike turns to hate and eventually a desire to see the person dead."

"In the process of obtaining protective fetishes, the wearer agrees that his enemy should die from occult-protective powers should he try to attack. When rivalry, jealousy, or a desire for revenge fills a person's heart, a shaman may be hired to kill, cripple, or humiliate the person in question. It is understood that a shaman has agreed to the death of a blood relative by occult means in order to obtain the occult powers for him or herself."

"Descendents of blood sisters produced competitive sub-groupings of the bloodline. Fear, suspicion, jealousy, revenge, chronic illness, physical disasters, and death are normally traced to these conflicts within the one bloodline."

"The Ngombo shaman, a clever, mysterious witch believed to possess magic powers of perception, is the one called to settle disputes by a process of trial. Once accused, the ndoki witch in question was executed publicly, poisoned secretly, or left to live out life as a rejected despicable marginalized person. Because someone is accused of witchcraft every time death occurs, the whole community is filled with suspicion, fear, distrust, and intrigue. Often harmony exists on a superficial level only because people are afraid of upsetting anyone who might possibly be an ndoki witch. All the latent suspicions are revived at the moment of crises."

Titi was alert and pensive throughout the summary. "He is right. If I were back in the village right now, I would be totally rejected. You would have screamed accusations at my family and me during Makiese's funeral. I would be facing a life of rejection and isolation just like my grandmother faced most of her lifetime. She was hated and feared by her own bloodline during most of her life. If I had faith like you, things might be different. I am not like you, Petelo. I would love to be like you, but I am not. I still live by the wretched rules Pastor Hedley described in his book."

Trapped

"I am sure that back in my village, everyone would believe me that I am a guilty ndoki witch, and behave accordingly. How I wish it were not true! If our baby reacted toward you as he did toward me, perhaps you would think as I do. Petelo, my mind is much clearer now because of rest and good food. I killed my baby, and I will be an ndoki witch until I die. I am trapped like an nsizi that has been crushed under the rocks of one of our village traps.

"Pastor Hedley does seem to understand how I think. He asked me if I had seen my demented grandmother in my dreams just as though he expected that I would. He asked me if I see Makiese accusing me as frequently as I did at first. It troubles me, that he expected me to be haunted by those dreams."

About dreams

"I will never forget what Pastor Hedley taught us about dreams because we had never heard anything like it before. His teaching was simple. The first principal idea was that whatever preoccupies our mind will then preoccupy our dreams. He taught us that dreams are like very important windows giving us a glimpse of the hidden feelings of our own hearts."

"He would tell you that you see your grandmother in your dreams just the way you think of her during the day. Your day thoughts become your night dreams. Your experiences through the day often dominate your dreams. Good dreams, as well as bad dreams, normally have been fondled in our minds during the day. You suspect that your grandmother slipped magic human flesh into your food to make you into an ndoki. He would say that what preoccupies your thoughts dominates your dreams."

"Petelo, I see her! She looks just as she did that terrible last week before she died! How would he explain that?"

"He often told us that our minds store all the pictures of everything we have seen in our lifetime. In class he would ask us to close our eyes and try to see a friend or loved one. We could all do it. Then he would ask us to try to see the picture of someone who had died. We could all do that too."

"He gave us examples from his own life. He was in here in Africa when two of his brothers died. He did not see them when their illness brought them close to death. He did not see them after they died. He told us that his brothers are always well and alive in his dreams, because his mind has no other photos."

"He told us of an experiment in the village. He projected a picture story on a big screen at night. One of the scenes showed a close up of an angry leopard about to attack. It was a dramatic story. At the end he predicted that the viewers would probably see a leopard in their dreams. In the morning he asked them to raise their hands if they had dreamed of an attacking leopard. Almost every hand went up. It proved that what dominates your mind will dominate your dreams." Pastor Hedley laughed when he explained that we have dream secretaries in our heads. If we have serious thoughts during the day, that would become her signal to prepare a movie while we slept that utilized all the necessary pictures from our files. He said our dreams are real because we not only have a lifetime of pictures stored, but we also have a lifetime of voices as well. The movie can be very realistic."

Titi was listening attentively. "What do you think he would think about my grandmother's appearances in my dreams? She never said those things to me while I was with her. She has only called me a ndoki witch when she has come to me in my dreams."

"You can ask him yourself, but I feel quite sure he would say that the horrible dream is simply a reproduction of your daytime thoughts. He always reminded us that our dreams often dramatize the thoughts and ideas hidden in our hearts without our conscious knowledge. From what you have told me, most people believed that your grandmother was an ndoki witch. It is possible that in your heart, you have agreed with them. I can't help but feel that Pastor Hedley's views could be right. I have slept in the same room with you all these days but have never felt the evil presence of your grandmother."

"I also see Makiese in my dreams too. Sometimes he is happy and healthy. More often I see him still, and motionless in that little coffin. Because I do not have the same fears, my dreams are sad but they do not terrify me."

"The very reason why I brought you here to this white man's home is because he is the only person I know who would not simply follow traditions and reject you. His classes opened a whole new avenue of thinking to me. I had always looked at dreams the way that everyone does until I read his book and attended his class. He knows how we think, but does not always agree with our conclusions. He was sure that you were having terrible dreams because people in your frame of mind usually do. He told us as pastors to always pay attention to the dreams because the dreams show what the person believes in his heart."

"You said that your grandmother made you a killer witch. He expected that idea to be reinforced in your dreams. When he heard that you had gone a long time without sleep, he would have suspected that you were terrified by dreams, and did all you could to avoid sleep, and the terrible nightmares it brought. In class he told us of people who stayed awake all night and only slept in broad daylight when they felt that ndoki witches would not dare to torment them. I think that his ideas are probably correct."

"Both in the book, and in class, he pointed out that, traditionally, the strongest evidence against an accused ndoki always resided in the dreams of the accuser. You know the basic rule. When two or more people see the same person in a threatening role in their dreams, that person who threatened them will be accused of being an ndoki witch. That is always enough evidence to convince the shaman, or the traditional judge, of the guilt of a person."

"Pastor Hedley's first step would be to see how important dreams are in the conclusions you have made about your guilt. He will never say that he must be right. He will just want you to consider another interpretation."

"Your grandmother and Makiese are no longer with us. From discussions in our classes I feel sure that he would be convinced that your horrible dreams find their origin in your troubled, grieving heart. He would be concerned about the dreams, because they tell him that troubling convictions are embedded in your heart. Because they are so deeply planted, he will understand that in many ways those troubling experiences are beyond your control at present."

"I am a little nervous to find a foreigner with so much understanding of the way we think and how our kindoki witchcraft works. He has even had to learn our language. Don't you find it strange? It must have taken him many years to learn what he knows about us."

"Personally, I trust Pastor Hedley very deeply. I can't prove that he is totally trustworthy, but, after hearing his teaching and, from what I have heard, I believe that he is my brother in Christ. In a way we are members of the same new clan that has Jesus as our Chief. Some of the younger students said that they had heard in the village that Pastor Hedley is considered to be 'black on the inside'. They think that he was one of our ancestors who were taken as a slave by the white men. They felt that his habit of asking so many questions about everything indicates that he is searching for his own clan roots. I don't agree with them. I think that God has given him love for us just the same way as he has given me a love for the people of the Dimba parish. No one makes me love them. No one pays me to love them, or yearn to see them put their trust in Jesus. That love is something God gives us. It is amazing but not complicated. I think that Chief Jesus rules the hearts of this couple who have taken us into their home."

"Petelo, to tell the truth I find myself trusting these folk more and more. You have prepared me for sharing my feelings with them." Petelo smiled and gave another suggestion.

"Do you suppose that God's Spirit might be increasing your trust?"

Coming upstairs for their meeting with Pastor Hedley, Titi admitted to Petelo that she was no longer nervous about meeting him because she realized that nothing she had said had produced any rejection that she could detect.

"What he knows about our way of thinking, he has learned from talking with hundreds of people entangled in every aspect of witchcraft. Because people have trusted him over the years, they have not felt embarrassed to tell him every painful detail of their struggles."

"You two look more rested," Pastor Hedley remarked.

After they were seated, Mama Fan put a plate of cookies on the coffee table and offered them a cup of tea. Titi and Petelo both agreed to have tea even though they considered it a breakfast drink.

"Petelo, I know that we met when I taught your class so I'm not a stranger to you. You already know how my mind works. Titi, you have every right to feel awkward talking with a white foreigner. You have no great reason to trust me. If I repeat some of the questions I have already asked, it will be with the hope that you might trust me a little more than you could at first."

"Please tell me again why you are convinced that you are a ndoki witch who took the life of your own baby."

Titi repeated her description of the death scene carefully.

"When my baby was dying he was hot and trembling uncontrollably in the grips of another convulsion. He seemed to scowl at me while he frothed at the mouth. He flailed his fists as though he was trying to strike me. He identified me as his enemy and stopped breathing. He died with a horrible look on his face. My baby clearly felt that I was his killer. The baby repeats his hateful gestures every time he comes to me." Titi's lips were quivering and tears were welling up in her eyes.

"Did you see him again last night?" Pastor Hedley asked gently.

"I only saw him during the lightning storm that passed by us in the night. He does not come as often as he did at first. My grandmother didn't come at all last night, when I stop to think about it. Perhaps that is why I feel a little stronger."

Convinced of innocence

Pastor Hedley looked intently at Titi. Engaging her eyes as he spoke decisively.

"I am personally convinced that you are not a ndoki witch, and that you did not cause the death of your baby. I can't prove my opinion. Neither can you prove yours. It is only the force of tradition that has convinced you because you loved your baby and never felt any desire to take his life. Sometimes traditions are wrong!

"From what you have said your baby had malaria and died having convulsions. You need to know that a white baby dying in a convulsion could well behave like your baby. You believe that his gestures were an act of accusation. I believe that he would have made the same gestures if I had been holding him. Whatever preoccupies the mind will dominate our dreams as well. You can't forget the way your baby died. You can't forget that his dying gestures seemed to be an accusation.

"When you relive those terrible moments, your mind asks you why you should be condemned by the baby you loved with all your heart. Your answer is totally logical. Your grandmother was thought to be an ndoki by most everyone. She was in a demented state when she died. She was the only possible ndoki from your bloodline in touch with you. You naturally felt that she had turned you into an ndoki witch.

"What filled your mind soon filled your dream. In your dream, your grandmother behaved as you had thought she might. The dream reinforced your thoughts during the day and determined what you would dream at night. All you ever received from your grandmother was love and wisdom. Will you judge her by the last few days of her life when her mind was not reasonable even for a moment?

"Titi, I agree that almost anyone of your friends would agree with your conclusion about yourself. They would agree sadly, that you must indeed be a witch just as you yourself have concluded. I cannot demonstrate which of us is right. My prayerful conviction is that you are innocent. Before God I believe you are innocent but I cannot prove it."

Titi was still listening intently as the Pastor continued.

"I recognize that none of us are able to change our minds about our deepest convictions just because we might want to or someone else is trying to persuade us. Of course, you wish with all your heart that you could feel innocent of the death of you beautiful baby."

"Oh Pastor, what a miracle it would be if I could be convinced rightly that I am not a ndoki witch and that I did not kill my baby. I feel I was tricked into becoming an ndoki. I would give everything to be freed from the power of kindoki witchcraft that has me trapped. I just can't jump out of my skin!"

Titi sobbed for a few minutes and then continued to speak.

"I know that according to our traditions I could go through a ceremony of cleansing directed by a shaman. I could take a vow that would theoretically make me incapable of ever acting as an ndoki. I would need to put a curse on myself, declaring that I would die first if I ever tried to take another life by my ndoki witch's power. My grandmother convinced me that such procedures are pointless. She convinced me that no one ever trusted such a person again. That ceremony did nothing to remove the guilt of the offender. I certainly could never trust myself to have another baby and run the risk of destroying it too. I am trapped even as my grandmother was trapped most of her life."

After her reasoned reply, Titi wept uncontrollably even refusing Petelo's comfort for a long time. Pastor Hedley simply sat quietly with his eyes closed pouring his heart out in prayer for this distraught young woman. He actually felt it was a good thing that she was pouring out her grief in their presence. Eventually he began to speak quietly.

"You have analyzed your situation well when you concluded that you are trapped. Truly, we can't jump out of our skins when it comes to our convictions. We can't remove the fears and anxieties from our grieving hearts. We are free to do many things, but we can't change our minds about important things, even when we want to.

You just pulled away from Petelo, refusing his attempt to comfort you. Nevertheless, you can't stop yearning for his love. Not many couples ever experience the depth of love God has given you. The only reason you tell Petelo to abandon you is because you love him and want him to have a happy life. You are sure that his life will be ruined if he stays with you."

Trapped with glimpses of hope

Sobbing, Titi spoke between her sighs. "Pastor, it is as though you are reading the deepest yearnings of my heart. It is so hopelessly true that I am trapped and can't even change my own mind. What ever can I do, except go on in total despair?"

"Titi, the good news is that God specializes in rescuing us from imprisonment by our thoughts and convictions. He is willing to forgive us when we need forgiving, and change our thinking when it needs changing. He is even able to change the desires of our hearts. He has the power to enable us to change our minds. Sometimes the changes are brought about entirely by his Spirit working with our spirits. Sometimes he uses other people to help us trust Him. Often his Spirit enables us to believe and trust true relevant teachings from Bible. When we allow God's marvelous Spirit to influence us, we may be surprised by the changes we discover in our thinking."

Mama Fan was smiling as she broke into the conversation. "This husband of mine would go right on until midnight if we didn't stop him once in a while. You have talked all afternoon. Now it is time to strengthen your bodies with the food that I just put on the table."

A few minutes later, with folk seated at the table, Titi surprised everyone by saying that she actually felt hungry for the first time since they came. Up to that time she had eaten dutifully to be polite, but that was all.

"I think the smell of beef brought back my appetite. We haven't eaten beef since we were married."

The meat was cut in thin slices and served with typical gravy made from the thickened juices produced in cooking. Onions and garlic were the only additional flavor. There was plenty of rice and a bowl of spinach.

"Now you are trying our kind of gravy," said Mama Fan. "We have often eaten the kind of gravy you folk make with palm oil, peanut butter, and hot peppers. Which kind do you prefer, Petelo?"

Being very diplomatic, Petelo said that he liked the kind on the table but really preferred what his wife made.

Mama Fan laughed. "We prefer your kind of gravy too but the palm oil sold in the market is not fresh and upsets our stomachs."

Titi's eyes brightened. "So that is the reason; all the time we were at school in Kimpese we had stomachaches after eating food with much palm oil in it. At Dimba we have had no problems at all. Of course, out there our oil is always fresh."

"The dessert tonight is something you may not like. I made some ice cream and it is always cold. I will give you each a little. If it seems too cold, let it melt."

Petelo tried a little and liked it, but Titi took one taste and quickly put the spoon back down.

"I have never tasted anything so cold. I will wait for mine."

Before they left the table, Petelo was asked to lead them all in prayers of thanksgiving. The sun was just setting and spreading a glorious crimson lining to all the puffy clouds in the West. As the sun slipped down behind the hills, they could spot the lights of Kimpese town in the near distance. Before they went down to their room, Pastor Hedley stepped out of the house and returned with a book.

"Please have a good look at the teaching in this book about 'Chief Jesus'. I prepared this book a few years ago to help people understand just how it is that Jesus can help change our hearts. We will talk about this after breakfast tomorrow."

It rained most of the night. In the morning, a misty fog hovered over the drenched vegetation. On their way up to breakfast, they noticed that the mango trees seemed to be shimmering as the sunrays came out from behind the clouds and bathed them with silver. From the verandah, they could watch the foggy mist disappear before their eyes. The last strip of fog followed the course of the Lukunga River, as it curved around the base of the Bango hills, then turned north to join the mighty Congo. It was this magic mixture of rain, mist and bright sunlight that gave life and vitality to thousands of precious gardens.

After breakfast, serious discussion began again with the reading from the Kikongo Bible, from First Peter Chapter three verses fourteen and fifteen. "Don't be afraid but proclaim Christ Jesus Chief in your hearts!"

After reading this short passage, Pastor Hedley prayed. "Chief Jesus, we are so thankful that you are willing to forgive us, clean our hearts, and then manage them. Each of us needs your management because there are so many things in our hearts that we can't change without you. Please rule and manage each of our hearts today so that we will be able to see things your way. Amen."

The Pastor asked about the book that he had handed them after supper. They both said that they had looked at it carefully.

"Those pictures of our hearts really helped me understand what you have been saying. I like the chief's chair with the leopard skin on it," Said Titi.

Titi grasps the central idea

"I don't think that my heart is like the ideal one. Chief Jesus is not managing my heart. The picture that fits me best is the one where the 'me' or my 'self' is sitting on the leopard skin-covered chair while the cross and dove, representing the available Jesus, is over in the corner. I can see that if Jesus, through his Spirit, really were Chief in my heart, He could manage my thoughts and help bring about any changes that were needed."

"This simple idea that you have grasped, is the most important idea that you will hear from me," explained the Pastor. "It is very simple and profound at the same time. Even a child can grasp the idea that we should ask Jesus to manage our hearts. Asking Chief Jesus to rule our heart is a prayer we may keep repeating for a lifetime."

"Our very first prayer when we first come to Jesus is just this; 'Chief Jesus rule my heart'. We would do well to begin every day of our lives saying; 'Chief Jesus, rule my heart.' Even on the day I am facing my death, it would be a most appropriate prayer. Because the Spirit of Jesus can actually interact with our spirits, deep convictions in our hearts can be changed for our good.

"Chief Jesus enables us to change in ways we can hardly imagine. The Spirit of Jesus is the only Spirit who can change our thinking for our good. There are other spirits, but their intent is to deceive, manipulate, and dominate.

"I don't think that a young couple can experience anything more heartbreaking than the death of their child. That grief alone is almost more than you can bear. Titi, your sincere conviction that you are destined to be a killer ndoki witch is a burden I can only imagine. I know that

I am personally powerless to change all this grief. This is why I keep recommending that you turn to Chief Jesus for the inside help you need. We all need Jesus to manage our hearts."

"Pastor Hedley, you have enabled me to picture clearly, what I believe with all my heart," exclaimed Petelo.

There was a glow of hope in Petelo's face as he spoke. "Often I show people a statement made by the Apostle John who was a close personal friend of Jesus. Let me find and read it in Kikongo."

First John, chapter one, verse, nine. "If we confess our sins, He is ready and qualified to forgive us our sins and cleanse us from every kind of evil."

"This truth has brought help to otherwise hopeless people. Jesus has done everything necessary to be qualified to forgive us from any kind of sin we can imagine. He forgives us, and is able to convince our hearts that we really are forgiven. After he has forgiven us, he is able to clean any kind of evil out of our hearts. I can see that you are right that that the prayer to Chief Jesus is at the heart of things. If Chief Jesus is ruling or managing our hearts, He can meet our deepest inner needs."

"Pastor Hedley, would you mind if we went down to our room for a while?" asked Titi. "If the things I have understood this morning are true, then there is a kind of Spirit power available in a way I have not understood. I can see the importance of what both of you are saying. I don't have that kind of faith yet, but I need to think about this for a while." Titi's face registered a tiny glimmer of hope as she spoke.

"Understanding is the very first and necessary step. I am delighted that you want to think about this and perhaps talk it over with Petelo. I will be working all day in my little office there beside the living room. Come up whenever you wish."

During the rainy season the weather only presented extremes. When it rained it poured down in torrents, with frequent thunderstorms. When it cleared, the sun was bright, powerful, and full of growing power for all vegetation. As Titi and Petelo walked out on the verandah, only puffy white clouds drifted above the Bangu hills. They decided to put their chairs out under a tree while they talked. Titi had important questions.

"Is it true that Jesus could help me? Do you really believe He can, Petelo?" There was a plaintive yearning in her voice.

"Titi, I really believe what I teach from the pulpit. The Spirit of Jesus can work in our hearts and change things we can't. I know that you can't imagine ever forgiving yourself. I am convinced that there is nothing in your heart that His Spirit can't change. You sometimes ask me why I work so hard in our villages. As you know, it is certainly not because of the money I earn. I guess I would say that Chief Jesus has given me a yearning to see people helped by trusting him. There is so much hatred and yearning for revenge in our villages after the teachings of Vunda. I feel that only Jesus can enable people to be truly reconciled. Yes, I am convinced that Jesus helps in making important changes, in our hearts. He begins when we ask Him sincerely to rule or manage our hearts."

Titi looked off to the green tops of the Bangu hills for a considerable length of time. In a somewhat apologetic tone of voice Titi confessed quietly, "Petelo I didn't understand the things we discussed this morning when I was baptized and joined our church. I believed everything the Pastor taught us about Jesus. I admired him and understood that it would be good for me to try to follow his example. I am beginning to understand how far I fall short from being the kind of wife you need. I admire your faith but I just don't have it yet. How can a woman who killed her own baby dare ask for help from someone sinless like Jesus?"

As usual, Petelo thought very carefully before giving his gentle reply. "Titi, you need to know that refusing to ask Jesus for help with your life is the worst thing you could ever do to hurt him. Listen to his invitation in Matthew eleven verse twenty eight." He read from his Kikongo Bible.

"Come to me, all you who are weary and burdened, and I will give you rest." (NIV)

Petelo smiled as he spoke." Can you think of any burdens greater than guilt, grief and hopelessness?"

"Petelo, you are right when you say that guilt and hopelessness are the worst burdens!"

Petelo smiled. "Can you see that Jesus actually asks us to bring him our burdens. When it comes having heavy burdens in your heart, you qualify to come to Him."

After lunch, Petelo told Pastor Hedley that he and Titi planned to study his book during the afternoon.

"Because I was in your classes and studied your book before, I think I can select the parts that deal best with Titi's questions. We will ask to see you if we have questions."

Pastor Hedley had a look of satisfaction when he explained. "Petelo, I prayerfully wrote that book to help people like you as you try to help others with their deep struggles. Folk need help to deal with the kindoki witchcraft that surrounds them like an impenetrable cloud. Here at our house you have uninterrupted freedom to work through a crippling struggle. We will be praying for you both. Don't forget that a good long nap can help you both to be rested and alert. You are wrestling with giants!"

Taking the advice, Titi and Petelo each had a refreshing shower before having a long nap. When they awoke two and half-hours later they recognized that their bodies and minds were still tired. The heat had become intense while they slept. Swirling dark clouds were rolling in from the northeast. Dust devils twisted in the yard making columns of dust that went up out of sight.

Picking mangos in a wind storm

"By the force of that wind I think we will have a serious thunderstorm within a half hour. Let's run out and collect mangos for Mama Fan. That kind of wind will certainly loosen up all the ripe ones. We will just have a few minutes before the rain hits".

Petelo grabbed a pail from the back porch and they had fun gathering the giant fruit that had been hidden in the deep leaves before being shaken free by the wind. From the mango tree they ran to gather fallen avocados. Their pail was full and overflowing when the rain hit. Scrambling onto the porch they knocked at the kitchen door. A surprised Mama Fan welcomed them into the kitchen. She was delighted with the fruit. Rain came down in torrents removing all thoughts of return to their room.

Lightning flashed, and thunder reverberated, as the storm followed the Lukunga River at the base of the Bangu range of hills. Both Petelo and Titi found it a strange experience to watch the fury of the storm through the large living room windows that afforded a panorama view. Any house, in which they had ever lived before, had wooden shutters that completely covered the window spaces because there was no glass in them. They felt reasonably safe because the lightning was following the river, a safe distance from them. Pastor Hedley and Mama Fan joined them to watch the storm as they often did.

"When the lightning gets close to us here, it always hits those high steel towers that carry the electrical power lines to Kinshasa. They are not damaged, and they keep us safe because they are the highest things around. Even our tallest trees seem to be safe since those towers were constructed. As they spoke, a blinding flash of lightning obscured the tower and made everyone jump with the crash of deafening thunder. It frightened everyone, but when it had passed on toward Kimpese town, Titi stammered out her observation.

"The lightning did exactly as Pastor Hedley said it might. She was rethinking all she had believed about lightning."

The rain was still roaring on the roof even though the thunderstorm had passed by.

"Let's make some mango jam. We have time before supper," Mama Fan suggested.

Both Petelo and Titi trailed Mama Fan into the kitchen. Handing each of them sharp knives, they all set to work pealing and slicing the ripe mangos. As soon as the large cooking pot was almost full, five cups of water were added and the pot was set on the stove. Titi was given the task of stirring the contents so the fruit would not burn on the bottom. Petelo spelled her off because the gas flame was hotter than the wood fires they used. As soon as the contents had turned into a bubbling mass of cooked fruit they worked it through a sieve to remove the fibers.

"So much sugar!" Titi's showed her surprise.

"For the jam to keep we need equal volume of fruit and sugar." Mama Fan explained as she watched Petelo stir it into the hot mass.

"This time when we boil it again you must really stir a lot because with all that sugar it can burn very easily. We will squeeze the juice of a lemon into our pot both to add flavor and to help the jam be less runny."

Titi and Petelo were still taking turns at the pot while supper was cooking. They finished just in time to sit down at the table.

"We will all get a taste of the jam when we have breakfast tomorrow." Mama Fan promised.

Hope

After supper, Pastor Hedley read from the Kikongo Bible again.

"This is one of the prayers of the Apostle Paul that has often encouraged me."

Romans, chapter fifteen, verse, thirteen, says this. "May the God of hope fill you with all joy and peace as you trust in him so that you may overflow with hope by the power of the Holy Spirit."(NIV)

"Notice that our God is called the '*God of hope*', the source of hope, who can enable us to have so much hope that we overflow with it. Do you see, Titi, that the Holy Spirit is the source of overflowing hope. It makes sense to ask God for hope. Hope is something we can't place in our own hearts simply because we want to. If God can heal our hearts, and produce fruit in our inner lives like love, joy, peace, and hope, we should allow him to manage our hearts. It seems to me that God is able to tend and develop our inner hearts, as though we were his private gardens."

As they walked slowly to their room, the night air was sweet and clean. The storm had rumbled off to the east leaving a cleansed world in its wake. Tree toads were singing shrilly with delight. Stars were set free from a cloudy prison and shone brightly in the moonless sky. As they stood quietly, they became aware of a swish, swish sound coming from every direction.

Petelo laughed. "Can you imagine that a million termites are dancing around us wiggling noisily?"

"They all dance at the exact same time. Who is their drummer?" Titi asked with a grin. "Since I was a child I have tried to picture their tiny drummer."

Because of their long afternoon nap, neither of them was sleepy. Together they examined the Bible references in the book Pastor Hedley had given them.

"One nice thing about a book is that it never gets tired repeating the same idea."

Petelo had a good way of explaining, without the slightest hint of impatience or intimidation. With her husband, Titi felt free to express her doubts and questions. When both of them yawned at the same time they agreed that it was time to sleep.

Petelo prayed aloud. "Chief Jesus, you ask us to bring you our burdens and exchange them for your rest. My heart aches for the wife you gave me. You are the only one we trust to have access to our hearts. Would you please work in Titi's heart and mind so that she can sleep without encountering her terrifying nightmares? Amen."

She fell asleep before he had finished his prayer for her.

Looking lovingly at her face, Petelo continued to pray. "Chief Jesus, you know that I can't change her heart or her feelings. I can't diminish her fears. I can't change her beliefs or her interpretation of life that she has embraced during a lifetime of powerful influences. I really need your wisdom to help her. Thank you for the deep love you keep supplying me. Her doubts and questions are honest ones on her part. We both need you managing our hearts from the inside. Thank you for the Bible and your living Spirit who can change opinions and feelings that are far beyond our reach."

Feeling a burden lifted from his shoulders, he slipped into a deep sleep.

The nearest roosters were too distant to awaken the young couple from their deep sleep. They weren't even disturbed by the pastor's dog that always barked when the hospital night watchmen passed.

It was Titi who wakened Petelo with her excited call. "Petelo, Petelo, my dreams were different. I saw my grandmother and it was the unforgettable day that she blessed me. I saw Makiese but he was well and nursing at my breast."

She began to weep gently, accepting Petelo's comforting arms.

"The thoughts that occupy our mind find place in our dreams," he whispered.

Although she was spared the horror of her nightmares, the dark reality of the death of their baby was still profoundly oppressive for both of them.

"Not only will my baby never nurse at my breast again, but he will always be dead when I awake each and every day. No matter what you or pastor Hedley say our baby is dead. My feeling of guilt still crushes me when I think about it."

Fresh bread

They had just finished getting dressed when a gentle knock sounded on their door.

"Petelo, I need to ask you to do me a favor." It was the voice of Mama Fan. "Would you please go to the wenze market for bread? I will leave the money here on the chair. Please buy the same as you did the day before yesterday. We need nice fresh bread to try out our jam."

Petelo was beside her before she had finished speaking. "I'll sniff out the very freshest in the market," he replied.

Whenever Petelo went for bread, he bought it from an Angolan refugee who had constructed his own bake oven. He always searched over the bread for the nicest pieces. He knew Pastor Hedley, and always spoke with him in Portuguese whenever he came by.

Breakfast was served as soon as Petelo returned with the bread. A generous bowl of mango jam occupied the center of the table. They were all anxious to try it.

Before they spread on the jam, Mama Fan made a suggestion that they try spreading a layer of peanut butter on the bread before they applied the jam.

"We will eat bread Canadian style this morning, just for fun. We don't have mango jam in Canada but we often spread whatever jam we have together with peanut butter to make a real treat with fresh bread."

There were smiles all around, as they tasted their handiwork from the previous day. They were pleased that they knew just how to make the jam themselves whenever they could afford the sugar.

"When I was at the Pastors school last year, Mama Wendy taught a number of the wives how to make this jam but I was sick and missed that demonstration. It will be nice to have something to share with other women when we get back to our village."

Even while she was talking of their return to the village, she recalled that those people would not want a Pastor who was married to an ndoki witch. She had been so preoccupied, she had not given a thought to the future.

After breakfast Pastor Hedley asked that they stay together a while because he wanted to explain some helpful scriptures.

"Petelo, I am sure that you have noticed that chapter fourteen of the **Gospel** of John is the foundation of much of the teaching in my book. This is part of what **Jesus** said to his friends the night before he was killed on a cross. In verse fifteen, he taught them **a** simple lesson. He told them that, if they loved him, they would obey him."

"It is helpful to notice that Jesus said that the way people could show their love for him was simply to do his will. When we pray our little prayer asking Chief Jesus to rule or manage our hearts, we are telling Jesus that we want to show our love by obedience and submission to him.

"When we request Chief Jesus to rule our hearts, we are meeting the conditions for the promises included in verse twenty-three."

Petelo read the verse from his Kikongo Bible.

"If a person habitually loves me, he will habitually keep obeying what I say. My father will be constantly loving him and we will come to him and make our home with him."

"In this teaching of Jesus," continued the Pastor. "We see just how a person can receive the immense benefit of having the Spirit of Jesus, or the Spirit of God, living within us in a perfect position to help us. We need help with managing all the thoughts, fears, and impulses of our hearts. Here we see Jesus promising his kind of inside help, right in our hearts where we need it most. Imagine what comfort his words brought to his friends over the hard years that followed."

At his request, Petelo read from Paul's letter to the believers in Galatia, a part of modern Turkey. Galatians chapter five, verses twenty-two and twenty- three from his Kikongo Bible brought new insights.

"The fruit of the Spirit is love, joy, peace, patience, kindness, goodness, faithfulness, gentleness, and self control."(NIV)

"The Spirit of Jesus ruling and managing our hearts from the inside will manage to produce so much love, joy, and peace in our hearts that those fruits will dominate our lives. As far as I can see, it is only the living Spirit that can heal our hearts from the inside. Before we can benefit from the Spirit's transforming work, we must be surrendered to Jesus as the managing, ruling Chief in our hearts."

Titi began to weep again quietly. "I have killed my son. How could I ever ask Jesus to do anything for me?"

"According to the verse from the Bible we have already studied, in order to find forgiveness, we must confess our sins. Pour out your heart to Jesus and ask him to assure you of your forgiveness."

Leaning toward her, Pastor Hedley asked gently. "Do you understand what I have been trying to make clear to you? Your whole future depends on your relationship with the living Spirit of Jesus."

"Pastor, you are telling me that Jesus wants to forgive me, then come into my heart to help heal me. I understand what both you and Petelo have been showing me. I understand but I am not yet ready. I am so thankful for all you are doing for me that I don't want to deceive you. I am just not ready. Your love and patience amazes me. You hardly know me, but I believe that you really do care about me. I guess that if you, a white foreigner, can love me and accept me as I am, so could Jesus. Right now I can go no further, but please pray for me."

Pastor Hedley stood quietly behind her chair, placing one hand lightly on her head while he prayed from his heart.

"Chief Jesus, please enable Titi to trust you enough to come for the profound help her heart needs. I know that your Spirit can enable her to grieve without bitterness. Only you can bring about the kind of changes she needs. Help her to know that you love her even more than her mother or her husband ever could. Please help her to trust you from the depths of her heart. Please, Chief Jesus, continue to fill Petelo's heart with your kind of love so he can both grieve himself, and support Titi while her heart is breaking. Your Spirit alone can bring the kind of hope she needs to enable her to smile through her tears. Please help her to know that you love her. Thank you! Amen."

The sunshine made the rising mist glisten as it hovered over the Lukunga River. Feeling refreshed after a night without even one terrifying nightmare, Titi suggested that they take a walk out through the fields of manioc that stretched out toward the hills. There was a well-traveled path used by the folk who tilled their individual plots.

"Petelo, have you ever seen people have their hearts changed the way pastor Hedley describes?"

"Do you remember old Chief Kongokula from Maki, who spoke at our Matondo thanksgiving celebration? When I first met him, he had a bitter heart filled with a lifetime of resentments and conflicts. Even his face was marked with lines carved by the misery and hatred, which made his solitary life miserable. All he knew about Jesus was what I taught him. After a heart to heart talk, I told him that he needed the ask Chief Jesus to rule his heart, bringing him forgiveness and peace."

"He was sitting up front in the little village chapel. Before the eyes of everyone, he knelt by his chair and prayed, asking Chief Jesus to rule his heart. He confessed that there were many things in his heart he did not want to keep there. In his case, one chief was asking another Chief to rule his heart, and show him what he should do."

"He was sincere, so the villagers began to see big changes in him. First he initiated a search for reconciliation with the refugees in his village. In Angola his tribe always felt superior to the tribes of the new refugees who settled beside his village. The very same day he asked for help to burn all his fetishes and teki idols. Now he tells people that he is no longer afraid, because he trusts the Chief Jesus who is changing his heart. He even declared that he no longer fears death because he knows that this Jesus, who promised to be with him always, will lead him across that bridge called death.

"I know that personally I had no power to bring about the changes we have seen in that elderly chief. Only Jesus could have removed the burdens of jealousy, hatred and fear, which once kept him as a miserable slave."

"Just as all cars were designed to have drivers at the wheel to steer them, I am convinced that God intended us to operate with His Spirit as chauffeur. I often tell the children that I am a sort of truck but Jesus is my driver."

Titi fell silent, preferring not to discuss the subject any further. They had walked a fair distance, so she suggested that they return to the house and do some washing, while they had lots of hot water and soap.

"This sun will dry everything quickly," Titi suggested.

As soon as they returned, Petelo asked Mama Fan for a big basin for washing their clothes. She suggested that they bring their clothes to the back porch and use the washing machine. This looked like an interesting adventure, so they agreed.

Titi had never seen a washing machine before, so she was eager to allow Mama Fan show her all about it.

"Was this machine invented by a woman?" she asked, but Mama Fan didn't know the answer.

Within a half-hour, all their clothes had been washed and rinsed. Instead of laying everything out on the grass to dry, everything was soon flying like flags from the long clothesline. They hoped that the wash would dry before the big rain cloud reached them.

"The afternoon thunder shower usually comes our way about four in the afternoon. We can't count on that though, so we will need to keep an eye on the sky." Mama Fan observed. "Do come in for lunch now that you are both here."

"Let's sit for a few minutes while Tata George finishes our lunch preparation. You will meet him shortly. He just got back this morning from his aunt's funeral in Matadi. He is an Angolan from near Songo. He helps with everything, and sleeps here in our house when we are away. Because he helps me, I have time to do other things. I'm a nurse, and his help enables me work part-time in the private clinic at the hospital."

A memorable chat before lunch

"Pastor and Mama Fan, you have been like wonderful parents to us ever since we came a few days ago. Something in my heart told me that you would accept us, if you could. I am sure you can see a lot of change in Titi since the first day. As you recall, she could barely speak then. It seems to me that God uses several ways and means to help us when we are helpless- people, truth from the Bible, his Spirit, and periods of time."

"You have made us feel like family. I think that Africa has had its influence on you. Not once have you asked when we would be leaving. I had always heard that White people had to have everything planned ahead. Our arrival was a surprise, and you have allowed us to stay indefinitely. You have shown genuine Congolese hospitality, and offered us your love unconditionally. Please continue to pray for us. We have decided that Titi is well enough now to go visit her aunt at Lukala. We will probably stay there for a while before we go back to Dimba. Depending on how she feels, I may go back first, leaving her with her aunt for a while. Titi is still pondering everything she has seen and heard while we have been with you. Your love and acceptance has helped her feel that God may be able to accept her too."

Pastor Hedley replied to Petelo's kind remarks. "We were encouraged to think that you trusted us enough to have come to our door. We travel in the Kimvula area about half of the time, so we feel God wanted us together, because we were home and available when you came. Titi, I know that God is not as rushed as I am. He is willing for you to take all the time you need to make a decision that truly comes from your heart. I would love to talk with you once more after lunch about an important idea that has come to my mind."

Tata George called everyone to the table and was pleased to meet the young couple. He soon discovered that Titi had lived only a couple days walk from his former home in Angola.

Titi was surprised to learn that the fried fish they were eating were actually tinned mackerel with all the tomato sauce removed so they could be rolled in flour and fried. She agreed that they could pass as fresh fish. Rice was familiar, but boiled lengi squash was a pleasant new taste. They had often eaten varieties of squash and pumpkin seeds but had never tried eating the flesh before.

"It seems to me I have been learning new things every day," Titi remarked quietly.

Promptly at three in the afternoon, Petelo and Titi came up for their time of discussion and instruction.

"I have observed, that, according to the traditions I have noticed among your people, there seems to be a deep-seated necessity to take revenge. Witchcraft is repaid with other acts of witchcraft, even if it must await the next generation. If there is a lack of personal power to exact revenge, a shaman will be paid to deliver a fatal curse."

"As far as I can determine, genuine reconciliation between enemies is most uncommon. Despite the elaborate ceremonies of reconciliation complete with vows and public handshakes, trust is seldom reestablished. When death strikes again, the old enemy is immediately the first suspect. Are we in agreement about this?"

After thoughtful silence, Titi responded. "Once more, I must concede that you have observed us well. Now that I think of it, deep trust seldom, if ever, is reestablished after someone is considered guilty of some kind of evil or vindictive act."

"We need to recognize that Jesus wants us to relate to our enemies in a very different way. Let's examine His teaching found in the gospel of Matthew chapter five, verses forty four and forty five."

Petelo read the passage from his Kikongo Bible.

"Make a habit of loving your enemies, and praying for those who treat you badly, in order that you may really be children of you father in the heavens, because he habitually shines his sun for the good people and the bad people and habitually causes the rains to fall on the wholesome people as well as the unwholesome."

"In your sad experience, Titi, the enemy you want to hate and destroy is yourself. You feel that, however unwillingly, you are the ndoki witch who took the life of the baby you both loved."

Power for forgiving one's self

"Please listen to my sincere request. Titi, I am confident that before long you will willingly ask Chief to take over the management of your heart. When you do, please ask him to enable you to forgive yourself. To be able to love others, you need to be able to forgive and love yourself. The Spirit of Jesus will enable you to do this, even though it seems impossible to you now."

"Often people fear and hate someone they feel is practicing kindoki witchcraft against them. The powerful Spirit of Jesus can remove the hate from the victim's heart. You may not like the person who does evil things, but you begin to see him as someone in deep need. Often they are people trapped by evil powers. When the hate is replaced by compassion for the enemy, fear diminishes or disappears. To hate an enemy is to go against the will of God. Only the power of the Spirit of Jesus can enable a person to have compassion, and begin to pray for an enemy's reconciliation with God."

"The Apostle John was a close personal friend of Jesus. Petelo, please read what he wrote in First John chapter two and verse eleven."

"Whoever habitually hates his brother (or sister) is in darkness, walks habitually in darkness, and doesn't know where he is going because the darkness (of hate) has blinded his eyes."

Pastor Hedley continued, "I have talked with people so overwhelmed by their hatred they could think of nothing else. Hatred dominated their lives, and they became irrational, because they could not think of anything but revenge. I have seen God change such hearts and set the person free to love again."

"As I understand you, Titi, you, as a loving mother, are consumed with the total rejection of Titi, the ndoki witch. As a result, you have become bewildered and blind. Part of you totally rejects the other side of yourself."

"If any of us could help you we would. We have been doing all we can. We love you but we can't liberate you. Hate seems to have a power of it's own that cannot be dislodged by will power alone."

"You have been brave and courageous all your young life. You have accomplished incredible things, in difficult circumstances. As I see it, you need the transforming love and hope-giving help of the living Spirit of Jesus to set you free."

Titi could feel her whole body trembling. She felt as though her mind was wrestling, the words had the ring of truth. There was a very long silence. Both Petelo and pastor Hedley had their eyes closed as they prayed fervently for Titi to find release for her overburdened heart. Their love was so strong, they all melted into silent tears.

"I can see the profound truth in what you just explained, Pastor," Titi said carefully. "You are right, I am sure. At least, I hope you are right. I wish I could experience all that you say the Spirit of Jesus can do with me. There is no true solution in our traditions. Some of our traditions have valid intentions, but lack the power. There is no lack of power for evil, even miraculous evil. Power to bring reconciliation never seemed to be available. Please continue to pray for me. Your certainty that Jesus will help me is perhaps my deepest source of encouragement at the moment. Pastor, I trust you and am amazed at the love we have experienced here. My reason tells me that only the Spirit of Jesus could give you and Petelo love for someone like me."

"Titi, I know that your grief and sorrow will not disappear. Jesus can help you bear these burdens, enabling you to have inner peace while your eyes are filled with tears."

Petelo spoke. "Pastor, this session has shown me that God had my people in mind when he inspired the writers of the Bible. I did learn a great deal in your classes, but now that you are reaching out to the girl I love so dearly, it all becomes intensely real. You have helped me with my fears, and shown me how I may help others who are unaware of what the Spirit of Jesus can do for a son or daughter of Africa. I will become a more useful pastor, thanks to these talks."

"The wash, the wash!"

Mama Fan's words catapulted everyone out the door to the clothesline. Each grabbed what he could just as the first big drops of rain arrived. They were all laughing as they pushed each other in out of the rain. Torrents of rain came down for about twenty minutes, then the sun appeared. It was all over as quickly as it had come. Petelo and Titi took their clean clothes down to their room so they could be packed for the trip to Lukala. He understood his wife's unspoken wish for time to ponder all that had been discussed.

"Have you ever noticed the big yellow book in my little library? Pastor Hedley wrote that book, too. It is called 'The Other Amazing Helper'. It is the only book of its kind about the Holy Spirit. He gave us each a copy of his eleven books and booklets when we were in his courses. I think I will want to read them all again after getting to know the author.

"While we were waiting for the rain to pass, Tata George told me that there is a special choir singing over at the chapel this evening. Would you like to go? "

Titi hesitated and then agreed that she would like to go if they could slip in at the back.

The last meal together

There was a hint of sadness around the breakfast table. Pastor Hedley needed to buy cement at Lukala, so he offered to take the young couple along with him when he went. The last prayer time together took place at the table after they had finished eating.

"I have met many people entangled in the twists and turns of that trap of kindoki witchcraft. I can't prove I am right, but I want you to know my conclusion. I have prayed fervently to know how to assess you.

"I am convinced that you are not a witch, Titi, and that you witnessed your baby's death, but did not cause it in any way! I feel compelled to tell you this, but I am not offended that you see it all differently."

Titi listened intently to the Pastor's conclusion. In her opinion, he was speaking the truth as he saw it. She had no feeling that he was just trying to console her. She would never forget the compassion and conviction with which he spoke. There was an aura of authority in his words. She yearned to be convinced of what she had just heard.

Petelo and Titi stood together holding hands as Mama Fan prayed. "Chief Jesus, we entrust Petelo and Titi into your care. Please help them to trust you every day. Please keep them safe, and prepare the hearts of the people of Dimba for their return. Please help Titi to trust you, no matter how much sorrow she feels in her heart. I ask you Jesus, because I am sure that you love her even more than we do. Amen."

The good-bye handshakes were exchanged silently with glistening eyes. It didn't take long for the red Toyota to arrive at Lukala, right in front of the Nogueira store managed by Sami and Lala. In addition to the one suitcase, Titi carefully carried her carton containing a half-dozen jars of precious Mango jam.

Fresh tears at Lukala

The moment Lala set eyes on Titi, they both began to cry. Mama Nkenda had told her all the details of the untimely death, but seeing the sad-eyed young mother, she could not contain her grief. Lala had become very fond of her co-wife's little niece.

"Why didn't you come and stay with us when you came from Dimba?" Lala asked in a plaintive tone. "We would have done everything for you, you know that!"

Petelo explained honestly and openly just why they had gone right by in order to seek the help of Pastor Hedley.

"I didn't know of anyone else who understands our traditions and yet would not treat Titi as a woman damaged beyond repair by kindoki witchcraft."

"Petelo knew what he was doing. I never expected to meet a white man who understands our traditions and allows people to hold opinions different from his own. They treated us as though we were their children. The Pastor encouraged us to sleep most of the first two days until we had gained enough strength to think reasonably again. He presented a number of important ideas that have set me to thinking new thoughts."

Unusual conviction

"He said one thing so forcefully and with so much compassion that I shall never forget him as long as I live. He told me that, despite listening to the detailed story of my baby's death, he had come prayerfully to the conclusion that I am not the killer ndoki I told him I was. He reasoned that babies die in similar convulsions in many lands where there is no thought of kindoki witchcraft. His convincing, compassionate eyes reinforced his words. I think that he felt that God had led him to his conclusions about my innocence. It was as though he was speaking for God when he told me I did not take my baby's life. I can't forget what he said, but I still don't know what to think. I am not through thinking about all this yet.

"I told him about my terrifying nightmares in which my baby accused me and my grandmother came back from among the dead to taunt me. Pastor Hedley showed me a new way of understanding dreams. He said that the ideas that dominate our minds while we are awake produce parallel dreams while we sleep. He feels that most of our dreams are produced in our own minds using our own thoughts and memories. He refuses to accept dreams as sure evidence of kindoki witchcraft. I must admit that, as my thinking changed, so did my dreams."

"The last couple of days he taught us from the Bible. He showed us that the Spirit of Jesus can really change us on the inside, even the deep thoughts and fears in our hearts. Petelo agrees, but I have been afraid to open my heart and ask Chief Jesus to manage and change it. I'm afraid that nothing will really happen, and then I will really be without hope. I can't handle any more despair than I already have. Lala, I am afraid. I don't dare have another baby if I will only eat it like I did the first one."

Titi's composure dissolved into quiet sobs. Lala and her aunt each took one of her hands as they wept with her.

"Titi, you are so open and honest. We don't know anyone like you. Any ndoki we ever knew denied everything. One thing is sure; you are not what we call an ndoki nsoki (ruthless witch). Your heart only knows how to love!"

"I am surprised that Pastor Hedley thinks that most babies in the world die without any activity of witchcraft. We have always thought just the opposite." Mama Nkenda remarked.

Petelo and Sami had been sitting outside. They quietly joined the women who were still deep in conversation.

"One day in class," explained Petelo. "Pastor Hedley told us that there are far more black people in America than the total population of Angola. The ancestors of those blacks were all slaves from Africa. The way they were traded and sold, their bloodlines were lost. No one knows his luvila (bloodline) anymore. There is no trace of our kindoki kind of witchcraft among them. He said that their babies die, but no one is accused.

"Pastor admitted that he could not prove that a particular death had not been caused by a ndoki witch. He went on to say that one God created all people, black and white. He said that all races die and he was not prepared to believe that black babies in Africa all die from witchcraft, while millions of others didn't. He concluded his reasoning by stating that he wanted us to agree that not all death was caused by kindoki. Accusation of a killer for every death is not reasonable, he said."

Petelo continued to repeat some of the things he had learned. "He is the only person I know who has given reasons to challenge some of our traditions. In my heart I do not believe that Titi killed our baby. That is why I brought her to hear his reasoning personally. I love her and intend to keep her as my wife." There were tears in his eyes as he spoke with total conviction.

Significant silence

Sami had been silent until he heard Petelo's resolve. "You are the first man I have ever met who wanted to keep his wife after she confessed to being a ndoki witch. She confessed to the killing of your baby. Any man I know would have beaten her to within an inch of death and then expelled her from his home. Why are you so different?"

The silence that followed was most uncomfortable, but no one spoke for a long time. Eventually Petelo gave his reply.

"The teachings of Jesus and the Spirit of Jesus manage my heart. The Spirit of Jesus has empowered me. I have no fear at all about keeping Titi. I pray that one day Titi will fully open her heart to the management of Chief Jesus. I love her. I will continue to pray for her but I can't change her heart. I am prepared to wait for the day that Titi's heart is set free."

Petelo's response disarmed Sami. He sat in reflective silence. Finally he let his thoughts flow freely.

"Petelo, you know that I have made no pretense of being interested in the church. I attended only a few times in Luanda when I heard that an outstanding choir was singing. I saw the church as something brought in by white men. I concluded that this Jesus was some white hero who had no thought of dealing with our deepest problems. The hatred and division that grows out of our religion of kindoki witchcraft is destroying us. I have never heard of any religion that could help us with these heartaches until now."

"I have consulted some renowned shamen in my lifetime. Each shaman demonstrated his power to us. I never saw any real power in the church. It seemed to me that the teachings of the church just skirted around our heartaches that come from our beliefs and practices. The church seemed to be helpful in good times only.."

"You seem to have an expectation that the Spirit of Chief Jesus can really do something in our hearts where our deepest burdens lie."

Petelo recognized the sincerity of Sami's observations. "My faith does not let us escape the ravages of death and tragedy. I cannot explain why God allowed my baby to die. We know he died from malaria. That does not remove the agonizing question of why malaria killed our baby while others are still alive."

Amazing commitment

"There are lots of unanswered questions for me too," Petelo continued. "It is God's Spirit that enables me to trust Him even when my heart is broken and my wife is burdened beyond all reason. I believe that it is that same Spirit that has convinced me that one day her broken heart will be healed and changed. I don't know just when Titi will be set free. I intend to wait and pray for that day."

Titi was visibly touched by her husband's words. He had never before explained his faith and attitude so thoroughly. His unswerving confidence brought her deep consolation. The whole room was moved to a kind of pregnant silence, full of potential. Hope was rekindled in their hearts. They felt the presence of the Spirit of God whether they recognized Him or not.

There was sadness in Sami's observation. "I don't know of any way a person tricked into becoming a ndoki can get free from that curse. Our tradition of self-cursing never works. If the Spirit of Jesus can really change a person's heart and mind, that is good news. I can see how that could be a real solution. How could a person ever be good enough to get God to do him that kind of a favor?"

"Your question is a good one. The only reason I can answer is because of the teachings of the Bible. I believe that it was God's Spirit who guided the writers of that book, with the result that we know how God thinks about many things. The only reason we have the privilege of having the Spirit of Chief Jesus to help us is because of his love for us. It is an amazing story. God wants us back in touch with him."

"We all value relationships with the people we love and trust. We ourselves love to be trusted. I think that each of us has learned to love Titi, no matter what she might do. We want to see her free from the crippling curse she seems to be under."

With glistening eyes Titi joined in the discussion. "Petelo is right when he says that we value our relationships with those we love and trust. In my heart, I yearn to be trustworthy.

I want to believe that Jesus can make that possible. Of course I don't want to be a threat to people. I know that I can't jump out of my skin and change myself. I wish I could have Petelo's confidence. None of the rest of us has ever seen an ndoki witch transformed the way I need to be changed."

"When you all surround me, I have glimpses of hope. I dread going through the accusations of my nightmares. For two nights now I have not seen the accusing dreams, thanks to God's merciful answers to Petelo's prayers."

Lala called from the kitchen. "I have water boiling on the electric plate. Let's make some fufu. I have some cooked beans in the refrigerator that we can heat too. We can celebrate with a tin of pilchard mackerel. You must be starving for some real food after eating with mindele (white people) all this time."

"Lala, that was our biggest surprise. We ate the same kind of food you eat. The only unusual thing was the way she cooked mangos and made a kind of pudding out of them. We made mango jam as well. Just one day, we tried cold ice cream. That was the only thing I didn't like. We ate rice quite often but, in general, we ate our kind of food.

"Can you imagine? Our little guestroom had its own bathroom and shower. I took a hot shower twice each day. Yesterday, I learned how to wash clothes in a washing machine. They were so kind and understanding. Without their help, I don't know what might have become of me. I just wanted to die."

While Titi was talking she and her aunt were pounding fufu in rhythm. Together, the women prepared a delicious meal in little more than a half an hour. Truthfully, it proved to be a wonderful reunion.

"Right now, I recognize how much I miss you all. I lived without you for so many years that I just love being with you. Even while she spoke, a plan was growing in her mind.

"Mama Mbuta, could we stay with you for a week and go to Dimba on the next market truck?" The delight in her aunt's eyes gave her all the answer she needed.

There were three roosters in the back yard that joined forces to organize the daily routine with an early wake up call to everyone. With girlish delight, Titi shouted her morning greetings to everyone.

"Once more, I slept without those devastating nightmares. Aren't you glad I married someone with real faith?"

After breakfast, Mama Mbuta, Titi and Petelo walked out to the little house by the Lukunga River.

"Sami has made you a really nice little house. It is good to see that you are comfortable. You have the whole roof covered with metal sheets, I see."

Titi had been worried that, with both Sami and Lala working in the store, her aunt might become a neglected, old first wife.

"Sami comes out here quite often. He sits in our little veranda overlooking the river. He says that it reminds him of his childhood days by the Lufu River in Angola."

The week went by quickly. Titi took Petelo to her special fishing place and together they caught some great fish. The high waters were far too strong for Titi, so she guided Petelo when he set their traps. She did not feel like facing the choir that first week, but Petelo enjoyed visiting with everyone again. Before he left for Dimba, they agreed that Titi should stay a couple of weeks more before she joined him.

On the appointed day, Petelo slipped away, shortly after the first rooster call, so he would be ready to travel when the truck left around four.

The pact

In the morning Titi felt sadness come over her.

"I miss Petelo already. I feel protected and safe when he is beside me. I know he will keep on praying for me. We agreed to pray for each another each morning at the second rooster call. My faith is not very strong, but he keeps telling me that Chief Jesus loves me just as I am. Once he told me that Jesus loved me too much to leave me as I am. I am thankful for his spiritual strength. I just doubt too much."

"Would you like to visit Ngunza Tulu? He sees in people's hearts and has the power to cast out demons. He uses our Bible and some of our hymns. Many people go to him when they are afraid to go to the Nganga Shaman. As far as I can see, church people ask the ngunza prophet to do the same work as the ngombo shaman used to do back in our village. His place looks like a little church, cross, pulpit and all."

"Mama Mbuta, what could the ngunza tell us that we don't already know. I don't need him to tell me that I am the ndoki. I need power to change. If he did not accuse me for the death of my baby, he would end up accusing you because you are the only member of our bloodline who even knows that I gave birth to a baby. The year that I was taking class at Kimpese in the pastor's wives school I made a decision not to consult any kind of diviner. They make questionable decisions about whom to hate. His or her reconciliation meetings are useless because no one trusts the person once accused. Reconciliation that goes no deeper than the lips is a waste of time, good goats, and chickens. What Petelo and Pastor Hedley believe is what I want to believe but I lack the faith."

Days seemed to pass like hours. It was wonderfully comfortable to be in the presence of her closest relative, her older mother, as she called her aunt.

"People as wise and sincere as Petelo and pastor Hedley both are convinced that you are not a killer ndoki witch. I think you should not spread your conviction of your guilt around here. All my life I have been taught by word and experience to think exactly the way you do. According to our traditions you are right in your interpretation. Since coming to Lukala a few years ago, I must confess that I have found reasons to doubt more than one of our traditions."

"A woman's intimate relationships with her husband are very important in any marriage. I was taught that I should have no relations with my husband from the time my tummy showed my pregnancy, until after the baby was weaned, about two years after its birth. Everyone knew that during that period a husband would procure a second wife, if he could afford one. Other men would find available women in the towns. All our mothers taught the rule with such authority that we did not dare to change. It is true that getting pregnant would stop the milk supply of the nursing baby. Sami learned in the city that there were protective measures that could keep the wife from becoming pregnant too soon. He told me to listen to him and offer him relationships or he would be unfaithful. I could not change, so he was unfaithful. He had a concubine in Luanda for years. She could not have children so he has no others."

"When he found a smart young woman who would help him with his business, and follow his thinking about relationships, he married her. Lala is a good woman and we get along well. If I had believed that I could follow new ways, I would not have spent years knowing that my husband had other women. Child, some of our traditions are being changed and challenged. It is much easier for good young people to remain faithful than in my day. Not many older men were faithful to only one partner. It was Lala who informed me about modern ways to avoid unwanted pregnancy."

Titi smiled before she replied. "I was afraid to tell you about the teachings on this subject that young couples were taught at Kimpese. I knew they were a change from what you were taught. We learned, as well, that we should not marry into either our father's or out mother's bloodlines. As you know, our elders encouraged us to marry our cousins in our father's bloodline. They did not know that both bloodlines become partners in forming a new baby. It is true that some of our traditions are being challenged. This is one of the reasons of conflict between the educated young people, and their elders. Young people are as convinced of some of these new ideas, as the elders are of the old. Mama Wendi warned us that frequent marriage of first cousins could increase some serious family defects as well as diminish intelligence. She was very convincing because the white people have overwhelming proof of this danger."

Talking about issues that married women face was a new experience for Titi and her aunt. They had deep trust and respect for one another. Mama Nkenda was very sincere about her new faith in Chief Jesus. Titi was pleased to allow her aunt to pray for her.

"I find it difficult to pray to the God who did not keep my baby alive," Titi said tearfully one evening. "I am all mixed up in my mind. I want to believe that Petelo and Pastor Hedley are right, when they think I am innocent. If they are not right and Chief Jesus cannot help me, there is no hope for me at all. Our traditions offer me nothing. On the other hand, why did Chief Jesus not protect our little son?"

Going to market was a happy experience especially on the days Titi and her aunt managed to have smoked fish to sell. Visits with the old choir members were encouraging. On more than one occasion they turned the choir practice into a sincere prayer meeting. They prayed that Titi would be restored to peace and joy again. Some prayed that she would soon get pregnant and have a new baby to console her. They had no idea how much she feared any thought of giving birth to another baby that she would inevitably kill because she was an ndoki witch.

One evening, as they were talking by firelight, Titi asked her aunt why she hadn't rejected her for being a witch. Her aunt's careful reply brought her some hope.

"You lived with us for a year before you were married. You visited us often during the year you were at Kimpese. You were with us after the baby was born. There was never a moment when you showed any hint of being an ndoki witch. If my mother made you a witch, you would have been a witch all the time you were with us. All I have seen in you are the best qualities I have seen in a young person. I suppose that I just can't believe that you are a witch, even though I know that my mother could have harmed you.

"The fact that Petelo and pastor Hedley do not believe you killed your baby has an important influence on me as well. I know that nothing can be more terrible for a mother than watching her baby die in her arms. Despite your strong arguments, I am not convinced of your guilt. Praying to Jesus is quite new for me. I have asked him to lead me in my thoughts. I feel no force in my heart that finds you guilty. Just as Pastor Hedley told you, none of us can get into your heart to change your opinion. Our words remain on the surface of your mind."

The resident rooster spent the night perched in the branches of the rapidly growing sanda tree. There was no escaping his morning wakeup ritual. He flew to the rooftop, vigorously flapped his wings, and alarmed the whole sleeping world with his vociferous crowing. In accordance with their parting promises, Titi prayed for her husband. She was sure that his prayers for her were much more powerful because she always felt a flood of Petelo's love and affection as though her were right beside her. One morning she recognized that she had not had her terrifying nightmares since the day before Petelo had returned to Dimba. *"It must be his prayers, that are protecting me,"* she thought after finishing her own prayer.

Dilemma and sound advice

"Mama Mbuta, I'm all mixed up in my heart. I yearn to be back with Petelo. At the same time, I can't even think of having another baby for the reasons that I have told you. What shall I do?"

An hour later at breakfast, Mama Nkenda gave her carefully reasoned reply.

"My child, there is no solution to your problems from our traditions. In the days of our ancestors you would either have been executed or sold as a slave by now. They would have gotten rid of you one way or the other. There never would have been any thought of your husband keeping you. Go back to Petelo. Do exactly what he tells you to do, get the help of the Spirit of Jesus. Do not have sex relations with him until you have some good reason to believe that you are free from the curse you feel is upon you."

"You have been vulnerable to all sorts of evil powers during your stay with your grandmother. She had all sorts of teki idols and fetishes, as you well know. You certainly need a powerful spirit to set you free! You can't change your own heart. All our lifetime we have tried to fight evil powers, by finding more powerful evil forces to protect us, and to get vengeance. None of those solutions have ever really blessed our people.

"Our traditional conflicts of kindoki witchcraft remind me of the civil war in Angola. Each side looks for better guns and bigger mines to destroy the enemy. The young soldiers are always afraid. There is a power of hate in war that makes people very clever at killing. In the end every soldier who dies is a child of Angola. Everybody loses over and over again. You have nothing to lose, and perhaps much to gain by discovering how our new faith can help us cope with our worst problem, the intrigue of kindoki witchcraft. Whatever you learn, I want you to teach me."

"I will follow your advice because it makes sense to me. If I can get out of this trap I am in and receive help in changing my heart, I suppose I could risk having another baby. I know that Petelo will help me. I think that his prayers have already rescued me from those heart-wrenching nightmares."

Mama Mbuta was nodding her head in agreement. "The pastor tells us that the church is a new clan, and Jesus is the Chief. I'm glad that Jesus works through the power of love, rather than the power of hate that we are accustomed to seeing in the traditions of our ancestors."

Plans for the return to Dimba

The truck that goes out to the Dimba market leaves at four in the morning on Fridays. To be assured a place, Sami had to contact the driver. Titi decided that it would be better to spend Thursday night with Lala and Sami because their store was very near the truck driver's house. It was always wise to be among the first at the truck so you weren't obliged to sit or stand over the wheels. The shaking was bad enough to make some people ill.

Sami had an alarm clock that woke up the household at three in the morning. Inside the store, they risked not hearing the roosters. In any case, the clock allowed one hour's sleep more than the roosters. There was no way to set a rooster to call at three instead of his routine two A.M.

The driver remembered Titi and saw to it that she was placed as comfortably as possible. A police officer rode in the coveted front seat. Having had three successive days without rain gave a reasonable expectation of arriving at Dimba market before nine in the morning.

Despite the bumpy ride, all eleven passengers fell asleep during the hour and a half drive to Mbanza Ngungu. The hum of the diesel engine through the early morning darkness helped folk recuperate some of the sleep lost earlier. Once they hit the rough dirt road, they were all awakened with a jolt when they hit the first really big hole. From then on it was far too rough to sit, so folk stood hanging onto the rack. Bending at the knees absorbed bumps that a person seated could not bear. The big old war surplus six wheel drive had no trouble navigating some very deep mud holes that would have stopped a normal truck.

After the old truck chugged over the top of the Ndoko hills the whole load of passengers gave a cheer. With that hill behind them, they could be sure of reaching Dimba. As the truck rolled into the market, everyone cheered again. Without the truck to bring in supplies and carry out farm produce, the market made no sense.

As soon as the engine stopped, Petelo, Mama Sala, and Tata Dioko were at the rear of the high vehicle to help Titi down the five-foot drop with her few things. Shaking her hand warmly, Petelo scanned her eyes to estimate her state of mind.

Mama Sala embraced her. "We missed you, child," she said with warmth. "We haven't stopped praying since you left. You look good. Mind you, you couldn't look much worse than you did the day you left unless you were dead."

Petelo and Titi went straight home because everyone had a lot of activity in the market. They hadn't had a truck since Petelo came two weeks earlier. Once inside the door, they embraced each other warmly. "I have missed you so very much. This house has seemed totally empty with both you and Makiese gone."

"I think I felt your prayers. Did you pray as you said we should?

"Your old rooster wouldn't let me forget." His answer came with his familiar chuckle.

"Petelo, you need to know that ever since you left I have not had a single nightmare! Will they begin again now that I am back here where my baby died?"

Taking both her hands in his, he replied. "It is still true that whatever preoccupies you thoughts may well show up in your dreams at night. You have a lot of memories associated with our little house. Coming back here, you can't help but remember Makiese. We will pray together at bedtime that the Spirit of Jesus will help you sleep without those haunting nightmares."

After a cup of coffee and a piece of the bread she had brought for Petelo, she asked if they could go to the cemetery. Their tears flowed freely as they held hands beside the little mound of earth. The simple wooden cross had not yet faded in the sunlight. They read the marker together.

"Pastor Hedley said that every life ended in death everywhere in the world. Somehow I had the idea that white people didn't die the way we do."

"There is a whole cemetery full of dead missionaries at the mission in Mbanza Kongo. Looking at the grave markers, and seeing how young those missionaries died left a deep impression on me. I knew that they died while making an effort to tell my people about Jesus. You must really believe that the Spirit of Jesus is available to transform black people to risk everything and die the way they did in those early days. I was in their cemetery when I asked Jesus to come into my heart." Petelo was still choked up as he spoke.

"Death is certain, but we never know just when its shadow will cross our path. We all cross over that bridge called death to get to the other side. I'm counting on Chief Jesus to be there to meet me at the bridge. He said he would be with us always. Knowing I will not cross the bridge of death alone is a great comfort to me. I have pictured Jesus taking our baby in his arms ever so gently. I know it is only a picture, but I am sure that Jesus receives us when we die. Chief Jesus will help us live, and eventually he will help us die and cross over the bridge with his help."

They stood hand in hand for a long time. "Makiese, I loved you with all my heart. My heart has never changed. If I killed you, it is because of a curse put on me that made me an ndoki witch. I couldn't stop your death because I didn't even know I was a witch. I only knew when you accused me, with your look and your thrashing fists. Baby, baby, I had no idea!" Petelo held her as she sobbed.

The whole village was at the market so their visit to the cemetery had been their own private pilgrimage. They were most grateful for the unusual solitude in the midst of the village.

"Petelo, I love you so dearly. I can't imagine that I should have such a wonderful husband. No one I know has anyone like you. I need you so much, and I am thankful to be home.

"Petelo, please understand that I can't be a real wife for you and satisfy your love. In Lukala my aunt helped me come to a conclusion. I can't risk giving birth to another baby until Chief Jesus is able to convince me that I am forgiven and no longer under the curse that has trapped into being an ndoki witch. I can't face the thoughts of giving birth, only to destroy the new life in my arms, It wouldn't be right. I would rather be childless with all the shame that brings."

He was still holding her when he replied after a long silence. "Titi, did I ever try to treat your body selfishly before we were married?"

Shaking her head quietly she replied, "Your respect for me made me love you because I knew I could trust you. My girl friends could not believe that even when we were all alone you never made the slightest sexual advances. They were sure you would never marry me if you hadn't explored my body. That was one of the main reasons I felt I could trust you as my husband. You have been so wonderful. I'm sorry, I'm sorry to deny you anything."

A most unusual promise

"I love you, and I will respect your request. I have no doubt about your love and I understand your fears. I think that your request is fair. I am counting on the power of the Spirit of Jesus to set you free of all these burdens. I am willing to wait as long as it may take. I just don't know how long it will take for you to trust Jesus as much as you trust me. I waited a long time for you to love me enough to marry me. Remember that I had no money, no family, and I was not born a Zombo. I had no possible way of meeting the requirements for even a traditional marriage. God enabled me to have you as my wife. I will wait and pray as long as it takes. Believe me, you can sleep beside me and I will never betray your request, because I love you.

"After we were married, you welcomed me and surrendered your whole self to me. I surrendered to you and we both began to experience the depth of love and trust we have for one another."

"Your relationship with Jesus has been honest and wholesome. You admire him and believe his teachings. You eventually surrendered to me physically and emotionally as an expression of your love and trust. In a spiritual sense, you need to surrender to the Spirit of Jesus unconditionally. It is vitally important that you allow His Spirit to manage your whole heart, because you trust Him. Just as our love has grown since we first surrendered in marriage, so will your trust of Jesus grow after you take what you perceive as the risk of allowing his Spirit to manage your most inner person. You took a big risk when you married me. I might have hurt you. Risking surrender to Jesus is risking allowing someone who is sinless to enter lovingly into your heart for your good."

"You can't trust me to always understand you, whereas Jesus will always see the very intentions of you inner heart. He will understand you better than you understand yourself. I can't be with you always. Often I will be away from you. Jesus, through his Spirit, can be with you night and day. I yearn to do many things for you that I can't manage. The Spirit of Jesus can do things for you what no one else can ever do. He can forgive you and enable you to feel forgiven. He can cleanse your heart. He can give you an endless supply of love, peace, and joy that does not depend on your circumstances."

Titi had been hanging on every word. "Why is it that I have so much hesitation to surrender to the Spirit of Jesus?"

"You may be afraid of being disappointed. It is true that the Spirit of Jesus will bring some changes very gradually. I think that you feel unworthy because you feel so guilty. We should feel unworthy of him. We don't earn his love we just receive it!"

"There is another serious factor. To whatever degree you are trapped by the dark powers of kindoki witchcraft, you need to know that evil forces are real. I know you have seen many displays of evil power in your life. Only Jesus has the spiritual power to set you free from forces that would want to hold you back from surrendering to Him. There is a civil war going on in your heart. You must choose the side of Jesus. Of course you have fears about surrendering to another power. My dear, if you don't surrender to the Spirit of Jesus, you still remain in the grips of a spiritual power that can destroy you. Refusing to surrender to Jesus is a far more serious failure or sin than anything evil you can imagine."

They sat in their two chairs still holding each other's hands. "Think of it, Titi, The Spirit of Jesus can totally defeat the power of evil in you, no matter what the source. Remember the verse we studied. 'When we confess our sins, He will forgive us and cleanse us from everything evil.' Confess anything his Spirit brings to your mind, and He will forgive you."

"I was reading from Ephesians chapter six, just this morning. The Apostle Paul makes it clear that people like you are in a struggle against what he calls '*against the powers of this dark world*' and '*spiritual forces of evil*'.(NIV) We need spiritual strength to defeat the evil satanic forces that oppose us. Titi, my dear, it seems to me that your struggle is what we should expect. The Apostle John said that the Spirit of the Lord in us is more powerful than any evil power. It is only safe to trust the Spirit of Jesus."

Titi leaned forward and kissed Petelo whispering gently, "I feel safe when you are with me. Perhaps it is because the Spirit of Jesus makes you so strong."

Acceptance by most of the village women

The snorting roars of the market truck warned them that their private talks were over. Less than five minutes later, the first of the marketers came by to welcome Titi home. Most of the women had decided not to take her declarations of being an ndoki witch seriously. They had all heard distraught people make extreme statements at a heart-rending funeral. Most of those who came to greet her had been praying fervently for her from the day she left.

"You two will eat at my house today. Tomorrow Titi must cook for her husband, so that I will not be accused of trying to lure him away."

This serious sounding statement was followed by Mama Sala's hearty laugh.

Because it was market day, the big meal was ready about four in the afternoon because it was taking the place of both the noon and evening meal. Mealtime was pleasant because they chose to eat together.

That evening Titi carefully gathered up all the baby clothes that they had managed to buy with their meager finances. Only the clothes he was buried in were missing. Placing them carefully and sadly in a plastic bag she was thinking that she would never use baby clothes again. Part of her heart told her that Petelo was usually right on spiritual issues. He had confidence that his loving wife's heart was going to be changed from the inside.

Titi had no reserve about sleeping with Petelo. She trusted him totally. He kissed her fondly as she snuggled next to him, comforted by his presence. As she expected, he kept his word.

"Can you believe that your loving restraint makes me love you even more than the free expression of passion?" Titi whispers.

Before they slept, Petelo prayed that during this first night back in their home, Titi would be free from her former nightmares. He asked the Spirit of Jesus to guard their minds and hearts while they slept.

Because they had gone to bed early and slept well, they were not startled by their faithful rooster's wake up call. There was plenty of rainwater for both washing and coffee, so no one jumped to get up.

"Petelo, your prayer was answered again. Here I am home where my baby died, but I didn't have a nightmare. The Spirit of Jesus is so kind to me. I have known women to be haunted by the same bad dream for a whole year."

They sat by the fire drinking their coffee. Their own fat peanuts tasted better than any they ate on their travels.

"You are visiting the villages, and I must get to work in our gardens. Let's finish our Lukala bread to celebrate our first breakfast together for two weeks."

"You just want to eat up the bread you brought me," Petelo said with a laugh.

Petelo packed his little sack in preparation for the day.

"I will get back as soon as I can, but it may be dusk before I arrive."

Titi explained that she would be working in her fields. She expected their crops would be overrun with the weeds that grow luxuriously during the hot rainy weather.

Unexpected kindness

Their beans were planted on the steep slopes that stretched up from the stream. Arriving at her bean patch, Titi looked all around thinking she was in someone else's garden. All the weeds were gone, the beans looked wonderful. An army of women had done all her farming for her while she was away. The manioc, the sweet potatoes, the late peanuts; every field was spotless. Mama Sala and her friends have done this for me, she reasoned. They don't think of me as an ndoki witch, or they never would have helped me.

Titi sat down on a boulder located right beside the rippling stream. Her heart wanted to pray.

"Heavenly Father, thank you for all the kindness you have shown me through the actions of others. I am so thankful that the Spirit of your Son led all these women to turn their back on our traditions and follow yours. They should have hated me, but instead, they worked hard to show me kindness. In my old village, you know what would have happened to me."

Tears of gratefulness began to flow freely as she sat surrounded by God's creative handiwork.

"I would have been rejected by my relatives and publicly insulted. My husband would have renounced me. His family would be insulting my family and asking that the bride price be returned because they had palmed off a ndoki witch on their son," Titi whispered to herself.

She remembered the lifelong rejection of her grandmother. She recalled pleading for her grandmother to be buried without the shame of having a pot of peppers covering her head. Most villagers were relieved when her grandmother was dead and buried. A thousand memories crossed her mind as she sat all alone.

Titi soon found herself talking to herself out loud, just the way she sometimes had caught her mother doing when she was a child.

"There is no help from our traditions. There is no solution for me unless the living Spirit of Jesus changes my mind and my heart. I have had the courage to do many different things in my life. I learned to read and write in just one year. I taught all the young people in our village how to read and write when I was just a child. I learned to stand in rapid waters to catch fish when no one else was catching any. I headed for the Congo without any idea as to how it would all work out. I challenged Sami to choose life, when he had chosen death. A young girl never corrects an adult man. I married a man who could not meet any of the traditional conditions for marriage. I have had lots of courage in the past. Why shouldn't I run the risk of allowing the Spirit of Jesus to take over the management of my heart and mind?"

Sitting in solitude, but surrounded by swirling memories and ideas, a new resolve was taking shape. A Bible verse memorized during her baptismal class came back to her mind and she repeated it aloud. "Come unto me, all you who are weary and burdened, and I will give you rest." *"These are the words of Jesus himself. I am burdened and no one else knows how to help me."*

Humble honesty

Only the sounds of the forest whispered as she began to weep quietly.

"Chief Jesus, please help me on the inside. I need forgiveness because I am the ndoki witch who killed my baby. My heart is filled with turmoil. I want to trust you like Petelo does. I don't have that trust within me, so please help me trust you to forgive me. Please change my heart any way you need to, so I can look at things the way you want me to. You have so much power, but you let me kill my baby. Jesus, I'm all mixed up, but I understand that you even love your enemies."

"Please forgive me, and change me. I don't know how you can do it, but please sit on the chief's chair in my heart. Jesus, I have asked but I don't feel anything. I yearn to believe that you hear me, but I can't tell. Please help me on the inside where I can't even help myself."

"If I don't find any changes in my thinking, I will just have to conclude that the whole idea about your Spirit changing my spirit is just a fable. I need to trust you, and I need your transforming power."

"Jesus, I memorized something you said."

"'If you love me you will obey what I command.'" (NIV)

"Jesus, just look in my heart and you will see that I yearn to do whatever you want me to do. Please forgive me for not risking surrender to your Spirit sooner. Please forgive me for taking Makiese's life. Please wash my heart. Throw out any thought, any evil power, you can see in my heart. You must do it, because I can't change myself. Only you know which things should be washed out of my heart."

"Until two years ago, I didn't know anything about you. Do you really know who I am? I'm sure that you don't need me, but I need you. I can't stand living with my guilt. I don't dare have another baby unless the curse of being an ndoki witch is removed from my being. I loved my baby, yet I killed him! Chief Jesus, can you see that I am trapped. I am someone I hate. I am someone I can't forgive. No one else but you has the power to change me into someone I can trust and love. Please, please, please, please Jesus, have mercy on me. Don't leave me as I am."

Titi fell silent for a long time and then began to pray in a whisper. "Jesus, I'm sure that you gave me Petelo. He loves me and I can tell that he does. It must be you who keeps replenishing the love in his heart. I have never heard of a man keeping, and loving a person like me. Why is it that Mama Sala and her friends love me and treat me like a daughter when I don't deserve it? You are putting love in their hearts, aren't you? Did you enable my aunt, Mama Mbuta, to love me when she knows the source of the curse in me?"

"Jesus, you must love me or else you would never have enabled those people to love me the way they do. People who love you love me! Especially Petelo, he has never once rejected me or punished me in any way. He risked being called an ndoki himself just so he could keep on loving me. Your Spirit is in him, isn't it? His best thoughts are guided by your Spirit, aren't they? You have placed people all around me to show me how you feel about me, haven't you?"

"Thank you, thank you for showing your love in ways I can't deny. You are loving me through all these others. Petelo's arms are yours in a way, aren't they? Chief Jesus, thank you for helping me to see your hands and hear your voice this morning. Please stay right with me because I need everything you promise."

"Jesus, now that I know you are with me and have been tugging at my heart all this time, I am willing for you to bring about other changes in me, whenever you see that the time is right. I can wait for things as long as I know that you love me unconditionally. I know that you have forgiven me all along. I can't imagine why I was so blind that I could not see that you were showing me your attitude through the people you have put in my life ever since my baby died. Jesus, my baby is with you. I will always miss him but I realize that he is fine if he is with you."

As she sat in quiet wonderment at the peace that seemed to remove all her burdens she whispered, "Chief Jesus, you have given me hope already. I am no longer afraid of the unknown that lies ahead. Thank you. I hardly dared to believe that you really could change a person on the inside."

A choir song came tripping into her mind, and she began to sing to the little birds bathing in the stream beside her.

"Ya toma zenga mu landa Yesu.
Ya toma zenga mu landa Yesu.
Mu vutuka kilendi ko!
(I have decided to follow Jesus.
I have decided to follow Jesus.
No turning back, no turning back!)"

As she found herself repeating this little song from her choir days at Lukala, she felt her conviction growing.

Changed

Titi had very little idea about how long she had been seated on the big rock by the stream. A look at the sun's position told her it was well past noon. Beyond doubt, the young woman who finally stood to leave was very different from the burdened person who first sat there in the morning.

The tasks of gathering food from her gardens and firewood from the forest seemed like child's play now that her broken heart was beginning to heal. With her gardens all weed free, she actually felt no rush. She decided she would prepare a really good supper for Petelo to celebrate her new beginning. As she gathered the food, she needed, she found herself speaking to Jesus now and again in a little natural prayer. "Something big has changed in my heart. Jesus, I see that you keep your promises."

Petelo's question

Supper was almost cooked by the time Petelo arrived home, shortly after darkness had settled in for the night. Coming into the little kitchen, he bent down and kissed her. "You have been on my mind most of the day. When I was walking over to Maki, I felt the need to stop and pray for you for the longest time. What was going on? Why did I feel such a need to pray for you?"

Shaking her head from side to side in an expression of amazement, she replied, "Petelo, I spent the whole morning thinking and praying down by the brook. The church women had pulled all the weeds from our gardens! Petelo, I have sincerely and thoughtfully asked Chief Jesus to take over the management of my heart. It was a long struggle. Petelo, now I know for sure that Chief Jesus can change a troubled heart. I have hope! I am free from my deepest fears! I don't have the same despair any more."

"It finally dawned on me that Jesus has been loving me through a whole circle of his faithful. I see in a new way that Jesus put the love you have for me in your heart. Without his management of your heart, you would never have put up with me. I couldn't even drive you away from me. Pastor Hedley and Mama Fan seemed to love me from the beginning. I finally saw that Jesus was loving me through them. My aunt, mama Sala and her friends, all of them have been loving me because Jesus enables them to do it."

"In my village, where I was born, where people really don't even know about Jesus, everything would have been totally different. The power of Jesus' love channeled through his followers finally reached my heart. Petelo, I can see the change myself. We have no reason to fear the future with this loving Chief Jesus travelling beside us and in our hearts. No one else could have changed me, Petelo. I have already told him that I am willing for Him to take whatever time he wants to change other things in me. A great burden has been lifted from my heart and mind."

Putting his arms around her gently, Petelo prayed. "Thank you, Jesus, for placing your love, peace, and hope in the heart of the girl I love so dearly. Thank you for beginning the changes she needs. Thank you for rescuing her from the evil powers that did not want her to come to you. I am so thankful that you will always be more powerful than any satanic power."

They were both hungry and the food was especially delicious. "Even your eyes have changed, Titi. I can see joy in them. How I have yearned to see you rescued from the dark despair that enveloped you."

They talked a long time before going to bed. As they lay in bed Titi embraced Petelo. "I'm not afraid any more! How did the Spirit of Jesus manage such a change in me? Petelo, I am no longer afraid to bear your child. With Him managing my heart, I am not afraid. Whatever I may have done has been forgiven. I know it in my heart! Petelo, I have been set free to be your wife again, even to become the mother of your child. How is all this possible?"

"People get trapped, but the Spirit of Jesus performs his rescue from inside our hearts and minds. This is why trusting Jesus meets us right where we are, surrounded by our traditions. The Spirit of Jesus is the Spirit of God who wants to rescue trapped people from every corner of the earth."

EIGHT YEARS LATER

Eight years later Petelo, and Titi came knocking on pastor Hedley's door in Kimpese. The pastor himself opened the door. "Do you remember us?" Titi asked. The pastor smiled and confessed that their faces looked familiar, but he couldn't remember just how they had met.

"Please come in and visit us a while."

"I am the young woman who came here with my husband just after our first baby had died. I confessed to you that I was the ndoki witch who had taken the life of my own baby."

A broad smile lit up the pastor's face and he called his wife into the living room. "Petelo and Titi, have come back for a visit after all these years," he told her.

"We have come back to say thank you for all you did for us during the darkest period of my life," explained Titi. "We have three wonderful children now. Chief Jesus is managing our lives. Pastor, your book has helped us rescue many people from the snare of witchcraft."

That priceless, unforgettable reunion was one of the most rewarding moments of your author's many rich years spent in Africa.